Courage, pass... ...rance
would mark each of them
as her mother's daughter. . . .

LEAH—Her gift for words propelled her into the bohemian life of Greenwich Village in the 1920s, a world ripe with intellectual and artistic ideas, wine, laughter, and love. Her passion and sensuality were fired by the love of two men. . . .

JO—World War II Britain was ripe for exposure, and Jo's stark photographs of the Blitz propelled her to fame. But behind the camera, her fairy-tale marriage to an RAF officer was a hideous masquerade. When had she run away from herself?

SARAH—A singer who lived for the spotlight, music calmed the discontent that pervaded her life. She embraced the sixties in all their kaleidoscopic glory only to discover that freedom was a prison—and the baby girl with her father's eyes only reminded Sarah of all she had lost. . . .

ANNIE—Growing up in the shadow of one of the world's most beautiful, enigmatic women, Annie found salvation as a comedian, sure that her sense of humor could make the world laugh. Bright, funny, lovely, she forged a special relationship with her great-grandmother that sustained them both through turbulent years. . . .

By Marcia Rose
Published by Ballantine Books:

ADMISSIONS
CHOICES
CONNECTIONS
SECOND CHANCES
SUMMERTIMES
ALL FOR THE LOVE OF DADDY
SONGS MY FATHER TAUGHT ME
A HOUSE OF HER OWN
HOSPITAL
LIKE MOTHER, LIKE DAUGHTER

LIKE MOTHER, LIKE DAUGHTER

Marcia Rose

BALLANTINE BOOKS • NEW YORK

Copyright © 1994 by Marcia Kamien

All rights reserved under International and Pan-American Copyright Conventions. Published in the United States by Ballantine Books, a division of Random House, Inc., New York, and simultaneously in Canada by Random House of Canada Limited, Toronto.

Library of Congress Catalog Card Number: 93-47124

ISBN 0-345-37572-6

Manufactured in the United States of America

First Hardcover Edition: August 1994
First Mass Market Edition: August 1995

10 9 8 7 6 5 4 3 2 1

For my mother,
who made me a writer,
and for my daughters,
who made me a mother

Acknowledgments

Grateful acknowledgment and thanks to the late Rose L. Lesnoy and the late Maurice Slonk.

To Judy Panitch, researcher par excellence, and most especially to Rose Novak, who, for seventeen years, was the other half of Marcia Rose and who contributed greatly to the creation of this story.

Prologue

June 18, 1990

Only ten minutes ago the sky over Willow Street was still the deep blue-black of nighttime, just the faintest hint of hazy white on the horizon. Now, suddenly, it had become a pale, nearly colorless vault curving over the world. Like the inside of an eggshell, Leah Lazarus thought, leaning on the sill, her arms folded on a pillow. Her elbows were always stiff these days. Arthritis. Bursitis. Some damn thing or other, put there to remind her that she might still be alive, at ninety-six, but she'd better not get too arrogant about it.

She inhaled the sweet-scented June air; the aroma came from the tree growing in front of her house. Every spring it gave out a gorgeous perfume. Funny, she'd been living there nearly fifty years and she'd never found out the name of that tree.

She supposed she should get herself dressed; Annie said she'd pick her up bright and early. God knows it took her long enough to put her clothes on these days! Annie had something special planned for today—a birthday present, she'd said; and Leah should make an effort not to be late.

But dawn was her favorite time, that magical hour when it had stopped being night but was not yet day . . . when the shadows went from purple to pale blue, and the very air was hushed with anticipation. She'd been up since three—that was happening more and more lately, her eyes flying open in the middle of the night, suddenly wide-awake, usually remembering something from years ago. Well, that shouldn't come as a surprise; she was deep into her book . . . not memoirs, that was too fancy a word. It was a book of *memories*, or rememberings. She was ninety-six today, and she remembered it all, even the bad parts. Oh yes, there were plenty of bad parts.

1

How It Was, that's what she was calling it, even though her agent shook his head sadly, saying he didn't know who would pick it up with that title. If the publisher insisted it be changed, well, then she'd see. In the meantime, *How It Was* was how it was.

Outside, a group of chattering strollers came by, oohing and ahing loudly over the pretty street, the old-fashioned houses, the venerable trees. At this hour of the morning! They should be ashamed of themselves; better yet, they should be in bed, sleeping, instead of cluttering up the streets and waking the neighborhood.

Number 202 Willow Street, a small frame house, painted pale gray with black shutters and door, looking a bit out of place in the company of its neighbors: wide, spacious brownstone houses built by rich merchants for their wives and large families. The brownstones were splendid edifices, monuments to prosperity, with ornate wrought-iron railings, carved lintels, and stone urns filled with petunias and portulaca. By contrast, number 202 looked sketched-in, like a child's drawing of a house; its front door in the middle, one uncurtained window on either side, and four upstairs windows, evenly spaced. The house's only decoration was a small stone angel, kneeling unobtrusively by the front door, and looking out of place, truth be told. But never mind, it had sentimental value.

Across the street in the brownstones, shutters were being thrown back and shades pulled up. Looking down, Leah could make out the numbers on the outsized wristwatch that young Annie had given her. Oh God, seven already? She'd better get going.

She pushed herself up and walked to the big dressing table, where she turned on one of the pink-shaded lamps. She had already showered and wrapped herself in a man's faded brocade robe. It was a kind of dusty rose now, though it had been deep maroon once. She always had loved the feel of the heavy silk, sliding against her skin; the older it got, the softer it became. Sometimes she thought she caught the scent of bay rum from its folds; but she knew that was nonsense. The robe hadn't been worn by its original owner for . . . what? Thirty years? She stopped for a moment to count, shocked to realize it was more like fifty years. God, that long ago!

She had bought the robe for Jim. Her hand went to the breast pocket and, with her fingertips, she traced the ornate embroidered initials, the ones she had ordered done by a seamstress in London.

She still remembered how her heart had pounded guiltily when Jim lifted the robe from the shiny Harrods box. But he had never guessed about that fleeting affair in London, and she had never told him about Emile. Now the embroidery was so faded, it could hardly be seen. But it could be felt. J.W.M. in ornate, thick script letters. Overstated, like Jim McCready himself.

Big Jim McCready, always larger than life. Once again she felt that odd little shock in her chest. Jim had been dead for so many years. Emile, too. And Joe Lazarus. Annie Bernstein. Everyone from her youth. Her life was becoming ancient history.

She fluffed up her damp hair with her fingers, without looking into the mirror. Her hair curled neatly and naturally; and she kept it cut short so she wouldn't have to fuss. God, in the old days, she had hair down to her *tush*! She laughed, remembering the time it took to wash; the time it took to dry. And then you had to brush it one hundred strokes every night, to keep it lustrous and shining. A woman's hair was her beauty in those days, perhaps her only beauty. No decent woman wore rouge or powder; you had to walk out into the world with the face God gave you. But you *could* fuss with your hair, pile it up, braid it, curl it, twist it.

She and Annie Bernstein had washed each other's hair at the Cherry Street Baths once a week, then had run home with their heads wrapped like Arabs. And while their hair dried, they talked about their dreams and their plans. They were no more than teenagers. But in those days, at sixteen, you were a young lady, a working girl, an independent woman.

Untying the sash, Leah let the heavy robe slide to the floor as she looked in her closet. She would put on something brand-new, she decided. Young Annie had gone with her last week to Loehmann's in Brooklyn, and Leah had bought several of the latest styles. They were back to pants now; she was glad for that. Who could worry about hemlines . . . below the knee, above the thigh, to the ankle! She pulled out the silk pants, the silk print tunic. Perfect. Her colors, too. After she dressed, she did a cautious foxtrot around the room—her knees were none too wonderful these days—singing "My funny valentine . . . Sweet comic valentine . . ." She might not recall names too well lately, but she still had all the words to any song she had ever known. She danced, singing, until she ran out of breath.

Laughing at herself for an old fool, Leah looked around her bedroom, a room so familiar to her that she would not have been able to describe it. She had lived in this house since the end of World War II. A long time. What did her room say about her? she wondered. A large bed, even though she slept alone these days. Opposite it a fireplace, which had never worked properly, its marble mantel overflowing with propped-up photographs, some of them portraits, others of families in slum rooms, all with that frozen expression people used to have when film wasn't that fast.

The room was crammed with too much furniture, too many pictures. But every single thing had its memory. The wine stain on the chaise from that time she threw a full glass at Jim and missed. The wooden rocker from the Lower East Side—the only remnant left from there. The walls were filled with art and photographs, old magazine covers from the Village days, playbills and posters announcing meetings and demonstrations and lectures.

Over the fireplace, where she had to face it every day of her life, was a large oil painting of a nude woman, a girl really, sprawled in a huge thronelike chair, looking up sulkily from under dark brows, a faintly provocative smile on her lips. Leah walked to it, lightly touching the canvas with her fingertips and smiling back at the young model. Jim had bought it for her—paid much too much money to a railroad magnate who had an entire roomful of nude women on his walls. "Now maybe you'll stay out of trouble," Jim had said to her the day it was delivered in its wooden crate. Giving him a big hug, she had answered, "Well, I do promise never again to take my clothes off in front of a man with a painter's brush in his hand." Leah supposed it was worth a lot of money now; Walter Morris was being "rediscovered" for the second or third time. But she would never sell it. Too much of her life was attached to it.

Leah glanced at her wristwatch. Annie would be ringing the doorbell in a minute, and here she was thinking about old nonsense instead of getting ready to go! She marched to the big lacquered dresser, the one she had bought at auction right after Jim . . . no, no more remembrances! She began searching through her jewelry drawer.

Ah, there it was, in a worn black box—her locket. She and Annie Bernstein had bought lockets for each other on their birthday in 1910. She had planned that every woman in her family would wear it; but it wasn't to be. She sighed, running her thumb over the front. Just barely, she could feel that there had been a design engraved there. Then she opened it and gazed at the two photos inside, brown and faded. She knew those pictures by heart: Annie Bernstein, fair and freckled, with the frizzy strawberry-blond hair always escaping the pins; and in the other, Leah Vogel, lips fighting a smile, her dark eyes, even in this old photograph, flashing with mischief.

Leah put the locket into her handbag. It was time to give the locket to young Annie. It *couldn't* be bad luck anymore; too many years had gone by. Annie should have it. Annie Diamond was a chip off the old block, a woman who wasn't afraid to take life by the hair and *pull*! Anyway, she was the namesake of the fair girl in the picture, and young Annie had never even seen what Annie Bernstein looked like!

Tears stung at Leah's eyes, so she closed them briefly. When she opened them, she found herself looking into the mirror at a tanned old woman, wrinkled, her thick cropped hair a blaze of white. As always, these days, her reflection gave her intense pain. How could this have happened to her so fast?

"No," she told the old woman in the glass. "No. You aren't me. You can't be me. Inside, I'm still sixteen, you know," she said, defiant. "Still a girl of sixteen."

1

June 18, 1910

It was a magical evening, the air soft with just a slight breeze from the ocean; the sky a blue so deep it looked like velvet. "Look, Annie." Leah Vogel pointed as the train swayed and bumped its noisy way through Sheepshead Bay. "Look how beautiful." Then her voice changed. "Ooh. *There!* Look, Annie, the lights. Look!"

They both turned in their seats to stare out of the train window, two pairs of eyes wide with wonder, two mouths slightly open. Their expressions were identical; otherwise, they were as different as day and night—the one fair and blond, the other with hair as dark and shiny as a raven's wing, and snapping dark eyes framed by thick black lashes.

"No matter how many times we see it . . ." Annie breathed. She reached out to hold Leah's hand. "It's like a . . . a . . . fairyland."

"Better than a fairyland, Annie! Coney Island!"

An island made of light and fire appeared out of the night. Glittering towers and gleaming minarets. Castles, shimmering in the deepening darkness. The glow reached up into the heavens; they said that ships at sea navigated by it. Leah believed it. She'd read that Luna Park's fantastic structures were outlined in a million electric lights. A million! How many were a million? She couldn't even begin to imagine such a number.

There was nothing like it anywhere else in the world. Everyone said so. They said that people from all over the world made a special trip to Brooklyn just to see Coney Island. Sodom by the Sea, the old fuddy-duddies called it. Never mind what the *alte cockers* thought; it was magical, magical! Once you were in Coney Island, all the usual rules were forgotten. It was the very edge of America, the outer border of Brooklyn—of New York

City, really. Here, land met sea and city met country; reality met dreams. Here on a Saturday night, you were in a world where anything, anything at all, was possible, and Monday was so far off you didn't even have to think about it.

Gazing at the luminescence that lit the sky, hiding the stars, Leah could feel her heart speed up. She could hardly wait to start their stroll on Surf Avenue. It was always exciting, with the young men making eyes at them, tipping their hats, perhaps coming over to start a conversation if the two young women did not look away or hurry on a bit faster.

"Oh Annie, it's a perfect night, a *perfect* night. I told you it would be . . . just for us."

Annie gave a great sigh. "You are always right, Leah."

It was their sixteenth birthday. On June eighteenth both Leah Vogel and Annie Bernstein had been born, far across the Atlantic Ocean in different cities in Russia. Little Russia, really; the Ukraine. The wonder was that they had met here, in America, in the Triangle Shirtwaist Factory, quite by chance. And now they were best friends, inseparable!

"I'm a lucky person, and that's why that nogoodnik, Morris Levinsky, put you next to me," Leah told Annie the first day they met. "I'm alone in this world and so are you. Don't you think there's a reason we met today? Listen, in the building next to where I'm living now, there's a room we could take together. At the Roths' place. Our meals we could take with Mrs. Katz downstairs. She's a good cook and I happen to know she's looking for boarders. If we share expenses, say, our seven dollars a week each will go a lot farther. What do you say?"

Well, they had done it, that very week. That was in March, and this was their first birthday together. What a celebration they had planned! First of all, they had each spent three dollars on identical gold lockets that opened to hold two pictures. They had even had them engraved on the back—such a spending of money, it nearly took Annie's breath away.

"Are you sure we should, Leah?" she murmured; but Leah waved away her friend's fears. "Maybe not," she said smartly, "but you only live once. So we'll do without lunch for a few days. It will be slimming."

That made Annie smile, but she said, "Men don't like girls who are too skinny, Leah."

"Feh! Who told you that? Aren't the latest corsets made out of rubber elastic to 'reduce the flesh'?" She put on a la-di-da tone as she quoted *Vogue* magazine. The other girls made fun of Leah for reading all the rich people's magazines—*goyishe* magazines—full of things they could never even *hope* to have. But she got all kinds of ideas from looking at the pictures and reading what the fashion mavens had to say. She was always right up to the minute.

"Men like *girls*, period," Leah insisted. "Looks are nothing in the end. What they want is a bit of liveliness, a little spunk, Annie!" She had read that in a magazine, too.

When her friend blushed, Leah was immediately sorry for her thoughtless words. Annie was so shy, she could hardly get a word out if a fellow spoke to her, and she was ashamed of this failing.

"I didn't mean you, Annie, I meant . . . in general." *In general* was one of the new phrases she had learned recently. At the Educational Alliance, where she attended a night class, the teacher had told her she was a natural at languages.

"In general?" Annie repeated, puzzled.

"That means it applies to everyone, all girls . . . not just bashful Annie!" At least that got a smile out of her.

So they had the backs of the lockets engraved; and Leah told Annie she should pick out what to say. Leah's said: "To Leah, 6/18/10, friends forever." Annie's said the same, except for the name. When the engraver had finished and handed them over, the girls couldn't get over the beautiful job he had done. He had written their messages in tiny, perfect, clear script, even adding flourishes to the ends of the capital letters.

He waved off their admiration, saying, "For two such lovely young ladies, a special job with a special price." And he charged them a dollar.

That was last week. They had waited until this morning, their birthday, to give the lockets to each other. Sitting on the edge of the swaybacked iron bed, still in their muslin nightdresses, their long braids messy from sleep, they had admired their gifts, the only real jewelry either of them owned. Leah had threaded Annie's on a length of pink satin ribbon; Annie had chosen bright red for Leah. Solemnly, as they said "Happy birthday" together, they put the lockets around one another's necks. And then they hugged each other.

That's when it occurred to Leah. "Pictures. We should have our pictures inside. Tonight, when we go to Coney, we'll look for a photographer."

Annie beamed. "Oh, Leah, how extrav—extrav— Oh dear, I forget how to say."

"Extravagant," Leah supplied. "Who cares? It's our birthday."

The train pulled into the station, shuddering to a halt, and the conductor yelled out, "Coney Island! Last stop!" As if anyone needed telling! Everyone poured off the train, heading for the stairs to Surf Avenue. There, the night's adventure would begin!

"So," Leah said, as they picked their way carefully down the steep steps, "who shall we be tonight?"

"You say, Leah. You always have good ideas."

"Okeydokey. We're nineteen, we've been in America eight, no nine years, and we're—" She paused, trying to think of the classiest sounding job that would be believed. "—we're telephone operators. No, wait. We're bookkeepers. For an insurance company." Her English teacher at the Alliance was a bookkeeper for an insurance company, so she knew that was a good job for an educated woman. Which, she promised herself fiercely every single day of her life, she was going to be . . . *they* were going to be. She and Annie. Educated women, beholden to nobody.

On the street they shook out their skirts and made sure their big hats were securely pinned onto their pompadours. It was a warm night so they were both wearing lawn dresses, Annie's pale blue, Leah's white. Skirts were getting more manageable these days, and you weren't expected to pad your hips, thank God. Although you still had to get laced into a corset. One day they were going to invent something that didn't squeeze the breath right out of your body, the way corsets did. But what could they do? The Gibson Girl was everyone's ideal, with her tiny waist and round bosom, and the only way to look like that was to wear a corset.

Checking each other out, they pronounced one another beautiful, and then they were ready to start.

"Remember to look for a photographer," Leah said. She meant it as a joke. Nowadays, you couldn't go a block without bumping into a traveling photographer with all his equipment, beckoning you over, promising an eternal memory.

Then Leah spotted him: a young man with a thick, curved mustache and twinkling eyes, a handsome devil, standing in front of his tiny booth, calling out, "Take your picture, ma'am. Take your lady's pictures, sir. Just a quarter, two bits, and you have a memory you can hold in your hands and look at forever."

When he saw Annie and Leah approaching, his smile deepened and he stepped out toward them, bowing from the waist. "Ah, not one but two beautiful ladies . . . the answer to my prayer."

Annie blushed and would have hurried on. The minute a man looked directly at her or spoke directly to her, she was full of trembling confusion. But Leah held her by the arm. She liked his looks, and maybe if she flashed him a nice smile, he might lower his price.

"And what prayer might *that* be, sir?" Leah asked, tipping her head to one side and sliding him a glance under her lashes in a way she knew drove the boys wild.

"Why, to have pictures worthy to be framed and displayed here in front of my shop . . . to show the world what a fine photographer I am." He lowered his voice. "But I must tell you the truth, ladies. Fine as I am, I cannot make a silk purse from a sow's ear . . . I need your beautiful faces in front of my cameras to make my beautiful pictures." He rolled his eyes and lightly kissed his fingers. "When I put your lovely faces out here, on this piece of black velvet, ladies, the public will *flock* to me, demanding I take their photos, too. So you see . . ."

"Yes?"

"So you see, I *must* take your photographs if I want to make a living."

"Oh, I see," Leah said, mock serious. "Then we get them free, since we're doing you such a favor?"

He threw his head back and laughed. "I only wish I could. But listen, I'll take pictures of both of you, two for the price of one, how's that? Could anything be fairer—except for your flashing dark eyes?"

It didn't surprise Leah that he was flirting with her; and she agreed quickly, before he could change his mind. When he motioned to Annie to sit first, calling her "Fair maiden," she thought Annie's face would burst into flame. But he was nice. He saw that Annie was not the kind who could give back the wisecracks, and he became softer, gentler with her, calling her ma'am and saying please when he asked her to tip her head or smile. He described her in terms that would make any woman blush, though, calling her crinkly hair the color of corn silk and saying her pale eyes reminded him of brook water. From the look on Annie's face, kind of glazed and wide-eyed, and from the way she kept giggling at his outrageous compliments,

Leah knew that her friend was falling for the fellow. Falling for his line.

Oh, Annie, she thought, if you didn't have me to watch over you, you'd really make a fool of yourself over this man, wouldn't you? Not that she could blame Annie, really. He was quite a charmer, with his quick smile and flashing eyes and always the right word on the tip of his tongue.

"And now . . . Snow White, with her lips like cherries and her hair like shining jet. . . ." Ah, now it was *her* turn. Well, he wasn't going to get to *her*. A lot of men flirted with her; a couple she had even allowed a chaste kiss or two.

And, once only, when she was not quite fourteen, she had had a taste of what they really wanted.

It was her first job. She glued feathers onto ladies' hats twelve hours a day, and once a month she helped the boss pay his bills because the fool could neither read nor write. When he needed to sign papers, he would sit her at the desk in his tiny office and come up close behind her—too close. It made her feel suffocated. Then she would put the pen in his hand, and with her hand over his, guide his hand so he could write his name. She'd never forget that name, not as long as she lived. Irving Moscow.

One day when she got up from the chair, he grabbed her, turned her around and began clutching at her, talking funny, making her feel queer and scared. Then he pushed her against the wall and kissed her, a horrible wet kiss.

But she bit his horrible tongue, and he shrieked like he was being murdered. Then he ordered her to get out. Inside, she was frightened because she feared he wouldn't give her a reference. But to her own surprise, she found herself saying, "Oh yeah? Well, I quit! I wouldn't work here for one more minute! And what's more, I think I'll write letters to all your customers and tell them you're just a stupid man who never learned to read and write!"

"You do and I'll—" He had stopped there, his face the color of a plum. And all her fear disappeared. He was scared of her. Of *her*! He couldn't even think what to say.

But she could! "You'll do nothing, you evil old man. You're too stupid to think of something to do! Give me my wages now!"

"You'll get nothing, my fine young weisenheimer. You'll get nothing from me!"

"My wages or I *will* write those letters. And when your cus-

tomers write to you, telling you they don't want to do business
with you anymore, you won't even know it because you're so
ignorant! I'll . . . I'll even tell the whores! And then they won't
buy from you anymore!"

Moscow blanched then. He really *was* stupid, she realized.
He had been sending her to the Brooklyn Navy Yard every Friday, and he thought she didn't know who she was meeting.
Leah always carried six hat boxes, each one with an egret
plume carefully curled inside, the boxes slung across her
shoulders, and gave them to a woman named Lil. Leah found
out quickly enough that she was delivering to the red-light district. Lil, who was one of the prostitutes, told her.

She had, apparently, given old Irving Moscow a real
shock—having threatened him with the loss of a very lucrative
business—because, in a minute, he had the cash box unlocked
and was counting out the dollar bills. Three dollars, a week's
pay. Then, as she stared at him, he reluctantly counted out
three more. Blood money.

She walked out knowing that there was power in words, real
power. And she knew something else, too: that there was
power in the way she looked; something that could make men
act foolish. She tucked both those thoughts away in the back
of her head. Who knew when she might need them?

In the meantime, she wasn't wasting her time on street photographers, no matter how good-looking and quick-witted. No
matter how full of graceful compliments. She answered his
questions—God, but he was full of questions—telling him the
fibs she and Annie had decided on. He believed her. And
why not? She knew she looked nineteen, not sixteen. And why
shouldn't she and Annie be taken for bookkeepers in their nice
clothes and new shoes?

But when she sat down in the chair and he touched the side
of her face to show her how he wanted her to hold her head,
she felt a tingle in her skin. She had to fight not to pull away
from his touch. And when he murmured, "Skin like silk," she
just tightened her lips and ordered her heart to stop jumping
around.

He disappeared beneath the black cloth, but continued to
talk. "So what are your names, ladies? Mine is Lazarus, Joe
Lazarus."

Leah was not going to give him the satisfaction of an answer, but to her surprise, Annie piped up. "She's Leah Vogel
and I'm Annie Bernstein."

He popped out from under the cloth a moment later. "I knew it. Your names suit you. Bernstein, Amber. Vogel, Bird. You're as golden in color as amber. . . ." That caused Annie to turn an alarming shade of pink. "And *you* . . . you remind me of a bird, ready to fly off if I come too close."

The nerve of him! Oh he was right, yes, but . . . well, Leah wasn't having any of it, that's all. Nevertheless, when he caught her eye, his lips twitching with a smile, she just couldn't help it. She burst out laughing. He was a devil! She'd better watch herself with him. "Are you finished with me, Mr. Lazarus?" Very cool and proper.

"I'll never be finished with *you*, Miss Vogel." Very low and improper.

She looked quickly away, hoping she wasn't blushing. "So," she said, to get the conversation back on a more businesslike track, "this is what you do for a living?"

"At Coney? Only on the weekends. I take photographs of the immigrants in the city. I have a publisher, New World Books. They're very progressive. They don't want just pretty pictures of happy families, they want me to go into the slums and show what it's *really* like. Then maybe the fat cats will reach into their fat pocketbooks for a change and see to it that good people, whose only fault is that they're poor and new in this country, don't starve to death!—forgive me, ladies, I sometimes get carried away." In an entirely different tone he added: "I'll have your pictures for you in five minutes. If you'll give me your lockets, I'll even slip them in for you."

Suddenly he was all business, and Leah was disappointed. She had liked his speech and wanted to hear more. She liked a man with strong opinions. She almost opened her mouth to tell him they weren't *really* bookkeepers, they were just sewing machine operators at the Triangle Shirtwaist Factory, and they *knew* what it was like to have barely enough to eat. But why was she thinking that way? What was he to her? Nothing. Still, it might have been interesting to have a discussion with this Joe Lazarus. At first, she would have bet he was as deep as a rain puddle and no deeper, with his lighthearted chatter and dandified clothes, but he had fooled her. Well, if he didn't want to talk, then neither did she.

So she just turned to Annie, chatting as if he weren't even there. And he went off into his little booth with their lockets.

"Oh, Leah, isn't he handsome?" Annie was all pink.

"What's the matter with you? You look feverish!"

"Don't say that. I only thought . . . well, he *is* handsome, Leah, and so nice."

"I'm sorry, Annie dear, I didn't mean to hurt your feelings. Yes, he is very good-looking, and has a good line of gab. But that's part of doing business, you know that. Doesn't every pushcart peddler always have the freshest, the sweetest, the cheapest, the finest? Well, then. I wouldn't take him seriously, Annie, I'm telling you."

"I'm not . . . I only thought . . ."

Oh dear, she *was* taken with the photographer. Poor Annie, she was awkward at flirting, and she did tend to think everyone meant what they said. *She* did, bless her heart. She was a good, dear person, and Leah was going to make sure she found herself a good, dear man, not an attractive heartbreaker like this one. Leah squeezed Annie's hand and said, "I can't wait to see how we came out, can you?"

Joe Lazarus was as good as his word. In a few minutes he emerged from his booth, grinning from ear to ear.

"It just goes to show what the camera can do—with the right subject," he said, looking into Leah's eyes.

Let her heart flutter like an imprisoned bird! She would ignore it. He was not going to get to her! But he was getting to Annie, who looked at him with goo-goo eyes, her hands clasped together in front of her heart.

"So let's see how right you are," Leah countered. He held out the lockets, opened, one in each hand.

When she looked, she couldn't help smiling. He was good, no doubt about it. It was Annie to the life, and looking very pretty, too, with a slight smile curving her mouth. Leah studied her own picture. Even in the tiny image, her eyes dared you to tell her no. He had got her, he really had! Even the little dimple to the right side of her mouth . . . yes, and the wisps of hair that always escaped and curled around her temples and ears. He had tried to make her give him a great big smile, but that would have revealed her chipped front tooth. No sense having *that* as a memory.

"You did good, Mr. Lazarus."

"Like I said, the photograph is only as good as the subject."

"And now, I believe, we owe you twenty-five cents."

"Don't run off so fast. If you stand here, it'll look like I'm doing a lot of business. Stay, and you can have the pictures for nothing."

It was tempting. She was intrigued by him. But this was

their birthday, and they had plans. "No, thank you just the same. We'll pay, like everyone else. We want to get to *Fire and Flames* in time to get good seats."

Annie shyly praised the pictures and thanked him a thousand times; Leah had to practically drag her away.

"Annie, Annie, listen to me," she said as they walked down Surf Avenue toward Luna Park. "He does this with every girl who pays for a picture. Believe me, it means nothing."

Stubbornly: "He was different with us. And, oh Leah, he's so much nicer than the fellows in the neighborhood. A real Yankee, and with his own business, too."

"Yeah, yeah, yeah ... Let me tell you something, Annie dear, they're all the same! But," she added quickly, seeing her friend's face fall, "maybe not, maybe not. So tell me, you think we should turn around and go back?"

"Well ..." Annie cogitated. "No, I guess not. It would be terribly forward."

"Yes, and we want to see *Fire and Flames*. Everyone says it's so thrilling."

"T'rilling," Annie repeated. "I ... I don't know, Leah. . . ."

"Oh, Annie, it will be good for you to see it. Really! It will strengthen you. It's only make-believe, and I'll be with you, and once you look at it, maybe the demons will go away and you won't have your nightmares anymore."

When Annie didn't answer, Leah took it for agreement. She quickened her step, pulling her friend along, and then there it was: the entranceway to Luna Park, glittering and sparkling. The tall twin towers, on either side of the huge arched opening, were outlined with bright lights. Giant letters of light spelled out LUNA PARK below a huge heart with the pronouncement "The Heart of Coney Island." Through the succession of giant arches you could see the towers and spires and onion domes rearing up into the night sky, all aflame with electric light, their orange and white and golden banners flapping and cracking in the sea breeze.

Leah and Annie joined the parade of people, dressed in their best, strolling past brightly colored buildings that looked like the castles in fairy-tale books. There was the mighty Electric Tower with its lines of rosette windows. And the Dragon's Gorge; and farther on, the elevated promenade with its outsized ducks' heads and fanciful plantings. On the lagoon near Venice, young people floated around in boats, laughing and calling to each other.

"Excuse us, ladies." A young man with curly carrot hair doffed his hat and bowed low. "My name is Nathan Goldman and this is my friend Harry Fink. We would be delighted if you young ladies would join us for a boat ride. What do you say? We're really fine fellows with steady jobs. Your mothers would love both of us." He laughed good-naturedly.

Leah liked his style. He'd be good for Annie; too bad he had his eye on *her*. She could tell. His friend Harry wasn't to her taste, being a bit on the fat side. And anyway, that photographer . . .

"Thank you so much," she said in her toniest voice. "But we're planning to see *Fire and Flames*."

"Say, we'd thought to do that, too. Perhaps you'd allow us to walk with you."

Quickly Leah said, "Certainly. That would be fine. My friend Annie Bernstein would enjoy having you as an escort." Well, give him credit; Nathan Goldman was disappointed but game. He crooked his elbow to Annie and very politely said he was delighted. As they strolled out of Venice, past the Japanese gardens with their quaint humpback bridges and parasoled ladies, Leah found herself laughing at the jokes Harry Fink told. So he wasn't much to look at! He was a lot of fun.

"They hire me sometimes to tell funny stories at wedding parties. And I read all the messages from the relatives who couldn't come . . . and I'll tell you a secret, most of them can't read or write English, so it's me who makes them up!"

Lining up to get their tickets into the show, Harry Fink noticed how Annie hung back. "What's the trouble?"

Leah pulled him off a little to the side and spoke rapidly, in a low voice. "Her entire family was wiped out in a pogrom. Those dirty Cossacks, it wasn't enough they killed everyone, just ran them through; then they put a torch to the house, set it on fire!"

"Momzers!"

"Annie was little then, and she'd been playing in the corn crib, so she hid there. But she saw the whole thing. She saw the fire eat up her house and her bed and her mama and her papa and her brothers and her sisters . . . ugh!" Leah shuddered.

"So, tell me, is it such a good idea for her to watch this? Even though nobody gets hurt, it's a real fire, you know."

"The way I figure it is, since everyone here is saved, it might be good for her to see that. She has terrible bad dreams about it . . . terrible. Screams in her sleep, and wakes up sweating."

"Poor kid."

"Well, I'll tell you something, Mr. Fink. Annie is like a sister to me, closer maybe. And I feel for her. But I agree with the Educational Alliance. Grow or go. There's not one of us didn't have hard times. What happened to Annie is horrible, but what's done is done. She can't change it, so she better forget it and go on with her life. Those of us who are smart enough to forget the past, we're the future of this country. We're the ones who are going to get ahead." She stopped, a little breathless.

He clapped his hands and grinned at her. "You got quite a mouth on you," he said, but his tone was admiring. "Maybe you could make a buck from it, you know what I mean? Like I do."

Leah laughed. "If someone would come along and pay me for speaking my mind, believe me, I'd take the job!"

"And if I had the money, believe me, I'd hire you!"

He was a pleasant young man, Leah thought, and comical. And he liked her. Secretly, she looked him over, listing everything good about him. But the impish smile of that photographer, that Joe Lazarus, kept floating in front of her eyes. *Gottenu*, she was as bad as Annie!

"So I'll come to you, Mr. Fink, if I ever need a new job." She watched his face fall; good, he got the message.

The line inched up, and finally they were able to buy their tickets and go in. Annie gave Leah one imploring glance, but then smiled over it. She was being very brave. Leah would make sure they'd go to see the *Streets of Delhi* next time— Annie loved the elephants and the dancing girls, and especially the music that sounded so much like old Jewish men at their prayers. Funny girl.

They crowded into their seats, facing the building, waiting, holding their breath, then gasping as flames burst out of the windows, first one, then another and another and another. Then—oh horrors!—people appeared at the blazing windows, yelling and screaming. Finally, the horde of heroic firemen with their hoses and their hatchets and their shiny coats and their safety nets arrived. By then the entire audience was hollering right along with the "victims." Leah had sprung to her feet without even realizing it and was yelling, "Go on! Jump! Quick! They'll catch you!" And they jumped, bouncing safely into the nets. The whole time, Annie clung to Leah's hand, nearly squeezing the blood out of it.

When it was over, and both of them hoarse from all the shouting and screeching, Leah was relieved to see that Annie was pink with exertion, not pasty and pale the way she was after one of her bad dreams.

"So, Annie, it wasn't so bad now, was it?" Leah smiled, rubbing the hand Annie had clutched.

"No, Leah, not so bad." Annie even managed a wavery smile. "I'm sorry to be such a baby."

"You're not a baby, Annie dear. You've had a hard life. But that's why we're here, you and me, in the Golden Land . . . to make a new life for ourselves and cast off the old! Yes, cast off the old, like a worn-out dress, Annie. Throw it in the rag bag and forget it! Remember, I'm lucky and my luck rubs off on you!" She rubbed her arm against Annie's. "You feel luckier now?"

Annie giggled, then grabbed onto Leah's arm as the crowd behind them, eager to get on to the next attraction, pushed along.

"Where are Nathan and his friend?" Annie said.

Leah looked around, although not too carefully. It suited her fine to lose them in the crowd. Nice young men, but the world was full of nice young men. "Never mind them," she told Annie. "If they want, they'll find us again. And there's still so much to see!"

On every side there were fascinating things to see. Premature babies kept alive in a new invention called an Incubator; Hottentots, real Hottentots, living in their own little village; camels, bears, elephants, "King" the diving horse. You could watch the fall of Pompeii or the great Johnstown Flood. You could come here every Saturday night for the rest of your life and never see it all!

Annie stopped suddenly. "Leah, Leah, look! Our pictures! He put them outside, for everyone to see!" Her voice quavered with excitement.

"What? Oh." Leah hid her smile. Cleverly, she had been guiding them back toward Joe Lazarus's booth. And there, much bigger than the ones in the lockets, were their pictures, hers and Annie's. But the photographer himself was nowhere to be seen. She had been hoping . . . never mind. He was good-looking but a bit of a weisenheimer, too sure of himself. Joe Lazarus and she were too much alike to ever get along.

Leah said, "Oh yes, very nice," and began to walk on. She knew that Annie, too, would have liked to stop a minute or two to see if Joe Lazarus would step outside. But they had better things to do, she and Annie. Firmly, she turned her back on their pictures and led the way to the Loop-the-Loop, talking as fast as she could.

"Look around, Annie! When you were in the Old Country, did you ever for even one minute dream that one day you would be in a place like this, walking by palaces and lagoons, looking at a million electric lights?" She laughed. "But here we are, you and I, Annie! Here we are, in this wonderful country where it doesn't matter what you are. Here you could be a Jew, a goy, a . . . a Hottentot, even! Who cares? You work hard, you save your money, you get an education, and there's no telling how far you can get! We're going to school! We're young. We're good-looking. We're both smart. Hey, Annie, the world is ours. Someday soon, we're going to be *teachers*, Annie, *ganser machers*, high-class ladies!"

Carried away by her own words, Leah threw her head back and laughed with pure pleasure, and in a minute so did Annie. They clasped hands and, without a word, began to twirl around like little girls, until they were both dizzy and had to stop.

"You know what, Annie?" Leah said, panting a little. "Every year, on our birthday, let's come back here, to Coney Island. . . ."

"To Luna Park . . ."

"To Luna Park. And go on the Loop-the-Loop and the Carousel . . ."

"And have our pictures taken!"

"Yes, yes, and have our pictures taken, every year, even when we're little old ladies, all bent over and shuffling along!"

Now *that* was a picture to make them laugh. And so they stood there, on their sixteenth birthday, holding hands and laughing like loons because life was so full of promise!

2

October 1910

Morris Levinsky handed out the pay envelopes and then, slowly, very slowly, took himself over to the elevator. Secretly, every eye on the floor watched him. Secretly, every mind cursed him for a mean little bastard, who always held off as long as possible before he rang the quitting bell. Some people, when you gave them a little power, it went to their heads. Levinsky was universally loathed.

Finally the bell gave its raucous peal. Every machine stopped at once, and the loud rasp that had dinned in their ears all day long stopped, too, though their heads rang with the echo for minutes afterward.

Five-thirty P.M., that's what the clock said; but Leah doubted that was really the time. The bosses had a way of setting the clocks so they'd get the most work out of their poor, overworked operators. Oh, well, no matter. It was Friday. *Shabbos nacht*, and their supper would be better than usual.

Leah stretched, still in the wooden chair, and looked over at Annie with a smile. They sat next to each other at their plant: the long wooden table, seventy-five feet, that held the double rows of sewing machines; fifteen on each side facing each other. Sitting across from them at the plant were Angela Gullo, who lived with her family in their building on Hester Street, and Celia Kaplan. Angie, they liked, but Celia was always putting on airs. She considered herself a cut or two above the rest of the workers because *her* family had owned a ninety-nine-year lease on a tobacco farm in Ekatrinaslav, and she thought that made her nobility. Feh! Who wanted to be nobility, anyway? Celia was just a poor girl, a factory worker toiling for wages, just like the rest of them.

Leah tossed her head and said, "Come on, Annie, let's go."

They pushed their way out to the end of the plant, making jokes with the other girls, shaking out their skirts, patting their hair. All over the room was the buzz of talk, the cheerful sounds of a workday over at last. The chairs scraped back, then scraped again as they were pushed in under the plant. Scrape, scrape, scrape. Laughing, joking, snatches of song.

"Hey you up there, let's get moving!" Leah called out. "Some of us have things to do and places to go!"

"Yeah, yeah!" came the good-natured answer. "So how come you don't flap your wings and fly, Miss Vogel?"

Leah laughed. Truthfully, there was no way to hurry out of the place. Not only were all the chairs crowded in, back to back, but wicker baskets full of work sat everywhere on the floor. There was only one way out of the ninth floor of the Triangle Shirtwaist Factory, and it was slow going. Never mind. It felt good to know that tonight was for Shabbos, tomorrow night for fun and dancing, and Sunday for sleeping. And for reading the English newspaper. Leah practiced all the time on the newspaper. Well, it was easier than some of the books her teachers wanted her to read. At least, in the *Tribune*, there were pictures and you could recognize names and you could guess a lot of words.

At the end of the row, she and Annie raced to the dressing room for their coats. The others yelled after them to watch where they were going—what was their hurry, where was the fire—but it was all in fun. As they put on their coats and prepared to open their purses so Levinsky could search them and make sure they didn't steal a thread or a scrap of cloth, God forbid, Leah began to sing a new song she had just learned. It was a catchy little number, and she had really enjoyed the way the song pusher on Fourteenth Street had done it, acting out the words. She had listened to "Down by the Old Millstream" three or four times, until she had it all memorized. The part she liked best was, ". . . you were sixteen, my village queen . . ." You counted out sixteen on your fingers; and then, for the next line, made a crown from your two hands.

"Do the whole thing!" Angela Gulla cried, and there was a little burst of applause. So they all stopped for a minute while Leah sang it, and pretty soon they were all singing. It was a big hit so everybody knew the words. As they filed past Levinsky, they were still singing, and even he gave a little smile.

Leah felt a light little pinch on her tush as she went by the foreman, but she wasn't going to give the *momzer* the satisfaction. So let him think he'd got away with something! Who cared?

The Greene Street door was open; she grabbed Annie by the hand and said, "Let's walk down. We'll be forever, waiting for the elevator." Hand in hand, holding their skirts up high, they skipped down the stairs.

They came out into a world lit red-gold by the setting sun. The air smelled of wine, and smoke from all the fireplaces and stoves, and of apples. On the street, people were bustling about, shopping, visiting, hurrying to where they were going. The buildings all looked like lighted candles glowing against the darkening sky. A delivery boy hustled by, singing "Ah, Sweet Mystery of Life" at the top of his high-pitched voice. In spite of everything, life was good.

"So, Annie, what shall we do this evening?"

"Eat! I'm starving!"

Leah laughed. "Well, Mrs. Katz is sure to have a wonderful supper for us, nu? It's Shabbos tonight and tomorrow's the special day of the week." She gave a little laugh. "Except not at Triangle."

"Nothing's special to Triangle," Annie agreed. "Except money."

"Absolutely! It's wrong that they diddle with the clock to keep us working an extra five minutes, maybe ten. What are we, animals? We're people, just like them. Think about it, Annie. Without workers, how does a boss make money? Who does the cutting and the sewing and the picking up and the putting down, hey? The boss?"

"No!" Triumphant: "We do!"

"Exactly! So why not treat us fairly? It seems to me that if they were nicer to us, we'd work a lot harder."

Annie giggled. "You sound like Celia Kaplan, you know that?"

"Me? Like that snob?" But she knew she did. Celia was Union . . . for all the good it did her. For all the good it did *any* of them. Last year there had been a big strike, started at Triangle. "You came after the strike, didn't you, Annie?"

"Yes, I missed it. Oh Leah, I wish I had been there."

"Don't be so sure."

Thinking about the strike, about how powerful all the women had felt, keeping the march on the picket line for more than two months, she shook her head sadly. The strike that had started at Triangle was crushed at Triangle. And all those brave women who spoke up at meetings and took a chance of starving, they had been defeated, totally, as if they had never done anything at all! Break her back again, and have it all come to nothing? No thank you! Not Leah Vogel!

"Remember, there's *still* no union at Triangle," she reminded Annie. "They were very brave and all, but . . . what good did it do? We're still an open shop and the union got nothing they asked for."

"In the end, the union will triumph," Annie declaimed. "Right is on our side."

Leah smiled at her but shook her head. "I wish I could be so sure. But look what happened to the girls who joined last year. They got locked out. You and me, we can't afford to get locked out, Annie. We have to save every penny so we can go to Normal School, and then we won't *need* a union . . . *Gottenu!* Quick! In here!"

In a flash she ducked into the doorway of a tiny tailor shop. The dim little man hunched over his mending looking up, gave a little cough. "Excuse me, I'm hiding out for a minute—" Leah had to laugh at the look of bewilderment on the man's face. Then out she went again, keeping herself behind Annie.

"What's got into you?" But Annie was laughing. She knew. "It's that Fink fellow, isn't it?"

"I keep seeing him."

"And why not? He lives in the neighborhood. He's got a right to be on the street, same as you."

"Well, the last time we bumped into each other, I got the feeling we weren't just bumping into each other accidentally."

"So he likes you. What's so terrible?"

"I'm not ready for that kind of stuff, Annie. You know that."

"Anyway, I don't think it was him this time." As they continued down the street, Annie added, shyly, "I only wish such a nice young man would bump into *me*—" She searched for the phrase she wanted and came up with it triumphantly. "—accidentally on purpose." She grinned, then sighed.

"Oh, Annie, it'll happen to you, I promise. It's . . . you don't put yourself forward, Annie, you try to sink into the background! You're not like that with *me*! I only wish some of these fellows could see and hear you when we're together. . . ."

"Well, it's different with you. . . ."

"And anyway, Annie, what of it? It's nice to flirt, it's nice to have someone pay attention. But Annie, what does it mean in the end? It means ... it means ..." She searched for the right example.

They were walking through the Italian section now, past all the exotic smells from the salumeria, past the little shop with the pastries in the window, little horns stuffed with cream. Italian women wore black, as if they were all in perpetual mourning. Whatever women made on the job, they handed over, no question. And women were nothing, Angela had told her. Women were there to serve men, to bear men's children, to make families for men.

"Look at all the women in Little Italy, Annie. Can you believe that Angie is going to look just like them in a few years?"

She expected an argument, but Annie surprised her by saying, calmly, "It's the same everywhere, Leah."

It was true; it was the same with Jews. Mrs. Katz was a tired old woman already, and she was, what? Thirty-five? Was that what God had put Leah Vogel here for? To serve some man she hadn't even met yet? To have babies, one after the other, to watch some of them die, and then die herself? But then why give her a good brain and a quick tongue? Surely God, who knew and saw everything, would not be so wasteful!

"But Annie ... you don't want to turn into Mrs. Katz!"

"Leah, don't be silly. I can't turn into Mrs. Katz!"

"Yes, don't you see? So Mr. Katz made eyes at Mrs. Katz, and Mrs. Katz felt all soft inside and they got married. And now look at her! Annie! Think! Mrs. Katz, old and withered, five children and another on the way, her hair already gray and she's not even forty. Annie! Don't you see what a trap it is for us?"

She could tell by the mystified look on Annie's sweet pale face that she didn't see it, not at all. Finally Annie said, timidly, the way she said most things: "But Leah, we're *meant* to get married."

"No we aren't!"

Stubbornly: "It says in the Bible. And everyone *does*."

"But Annie, we don't have to! We can be different."

"I'm just afraid ..."

"Yes? What? What are you afraid of?"

"Of ... I don't know ... of getting old and being all alone."

"All alone! What an idea! You'll always have *me*, Annie! I'll look out for you! Who needs a man, anyway? Who needs a union? Who needs other people?"

Not me, she thought fiercely, not me. She didn't need anyone to take care of *her*. She'd been taking care of herself ever since the day her mother gave her away.

The voyage from Rotterdam was stored in Leah's memory in pieces. Well, she was only six. One piece was the noise of the engines. Another was the smell: rotting fish from the herring barrel, human sweat, blood and excrement. And she remembered her mother's magical incantation: *Soon we will see Papa.* She had no real memory of her father then—he had left long before for the Golden Land—but she knew he was very important. Back home, in Kiev, he was constantly evoked. Her aunts, her mother's friends, her grandmother, always told her to behave for her papa, so he should be proud of her when he saw her at last.

Mama spoke of him all the time. When they sat on the deck of the ship with the other women, Bella would say proudly, "Ours was a love match. No *shiddach*, no matchmaker, for Jake and me. For us it was Fate. He saw me at the market one day, in my blue dress, and that was it for him. He told my father of blessed memory that he was going to marry me, and if Papa would not give his blessing, we would run away together!"

There were always gasps at this audacity, and Mama would nod, lifting her head proudly. "I was hiding behind the curtain in the doorway, and let me tell you, my heart was beating so hard, I thought it would jump right out of my chest." Here, she would always put her hand over her heart and smile.

From listening to her mother, Leah knew that Jake was a handsome devil, a man like no other man, so lean, so dark, with thick curly hair—such a man, such teeth, such eyes, such strong hands! "It has been five years of torment and torture, five years of longing, of burning. . . ." The other women laughed; they told Bella Vogel she was bewitched. Some of the women made signs with their hands or spit three times over their shoulders, to ward off the *ayin hora*, the Evil Eye. You married a man because your parents chose him for you. You married him because to be married was a mitzvah. You married him because he was a scholar or because he had a cow or a little land . . . or you married him "because he was there and he didn't say no." To be *in love* with your husband, that was strange and probably dangerous.

But when the other women laughed and teased her, Mama

would toss her head and say, "I don't care what you think, it was *baschert*, it was fate. The Gypsy saw it, written in my palm."

A caravan had come through Bella's village the year she was twelve; and she had snuck out one afternoon, to have her hand read. The Gypsy crone— "All wrinkled, Leah, dark and wrinkled like a walnut, but still with most of her teeth, and wearing so many bracelets and necklaces that jingled and jangled whenever she made the smallest move!"—had beckoned to Bella, taking her hand.

"You are a beautiful girl," she told the wide-eyed Bella, after studying her palm. "And a lucky one, too, my dear. You will be greatly loved by a dark and handsome man. You will travel the world over and you will find great treasure."

Mama had told Leah that story, over and over. Mama said the gypsy fortune-teller had made her a promise and—what do you know?—so far, it was all true. She was lucky and she was greatly loved by her dark and handsome Jake, even though they had been parted so long, and she had even found the treasure.

"And you're beautiful, Mama, don't forget that part!" Her mother always laughed and tossed her head, but her mother *was* beautiful. Many people said so. She had hair the color of polished mahogany, a deep rich wine-brown, and stormy gray-green eyes, and tiny dots of freckles over the bridge of her nose and her broad cheekbones. "You are, Mama! You're more beautiful than a princess!"

"And you, Leah Masha, are my treasure!"

That made her feel so important, to be called her mama's treasure, to be held and hugged. But Mama's mind was often elsewhere. When Leah lay down to nap, Bella would wrap her shawl around her shoulders and go "upstairs" where there was fresh air and company . . . and, sometimes, she would forget to come back down to get her. Leah hated falling asleep and then waking up all alone. The heavy thudding of the ship's engines sounded to her like great heavy beasts crashing through a forest, coming closer and closer. "Mama!" she would call. "Mama!" Sometimes, Leah went looking for Mama; and sometimes she found her, sitting on the deck or standing at the rail, looking out over the endless silvery water, talking, talking, talking. Night or day, it didn't matter. Bella Vogel spoke of her anguish to anyone who would lis-

ten. Jake. My Jake. It had taken Leah a while to realize that
"my Jake" and "your tateh" were the same person.

Leah tried to remember her tateh. She remembered, vaguely, being tossed in the air; she thought she could remember
his laughter. Mama sometimes sang her a little hand-clapping
ditty—*"Potche, potche, kichalach"*—Clap, clap your little
hands—and she told Leah that her tateh always played that
game and sang that song to her. But although she tried very
hard to see him in her memory, she couldn't. She had no idea
what he looked like, except that Mama kept saying that
she, Leah, looked exactly like him. Whenever she said that,
she would hug Leah close, but it wasn't Leah's name she
murmured over and over. It was Jake, Jake, my Yankele, my
Jake.

Finally, there came that bright shining day when the sky and
the air were crystal clear and everyone came onto the deck,
even the sick ones who usually stayed below, moaning. It had
been raining for two terrible days, and then, like a miracle, the
rain had stopped and the clouds went flying across the sky,
turning into white tatters. On deck it was windy, and all the
women's skirts snapped back and forth, making a cracking
sound like laundry on the line. There were birds, swooping and
crying, and everyone was smiling.

Someone yelled, "There she is! The lady!" and everyone
went running to one side of the ship. A man's voice shouted,
"Be careful, you fools, you'll tip us over."

The deck slanted alarmingly, but who cared? Mama took her
hand and they ran, too. Mama said, "Keep this in your memory forever. It's America! And soon we will see Papa."

But when Leah tried to see what America looked like, she
could see nothing at all but a sea of legs and boots and skirts
and long, rusty black coats. She was too little, and there were
too many people crowding in front of her.

She began to cry. "I can't see America, Mama. I want to see
America! I want to see Papa!"

A pair of hands came out of nowhere and scooped her up,
holding her high over everyone's head. She would never forget
the surprise. Looming close to her was a giant green statue, a
woman with a stern face. She said something that made the
man who had picked her up roar with laughter. She remembered his big voice, his funny Polish accent as he told her, in
Yiddish, "No, no, *bubbele*, that's not America. That's the lady

with the lamp, the Statue of Liberty. Look past her . . . *that's* America!"

And then Leah saw the Golden Land; so many buildings rising up out of the ocean. How did they float? In the distance, a bridge, and more buildings, many more. And boats, with sails, with smokestacks, big boats, little boats, going back and forth, so busy.

Mama told her to put it into her memory forever, and she had. For the rest of her life, no matter how many magnificent sights she saw—and she had seen plenty—nothing ever struck her with such amazement.

"Leah!" Annie was laughing at her. "You're walking right by our building! Where is your mind?"

"Far away and long ago," Leah said, and then, with a wave of her hand, "Nothing, nothing. For some reason, I was remembering coming past the Statue of Liberty, to Ellis Island."

"Ellis Island!" Annie wrinkled her nose and spat three times—ptoo! ptoo! ptoo!—for good luck.

"Listen, it wasn't so wonderful at Ellis Island, but it brought you into the Golden Land, right? So there's no *ayin hora* looking at Ellis Island. There's no *ayin hora* in America, Annie! We left all that *narischkeit* behind, in the Old Country!"

At six sharp they presented themselves at the Katzes' place: three rooms, instead of their two, and facing the street rather than the gloomy courtyard. They had washed and changed into fresh shirtwaists for the Shabbos meal.

Leah found the whole ceremonial rite tedious and boring. So Mrs. Katz got to put a scarf on her head and bless the candles for the Sabbath . . . so what? Queen of the household! When Mrs. Katz's head was bent into her folded hands, you could see the back of her neck, how fresh and young the skin still was. But when she turned around! Her face was lined, grooved with worry and hard work, and when she smiled, which was seldom, she had to cover her mouth and duck her head, because so many of her teeth were missing.

Tonight she seemed even more weary than usual; but, as usual, her jolly husband did not notice.

"So, come on, Selma, what are we waiting for? The Messiah?" David Katz laughed loudly and clapped his hands. "We're hungry. Here we got three *working* people, you understand?"

"You think maybe Mrs. Katz didn't have to work, to put this

meal on the table?" Leah countered. Annie was scared to answer him back, but she wasn't. He wasn't a bad man, just thoughtless. He liked to laugh and joke, and he enjoyed it when Leah joked and laughed with him.

"What, her? Mrs. Katz has been cooking supper so many years, it practically cooks itself."

"Oh, really? Cooks itself? That's a wonderful invention, Mr. Katz. Maybe you should sell it! I know three hundred women would buy it, never mind the price!"

He threw his head back and roared. "Caught me! Okay, you're right and fair is fair. Selma, we thank you for working to make this delicious meal."

Little Mrs. Katz colored deeply and she smiled her tiny little smile, the one that hid her missing teeth. She was almost pretty when she smiled. "It's nothing," she said in Yiddish, and of course, immediately Mr. Katz had to make jokes about it.

"You see?" he said to Leah. "I was right! Even my wife says it was nothing! Nu, Selma, not so?"

"Okay, okay," Selma Katz said, but her eyes were baffled.

It really was mean of him to tease, because his wife didn't understand English very well. But on the other hand, Leah thought, why didn't she learn? It wasn't so hard, only at first. You had to *make* yourself talk English, even to the shopkeepers who would just as soon stick with Yiddish, and pretty soon it began to sound right. Even Annie, with her heavy accent, kept trying. So if Mr. Katz made fun of his wife, maybe in a way she deserved it.

Tonight, though, having had his amusement, he ignored her, and they had their supper in peace. The food was good; it was always good. No matter how little she had, Mrs. Katz managed somehow to stretch it out and make it seem like more. Tonight they had hot borscht with little shreds of meat and thick strips of cabbage; boiled beef, a small piece each, but very tasty, and plenty of potatoes, carrots, onions, beans, and thick gravy. And two huge braided challahs, for the Sabbath. Since it was October and apples were cheap, they had apple cake with their tea.

Once the meal was over, Leah said, "Annie, we can't stay long." Annie loved to play children's games with *der kinder.* That meant Leah would have two choices. She could help Mrs. Katz clean up—after a whole day sewing!—or she could stay at the table and match wits with Mr. Katz. Neither appealed to her tonight. Why Annie liked being with the horrible children, who always spent the entire meal kicking each other under the table, Leah didn't know. But she did; Annie's whole face lit up when she was with them.

Leah was dying to say good night and get out of there, but she reminded herself that poor Annie deserved a little of what she wanted, after all the terrible things she'd been through. Annie had told Leah a little about her life. How, after her parents' death, she had lived with a cruel aunt and uncle and had run away. How a man had rescued her, only to take advantage of her and force her to submit to him.

Leah had said, "Really? A man *did* it to you? So, tell me, what was it like? Was it nice?"

"It hurt. It was awful."

"It hurt? Oh Annie, how terrible. I wonder why so many people seem to like it?"

"I don't know. Maybe only *men* really like it!" Annie had told her.

And yet, Leah was positive that women liked it, too, longed for it, cried for it—the way her mama had cried for her Jake. Yet, here was Annie, saying she thanked God every day that she had escaped, and that it scared her to think about letting another man anywhere near her.

"A penny for your thoughts," Mr. Katz teased. Leah nearly jumped out of her chair. For a change, she had no ready answer. She could *never* say that she had been thinking about a man's . . . *thing*! She felt the heat climbing in her face. "Hoo-ha!" Mr. Katz laughed. "I think I can guess!"

He'd better not be able to guess! Leah got to her feet in a hurry. "Come on, Annie, it's time we left." She didn't wait for the other girl, but went racing out the door, the sound of Mr. Katz's laughter following her down the hall.

3

October 1910

Twenty-three Norfolk Street, corner of Hester, was no palace. Four apartments to each floor, two toilets in the hallway, tiny rooms, cramped and cold, with only a couple of windows to let in a light that was eternally gray and dingy. Their room was in the back of the Roths' apartment. But their little place, Leah thought as they walked in, was so much nicer than the Katzes', though it was just the one room. She and Annie had made themselves a beautiful coverlet from scraps and remnants and all the shelves were edged with ruffled material. And at least the toilet was just a few steps down the hall, not out in the courtyard like in her last place, where she had to go stumbling down all the stairs and outside, even in the freezing cold or pouring-down rain.

It was Saturday, and Leah and Annie had gone before dinner to the baths on Cherry Street for their weekly bath. If that's what you wanted to call it. For two cents you got a towel and a sliver of soap. Then, averting your eyes, you got into the big, round, communal tub where the water was always gray and felt greasy. You just had to pray you didn't get someone else's bugs, in that water. But so? At least you were wet!

They had washed each other's hair while the slippery little piece of soap kept spurting out of their wet hands. That always struck them as hilarious. Then they brushed each other's hair until it was shiny. Annie's thick curls always tried to resist the brush, and she would yell "Ow!" but add quickly, "No, don't stop. Pull!" In the end, it was no use. Annie's hair would kink up and curl tightly, no matter how long she brushed or how tightly she yanked.

"Never mind, Annie," Leah would say. "You have natural curl, and when you put it up, it *stays*. Not like mine, that slips

31

right out of the pins. By the time I'm finished with one dance, my pompadour is all crooked and half the pins are out."

"It doesn't matter about your pompadour. You're so pretty, Leah."

"And so are you. You want to know your trouble, Annie? Your trouble is you don't have enough faith in yourself. I know, I know, you've had a hard life and a lot of things have gone wrong. But now you're with me, Annie, and I'm lucky! And that means you're going to be lucky, too." But Annie always looked as if she didn't quite believe it.

She'd never forget the day Morris Levinsky put Annie at the machine next to hers, in the factory. The girl was a wreck, you could see that with just one look. Eyes downcast, hardly able to squeak out a "Yes, sir" when Levinsky explained to her what she had to do and then barked, "Understand me? *Verschtayst, du?* You'd better do a good job!"

"I will do my best," Annie said in her soft, tentative voice; only with her heavy accent, it came out, "I vill do mine bast." Instantly, Leah decided she would help this girl with her English.

She smiled. "You're a *greeneh?*"

The pale skin flushed. "My English is not so good. I try . . . I, how you say it, I practice, but—"

"Never mind, I'll help you."

"Oh, I cannot never sound so good, like you."

"Say, I've been here ten years. That's why I don't have an accent. Not because I'm anything special." But Annie Bernstein looked dubious. Just then Levinsky gave a holler, and Leah said, "We'd better start working or Horrible Morris will move you away."

At the lunch break, Leah turned to the new girl and said, "You'll come with me and we'll get what to eat. I'm Leah Vogel."

"I am Anna Bernstein—called Annie."

Leah took Annie Bernstein down the street to where Mrs. Silverman cooked knishes in her kitchen and sold them to the working girls in the neighborhood. You could get also a glass of tea. Though they ate their midday meal together, when the quitting bell clanged, Annie got lost in the bustling crowd and disappeared. But when Leah got out onto the street, she looked behind her. Sure enough, there was Anna Bernstein, lagging along, all alone, looking lost. Leah waited for her, and when she got close, said, "Nu, Annie? Where do you live? I'll walk with you."

First Annie smiled, but the smile wavered, and she suddenly burst into tears. "You have no place to go," Leah guessed.

Annie nodded, crying even more. And then she told Leah the whole story, how she had run away from her cruel relatives. How she had been tricked by a man who had promised to help her, and how she had gathered all her courage to escape from him with nothing but the clothes on her back. "I have nothing!" she wept. "Not even another dress!"

"Listen to me. You'll come with me tonight, and tomorrow we'll look for a bigger place. How about that? Tomorrow we'll go to Deena the pushcart lady and find some clothes for you. She has good used clothes, some of them from rich women, and all dirt cheap. You'll see . . . I'm a good *hondler.* I'll get you a bargain!"

And that was how it began. Leah just wished that Annie had a bit more gumption, wanted a little bit more out of life. But her dreams were ordinary dreams: to marry a man who wouldn't beat her, to have children, to keep house and be a good wife. It took all Leah's powers of persuasion to get Annie to stay in English class. She had to go with her every time to the Alliance, and keep reminding her to study because they were going to be schoolteachers. Be *somebody!* Not just some man's wife!

While they dressed and put up each other's hair, Annie said, "Mr. Katz, I wish he wouldn't joke with me. It makes me feel bad. I don't know what to answer to him."

" 'Answer him' . . . no 'to,' " Leah corrected automatically.

"I don't know what to answer him. I am not liking it."

" 'I don't like it.' Actually, Annie, Katz is better than most men. At least he loves his daughters. You don't hear him complaining they're no good for anything, that a man needs sons. Most of the men around here, they still think like in the Old Country, they're supposed to *daven* all day long in *shul,* talking to God. And meanwhile, who is doing everything else? Tell me, Annie, who?"

"I don't know, Leah."

"Their wives, Annie, the *women!*" She pulled the waist cincher too tight in her fervor, and Annie squeaked a protest. "Sorry, Annie, but just open your eyes and look around you! Mrs. Katz, Annie. Doesn't she always have piles of home work to do? Putting collars on shirts, that's what she does after she cooks, after she serves the meal, after she cleans up, after she puts the children to sleep. *Then* she sews. And look at her! Worn-out, missing half of her teeth! Not me, Annie, I swear to God that will not be me! And if I have to drag you by the hair, it's not gonna be you, either!"

"I only want a family of my own," Annie said. "That's enough for me."

"Listen, in the State of Washington—that's a state way out West, not Washington, D.C., where the President is . . ." Leah was proud of her knowledge. Well, you had to know a lot of these things if you wanted to get your citizenship. And she did! "It's thousands of miles from New York, but it's still part of America."

Annie shook her head at the wonder of it, the immenseness of the Golden Land. "Are there Jews there, in the State of Washington, Leah?"

"I'm sure there are! But what I'm trying to tell you, Annie, is that the State of Washington just gave women the right to vote. Do you realize what that means? That a woman can vote, in the State of Washington, just like a man!"

"I don't want to vote," Annie said, "I want to get married and have a family of my own."

"I'm your family," Leah said firmly, so firmly she almost believed it herself.

At last they were ready to go to the dance hall, wearing their best dresses of bombazine. Annie's was blue and Leah's wine-red. They had stopped that afternoon at the little shop where Mr. Marcus sold dry goods and bought new ribbons for their lockets, to match the dresses. They tied the lockets around each other's neck and then put their heads close together to look in the mirror.

"You're so beautiful, Leah!" Annie was always saying that.

"So are you, Annie dear!"

"I'm not so smart like you, Leah, but I have eyes."

"Poo! To me you're beautiful, and that means you're beautiful."

They were both laughing as they went running down the stairs and out of the building. Though it was a chilly night, several of the grandmothers and grandfathers were sitting in front of the building, complaining to each other about how awful their children treated them. Leah always wanted to stop and ask them, What would they do if their children didn't take them in, give them a bed, and put food into their mouths?

Then they would starve or freeze to death, and *then* she'd like to hear them complain!

Loudly, she said, "Come on, Annie, let's get away from here. I get sick from all the *kvetching!*"

"Leah, you shouldn't talk like that in front of them!"

"Well, what is it they want, anyway? Agh, who needs them? I'm glad I don't have a mother or a father to bother me!"

"Bite your tongue!"

"Oh, Annie! Such superstition!" But she had to admit, she had felt a twinge when she said it. Maybe her mother was still alive. She didn't know for sure. She could be living in this neighborhood; maybe they passed each other a hundred times and didn't realize it. Or didn't recognize each other. Would she know what her mother looked like after so many years? Would her mother know *her?*

As for her father . . . her mind went skittering away from him, as it always did. Still, she remembered clearly how they had to wait for him, on Ellis Island. He wasn't there to meet them. Her mother ran back and forth, looking through the screen for him, wringing her hands and calling on God to protect her from the perfidy of men.

They had to stay the night on Ellis Island. They had to eat in the huge, echoing dining room with the long, heavy tables and so many strangers, so many different languages being spoken! Leah liked Ellis Island. It didn't stink of rotten fish, like the boat, and at last she was free of the dreaded clanking and thudding of the ship's engines. And there were other children; they played together, making up games without words. The other mothers smiled at her and patted her cheeks. She had already forgotten the little house outside Kiev, the rutted road and the vegetable garden out back.

Her tateh would soon come to get them, and then her mother would stop moaning and they would all live happily ever after. She prayed for it; it was so terrible when her mother was unhappy.

He must have come and it must have been a joyous reunion; but she couldn't recall it. One minute he wasn't there, and the next thing she remembered was getting off the ferryboat in New York and walking between her father and Mama as they talked above her head. The city! The noise, the din, the stink of fish—again! For a long time she thought rotting fish was the odor of the Golden Land. Shouts from sailors aloft in the rigging of ships, sirens screaming, bells ringing, wagons piled

high, rolling—in all directions, it seemed to the little girl—
pulled by large, snorting horses and driven by men who hollered and called out in words she had never heard before.

There were so many boys, she remembered; boys in knick-
ers and caps, pointing at her parents and hooting and calling
out in a strange language. She moved in closer to her father's
leg; she remembered him looking down at her, smiling,
squeezing her hand.

"Carry her, Jake. She's so little."

"A big girl like this? Carry? What do you say, little one?
Shall Tateh carry you like a baby?"

"Oh, yes!" He bent to pick her up, laughing, and there she
was, high above the strangeness and the din, safe at last.

Soon they came to a big wide street, lined with tall buildings and jammed with horses, wagons, carts, and people, hundreds and hundreds of people, all moving as fast as they could,
bumping into each other, yelling, shrieking, shouting. Over her
head a rumbling monster belched smoke and sent showers of
fire down on them. She began to cry and hid her head in
Tateh's shoulder, sobbing, *"Vilde chaya, vilde chaya!"*

"Sha, sha mameleh. It's only a train. Can you say 'train'?
It's the elevated subway. A machine that people ride on. Soon,
I will take you on a ride and you will see it's not a wild animal
at all. Okay? Okay?"

It was the first time she had heard that word, and, timidly,
she tried it out. "Hokay."

Tateh laughed and kissed her. "You'll do fine, my pretty
grineleh, my adorable greenhorn! You'll do just fine in America!"

And she had, but no thanks to him! As usual, her anger was
the signal to stop thinking about him. She was relieved when
Annie started talking about the Edison phonograph they were
saving up to buy. Annie loved all dance music, the faster the
better; she was a very good dancer, too. It was such a surprise.
The girl who could trip over her own feet, who constantly
bumped into things and knocked things over, who seemed not
to know where her own body began and ended . . . put that girl
onto the dance floor and start the music, and she was transformed. Annie's feet didn't have to think where to go, they just
went. But she couldn't sing, couldn't hold a tune at all; and
worst of all, couldn't hear when she went off. Leah didn't have
the heart to tell her, but how she suffered whenever Annie sang
along with her!

Between the two of them, the singer and the dancer, it was no surprise that their favorite fantasy was having enough money to buy one of the new Edison phonographs. They had been shopping way uptown, and on Herald Square there was a tall building with a huge sign that had a picture of the phonograph on it, and in big letters, THE EDISON PHONOGRAPH PUTS MUSIC IN EVERY HOME.

Those were magical words to Leah and Annie. If ever there was something they wanted, it was to have music in *their* home. Leah knew they couldn't afford it; but Annie was a different story. To her, all dreams were just a step away from reality. So, for a week she went without lunch to save money, until she fainted over her work one afternoon from hunger. Leah had to scold her.

"No more starving yourself, you hear me, Annie?" she said. "I'll save along with you, and before you know it, we'll have our Edison. But no more going without meals! Is it a deal?"

"Is deal," Annie agreed. Her English was still mostly a matter of sometimes yes, sometimes no. But, Leah told herself, it *was* improving, no matter how slowly.

The streets of the Lower East Side were alive on Saturday night. The day of rest, prayer, and contemplation was over and it was time to play . . . or, for some, time to get back to work. Many of the factories that closed for Shabbos opened as soon as the sun sank in the west; and the streets that were empty of men all week long once again filled as they went back to work so their children wouldn't starve. Peddlers were back out, hawking their wares; bakeries were open; and young people, dressed in their finery, crowded into the many dance halls that lined Delancey Street, Hester Street, Norfolk Street. Every other building had a dance hall on its second floor where, each Saturday night, musicians played the latest tunes from shows, both Yiddish and English, and from the song pluggers' new hits.

As they strolled along, eyeing the young men who eyed them, stopping to admire a piece of material or a hat, they could hear the sounds of fiddle and saxophone and accordian, tootling "Let Me Call you Sweetheart" and "Minnie the Moocher" and "Put Your Arms Around Me, Honey, Hold Me Tight."

Annie tugged on Leah's arm, her feet tapping impatiently every time Leah stopped to look at something or to talk to someone.

"Come, Leah, they're starting already. All week, I wait to dance Saturday night. Come, come!"

Leah let herself be dragged along. She did not want Annie to know that she hung back, always hoping to see Joe Lazarus. She wondered if he lived around there; if he liked to go to the dances on Saturday night. Oh, how she hoped so! It was stupid of her, she knew that. Joe Lazarus had a business in Coney Island and he probably lived in far-off Brooklyn. Anyway, what was Joe Lazarus to her—other than the man she kept thinking about and dreaming about and looking for every time she went out?

So, up the flight of stairs they went, and into the dance hall. Chairs were lined up around the walls, with boys sitting and standing on one side, girls on the other, leaning into each other, chattering and giggling, while their eyes roved along the line across the room.

No sign of Joe Lazarus, of course; but Leah was not surprised to spot Harry Fink. He grinned broadly when he saw her and came right over, bowing from the waist and asking her if he might have the honor and the privilege. She couldn't help laughing at him, he was so good-humored and full of fun. And she knew he made sure to be where she was, whenever he could.

"You do do the turkey trot, Miss Vogel?"

"Of course." Who didn't do the turkey trot? It was all the craze. "*I* don't think it's indecent, Mr. Fink, do you?"

"Me? I think men and women should *always* dance so close."

They laughed and began to dance. "I read that Mr. Bok, the editor of the *Ladies' Home Journal*, fired fifteen girls on the spot when he found them dancing the turkey trot during their lunch break," she told him.

"People are crazy, you know that? Especially when they get old! Well, we sing a little song about that," he said with a laugh, and held her closer to sing in her ear: " 'Rosie, Rosie Rosenblatt . . . don't you do that turkey trot!' But we do it, don't we, Miss Vogel, because we're real Yankees and we do all the animal dances. The grizzly bear . . ."

"The bunny hug," Leah added, and again they laughed.

Harry Fink wasn't a very good dancer, but he had sharp remarks to make about everyone else on the dance floor, and he kept her so amused, she hardly noticed. It was too bad she couldn't warm up to him; it was a real *shandah*. But either the spark was there or it wasn't. In the case of Harry Fink, it wasn't.

He noticed Annie's dancing; everyone always did. "Wow, look at your friend. She's terrific!"

"So why don't you ask her to dance?"

"I'd rather be with you and have my toes trampled."

"The nerve of you! I haven't stepped on—oh. A joke."

"A bad one, I see. I'd rather be with you in any case."

"I'm sorry to hear that, Mr. Fink. I'd rather you danced with my friend Annie."

He turned red, and she was instantly sorry she had been so blunt. He seemed so lighthearted, she hadn't thought he would be hurt. "I guess you can't be plainer than that. I should be grateful. But I'll tell you something, Miss Vogel, I'm not."

"Listen, I'm really sorry—"

He waved off her apologies. "Yeah, yeah. Maybe you should try to be a little more careful with that mouth of yours. But I'll take your advice, anyway." And he was gone, leaving her standing like an idiot in the middle of the floor, while he bowed to Annie and said something that made her blush.

The rest of the evening was just like it always was. Leah danced, chatted, smiled, she danced some more. Why could she never seem to find a man to please her? The girls at the factory said she was too picky and particular; maybe they were right. But she didn't want to take just anyone, she didn't want to settle for a man who was just all right. She wanted her head to spin and her heart to stop ... she wanted fireworks and shooting stars and ... and *everything*! It might be Joe Lazarus could give her all that; but it didn't look like she was ever going to see him again, so she might as well forget him.

Several of the young men asked to see them home, but in the end she and Annie walked by themselves. She knew Annie was disappointed, but Annie just had to set her sights a lot higher, that's all.

You'll see, Annie, Leah silently promised, marching along, pulling the other girl with her. One day, when we're little old ladies looking back on lives full of success and independence, then you'll realize. Then you'll say, "Leah, you know what? You were right all along."

4

March 1911

It was a regular Saturday, quitting time four forty-five. As usual, Levinsky took his sweet time handing out the pay envelopes and ringing the quitting bell. Annie was particularly high-spirited today, Leah noted, and she guessed it was on account of Jack Kamenetsky. He was the baker Annie had met at the dance last Saturday. Jack was definitely interested, and Annie found him wonderful. Of course, Leah kept telling herself, Annie wasn't going to *marry* him. When she asked, Annie said, "I'm not even sure I love him, Leah, so how could I think about marrying?" But she wouldn't look Leah in the eye and she blushed deeply.

Annie was very happy this afternoon, humming a little tune as they got ready to leave. Leah was probably the only one who could recognize it as "Oh, You Beautiful Doll." She hoped she wasn't going to lose Annie to *narischkeit*; nonsense.

It was time for them to be on their way, out of there permanently. She was sick to death of sitting at the machine almost every day of her life, rocking back and forth, mindlessly sewing whatever was handed to her. She was beginning to feel like a machine herself!

But she didn't like dwelling on it, so she took up the song: ". . . you great big beautiful doll . . ." Leah warbled, just as if she and Annie were both on top of the world.

"Ever since you bought yourselves that Edison phonograph, you have to show off how many songs you know!" Angie called out, and Leah waved to her without answering. She was also tired of all the wisecracks directed at them everytime she and Annie did anything different to make their lives better. How could the rest of them settle for this tedious, backbreaking excuse for existence?

She was sick of it all, of everything always the same: the slow single-file move through the narrow doorway, while Morris pawed through their purses; the dash into the dressing room to snatch up their coats; and then, down the stairs and out.

Then, today suddenly, it was horribly different. There was a crackling sound, and a terrible heat, and screams rose up from the eighth floor. When they rounded the landing, flames leaped up at them, swaying and panting like living things.

Leah had only one idea: Get out, run, escape! "Come on, Annie! As fast as you can! Hold on and *run*!"

Gripping the railing, Leah raced down, past the heat and the fire, skidding and sliding, willing herself to stay upright. She was alone on the stairs, her heart was pounding in her chest, her ears, her mouth. Where *was* everyone?

She was so sure Annie was right behind her; Annie was always willing to follow her. But then she realized there were no footsteps behind her. She stopped, breathing hard, and turned, her whole body quivering.

"Annie! Annie!" No answer. No Annie. Of course not! She was a *dumbkopf*. Annie had probably stopped in her tracks, frozen, the minute she saw those hungry flames. Then where was she? Why wouldn't she answer?

"Annie, Annie!" Leah screamed at the top of her lungs. "Annie, answer me!" Nothing.

She had to get her. Gathering her skirts high, she began to take the stairs back up, two, three at a time. Suddenly, a bulky form moved in front of her. She looked up, dazed. A fireman in his oilskins and big hat. "You can't go up there."

"My friend!" she cried, frantic. "My friend. I have to go get her!"

"You can't go get her, miss. And if you want to stay alive, turn around, go back down!" As she hesitated, he gave her a little push. "Down!" he barked.

So, down she went, sobbing. She had no choice. She passed other women, shoving at them to get them out of her way. At the bottom she stopped, suddenly aware that one side of her coat was scorched. When did that happen?

Firemen stood at the bottom, blocking the doorway, waiting while a few others came running down the stairs. One woman's hair was on fire, and the minute she stopped, the others used their hands and scarves to smother it. The smell was horrible. Then the firemen opened the door and led them out into the street, telling them, "Go home. Go home."

Leah went only as far as the sidewalk. There, she waited, stopping everyone who came out or walked by. "Do you know Annie Bernstein?" "Have you seen a tall fair girl in a blue coat and shiny brown boots?"

Annie had buffed those boots with her own hands, last night. She loved pretty shoes, and she had bargained with a pushcart peddler with all her might to get them for fifty cents. She had neat little feet, and she was proud of them. Shoes and boots were her great weakness, maybe her only weakness. Leah began to cry, like a lost child. Where was she? Annie! Annie!

"My friend Annie Bernstein? Did you see her? Is she all right?" But everyone either shook their heads or walked by her as if they couldn't hear.

Then a strange sound rose all around her, like a melancholy wind rising. Everyone on the street was looking up, and she looked up too. And cried out. It was so awful. Girls were crawling out onto the window ledges, bunching their skirts up carefully. Then, holding hands, with loud cries, they jumped, one by one, two by two, from windows that were filled with roaring flames. Not Annie, please God, not Annie! The thought of Annie, paralyzed with fright in the middle of the heat and the greedy roar, wrenched Leah's heart. She heard a voice screaming, "No! No! No!" It was her voice.

The *thunk . . . thunk . . . thunk* of bodies hitting the sidewalk was awful. How could it be, that you could hear soft bodies, when all around there was banging and screaming and shrieking and the loud crackle of the fire as it consumed everything in its path! And then the dreadful sound stopped because bodies were falling on top of bodies, silently. She did not know if she could stand much more. A sour taste rose in her throat and she wanted to vomit. But she couldn't; she had to find Annie.

Firemen were running to the pile of bodies, lifting them, carrying them across the street, stacking them neatly. *Neatly*. The thought gave her the shudders, but she ran to them, pushing aside dead hands and dead feet, searching. She looked into faces without any signs of violence on them, but without life, looking for Annie's face. She began to shove at the limp heavy bodies, trying to roll them over. Suddenly, she shrieked and pulled her hand away, because something was stirring there. Then she scolded herself, not a ghost, not a spirit, but a miracle. Someone was still alive! With all her strength she shoved aside an inert body to find underneath a dark-haired girl, a bruise on her cheek, her dress dirty, but breathing. "Miss," Leah said, bending close. "You're going to be fine. I'm going to get help."

The girl's lips moved, but only the feeblest of whispers came out. Leah bent so that her ear was next to her mouth; but she could make out nothing.

She got up, ran to a policeman and told him that there was a girl over there, still alive. "Thanks be to God. Henry! Get a stretcher and hurry!"

Her heart hammered with hope. Maybe Annie, too, was still alive. If God could save this girl, surely He could save Annie Bernstein. Annie had been behind her. So did she jump? Wouldn't she have seen Annie jumping, recognizing her bright red boa? But she could have dropped the boa, lost it. Maybe she went out another way. Maybe she was searching through the crowd even now, calling her name. Yes, any minute, now, Leah would hear her, calling.

But then she saw the boot, the familiar russet button boot, the sole recently retipped, and a painful sob tore from her throat. Annie's boot, she'd know it anywhere. And next to it, the other foot with the boot gone, the brown stocking with its neat mend . . . Annie. There were . . . others . . . on top. Wailing, Leah clawed through the other bodies, pushing and shoving with newfound strength, shuddering and shivering, but determined.

Finally she had Annie, lying there, looking so . . . regular, so normal, just like she was sleeping. Maybe she was still alive. She *had* to be. "Annie, wait here, Annie don't move!" Leah got up and ran, splashing through the puddles, to a nearby group of men. Some of them were firemen. She tugged at the nearest one's arm. "Come! Come! Hurry! A girl is alive!"

They came in a hurry, but even so, she beat them. She stood, her knuckles in her mouth, crying and praying as they carefully lifted the other bodies away from Annie. When they placed her on the ground, Leah saw that Annie's shirtwaist was torn and . . . her locket was gone! Who would steal from a dead girl, who?

Falling to her knees, she felt under the skirts for the little bag of money Annie sewed into her petticoat. Gone!

She turned her face up to the men, trying to shout, her voice weak. "They've taken all her money! And her locket! I have to find the locket! She'll be so upset!"

Strong arms lifted her up, put her on her feet, and a kind

voice said, "I'm very sorry, miss, someone must have done it when we first laid her out here."

"She'll have a fit! Who would take a poor girl's money, a poor girl's locket! The money maybe she could forget, but we *have* to get her locket back!"

"Miss . . ." Strong hands tried to make her move; she wouldn't. "Miss, please. Your friend isn't going to miss her locket. I'm very sorry, but your friend is . . . gone."

"Look, I have one like it! We bought them together! It's very important! Very important!"

"Look, miss," a policeman said. "We're going to clear the area now. It could be that we'll find your friend's necklace. This is a terrible thing, terrible, terrible. But you must go home now. Do you have someone to walk with you?"

Then it hit her, like a fist in her chest. Annie was dead. Annie was dead. She had no one to walk her home; in fact, she would never have someone to go home with, never again. She slumped to her knees and began to weep again, holding her face in her hands.

When she looked up, she promised herself, she would not see Annie's face, mouth agape, eyes shuttered; it would not be Annie's body, hardly touched, hardly singed, but still, so still. It would all be nothing but a bad dream. But when she lifted her head from her hands, it was still horribly the same. The fire engines snorting and clanging like huge beasts; the horrible odor of burnt flesh and burnt hair; the sounds of charred timbers cracking and falling inside the Asch Building; the sounds of the bodies hitting the ground. The bodies! Her friends, women she worked with every day . . . Angie, Celia, Fanny, Rosa, Dorothy . . . Annie, dear God, *Annie*!

A wave of heat swept through her body. She thought she would topple over in a faint. She wanted to faint; she wanted to die. She threw her head back and opened her mouth and wailed. Not Annie! Not Annie! They had so many things to do, so many things to talk about, so many plans! They were going to move in the fall!

"What am I going to do?" Leah sobbed. "What am I going to do without you, Annie? Oh, Annie! Please!"

Everyone thought Leah led Annie around by the nose. But they didn't know how much she needed Annie, needed her smile and Annie's faith in her, her total trust, her tenderness. Oh God! In the night, when Leah had her worst dream—the one where her mother smiled at her and reached out her hand

and, just as Leah was about to grab hold, her mother began to fade away until there was nothing, nothing at all—she would cry out and sit up in the bed, drenched in cold sweat. And Annie would hold her and rock her, like a baby, smoothing her hair and singing a Russian lullaby. Oh, how beautiful it always sounded to Leah! And now, never again to have that warmth, that comfort! She had lost her best friend, her family; she had lost everything!

On her knees by Annie's body, Leah wept loudly, shaking with grief, her chest wracked with pain. It felt like the end of the world. It *was* the end of the world.

"I'm so sorry, miss, but you must leave the area." The policeman still stood next to her. She had forgotten his very existence. He helped her to her feet and she swayed unsteadily.

She saw the photographer then, darkly silhouetted against the flames and spurting water, his camera in his hands. He was taking pictures of *her*, she realized. He dared to poke his rotten nose and his rotten camera into her grief to make pictures out of it, for strangers to gawk at! Oh God, the *momzer*, the bastard!

A cry was torn from her vitals, a howl of outrage and fury. All of a sudden the legs that had felt as limp as dishrags a moment earlier were carrying her at a run, right for him. She would kill him. She would scratch his eyes out of his head. She would tear him apart with her own two hands!

She flung herself at him, beating at him with her fists, shrieking sounds, not words, tears streaking down her face. She reached for his hair, knocking off his hat, and pulled with all her might. But he was stronger than she. He grabbed both her hands, holding her away from him, shouting, "*Genug*, enough, enough already! It's okay. I didn't take any pictures of you! I didn't take any pictures of you! Do you hear me? *Do you hear me?* I didn't take your picture!"

All at once she ran out of steam and went limp. He threw his arms around her to keep her from falling. He told her it was going to be all right, it was going to be fine. She shook her head and wept. Nothing was going to be fine; everything was wrong, everything was finished, she had nothing!

He half walked, half dragged her around the corner, where it was a little bit quieter, and sat her down on the front steps of a building. He sat her next to him, holding her while she sobbed against the rough wool of his overcoat.

Finally she was able to stop, and she pulled away from him.

"Thank you," she managed, her voice clogged with tears. "I . . . it was too much—"

"I understand. Believe me. Here . . ." He wiped her eyes and her wet face with his handkerchief, his touch firm yet gentle. She was grateful not to have to think or move or do anything. She let him smooth the hair away from her cheeks and button the top button of her coat, for she had begun to shake and shiver as if caught in a terrible icy draft. Her teeth chattered.

Again he held her until the chill had passed; and when it did, she was able to look him right in the face.

"Why, it's the little bird who flew off so fast and never returned," he said. "I'm so terribly sorry, Miss Vogel. Was it . . . your friend? The fair-haired girl?"

His use of her name startled her into awareness, and now she really looked at him. Joe Lazarus. What a cruel God, to bring him to her side and take Annie away, all at the same time. Her hand flew to her neck, to make sure the ribbon was still there. Her locket at least was safe, and with it the only picture of Annie she had . . . would *ever* have.

"Yes. My friend. Annie." That was all she could get out. The tears she had thought must be used up started once more. "She's dead! She's dead!"

"Oh my God, I'm so sorry for your trouble! I'm so sorry. . . ."

"They stole her money! They took the locket from her neck!"

"The *momzers*! Don't worry, I'll be watching for it. You can count on me. I'll go to all the hockshops. If it's there to be found, I'll find it. I'll make it okay for you, I swear."

"I have to get her! She has to have someone to—" Her throat closed, but she forced the words out. "—to bury her. And I'm the only family she's got!" Leah struggled to get to her feet. Her head was spinning.

"We'll do it together, Miss Vogel."

"Me and . . . you?"

"Me . . . and you. Yes. So, shhh, don't think about it anymore."

He held his arms out, and without thinking, she crawled into them, sobbing aloud like a child, feeling safe in his embrace, warmed by his body heat and comforted by his strength.

5

October 1913

"Indian summer on Barrow Street! Just look at those leaves! Just look at the blue of the sky! It makes you want to write poetry. No, it makes you wish somebody'd invent color film for the camera!" Joe Lazarus leaned dangerously far out of the third-story window and breathed in dramatically.

"Joe!" Leah protested, coming in from their bedroom at the back of the apartment. "For God's sake! You'll fall!"

He hauled himself obediently back inside and, turning to her, gave a little whistle. "Wearing your pneumonia blouse? You'll have them buzzing at Bertolotti's."

Leah gave him a little smile, preening. She had on the latest style, a V-neck tunic over a very narrow ankle-length skirt that forced her to walk in mincing little steps. That always made Joe laugh. "Amazing," he kept saying, "what women will put up with for the sake of fashion!" And what about those high starched collars men had to wear! Now, he was teasing her about the V-neck on her blouse. The low-cut vee had inspired every preacher and prude in the country to rail and rant about the depths to which modern woman had sunk, about how demeaning and disgusting it was. So of course it pleased her to wear the blouse often.

"The crowd at Bertolotti's wouldn't notice if I walked in stark naked," she said, putting the second ear bob into her ears. "Nothing surprises them. Or at least that's what they pretend."

Joe put his arm around her to pull her close. "You, my lovely Leah, are *full* of surprises!" He nuzzled into her neck, then said, "Those damn earrings. I want a nip of your plump little earlobe . . . my favorite part of you . . . well, my second-favorite part. . . ."

"Joe! Stop! I just got dressed! Come on, you loon! Let me

47

be! And go get dressed! I'm starving!" But she was laughing, and as he walked into the back room, he was, too. Life with Joe Lazarus was full of laughter. A little disorderly, but fun. Who would have thought it? she marveled. Little Leah Vogel from the Lower East Side, in a flat in Greenwich Village and living in sin, yet! Two years ago, a sewing machine operator in a factory, toiling for wages, scrimping along, boarding with a family as poor as she, owning three dresses, a phonograph, and not much more.

And now! She looked around, filled with satisfaction. "Put your arms around me honey, hold me tight . . ." she caroled, hugging herself. Didn't she always know she was lucky?

She loved this flat. They had the left half of number 35 Barrow Street, which amounted to a large front room, a back bedroom, and a windowless space in between that contained a small gas stove, sink, and a little cabinet with the toilet. But to her it was a palace. No more walking down the hall, hoping you won't bump into the neighbors! And when you looked out of the big arched window, you didn't see the dingy back of another tenement; you saw the curve of Commerce Street as it met Barrow, the trees and the narrow, pretty houses crowded into the bend, huddling up and cuddling up—just like the song. They weren't far from the Lower East Side if you counted in miles . . . but what a difference! Everytime she woke up and realized where she was, her whole body was flooded with happiness.

It was funny about her and Joe, about how they came to be living together in an apartment in the Village, living the Bohemian life. It began right after the fire. Joe had taken to hanging around, making sure she was okay. He was like a pal. He never touched her, although, of course, she wished that he would. She dreamed of his lips on hers, prayed for it, longed for it. He was so handsome, so clever, so quick; he was going places, she just knew it. He was the man for her. So why couldn't *he* see it? Why was he so blind?

But it seemed as if Joe had different ideas about her, and none of them romantic. Joe insisted that she had a way with words . . . no, that she had talent. "Yes, I'm talking about your big mouth, Leah! Use it! It's a gift, I'm telling you."

"You think maybe I should tell jokes at bar mitzvahs and weddings?"

"No, I'm talking about important things."

"For instance?"

"For instance, I think you should put it in writing—the way you feel about the Triangle fire. You were there, Leah, and the way you describe it . . . well, I can see it again, and smell it. I can feel what you're feeling. Write it down!"

"Put it down for what? For who? Will it bring Annie back?" The mere mention of Annie's name made her voice quaver.

"Words make a difference. Believe me, I wish I could use words the way you do. But I can't, so instead I take pictures. And I don't know how much good they'll do until they finally figure out how to print photographs in the newspapers! Wait!" He snapped his fingers and began to grin. "I've got it! Write a letter to the editor, to all the editors! I'll get the names and addresses, I'll even mail them for you!"

Well, he nagged her, he pleaded with her, he yelled at her. So finally she did it. Wrote a fiery letter to the *Tribune*. "We are poor girls," she wrote, "who slave six days a week in the factories to avoid a life of shame. And they give us a firetrap to work in. Then we go home and the same landlords give us a firetrap to live in! Why is there no safe place for us? We are condemned to two kinds of Hell!"

She ended her letter saying she hoped that the acquitted Triangle owners would rot in Hell, and with a plea for new regulations for building owners. Not only did the *Trib* print it, every single word, with her name at the end, too, but they made a special box for it. The headline read: ONE OF THE FIRE'S VICTIMS SPEAKS OUT AGAINST 'TWO KINDS OF HELL FOR WORKING GIRLS.' The editor wrote a little about her and her letter and urged the city fathers to reform New York's building codes and insurance laws.

As if that wasn't enough, her letter brought in so much mail that the editor wrote and asked her to come by his office. He wanted to do a *series*, six or seven stories on shop girls, their exploitation by the greedy bosses, their struggles, their lives. A Yankee newspaper, in English, and they wanted the thoughts of an immigrant girl! No wonder it was called the Golden Land!

The day she met with the editor, Leah went home like one in a dream, floating above the ground, her head in a daze. Joe was on the stoop, waiting to take her to supper, his hat tipped at its usual cocky angle. He didn't see her, so she was able to study him as she approached. She loved the way he looked, his thick hair and mustache, his quick grin, his twinkly eyes. In fact, she loved all of him. Not that she'd ever let *him* know.

When he looked up and saw her, he smiled. His smile

slowly broadened, and he got up to go to her, his eyes never leaving hers. She stood where she was, barely able to breathe.

He didn't even say hello, just, "Come, Leah. It's time for you to see my place." He took her hand, holding it so tightly it hurt a little. But she dared not say anything, for fear he would let go of her, and she did not want him to let go. Not ever.

He headed uptown at a furious pace; she had to trot to keep up. That day, she got her first real look at the Village. She thought it was beautiful, a real neighborhood, old and peaceful, where real people lived. She had known where it was, of course; she had walked to Washington Arch with all the others, the day of the Triangle Fire funeral parade. But it seemed very different, walking up Waverly Place hand in hand with Joe Lazarus. He had tucked her arm under his, and she could feel his muscle under his coat. A small shiver crawled up her back. She knew something was about to happen. She could feel it, like a heat in her blood. Everything else left her mind, everything, even her writing assignment from the newspaper.

Joe's flat was at the top of an old building on West Eighth Street; a cramped studio overflowing with papers, crowded with equipment, smelling strongly of photographic chemicals. He swept away the clothes heaped onto his bed, and then he turned to her. She stood waiting, her heart hammering in her ears.

"Leah, I think . . . Leah, I've been thinking . . . oh hell. Leah, I love you. I love you. Am I a fool to think you feel . . . the same?"

She could not speak. She stared at him, her eyes filling, shaking her head. No, no, a fool you're not.

"Oh God! I've been waiting . . . so long!" He wrapped his arms tightly around her, bending his mouth to hers, kissing her urgently, sucking on her lips and moaning a little. She was so dizzy and breathless, she was sure she would fall to the floor in a faint if he let her go. But he did not let her go. Still kissing her and murmuring incoherent words into her ear, he walked them together to the bed, and together they fell onto it.

She could never remember how her clothes came off her body. She did remember him peeling his own clothing away, layer by layer. He was very muscular—his shoulders and upper arms bulged out—and very hairy. And of course she remembered her first sight of his cock, engorged with blood, standing straight out from his belly, twitching a little. All she could think was *oy, Gott*, how does he expect to get that great big thing into me?

The pain was nothing compared to the wonderful sensations he brought out in her. She bit her lips and refused to cry out. He buried his head in her neck and pushed into her with great thrusts, groaning with pleasure, muttering sweet things in a strangled whisper. When it was over, he fell asleep, and she lay on his bed, hurting, a little disappointed—was this all there was to it?—but supremely happy. Because he loved her, he really loved her. And after this, surely they would get married.

Moving through their front room now, straightening pictures on the wall, waiting for Joe to finish shaving, Leah shook her head at her former, naive self. What a ninny she had been to think about marriage! Everyone in the know said marriage was a trap that only led to dishonesty between men and women. Wedlock was a false convention, bourgeois and unequitable.

At first she hadn't quite gone for it, but now she was convinced. After all, these were modern times and she was a modern woman. And how much better it was, the way she and Joe lived like equals, each loving the other, each free to love others. Nobody was forced to pretend; nobody was enslaved forever to a relationship that had gone dead. It was the way everyone they knew thought and lived; and she agreed that it all made perfect sense. The only trouble, as she had found over the last year, was that she was still full of stupid, bourgeois jealousy.

Women were always after Joe. He was so alive, so full of fun. And when they sat on his lap or ran their fingers through his thick, dark hair, she could feel a solid weight settle in her chest.

"Why don't you push them away?" she asked him. "Why don't you tell them you belong to me?"

"Leah, darling, nobody can *belong* to another person. That's called slavery, and Mr. Lincoln put an end to it, remember?" He pulled her close to him. "My sweet Leah, I don't have to push them away. They mean nothing to me. They don't affect me at all, none of them, whereas *you* . . ." Taking her hand, he put it on the hard bulge between his thighs. In a minute they were in each other's arms, undressing each other, kissing whatever happened to come nearest their mouths, laughing as they made love.

She knew he was in love with her, just as she loved him. The proof, Joe kept telling her, was the fact that they were faithful to each other "without a marriage license, because we don't need a piece of paper to tell us how we feel. And that makes it even better, don't you see that, sweetheart?"

She always said yes, she saw it. But when Jane Armstrong the actress, so beautiful, so flirtatious, wound her arm into his and called him her Gypsy man, saying, "You would look so beautiful with gold earrings, Joe Lazarus, and a bright scarf tied around your head . . . wouldn't he?" giving Leah a laughing look, her bright red lips pouting, Leah found herself wishing, no *longing*, for a rabbi to say the blessings over them so that all the Jane Armstrongs would know that Joe Lazarus was *hers*.

Don't be silly, she scolded herself now, still waiting for him to get dressed. Joe *is* yours, and he loves you. Restless, she studied his photographs, hung on every wall. Dramatic shafts of dusty light; cracks and holes in a wall, taken up close so that suddenly they weren't the signs of poverty, they were interesting designs. And the group of tenement boys dressed like ragged Gypsies, leaning on each other, grinning. They looked so devil-may-care, so cocky. But she knew they were probably hungry, every one of them. Leah wasn't so sure it was such a good idea, making poverty look artistic, so that you almost forgot people were actually forced to *live* in those hovels; that real rats lived in those dramatic-looking holes; that those boys were poor and cold in their picturesque rags.

But she seemed to be the only one who felt that way. Joe's pictures were published in established magazines; and now that Leah was a muckraker, going into the slums and sweatshops to expose their hidden horrors, she was, too. She really preferred the small radical magazines, though. You didn't have to be careful how you said things. You could tell the *whole* story, and the editor loved it.

Alongside Joe's photographs hung drawings and paintings by their friends, even a sketch on a linen handkerchief, done one lunchtime by Herb Roth, between the salad and the dessert. Next to the front door hung a huge canvas, all bright clashing oranges and greens and purples, dominating the wall. The painting was crowded with big naked women; women with large sagging breasts and bellies, huge lumpy hips, and giant thighs. Leah could hardly bear to look at it; there was something spoiled about the colors, and the nude women always made her think of rotting meat. It was labeled *Call to Arms*, and she hated it. Nevertheless, she ran a finger over the scrawled signature on the bottom: Walter Morris. She loathed the painting; *and* the painter.

At last Joe was finished and they went out into the rich golden sunshine and sweet winy autumn air. He fished in his pockets and came up with a handful of small change. He gave a sharp little whistle. "Well, I guess we'd better stick with the fifteen-cent lunch and a bottle of Angelo's dago red," he said. "Harper's paid me, but that went for the rent and supplies. As for Jim McCready . . . he's always got an excuse."

"*The Future* isn't commercial, Joe. And Jim always pays in the end." She felt a bit proprietary about Jim McCready; he was *her* most faithful publisher. In fact, he had recently asked her to write for *The Future* every month, on a regular basis, and he was going to put her name on the masthead as Contributing Editor.

Joe snorted at the title. "Sure! You go into that cramped basement on Little West Twelfth Street he has the nerve to call an office, and you slave for him! That's what you contribute!"

She disagreed. She did not consider reading manuscripts slaving, nor licking stamps, nor running to the post office, no, nor even sweeping the floor from time to time. She liked doing chores at *The Future*. It was like a family there; a family where everyone believed in the same things. When enough copies were sold, they all got paid and Jim brought wine to celebrate. And when sales were down . . . well, they all took less, even Jim.

"He always pays in the end," she repeated.

"Well, let him pay in the middle!" Joe laughed loudly. "In the middle of the month! Get it? Not bad, eh?"

They took Barrow Street to Bleecker, where people in all sorts of costumes and getups bustled back and forth. There were people from all over America, freethinkers, socialists, communists, with every kind of idea, every kind of notion. And yet it was so quiet; not like the Lower East Side, with its din of Yiddish and Polish and Russian, the shouting, the yelling, the selling!

"Say, speak of the devil, there's McCready across the street! Come on, Leah, let's catch up with him and rag him about not paying us! I bet he'll stand an extra bottle if we make him feel bad!"

Joe didn't mean it; he didn't say a word to Jim. He liked to talk tough, but he was a softie. He knew how hard it was, trying to make a living from your art. Jim lived on West Fourth, in a room at the back of someone's house. He claimed that was all he needed, but Leah knew it was all Jim could afford. Nearly every penny he had went into the magazine.

They continued on their way, greeting friends, discussing the rally in Rutgers Park, where both "Big Bill" Heywood and Eugene Debs had spoken. Maurice Becker had done a cartoon of the rally for the next issue of *Future*, and Jim was really excited about it.

"Dammit, Becker's the number-one cartoonist as far as I'm concerned. And I'll tell you, I'm flattered that he's given me a drawing. He usually saves them all for the socialist rags."

"And what do you call *your* rag?" Joe laughed.

"A muckraking instrument, my boy! The shovel that will bury those sons of bitches who think they can take advantage of the downtrodden. We're the voice of the poor, Joe. We're gonna teach them that they *do* have power and it's called the *vote*!"

They were still talking animatedly as they walked into Bertolotti's. The trio was greeted with enthusiasm by Angelo, in shirtsleeves and braces, his ever-present derby hat sitting squarely on his head. Angelo led them to their usual table. Another of Jim's writers was already there, next to the dancer Lenore Hutchinson, who—even sitting down—towered over him by a foot. Not that they were a couple; no, for Lenore was not interested in men. In fact, she was after Leah—or so she said. To tell the truth, it made Leah very uncomfortable, although she would never admit it. It would be like announcing to the world that Leah Vogel was still an ignorant little immigrant girl from the Lower East Side and not really part of the Village freethinkers. So whenever Lenore leaned close and murmured, "Whenever you get tired of Joe . . . I'll be waiting," Leah just laughed. And moved away as soon as she could, without being obvious. She couldn't imagine what two women *did*; but she was sure if she found out, it would not appeal to her.

Mama Bertolotti came bustling up to the table, bringing another bottle of wine and glasses, and took their orders for three fifteen-cent lunches. In a minute bowls of thick, steaming minestrone soup and a giant basket of bread and butter were set in front of them.

Angelo came over. "Joe, what's this? The cheap lunch? But just last week you gave me that beautiful hickory stick with a dog's head carved on it. What do you do? Gamble away your money?"

"No, this cheapskate editor here won't pay up on time!"

"I pay up! I pay up! You should consider it enough to know that the best minds in New York City will be seeing your work, instead of the dull masses who buy the *Saturday Evening Post!*" Jim McCready's voice was a rich basso that carried for three city blocks. Inside the restaurant, it caused the glasses to rattle.

Jim was a flamboyant figure anyway, being well over six feet tall and two hundred sixty pounds of solid flesh, with the high color, copper-colored curls, and down-slanted eyes typical of some Irishmen. He was blunt and opinionated, but people didn't mind, since everything was always said in high good humor and with great charm.

"I find it fascinating that Angelo collects walking sticks," Leah mused aloud. "I wonder what Dr. Freud would make of that?"

Angelo waved dismissal. "Freud! Freud! Who is this guy, anyway? Everybody who comes in here, they're telling me all about their complexes! Freud says this, Freud says that! When I'm gonna see this fellow Freud?"

He laughed and went on to the next table, where a scrawny young man, pasty and unhealthy-looking, sat. He was an anarchist who came every day to be fed by the good-natured Bertolotti. Angelo loved every one of his regulars; and if anyone asked him why he gave away so much of his livelihood, he shrugged and said, "What? I'm going to let a friend go hungry when in my kitchen is so much food?"

There was another man eating on the house, as usual: the painter Walter Morris. Leah tried very hard not to look his way; but it was as if he had her tied to a cord and kept tugging at it. She couldn't help herself. She glanced over to find him gazing intently at her. As soon as their eyes met, his lips curled in a little smile and one black eyebrow went up. She looked quickly away. Taking a deep gulp of her wine, she joined the conversation, which had moved to Charlie Chaplin. Everyone thought he was so wonderful, so funny. She did not.

"There's nothing funny in poverty!" she proclaimed.

"Leah's right." The voice was Walter's; he was sliding into a seat right next to her, *right* next to her, his arm pressing against hers, his leg pressing against hers. "But of course," he went on smoothly, "Leah doesn't realize that we laugh at Charlie Chaplin not because he's funny, but because he makes us uncomfortable. It's nervous laughter."

"More of that Freud stuff!" McCready scoffed.

"Freud has nothing to do with it. As an artist"—Walter put just the slightest emphasis on the last word—"I understand how ordinary people react to strong emotion."

"Oh really?" Lenore demanded coolly. "And what might that be, wise one?" She had disliked the painter since the day he did a cruel imitation of Isadora Duncan, right there in Bertolotti's, using a paisley shawl snatched from a hook on the wall. He found modern dance very amusing. But Lenore worshiped the great Duncan and danced in that style; so she hated him.

Walter gave her a sly smile. "Most people are ill at ease with any powerful feeling. Watch what happens whenever the subject of sex comes up. . . . See? Leah is blushing, McCready is shifting in his seat . . . and as for you, dear Lenore, your eyes are throwing daggers at me."

With every word, he seemed to press in closer to Leah. She could smell turpentine and, faintly, soap, or maybe hair pomade. She could feel the heat from his body.

"Just because you live in the House of Genius doesn't make you one!" the dancer snapped; but he just laughed at her.

"At least I can recognize genius when I see it and when I hear it. Weren't you the one so shocked at Stravinsky's *Rites of Spring*? How can a woman who calls herself a *dancer* have so little respect for a great and innovative piece of music?" Without waiting for an answer, he turned to Leah. "Oh yes, the ancient Greeks knew how to worship the forces of life!"

He looked at her so meaningfully, she had to drop her eyes. Why didn't Joe say something? Was he deaf, dumb, and blind? He was right across the table; there wasn't a chance he had missed what was going on. Didn't he care that she was squirming in her chair? God knows what would happen if Walter Morris kept on after her like this.

But Joe seemed oblivious, eating his bread and soup with relish and then finishing Leah's bowl when she declared herself not hungry. The others continued chatting while Leah fumed in silence. Walter's knee was definitely pressing against hers. She had already moved away twice. One more move and she'd be in Jim McCready's lap. She refused to look at Walter Morris, but she could *feel* him grinning at her discomfort.

At last Joe was finished. Wiping his mouth carefully with

his napkin, folding it neatly, he put it gently down on the table. Then, without warning, he reached over and grabbed Walter by the kerchief around his neck, yanking him half across the table.

"Say, Morris," Joe said in a mild voice, ignoring the buzz that went up from the others. "I've got an idea for you. Stop bothering my girl and get one of your own. That is, if one will have you . . . which I doubt. Unless, of course, you begin to bathe regularly."

The table had gone completely quiet. Even Lenore was silent; her jaw had dropped open. Leah wanted to stand up and cheer. Oh, that Joe! Pretending he didn't notice, and all the time he was seething with jealousy. He was so . . . so manly. And he loved her, he really did, he was ready to fight for her!

Walter Morris gave a crooked grin, cool in spite of his awkward position. "Say, Lazarus, you don't have to choke me to death. I was only being friendly." And, as Joe loosened his grip, allowing Walter to sit up and rearrange his clothing, he added, "I just thought Leah might like a little company, that's all. Seems to me you ignore her more often than not."

"Ignore her, do I? Well—" Joe pushed back his chair and came quickly to her side. In one swift movement he lifted her to her feet, bent his head, and covered her mouth with his. Leah could hear their table, and then others nearby, clapping and cheering them on. At first it was just another kiss. But then, all of a sudden, it changed. His lips softened and he pulled her into him. Leah felt herself flood with desire, right there, in Bertolotti's! She pulled back from him, laughing a little.

Joe's eyes were smoky with heat. "Excuse us," he said, "me and my girl have some urgent business to attend to."

Leah felt herself turn crimson, but she felt so loved and protected that she didn't care what anyone thought! As Joe put his arm around her shoulder, urging her toward the door, she couldn't resist one last triumphant look at the scowling Walter. Then out they went, together, she and Joe, heading home to bed. In the middle of the day! Who needed a marriage certificate?

6

February 1914

Inside the Lafayette Café all was warm and cozy, fragrant with the mingled odors of coffee, brandy, and good hot food. Leah and Joe lingered over brandy at their marble-topped table, unwilling to venture back out into the ice-edged drizzle and fog that had been hanging over New York all day. Even though Joe was hidden behind his evening paper, absorbed in the news from Europe, his leg was pressed against Leah's, as if to say, I'm with you. She was content. Almost.

At least tonight they were together and Joe showed no signs of leaving. No pulling out his pocket watch every few minutes to check the time, no restless stirring in the chair. It had gotten so that she watched him constantly, poised, edgy, waiting for that moment when he would get up, give her a kiss, and announce, "Well, I'm off. See you in a little while."

But sometimes that "little while" stretched out to the middle of the night, when he would tiptoe into the bedroom, and with him would come the faint smell of strange perfume.

Last Tuesday he hadn't come home until morning. She could no longer hold her tongue. Sitting up in the bed, her voice cracking with emotion, she said, "Where have you *been*, damn it?"

"I met a young lady at the Liberal Club, a girl from Vassar, and . . . well, we all went downstairs to Polly's for a late supper and I . . . took her home. I guess we had a bit too much wine, because I fell asleep. I'm sorry."

"You're sorry! Sorry for what? That you overslept? Not that you spent the night making love to another woman? A woman you just met!" Then she burst into tears. "Why are you doing this to me?"

He took her in his arms and said, "Leah, I thought we had

58

an agreement. Don't you remember? We said we were both free to come and go as we please."

"But I don't understand! I thought you loved me!"

"I do, darling! This girl . . . she meant nothing to me. She was there, I was in the mood, she gave me the eye, and we did it. But it's you I came home to. It's you I'll always come home to. You know that. As for her . . . I've already forgotten her."

By that time she was hysterical. "*I* haven't! I can't!"

"Leah, Leah, please stop crying. It's not worth it, really. I love you. So . . . please, Leah."

"You never came home at all last night! I thought you were . . . I was sure you were *dead*!"

He held her closer. "I'm truly sorry, Leah. Will you forgive me? I promise I won't do that the next time."

The next time! The words lanced her heart like daggers. How could he love *her* and still want to go with other women?

In the café, Leah sipped at her coffee. Well, she was no longer the innocent little shop girl she had been when he first took her into his bed. She was nineteen now, nineteen going on twenty, a grown woman. And she was a quick learner, always had been. She had ideas of her own. Joe should know that by now. But men were stupid about some things.

She began to hum a new song she'd heard them plugging the other day at Schirmer's, "Keep the Home Fires Burning." Joe had snorted at it when she sang it last night. "What old-fashioned, sentimental drivel!" he'd said. "Sing something more lively, something by Irving Berlin!" And he had bounced around the living room with her in a lively two-step, laughing. But tonight he didn't comment, he didn't seem to even hear her, he was so engrossed in his newspaper.

His head came up with a snap, however, at the sound of Jane Armstrong's velvety voice. "Why, it's the lovebirds, alone together as usual. Mind if I make it a threesome?"

Joe rose swiftly to his feet, pulling out the chair for her, a broad smile on his face. "Three's not a crowd when it's the delightful Miss Armstrong, now appearing with the Waverly Place Players in the heartrending melodrama, *More Sinned Against than Usual*."

They both laughed merrily, while Leah forced herself to smile. Other women, a vague notion easily pushed to the back of the mind, was one thing; Jane Armstrong, a willowy and seductive actress, with large, heavy-lidded blue eyes that seemed to promise everything, was another. Jane slid into the chair Joe held for her and bestowed an enigmatic smile upon Leah.

"You're looking lovely these days," she murmured, and then turned to Joe, saying, "The entire troupe is looking forward to seeing the pictures you took of us."

That was news to Leah, and she gave Joe a hard look. His eyes dropped. He hadn't mentioned photographing the Waverly Place Players, and suddenly Leah knew why. Not only because he had been with Jane, which was bad enough, but because he had done it on the cuff. And he complained all the time about their lack of money!

"Yes, I can barely wait to see those pictures myself," Leah said in her sweetest coo. "I hope you gave them a good price, Joe, since we're all struggling artists together."

Joe was silent and Jane Armstrong smiled a little, putting a proprietary hand on his arm. "He didn't charge us a thing, isn't that too wonderful?" she said in almost the same coo. It was very hard to tell when Jane was being insulting, since that tiny Mona Lisa smile never seemed to leave her lips.

"Perhaps," Leah said, "he'll take it out in trade."

Jane gave a little intake of breath, and Joe said, "Leah!" turning quite red.

"Free admission to all the shows," Leah finished, giving her own minuscule smile. "That's all I meant, Joe."

Jane gave a tinkly little laugh. "Of course, Joe gets free admission . . . and you, too, Leah. Just give my name at the door, any time."

Leah was saved from replying by the arrival of Walter Morris. He yawned and stretched. He was the least self-conscious person Leah had ever met. He just didn't care what he looked like or what anyone thought. "I fell asleep, reading the newspaper on a divan in there," he said, pointing to the bar area. "Mind if I take a drop of brandy to wake me up?"

Without waiting for an answer, he sat himself next to Leah, pulling his chair closer. As he put his arm across the back of her chair, his fingers grazed her shoulder. Joe stared for a moment, his eyes stormy, but instead of saying anything, he turned back to Jane Armstrong.

"You can drink from my glass," Leah said, feeling intrepid. She didn't care what happened, Joe was going to get exactly what he deserved.

Walter Morris had been haunting her thoughts lately, anyway. Not that she welcomed his image; she didn't, but it came anyway, even into her dreams. He looked like Satan to her, with his thick black satin hair, a lock always falling on his forehead so that he had to toss his head, like a spirited horse, to get it out of the way. And those deep-set dark almond eyes! The backs of his muscular hands were covered with wiry black hair; the tips of his ears were pointed, like a faun's.

He was evil; there was no doubt he was evil. Otherwise, how could she love Joe the way she did and still be falling under his spell? One of these days, Walter Morris would put out a lazy hand and take her, and she would disappear, melting totally into him. Just thinking about him made her go hot, then cold.

And Joe, who was oozing charm all over that blond seductress, wouldn't stop Walter *this* time, she was sure. She was glad she had put on the locket tonight. It looked old-fashioned, but it was her lucky charm. And from the way her heart was skipping around, she had a feeling she might need luck.

Joe got to his feet and said, "Well, I'm off." Leah felt a stab of pain, but she pushed it away. She had hoped . . . But never mind what she had hoped. Free love was *free*, and you could not shackle a free man and force him to stay with you. But the same went for a woman, she thought fiercely.

She looked directly at Joe. He could still change his mind. Then Walter Morris laid his hand over hers. Joe's lips quirked and tightened, and he said loudly, "Come on, Jane, let's see if we can find some fun." To which Jane said, "Oh, we can, Gypsy Joe, we certainly can." And they were gone.

Leah turned to Walter Morris, putting her other hand over his. It was the first time she had touched him, and she saw by his quick glance downward that he was surprised.

"You've been asking me to pose for you, Walter."

"As I recall," he said with a lazy smile, "you said you weren't ready for that."

"Now I'm ready."

The painter pushed himself to his feet. "Good. Let's go."

His studio was the attic of a crumbling building on Bedford Street, forgotten by time. The attic was a huge room with heavy beams and a ceiling that slanted with the roof. The place was crammed with paints and brushes, jars and bottles, canvases. Its many windows were all dirty, and a lot of dust puffed up as Walter moved tarps and shawls and piles of his own clothing. A sink stood in one corner, filled with dirty dishes. Near it there was a folding screen. Once, the place had been painted a chrome-yellow, but now every wall was covered with grime and large angry-looking paintings. A bed was pushed against the back wall—shameless, Leah had looked for the bed first—covered with dirty linen. Would she have to lie down on that mess?

Walter didn't ask her if she'd like a cup of tea or even a drink of water, didn't look at her at all or offer her a chair; he just put a fresh canvas onto the easel and begin to collect tubes of paint and brushes and a large palette. When she'd begun to think she might as well leave for all the attention she was getting, he turned and said, "Get undressed."

"Undressed! You mean . . . all my clothes?"

"Of course that's what I mean." When she stood there, not sure what to think, he added, "There's a robe. Behind the screen. If you're really that modest."

Leah felt shock roll over her. All his smiles and nudges and winks hadn't been . . . well, they hadn't been what she had thought. He actually wanted to *paint* her. Of all the nerve! And then she thought, So? And why not? She was here, wasn't she? And she'd be acting like a complete idiot if she squeaked and squawked and ran off. Besides . . . Joe had made her mad.

The robe behind the screen was a cheap material, printed with huge cabbage roses in a terrible shade of pink. And it smelled of perfume; not a perfume she liked, either. But she stripped off her clothes, folding them neatly and putting them on a stool. Then, wrapping herself in the robe, she took a deep breath and walked out.

His eyes never met hers at all. He barked orders: stand this way, move that way, no not like *that*, woman, with the knee *bent*. Now take the robe off. Take it *off*, Leah. What's the matter, has your nerve deserted you all of a sudden?

Disconcerted and a little hurt, she untied the belt and let the robe slip down around her feet. Even then his eyes seemed not to see her, but something around and beyond her. She felt . . . not quite human, somehow.

It was surprising, how easy it got to be, to stand naked in front of a man, turning her body a little this way, twisting a little that way, lifting her head, dropping her shoulders. Once he started painting, Walter talked constantly.

"I've wanted to paint you for so long, Leah. I can't believe how patient I've been. How quietly I've waited for you to say yes. I've painted you in my mind, over and over again, a hundred different ways. . . . In my imagination I've turned you around, bent you forward and backward, painting you and painting you. . . ."

She had to stop listening to him. *Paint*, she realized, was just a substitute word for *fuck*; and as he continued to describe ways he had thought of *painting* her and how many times he would like to *paint* her today, how *painting* her had become an obsession with him, how he dreamed about it . . . she felt her nipples hardening. Stop it, she ordered, but it would not stop. There was nothing she could do about it—except pick up the robe and put it on. But if she did that, he would surely . . . She wasn't sure what he would surely do. She just knew she was mesmerized, frozen, with shivers running up her spine, while a glow started between her legs.

At some point during her confusion, he looked directly at her and she thought he smiled. She couldn't be sure. To cover her nervousness, she tried to talk about something impersonal—and for some outlandish reason, all she could think of was the Wobblies.

"Sorry," Walter interrupted her babbling in that bored drawl of his. "Unions don't interest me. And I never read McCready's rag. It's too deep for me." He gave a short bark of a laugh. "So I have to admit I've never read your stuff, Leah. But they say you're damn good, and I believe it."

He didn't continue, simply kept on painting. Then, just as she thought her left leg would fall asleep, he stopped, grunted, and said, "Okay. That's it."

"It's done? May I see it?"

A shrug. "Suit yourself!"

Well, of course he didn't care what she thought about it. It was just going to be another one of those grotesque women he was always putting on canvas. That's why she'd been so sure his invitation to "pose" was just a cover for seduction. She was going to look, anyway.

But to her amazement, it was *her*. "Oh my God," she said. "It looks just like me!"

He grunted.

"But . . . people could recognize me!"

"What do you care? This is art, Leah! You've been immortalized on canvas. Centuries from now, when the flesh has long melted from your bones and your lovely face has gone to dust, people will look at this and think, 'How beautiful.' "

He thought she was beautiful! "But . . . my friends. Joe. Oh my God, Joe. He must never know. Promise me you'll never show it."

"Don't be a child! Of course I'll show it. It's very good."

To her horror, she began to cry. She didn't want to; the tears just came, unannounced and unasked-for.

"Now you *are* being childish. But all right. I won't hang it. I'll turn it to the wall. I'll paint over it the next time I need canvas and can't afford new." As he spoke, he plucked the canvas from the easel and took it to the back wall, placing it in the shadows. "There. Does *that* satisfy you?"

It was over. She could get dressed now, she was free to go. "But before you leave, I wonder, could you spare two dollars? I seem to be out of pocket this week."

She had it and she gave it to him; he accepted it with a nod of thanks. She began; "Well, then, if there's nothing more you want from me . . ."

"Nothing . . ."

"Then I'll be on my way."

Leah started to dress, but she kept waiting for Walter to say something. After all these months of dogging her every move . . . ! What was it all about, then? What had he been after? Her two dollars? Her naked body painted on a stretched piece of cloth? But then he touched her arm.

And there he was, totally bare, a lock of his hair falling over one eye, paint smudges on one cheek, smudges the color of *her* skin and *her* nipples and *her* hair.

His look was charged with heat. He didn't say one word, just grinned at her as he pulled her in, his mouth already greedily on hers.

7

August 1914

"We are gathered here this evening in the very elegant and *costly* Brevoort Café to honor a very special occasion," Jim McCready intoned, raising his glass. "I am proud to announce that the Society for the Suppression of Vice has denounced our very own . . . Leah Vogel!"

If he thought the entire table would burst into applause, he was doomed to disappointment. Nobody was paying attention—not even Leah. Everyone was listening to the boisterous young men at the next table arguing loudly over whether or not America should go to war. War was the topic of the moment, and had been since the fighting in France had started on the twenty-eighth of June.

"Go fight the Hun? What for? My grandfather is German. I might find myself pointing a rifle at my cousin!"

"Don't be a complete fool, Edwin! If we don't fight them now, in France, we'll end up fighting them on the streets of New York!"

"The French are good fighters. And anyway, it's *their* war."

"I say we fight for democracy, *wherever* the battlefield!"

The last pronouncement was greeted with a mixed chorus of cheers and boos. Leah twisted around in her chair, outraged, and called out, "Don't you think we have *enough* problems right here at *home*? Problems that aren't being taken care of? Don't you know what's going on in your own city? The people who are living in alleyways, eating garbage, struggling to just keep *clean*? Democracy!" She snorted. "Ask the women of this country if *they* enjoy democracy! Are they even allowed to *vote*?"

The noisy young men all stopped talking at once and gaped at her with identical expressions of stupefaction. It was clear

they thought her quite mad. Men and their wars! Since the war
had begun that's all you heard from the male sex: army, fighting, guns and ammunition, generals, battles, battleships and airplanes. Well, as far as *she* was concerned, they were all
meshugah!

Jim McCready's big hand turned her around. He was laughing. "Our apologies, gents," he said. "But you see, this little
lady is a journalist. She has an opinion on *everything*!"

"Well, and what's wrong with that?" Leah was aware of the
color and heat in her cheeks, but she had had several glasses
of wine so she didn't care. "Why shouldn't I have opinions?
Because I'm female? I am the equal of *any* man!"

The last sentence was spoken by everyone at the table—
everyone but Joe, that is—word for word, right along with her.
For a moment Leah was furious that they would ridicule her in
public; but then she realized how funny it was. She must have
been spouting that same speech over and over. Why, she was
as bad as the men who couldn't stop chewing over the war!
She began to laugh.

"Oh God, have I become a total bore? I'll kill myself!"

"No need," Jim soothed. "But you might let up on us a bit,
you know. We were *all* at those rallies for feminism. We all
heard it. . . ." He changed his voice to a falsetto and chirped:
"We must liberate the modern woman from her bondage. . . ."

"Well, it suddenly occurred to me that night that the women
I write about are not the *only* ones downtrodden by society.
Even I—"

Jim and Joe and the others—four writers, two cartoonists,
and a typist, all from *The Future*—hooted and laughed and
banged their glasses on the table.

"You! Downtrodden! You're the least trod-upon female I
know!"

"Just because I have a mouth, don't be fooled. I suffer all
the indignities—"

"You know what, Leah?" one of the writers said. "You
could run for mayor of New York!"

"Run for mayor!" she repeated bitterly. "They won't even
let me *vote* for mayor. Women are too *emotional*. Our minds
are too *soft*." She stopped. She had had too much to drink and
her tongue was thick. "But this is a *celebration*!" she reminded
them. Reminded herself. "I guess if the Society for the Suppression of Vice denounces me personally, by name, I'm not
doing *too* badly!"

"Bravo!" Joe cried. "I'll drink to that!"

"Another country heard from!" McCready said, his eyes hard but his tone light.

Everyone was aware that Joe had been hitting the booze like crazy lately. He was mad as hell at her. Could she help it that she was making more money than him? What was the difference which one of them made it; didn't they share everything? But he didn't see it that way. He'd been in a foul mood for the past six months. Well, maybe the money was *all* of it.

When Joe reached out for the bottle again, Jim McCready put his great fist around it. Holding on, Jim smiled and said, "Don't you think you've had enough, me boyo?" His tone was light as a feather, but his use of the Irish lilt, which had almost entirely disappeared from his speech, was a sure sign that he meant business. If he hadn't been a little tipsy, Joe would have realized. But he was past noticing any subleties. Angrily, Joe tugged at the bottle.

"*I'll* tell *you* when I've had enough, McCready!"

Still smiling broadly, Jim released his grasp on the bottle so suddenly that it tipped over, spilling wine all over the table-cloth and all over Joe as well. Joe leapt to his feet, swearing and dabbing at his trousers with a napkin. Jim moved next to him, as if they were pals, smiling, urging him to the back of the restaurant where they could get some water and wash away the wine before it stained.

Everyone at the table knew it had been done deliberately, and nobody would look Leah in the eyes. She was mortified, but at the same time relieved. The wine bottle was nearly empty, anyway, and maybe when he came back, Joe would be in a better mood.

Well, he *was* quieter when they returned, although his eyes were downcast, so Leah couldn't see what he might be thinking. She looked a question at Jim—What did you say to him?—but he shook his head slightly and stood to propose his toast again.

"It's not every little magazine in New York can claim it's been banned by the Society for the Suppression of Vice! I say three cheers for us and three more for the author of 'A Woman's Right to Her Own Reproduction.' I give you Miss Leah Vogel!"

"Leah!" they all cried in unison. Joe joined in. Smiling again, he reached for her hand and bestowed a kiss on it.

"I say three cheers," Jim went on, "for the little lady who,

according to the fine folks at the Society—" Here, he closed
his eyes and intoned from memory. " '—cares only for her
own lustful, vice-ridden crowd of so-called friends who live in
that den of iniquity and sin, Greenwich Village. Does she not
realize, poor woman,' " he quoted, his voice brimming with
amusement, " 'that these people will leave her in the
gutter—' " He was laughing so hard, he couldn't go on.

Someone else picked it up: " '—the fitting place for all
wicked, promiscuous females!' "

Now they were all laughing. Leah was warmed that all her
friends had memorized the condemnation, and that they all
found it hilarious. The article had aroused a great deal of comment, pro and con, mostly against. It always amazed her how
mere words could arouse such powerful feelings! Hundreds of
letters had poured into the magazine's office—men offering to
meet her at dawn for duels or else offering to meet her at night
for sex. Just because she used words like "penis" and "va-
gina"! Just because she listed and described methods of contra-
ception!

Even the *New York Times* had run an editorial denouncing
her article, saying they could not quote from it because the
words she used were "not fit for a family readership such as
the *Times'*." When Jim handed it to her, the harsh words had
made her flush with embarrassment; but Jim had said, "Let
them say their worst. Only let them get your name right. And
the magazine's, too, of course. It's not every woman gets her
name into the *New York Times.*"

"As one of Leah's sinful, so-called friends," Lenore cried,
lifting her glass, "*I* condemn their goddammed condemnation!"
Her voice was beginning to slur, too. They were all putting the
wine away at a great rate, Leah thought.

"I'll drink to that!" Joe cried, and gulped down his wine.
"And to promiscuous females, long may they wave . . . or
whatever!"

Leah sighed as she raised her glass high. "Ladies and gentlemen, I give you sin!"

"Sin!" they all responded, and everyone drank.

"Iniquity!"

"Wickedness!"

"Lewd and lacivious!"

After each toast, a gust of laughter and a gulp of wine, until
her head was spinning. But she kept her smile bright and refused to look in Joe Lazarus's direction.

The fun went on, with each one at the table trying to outdo all the others' toasts. By the time Walter came up behind her, giving her a kiss on her ear and reaching around her to take the glass from her hand to drink, she was tipsy. But not too intoxicated to know that Walter was putting on a big show of affection to make Joe crazy. And he was succeeding; Joe's face was flushed an ugly plum color.

Walter squeezed in next to her, putting his hand on her thigh, very high up, his fingers hidden suggestively between her legs. Sometimes, when he was really boozing, he would reach under her skirt and actually fondle her there, never so much as glancing at her, just smirking to himself like the devil he was.

"What if someone should see?" she would protest later.

"Then they'll know you're mine." He would bring his face very close to hers, smiling. "All women have cunts. That's why men want them . . . for fucking."

"But I don't like you doing that in public."

"Oh yes you do. I can feel your pussy getting wet."

He always used the coarsest words to her, and she always tried to act as if they didn't offend her because she knew he liked seeing her embarrassed. Sometimes she hated him for his crude ways; then, she would wonder what she was doing with him.

But when they were alone and he put his hands on her, something happened to her. She became a shrieking, clawing animal, digging her fingers into his back and buttocks, pulling him closer, clutching at his erection, shoving it in, trying to push him even deeper into her, sobbing, begging him for more, for more, for more, using all the words he had taught her. Thinking about it made shudders zigzag down her spine. It was like a horrible drug. Every time she left his filthy bed, she was filled with self-loathing. Every time, as she ran down the stairs, she promised herself, Never again.

But it was all a lie. Even now, at the dinner table, surrounded by her colleagues, and with Joe nearby, she could feel the sick excitement climbing through her loins. But tonight it was mixed with something else . . . apprehension, perhaps. Ever since yesterday afternoon . . .

When she had gone to his place, there was another man there, lounging on the bed, sipping whiskey. Leon Cavalier. She had remembered his name after a moment. She'd seen him around;

and one day, Walter had introduced them on the street. He was a painter who made a fair living doing portraits of wives and children for well-to-do merchants. He would also, for a little extra, Walter had told her, paint some authentic-looking "ancestors" for those who were eager to climb the social ladder. And, Walter had added with a sly twinkle, for a lot extra, he would paint the merchant with a lady of his choice, in the nude, doing whatever struck the merchant's fancy. Six poses in meticulous miniature and explicit detail. From life, of course.

"I don't believe it!"

"Ah, my dear Leah, but it's true. I hope you don't think we all *like* living on the cuff. I'm only sorry I didn't think of it myself."

"How horrible!"

"Think of it as a safeguard for the sanctity of marriage, Leah. The gentleman finds himself randy as a goat, and his good wife cannot satisfy him. Presto! He goes to his secret cache, he pulls out his collection of paintings, gazes upon them, remembering better times, and soon he has matters well in hand!" He gave a bark of laughter, nudging her to make sure she got the pun. "No fears of disease or discovery—and he hasn't even left his house! Why, if you think about it for a moment, you can see that Leon is keeping the men of the middle-class from straying!"

"Well, I think it's disgusting!"

"Do you?" He had regarded her for long moments, until she felt quite uncomfortable. Then he smiled and said, "Well, we'll see, we'll see."

And here was Cavalier, in the flesh, reclining on the bed that was still rumpled from their passion the night before. Leon Cavalier was very fair, his hair almost colorless and his eyes thickly lashed in white, like a rabbit's. He greeted her politely, but he looked her over boldly and appreciatively.

The back of her neck prickled. "I'll come back later," she said. "When you're alone, Walter."

"Not at all, my dear. I am pouring you a glass of sherry this very minute. Come. Chat with us. We have been longing for female companionship, haven't we, Leon?"

Leon Cavalier patted an empty space next to him on the bed. "Longing," he repeated in a lingering tone that sent shivers up her arms. "Sit here, Leah. I may call you Leah?" But he didn't wait for her to say yes or no. "Walter has told me so much about you. I'd like to get to know you better."

Leah stood where she was. She did not want to sit on the bed next to him, with his lazy eyes and mocking smile, and she certainly did not want him to get to know her at *all*. She glanced over at Walter, for a clue, but his back was turned to her.

So she sat down, as far from Leon Cavalier as she could get, bolt upright, looking straight ahead, her hand enfolding the locket she still wore from time to time for luck. She could feel his strange colorless eyes on her. And then, deliberately, he shifted his position, so that he was right next to her. He smelled musky.

"She's a looker, Morris, you were right about that."

Leah said nothing. Then she felt his hand on her head and she turned to him, startled and angry.

When he took his hand away, he had three of her hairpins! She put her hand up and felt where he had loosened her hair.

"I wanted to see what it looked like down," he said, as if men loosened the hair of strange women every day of the week. "It's really black, isn't it, not just dark brown? But of course, you're a Jewess . . ." He reached out and took her hair in his hands, fondling it. Leah felt paralyzed. She did not want him touching her, but neither did she want to make a complete fool of herself by leaping up and demanding the return of her hairpins.

"Walter . . ." she pleaded.

But when he turned, he said, "Yes, why don't you take your hair down? It's so beautiful." He smiled at her, but his eyes were blank. Couldn't he see what was happening? Could he see that this man was . . . What *was* he doing?

"Mr. Cavalier," she began. "I really don't—"

But he interrupted her, saying, "Leon. Please call me Leon. Or Lee. My friends call me Lee. Lee . . . and Leah. We were meant for each other." He took out the rest of the pins and put both his hands into her hair, shaking it out, smoothing it!

Leah's heart gave a jump in her chest and she leaped to her feet. "Mr. Cavalier! Walter! Walter, stop this!" She ran to him, and he put an arm around her shoulder. She leaned against him, panting a little.

"Leah, my dear, whatever is the matter? Haven't I told you that Leon is not only an old friend of mine, but a very fine painter? I have asked him to do a series for us, and he is simply looking to see how best to show you off. . . ."

"No!" Shudders ran down her spine.

"Whyever not? I assure you, Leon is a splendid painter. Show her the Hitchcock pictures, why don't you, Leon?" He gave her a little push.

She held herself very straight and walked to where Leon Cavalier stood, spreading some small canvases, perhaps eight inches square, out on the bed. A horrible excitement enveloped her, rising through her throat and nauseating her.

The pictures were beautifully painted with tiny brush strokes. They were, as Walter had said, meticulous in their every detail. The man was heavy, his upper body covered with hair, his outsized penis erect and darkly engorged. His companion, a young woman with straight yellow hair, looked tiny and fragile next to his bulk. They were on a bed heaped with pillows; and each little painting showed them in a different position. Leah looked, horrified but curious. There was one in which the girl knelt with her buttocks raised, her head hidden in the crook of her arms, while he pushed his member into her. His head was back, his hair tousled, his eyes closed, his teeth bared in a heated grimace. To her horror, Leah felt her loins burning and a rush of wetness.

Leon Cavalier's laughter brought her to her senses. "She'll do just fine, Morris!" he said, and reached out to touch her.

Leah did not wait to find out what he had in mind. She ran to the door and down the stairs, panting and sweating. She walked for miles through the familiar Village streets, willing her heart to stop racing, trying to keep her mind from going back again and again to those pictures. Walter and her, on his bed . . . while Leon Cavalier did what? Made sketches? Rearranged the poses? And then what? She thought she knew. Then he would strip and join them. She took a deep breath. The real revulsion was that such thoughts thrilled her. Part of her wanted it to happen. What kind of woman *was* she?

Leah had managed to put the whole incident away, somewhere in the back of her head, until this very moment, when Walter curled his hands around her thigh.

She looked around the table, at all the familiar faces flushed with wine and with their feelings of victory. This was her life, a life of writing and intellectual companionship, a life with love in it and self-respect and thoughtfulness. The man next to her, with his hand under cover of the tablecloth doing disgusting things to her while he chatted and laughed and smoked a cigarette . . . he was evil, he would drag her down, down, down, until she was no better than a whore.

She reached down, pushing his hand away, then stood up, her glass raised. "To friendship!" she toasted, and drank the glass down. Everyone followed suit.

"To love!" Walter said, smiling up at her knowingly.

There was a choked sound and then a glass of wine came flying through the air, spraying the tablecloth with spots and blobs of pink and finally crashing into a thousand pieces not far from where Walter Morris sat.

It was Joe, a furious red-faced Joe, who, having sent his glass sailing, picked up someone else's and slammed it onto the table, shattering it and two plates as well. Shards of glass and china flew everywhere, and people at the table pushed back chairs and got out of the way of his rage.

"Love!" he bellowed. "Love! And what would *you* know about love, you whoremaster, you piece of filth!" With the last words, he launched himself across the table, right at Walter.

It wasn't much of a fight, even Leah could see that. Joe was too drunk, and Walter too surprised. Neither could do more than hold onto the other. But hold on they did, in a travesty of embracing lovers, reeling across the floor, bumping into tables and waiters, to the sounds of breaking dishes and clattering silverware. The manager and two waiters leaped upon them, shouting at them and trying to pry them apart. Finally, still joined together, sweating and straining to get a blow in, the two men fell with a crash to the floor. They rolled apart, panting. There was a sudden silence, and then a buzz as everyone in the restaurant began to talk.

Leah ran to help Joe. In the background the manager was complaining, decorously, of course, about the mess and the broken crockery. And the restaurant's reputation. "The tourists! Think of the stories they'll take home! I'll be ruined, ruined!" His voice was joined by Jim McCready, apologizing, offering to pay for the damage. Jim assured the manager that the tourists would love the fight. "No blood," he exclaimed. "And it's over a woman. Why, man, that's why they come to the Village—to see the Bohemians act up as they'd never dare themselves!"

Jim would take care of everything; he always did. And Leah could go where she really belonged, into the safety of Joe's loving arms. She flung herself at him, hugging him fiercely. "Joe, are you all right? Did he hurt you? Please forgive me!"

"You're back, at last you're back," Joe said, putting his arms tightly around her and burying his face into the curve of her neck. "Oh, Leah, you've got to forgive *me*. It's you I love, only you. Those others ... they never meant a thing. Jane Armstrong ... I didn't even like her. It was just ... I don't know *what* it was. I've been a damn fool! I don't want free love, not if it tears us apart. To hell with it, Leah! Leah, do you hear me? To hell with free love! It's just you and me from now on, just you and me!"

Oh God, it was such a good feeling, to be in Joe's arms, to smell his good smell and feel his good warmth and know she was safe. *Safe.* She sighed deeply and closed her eyes as Joe began softly to sing in her ear, ". . . and when I told them how beautiful you are, they didn't believe me . . ."

They were singing together, arms around each other's waists, as they left the restaurant; and she knew. This was it, the two of them, Joe and Leah, forever.

8

June 1915

"So, Miss Vogel, I understand you do a little scribbling?" Bertha Lazarus leaned forward so she could see past her husband's protruding paunch. They had started out trying to walk together—Joe, Leah, his parents, and his sister Zelda—but five across wasn't possible, not in the Village on a sunny Sunday. So Mr. and Mrs. Lazarus walked arm in arm, with Leah trotting alongside—like a puppy dog, she thought. Joe and his sister lagged behind.

Joe's parents were an imposing pair: Isaac round as an egg, like Humpty Dumpty, with a big head, big mustache, big jutting jaw, and big booming voice. Bertha Lazarus was quite a bit taller than her husband, curvaceous and animated.

Zelda took after her papa, with the same thickset body and

heavy chin. Leah wondered why her mother had dressed her in a long tunic top and narrow skirt that strained at the seams and made her look even dumpier. Why did the top have so many ruffles and bows? Why so many ribbons and flowers on her hat? Why three bracelets and every pudgy finger adorned with another huge flashing ring? Zelda walked with an awkward little stoop, as if she would like to shrink inside her ill-fitting, fussy clothes; and every ten steps or so Mama would interrupt herself to turn and say, sharply, "Zelda! Shoulders back!" Without even bothering to see whether or not she obeyed.

Poor Zelda. Eighteen years old and not married, "not even a nibble," as Bertha had already said several times. Whenever the subject of Zelda's maidenhood came up, her mother would slide her a look and shake her head a little, sighing. Joe got his vivid good looks from his mother, you could see that in a minute. Both had wavy dark hair, flashing eyes, and brilliant smiles. But Joe was genuinely good-natured, not a mean bone in his body. Whereas Mama . . . well, Leah wasn't so sure.

When Joe introduced them, she had given Leah a sugary smile and her hand, encased in a white kid glove, and said, "Bertha Lazarus," loudly and clearly, as if announcing the final destination of some long, arduous journey. And then almost immediately began asking rude questions that were really just impolite comments.

So, Miss Vogel, I don't suppose you'd be related to the Bernard Vogels of Westchester? And then answering herself: *No, they're very important, socially.*

Won't you be uncomfortable out in public without a hat, Miss Vogel?

Oh my, Miss Vogel, is that how we are all to wear our hair? Staring at Leah's Castle Clip, absolutely scandalized to see a woman with short hair.

And calling her articles "scribbles" as if they were a frivolous little hobby!

"Well, Bertha, I do more than a *little*, and most people don't consider it 'scribbling.' I'm a writer, for magazines and newspapers."

Leah could feel Joe's eyes boring into her. If she looked over at him, she knew he would be glaring, but she was going to ignore it. She knew she was being contrary. Bertha Lazarus was the sort of woman who expected a great deal of fawning and groveling. Calling her by her first name, without being invited to . . . that was not the sort of behavior Bertha Lazarus was accustomed to. Too bad. Bending the knee before this handsome, overdressed woman, even if she *was* Joe's mother, was not Leah Vogel's style.

"Oh yes, now I remember. Joseph said something about your work . . . you write those pieces about the poor that are supposed to make the rest of us empty our pockets from pity. Well . . ." A smug little laugh. "I can tell you right here and now, Miss Vogel, you wouldn't move Mr. Lazarus to dig into his pocket, not in a million years!" Again the laugh with its nasty edge. "No matter how good you may consider yourself."

Leah smiled and wished the woman six feet into the ground. But silently. She would love to say, "Oh, is Mr. Lazarus able to reach into his pocket when his pants fit so tight?" But she wouldn't do it. For Joe's sake, she would try to hold her tongue.

Before his family arrived, he had begged her, "Please, Leah, do me a favor, darling. They're not easy, but they're not so bad when you get to know them. Try to be nice. It's taken me long enough to get them to even *meet* you."

She knew all about that! According to them, she was a Fallen Woman, a tramp, a trollop, not worthy of the son of Isaac Lazarus, button manufacturer, self-made man. He had announced to his son that he would *never* allow his hand to touch that of a woman who had no greater self-respect than to sleep with a man not her husband—even though the man not her husband was his only son and heir. If his son wished to maintain family ties, he should come to the Bronx, and there he, and he alone, would be welcome.

Well, Papa had eventually come around; his curiosity overcame his so-called morality. Joe had told Leah about his trip uptown to the Optima Club on 238th Street—"filled with fat, wheezing merchants, all of them red in the face from too much port wine, but *rich*, Leah. Oh God, so much *money*!"—to take lunch with Papa, to discuss Joseph's, um . . . irregular alliance with "that woman."

"I had to listen to the latest news on button prices. That was difficult. Then I had to hear a lecture about how far I have gone astray, which was worse. The hardest part of all was staying awake, Leah! But I had to, because I wanted my turn to talk and to convince him to *meet* you. He didn't have to approve of you or like you, I told him, 'but you will do both, that I promise you.' Now, there's nothing my papa likes better than to see a man show spunk and spirit, and I was the spunkiest, most spirited fellow you have ever seen. So he said yes."

But Isaac had refused to put one foot over the threshold of their domicile, nor would he have her presence disturb the sanctity of his home in the Bronx. The condescending *momzer*! One holiday when the three of them were at a hotel in the Catskill Mountains, Joe had taken her. She found the Bronx raw and ugly, in spite of all the grass and flowers. There were so many new buildings, all of them huge edifices that loomed over you and put dark shadows on the streets. Anyway, such large buildings looked ridiculous, sitting in the middle of fields and meadows. The Bronx, Leah had remarked to Joe, must have been lovely countryside before the builders ruined it.

"Ruin!" He had laughed. "On the contrary, Leah darling, you and I are looking at the future of New York City! Since they brought the subway out here this year, people are moving uptown like they just invented it, hoping for a blade of grass, the sight of flowers, some fresh air."

Everything was on such a grand scale, you'd think the Bronx had been built for a race of giants. Streets were wider. The building where Joe's family lived looked like a mansion, no, a castle, embellished with hand-carved stone; it even had gargoyles on the upper floors, like a cathedral. The front entrance was twelve feet high, with massive wooden doors, and the lobby was cavernous. If you didn't whisper, your voice echoed.

The Lazaruses lived in a flat of five large rooms with central heating, gas and electricity. The landlord had put in a range and refrigerator for them. There was even a telephone in the building, managed by the janitor's fifteen-year-old daughter, who took a nickel for each call she placed.

Of course, such a place cost big money: twenty-seven dollars a month. Leah couldn't see it; they were so far uptown, they were nearly in Yonkers. Poo! she thought. Who needed a lobby the size of a ballpark, if you were so far from where everything important happened!

The Lazaruses' apartment was ugly, too, carpeted with dark Oriental rugs, crammed with dark furniture, hung with dark velvet draperies and many oil paintings of dubious value in ornate gilded frames. These people had obviously never heard of modern art or batik fabrics or simple furniture.

"I keep thinking I should whisper," Leah had said to Joe. "And walk on tiptoe."

"Really? Why?"

"It's like a funeral parlor . . . a fancy one, of course. . . ."

Joe gave her a smile, but she knew he did not like her saying it. More tiptoeing, she thought. He had run from his family; he didn't like them particularly. And yet she couldn't say
a word about them without him getting his back up.

Today, too. She was trying to do her best; but she was not
going to toady, not for anyone. She had been snubbed, as if
she weren't even worth considering. But here all the Lazaruses
were, walking along Barrow Street, gawking at the Villagers,
just like all the other tourists who came hoping to have the
Bohemians shock them. And Joe's father, Isaac, took every opportunity to ogle her as though she were for sale.

"Oh, I consider myself only an ordinary writer," Leah answered Joe's mother, in her sweetest voice. "It's my readers
who keep demanding I write more, my editors who keep raising my pay. So what can I do?" She widened her eyes at Bertha Lazarus, who made a little sound in her throat but did not
answer.

Leah thought of the little secret she knew. In the baronial
living room of the Lazarus apartment in the Bronx, hanging on
either side of the elaborately carved bookcase, were paintings
of a woman and a man in the dress of a well-to-do merchant
and his wife from the early nineteenth century. There was
something about the paintings' style, something that nagged at
her mind.

"Who are those people?" she had asked Joe.

"My mother says they're her great-grandparents or great-
greats . . . I never can remember. Discovered in an attic of an
aunt or a cousin just last year. But . . . who knows? My mother
tells st— My mother has a vivid imagination," he amended.

Leah walked over to look in the corner, where painters usually put their signatures. She had a feeling . . . and there it was:
very tiny, but definitely a courtier's plumed hat. That was how
Leon Cavalier signed all his paintings; Walter had pointed it
out to her one day at a gallery. So the rich and snooty Mr. and
Mrs. Lazarus had "ancestors" painted by one of Greenwich
Village's better pornographers! It was a lovely little joke, and
Leah intended to keep it for herself. Unless she needed it, of
course.

Apparently Bertha Lazarus had decided it might be wise to
change the subject. "Zelda," she said in the sharp tone she reserved for her daughter. "Come up here and walk with us.

Your father wants to talk to Joseph." The girl obeyed, and was walking between them when Bertha barked again: "For God's sake, can't you remember for more than a minute? Shoulders, shoulders!"

"Mama, I am holding my shoulders back and it hurts."

"Nonsense! You'll never find a husband by complaining!" To Leah, she added, "The man who wins my daughter's heart will be very lucky, Miss Vogel. She is an heiress. But an heiress who will *not* stand straight!" This last was snapped out so ferociously that several strollers turned to look.

Zelda's eyes flooded. Leah felt sorry for her. "Look, Bertha . . . Mrs. Lazarus . . . Zelda is standing perfectly straight, see?" Leah said earnestly. "Her shoulders curve forward a little—" She thought fast. "—the way the ancient Greeks considered proper and beautiful in a woman of quality."

"The ancient Greeks?"

"They called it the Curve of Femininity." Quickly, before the woman asked too many more questions about something that had been born in her imagination only minutes ago, Leah went on. "What you should concentrate on, in my opinion, is Zelda's beautiful big eyes. I could show you how to make them look even bigger, Zelda, with kohl. . . ."

"Coal? What nonsense!"

Leah gave a little tinkle of a laugh. "No, no, Bertha, not c-o-a-l. K-o-h-l. The ancient Egyptians used it. You can see it at any museum. All the busts of royalty, yes, even the kings, you see the eyes outlined in kohl."

"You're quite the authority on ancient customs, aren't you, Miss Vogel?"

"I *am* a writer, you know." Another gay little laugh. "And I know beautiful eyes when I see them—that I really *am* expert at."

Mrs. Lazarus peered at her daughter's face. "Yes . . . well, the eyes *are* quite nice. Kohl, you say. Where could we . . . ? I mean, if I should decide to do it, where could we find kohl?"

"In a pharmacy. That's where I buy mine. But I'd be glad to save you the trouble. Before you leave, why don't I give Zelda a little potful of mine, and a brush, and show her—show you both—how it's done."

Zelda gave Leah a look of such melting gratitude, she almost blushed from it. "I never knew I had beautiful eyes before."

"Don't talk nonsense, Zelda. Of course, you knew! Your papa and I have told you so, dozens of times!"

"I don't re—"

"Dozens of times!"

"Yes, Mama," the girl said; but to Leah's astonishment, she gave Leah a look that said, as clearly as words, *No, Mama, I don't, Mama, and Mama, you're a liar.* In a moment it was gone. But it seemed the lumpen Zelda kept a little spark of fight hidden away. Well, good for her.

Bertha had already forgotten her cruel words. "Kohl . . ." she repeated. "But . . . I wonder . . . is it quite, um, *ladylike.* I mean you say you use it . . . and you look . . ."

Leah knew that when she had first come downstairs from the apartment to meet Joe's family in the street, she had shocked them. Poo, what did they know about style, up there in the Bronx? She was wearing the latest rage, a simple sack dress, trimmed in braid and fringe and made of the nicest silk, but she knew it had thrown these overstuffed and overdressed *nouveau riche* into a tizzy. "That's right," she wanted to say, "no corset. Aren't you jealous?" Of course, Leah said nothing, just pretended she didn't notice their stares and their open mouths as they took in her bobbed hair, her loose-fitting dress, and her *sandals. No lady wears sandals:* the words might just as well have been written across Bertha Lazarus's broad forehead. That's right, and no lady wore rows and rows of beads along with an old-fashioned gold locket on a chain. But Leah Vogel did! And looked much nicer than those two mincing along in their tight, narrow skirts and high-button shoes!

"So, Miss Vogel, how long did you say you and Joseph . . . er, know each other?"

"Five years. But we didn't live together until two years ago, if that's what you mean."

"No, that's certainly *not* what I mean." The older woman made a fierce face, gesturing with her elaborate hat toward her daughter, as if to say, *Not in front of the child.* Leah caught Zelda secretly sticking her tongue out at her mother.

When they got to Sixth Avenue, Joe herded them across the street, pointing out places of interest—as they headed for West Fourth Street to look at its "quaint" little shops—like the Paint Box Art Gallery and the Idée Chic Tea Room. All along the way, they kept being bumped by people who were busy looking at their guidebooks and maps for art studios and garrets.

The five of them continued toward Washington Square.

There, they would stroll from stand to stand so the Lazaruses could look for souvenirs of their visit to "Manhattan's Montmartre."

Along the way, Bertha spotted a downstairs tea shop, its tables draped in Spanish shawls, its walls painted a bright chrome yellow. Candles stuffed into bottles cast dim light and created deep shadows. All the better to hide the cracks in the walls and dirt in the corners, Leah thought.

"Oh look, Ike, how sweet! Can't we go in?"

Isaac gave a quick look and dismissed it with a disdainful wave of his hand. "Joseph is taking us to a proper restaurant for lunch. . . ." He looked to Joe to finish his thought. He did a lot of that, Leah noted; and she also noted that Joe was right there, ready to provide whatever his papa could not remember. Well, the man hardly listened. He spoke and then he turned his attention elsewhere. Leah could not imagine having a real conversation with him.

"The O'Neill and Bristol Oyster and Chop House, Mama," Joe said. "You'll love it. They still have some gaslight there and a lot of big old aspidistras. I know you like them. And the food is really good."

Leah knew he meant plentiful. O'Neill and Bristol was known for the huge quantities of food served. And from the look of him, Leah thought, that was right up Papa's alley.

"Joseph and his father are close . . . *quite* close," Bertha Lazarus said. When Leah did not respond, she charged ahead. "Well, you can understand that. Three daughters and only one son. Sons are important to fathers, you know. That's why we had always hoped that Joseph would marry and have a son of his own. You know what I mean, Miss Vogel."

"No, Bertha, I'm afraid I don't know what you mean. Why is it important for Joe to have a son? He doesn't seem to want one."

"Every man needs an heir, Miss Vogel. Time is passing, and if Joe isn't careful, we won't have our grandsons." Her tone was coy, but her eyes were as hard as flint.

"I'm sorry, did I misunderstand? I thought Joe's sisters had sons. . . ."

"Yes, but the *name*, Miss Vogel, the *name*." As Leah seemed not to get her meaning, she added, "The Lazarus name. My daughters, of course, are no longer Lazarus."

"You mean, a grandson doesn't count unless he has the right

last name?" Leah couldn't help it; her voice was getting tight
with irritation.

"Now, Leah, that's not what Mama means at all. Mama
loves all her grandsons," Joe chimed in.

"Of course I do!" Bertha snapped, glaring at Leah as if the
whole idea had been hers in the first place. "Of *course* I do!"

"Leah didn't mean it the way it sounded, did you, Leah?"

Leah opened her mouth and closed it, opened it again and
then decided to hell with it. She hated these people, *hated*
them. She was watching her lighthearted, devil-may-care
sweetheart turn, in front of her eyes, into a dutiful little boy.
Why? Why was he bowing and scraping before them? He always made such jokes about them. She didn't understand!

Leah sighed, and gave Bertha Lazarus her best smile. "I
can't imagine how you could think I would ever accuse *you* of
a lack of feeling, Bertha. You are so obviously a woman of
sensitivity."

"I accept your apology, Miss Vogel. And I hope that now
you grasp the importance of not losing the family name."

Whether she grasped it or not was never to be known. At
that moment—happily, Leah thought—Lenore Hutchinson and
her dear friend Hortense Detweiler came striding toward them,
arms open, big smiles on their faces. Both women wore trousers, silk embroidered shirts, and handwoven sashes, bowler
hats on their heads. Even as she cried out greetings to them,
Leah was aware that Bertha Lazarus had stopped walking and
was staring at them, aghast.

"Joe! Leah! How divine!" Both Lenore and Hortense had
taken in the scene with one look: the uncomfortable Leah, the
squirming Joe, the overstuffed, overdressed threesome; and
they had decided to put on their best Bohemian act. There
were hugs and kisses and exclamations, a great deal of posing
and posturing—even a bit of an English accent from Hortense,
who came from Michigan. Leah wanted to giggle; it was delicious. When they were introduced to the Lazaruses, they all
but bowed from the waist, and Lenore, who could be wicked,
actually kissed Bertha's hand.

"We're off to the suffrage meeting in Cooper Union. Anyone like to come with us? No? Well, take these—" Laughing,
they handed out leaflets. And then they were gone, like a
whirlwind spinning through, lifting Leah up, then putting her
down and speeding off.

"Well!" Bertha Lazarus said. Color was returning to her

cheeks. "Well, I never . . . ! Joseph, those creatures *were* both women, weren't they?"

"Yes, Mama, dancers. Very well-known dancers."

"*I* don't know them. And are they . . . ? No, I don't want to know. I don't think I could *stand* knowing."

Leah looked over at Joe and, to her relief, he gave her a wink. Maybe she would be able to live through the rest of this day, after all.

Lunch was plentiful and good, and both Mama and Papa approved of the slightly old-fashioned look of the restaurant. Isaac Lazarus polished off the last crumb of his dessert, belched, patted his belly and took out an ivory toothpick, which he proceeded to use—behind his hand, as was considered genteel.

When he was quite finished, he sat back and said, "Well now, I understand that there's real genuine art for sale down here at good prices. Is that so, Joseph?"

"Yes, sir. Greenwich Village is the source, Papa. What were you thinking of?"

"No photographs. That's not art." Leah looked to see how Joe took that. He just lowered his eyes and tightened his lips. "No, what I want is *real* art! Oil paintings, like your mother's ancestors. Something big and grand. What do you say, Bertie?" he said to his wife; it was the first time he had addressed her directly since Leah had met them. "You've been wanting a painting to match the new sofa in the living room. Joseph, do you think we could find something in blue?" Eating had not only improved his disposition, it had apparently rendered him capable of extended speech.

Instead of laughing at the idea of using art to match furniture, Joe very seriously assured his father that probably they could find something in blue.

"Something on the lines of Maxfield Parrish or maybe that new fellow, what's his name, Joseph?"

"Norman Rockwell?"

"That's the fellow. I like them. Their pictures are always so true-to-life, and I say if you're going to have a picture on your wall, it should be true-to-life."

"I'm certain we can find you an artist who paints true-to-life in blue, Papa."

"Good . . . and if we find a painter who did something nice in blue, why, maybe we'll ask him to do a family portrait. I do like a nice big family portrait in oils, don't you?"

Leah brought her wandering thoughts back. "If it's nice big oil paintings you want, you're certainly in the right place." Let them buy two oil paintings, let them buy six! With all the friends she and Joe had who struggled to make a living painting, why shouldn't these rich idiots help?

And so, when they came out of the restaurant into the sunshine, they went looking for art galleries. On the way, Papa insisted upon stopping and listening while two streets musicians finished a rendition of "I Didn't Raise My Boy to Be a Soldier." Antiwar feeling was running high in the Village. He then gave them a lecture on the glory of war, and a dime.

Suddenly Isaac announced: "There's one!" A few steps away a sign pointed upstairs to the Unity Art Gallery. Leah was not familiar with the Unity. But that meant nothing; new galleries opened every day.

They went up a steep flight to the second floor gallery, which consisted of three small low-ceilinged rooms. The walls were covered with paintings, and with sinking heart Leah recognized them at once as Walter Morris's new cubist works. Then she saw, in the next room, facing the entrance and bigger than life, one of his outsized garish nudes. Oh God! Her pulse began racing as she looked around to be sure Walter wasn't there.

"Joe," she said, trying to keep her tone light, "I don't think these paintings will suit your parents at all."

"Not at all," Papa boomed, moving inexorably past the cubist canvases in the first room, toward the huge nude. They all followed, Leah bringing up the rear.

Suddenly, with a jolt that felt as if someone had punched her in the middle of her chest, Leah stopped stock-still, then she turned cold right down to her fingertips, and a strange humming began in her ears. Was she going to faint? She certainly hoped so.

Oh dear God, there it was. No, there *she* was. Damn Walter! He had *promised*! He had promised to destroy it, to paint over it. He was a liar, a diabolic, malicious liar! She was going to die! Her throat had closed up. She could not utter a single word.

The young woman looked so *large*, up there on the wall, framed in gilded wood, the flesh gleaming with youth and health, one soft hip thrust out, the pink nipples on the breasts tight, the pouting lips on the face—on what was unmistakably, without a doubt, *her* face—curled seductively.

It was utterly silent in the room. No one spoke. No one seemed to be breathing. Leah could hear the hurried beating of her heart like a drum's tattoo. She could not take her eyes from the painting. She could not think. She wanted to kill Walter Morris with her bare hands.

And then, a little too calmly, and loudly, Joe said, "Well I think that's all we need see here. I know a much better place, Papa, with many blue paintings."

They all turned and walked out and went down the stairs without another word. Down on the street, Joe began walking rapidly, and they followed him, without asking where he was going. The silence was taut with unspoken accusations.

Abruptly, Isaac Lazarus stopped and rounded on his son. "So, Joseph, this is how you repay me for my years of investment in you!"

"Papa, I—"

"Be quiet! Fifty dollars I send you, every month, every month for years because a photographer cannot make a decent living, because it takes *time* to become known. Fifty dollars I send you each month, and when I ask you to find a nice Jewish girl to marry, do you listen? No, you get yourself a harlot, a whore who poses bare naked for strangers and allows her pictures to be put on public walls for everyone to see!

"Have you no shame?" That was for Leah; but he did not wait for an answer. He turned back to Joe. "Women are a different race from men, Joseph! All your life I tell you that, but you will not believe me. Women are put on earth for one thing and one thing only—to be a man's wife and bear his children. Do you see what happens when you go against God's will? Look at the women in this hellhole, running around the streets, dressed like men! Women smoking! Women drinking in bars! Women painted like common sluts!"

He turned once again to Leah, glaring at her as if his eyes could shoot daggers into her and kill her on the spot.

"For years, my brothers have asked me when will my Yussele begin to give me a return on my investment! Do I have an answer for them? I have no answer for them. I bend my head in shame because my only son is a wastrel and an ingrate, who takes my money and spits in my face!

"It is done! It is over! No more *schtupping* you with money! Not until this whore is out of your home!"

"It's my home, too!" Leah couldn't believe it was her voice, shouting like that, without so much as a quiver. "And it's my life! You have nothing to say about what I do, *nothing*! And for your information, I don't take money for doing it!"

Isaac turned the color of a plum and made a strangling sound, so that his wife quickly went to him, her hand on his arm.

"A *pisk*! A *nafke*!" He spat on the ground. Leah heard Zelda give a little gasp; nobody else said a word. "My son will come to his senses," Isaac Lazarus roared at her. "And until he does, not one more penny, not *one*!"

"Papa! Please!" Joe cried; but the old man wheeled around and strode away. His wife trotted alongside him, talking rapidly to him. Zelda started after them, then came running back. She gave Leah a swift hug and in her ear, so softly Leah might have imagined it, whispered. "*I* think you're grand. I hope Joe marries you." And then she was off, at a run, to join her parents before they noticed she had stayed behind.

"Papa! Please!" Leah mimicked, her voice heavy with contempt. "So, your papa has been keeping you all these years. And you had the nerve to pass yourself off as an artist, independent of society! You're a fraud, Joe Lazarus! I don't know you! I guess I never did." She blinked back tears. She would *not* cry. She would *not* seem weak and . . . and womanly.

She turned from him and walked rapidly up the street, not even looking where she was going. She didn't care, just so long as she got away from him. She could hear his footsteps, running behind her, and he called out, "I'm a fraud!? What about you? Posing in the nude and never telling me! Just how do you think I felt, seeing you on that wall for all the world to look at and desire!'

As Joe caught up with her, she quickened her steps. "My body is mine, to do with what I wish. You were the one who wanted freedom. But when *I* took it, that was another story, wasn't it?"

"Your big mouth nearly gave my father a heart attack. He has a bad heart, you could have killed him."

They were both panting a little, quickening the pace as they walked, not looking at each other. "What a pity that would have been! To kill the goose that lays the golden egg!"

"We couldn't live if it wasn't for the money he gives me!"

At their building on Barrow Street, they fought over who would open the door. Joe won and Leah took the opportunity to rush past him up the stairs. But he was right behind her.

At the door to their apartment, he held onto her arm. "Leah, I only took the money so we could afford to live together!"

"Like hell you did!"

"Goddammit, are you calling me a liar?"

"Goddammit, Joe," she cried, pulling away and rushing past him into the flat, frantic to get she didn't know where. "I'm calling you a man I thought I knew but now I think I don't even know if I know!" She stopped, realizing how ridiculous she sounded. "Joe, I don't know *who* you are anymore!"

She burst into despairing tears, burying her face in her hands. His arms went around her, he murmured into her ear, kissing her neck, her hair, whatever he could reach.

"Leah, it's me, it's me, don't worry, I haven't changed. I'm the same Joe Lazarus, you'll see. It's me, the man who loves you."

He was getting to her; he was definitely getting to her. He was a charmer, and wasn't that why she loved him? "But you lied to me, Joe."

She could hear the grin in his voice. "No I didn't; I just, er . . . neglected to tell you something. Please, sweetheart, that's not lying. I knew you wouldn't like it, and I was afraid I'd lose you. And my family . . . my mother and my father . . . Now that you've met them, you can see what I'm up against. Can't you?"

"Oh, Joe, it was so *awful*!"

"I know, I know . . ." His hands were busy on her clothing, his lips on her throat and her earlobe as one by one he removed the beads from her neck. "*They're* awful," he murmured, his voice thick with heat. "But they're my family, Leah. . . ."

And she was just going to have to put up with them, she supposed. But now Joe was peeling the shift dress from her, throwing it across the room; he was dropping to his knees, kissing her belly, stripping the panties from her hips. All thought came to a halt as he unbuttoned his trousers, as he fell to his knees between her legs, pushing them apart, as he thrust himself, stiff, ecstatic, engorged, into her, panting, grunting, his eyes looking into hers as he drove into her faster, faster, faster, as he pumped his life into her. Trembling, both of them clinging tightly to each other, they fell together onto the carpet.

Suddenly they both began to laugh. "Oh God," Joe said. "The look on his face when he realized the beautiful girl in the painting was *you*!"

Leah had been picturing the same thing, exactly the same thing! Nothing mattered, none of it counted, except that they had the same thoughts, that they were soulmates. What did she care about his family? What could they possibly do to them? They couldn't be harmed, she and Joe, just as long as they stuck together. Because as long as they stuck together, *they* were a family, and to hell with everyone else.

9

September 1917

Leah's anguish was deep and cold, like a block of ice sitting in the middle of her chest, chilling her blood and numbing her. Yet, in spite of being dead inside, she could not stop weeping tears that were salty and hot, like life. She stood in the middle of the kitchen, wailing like a child, unable to stop.

She was only dimly aware of Joe, on his knees in front of her, his arms wrapped tightly around her legs, his voice supplicating.

"Leah, darling, please. You knew I was going to sign up. We went through this whole thing already. Can't you be proud of me? All the other women are proud of *their* soldier boys." He got to his feet, brushed off the knees of his trousers, and grinned. "And think how good I'll look in a uniform."

From a great distance she heard his voice, realized he was trying to make her laugh. She didn't care. She was sick with her anger and her fear.

"No! Again you're leaving me! No! I can't bear it!"

"What do you mean again? I've never left you. If you're bringing up that free-love nonsense from the past—you know that's all over with, that it was just . . . ! Leah, for God's sake, make sense! At least stop the crying, you'll make yourself sick!"

Where were all the tears coming from? In one little corner

of her mind she saw herself: tightly hugging herself, her nails digging into the tender skin of her upper arms; barely feeling the pain, wondering if the marks would bleed, and wondering why she was crying as if her heart would break. . . . And then the world went blank and she fainted.

When she opened her eyes, she was curled on the couch. It was only a few moments later. The autumn sun was slanting through the window right where it had been before—when Joe had come in laughing and shouting: "We're going! We're going to fight the Hun at last!"

Leah moaned and turned her head, pushing her face into the prickly tweed, her eyes squeezed shut again.

"Leah. Sweetheart." Joe's voice, tender and tentative.

"How could you? How *could* you?" Her tears began once more.

"Leah, how could I *not*? We're at war, my darling, it's every able-bodied man's duty to go."

She struggled to push herself upright, made strong by a surge of anger. "Men are going to be called. When that happens, it will be soon enough! You could have waited!"

"Wait? Are you *meshugah*? If I wait, it'll be all over before I even get there!"

She saw that he was balanced on the very edge of the couch. One quick push from her and off he fell, tumbling onto the floor, yelling "Hey!" in surprise.

"You really are selfish, Joe! You're so afraid you'll miss the 'fun'! What is there about shooting guns and pushing bayonets through people that appeals to the male sex, anyway? And not one thought to me! What about me? What am I supposed to do while you're gallivanting all over France, playing at war? How am I supposed to make my way alone?"

Joe picked himself up off the floor, taking care not to get too close to her. That almost made her laugh; but she was damned if she would. The nerve of him! Going off to fight the Kaiser for no good reason except it was an adventure!

"What does it solve?" she demanded. "What does war do, except kill people?"

Leah knew she was in the minority. It seemed like the entire city of New York was war-crazy—even the theater, even vaudeville. All you heard on the streets and in the dance halls and on the stage were war songs. They brought down the house, people leaping to their feet and cheering. But not Leah Vogel, not she. When they went dancing, she always asked for

"Oh, Johnny, Oh," or "For Me and My Gal," or "Darktown Strutter's Ball." Something lively you could tap your feet to and sing along with; something to blot out the talk and head-lines about the Kaiser and the trenches and the Dardanelles!

Joe was saying earnestly, "Leah, listen. We already had this out in June—remember?—when I signed up for Selective Service."

"Remember? How could I ever forget? How could you do a thing like that, without even *telling* me!"

"Peace, woman! What's done is done. Where's your patrio-tism? You know what that poster says, 'Uncle Sam Wants *You*.' Well, I looked into that stern, fatherly visage and found myself saluting and saying 'Yes, *sir*!' You wouldn't want me to be a shirker, would you, Leah?" He tipped his head to one side, giving her that lopsided grin she loved, hoping to coax a smile from her.

"I suppose not. But still . . . to go off just like that and leave me all alone, a helpless woman . . ."

He burst into laughter. "You, helpless? Since when? You go into the worst neighborhoods in New York, alone and absolutely fearless. When I objected to you going to that shantytown under the bridge, what did you say to me, hey? You said you were perfectly fine, thank you very much, and just because you were a woman that didn't mean you were a weakling. Well, now, didn't you? Didn't you?"

Yes, of course, that's precisely what she had said to him. But this was different. He was deserting her to go play at soldiers. He was going, not sometime, not someday in the fuzzy future, but tomorrow. *Tomorrow.* She was angry, but most of all she was afraid. Of what, she wasn't quite sure, she only knew that a knot of apprehension had been sitting in her belly since the fifth of June, that terrible day when hundreds of thousands of young men had joined the army in a fit of patriotism. And Joe Lazarus among them.

"I know I said I'm not a weakling," she told him now. "I just don't understand how you can go off so easily, with a whistle and a wave. Don't you care about me? Won't you . . . miss me, Joe? Don't you love me?"

She watched the melting look glaze his eyes. He walked over and sat next to her on the sofa, gathering her into his arms.

"You know how much I love you."

"But Joe, you might . . . you might get hurt."

He kissed her earlobe and then the soft curve under her ear, sending shivers down her spine. "Don't be silly. Once the Americans get there, the war'll be over in a month! Everyone says so." His lips moved to the hollow in her throat.

"How do you *know* that? What if it isn't?" she persisted.

"Everyone says so . . ." His voice had become husky and his kisses more ardent. He was tugging at the ties on her blouse. "I'll be back before you know it . . . sweet Leah. . . ."

But what if you don't come back at all? The thought came, unbidden, bringing with it a dreadful chill, and she quickly pushed it away. And then, for the first time in years, a picture of her mother came flashing into her head. It was eerie: she could see every detail, down to her gold ear bobs, the blue hat with the flowers, her mother's sad eyes, filled with tears. She could even smell lilies of the valley. Her mother loved them. She had forgotten that totally; but suddenly, the scent was sharp in her nostrils, startling her.

She must have moved in Joe's arms; he stopped his caresses and pushed her away a little, to look at her. "Leah? What is it?"

"Nothing. Nothing. Something." She strained to bring back the picture of her mother, but it would not come. "Never mind, it's gone now."

She lifted her face to him, offering her lips, desperate now to be close to him, as close as she could get.

The sun was shining brightly on Brooklyn. Leah picked her way along the tracks of the Flatbush Avenue Terminal, walking past car after car of the train, peering up at the windows, looking for Joe. His group had crossed the East River this morning to board a train that would take them all the way out to Yaphank on Long Island, to Camp Upton, to boot camp.

"They'll train us there," he explained to her. "They'll show us how to shoot and use our bayonets." His voice was eager and excited; how she hated that.

A long line of women, all ages, sisters, mothers, wives, sweethearts, inched its way along, every woman with her head tipped back, looking up at the windows for her own soldier boy. There was an excited buzz of conversation; over it, every once in a while, a name would be called. Hank! Johnny! Alfred! Tom!

Where was Joe? The sun was so bright, it dazzled the eyes, and when she looked up at all the heads stuck out of the windows, they all looked the same, the young men all wearing their uniforms, all with their hair clipped short.

But then there he was. There was no mistaking the thick black hair, the impish grin, the crinkling eyes. Joe! Her heart flooded. She still felt the same thrill as when she had seen him the first time. Nineteen ten. Only seven years? How long ago it seemed now, a different world, and she a very different Leah.

"Joe! Joe! Here I am!"

He grinned when he spotted her. "How could I miss you?" he called, shoving his head and shoulders out of the window. "The prettiest girl in the place!"

"I was afraid I wouldn't find you!"

"Well, I knew you would." She looked around, theatrically; and he said, "What? *What?*"

"I thought for sure your mama and papa and your sister would be here to say good-bye to you. What happened? Did they find out I'd be here and decide to do without a farewell?"

He flushed. "Well . . . as a matter of fact . . ."

"As a matter of fact *what*, Joe?" And then she knew. Last evening, their last night together, he had gone off for several hours. "I'm going to walk the streets and say my good-byes to everything," he had told her. "You understand." He even took his favorite camera. Of course, she had thought, the artist says good-bye to the world as he knows it. She could almost see the picture story, laid out for the Mid-Week Pictorial of the *Times*.

But now she knew better. He really had gone up to the Bronx, to bend the knee before Mama and Papa, pretending right along with them that she did not exist, did not share his life, was not a person, in fact! He had promised he would never visit them as long as they refused to see her.

"You broke your promise! I don't believe you!"

"Leah! They're my parents!"

"They hate me! They won't even change now that you're going and leaving me alone! I call that heartless. I call *you* heartless! And to think I believed you loved me."

"Leah! Please don't be angry. Of course I love you. But my mother . . . my father . . . my sister . . . how could I go off to boot camp without saying good-bye?"

"You could have said, 'Come to my house, where Leah also lives, and there I will say good-bye.' We've been together for years, Joe. They should be used to it by now."

"Oh God! Don't make me choose! It makes me feel so bad!

Look, Leah, in time they'll come around, you'll see. And listen, please stay in touch with Zelda, would you? She adores you. Will you? Please?"

"With Zelda, yes. Okay. But only with Zelda!"

"That's my girl! But you'll see me first. As soon as they give us our first leave, I'll be running back to you!"

A loud hiss of steam shot out from beneath the car, followed by the unmistakable clank of a train preparing to move. Then from up front, tooting, bells ringing, and more spurts of noisy steam. Oh God, he was going! He was leaving!

"Joe! Joe!" She stood on tiptoe, reaching to take his hand; and he leaned out as far as he could; but there were so many other men trying to push out of the small window, trying to say their farewells. She jumped up, their outstretched fingers strained to touch, but they could not quite reach.

"Joe!" she called as the train started to move, trying to fight back the tears that sprang into her eyes. She wanted to say something to him, but she didn't know what.

And then there it was again: the memory. But now she remembered all of it.

She is seven years old, dressed in her very best dress, a pretty blue coat and matching bonnet, holding her mother's hand. Her mother is also wearing a blue coat, a blue hat with pretty flowers on it. Her kidskin gloves feel slippery and not real, not warm like skin. She does not like the way the gloves feel but when she tries to get her mother's attention, she cannot. Her mother is looking somewhere else, her head turned away. Leah can see only the curve of a cheek, the tip of the nose, the tendrils of dark hair that have loosened from the combs.

"Mama! Mama! Where are we going?"

There is no answer and they continue walking—just a little too fast for Leah's short legs. She is forced to trot to keep up and, after a while, she begins to whimper. But her mother pays no attention, just keeps tugging at her, keeps saying, "Hurry, hurry."

Where is her Mama taking her and why is she wearing her *Shabbos* dress? When she asked this morning, Mama only shook her head and said, "You ask too many questions."

"Mama, are we going to Papa now?" Where is Papa? *Where is her papa?* She is frightened, without the words to describe what of. She is tired and out of breath. Her arm hurts where Mama tugs at it, and she needs to make water.

"Mama, am I going to see my papa now?"

They stop walking and Bella's face turns down to look at her. An angry face. "Hush up, you stupid child! No, you are not going to see your papa now!"

To her horror, her mother begins to weep, right there in the middle of the street. People stop walking and turn to stare at them.

Her mother looks around, her face twisted with anger, and she screams at them, in Yiddish. Not in English. Her mother never learned more than a few words in English.

"What's the matter with you? You never saw a woman cry before? You've got nothing better to do but stand in the street and stare at me? If you can't have *rachmonos* on me, at least think of the child!"

It is all emblazoned on Leah's memory: the pant legs and boots and long skirts, dust on the hems, the high-heeled shoes, the ruffled edge of a folded parasol. People standing still and then finally moving away. There's a tug on her arm, and once again they are marching along and she has to scamper to keep up.

She has trouble climbing the long stairs and at last Mama lifts her up to carry her to the top. Then Mama is hugging her close, whispering in her ear, "I promise you, *shayfele*, one day you will understand. I love you, you hear me? You are my treasure, you hear me?" Squeezing her, covering her cheek with kisses and tears, tears and kisses.

She puts Leah down, and squatting next to her, straightens her bonnet, tucks in a stray curl, adjusts the coat, pulls up the cotton stockings.

"Very pretty. You are a very pretty girl, Leah. Always remember that. Pretty and quick-witted. You will do well in this world, if you learn never to trust a man."

"Where are we?"

"The train station. One hundred twenty-fifth Street station." A train station. Yes. Leah has been on the train. It is very clickety clackety, loud, and you get thrown from side to side.

"Are we going on the train, Mama?"

Her mother does not answer. She pins something to Leah's coat, a thick folded paper, and then stands straight and takes Leah's hand again. "Just a few minutes, *shayfele*, just a few minutes more." Once again her face has turned to look somewhere else, somewhere Leah cannot follow.

A woman with hair the color of carrots, skin the color of

milk, little orange dots all over her face, comes clambering up the steps, looking around, a little out of breath. When she sees them, she smiles right at Leah. Leah does not smile back; the woman is a stranger.

"Mrs. Vogel? Mrs. Bella Vogel? I am Lucy Jacobs of the Hebrew—"

"I know, I know who you are. Good. Here. This is Leah. She is seven. I cannot—"

Leah hears her mother's voice crack, feels her mother letting go of her hand, and then, without warning, Mama is running, running away, away from the woman, away from her.

"Mama!" She must run and catch up with her. But the woman holds onto her.

"Be careful, little one! A train is coming!"

The smoke-belching, spark-spraying monster screeches and squeals and thunders as it comes racing toward her. Leah shrinks back, close to Lucy Jacobs, who picks her up. Held high in Lucy Jacob's arms, Leah can see Mama again, and as the train shudders to a halt, Mama climbs into it and disappears.

Leah calls and calls to her. Even after the train leaves the station, she struggles in Lucy Jacobs's arms, crying for her mama to come back, come back, don't go, wait for me, wait for me, come back . . .

But Mama did not wait. And Mama did not come back. And here I am again, Leah thought, blinking back tears. Watching a train take away someone I love. I never saw her again, never. Will I ever see Joe? My darling Joe? Oh God! The next moment, his car had gone around a curve, the open windows sprouting dozens of waving arms and tiny American flags. Leah trotted alongside, letting the tears streak down her face. But she couldn't see him; she had no idea which arm was his. The train quickly took on speed and she was out of breath. She had to stop running. Her chest was heaving, her heart pounding heavily and hurtfully behind her ribs. She stood and watched, helpless, as the train became smaller and smaller, moving inexorably away from her, finally becoming a little dark dot, and then disappearing from sight.

He was gone, gone. He had really left her. And he had left with a lie. He said, "Don't make me choose," but it seemed to her that he had already made his choice. His horrible parents, who understood nothing about him, were more important to

him than she was. Was this her fate, that everyone she loved
left her? Well, then, she was going to have to learn how to live
without love, somehow.

She turned to leave the terminal to go home. No, she decided, not home. The office. Jim would be there; he almost always was. Jim could be a big bully sometimes. He was always
stony broke and behind on every bill, and he was stubborn as
a mule. But today the thought of him sitting in his swivel
chair—big, solid, immovable, unchanging, chewing on the
stump of a cigar—gave her a wonderful, warm feeling of secu-
rity.

She'd go to the office and they would talk and talk. Maybe
even about Joe. Jim would tell her she was behaving like a
typical woman, silly, romantic, and unrealistic. "You're better
than that, Leah, you can rise above your unfortunate sex." And
somehow, in the end, he would make her feel better; he always
did.

10

August 1918

It was so hot! The front door of 35 Barrow Street was propped
open in the hope of catching a breath of air. Fat chance! Even
though the morning's paper said "not as warm as yesterday,
with light winds," it felt every bit as hot as yesterday—and the
day before and the day before that. As for winds, they were
nonexistent. Not a leaf on any tree stirred. August in New
York was somebody's bad dream: sweltering, hot, humid, and
heavy, so that you felt as if you were walking through water.
Especially her, especially now, pregnant and clumsy.

How different the weather had been the night she and Joe
made this baby. New Year's Eve, frosty and full of snow, their
breath like twin plumes in the lamplight as they strolled home
from a celebration at Bertolotti's. They had felt so lucky that

Joe had been given a weekend pass and they could see 1917 out together. Joe had pulled her closer and said, "Oh my God, Leah, I just had an awful thought!"

Alarmed, she stopped walking. "What?"

"We haven't made love since last year!" And he laughed at the look on her face.

Later, when they were entwined on the bed, his eyes had been blazing, his lips pulled tight against his teeth in passion. No laughs then. All night long they kept waking up and making love. In the morning she was sore and tender, and exhausted; still, they turned to each other ardently once again. As if they were both afraid that this time might be the very last. That's how everyone was making love: as if it might never happen again. That's what war did.

And war took the men away. In March, Joe had left on a troop ship. A brass band played marches at the pier, and the dock was full of women waving and crying and blowing kisses to the olive-drab mass of men far above on the decks. Leah kept smiling, just in case Joe could see her, but all the time she was fighting her morning sickness, willing the toast and tea she had forced down for breakfast to stay in her stomach. The doctor had told her the nausea would disappear soon. "My guess is that this is another New Year's Eve baby. We always get plenty of those. The champagne does it. Well, by April Fool's Day you should be feeling a whole lot better."

A baby was the last thing Leah wanted, with Joe off to France any minute; but he seemed happy about it. "I'll have a whole family to come home to, sweetheart, you and a pretty little girl who looks just like you." He had laughed when she said, "Not if your mother has anything to say about it. She wants a boy." "Well," Joe said, "she *doesn't* have anything to say about it. And anyway, she'll love this child, boy or girl, I promise you."

One thing had come true: by April, that ever-present sick feeling was gone. In fact, for a while Leah felt better and more energetic than she ever had. But now, in her eighth month, the child was a heavy weight that pressed on her bladder and bent her back. She felt bloated and bulky and not at all attractive.

Ungainly or not, in spite of the heat and humidity, she went down the stairs at a run. She could see the familiar envelope from Over There on top of the pile of mail. A letter from Joe! Her heart lifted. It was going to be a lucky day.

The first auspicious sign was the photograph she'd spotted

in the morning's *Times* Mid-Week Pictorial. It showed the Second Division, Joe's division, moving along a French road. Men on horseback were accompanying a wagon train of ammunition; and in the background a long double line of men raising a cloud of dust as they marched. Joe's division . . . maybe he was somewhere in this picture, maybe he was one of those faceless men way in the back. Look how the ones in the front smiled; Joe would be smiling, too. All the photographs of the AEF showed grinning, cocky young men who looked as if they hadn't a care in the world. They looked as if they were on their way to a party, not to a battle.

Maybe Joe was there the day the photographer shot this scene. Wait a minute, what did she mean, *maybe*. She was sure of it; she had kissed the tip of her finger and touched the photograph. Anyway, thinking so comforted her.

Leah smiled with anticipation. Joe's letters were usually long, full of his thoughts and longings, but they also contained vivid word-pictures of the French countryside and his comrades. She loved his letters. If she couldn't have him, then let her have his written words! Each one of his letters had been read and reread so often, the paper had gone quite thin and had a strange grayish look to it. If she weren't careful, she'd wear the ink from the page!

She clutched the small bundle of mail, put her hand on the railing and looked up the stairway. It seemed endless, so many steps. But that was only because she was so heavy and clumsy. The child she carried was huge, or anyway, that's how it felt. Her belly was enormous, a huge solid mass that she had to push along in front of her; it was part of her, yet separate. It was very strange, but rather exciting, especially when the little one in there began kicking and moving around.

But it was very definitely not exciting to contemplate climbing the two long flights to the apartment. There had been days, in the past few weeks, when she'd thought she would *never* get to the top. The usual end-of-summer heat had settled in, like a steaming stolid beast, crouched on its haunches over the city, panting damp hot air into the baking streets. She found it difficult to move or breathe.

But a letter from Joe! For that she would gladly make the long climb. Sometimes, if Joe wasn't too exhausted or too fed-up or too bored, he would write long passages describing the ways he would make love to her when he got back. She would sit there with her loins flooding, her engorged sex pulsing, feeling the heat rise in her. It had been so long! So long! Even with that awkward protuberance she carried in front of her, even with her belly button turned inside out from the stretching skin, even though she could no longer see her feet and could only fit into shifts and chemises made for fat women . . . even so, she sometimes moaned and wept with her desire to feel him, hot and stiff, entering her. How she missed him!

Slowly, grunting with the effort, she pulled herself up the long stairway by grabbing on the railing. By the time she was at her door, she was puffing, sweat streaming from her armpits and under her breasts. As soon as she paused, the child within her began to turn itself, squirming and kicking. She could see her distended belly pulsing and throbbing; she could even see little knobs pushing out. Elbows? Feet? She didn't know. She could not wait for this child to get itself born and leave her be.

She let herself in and, picking up the paper Japanese fan she had dropped onto the desk on her way downstairs, began fanning herself vigorously. There was a pitcher of lemonade in the fridge. She shuffled in, poured herself a glass and carried it back out into the living room, rubbing its frosty sides on the back of her neck.

She sat in the rocker, waiting for the kicking and pushing to stop. Lately it started whenever she rested. "I hope you are better-behaved when you're here," she said to the unborn baby. "Or you and I will have trouble."

It couldn't be very long now; the taut belly that had so long ridden high on her body, making her gasp for breath, had shifted. The doctor said the fetus had dropped. She would go into labor in a week or two, he'd guessed. It couldn't be too soon for her.

She took a sip of lemonade and then slowly, slowly, opened Joe's letter. It was dated "end of June" and began:

My darling Leah and baby. I write this, sitting in the hole made some time ago in a garden wall by a German shell, with the smell of springtime all about me. France is a beautiful country; I can see why the Fritzes want it. They say the roads we travel on were built by the ancient Romans; can you imagine? Seems strange to be marching where Caesar's legions marched, before the Christian Era, and believe me, Leah, the roads are almost as good as the day they were built. Think of it: in little old New York, anything over six months old is considered out-of-date! You wonder if I am practicing French so I can teach you when I come back. We don't see much of the Frenchies, in the Second, except to pass them running south as we slog on to the north to meet the Hun. I think I wrote you already how we kept seeing thousands and thousands of refugees on the road, all of them yelling *"La guerre est finie!"* The war is over! You see what a good boy am I; I checked on the spelling of the French and am assured that it is *parfait* (perfect).

Well, the latest story is that the First Division bumped into a French general on their way to the battlefield and began pumping him for information. It seems the only answer he had—to everything, Leah—was *"Je ne sais pas,"* or, in good old American lingo, "Dunno." And when they said, "And where are you going now, General?" he laughed and said, *"La soupe!"* That, I am sure, needs no translation, my pet . . .

Leah put the letter down in her lap and forced herself to look out of the big arched window. She had to ration the letter; otherwise, the whole thing was gulped down within just a few minutes . . . and then she had to wait days, sometimes weeks, for the next. Not that she stopped living until she heard from him, not at all; she had plenty to do. She was working on a story for the *Saturday Evening Post*, called "The Girls They Left Behind," about some of the wives and sweethearts and mothers of the nine million men who signed up for the army last spring right along with Joe Lazarus.

She had started her interviews, thinking they would be full of sad stories of wistful wives sitting home canning vegetables and fruits in order to "can the Kaiser," like it said in all the posters. But what she found was very different. Most of the women she talked to were filled with patriotic fervor. They knitted for the war effort, yes, and they canned and they religiously kept Meatless Mondays and Gasless Sundays, just as the President had asked. But it didn't end there. So many of them were on their way to join the Women's Corps or the Red Cross, and go overseas to drive ambulances or run telephone switchboards for the Signal corps or act as interpreters. Leah was against the war, she couldn't see what business America had in it; but she had to admire those brave women, willing to take the same chances as their men.

And she had to admit, all the posters and the music and speeches were beginning to get to her. Nowadays, when she sang along to George M. Cohan's "Over There," she found herself thrilling to the martial beat, and yes, even to the message: *The Yanks are coming! The Yanks are coming!* She'd seen the show three times; and each time, she'd found herself rising to her feet, applauding like mad and screaming, like everyone else.

Jim couldn't get over it. "I thought you were too smart to get caught up in jingoist nonsense."

But she told him, "I'm not caught up, Jim. It's the music, that's all. And Joe, of course. I mean, Joe *is* over there."

"Sure, kid, sure. I didn't mean it was *all* nonsense . . . just the war part, the killing part!" And he patted her hand.

She hadn't put her life away just because Joe was gone. She was busy enough; and she had the company of their friends. It was this pregnancy, and the heat, that made her feel time was crawling.

Quickly, she picked up the letter and resumed reading.

. . . God, we've covered over 50 kilometers in the past three days! I can't say where we've been or where we're going, but I can tell you we were hauled by truck in the dead of night to get here. When the sun rose this morning, we could hardly believe our eyes. There is no sign of war here, none, just gently rolling hills, and all the spring crops growing. I wish I could see you right now, this morning, your face all flushed with sleep, like a baby's. I miss you, my darling Leah.

But I must say I wouldn't miss this adventure for the world. Wait till I get back; the stories I'll have to tell you! I only wish, sometimes, that I was carrying a camera instead of a rifle. We're stuck where we are; no big offenses for the Infantry, say the officers; our artillery is needed for the Marines. The Marines! They say the Marines are getting all the credit for beating back Jerry. Once I'm home, I'll set them straight!

Once again she put the pages down, her eyes stinging with tears. You miss me but you wouldn't miss this adventure. Oh, Joe, and here I am, having our baby all alone, living our life all alone. He always ended his letters with love to her and to the child, adding, "I'm sorry to be away from you at this time. Please be proud, because I'm doing what has to be done to defend democracy and the grand old flag."

On the nineteenth of May, after the AEF had won some battle or other, the *New York World* printed a big cartoon showing a grinning American soldier brandishing a German helmet, standing astride the entire town of Catigny. She realized they had to show this as a splendid victory; but it had made her feel ill. The destruction of an entire town! In the drawing, hundreds of frightened women and children cowered behind the jubilant Doughboy, little ones whose mothers might have been killed in the shelling, little ones alone and helpless, crying for a mother who would never come back. She shivered. It was too horrible to think about.

The doorbell rang, then rang again. She leaned out the open window to shout down: "Hold your horses, will you?" But the words caught in her throat when she saw it was a Western Union messenger on his dusty bike, squinting up at her.

"Miss Vogel?"

"Yes?" Silently, she promised herself that if Joe got back, *when* Joe got back, she *would* marry him. She knew the promise was a pact with God, to make the telegram not say what she was sickeningly sure it would. Please. Don't let him be badly hurt. Please. Don't let it be about Joe. Please. I'll marry him, I'll be Leah Lazarus and my child will not be illegitimate.

The boy waved the telegram at her wordlessly. Please, God, she thought as she ran clumsily down the stairs, out of breath before she even started. She felt as if she were drowning for lack of air.

Downstairs, she reached her hand out for the telegram and dared to look straight at the messenger. His sad eyes told her the message before she looked at the words. And when she finally could bring herself to look, she began to scream.

Joe was dead, killed at Chateau-Thierry. But he couldn't be; she would not believe it. But he was, and it was all Jim's fault. It was Jim's voice that kept telling her, over and over, Jim's voice that she had to get rid of, destroy. And then it was Annie who was dead. She saw her peaceful face, not looking dead at all, not a mark on it, just one little smudge of dirt across her nose, so how could she be dead?

Then, somehow she was back at the Hebrew Home for Orphans and she was out in the park with all of her group and Miss Shapiro, too! Oh, it was so lovely to see Miss Shapiro. They were ice-skating. It was cool, so cool . . .

Leah sat up, wide-awake and weeping. She did not know

where she was, didn't recognize anything. Then Jim came rushing into the room and it became her bedroom, familiar, comfortable, unchanged. Except for one horrifying thing.

"Jim! Oh God! He's dead! They're all dead!"

Jim came to her, sitting on the edge of the bed, and scooped her into his arms, smoothing her hair with one big hand, saying, "Shhhh . . . I know, I know . . . That's the girl, cry your heart out."

That startled her. She pushed away from him. "You're supposed to tell me *not* to cry, Jim. You always get it wrong!" She started to laugh, but it quickly turned into wailing and she began weeping again.

He continued to croon to her, rubbing her back and wiping her wet face with his big handkerchief. When she had quieted down a little, he let her go and answered her, "No, no, dearie, I knew what I was saying. For two days, nearly three, you've been lying here all curled up like a little shrimp, your eyes closed, moaning, but never a sign of knowing I was here. You refused to eat, too, though you would take a few sips of water. I can tell you, I've been worried about you. Another hour and I was going to call your doctor. Those tears were the first signs of life in you. . . ."

"Two days, almost three? But that makes it—"

"Friday. Yes, indeed. It's Friday."

She sat up feeling dizzy. "I don't believe it!"

Jim began to laugh. "And I don't believe *you*! Eight months gone with child, in a trance, making me fret and worry. Mind you, I haven't been out of this place since I carried you upstairs. And all you can do when you finally come to is call me a liar!"

"You? Carried me?"

"It wasn't easy, let me tell you. That's a fine big fellow you're carrying."

"Fellow! Isn't that just like a man! Well, for your information, it's going to be a girl. That's what Joe ordered and that's what he's going to get." And then desolation swept over her again. "Oh Jim, he's gone! My Joe is gone! My baby doesn't have a father and Joe is dead! Oh God, why couldn't I have died, too?"

Taking a cloth from a bowl of water, Jim washed her face, clucking at her, pushing the nightdress away to get the back of her neck. She closed her eyes, feeling the throb of pain behind her eyelids, and let him minister to her.

"Jim, how did you find me?"

"When you fainted, you scared the Western Union boy half to death. He went flying out into the street, yelling for help, and your landlord came out to give him hell. But when he heard what had happened, he sent the boy running to get me at the office. And here I am, your humble and obedient servant."

"Oh, Jim, how can I ever thank you?"

"Aw . . ." He waved this thought away and said, "Listen, do you hear the thunder? They say it'll rain today and cool off this inferno of a city."

But I'm comfortable, she thought, and then suddenly realized. "But I'm in my nightgown!"

"Why, so you are."

"But— But that means . . . but that means that you—"

His face betrayed no emotion at all. Evenly, he said, "That's right, Miss Vogel, I carried you upstairs. I undressed you. I put a nightdress on you and I put you into your bed."

"Oh God!" She buried her face in her hands.

"Now, don't be silly. I hardly looked at you. In fact, I might say I didn't look at you at all. I was too busy trying to figure out how the damn thing went on."

"Oh God, the way I look, all huge and ugly . . . !"

He threw his head back and laughed. "Well, you're back to yourself, that's for sure, if all you're worried about is how you look and not that you've been compromised."

"Compromised? By *you*? Oh Jim, that's funny!"

"Oh, is it?" The laughter wiped away and his face resumed its placid blankness. "I'll have you know that, in spite of my years, Miss Vogel, I am still considered something of a fine fellow."

"Oh Jim, I didn't mean—"

"Oh Leah, yes you did. But that's all right. That's one of the things makes you a good reporter, Miss Vogel, your ability to slice right through the murk of emotions and get to the truth."

"By the way, Jim, I'm Leah *Lazarus* now."

A thick black eyebrow shot up. "Whatever for? If you didn't give a hang about convention when Joe was . . . *before*, then why now?"

"I . . . I don't really know. It just seems right. And Leah Lazarus has a nice ring to it, don't you think?"

"Oh, sure, sure. And you know that it was Lazarus who rose from the dead. . . ." Her eyes filled with tears, and quickly Jim continued his washing; for all the world, she thought, like a mother cat cleaning a kitten.

So she changed the subject. "Actually, Jim," she said in a mock serious tone, "I want to take the name because I have these wonderful *ancestors*. . . ." And she told him about Leon Cavalier—not quite *all* about Leon Cavalier, but the Lazaruses' fake ancestor part. It made Jim laugh; well, that's why she told him.

"Seems to me," he said, "I've heard a different kind of story about the special paintings Cavalier does. But you wouldn't know about that."

"Oh yes I would. Walter Morris told me."

"Well, it's all very interesting, very interesting, indeed. And how do you think Isaac and Bertha will take to your carrying their sainted family name that's so precious?"

"I don't know and I don't care!"

"That sounds like the Leah Vo—Lazarus I know!"

Talking with Jim that way, she began to remember bits and pieces of his caring for her, lifting her up, shifting her in the bed, urging her to take a little, just a little—of what, she didn't know—of carrying her, singing to her and reading to her, telling her that she had to get better, not to worry.

"Oh God, Jim, I was really gone, wasn't I? And you took care of me."

"Guilty as charged."

"Oh, Jim, you are so—" She searched for the right word, finally found it. "—so motherly."

"Motherly!" he spluttered. "God deliver me from *that*, if you don't mind! Motherly! Motherly!" But crimson stained his cheeks and, while his voice was gruff, a smile twitched at his mouth.

Again her hand flew to her bare throat. "My locket! Where is it? I *was* wearing it when you . . . when you . . ."

"Yes, you were wearing it. And I took it off and put it into your jewelry box. I was afraid you'd choke yourself."

"Never mind that." She felt her hair. A rat's nest. "Be an angel, Jim, would you, and bring me my hairbrush. And the locket."

When the locket was once again safely around her neck and she began to brush her hair, she sat down carefully on the bed.

"Tell me, Leah, who's this Miss Shapiro you were calling out to?"

Miss Shapiro sliding along the glittering ice. It had been

lovely to see her once more, even if it was only in a dream. "A teacher at . . . at school."

"Well, of course at school. That's where teachers generally are."

But my school was somewhat different, Leah thought. She had never wanted anyone to know she had been at HHO.

"Elementary school, then?" Jim went on.

"Yes, yes, of course. I never went further than sixth grade, you know that. I left and went to work."

"Which school?"

"What do you care?" But that was a giveaway, too. Better to just answer casually and calmly. "Well, if you must know, P.S. 267."

"In Harlem?"

"That's right."

"A hundred thirty-sixth Street and—"

"Yes, dammit! Now can we talk about something else?"

"Leah . . . that was the public school inside the big Jewish orphanage. Were you in that orphanage? Is that why you're so touchy?"

Her eyes felt sunk deep into her head, and her head was pounding; but she managed to give him level stare for level stare. Damn his Irish curiosity. "Do I ask you questions?" she demanded.

He did not answer her, nor did he change the expression on his face; but he gave himself a brisk little nod, as if to say, Well now I know. He resumed washing her arms, but she stopped him. "You're getting more water on the quilt than on me."

"Whoops. Sorry." He slid on a puddle he'd made on the floor as he took the pan away. "I'll be back in a minute, Leah, with soup. You've got to eat something."

"I'm not hungry!"

But when he came back into the bedroom, carrying a tray with such awkward care, a tray with a steaming bowl, a napkin, and a teaspoon, her heart went out to him. He was so dear, such a good, kind man. Even in that florid Irish way, good-looking, for when he smiled, his eyes twinkled and dimples appeared in his cheeks.

But a klutz. As he approached, taking gingerly steps, he tripped over the corner of a rug and the bowl of soup went flying through the air. It was almost beautiful, the golden curve of the soup as it leapt out of the bowl, arcing gracefully before splattering onto the rug and all over the bedclothes.

"Oh, Jim, I think I'd better pull myself together before you kill me." She was grateful to find herself laughing. When she looked over at him, the shamefaced look had disappeared from his face and was replaced by a pleased grin. *"What?"* she demanded.

"I did it. I brought you back to the land of the living. With my two left feet and a bit of the famed McCready grace, I have made you laugh, by God!"

"You needn't be so pleased with yourself," Leah said.

"I'm not. I'm thinking, good, now I'll have someone to accompany me to the Liberty Theater to see *The Birth of a Nation* . . . yes, that's right, I'm thinking of taking you. It's quite wondrous, so I hear, and they have not just an ordinary organ in the theater, but a full forty-piece symphony orchestra, mind!

"Yes, and I'm also thinking now that you're back to yourself, I need you to get over to Margaret Sanger's newest clinic. They've done it again—sent in a policewoman, disguised as a real person—" He paused to laugh at his own joke. "—and they've closed the place down again!"

"But how can they? Wasn't the law changed so that having too many children could be considered a disease?"

"Yes, m'dear, but since when does an insignificant matter like legality make a difference to her enemies? And now, of course, several of her workers have decided to go on a hunger strike . . . and you know what *that* means! Nice young women, guilty of no crime whatever, put into manacles and force-fed! Just because they believe in birth control. Does it sound like a story you'd like to cover, dear Miss Vo—pardon me, Mrs. Lazarus?"

Did it! He knew her answer! In her head she was already on her way to the Women's House of Detention, only a few blocks away. She could feel enthusiasm surging through her like a flood of life.

And then it struck her: the joke. She looked pointedly down at her protruding belly and, after a moment, a bit puzzled, Jim stared there, too.

"What? What is it?"

"Are you sure," she asked sweetly, "that I'm the ideal person to do a story on birth control?"

The next moment they were both yelling with helpless laughter. And that's when it started. The cramping pain that took over her belly and back, shutting off her laughter. "Oh . . . ow!"

"Labor pains," Jim said calmly, nodding like a sage. "Come on."

"Come on? What are you talking about?"

"About getting you dressed decently and to the hospital where you obviously belong. I'll get you a dress. . . ."

"And a change, too, and a clean nightdress. My robe, a hairbrush, cold cream . . . oh dear, I'd better do it myself. You'll forget something important. Hand me the red dress from the closet, would you, Jim dear? No, wait. The blue linen, the pale one, right . . ." She had to stop, to wait for another labor pain to pass.

"Be warned, Leah," Jim said, his voice stern but his eye eyes full of laughter. "You may be able to order me about, but that child in your belly has a mind of its own. Yes, I think you may have met your match at last!"

11

September 1918

The glow of well-being that filled her entire body was amazing, absolutely amazing. Leah was sure she was as radiant as Coney Island, sparkling, shimmering, able to be seen from great distances. Even the baby—*her* baby, her daughter—*her* daughter seemed vivid with light. Leah looked down and, as happened each time, felt a little shock of delight. That huge swelling she had carried in front of her for so long turned out magically to be this tiny perfect person, with tiny fingers, tiny fingernails, tiny feet, huge eyes, and a sweet little pink rosebud of a mouth that curled and pouted and, often, opened wide to emit high-pitched yells. Leah was enchanted with all of it, even the cries.

And from the look on Lenore Hutchinson's face—half awe,

half dismay—as she eyed mother and child from the foot of the bed, they might very well both be enchanted. Lenore hadn't even bothered to remove her hat or coat, coming close to stare at them, the hothouse flowers she clutched in one hand forgotten.

"I don't believe it," Lenore said finally. "You, a mother."

"Yes, it's amazing, isn't it?" Leah grinned and sneaked another peek down at the little miracle wrapped in a blanket. Out of the haze of pain and pushing and mess, had emerged this beautiful little creature. "Look, Lenore, come here, look at her skinny arms and legs. . . ."

Lenore leaned over the foot of the bed. "Her skin is so pale," she said, "almost blue, like milk."

"Like my mother," Leah said proudly. It was nice to be able to claim a mother at last, like a normal person. "Her hair, too . . ." She pulled back the blanket to reveal a fuzz of auburn.

"Imagine," Lenore murmured politely. "And you and Joe both so dark . . . oh, I'm sorry, Leah."

The mention of Joe brought tears to Leah's eyes; it always did. With Jim, it was okay to cry, but not in front of anyone else. She blinked rapidly, saying, "No, no, it's all right, honestly. The nurses tell me that all new mothers cry a lot. Everything seems to bring on tears. God, Lenore, I'm leaking from *everywhere*!" And that made them both laugh. "The flowers are beautiful, Lenore. If you ask, one of the nurses will put them into a vase for you."

"Oh really? And then where will they go?" Lenore asked. She had a point; every flat surface was covered with containers full of flowers. Their friends had come, all agog, to see what she had accomplished; and all carrying bouquets; Jim, too. He arrived twice a day, his arms always loaded with blooms.

Finally Jim told them to take half a dozen vases to the children's ward. "As a matter of fact, nurse, I'd like it if you could make sure each child gets a flower of its own." For some reason, that made Leah cry, too; so he quickly added, "Don't worry, Leah, we won't tell Head Nurse Harwood we did anything *nice*."

Head Nurse Harwood was the joke of the maternity ward. Although often invoked by the other nurses—especially when they were telling you you had to eat your Cream of Wheat or had to get some rest—she was largely invisible. The head nurse was too busy with arcane matters having to do with "her babies" to visit the mothers. Leah wondered aloud to her nurses whether Head Nurse Harwood really existed.

Her personal favorite was a lively young nurse named Florence, who wore a cap atop her curly head with wings so wide it looked as if it might fly off at any moment. Florence assured Leah, "Oh, yes, Nurse Harwood really exists, I can tell you that." And rolled her eyes, adding, "She exists to keep us on our toes, Mrs. Lazarus. And off our feed."

Finally, yesterday, she had come into Leah's room, a matronly figure of a woman, crackling with starch. "I am Head Nurse Harwood," she announced, after a swift and thorough examination of the room. "I came to see for myself the fount of this flower business. Most particularly, I wish to thank your husband for his thoughtfulness," Turning to Jim, she tried hard to smile sweetly. It was a bit difficult; her graying hair had been pulled back so tightly that her features were stretched and rigid. "The children love pretty things and, alas, they don't often get brought flowers. So we thank you, sir. Ah, I see that the baby has your Irish coloring, sir, just look at that red hair."

Poor Jim; he looked quite nonplussed, but pleased at the same time. Leah had to speak up; she let Nurse Harwood know that her "husband" had been killed in France and the baby's auburn hair was the same color as her grandmother's, "my mother's."

"Oh, I'm sorry, I'm sure, Mrs. Lazarus. Of course, of course, how silly of me. I'm so sorry . . . about your husband . . . a natural mistake . . . I didn't realize Jews had red hair."

She bustled off, with Leah calling after her, "Well, they do!" But she was laughing. Nothing could make her angry, not even Head Nurse Harwood. But when she turned to share the joke with Jim, he was looking out the window, his broad back turned to her. She had hurt him again; she was sorry, but really, she could not change the truth.

Well, that was yesterday, and no doubt Jim had forgotten all about it by now. She wanted no unhappiness around her. In her second week at the hospital, she was still floating. "Say, Lenore, don't you want to see her up close? Hold her, maybe?" she asked.

"Oh, no! This is fine. I'm afraid I'd break her. She looks just beautiful, though. Leah, do you realize, you're the first of our crowd to do this? Have a child? It's going to change everything."

"Not a bit! I'm going to be doing exactly the same things I

always did. Interviewing, writing, following leads. Everything.
I'll just take her along in a little basket or something!"

At that moment Nurse Florence came sailing in to take the
baby away for a bath. As soon as they were gone, Lenore said.
"Now you look normal. Ah, and here's Jim. And Jack Murray,
too!" She sounded positively relieved.

Jack had a studio in the Village, where he painted portraits.
Sold them, too. Unlike most of the artists they knew, Jack
made money. He was carrying two huge armloads of roses.
"Oh God, Jack, they must have cost the earth! But they're gorgeous! Jim, you'll have to go charm another water pitcher
from the nurses."

Jack went over to give her a kiss, then looked around, a big
goofy grin on his face. "Isn't something missing? A baby, it's
been rumored?"

"She was just taken away to have a bath, but sit down, the
edge of the bed is fine, Jack, it's not *catching*."

"What's her name?"

Jim, coming in with two pitchers, said, "Leah can't decide.
Did you ever hear of such a scandal? The child's over a week
old and is still being called Hey You."

They all laughed, and Leah said, "I think it'll be Josephine.
Josephine Bella. After Joe, of course, and my mother. But it
sounds such a big mouthful for such a little thing. . . ."

"She'll grow, she'll grow." Jim stuffed flowers into pitchers
and sat on the other side of the bed. The Lazarus clan walked
in then, dressed to the nines and—wouldn't you know it, Leah
thought—bearing flowers.

"Dear Leah!" Bertha handed her bouquet to Zelda and bent
to give Leah a kiss on the cheek. "Our congratulations. We'd
have come much sooner, but hospital visiting hours don't quite
match Mr. Lazarus's free time. But today I *insisted*. I said,
'Your granddaughter, Ike! All we have left of our dear Joe!' "

When she paused to allow one perfect tear to run down her
cheek, Papa Lazarus was able to mumble something that
sounded like "Very proud, very pleased."

Leah introduced everyone, trying hard to keep a straight
face. She could see that Joe's parents disapproved of everything they saw—beginning with the dozens of bouquets and
ending with her friends . . . not to mention herself, "that
woman." Yet, there was no question she had just given birth to
their grandchild, and they were obliged to make an appearance,
like it or not.

Now, having given her speech, Bertha busied herself with their flowers, trying to fit them into every receptacle and failing.

"Oh dear, you'll just have to ask the nurses for a vase, Zelda. *Now!*" she added meaningfully. Zelda, beaming and pink in the face, had bent to kiss Leah, but at that imperious "Now!" she obediently scurried away.

Bertha, who had not stopped talking, eyed the three visitors surrounding Leah, her eyebrows up expressively.

"When *I* was a girl, a man was never allowed to sit on a lady's bed," she remarked.

Leah almost laughed aloud. Jim and Jack both sprang up as if someone had jerked them with a string, both flushing.

"Look, Leah ... it's time I got back to the studio," Jack stammered. He bent to kiss her, then thought better of it and beat a retreat. Lenore and Jim began to talk together about how busy they were and how the Lazaruses would have a great deal to talk about. They said, "So long, Leah, we'll see you later." And they were gone.

"Well, your friends were right about *one* thing," Bertha announced. "We have a great deal to talk about."

Uh-oh, Leah thought. What now?

Zelda came in with a glass beaker. "This is all they had left. Leah's the talk of the nursing station. They say she's had more flowers than any of the other mothers."

"That's nothing—" Bertha started, but Zelda went on.

"They let me see the baby. Oh, Leah, she's so pretty, not wizened or all red like some of them. Mama, you should go see her. Papa!"

"We'll be seeing plenty of her, don't you worry. Right now, we have important business to discuss. Sit down, Zelda."

Leah patted the side of the bed. But Zelda gave a tiny shake of her head and sat meekly on the one hard chair.

Papa Lazarus cleared his throat, but it was Bertha who spoke. "We're so delighted that you've taken Joe's name, Leah. But in spite of that, you are, after all, still an unmarried woman, all alone in the world. . . ."

"Not quite alone," Leah said, echoing the sugary tones. "I have my friends. And the baby. My daughter."

"Just my point, Leah. The baby. There's no possible way for you to take care of her ... I'm talking about earning a living now, not changing diapers and giving baths. . . ."

"Excuse me, I earn a very good living."

"Excuse *me*, Leah, you *used to* earn a very good living. But with a child, you'll have to stay home to care for her. You do take my meaning, don't you?"

"No, I don't take your meaning. I intend to take her with me."

"Take her with you!"

"I don't work in a filthy factory, Bertha. I'm a writer. Where I go, she can very well go, too. And if I think she shouldn't ... well, there's always Jim or one of my friends to watch her for a while."

"Absolutely not!" That was Papa, coming out of the corner, and turning quite purple. "Strangers ... *men* ... and not even Jewish ... taking care of my granddaughter? Out of the question!"

"I'm sorry to tell you this," Leah said evenly, "but you don't have a say. She's my child, mine and Joe's."

"Since our son chose not to marry you before he went off to fight and die for his country— Now, now, Mother, try to keep your composure. . . ."

Leah felt like one of those head-bobbing toys, turning in disbelief from one to the other. Bertha was dabbing at her eyes with a hankie, the perfect picture of a grieving mother in her stylish black silk. "Well, my dear," she said, "it was obvious, wasn't it, that he never intended to make an honest woman of you. We're doing you a favor. . . ."

"What favor exactly are you doing me?" She could taste the bile rising in her throat. They wouldn't dare!

"We are willing to take this child of Joe's and raise her the way he doubtless would want her raised ... the way he was raised. In comfort and luxury, with the best of everything."

"Not only that," Isaac said, looking very pleased with himself, "but I would be willing to continue Joseph's, ah, allowance to you ... cushion the bumpy path a bit."

Leah smiled sweetly and said, "Oh? But I thought you were only interested in a male child."

Bertha Lazarus fiddled with her handkerchief, her lips twitching in anger; but she kept her voice even. "My dear, what a dreadful thing to say. Wherever did you get that idea? Of course, your parents were immigrants, weren't they? From ... Eastern Europe? They do have such backward notions, in those countries. . . ."

"You don't speak of my parents!" Leah blazed. "Don't you dare say a *word* about them! Not one word!"

Something in her face rang a warning bell; Bertha backed off, stammering half apologies. "I can see you're not quite back to normal yet, my dear. A bit excitable. But you *will* think about our offer, won't you?"

Through gritted teeth, Leah answered, "I'm going to try very hard *not* to think about it at all! You cannot buy my baby, and that's flat!"

Both of them paled, and Bertha's mouth silently formed the word "buy." She began to choke and cough, which brought Isaac to her side, pounding on her back until she cried for him to stop.

"Joe's child belongs with his family, where he would have wanted her to be. She's a *real* Lazarus—unlike some others who think nothing of taking our name under false pretenses." Bertha's voice was thin with fury.

"I never pretend we got married," Leah said to her. "I don't tell lies. But, you see, the people *I* know would never ask. The people I know don't care."

"We'll continue this conversation at another time, dear, when you're more ... yourself." Leah did not answer, just kept a smile plastered on her face. "Zelda, get up, we're going. Isaac!" At the door, Bertha turned. "At least you'll have the decency to name her Josephine Blossom—after my mother. Joe promised me."

"Josephine?" she said slowly, as if she had never heard the name. "No. I don't think so. No, not Josephine. I find it an ugly name."

And now it was Isaac's turn. "If you don't name this child in my son's honor, she will never get a cent from us."

Leah just gave him an enigmatic smile and said in honeyed tones, "Let me tell you something, Mr. Lazarus, Mrs. Lazarus—I don't care about your money. What I care about is that you leave, and quickly before I scream and bring all the nurses!"

When they stood where they were, looking stupefied, she opened her mouth and began to shriek. In a moment they had disappeared. But not before Zelda turned and gave Leah a lighthearted wink and the thumb's up sign. At that moment Zelda looked just like Joe.

12

April 1920

"Vote? Women vote?" Mary Markowitz, a thin, pale woman who was probably in her late twenties but looked totally worn out, pushed some of her lank mousy hair in back of her ear and shrugged. "*They* don't care what women think!" She did not sound at all perturbed by the thought; in fact, she smiled as she said it, glancing down at the baby who suckled listlessly at her breast.

Leah scribbled notes. Mary Markowitz might be dirt poor and totally uneducated, but Leah Lazarus was determined to give her a voice—in a magazine where thousands of people could read it. She was still amazed that *Beautiful Womanhood* had liked her idea of comparing the lives and ideas of two women, one well-off and the other not. But "both," the editor had warned sternly, "decent women . . . ladies, you understand, with hopes and dreams. Mr. Macfadden likes people with, um . . . 'glorious experiences'. . . ."

"Yes, Mary," Leah said now, "often men don't care what we think. So what do you think we women can do about that?"

"It's no use, miss. Men have always run the world. And I say, let 'em. Why, the world's more of a mess than my kitchen!"

Mary laughed, looking surprised at her own wit, making a vague gesture that took in the battered furniture, the worn linoleum, the naked electric bulb hanging from the ceiling. Leah still remembered the little room she and Annie had shared, the dank, dark little hole they were so proud of . . . not so different from this. You'd think things would have improved in ten years! Nowadays everyone had electricity, and toilets were all inside, the city moving rapidly into the modern era—or so the newspapers would have you believe. But just look at this place!

Leah stifled a sigh and scribbled, "Wld more mess than m kitch." Her job wasn't to better Mary Markowitz's lot in life; it was to find what glorious experiences Mary was able to wring from a miserable existance. Besides, what she had just said about the worth of her vote was not so different from the thoughts of Amy (Mrs. George) Reardon, 18 West Sixty-ninth Street.

Amy Reardon, with her fashionable boyish bob and wool crepe shift belted around her narrow hips, couldn't have looked more different from Mary Markowitz. Yet, Amy, too, had given the same shrug and said, "Vote? Does it matter? I suppose so. George will like having two votes instead of one. He'll tell me who." And when asked if she wouldn't like to have a bit more say-so, Amy answered, "Oh, I have plenty of say-so where it really matters. Our social life, the children's schools, where we live. All those politicians . . . so boring."

"If you vote," Leah said to Mary Markowitz, "if all women vote, then maybe we can get the things *we* want done."

"Maybe. Probably not. Anyways—" A faint smile flickered over Mary's pale lips. "—how could I run the world with all these little ones to take care of?"

Leah leaned forward and said earnestly, "Women don't *have* to have so many babies, Mary. There's birth control now and—"

Mary Markowitz turned scarlet. She looked almost pretty with color flooding her face. "Harry likes . . . he likes nothing between us but air. That's the way he likes it." The blush deepened; and yes, she was definitely smiling to herself. Here, at last, was a real-life glorious moment for *Beautiful Womanhood*.

"And you? Is that the way you like it?"

"Well, I must say . . . there aren't too many whose husbands still . . . come to them, not after the first couple of babies. Mostly, they just want to go out and drink beer, maybe find another woman. But it's different with me and Harry." Now she looked alive; her eyes shone. "We've got something special."

Leah leaned forward, across the table, and said, "That doesn't happen too often. Why do you think you and Harry are so blessed?" She began to write as fast as she could. At least Mary Markowitz had good sex—or thought she did. Much better than Amy, her middle-class counterpart uptown whose most glorious moment had something to do with a dance contest.

No matter, Leah decided it was a stupid article. Why had she ever thought it was a good idea? She'd interviewed six women, and not one of them wanted to think about anything outside her own little world. It was as if they were wrapped in cotton wool, totally unaware of the poverty and hunger around them. Sometimes it seemed that the country had gone backward since the war.

Leah remembered how joyous everyone had been, that bright September day in 1919 when the grand victory parade came through the Washington Square Arch and up Fifth Avenue to the park. She had cheered for the memory of her sweet Joe, dead and buried in France, while tears streamed down her face. And when she glanced around, everyone looked the same: smiling, so proud of their mighty victory, their stalwart soldiers; but at the same time weeping for all the young men gone. Winning the war offered *hope*. So everyone hugged everyone else, glad it was over and that the world could go back to normal.

But there was no going back to normal. As Jim wrote in last month's editorial column: "Keeping the world safe for democracy has left us with an entirely different world; it's unfortunate that nobody seems to have made note of it."

Well, some people had. There had been so many strikes, first the bricklayers, then a general strike, and now the railroads! Mary's husband was a union man, a bricklayer, and the bricklayers had been on strike for months. He spent his days at the union hall with his cronies, waiting for what? A miracle, maybe.

And there *she* was, a baby at the breast, two or three more swarming around on the floor, her belly big with another one, very little food in the larder and very little hope of any.

To hell with it, Leah thought, and got up, gathering her papers together. It was nearly four o'clock, and she had to get back to the Village by five-thirty.

"Come, Jo," she said, bending to pick up the auburn-haired little girl sitting on the floor, playing with Mary's children. How different *her* child looked; how rosy and well-fed, compared to the others. "We have to get to Jack Murray's studio for Mommy's next job."

Joanna came to her with a ready smile. She was a good, sweet-natured baby—unless she had her mind set on some particular thing. Then you couldn't budge her. Leah liked to joke that Joanna's first word had been "No!—and she's been using it regularly ever since." But really, she rather admired her. Imagine, not even two years old and already a mind of her own!

"Say bye-bye," Leah said, and the baby waved her hand, echoing the words. "Bye-bye."

"Your baby's such a darling little thing," Mary Markowitz said, smiling at her. "Good as gold. Not a squawk out of her when the others made out she was their baby and fed her all that pretend food. I'll bet she's the apple of her daddy's eye."

"Her father was killed in France."

"Oh dear. I'm so sorry."

"Agh, I didn't mean it to come out that way. I—I'm used to it now. But thank you, thank you."

Suddenly Leah needed to get outside into the fresh air. She bustled out, saying she'd get in touch if the article was published.

In the street, she leaned against the building for a moment, taking in a deep breath, letting it out slowly. Oh God, how easily she could have ended up like the woman upstairs! Most of the men she had known in the old neighborhood and at Triangle were working men . . . union . . . "Reds," if you wanted to call them that. What if she had *married* one of them and he went on strike? Or had been deported? What if she, too, had three or four children and no way to feed them? She'd have had to give them to the orphanage. . . .

Like a door opening unexpectedly onto a brightly lit scene, she suddenly recalled the huge echoing dormitory room at the Hebrew Home for Orphans. The high ceilings, the ugly lights hanging from them. Six rows of metal beds stretch the full length of the huge room, all painted white. Everything is white, the sheets, the blankets, the cotton spreads, everything tight, tucked in, clean, bleached, sanitary. She is next to her bed, standing still and straight and tall, as are all the other girls. There isn't a sound in the place except for a cough here and there, muffled quickly.

The monitor stands in front of the room, a big, heavyset Polish girl named Vashti, but whom they all call Piggy because her nose tips up so you can see the two round holes of her nostrils. Also because she is mean. Piggy likes to tiptoe into the dormitory in the morning and yank the sheets from the first four or five girls she can get to, rolling them abruptly onto the floor. They always cry out, and that wakes the rest of the room, and everybody sits up in bed to see Piggy, hands on hips, laughing loudly. Leah tells her best friend that when Piggy laughs like that, she looks like a *hazzer* opening its mouth to be fed slops.

But what Leah sees now is the end of the day, not the beginning. They are all standing there, each girl next to her bed, not a peep out of any of them or Piggy will make them sorry.

And then it begins. "One!" Piggy hollers.

Every pinafore on every little girl comes off, is folded and put on the metal chair that stands by each bed. Quickly, quickly, before the next number.

"Two!" All smock dresses go over all heads, are folded, are put in the chair seat. They all sit.

"Three!" Right shoes come off, hit the floor.

"Four!" Left shoes. *Thunk*, onto the floor.

"Five!" Right sock. Uh-oh, one of the girls forgets and takes off the wrong sock. Piggy's baleful glare focuses on her, like a thousand daggers, and they all hold their breath. Sometimes she hits you for a mistake like that. But this time she just sneers and yells out, "Six!" and they all concentrate on the left sock, grateful for small favors.

Leah shivered, remembering. That she could even *think* about a child of hers in such a place. She bit her tongue, against the Evil Eye, and reached under her blouse to finger the locket. She was lucky. Something always came up. Like the deal she had made with Jack Murray. It was fun and it brought in a little extra. And she could use the money, the way sales of magazines were slipping.

Jim had been talking a lot lately about a new idea he had, for a magazine that was mostly pictures. "Just look how popular the movies are." But getting the backing hadn't been so easy, and Leah was afraid she'd have to find another way to make a living. Then Jack asked her if she'd like to do some acting in his studio, for money.

"Saved in the nick of time!" Jim joked. "Again!" But she didn't laugh; she didn't want to scare her luck away.

She hefted the baby to her shoulder and walked down the block, dancing a little—Joanna was heavy—and singing "Look for the silver lining . . . whenever clouds appear in the blue . . ." The baby loved her to sing; she smiled and patted Leah's cheek. As they rounded the corner by the bus stop, a man stepped out of the shadows, directly in front of her, so close she had to take a couple of steps back. Instinctively she tightened her grip on Joanna.

She knew what he wanted. "I'm poor myself, not even a nickel to spare," she said, preparing to continue on her way.

But he was no bleary-eyed drunk looking for pennies to buy more Sneaky Pete. His pale eyes were menacing as he advanced on her, moving forward for every step she took back.

"You can forget that bunk! Hand it over, sister, or else I'll have to hurt you! And maybe your kid, too!"

The thumping of her heart in her chest was so loud, she was surprised he didn't hear it. But she would die before she'd let this ragged heap of nothingness know she was scared!

"You should be ashamed of yourself, picking on a woman and a baby! The Salvation Army is right down the street. They'll give you warm clothes and a meal. . . . Now, back away and let us be!"

She was as surprised at herself as he was. He blinked and wavered, and she just strode right past him, her heart still hammering. She did not dare look back, but when she saw the bus coming, she ran to the corner, waving at the driver to wait.

She didn't feel really safe until she was in a seat, with Joanna on her lap. And then, she couldn't help it, she had to grin, she was so pleased with herself. "There, Jo, you see? If you just stand up for yourself, nobody can hurt you."

The child stared back at her, so solemn, as if she could understand every word. She had large amber-colored eyes, with flecks of green in them. Beautiful eyes, just like Bella Vogel's. Leah had almost forgotten what her mother looked like, until Jo came along. Now, everytime she looked at her daughter, she was reminded of her mother. Sometimes it hurt. But mostly it just made her swear to herself that she would never leave Joanna, never, not for any reason. Not if they both had to die of starvation.

As they rode uptown, Jo looked out the window, trying to say the names of everything she saw. She had started to talk early; everyone teased Leah, saying the baby had inherited her mother's mouth, if nothing else. Right now Leah was grateful for the babyish chatter that required no response; it gave her time to compose herself, to try to erase the man, the desperate look of him, his awful stench, from her mind.

At Washington Square she got off the bus and headed quickly for Jack's studio on Macdougal. The tourists always started coming in just before dinnertime, and she had to take her pose before anyone got there; so she half ran, with the baby bouncing on her hip and giggling.

Leah wasn't quite sure how or when the open-studio idea had started, but she thought it very clever, even though Jim found it hilarious. Lots of her friends were doing it. Various artists in the Village had started to open their doors to the general public ... to the *paying* public was more to the point. From six to nine P.M. thrill seekers from the Bronx and Brooklyn could climb the stairs to Jack's studio on Macdougal and see a real artist at work, while the "guests" lounged around, chatting and drinking. They could wander around the place, looking at the paintings and sculptures, and it was hoped they might even buy something. Cheap wine was included in the entrance fee, as well as atmosphere: dim lights, lots of candles stuck into wine bottles, a guitarist playing "Japanese Sandman" or "Whispering," and six or seven Village characters for local color.

That's who she was: one of the characters, part of the background of this carefully staged "reality," dressed in a silk chemise, dyed vibrant crimson and purple, with a load of Gypsy bracelets up one arm, smoking a cigarette in a long holder. She didn't really smoke, but she was awfully good at putting the holder in her teeth, lowering her eyelids and gazing out at the visitors with smoky disdain, just like Theda Bara. And they fell for it!

Jack himself was always seated at his easel, working on a painting—usually of a carefully draped female.

Jack's place was even on the list of Things to See in *The Little Guide to Greenwich Village*, where it was called "An Open Invitation to an Atelier Party on Macdougal Street."

When she got to Jack's building, Leah climbed the steep staircase as quickly as she could with her burden. "Jack! Jack!" baby Jo chortled. She loved it there. Everyone fussed over her, and Jack let her play with all his old brushes. She would happily munch on a chunk of bread and a piece of cheese, and at some point burrow into some pillows on a couch or the floor, and fall asleep.

By eight o'clock the place was crowded with gawkers, and the baby fast asleep in spite of the commotion. The usual number of women had asked her, in low voices, how it felt to go without a corset. The usual number of men had done the same, only loudly. She was waiting for someone to ask her to point the way to a speakeasy, a "third sex" bar, an opium den, or an abortionist. They were always so eager and ashamed, and always so condescending at the same time. It was ridiculous.

She covered a yawn with her hand—she had been up for fourteen hours—when her eyes popped open as wide as her mouth. Oh my God! It couldn't be! But it was: Joe's parents, Bertha in the lead, with another overfed couple. That was all she needed!

Leah considered disappearing into the back of the studio; she considered throwing the shawl over her head; she considered falling to the floor and pretending to be asleep or drunk. But then she stopped dithering and sat up straight and tall—she was seated at a little round table, toying with a glass of wine—and waited for them to spot her.

Since that first visit at the hospital, Bertha had not given up. She wanted the baby and did her best to wear Leah down. She called on the telephone, she wrote letters, and about twice a month she came to the apartment on Barrow Street. Leah knew what she was looking for: signs that a man was living there. Well, no man was living in her apartment, although she was very tempted to borrow one of Jim's robes and fling it over the couch, just to give the old bitch something to sniff about.

And here she was, big as life and twice as ugly, at Jack's. As beautiful as Bertha's face was, it was becoming etched with her bad temper and suspicious nature. Also, Leah noted with pleasure, she had grown quite fat and was puffing from the climb, her face pink with exertion.

A moment later the flush deepened, as she caught sight of Leah. She quickly turned and, behind her hand, whispered to the others in her party. Leah felt all of their eyes directed to her. Not knowing what she wanted to do, she smiled brightly and gave a little wave with the cigarette holder.

Bertha Lazarus was by her side in a moment. "I might have known I'd find you in a place like this!"

"Why hello, Bertha, and might I say the same of you," Leah murmured, holding the other woman's gaze.

"Just what is *that* supposed to mean?"

"I mean a place like this is meant for tourists from the Bronx." She smiled. "The artist happens to be a friend of mine. Would you like to be introduced?"

"The Franks—our friends—brought us here. They thought it would be fun to see—" She glanced down at the tourist guide clutched in her hand. " '—dainty elves and stern women.' But the first person we see is . . . the mother of Joe's child!"

"If you don't like the mother of Joe's child being here, Bertha, I suggest that you send money for her support. I get paid for being part of the scenery, you know. It's honest work. And we need it."

"You get *paid*? How disgusting!" The dark eyes swiftly scanned the room. "I'm only surprised *you* aren't the one draped in a sheet, posing."

Anger was rising from her stomach to her chest. "Not as long as I have Joanna with me."

"Joanna? Is here? With you? Now?" Bertha's hand flew to the middle of her chest . . . where a heart would be, Leah thought, if she had one. "Where? Where is my poor baby?"

"She's not poor and she's *not* yours, and let me tell you something—" It was strange to be shouting in a whisper. "—she never will be. She's my child. You have no right to keep bothering me. If you don't stop, I'll get a lawyer. Do you hear me? I'll make sure you never see her again!"

Bertha glared at her, her chest heaving. She bent low so that her narrowed eyes were on a level with Leah's. "We'll see about that. We'll just see! We'll see who is believed by the Law!"

Like a ship in full sail, Bertha turned and moved majestically away. What she said to the others Leah could not hear, but they all followed her, like small boats drawn by her wake, out the door and down the stairs.

Though Leah kept the smile on her face, inside she had a sinking feeling. Village vice might be attractive to the Smart Set, who considered the area their own private Latin Quarter, but to the Irish cops and Irish judges? Sodom and Gomorrah. She should have known better than to lose her temper at that woman! Who knew what Bertha would do?

Craning her neck, Leah made sure Joanna was still curled up in the corner. Of course she was, her tousled auburn head glowing russet in the soft candlelight, her thumb in her mouth, just a curve of a plump pink cheek showing. Joanna was fine. They were both fine. There was nothing to worry about. But maybe she shouldn't be so quick to turn Jim down every time he told her he wanted to take care of them.

"Leah, every woman needs a man," he'd insisted.

"This is 1920, not 1820, Jim."

"Every law on the books says you don't exist unless you're someone's wife, Leah darlin'. Look, I only want to help you

and the baby, so nobody can ever come along and accuse you
of not being able to take care of her."

Tonight, suddenly, Leah realized he was right. If Jim were
living with them on Barrow Street, if they were a family, Bertha Lazarus could stamp her feet and tighten her lips all she
wanted, but she would never be able to force Leah into anything.

Just then, Jim appeared in the doorway, his eyes seeking her
out. He always came on the nights she worked, so she
wouldn't have to walk home alone with the little one. Or—she
suspected—with some interested man, either. She met his eyes
and they smiled at each other. Nobody would dare bother her
in the company of this big burly man. Everything about him
was exaggerated; his hair was longer and thicker, his mustache
heavier, his shoulders broader, the dimple in his chin deeper
than that of ordinary men. Jim McCready was a man to be
reckoned with!

Maybe he was right; maybe she and Joanna needed him.
Maybe he was the answer. Maybe tonight she'd tell him yes.

13

June 18, 1922

Everything was so beautiful on the new subway line—the
Brooklyn Manhattan Transit Company, which everyone called
the BMT. All the stations were lined with tiles, each station
with its own color scheme, everything sparkling and well-lit.
The very latest word in modern design. If you looked carefully,
as you whizzed through, or when the train stopped, you could
see that each station had a line of tiles with a symbol: a sailing
ship, a paddlewheeler, a bird, City Hall, each station different
from the last. The first stop in Brooklyn, the Borough Hall–
Brooklyn Heights station, had tiles with a picture of Borough
Hall on them.

Joanna was amazed; she kept turning her head, crying, "Look, Mommy! Look, Jim!" about everything.

Leah wasn't really listening to Joanna; she was too full of memories. Every June eighteenth she had boarded the train for Coney, to keep that promise she and Annie had made to each other on their sixteenth birthday, to come back every year; but she never could bring herself to get off. Was it really twelve years ago that they had come and had their pictures taken? *Twelve years?* So long ago. She hadn't even really wanted to come today; but Jim made her.

"Didn't you promise your friend you'd go back every year? You can't break a promise to the dear departed, my girl. It's bad luck—that's what my old granny always told me. And how can you keep Jo from the place, when it's where you met her father?" he wheedled. "Come on, now, it'll be fine, you'll see."

She fingered the locket, dug up from the bottom of her jewelry drawer for this occasion. There was a time when she had worn the locket around her neck every day; and then, after a while, she wore it for luck. Finally, she took it out only on her birthday. And then, somehow, it just slid down under all the other necklaces and bracelets and beads in the drawer.

As soon as the excursion was planned, she went searching for it, but it was nowhere to be found. She was convinced it had been lost or stolen, or accidentally thrown away, and became quite frantic, pawing through all her dresser drawers, throwing lingerie and stockings onto the floor, sobbing in frustration. Finally, she remembered putting it in the second dressing table drawer, behind her scarves. And there it was! She sat staring at herself in the mirror, weeping tears of relief and chagrin.

Jim had taken it away then, and brought it back polished and hanging on a brand-new heavy gold chain. She was sitting at her dressing table, brushing her hair, when he came in and, without a word, hung it around her neck. The chain was so long, the locket nestled itself deep between her breasts. And it was gorgeous, the faceted links flashing in the light.

"Oh, Jim! You didn't have to do that! Annie and I always went out and bought ribbons—" Out of the blue her voice choked with tears and she couldn't go on.

Jim had put his big hand on her shoulder, his eyes warm as a puppy dog's, meeting hers in the dressing table mirror. . . .

Leah turned to Jim as the train clattered through Brooklyn,

past the springtime greenery of fields and woods and the occasional farm. "Bertha called me this morning."

"What does the old witch want now? Her pound of flesh?" Leah poked him. "Not in front of Jo."

"Jo's deep in dreamland, don't you worry." The four-year-old had fallen asleep in Jim's lap. "But why be so careful? They don't give a hoot in hell what they say about *you* in front of Jo."

"Just because they're stupid doesn't mean I should be. Anyway, let me tell you . . . they want her for a month this summer when they go to the Catskills."

"I can see where that's a problem. Jo would probably love the mountains. But on the other hand . . ."

"But on the other hand . . ." Leah agreed. "Although, I must say, Bertha's being very careful with me these days. She said she'd take whatever time was available. Sweet as pie."

"I guess you put the fear of God into her."

"Don't I wish!" Leah said. "But you can't trust that woman. She's devious. Wait till you hear—"

"Oh come on, Leah. Wasn't I there when Jo came home and said Grandmama told her Mommy doesn't really love her? Wasn't I right next to you, holding your hand while you phoned her, screaming into the mouthpiece? I'll never forget it. 'If I ever hear you've said that again, you'll never ever see Joanna! Not as long as you live! Not if I have to move to California!' "

His imitation of Leah in a high temper, her voice climbing the register with every word, was perfect. She had to laugh.

"I don't understand why you let them see her at all, Leah. All they ever do is stab you in the back. It's not like you to take it lying down."

He knew her, all right. "Ah, Jim, it's so complicated. . . ."

"But why *do* you keep sending Jo to them?"

"Joe asked me to. When he found out I was pregnant, he wrote me a long letter. He said he realized how ignorant and closed-minded they were, and he didn't ask me to forgive them, no. He said his father could be 'very good' to the baby—he underlined *very good*—but not if I estranged myself from them. Oh yeah, it made me mad. 'If *I* estranged myself'! As if *I* were the snob!" She took in an exasperated breath and let it out loudly. "Never mind. It's his family and he's dead, and I feel I shouldn't cut them out. Family is important. Don't I know it, who have none!"

"Ah, Leah, don't think about that, not on such a beautiful day." He gave her a soft look, and added: "The three of us could be a real family, you know. Just say the word."

Leah shook her head. "I'm not the marrying kind, Jim. But listen, something's—"

A quick movement of his head warned her, and she looked down. Joanna was no longer sleeping; she was sitting very quietly, listening to every word, her amber-colored eyes wide.

Luckily, the train came to a screeching halt just then, and they were at the end of the line—Coney Island! Descending the stairway, they both held tightly to Jo's hands. She was so excited, she was in danger of bouncing herself right over the railing. There were so many eager visitors getting off the train and pressing to get down in a hurry, a child could easily be trampled.

"Where to, Miss Jo? A little bite to eat?" Jim asked when they got to the street, his glance meeting Leah's. The child had been clamoring to try a Coney Island hot ever since they told her they were planning this trip. Right across the street stood Nathan's, a throng almost hiding the outdoor counter.

"The carousel! The carousel!"

Jo loved carousels, even the tiny tinny ones carted around on a truck by a team of horses, going from block to block. Leah had told her all about the famous B & B Carousel on Surf Avenue. Now that they were here, and it was all so familiar and yet so different, it suddenly occurred to Leah that B & B might have closed sometime in the past twelve years.

As they walked along, Leah marveled at the crowds. She and Annie had thought there were so many people when they had come here in 1910. Now, you could hardly walk for the throng; it was like swimming against the tide. She was a bit surprised; after all, the days were gone when Coney Island all lit up was cause for amazement and wonder; the whole city had electricity now.

The BMT, Jim pointed out, that's what had done it; the subway gave everyone in New York the opportunity to make the trip for only a nickel. Well, they were certainly taking their opportunity, Leah thought as she was jostled and elbowed and bumped. Jim had put Jo on his shoulders, so at least she was safe. It was no longer the same sort of crowd. On her sixteenth birthday, everyone had been all dressed up; the women carried parasols and all the men tipped their hats. Now the crowd was rowdier, rougher, not so well-dressed. Leah gave herself a

swift once-over in a shop window as they walked by: her tai-
lored blouse and narrow skirt were right up to the minute, and
very smart. Her new shoes she loved; she'd found them at
Bloomingdale's, only $3.69, brown leather with a strap across
the instep and a curved heel. They were so pretty, and she had
a well-turned narrow ankle. Only, looking around, she almost
felt overdressed.

She'd forgotten how rasping and nasal the Brooklyn speech
was. Couldn't they *hear* themselves? No wonder all the vaudeville comedians imitated them for laughs! And they thought
nothing of pushing you aside if you weren't moving fast
enough. She yelled "Hey!" a couple of times; but nobody even
bothered to turn to look at her, much less apologize!

Judging from the flirtatious laughter she kept hearing, Coney
was still the place where, for an hour or two, you could be
whoever you wanted to be, dream whatever dreams you
wanted to dream, and forget the rules. Even so, much of it was
changed. Dreamland had burned down, the same year as the
Triangle fire. The pygmies were gone, and the babies in their
incubators. But Steeplechase was still running, and Luna Park.
The Wonder Wheel you could see from blocks around, soaring
135 feet into the bright sky, so airy and graceful to look at,
made of iron latticework, its swaying chairs seeming to dangle
from silken threads. And there was the carousel, looking just
the same as her memories of it.

"Mommy! Mommy! Look! The horsies! I want the blue
one! Please, Uncle Jim, can I ride the blue one?"

"May I," Leah corrected automatically.

"*May* I, Uncle Jim?"

"You may and you can, my little leprechaun." He lifted her
down and they all got onto the wooden floor of the merry-go-
round, lifting Jo onto a gorgeous steed, beautifully painted and
decorated, its dainty legs frozen gracefully in a gallop.

Soon the wheeze of the calliope started "The Skater's
Waltz" and the carousel was moving, around and around. The
horses began to plunge up and down, up and down, while all
the children squealed with pleasure.

Leah was taken back, to another carousel in a different park.
How old was she? No more than eight or nine. They had all
caught a trolley, marching two by two, boarding two by two,
sitting two by two. Where was that park . . . ?

* * *

How she loves the feeling of herself, rocking on the horse as it moves; it feels so real to her; she sways a little in the saddle and hangs on tightly to the reins, imagining it's a real horse "out West," wherever that is. She doesn't know, but it's where cowboys and Indians come from. She knows she must get the brass ring. She has seen other children grab it, and heard their cries of triumph. They are bigger and older, but she can get it, she knows she can get it. And if she catches it, that means her mother will come—soon—and get her.

When she comes around again, she stands up and she stretches, she thinks she might leap from the horse and float right into the air. And maybe she *can* leap and float; because next thing she knows, her hand is wrapped around the thick, cold, heavy ring. She has it. She *has* it! She is magical. And then she hears one of the workers from the Home say, "Look at that! How do you suppose she did it? She's so small!" And the answer: "Luck, pure and simple!"

Well, Leah thought, as the B & B Carousel slowed and stopped, she *was* lucky, always had been, in a way. She'd had her share of hardship and heartaches, but hadn't she always landed on her feet?

"Okay, kiddo," Jim said to Joanna. "We've done the carousel. What's next? Nathan's for a Coney Island hot? Or straight to the Wonder Wheel?"

"Wonder Wheel! Wonder Wheel!"

"Matter of fact," Jim remarked as they headed for the boardwalk, "we probably shouldn't eat before we ride the thing."

"Why not, Jim?"

"Never you mind, never you mind."

They joined the line at the giant circular web, a long one, and looked around as it moved slowly up to the ticket man. The sky was darkening, just enough so you could see the thin slice of moon and the evening star looking odd in the middle of the blue, looking, she thought, as if they were in too much of a hurry to wait for nightfall. It wasn't often you got to think about the night sky, when you lived in the city, with all the bright lights and tall buildings. But out here, where both land and sea began and ended, the sky was enormous.

"Leah! Stop daydreaming. It's our turn," Jim said, laughing.

They climbed into the car, and right away Leah knew she was in trouble. As soon as they sat, it rocked back and forth, and her heart went flying into her throat. The merry-go-round was her speed: a gentle movement, not too fast, not too high.

A minute later, as they soared into the heavens, Leah felt as if she were on the edge of a precipice with the whole empty world yawning in front of her, only the slender bar across the front of the seat keeping her from floating off into space. She swallowed and gripped the bar, trying not to show her panic. She didn't want to frighten Jo—although, from the sounds of her daughter's laughter, Jo wasn't scared at all. Leah couldn't even turn her head to look. She could only sit absolutely still and hang on for dear life.

Spread out before them was all of Coney Island, with the trees and fields of Brooklyn behind, and beyond them, the ocean. The edge of sky was a deep purple fading off into shades of blue. Beautiful, Leah thought, holding on to the thought, holding her breath.

The great wheel came to a halt just as they reached the top. And their seat slipped and slid, plunging down and out, while the ground below flew by in a blur. Leah heard herself gasp— she wanted to scream, but no sound would come out of her throat. She could hear Jim's laughter, but she couldn't even be angry about it. Her whole body was quaking with the effort to keep herself from falling out, into the abyss.

"Mommy, look, there's a ship! It's so small, it looks like the one I play with in the bathtub!"

As Jo turned to her, pointing, she set the seat rocking and Leah's chest constricted.

Tightly, she said, "Very pretty," but she could see nothing but danger. She could feel Jim leaning out—*leaning out!* the effrontery of it!—to peer at her.

"Are you scared, Leah?" From the sound of his voice, he could hardly believe it.

"No." Said through gritted teeth. Leah forced her lips into a smile; she hoped it was a smile. She had often wondered why people panicked. Now she knew. Panic was precisely what she was feeling; if she thought she could survive, she would jump out of this infernal thing now! Desperately, she needed not to be here, up so high, so exposed. Desperate: that was the word. She recalled herself forcefully telling Annie that it would be good for her to face the fire she feared so horribly, and she was ashamed. Annie, I'm sorry; I had no idea.

And then, with grandeur, the great wheel began to move again, they were over the crest and moving down.

At last it was over and, with shaking knees, Leah could step onto terra firma. The operator held his callused hand out to help her, and never had the touch of another human felt so dear.

"Let's go have something to eat," she suggested brightly.

But Joanna wanted to go up again. "Please, please, oh Mommy, please let's go up again. It was so . . . thrilling."

"Come on, Leah, any four-year-old who can drag a word like 'thrilling' out of her vocabulary deserves another ride on the Wonder Wheel, don't you think?"

"All right. But you take her, Jim, I've had enough. God, she's fearless, isn't she?"

"Look who's talking!"

"Brave I am, fearless, no."

"Just what are you afraid of, I'd like to know."

"None of your business. Just go, go!" She laughed and gave him a playful shove.

Later, when they got to the wooden stand on Surf Avenue where Nathan sold his Coney Island hots, the crowd was fifteen deep and impatient. Jim hoisted Jo onto his shoulders. They stood near the stand to eat, and then Jim went back for more. Delicious! They agreed that Nathan really had a good idea—and you didn't even need a plate.

As they headed for the boardwalk again, Jim asked Joanna, "Remember our surprise?"

She looked up at her mother, giggling. "For your birthday, Mommy."

"A birthday surprise is the best surprise, *shayfele*." The Yiddish word, all but forgotten, came popping out of her mouth.

"What's . . . shayf'lla mean?"

Leah bent down to pick up her daughter. "My mama used to call me that."

"Tell me about your mama, tell me a story."

Leah put her down. "Some other day." There was a strained silence, so she smiled at both of them and said, "Do you know, I have no idea what *shayfele* means?" A little laugh. "I didn't even know I remembered it. So. Let's have my surprise, what do you say? After all, today *is* my birthday."

They strolled slowly past the line of booths: saltwater taffy; gold-colored necklaces and bracelets—"guaranteed to turn your skin green," Jim said—funny hats, cotton candy. Joanna hesitated for a long time in front of a machine featuring an animated Gypsy woman. For a penny she would tell your fortune, on a little card that slid out of the slot. But no, that wasn't good enough. And the penny machine with its crane that let you try to scoop up prizes with balls of chewing gum . . . that also took Jo's fancy, for a minute or two.

But it wasn't until they came to the dolls on sticks that she stopped and said, "That. I want that for my mommy's birthday." They were cheap celluloid dolls with their cheeks painted bright pink and their hair painted bright yellow. But glued onto the back of each head was a feather headdress, a fan of real feathers, dyed in garish colors. And the entire body of the doll sparkled and glittered in the bright electric light. Joanna could not take her eyes from the line of dolls.

"Please may I have a doll," she said to the vendor, a middle-aged man with tired eyes and a jauntily tipped straw boater.

"Of course, you may, little lady! Which one suits your pleasure, hey?"

After several careful moments of examination, she pointed to one wearing bright crimson.

"That'll be fifty cents, little darling."

Joanna unfisted the quarter she had been holding ever since they left Nathan's and held it out.

"That's only twenty-five cents, sweetheart. You need to give me another two bits."

"This is the only money I have. Please may I buy a doll?"

"I'm sorry . . ." As the man turned to put the doll back and Jo's lips began to quiver, Jim reached into his pocket. But Leah stopped him.

"No, Jim, if a quarter's what she has, let her learn what she can get with it. It's time she knew money doesn't just fall from the sky, anyway."

Leah fully expected the little girl to begin to cry, but instead Jo said, "That one over there, with the blue, she has a broken feather. Will my money buy *her*?"

"Look, little lady, the price is fifty cents. If I sold my dolls for two bits to every little beauty that comes along, I'd be broke."

"But her feather is broken. Nobody will buy her." The two of them locked eyes and stared at each other. Then, sweetly, reasonably, Jo added: "*I* will." Her hand, the quarter lying on the palm, was proffered once more.

The doll seller burst into laughter. "You're a stubborn little thing, ain't you? But smart. You got a *pisk* on you, a real mouth. How old is she?" he asked Jim.

"Four years old," Jo answered him. "And it's for my mommy's birthday. She's twenty-eight."

"Well, then, how can I say no?" He reached for the doll with the broken feather, then laughed again, and instead handed her the red one. "Here you go. And a happy birthday to you, ma'am."

When Joanna handed over her prize, Leah picked her up and gave her a big hug. "I'm very proud of you," she said. "You stuck to your guns. And now you see, it pays to stick to your guns. Don't ever let *anyone* tell you it can't be done, okay?"

So it was a happy child who fell fast asleep on the train going home, and had to be carried upstairs. Jim set her down on the sofa in the front room, where she curled up tightly, covered with the Spanish shawl Leah kept draped over the top of the piano.

"How do you like *them* apples?" Leah joked. "The guy was right—she's got a mouth on her."

"Like mother, like daughter."

"I guess she'll never—" The phone rang, sounding shrill and demanding in the quiet. "Now who . . . ?" She picked up the receiver quickly, before the noise disturbed Jo. "Hello?"

"Leah, I have to talk very fast. Mama thinks I've gone to the store for milk for breakfast coffee, but we really have a whole quart and if she ever finds out I've called you, well—"

"I know, I know," Leah interrupted. "What's up, Zelda?" She had become used to these hurried phone conversations; and to Zelda's breathy whisper, even though she was nowhere near her parents when she called. "And talk a little louder, would you? Sometimes I can't hear you."

"Oh, Leah, they're going to *buy* Joanna!"

"Excuse me?! They're going to *what*?"

"Buy her . . . that is, they're going to try to buy her."

"Buy my daughter from me? Is that what you're saying?" Leah and Jim stared at each other, unbelieving.

"Yes. They talked to Sidney Harris—their lawyer—they talked to him all evening yesterday, and I listened and I heard them say, 'You can go as high as five thousand dollars. But that means we're allowed to adopt her, be sure you put that in,' they told him. He's going to send you a letter about it. Leah, I really have to get back—"

"I know, I know. Zelda, thanks. I don't know what I'd do without you."

"I love you, Leah, and I know Joe wouldn't want them trying to buy his baby away from you."

Leah put the receiver back in place and turned to Jim. "Can you believe it? They're going to offer me five thousand dollars for my baby. Five thousand! They have more gall than brains, I'm telling you!"

Jim stuck a cigar into his teeth and lit it, puffing furiously. "At least they put a high price on her. Only kidding, only kidding."

"There is *no* price on her!" Leah paced the floor, shaken and feeling vulnerable. A mother who would sell her baby was a mother who should go straight to hell. And a grandmother who would ask her to do it was just as bad, maybe worse!

"How could they think I would give up my baby? How *could* they? Why do they think I fight for birth control? I want every child to be a *wanted* child, that's why! Look at all the abandoned children left in churches and in synogogues and in front of hospitals and, oh God, in garbage pails!" And at orphanages . . .

Suddenly the tears came pouring out of her, the sobs welling up so hard they hurt her chest. Jim was there in a second, his arms around her. She pushed her face into his broad fleshy chest, into the buttons of his vest, and let herself cry. They were so awful! How could they think of taking Jo away from her? She would die first!

After a while Leah pulled back, wiping at her eyes with the back of her hand. "Listen, Jim. Can they make me?"

"Make you sell Joanna? Good God, woman, of course they can't!"

"I mean . . . because Joe and I were never married . . . does that give them rights?"

He snorted. "There isn't a court in this land won't give a child to its mother over the grandparents. Even over the father."

"I hope you're right, Jim. But I can't help thinking . . . in that case, why do they keep on trying?"

"Why? Because they have the money and they have the lawyer, so what have they got to lose?"

"And because they hate me. They *hate* me, Jim. Well, let them and be damned to them! If they want a fight . . . they've *got* one!"

"That's my girl. Don't get sad, get sore! They can't make you do a goddamn thing you don't want to do."

She pulled gently out of his embrace and went to check herself in the mirror. A red-eyed mess. She found herself meeting Jim's gaze in the glass. His eyes were pleading.

"Listen to me, Leah. Let's get married. You know I love you. I'll adopt Jo. I love her, too. Come on, Leah, what do you say? I'll take good care of you. I'll get you to love me, you'll see." She couldn't answer him. "They'll never give up, you know, as long as you're on your own."

"To hell with them!" Then she softened. "Aw, Jim, it's not you. You're the best friend I have. I *do* love you. But I made myself a promise that I'd never marry, and I'm sticking with it."

"Okay, then let's live together. We could always tell them we're married. Who's to know?"

Thinking about it, Leah began to smile. It *would* be a delicious joke on those hateful Lazaruses with their bourgeois rules and phony gentility.

"Okay then, let's do it." Saying it surprised even her.

"You're joking!"

"No, not at all." She couldn't quite meet his eyes. "Your place is far too small so you better figure on moving in with us."

"You really *aren't* joking!" She couldn't be sure, but she thought his eyes filled. Quickly, she turned around to face him. He looked . . . the only word was *blissful*. She gazed at him for a moment, thinking, I'll be looking at him for a long, long time. It wouldn't be so bad; at forty-something, he was still a fine figure of a man, big, broad, barrel-chested. The thick copper hair had darkened but the big mustache was as red as ever. And the pale eyes shone with love. Taking in a deep breath, telling herself, *here goes*, she marched over to him and lifted her face for a kiss.

He tasted of cigar and something minty, but it was nice. His lips were firm and warm, and when his mouth opened and his tongue began to explore and a groan of pleasure came up out of his belly and his arms clamped around her and drew her into his solid strength, she found herself weakening, melting, clinging to him for dear life.

And then a little body was butting against their legs, and, down at waist level, a little voice demanding, "Me! Me!" But as she laughed with Jim and bent to pick the child up and include her in their embrace, Leah wondered: Even the two of us, can we protect Jo from them and their lawyers? And then, fiercely, Yes, we can, we can! We must!

14

October 1924

Leah heard them coming up the stairs after school: Jo and her little friend Peggy Powell and Inez, Peggy's mother. Inez was a prig and a prude; her eyes widened at *everything* in shock, but she was willing to go anywhere, even 35 Barrow Street, to provide her shy little girl a friend to play with. Also, she thought Leah was glamorous, being a writer and a Village character.

Leah put down her pen, stacked her papers and stretched her back. It was time for a break, anyway. Inez knocked; she always knocked. But she knew that the door was open. "Out in a minute!" Leah called, putting the big gray cover over the typewriter. "Come on in!" Inez had been there often enough to sit herself down and be patient, although she still didn't know how to make herself a drink.

By the time Leah joined them, Jo had gone into the kitchen and brought back the cookie jar, an apple, and a sharp knife, which she was using to cut the apple into slices. Alarmed, Inez got up and said, "I'll do that, Jo."

"I know how."

"It's very dangerous for a six-year-old girl to be using a sharp knife. You could cut yourself." Inez tried to take the knife away, but Jo just as firmly held onto it.

"I know how. Jim teached me."

"*Taught*, sweetheart," Leah said loudly, strolling in. "Hello, you beautiful girls, are you smarter than when you left for school this morning? Hi, Inez, it's all right. She really does know how to use a knife without cutting herself. Ready for a cocktail?"

"You must have your own private bootlegger, Leah."

"That's right, I do." She laughed, tossing her head. "To hell

136

with Prohibition, *I* say! I'd like to *see* the government that could tell *me* what to drink! It's bad enough to have our government climbing into bed with us, seeing if we dare use birth control! How about a sloe gin fizz?"

"Sounds yummy." Inez tossed her own head. Leah had noticed how much Inez copied her, and she wondered if Inez realized it.

"Cigarette?"

"Sure. What brand?"

Leah made a face. "London Life Turkish."

"Are they strong?"

"I wouldn't know, I don't smoke. But Jim does. They smell strong, I can tell you that."

Inez shook her head. "Just the drink, then. If Tim ever smelled smoke on me ... !" She followed Leah into the tiny kitchen.

Leah wore a silk dress, dyed in a pattern of swirls and curls, sashed around her hips. She had tied her shoes with ribbons that matched, instead of laces. She thought she made Inez, in her fashionable navy-blue middy and pumps, look like a frump; and, Leah guessed from her envious glances, so did Inez.

They went back into the front room carrying their glasses, to find Peggy and Jo and a whole family of dolls settled down on the carpet. The minute they sat down with their drinks, Jo said, "I did too see *Mad Love* in the moving pictures, didn't I, Mommy?"

"Yes, you did."

"My daddy doesn't allow me to go to the moving pictures," Peggy said, making Inez flush. She didn't like having her husband shown up as a pompous bore, which he was. Leah had met him just once, at City and Country, where the kids went to school. Once was enough. He nearly dragged poor Inez away, so eager was he to get her away from Leah's evil influence: Leah could see it all on his face. She'd bet a hundred bucks Inez never admitted how often she was here, or how long she stayed.

"Well, Uncle Jim and Mommy *always* take me with them to the moving pictures, don't you, Mommy?"

"Not quite always, sweetie pie."

"Uncle Jim says he'll take me to see Charlie Chaplin. But I love Pola Negri. When I grow up, I'm going to look just like

Pola Negri and be in the moving pictures and have men fall madly in love with me."

Leah began to laugh at this, and after a moment Inez did, too.

"And when I grow up, I'll get married," Joanna went on, "I'm going to marry Tommy Ramey."

"Tommy Ramey said he's going to marry *me*," Peggy protested.

"He can marry both of us, Peggy."

"No such thing!" Inez nearly choked on her drink. "A man can only have one wife, you know that, Joanna."

"Let's sing 'Barney Google,'" Jo suggested. She was obviously bored with the whole subject.

"If you ladies are going to sing," Leah said, "I want you to go into the back room to do it."

"Then we won't sing," Jo announced firmly. Leah noticed the look on Inez's face. Inez did not approve of letting children hang around and listen to grown-up conversation.

"What were you working on when we came in?" Inez asked politely. "One of your articles about free love or anarchy?"

A polite smile. "My articles are usually about the lowly state of women in this country, Inez, a subject *all* women should be interested in. But no, today I just finished a silly love story for a silly magazine. . . ."

"Have I ever heard of it? I *love* love stories!"

"I think so. The *Saturday Evening Post*."

"Oh, Leah, that's so exciting! The *Saturday Evening Post* is going to print a story by you? You'll be famous!"

"Perhaps, but none of my friends will ever know it. I'm writing under a pseudonym. Lee James . . . the James part is for Jim. Clever, huh?"

"Very. But I don't understand why you need a different name."

"Because I'm a serious writer in need of money, and in order to make money, I've written a silly short story about how an immigrant girl finds love in the slums of New York, for a silly bourgeois magazine that thinks the Lower East Side is *romantic*. They wouldn't have touched the article I did on the shame of child labor, nor my piece on the abandoned children who live on the streets and in the sewers of this supposedly civilized city!" She could hear her voice getting louder, so she stopped. "I guess most people don't want to hear the bad news, do they? They'd rather not know."

"Well, I think it's a shame the *Post* won't publish your serious work. So many people read it! And . . . I'm sorry you're . . . short. Can I help?"

"Inez, that's so sweet. But no. We'll manage, we always do. Jim's in the throes of setting up a new magazine, a new *kind* of magazine . . . it's going to be very exciting. Then we'll be so rich, we won't know what to do with all our money. But in the meantime . . . I write romantic short stories and . . . high-class pornography."

It took Inez a minute or two to take in the last word. "Did you say . . . por—" She couldn't repeat it; and her eyes were bugging right out of her head.

"Pornography. High-class stuff, of course, tasteful. Yes, you'd be surprised how easy it is to write. They pay very well."

Inez gulped down her drink, hardly knowing what to say or even where to look.

"Really, Inez, it's not much different than writing anything else, except of course for the details. . . ." She gave Inez a mischievous smile, and a moment later Inez laughed, too.

Still, it wasn't long after her confession that Inez took her daughter and left. Leah chided herself for mentioning the pornography but she could never resist shocking Inez Powell. The woman had a face like a mirror; you could read every thought that passed through her head. She was a fool, and Leah Lazarus had no time for fools. But Jo needed friends, so she acted the part. It was a relief to just be herself, now that Inez had gone home.

"Well, Jo, what shall we do now?"

"Are you finished, Mommy?"

"All finished!"

"Then I want to dress up, Mommy. Let's play going to the theater. Please?"

"Okay, but let me call the magazine first, and have them send a messenger."

When the knock came on the door an hour later, Joanna was resplendent in one of Leah's chemises, a feather boa around her neck, a plumed hat on her head, her cheeks and lips rouged, a black outline around her stormy green eyes.

She was seated on an outsized ornately carved chair, almost a throne, which Jim had spotted months ago in the street. They'd brought it upstairs and fixed it up. It was their theater seat. Leah, in bright red Chinese pajamas and blackface, was standing in front of the fireplace singing, "Toot, toot, Tootsie, goodbye, toot, toot, Tootsie, don't cry," imitating Al Jolson, whom she had seen doing it on stage in *Bombo* last year. Jo loved the song; whenever they played theater, that's what she usually asked for, although lately "Barney Google" was making inroads.

When she heard the knock, Leah marched to the door, still singing, and flung it open. The messenger, a young boy, no more than ten or eleven years old, stood there amazed.

Leah had to laugh; he looked so stunned. And then she had a flash of seeing this scene through his eyes. He knew he was to get a manuscript and bring it back to the office. What could he have expected? A man, probably, in shirtsleeves and suspenders, a dark-paneled room heavy with velvet drapes and leather and all those other male notions of decor. And what did he find? A room painted bright yellow, its walls covered with art and photographs; a mad mix of furniture, some of it painted, some of it covered in batik; and the pièce de résistance, two costumed females, one of them singing a song at the top of her lungs. And then Leah remembered her blackface. No wonder he stopped and stared, the poor kid.

"Yes, this is the right place. You just wait there." She ran into her writing alcove, grabbed a thick envelope from the desk, and hurried back to put it into his nerveless hand.

As soon as he had turned to go back down the stairs, she realized that she had just given him "1001 Nights of Ecstasy" instead of "Annie Finds Love." Oh my God! Just imaging that manuscript in the hands of the editors of the *Post*!

"No! Wait!" She nearly startled him into falling down the steps. "Don't move. I've given you the wrong envelope." In a moment she had done the trade.

"This one," she said, still laughing, "is much too naughty for the *Saturday Evening Post*!"

She hadn't thought his eyes could get much wider, but they did. She couldn't resist giving him a wink. He turned and bolted down the stairs. He wouldn't forget this visit soon!

But his intrusion reminded her that it was time to stop playing and wash off the paint. "Soon it'll be time for dinner, sweetie, and we want to be ready when Uncle Jim comes home, don't we?"

"What are we going to have tonight?"

"I don't know . . . you choose. Chinese? Sandwiches? Spaghetti and meatballs in Little Italy? Or Mori's."

"Mori's. Mori's. And can we walk by the gas lamps?"

"If you promise to eat your whole dinner."

"Promise."

While she was creaming the rouge and kohl from Joanna's face, the little girl said, "Is today Friday?"

"Yes. Why?"

"How many days to Saturday?"

Leah knew what was worrying her. Two Saturdays a month, Zelda came down from the Bronx to take Jo to her grandparents for the weekend. Joanna did not like going there. Leah hated to let her go, it always made her feel very uneasy, but how could she say no? Ever since she had turned down their five-thousand-dollar offer—in no uncertain terms and with a threat in her voice—they had been behaving themselves.

"You know tomorrow is Saturday, sweetie. Zelda will come to get you tomorrow morning, and then the very next day it will be Sunday, and Zelda will bring you back."

Like a little parrot, Joanna intoned: "I must say Aunt Zelda, not just Zelda. I must curtsey like you taught me and say please and thank you. I must be very quiet and not tell anything. . . ."

Leah stopped wiping Jo's face and, kneeling so their eyes were level, said, "Honey-bunny, listen to me. Just be your own self. I don't want you to look so worried. Your grandparents like you to say those things, but if you forget, they'll still love you."

"Not Grandmother." Jo sounded so sad and so sure, Leah couldn't help laughing.

"Oh, Jo, I know she's a tough cookie, but I also know she'll love you, no matter what."

"She always says to be a good girl. She always says I'll learn how to be a good girl when I live with them all the time and I'm *their* little girl. I'm *your* little girl, aren't I, Mommy? I'm not their little girl!"

Leah pulled the child close to her. "That's right, you're *my* little girl, and you always will be."

"Promise?"

Leah tightened her hold. "Promise."

Jo's tone changed, just a little. "They said that when I come to live with them and be their little girl, I can have a pony."

Oh, those *momzers*, with their bribes and blandishments! Did they really think it would *work*? They were stupid, stupid!

"But you don't want to leave Mommy and Uncle Jim, do you, Jo?"

"No, Mommy. But . . . it would be nice to have a pony."

Startled, Leah pulled back and was both surprised and relieved to see that Jo was only making a joke. A chip off the old block! They both burst into laughter; and Leah gave her a hug, saying, "And anyway, Jo, who needs a pony when we have the subway?"

15

December 1924

Six o'clock. A dark moonless night with lazy snowflakes beginning to fall, beginning to thicken. Outside, total darkness, except for the street lamps, and the Christmas lights gleaming out of windows in the curve of Commerce Street.

"Jim, what time is it?"

"Three minutes past. Leah, for God's sake, sit down and have a drink and stop wringing your hands. Joanna's fine. See how it's starting to snow? It's probably heavier up in the Bronx."

"So why haven't they called? They have a telephone!"

Leah got up and began to pace nervously back and forth. There wasn't a lot of room. An eleven-foot Scotch pine stood in one corner, hung with shiny ornaments and small white and red candles, a huge silver-gilt star at the very top.

Jim had dragged the thing up the stairs a week ago, announcing that this was their Christmas tree. Christmas tree! Leah had stared at it. A Jewish girl with a Christmas tree? But to be truthful, she had always thought them beautiful, glittering with gold and silver, gleaming with candlelight, the dark branches sweeping out like a grand green ball gown. She would walk slowly past the *goyishe* houses, catching glimpses of Christmas trees through parlor windows, envying the glow and warmth of the scene: the candles and the wreaths in the windows, the swags of greenery, the piles of brightly wrapped and ribboned boxes hiding the bottom of the tree. It had all looked so ... familyish, happy and complete.

So she had flung herself into decorating the tree, picking the perfect spot for each ornament, lifting Jo up to loop the strings of cranberries over the high branches. They had strung them together one afternoon, using big needles and waxed string. And Joanna had made a paper chain at school....

"Dammit, Jim! Look at me, I'm a nervous wreck! Where *is* she?" Her chest was constricted with dread. "They've been in an accident!"

Jim gave a bark of a laugh and ran his fingers through his curly hair, making it stand up in wild disarray. "Christ almighty, Leah, what are you talking about? *Accident!* What sort of accident?"

"An automobile accident! I don't know! I just have ... a feeling. You know how they're always promising her they'll give her a pony ... What if she fell off a horse and hit her head?"

"Pipe dreams, that's all the horse talk is, and you know it!" He had been standing by the window, looking out at the empty street below. Now he came to her, tipping her head up with a finger under her chin. "Listen to me, Leah. Jo is fine, just fine."

"Then where is she? She was supposed to be back at five!"

"They're held up, that's all. They've been late before."

Stubbornly: "Never this late."

"It's snowing."

"Jim, they are *very* late."

He gazed down at her, his expression a mix of tenderness and exasperation. Then he blew a noisy gust of air out between his lips and said, "All right, then, let me make a few calls, find out if there's been a tie-up on the roads or anything."

He stood at the entrance to the kitchen, leaning against the jamb, his bulk filling the entire doorway. The receiver looked dainty in his big hand. He had some trouble getting an operator; but then, someone answered and he asked to be connected to the *New York Daily Mirror*, where he had several friends.

She knew she should listen in, but she couldn't concentrate; her mind was wheeling this way and that, and her head was filled with inchoate fear. She reached down to a pile of magazines on a table and picked one up, leafing through it. Her eye was caught by a Kodak ad and tears immediately flooded her vision. The last time Jo had gone to the Bronx, she had come back, all excited, saying Zelda had promised her a Kodak camera of her own, for Christmas. She could hardly wait for the weeks to pass, to go back for it. Finally Leah had said, "If you want a camera so badly, Jim will get us one."

But Jo would have none of *that*. "No, Mommy. I wrote a letter to Santa. Santa is going to bring me a very special camera, a new kind for little girls to use, with film and everything. Zelda let me use her folding camera and I took pictures and she showed me them! I want my own very special camera."

Where *was* she? Leah flung the magazine down and turned to find Jim putting on his overcoat and hat.

"The roads are still clear, nothing doing anywhere. And—" He paused, clearly unwilling to go on. "—and don't worry about it, sweetheart, but . . . there's no answer at the Lazarus apartment. I let it ring twenty-two times. So . . . I'm going up to the Grand Concourse to see if I can find out what the hell is going on."

"I'm coming, too."

He put a hand on her shoulder. "No, Leah. I realize how you're feeling, but think a minute. Someone has to be here, if they should show up . . . *when* they show up."

He was right, of course. But it was so horribly quiet in the apartment after he left, so horribly empty and echoing. Leah walked from room to room, touching her favorite things for reassurance. She was wearing the locket today; now she took it off, opened it to gaze at the two browning photos, and thought of the man who had taken the pictures.

Here I am, Joe, she said silently, waiting for our daughter to come home from seeing your family. Can you believe that? She tried to remember how he looked and sounded and smiled, but it was no use. She had pictures of him, of course; she had the last one taken of him—in his uniform, his cap tucked under his arm, his expression serious, but a twinkle in his eye. No army in the world could erase Joe's good humor.

That photograph had been on her dresser in a frame until the day Jim moved in. She had asked him if the picture bothered him, and she would never forget the big broad smile, frozen on his lips, as he said, "No, of course not." At that moment she realized Jim McCready was terribly, painfully, in love with her, and would never say so because he knew she could never feel quite the same.

She went at once to the dresser, took the picture, and put it in her lingerie drawer, turning to look Jim in the eye. "There," she said. That was all.

He did not speak. He strode over to her, pulled her up on tiptoes to kiss her deeply, then scooped her up as easily as if she were a child. When he laid her down on the bed and began to undress her, kissing each portion of bare skin as he uncovered it, she tensed, preparing herself. He was so big, and so fervent in his passion. Sometimes as he pushed into her, his great hairy body looming above her, she felt she might be torn apart. And when he was close to his climax, his member stiffening and swelling, filling her up, stroking her everywhere at once, she would find herself screaming. Pleasure or pain? Maybe both.

But that time it was very different, slower and gentler, to begin with, tender and sweet, building slowly, so slowly, stroking and rubbing, then plunging and thrusting, and then—as she began to whimper, her hands on his buttocks forcing him in deeper, pushing her body up to meet him—she was swept by a fainting feeling, a rush of heat. Her whole body began to tremble uncontrollably, and her loins flooded over and she was taken by a pulsing that went on and on.

When it was finished, leaving her limp, exhausted, but still ravenous, she opened her eyes to find Jim looking down at her, smiling. "Well?" he demanded. She was surprised to find herself, in a croaking voice she could hardly recognize, pleading, "Do that again, Jim, again, again!"

Oh, and he had. Again and again, each climax piercingly sweet, while time and thought came to a halt. She had no idea what the hour was when he finally collapsed over her. Groaning, he said, "I'm afraid I'm finished, sweetheart . . . for a while, anyway."

Lying next to him, she thought how strange it was that Jim could create such sensations in her body! She had been crazy about Joe and he had never made her feel this way. Even Walter . . . she had been obsessed with Walter, but even in his arms, never had she been overtaken like that.

She stood now, shivering a little, staring sightlessly at the window that reflected the glittering Christmas tree, and wished Jim were there. She would go to him and put her hand on him and he would be instantly ready for her, and then she could lose herself, forget everything, everything in the world. . . .

But how could she? How could she forget that her baby, her

darling, her little girl was missing! How could she let her mind drift into thoughts of lust when her child might be lying dead in a ditch! What was wrong with her?

She walked to the window, looking down where Commerce Street curved into Barrow, to see everything covered with a thin blanket of snow.

She let her head rest against the cold windowpane, maybe it would blot out the heat in her. Please God, let her be safe, just let her be safe. . . . Oh, Jo, my sweet little girl, where are you?

An hour passed in slow thick ticks and tocks from the clock on the mantel. But Leah still stood by the window, her arms wrapped tightly around herself, mutely praying . . . saying silently in her head, over and over again, please, please, please. There was something about the quiet, the darkness, the waiting, the sound of her own heavy heartbeats, something that haunted her . . .

Waiting for Papa to come home. So long ago, waiting for Papa to come home. Curled up on her little bed, eyes wide open, staring at the blackness, pretending to herself that she was falling asleep. But she wasn't. She could hear her mother, in the other room, weeping with strange stifled sounds into her pillow. Until the door quietly opened and the floor squeaked with his soft steps. He always came in to see her, bending in the darkness to kiss the top of her head. Then she would fall asleep.

He was so sweet and so loving, her papa. He took her on long walks uptown. With him, she saw Little Italy for the first time; saw Greenwich Village for the first time. Did he take her to Chinatown? Vaguely, like a dream, she remembered seeing the Village and marveling at the trees, the dappled sunlight on the pavement, the sparkling houses with bright painted doors. The quiet, that's what she remembered most, so different from the constant clamor of Orchard Street and Hester Street and Norfolk Street.

Papa always told her, "Look, *shayfele*, look, this is how people can live. This is how *we* will live one day." Papa always spoke to her as if she were another grown-up person.

But she was, after all, only a little girl. There were nights, she suddenly recalled, when the door did not open and there were no footsteps. Nights when she stared endlessly into the dark, her heart thudding slowly in terror, thinking please please please, let him come home *now*. She would fall asleep eventually, but in the morning she would still be frightened and she would run to the big bed to check. And be flooded with relief to see him, lying on his side, his mouth open in sleep, the stubble dark on his face.

Then, one morning, he was not there, and when she cried out to Mama, she saw reflected on Mama's face her own terror . . .

Leah made a noise in her throat and turned swiftly away from the window. There was no reason for terror now; she wasn't that little girl, lying in the dark, afraid of only God knew what. She would sing, hum, make some noise to stop such thoughts. She began to pace the room, but the only song she could think of was "Who's Sorry Now?" She wanted something happy, jazzy. . . .

The phone rang, and she nearly jumped out of her skin. She picked up the receiver, her heart thumping.

"Jim?"

"Sit down, Leah."

"Oh God! What's happened? What have they done to her?"

"Nothing, nothing. She's fine. But . . . you were right, all along, about them. They've moved and taken her with them."

"Those *momzers*! I knew it! Where? Where? I'll go and wring both their necks! Just tell me where they are!"

"They didn't leave a forwarding address, Leah. The neighbors say they loaded up the car with suitcases and drove away, right after dinner, around two in the afternoon."

"Jim, we've got to find her! She must be so scared! Those bastards, may they rot in Hell!"

"Don't you worry. We'll find her. Look, I've got the cabbie waiting for me. We'll come right back downtown. You call the police. Tell them everything you can think of and then when—"

The doorbell shrilled and she interrupted him. "Don't hang up! Someone's here! Don't hang up!"

She flung open the door to find a Western Union boy, very young, with a runny nose, standing there. He was holding out a yellow envelope. How she hated the sight of it. Yellow envelopes brought only bad news.

"Leah Lazarus?"

She snatched the telegram from him, slammed the door, and ripped the envelope open.

"Jim? Listen. They sent a telegram. 'We have Joanna Do

not worry she is in good hands and very happy.' That's it. No signature."

"Where'd they send it from?"

She looked. "The Bronx."

"Damnation! Not a clue . . . except one neighbor said he was sure they were heading north, maybe into Westchester."

But Leah wasn't listening. She was reading and rereading the block letter words, as if she could transform them by sheer force of will. But they remained, unchanging. . . . IN GOOD HANDS AND VERY HAPPY. Yeah, yeah! . . . DO NOT WORRY . . . Over her dead body!

"Jim?" she said into the telephone. "Jim, come home. Quick! We don't have a minute to lose! I've just had a great idea! We'll give the story to all the papers! A real tear-jerker! Complete with an interview with the weeping mother, what do you say?"

"What do I say? I say you're a genius, my girl! And I'll be right back to help you plan it, so hang on!"

The next morning, upstairs in the magazine office on West Eighth Street, she could hear the impatient buzzing of reporters' voice all the way from the ground floor.

"They're here, Jim!" She clutched his arm. "And—" She consulted her wristwatch. "—right on the button. Oh, that old witch Bertha will be sorry she ever tangled with me!"

"Leah, Leah. Remember what we discussed. You're the pale, wan, frantic mother, her only child stolen from her. If you talk to them with blood in your eye, it'll spoil the picture."

She had forgotten, for a moment, in her excitement. She turned to him. "How do I look?"

"Pretty awful. The sight of you should really pluck their heartstrings."

She tried to smile, failed, and turned away quickly. Marching to the door, she opened it to the thunder of eager feet rushing up the steps.

There were nine or ten reporters, including a photographer with his big Rollei, chattering amongst themselves as they climbed. The minute they heard the door open, they looked up and began asking her questions, all at once.

"Hold your horses, everyone." Jim moved in front of her. "Mrs. Lazarus is understandably upset about the events that have transpired. We'll talk to *all* of you, but let's have a little decorum here."

Jim spoke firmly, and just as firmly pushed Leah toward the

chair behind the desk, while he held the door open for the reporters.

She waited until they had all filed in. "You've heard—Jim's told your editors—my child has been kidnapped by her grandparents," Leah said, and her voice broke.

"What do you mean—kidnapped, Mrs. Lazarus?"

Her eyes flooded over. Jim went and put his arm around her shoulder. "She means they've taken Joanna away and are hiding her."

"You don't know where she is? No idea?"

"No idea at all. They sent a telegram—" Jim let his voice drop. "—after keeping this poor frantic mother here waiting for *hours*, not knowing if her little girl was alive or dead. . . ."

The pencils all scribbled twice as fast.

"Why would they do a thing like that?"

Jim gave them a knowing smile. "Oh, come on! We live in the Village. Leah goes out alone at night to get stories. She has her little girl in the City and Country School. . . ." His voice was heavy with sarcasm. "Pretty shocking, eh? Well, to Joanna's grandparents, everything about Greenwich Village is shocking. But then what can you expect from Bronx provincials who don't even know it's against the law to kidnap someone else's child!"

"Hey, Jim, can we quote you?"

"You bet you can!"

Leah smiled a little. "I'll try to forgive them, providing they return my little girl to me *immediately*." Again the pencils flew and a flashbulb went off.

A few minutes later, as they planned, the phone rang and Jim went to answer it. He spoke rapidly and then turned back to the group with a huge grin.

"I've spoken to my old friend, Jed McAllister, Judge Jed McAllister, and he says— But I hadn't ought to quote him without his permission. I'll talk to him again later, and then . . . Now listen, I hope you put headlines big enough to be seen in Mr. and Mrs. Isaac Lazarus's hideout."

"Hideout! That's good, Jim," one of the reporters said. "Goes with bandits."

"Damn right. And it's accurate, too. Who but bandits take your most precious possession under cover of darkness and steal away to a secret place where nobody can find it? Oh, they're bandits, all right! The only difference, gentlemen, the big difference, is that their loot is an innocent child of six

years. Six years old and snatched from her mother without a
word of warning. Think of it, just think of this poor child,
alone and lonely, crying for her mother and being told to be
quiet lest someone hear! She's already lost her father, to the
Boche guns in the Great War. Now, is she to be robbed of her
mother, too? I swear, it's enough to bring tears to the eyes of
a strong man!"

"Say, Jim, can't you give us a hint what the judge said?"

Jim smoothed his mustache thoughtfully. "Well . . . all right,
but for God's sake, don't mention him by name. Just say a
noted justice says we must have a writ of habeas corpus. But
gentlemen, I ask you . . . where on earth are we to serve it,
when we have no idea where these heartless people have taken
the child?"

"You're our only hope," Leah said, her voice quivering
with emotion. "The power of the press may smoke them
out! At least we can get a message to them. *Bring my baby
back!*"

She didn't need any coaching from Jim; she burst into tears
all on her own. *Bring my baby back to me!*

16

December 1924

Zelda took the newspaper out of the rural mailbox and held it
with cold and shaking hands, staring at the big black headlines.

'BRING MY BABY BACK,' PLEADS DISTRAUGHT
WIDOW OF WAR HERO

- Paternal Grandparents Kidnap Child and Disappear / Police
  to Search Wide Area
- Writ of Habeas Corpus Sought as Mother Asks Public's
  Help in Finding Where 'Little Jo' Is Hidden

Oh God, oh God! Zelda wasn't sure what a writ of habeas corpus was, exactly; but she knew it had to do with the police. Oh God, what had her mother done? They were on the front page of the *New York American*, the front page!

Even though her hands were numb with cold, Zelda opened the paper to page six, where the story continued. And then she groaned aloud. There were drawings of her mother and her father, and one of Jo, too, set in an oval shape off to the side. The caption read: "The Abductors: Disguised as Loving Grandparents. The Question: What Do They Want?" *Abductors!* Her heart began to thump rapidly, as if she were already running from the police.

Slipping a little on the frozen paving stones that made a crooked path to the front door, Zelda scampered into the house. It might have been a dear little house—if Joanna weren't so upset and crying so much, if her mother weren't so bad-tempered, and if it hadn't turned so bitterly cold. They had fires going in all the fireplaces and it was still bone-chilling.

Papa had already pronounced this whole hideaway idea nuts and had gone tramping off. To where? "Into the town," he said.

"Well, while you're there, you might as well get me the latest copy of *Beautiful Womanhood*," Mother said.

His answer was to slam the door.

Into the town. How much of a town was Rye? Zelda had no idea. The little house they were renting was way out, near a country club. Near two or three, in fact, all of them empty and deserted, of course, it being winter. It seemed to Zelda that Westchester was just one big country club, with only a few houses scattered here and there. She would love to take a walk, and so would Joanna—maybe they would actually see another human being—but Mother would not allow it. "What if you should be seen by somebody who knows us, you silly goose?" Who would know Zelda Lazarus all the way up here in Westchester? Nobody knew her in the Bronx!

Zelda ran into the kitchen, where Mother was sitting by the stove, drinking tea and reading a book. Jo sat on a braided rug on the floor, where she had been ordered to play with a jigsaw puzzle. The house was like a doll's house, Zelda thought, with tiny rooms and low beamed ceilings and funny diamond-paned windows high up in the walls. It was dark inside and cramped; but when she'd said so, Mother informed her that this was Tudor style, "inhabited by the upper classes in England, and when you know nothing, say nothing."

Zelda sat down at the table, opposite Mother, and rustled the newspaper to get her attention. Mother often pretended she didn't know when she was there. Her mother thought she was stupid, but Zelda had come to realize that she wasn't.

She cleared her throat and rustled the newspaper again. Now Mother's eyes came up and she frowned.

"Well? Speak up, Zelda, don't just sit there like a deaf-mute!" Silently, Zelda turned the paper around so Mother could read the headline. But Mother didn't want to see anything; she wanted to yell at her. "Did you hear me, Zelda? I swear, I don't know what's happening to your mind—if you have one! Speak, will you? Speak!"

Okeydokey, if that's what Mother wanted: "You're on the front page, Mother. 'Grandparents Kidnap Child and Dis—' "

"Quiet, you idiot! Do you want her to hear you?"

Zelda smiled a tiny smile. "You told me to speak."

"Oh, for God's sake—!" Bertha snatched the newspaper from Zelda's fingers and rattled it open, her lips tightening as she read. "That slut . . . So this is her game, is it? Well, she'll learn she can't get away with slander! Get your father."

"He's gone to town."

"Well, go *get* him and bring him back!"

"Mother, I don't even know which way it is." Nor do you, she thought, but did not say it.

Her mother's face paled, then reddened, and she made a strange sound in her throat. Joanna looked up from her puzzle. "Grandmother? Is my mother coming for me?"

"No! I've told you, your mother doesn't want you!"

"Yes she does, Grandmother! Mommy is worried about me, she always worries about me if I'm late! I want you to take me home! Please, Grandmother!"

"I've told you and told you, Joanna, we're going to take a lovely trip and then you'll have a pony. Won't that be nice?"

"I don't want a pony. I want to go home. Take me home."

Mother became very, very still, her upper lip twitching. Zelda's hand flew to her heart—oh God, now there would be trouble! "Your mother does not want you back, you stubborn child!"

"You're telling a story!" Jo glared at Mother. The nerve of her, Zelda thought, awed. Jo was brave beyond belief. Well, of course, Leah was the same way. Zelda envied them achingly.

"How dare you, you little ingrate! Don't you realize what I'm saving you from?" Then, thinking better of her angry tone, Mother cleared her throat and put a smile on her face. "Now, darling, don't you worry about a thing. We won't be here forever. . . ."

"It says in the newspaper my mommy is looking for me."

Mother quickly folded up the *American* as small as she could. Too late, Zelda thought. Her mother seemed to forget a lot of little things, lately. Like the fact that Jo could read.

"Grandmother, it says in the news—"

"Well, the newspaper is wrong!"

"But Grandmother—"

Mother's voice became sugary, always a danger signal. "If we don't stop bothering Grandmother with silly notions, we'll have to go play alone in our bedroom, won't we?"

The upstairs bedrooms were poky and small and dark, and they were freezing cold. Joanna went back to her puzzle, her head bent; but Zelda could see that she was crying. A surge of anger came welling up into Zelda's throat; automatically, she pushed it down.

Mother sat without speaking for another minute or two, tapping her fingernails on the table. Then she asked, "How would you like to take a walk into town, Joanna, with Auntie Zelda? You can look for Grandfather and tell him he must come home and . . . I'll give you a nickel for some candy, how's that?"

It was so good to get outside, all bundled up, breathing in the clean, frosty air, their boots squeaking on the clean snow. They had to walk in the road; there were no sidewalks, no pavement at all. But it seemed safe enough; there were only a few automobiles, and it was so quiet, you could hear the roar of their motors approaching long before they went spluttering by.

Down the road they went. They walked along together, Jo singing away like she didn't have a care in the world. They sang "Barney Google," and then they sang "Yes, We Have No Bananas," and then they sang "Barney Google" again, four or five times. Jo's voice rang out in the frosty still air like a bell. Hard to imagine this was the same child who had wept into her pillow half the night.

Zelda had worried that her mother would forget the promised nickel. She knew if she reminded her, Mother's eyes would narrow suspiciously and she would say, "And just why are *you* so interested in the child's money, may I ask?"

But Jo put out a gloved hand and said, "Please, Grandmother, may I have the money?" so Zelda could breathe easily. She had an idea of what she would do with that nickel, but if they didn't see some signs of civilization pretty soon, she was going to have to give it up.

At last, there was another road joining this one. A big round black iron mailbox stood at the corner, mounted on a post, a name painted on it in white. EARHART. Oh God, it had to be her! Yes, of course it was. Zelda had totally forgotten that Amelia Earhart came from Rye, New York. Zelda had read all about Amelia Earhart and she admired her to pieces. She often dreamed that she would make friends with the aviatrix and she would learn how to operate a plane and, pilots together, they would fly away, high up in the sky, all over the world.

But as they walked away from the mailbox, Zelda laughed at herself. What was the use of foolish dreams like that, when she wasn't even allowed to learn how to operate an automobile! She had asked Papa to teach her, but Mother quickly put an end to that. "What a stupid notion . . . why, the very idea of you, as an automobilist . . . !" Just thinking about her mother's laughter made her cringe.

Soon they could see a cluster of buildings, not far off, down a steep hill. They followed the road, walking past a Y. and then a firehouse next to a curving lane that took them to a broad village green. Zelda asked a passing man what the wide thoroughfare near the green was called, and he looked at her as though she was an idiot. "Why, the Boston Post Road, of course."

Zelda paused to think. Jo was chattering and asking questions, which Zelda answered with half her mind. She was looking for a telephone booth. She thought she saw the blue and white sign with the bell on it down the street.

"Come on, Jo," she said, and made a left turn.

"Where are we going?"

Zelda laughed. "I'm not quite sure, Jo. I've never been here before."

"Are we going to find Grandfather?"

"If we can." But that was not in her plans. The telephone sign she'd seen before was on a store, and she paused. Mother would never forgive her; her life would be a living hell forever and ever. Her eye roved over the notices posted in the big front window, trying to think. The *Rye Chronicle* announced its new advertising rate schedule. The Rye Playhouse listed the moving picture playing this week: *The Hunchback of Notre Dame*. A notice demanded, in heavy black print, that the village allow "the establishment of a station for the New York, Westchester, and Boston Railroad on North Street, for the residents of West Rye."

And right under that, the timetable for the New York, Hartford & New Haven Railroad, showing it took only forty-three minutes to Grand Central Station from the Rye station.

For one bold, beautiful moment, Zelda imagined the two of them, she and Jo, boarding the train and steaming down to the city. But then she shook her head. Foolish thought, foolish dream.

Zelda stood there so long without speaking that Joanna tugged at her hand and demanded to know what she was looking at.

On an impulse, Zelda said, "How would you like to go home to your mother and Uncle Jim?"

But instead of a great big smile, Jo burst into sudden tears. "Why doesn't my mommy come and get me, Zelda?"

Zelda swallowed hard. Then she bent and put her arms around the sobbing child and said, in almost a whisper, "Because she doesn't know where you are." Well, it was out. The truth. Oh, the fat was in the fire now, and she was going to have to go through with it. If she could find the courage.

"Why don't we tell her? Oh, please, Zelda, let's tell her! Please, please, Zelda, let's tell my mommy so she can come and get me! I miss her, Zelda, I want to go home!"

"I know you do." Zelda straightened up and gazed through the window at the telephone inside. Did she have the courage to face her mother afterward? And then she thought, what if Jo were really her own little girl, as she liked to pretend sometimes? How would she feel, not knowing where her little girl was? Wouldn't *she* be walking up and down in her apartment all night long, wringing her hands and weeping and longing for a word, just one word to tell her where her little girl had been taken?

Zelda sucked in a deep breath. "All right, Jo, let's do it. Let's tell her."

"Really, Zelda? Really and truly, no fooling?" Jo jumped up and down in excitement.

"Really and truly, no fooling," Zelda said. She put her hand on the store's doorknob and turned it.

"And if Grandmother yells at you, you can come home with me."

Tears sprang to Zelda's eyes and she thought, This little girl knows more than Mother and she's only six. Suddenly, Zelda realized the whole ridiculous enterprise was truly crackbrained. They couldn't keep hiding Jo forever. Jo would end up hating them all. And, Zelda thought defiantly, with good reason!

When the operator said, "Number, *plee*-uz," she was ready in a firm voice, "Operator, I want to call New York City. I'm sure they will pay for the call. Yes, yes. It's Zelda. Quite sure." And, gathering courage, she added, "And . . . hurry, would you, operator? It's very important."

Leah answered almost instantly. "Yes? Hello?" interrupting the operator impatiently, "Yes, yes, I accept the charges. Hello?" Zelda pictured her sitting by the phone, staring at it, willing it to ring, willing it to tell her where Joanna was.

"Leah—" Her voice came out a croak and she had to clear her throat. "Leah, listen, it's Zelda."

"Where is she? Is she all right?"

"Jo's right here with me, and she's fine."

At that moment Jo began to cry, calling out, "Mommy!" so Zelda had to give her the receiver, lifting her so she could talk into the mouthpiece. Not that she talked much, mostly she cried.

Zelda put her back down, saying, "Jo, I'm going to tell Mommy and Jim how to find you. So please try not to cry or Mommy won't be able to hear me." Her heart was thumping like crazy; she kept expecting her mother's hand to land on her shoulder, or her father to walk by, see them, and come running in to rip the telephone off the wall.

"We're in a rented Tudor house in Rye . . . Rye, New York, in Westchester, near a country club. North Street, I think it's called. A little house, cream with brown timbers, not far from Amelia Earhart's mailbox . . . on a corner. . . ."

Leah repeated every word, obviously writing it down. "Zelda, you are an angel from heaven, and I don't know how I'll ever repay you for this," she said, "but I will, if it takes me the rest of my life."

"We drove up in the dark, so I'm not sure of anything—but they're careless what they say in front of me. . . . But, oh God, I only wish I could be more sure of the directions. I feel so stupid!"

"As far as I'm concerned, you're a genius! Don't you worry

about a thing. Jim will find the house. He can find *anything*. We'll catch the next train out there, with the writ, so they'll *have* to give her back to us . . . so, oh God, Zelda, I'll see you soon!" Leah's voice broke and she hung up.

Well, I've done it, Zelda thought. I've done it. And now? The next few hours loomed in front of her like a great yawning abyss, full of danger. But she had done it!

"Come on, Jo," she said, taking the little girl's hand. "Let's go back home and wait for your mommy."

17

February 1925

"Mrs. Lazarus! Leah! Over here! Duncan of the *World*! What do you say to the charge that you're an unfit mother?"

"Is it true that you've never married?"

"Leah Lazarus! The *Times*! Do you know who leaked this—?"

"Mrs. Lazarus, we understand the artist Walter Morris will testify against you. You have any idea what—"

Flashbulbs popped and blazed in Leah's eyes. She blinked and looked away; but too late, colored round spots danced in her eyes, so she couldn't see the reporters who crowded around.

"Now, now, ladies and gentlemen, you really must be patient. And take pity on Mrs. Lazarus, would you? Understandably, she hasn't had a decent night's sleep since her child was kidnapped." Fin O'Toole—Finian John O'Toole, Esq., more properly—had a stentorian voice and a powerful presence. But nothing was going to stop the press this morning. The press, Leah thought, had its teeth into a human interest story; and it was not going to let even Fin O'Toole intimidate it.

"Mr. O'Toole, sir, the opposition says it isn't kidnapping. They say they were *saving* the child from—"

"The opposition be damned! The opposition is whistling in the graveyard, gentlemen, and you may quote me. They're making a great deal of sound and fury, signifying nothing."

"Will Mrs. Lazarus be taking the stand?"

"Much too early to say *what* Mrs. Lazarus will be doing . . . except, of course, that when this is over, Mrs. Lazarus will be taking her daughter home with her."

Pencils flew over pads, and the cameras were aimed at O'Toole's well-fed Irish face, with its heavy white brows, thick white hair, and deep set eyes, which gave out little flares of bright blue. The lawyer straightened his back and posed briefly, allowing a grim smile to pull at his mouth. Then he scowled and, pulling a heavy gold pocket watch from his vest pocket, announced: "We'll be late, and His Honor does not suffer fools or lateness gladly."

So saying, he took Leah's elbow, nodded to Jim, and headed for the courtroom door. The reporters, not about to give up so easily, trotted along behind them.

"Will little Joanna be here again this morning, Mrs. Lazarus? And will you be allowed to speak to her this time?"

Leah came to a halt and turned. "I hope she will. And, in answer to your other question, I'd like to see anyone try to stop me!"

Fin hustled her along. "Now, now, my dear, I thought we agreed. No histrionics. You must appear to be calm, ladylike, and motherly. You must be vigilant against any desire to show temperament. Remember, my dear, Judge Gerald Phelan still thinks women should be kept barefoot, pregnant, and out of sight. We're going to have one hell of a time getting him on your side as it is."

Leah turned to him and said, fiercely: "But we'll do it, won't we, Mr. O'Toole?"

"Assuredly. You are the child's mother and there's the beginning and the end of it. You're not to worry, my dear Leah, you're to follow my instructions and look as proper and demure as you can. . . ." Here he winked at her, to show her he was only kidding. The wink and smile were gone in a flash, though, and it occurred to Leah that perhaps Judge Gerald Phelan wasn't the *only* man made uneasy by independent women. But Fin O'Toole was supposed to be the best, and she would put on a sunbonnet and apron and wear a dress down to her ankles if it would get Jo back.

It had been hell, not knowing where she was. The morning

Zelda called from Rye, Leah was sure it was all over. She was jubilant. She and Jim had boarded the very next train at Grand Central and hightailed it out to the house in Rye. The house was right where Zelda had said it was. But *they* were gone.

No clothes were there, no toilet articles, no suitcases. The house was empty, although there were newspapers and magazines scattered on tables, and the remains of breakfast were still in the kitchen. Even the pan used to fry eggs that morning sat on the stove, the fat coagulating. A fire still smoldered in the living room fireplace.

"Damn! They can't have left more than half an hour ago," Jim said. "And no way for us to even find out in which direction!"

Leah had had to wait almost a whole week until Zelda called again, her nights filled with nightmares and stabbing stomach pains that the doctor said were from nerves. He gave her a tonic and told her to take it easy. How could she take it easy? Where had they taken her baby? What if they went to Europe and she never saw Jo again? The thought made her stomach hurt even worse.

But then, at last, the phone rang and it was Zelda, sounding even more frightened than the first time. "Leah, they'll *kill* me if they find out. It was Jo who told them. She didn't know any better. But this time I'm by myself. You don't know what I had to do to get away—never mind." She spoke rapidly. They were still in Westchester, in a small hotel on Long Island Sound, in Mamaroneck.

"We'll be there in a couple of hours, Zelda."

"Leah, they won't let you in. They won't talk to you. My mother . . . my mother is determined, Leah. You don't know my mother when she's angry. She's angry now." Zelda wouldn't give the name of the hotel. "I'm afraid, Leah, afraid Mother will . . . do something to Jo if she feels threatened. So, Leah, don't try anything rash. Please. I just wanted you to know Jo's okay." And she hung up.

That's when Jim went to Fin O'Toole for advice. They were to stay away from the police. "Flatfeet take too much time to do anything, and anyway, they make too damn much noise," O'Toole instructed. "They very well might give warning, in their zeal. And God knows we don't want these characters getting away."

O'Toole got in touch with a private detective up in Westchester. It didn't take *him* long. Within three days of

Zelda's call, he knocked on their door in the hotel; when Bertha answered, he said he had special delivery for Mrs. Isaac Lazarus. She put her hand out, and what he put into it was a writ of habeas corpus, demanding "that Isaac and Bertha Lazarus bring up the body of the infant Joanna Lazarus on February 11, 1925, before Justice Phelan of the Supreme Court of the City of New York, to answer the allegation that the infant had been wrongfully restrained and detained against the wishes of the Relator Leah Vogel Lazarus, the mother and guardian of said infant."

February eleventh: that was yesterday, the day of the preliminary hearing. Leah and Jim had come half an hour early. Leah wanted to see Jo as soon as they brought her in the door. She was going to give her such a hug and a kiss! She could barely contain herself; she felt she might crawl right out of her skin, pacing back and forth, heart hammering and stomach knotting, constantly wiping her damp palms on Jim's large linen handkerchief. Even though it was a cold day, she was perspiring heavily.

When the Lazaruses arrived, however, Leah couldn't get near Joanna. "My own child!" Leah protested. But Fin told her to be patient and let the wheels of justice turn. Jo called out to her. Leah could see Jo really wanted to come to her, but Bertha held onto her tightly. Bertha and Isaac were surrounded by three lawyers. Zelda was not with them.

Leah kept staring at Jo during the hearing. She looked so familiar, yet so different. And it wasn't just that Bertha had pulled her thick, curly auburn hair into two tight braids and put her into a fussy blouse and pinafore and white stockings. She looked taller . . . older. . . . With a start, Leah realized again how much her daughter looked like Bella Vogel. The thin elegant nose, spattered with freckles, the high cheekbones, the full mouth. Oh, she had always known there was a resemblance. Nevertheless, it was a peculiar sensation, seeing her mother's face on Jo. Finally she had to look away, it was too painful.

Sidney Harris, the Lazarus lawyer, an older man who fiddled with his pince-nez and rocked on his heels whenever he wasn't talking, gave the judge a thick sheaf of papers. It was a Return and Answer to the writ, and it was thick because it had attached to it a dozen or more affidavits.

All of the papers were read aloud, and at the end of it Leah didn't know whether to weep or throttle Joe's mother, and to hell with the consequences. The bitch was saying that her son had *wanted* his parents to have his only issue to raise, and the proof of it was he had never married the mother.

"That's only because *I* wouldn't!" Leah cried. But she was told she was out of order, and nobody seemed to pay the least bit of attention. What came next was worse anyway, far worse. The affidavits all said she had no right to Jo in any case, because she was an unfit mother with low morals who had neglected her child.

Leah stood in a daze, listening with disbelief, shaking her head. Who was this woman they were talking about? This woman gave the child a sharp knife to use. She made the child prepare her own meals. She put rouge and powder on the child, and spoke of pornography in front of her. She kept the child up until all hours in an artist's loft that was really a saloon.

But that's not true! But I was with her! she wanted to shout. *But there were reasons! But that's only half true!* However, if she made even the tiniest move, Mr. O'Toole gave her a look that said, Keep still, Leah.

It was hard to keep still. The Lazaruses had been to everyone Leah knew, *everyone*! Even to people she didn't know! A Mr. Thomas Harrigan had signed an affidavit.

"Who's *that*?" she whispered to O'Toole; and he whispered back, "A messenger boy from *Saturday Evening Post*."

A messenger boy? Oh God, the day she and Jo were in makeup. What were they *doing* to her? Mr. Ira Haile? She shot a questioning look at the attorney. "Private detective." Oh God, they were truly terrible. She had thought so before; but she had also thought there were things they would never do. Now she knew they would stop at nothing.

As lawyer Harris droned on, Leah's head swam with the details, addresses, dates, and names. It was amazing, the people who were willing to swear, depose, and state that she had mistreated her own daughter. Inez Cooper. Inez, whom she'd always thought of as a friend. And her favorite editor at *Women's Home Gazette*. And the teachers at Jo's school. Even Jack Murray, for God's sake!

A little choked sound came up out of her throat. Oh, those *momzers*, Bertha and Isaac, those low-lifes! To go crawling around in her life, digging up the past, asking questions of people she didn't even see anymore. At least there wasn't an affidavit from Walter Morris; they hadn't got to *him*. She could hardly wait until this ordeal was over, so she could talk to her reporter friends and straighten out these stories, these *lies*!

But at the end of the preliminary hearing, when they came back out into the hallway, there were only a few people standing by the courtroom, and none of them were newsmen. Leah was disappointed.

"Jim, where is everybody? Don't they want to hear *my* side?"

"You just wait," Jim said, sounding grim. "There'll be plenty of our brothers and sisters of the press tomorrow, when we go into the courtroom. That's the real stuff, sweetheart. This was just the prelim. Yes, mark my words, tomorrow morning you'll be beating them off with a stick."

Well, here it was, tomorrow morning, and sure enough, they were all here. They fought their way into Courtroom 334, where the seats were filling up with newsmen and spectators—even the jury box. "But Jim," Leah said, "how did they know to ask those questions? How can they know so many details? Wasn't yesterday's hearing private?"

"So it was, so it was." He didn't look at her, but even in profile, she could see the sly twinkle in his eye. "You wanted to be able to tell the press your side, didn't you?" Jim went on.

"Yes, but—"

"Yes, well, all I can tell you is that somehow in the dark of night, copies of the Answer and Return, and the affidavits as well, all found their way to the city desk of every paper in the city."

"Jim, you didn't st—"

"Hush now. I did nothing, understand?" He turned to give her a stern look, but he couldn't stop the smile that tugged at the corners of his mouth. In spite of the gray in his mustache, he looked like a mischievous boy. "They just got up and walked, I guess, all on their ownie-o."

"Jim, I'm not at all sure I want them seeing all those lies—"

The twinkle disappeared. "Look here, my girl. If you want to clear your name, you have to answer those allegations, that's what Fin says. And when you do, every reading person in New York City will know the Lazaruses for liars."

In a loud whisper she said, "But what's this about Walter testifying against me? They didn't mention him yesterday."

He shrugged. "Damned if *I* know." And then O'Toole shushed them. There was a stir in the courtroom, and Leah turned to see Bertha, wearing a simple dove-gray dress and a black cloche hat—an outfit that was almost the twin of Leah's—striding down the aisle, Isaac right behind her, and Zelda, also in black, behind him. A murmur rose from the spectators and a buzzing from the knot of reporters huddled into the jury box when they saw that little Joanna was not with them. The newsmen were obviously hoping they could see the adorable little girl crying or holding her arms out for her mother, or something. Tears formed in Leah's eyes and she ordered herself sternly to stop thinking about Jo, about the reporters, about anything but what went on in the witness chair.

Inez Powell was the first witness called. Sid Harris all but bent the knee to her; his voice was fawning.

"Mrs. Powell, you know Mrs. Leah Lazarus, do you not?"

"Yes."

"You have known her for how long?"

"Our daughters are friends . . . *were* friends. I could never let my Peggy go back to that den of iniquity, now that I know—"

Fin O'Toole was on his feet. "Move to strike!"

"Strike that," Judge Phelan ordered the stenographer. "Mrs. Powell, kindly restrict yourself to direct answers of the questions put to you."

"Yes, Your Honor."

Leah sat forward on her seat, her hands folded together tightly on the table in front of her. She stared at Inez, silently daring her, *Just look over here and meet my eyes, you ninny.* But Inez acted as though she didn't know Leah was even in the room, while Sid Harris led her this way and that. Yes, often when she walked the children to the apartment on Barrow Street, nobody was home to greet them. Yes, the door was unlocked and Mrs. Lazarus had told her she often left it that way. No, Joanna was not disturbed at her mother's absences. No, Mrs. Powell was not about to leave two little girls alone in a flat; she stayed until Mrs. Lazarus finally got home. Yes, Mrs. Lazarus drank. What? Cocktails, mostly. She favored a sloe gin fizz. The child, Joanna, was invited to stir the drinks, to pour them, and to serve them. Yes, her mother often let her take a sip . . . and she made the children their own "cocktails" from fruit juice and club soda, so they could pretend to be drinking, too.

When O'Toole cross-examined, he went over every single detail all over again, saying, "But it was only play, was it not, Mrs. Powell?" "Did you object at the time, Mrs. Powell?" "A cocktail shaker, in and of itself, is not an evil object, would you agree, Mrs. Powell?" Inez was forced to answer him truthfully, but it was clear that her disapproval was real. From the look on her face, Leah decided that Inez had been wanting to say those things for a long time. It went on and on. Leah longed to stop listening to the endless lists of things she had done wrong. But she couldn't; she felt compelled to hear it all.

Mr. Thomas Harrigan, aged thirteen, his wavy hair slicked down with water, the combs marks still showing, fastened his eyes on the lawyer and said Yessir and Nosir. He went to pick up a manuscript, and that lady sitting at the table over there—yes, Mrs. Lazarus, he supposed—she opened the door.

"Nearly knocked me over with shock, sir." That got a laugh, which Justice Phelan frowned into silence. "The little girl was all painted up, like, with rouge and powder and black stuff around her eyes, and the lady . . . well, she had burnt cork all over her face. . . . "

"Are you saying that Mrs. Lazarus was . . . in *blackface*?"

"Yessir, she was in blackface and a pair of . . . pajamas—" He blushed. "—and the lady laughed and handed me the package, and then a minute later came after me with a different package and said this one was too dirty for the *Post*."

"No, I didn't," Leah murmured to O'Toole. "I said 'naughty.' "

"What was it?" O'Toole asked.

Leah hesitated, then took the notepad in front of her and scribbled *pornography*.

O'Toole flushed a deep pink, and snatched the piece of paper. He crumpled it, thrusting it into his pants pocket. Then he wrote a message to her in clear block letters: TELL NO ONE. *NO ONE.* UNDERSTAND? Leah nodded and watched as he crumpled up the second sheet of paper. Did he really think he had to *tell* her that?

When Fin O'Toole started his cross, he just asked the boy if he was *sure* Mrs. Lazarus had said the other manuscript was dirty. Well, it was something like that. Could she have said, for example, "Naughty"? The boy beamed. Yes, yes, that was it. O'Toole appealed to the judge: "Now, Your Honor, naughty can mean many things, as I'm sure you know, especially when we're talking about the *Saturday Evening Post*, a magazine which, as we all know, hasn't yet figured out how babies are made." That got another laugh, and another scowl from the bench. "Excuse me, Your Honor, I am far from finding any of these ... stories ... amusing. On the contrary. And I submit to you that, by forgetting the exact word, by *mistaking* Mrs. Lazarus's word, this young man may have done my client a dreadful disservice." And he let it go at that.

Next they called Philip Lewis, an editor for one of the progressive magazines. Leah relaxed. She did muckraking for them—good, solid, serious works about social ills. Phil Lewis liked her work; he couldn't possibly say anything bad about her!

But to her dismay, he *could*. Oh, not that he wanted to. Anyone could see that he was unhappy telling the truth and having it twisted out of shape. Yes, Leah Lazarus wrote stories for him. About what? About social problems. Like prostitution? Yes, like prostitution. And for her reportage, Mrs. Lazarus goes into some of the city's seamiest neighborhoods, is that not so? And for her stories, does she not speak to people of, er ... doubtful character? And does she not take her child, Joanna Lazarus, with her on the, ah ... interviews? I believe so, but I have no way of— Just answer the question, please.

So, in the end, shooting her a look that asked her to forgive him, the editor gave Justice Phelan a very strong impression that she dragged Joanna into dives and brothels all the time.

Fin O'Toole stood, facing Philip Lewis, and said: "Mr. Lewis, would you please tell the court *why* Leah Lazarus did several stories on brothels in New York City?"

"Why, to expose the owners of the places, businessmen who—"

"Objection! Objection!" Harris was on his feet, his face purple. "Irrelevant and immaterial. Move to strike!"

"So moved," said Justice Phelan. "Mr. O'Toole, kindly have the witness stick to the point."

"This line of questioning *is* to the point, Your Honor. There has been an effort to paint my client as a woman who would willfully, and perhaps for prurient reasons, go into a house of ill repute. Mrs. Lazarus is a well-known and highly regarded writer, Your Honor, and often goes to places not frequented by your usual lady—as would any good reporter. She has written several articles on prostitution over the years without anyone saying boo—"

"I said, stick to the point, and in my opinion, the point is not *why* she went or even how many *times* she went—but *that* she went. And whether or not her child was with her."

Fin nodded curtly to the judge and continued. "To your

knowledge, Mr. Lewis, did Mrs. Leah Lazarus ever take her daughter Joanna with her when she was interviewing prostitutes?"

With a look of relief: "No."

O'Toole smiled a knowing smile and said that would be all. But Harris demanded a rebuttal, and asked whether Philip knew for certain that she did *not* take the child such places.

"I wasn't there, of course. But I do know—"

"No further questions."

O'Toole got one more chance, and in his surrebuttal managed to elicit the fact that, when Leah had finished her interviews with the prostitutes for one particular story, she had come directly to the magazine office; and that she was alone. And that it had been a school day and Leah was in a hurry because it was almost time for Joanna to be coming home. So it didn't seem likely, did it, that the child had been with her? No sir, it did not.

The judge called a recess after that, for lunch. Leah got to her feet, surprised at how cramped her muscles had become. And when they emerged into the hallway, what looked like a hundred shouting reporters and photographers converged on her, flashbulbs popping and glaring.

"Mrs. Lazarus, is it true . . . ?" "Do you refute the statements of . . . ?" "What do you think of the story . . ." Their voices tumbled over each other. "The messenger, was he making it up?" "What do you think of friends who testify against . . . ?"

She opened her mouth to answer; she *wanted* to answer. But O'Toole swiftly took her arm and said, "No comment, ladies and gentlemen. Mrs. Lazarus is understandably shocked by the perfidy of . . . some people. Her name will be cleared, you have my word on it. In the meantime, no comment."

How they got her out of there, she would never know; but somehow, pushing, shoving, yelling, smiling all the while, Jim and the lawyer, one on either side of her, made their way out of the courthouse and into the chilly sunshine-filled street. People were scurrying around, secretaries in their cheap fur-trimmed coats, lawyers in suits, messengers, fellows pushing hand trucks. It was lunchtime in New York City. That square, dim room upstairs with the two American flags and the gilt lettering that said In God We Trust, had become her whole universe; and it felt strange to be out in the fresh air and to discover that the rest of the world had just been going about its business as usual.

"How about getting one of the whores to testify that you were there alone with them, Leah?" O'Toole said as they pushed their way through the crowd.

"Impossible. I promised them all anonymity. Otherwise, they wouldn't have talked to me at all. Oh my God, I'd never get another interview in the underworld again if I—"

O'Toole laughed. "All right, all right! But it *would* help our case."

"You'll have to find another way."

Leah just picked at her lunch; she had no appetite. Over dessert—great slabs of apple pie, which the men ordered and ate with gusto—O'Toole remarked: "Walter Morris is up next, Leah. I understand you, um . . ."

Her head snapped up. "You understand *what*, Mr. O'Toole?"

"Easy now, girl, easy. I'm on your side, remember? Did you pose in the altogether for Mr. Morris? And was the resultant painting put up for sale in an art gallery called—" He shuffled through some notes.

"Never mind," Leah said. "Yes, I did and he did. And, for your information, we were lovers." She could not look at Jim, but she felt his gaze burning into her. "You might as well know it first," she added defiantly, not sure which of the two men she was really talking to. "God, it was all so long ago. It was while Joe—Joanna's father—was still alive. He was . . . we . . . I was getting even with him for something."

O'Toole's bushy eyebrows went shooting up. "Aha! And was your daughter yet born?"

"Not even a twinkle in her father's eye."

"Excellent, excellent . . ." He took out his little pad and a pen and wrote quickly.

She looked at Jim. How sad his eyes were. "I'm sorry all these . . . things have to come up," she said.

There was a long silence, which she was forced to break. "I don't know why Walter's testifying against me, although I can guess. He always was a vindictive sort."

The lawyer shook his head, and swallowed the last bit of his pie. "For your information, Leah, Mr. Morris refused to give an affidavit. He's been subpoenaed, which is good news for us. He's been forced to appear . . . not so vindictive, after all, eh?"

Sure enough, when Walter sat in the witness chair that afternoon, he looked directly at her, giving her a jaunty wave and a big grin. He was immediately reprimanded by the judge.

"Sorry, Your Honor. But I haven't seen the lady in a long time and I thought—"

"Your job is not to think," Justice Phelan barked. "You are here to answer questions. There'll be no more of that in my courtroom, is that understood?"

"Yessir, Your Honor."

If Leah had been able to smile, she would have.

"Do you know the relator, Leah Lazarus?"

"Yes."

"And did Leah Lazarus pose for you in the nude?"

"Yes, but that's not so unusual—"

"Just answer the question, Mr. Morris. And did Mrs. Lazarus allow this, ah . . . portrait to be put up for sale in an art gallery in Greenwich Village?" Harris was smiling.

"She allowed nothing. I did it behind her back . . . and I really regret that, Leah."

"Did I not tell you, Mr. Morris," thundered the judge, "you are not to add your personal comments. We are not having a conversation here, sir. We are engaged in a serious court proceeding."

"I thought I was supposed to tell the truth, the whole truth, and nothing but the truth, Your Honor."

"You are, sir."

"But Your Honor, this gentleman here is not allowing the whole truth. He just wants little bits of the truth, so he can defame Leah here, who never wanted to pose in the first place—"

"Mr. Morris! You will be quiet, sir, or I will hold you in contempt!"

The entire courtroom hushed after that; and Sid Harris got Walter named a hostile witness, which seemed to mean that he could badger him as much as he wanted.

"Did you and Mrs. Lazarus have relations, sir?"

"You mean aunts and uncles? Yes, I imagine we both—"

"Mr. Morris, you have been warned. I think you would not like to go to jail for ten days. Answer the question."

Sweetly: "Would you mind repeating it?"

It was no use. He was under oath and he had to answer. So he said it. "Yes, at one point, we were lovers."

Behind her, Leah heard a commotion, and then Justice Phelan was shouting that the members of the fourth estate had better stay in their seats or they would be forbidden in the courtroom.

Leah put her head in her hands. She was getting a horrible stomachache. She could just imagine the headlines. Oh God, what if Joanna saw the newspapers, saw all this scandal printed about her mother? Then she lifted her head and opened her eyes. She had never been a coward. If Jo read the stories, she would explain them. She wasn't going to pretend to be someone she wasn't; and her child had better know who her mother was.

"I want to get on the stand," she wrote on the pad, and pushed it to Fin O'Toole.

We'll see, he mouthed; and at that moment Mr. Harris finished with the witness and it was their turn.

"Mr. Morris, you are an artist of some renown, is that correct?"

"I make a living at it . . . a good living. About renown, I'm not so sure . . . oh, very well, yes, I am an artist of some renown."

"And you have taught art classes at Pratt Institute in Brooklyn and Columbia University in New York City and at the Art Students League in New York City?"

"Yes, sir."

"What are these classes called, Mr. Morris?"

"Life classes."

"Life classes . . . ah . . . and what exactly does that mean?"

"Painting nude models from life, sir. It's a common practice . . . always has been."

"And the men and women who pose for these classes . . . how would you characterize them? Are they low-lifes . . . do you go to taverns and brothels to get them?"

Walter laughed his short bark of a laugh. "Of course not. Usually, they're students or artists. Not many of us manage a living from art, you know, and it's one way to pay for the groceries."

"So posing in the nude for a well-known artist, with or without his class, would not be considered improper?"

"Hell, no."

The judge's gavel banged down the ripple of laughter, and he said, "I cannot see where you are going with this line of questioning, Mr. O'Toole."

"Took the words right out of my mouth, Your Honor," Har-

ris said; and the judge gave him a severe look—but no reprimand.

"I am showing, Your Honor," O'Toole countered, not at all
flustered, "that my client, in posing for Mr. Morris, was doing
nothing immoral, but was simply helping make ends meet."
Smoothly, he turned back to Walter. "When Mrs. Lazarus
posed for you, Mr. Morris, was she married?"

"No, sir, she was not."

"Did she have any children?"

"No, sir, this was well before."

"Was she over twenty-one years of age?"

"Why . . . yes. I think so."

"So. Mrs. Lazarus, at the time she posed for this painting,
was, as we say, free, white, and twenty-one. That is all."

Mr. Harris just waved his hand in dismissal; there would
be no redirect. Then he asked to bring in a new witness,
with new proof of Mrs. Lazarus's unfitness to raise a child.
What . . . ? Leah watched with a mixture of interest and anxiety as the short blond man with an almost-invisible mustache
took the oath and sat.

His name was Ira Haile and he was the proprietor of the
Acme Detective Agency. Why had they called *him*?

"And when you searched those records, Mr. Haile, did you
find any information?"

"Yes sir, I did."

"And exactly what information did you find, sir?"

There was something in Sid Harris's voice, a ring of im-
pending triumph, that made Leah sit up straight.

"I found that Leah Lazarus's father died of self-inflicted
gunshot wounds, and that, several years later—three, to be
exact—her mother, Bella Vogel, died in Mercy Hospital."

"Mercy Hospital. And what kind of hospital is Mercy, Mr.
Haile?"

"A lunatic asylum."

What? What was he saying? Bella Vogel, her mother, in
a—no! *No!* Her father *shot* himself?

"No! That's not true!" The words were torn from her throat,
and without volition she found herself on her feet. "No, no!
Why do you tell these lies?"

But even as she shouted the words, she knew, suddenly. It
was true. It was true. Fragments of memory flooded back, all
in a jumble. And then one: the strange dark room in the
strange dark building, they walked up many stairs, and Papa

lay on the floor, there was blood all around, and her mother was shrieking, "You see how your papa loves you! He shoots himself! Remember this! Remember your whole life, how men destroy the women who love them!" But it was Papa who was dead. *Dead.*

Remember this, Mama had ordered. But she would not obey. She put it away, far away, she turned her head and she ran away from Mama, down the stairs, with Mama screaming after her, like a crazy woman. *Like a crazy woman.* Oh God!

Everyone seemed to be talking at once, while the judge pounded his gavel and called for order. Leah stood very still; she felt dead. O'Toole said something, and then he and Jim took her arms, pulling her to make her lifeless legs move.

Out in the hallway, the lawyer shook her. "Leah, Leah, for God's sake, pull yourself together, woman. Don't you realize it gives them ammunition? Do you want to lose your child?"

Leah looked at him. It took a minute or two for her to take in what he was saying. Then, in a hollow voice she did not recognize as her own, she said, "What's the difference? They've taken my mama and papa away from me, why not my child, too?"

18

February 1925

It was past midnight and still no Jim. He had been gone for hours. Around seven he'd gotten a phone call. After talking for a few minutes, an odd little smile appeared on his lips. Then he told her, "Leah, this could take a while. Don't wait up for me." But how could she sleep, with so much on her mind?

For the twentieth time Leah went to the window, rubbed a space in the frost, and looked out. The street below was empty. No sight of Jim.

She walked to the other side of the room and fingered a

book. Maybe she should read. But she couldn't. Her head was filled with fragments, pieces of memory; and she was trying so hard not to let any of them out from wherever they had been hidden all these years. No! She didn't want to remember, she didn't want to know.

She went to the piano and picked up the sheet music from *Rose Marie*, "Indian Love Call." She loved the song; but who could sing it? She fingered through the rest of the sheet music, opened one, picked out the tune with one finger and sang along softly: "Show me the way to go home, I'm tired and I want to go to bed ... " God, yes, she was tired, but where in the world was home?

Her mother, dead in a lunatic asylum! Oh God! And she never knew. She should have been there with her mother. She had been so hurt, yes, and angry, too, that her mother was able to leave her without a backward glance. But if Bella was ... if she had gone crazy from grief ... maybe she had forgotten who she was, maybe she couldn't remember she had a daughter she called her little treasure.

What could she remember of her mother, in the little flat on Essex Street? Her mother often had a wet rag tied around her forehead, to cure her headache. But she was brave about the pain, making jokes about it. The women in the building all came to their flat and sat in their kitchen, drinking tea, talking while they did their mending and crocheting. Leah remembered all the hands, always doing something very fast. There was always the sound of women's laughter, and Mama would sometimes pick Leah up and put her on her lap, brush her hair, squeeze her.

But when Papa walked in the door ... Leah had an image of the room emptying, of all the women scurrying out of the door, their long skirts belling out, leaving a trail of giggles. And of Mama, hands flying to her own hair, fussing with it, running to him, taking his coat, laying a hand on his cheek, gazing into his eyes, asking how did it go today, Jake? Was it better? Could she get him a nice glass of tea, some schnapps? Could he give her a smile, just a little one?

Now she remembered. Her father took a gun and shot himself dead. He didn't even leave a note. Why? Why did he do it? Why did he leave them all alone? Maybe he had hated the way he was forced to earn a living, with one back-breaking job after the other, but never anything that used his intelligence. The last job Leah could remember him having was pushing a scale on wheels up and down the streets, weighing people for a penny. Before that, he had run a candy store, but something had gone wrong. She remembered that vividly because, child that she was, she was angry when there was no longer any candy.

But . . . suicide! He was such an *alive* man. They took long, long walks; they walked everywhere a little girl's short legs could go. He showed her that the dirt and the noise of their neighborhood was not the whole world. He told her she was smart and quick and she could do anything, anything at all. Just go to school and learn, you understand? In the Old Country, they wouldn't let you because you're a girl. But here, in the Golden Land, a woman can go to school, can become even a schoolteacher! She remembered his crinkly eyes, dark eyes like hers, his thick dark hair, like hers, the feel of his hard, callused palm against hers.

Leah pounded a fist onto a side table. The pain felt good; it was real and immediate and it held her attention. Then she didn't have to wonder why both her mother and her father chose to leave her all alone in the world. She drifted into the kitchen and ran the cold water over her hand, a red welt forming on the side. She looked at it and began to cry.

Why was she cursed like this? Everyone she loved, she lost. Her papa. Her mama. Annie. Joe Lazarus. And now her child, her Jo! She stood by the kitchen sink, bent nearly double, her head resting on the porcelain lip. She didn't see how she was going to bear it much longer. How could they dig into her life—it was *her* life—and drag up things even she didn't know. They should rot in Hell! The judge would *never* give Jo back to her now! Even Fin O'Toole was worried. Her poor baby, she must be so scared, wherever it was they had her hidden!

And where had Jim gone to? She walked back out into the living room. The big clock said twelve-twenty. Was she going to lose him, too? Where *was* he?

Jim sat in an overstuffed chair in the lobby of the Broadway Central Hotel, smoking a cigar, smiling to himself, his eyes on the bank of elevators, waiting. He was relaxed for the first time in days. Weeks. Well, he could afford to be patient now. Every few seconds he patted his seersucker jacket, loving the crackle of the folded sheets of paper he had in his inside pocket. Ah. The brass pointer above the second elevator was moving in an arc and stopping, yes, on the fourth floor. Good. That would be

Isaac now. Jesus, the man must be in a cold sweat! Jim chuckled to himself. The old reprobate! It was no more than he deserved!

For just a moment Jim wondered what was going to happen to Zelda when this was all over. Poor thing, it had taken every bit of courage she owned to call him this evening.

"Mr. McCready, I . . . I know something. Something bad. I stayed awake all last night. . . . He *is* my father . . . but it isn't right, what they're doing!" Her voice, which had started as a kind of hoarse whisper, was getting stronger and clearer with every word. "I've made up my mind. Can you meet me?"

"Where are you?" The whereabouts of the Family Lazarus had been carefully guarded by their lawyers.

"The Broadway Central Hotel. Do you know where that is?"

Right in the neighborhood! The gall of those people! "I know where it is, Miss Lazarus. Do you want me to meet you in the lobby?"

"*No!* No, no, no. If they ever saw me . . . No, I thought maybe you could suggest another place, not too far from here. They don't let me— I'd better not be gone too long or they'll get suspicious."

"The lobby of the Lafayette Hotel. Is that all right? It's six blocks to walk. . . ."

"Just tell me where, Mr. McCready. I'll get there."

He gave her the directions and then asked, "Miss Lazarus, I'm curious. Why me? I mean, why aren't you talking to Leah about this . . . thing, whatever it is?"

Her voice was grim. "Believe me, Mr. McCready, this is a job for a man."

He found Zelda sitting in the farthest corner of the lobby, a pathetic figure, obviously trying to make her big-boned body small and invisible by hunching over. When she saw him, she started to smile, then wiped it away quickly. He pulled a chair close to her, but not *too* close, and put on his best avuncular face. She reminded him of an animal, tamed but not domesticated, wary, ready to bolt. And he did *not* want her bolting.

"Now, then, Miss Lazarus. I'm all ears."

Zelda's eyes darted around the room and she licked her lips. What was it about her look and her posture . . . and then he had it. She looked like a scared child. What was she? Twenty-five? Leah's age or near it. A grown woman, but a woman who had never been allowed to really grow up. And those par-

ents now wanted to do the same to spunky little Jo? Over his
dead body!

"Come on now, Zelda . . . I can call you Zelda? Good . . .
I know this is tough for you. But it's even tougher on Leah.
Not to mention Jo. She's okay, isn't she?"

"Oh, yes, yes. She wants to go home, of course. But this
isn't about Jo." She paused, licked her lips again, drew in air,
let it out in a long sigh. "It's . . . my father, actually."

"Your father . . . yes? Go on. Please."

"At least . . . I think so. Look, Mr. McCready," it came out
in a rush, "I think you should go talk to a man named Leon
Cavalier."

The name was familiar. . . . "The artist?" Of course, the fellow who had painted phony ancestors for the Lazarus living
room.

"Yes. He's been calling my father all week. And when he
does, my father . . . turns very pale. My mother doesn't notice,
but I do. And then he—my father—goes out and won't say
where. Last night I took his coat out of the closet when he was
ready to leave and I felt something in the pocket, it was a thick
envelope, and when I looked inside, it was stuffed with money,
Mr. McCready. I didn't have time to count it, but it was a lot
of money, maybe a thousand dollars. I think my father is giving money to Leon Cavalier. . . . I think he's being . . ."

"Blackmailed," Jim supplied, and she nodded.

He sat very still for a minute or two and then got up.
"Zelda, this may be very important. I understand that you're
concerned for your father. And that this could get you into
trouble. My lips are sealed, I promise you. Never a whisper of
your name. But I have to run—there's no time to lose."

And down he went, fairly flying through the Village: Eighth
Street, Greenwich Avenue, Waverly Place, Minetta Lane . . . in
one hangout and out of the next, asking if Cavalier had been
in, where he could be found. He wasn't to be found at 14 Barrow, nor in Jolly's, nor Romany Marie's. But there *was* a familiar face in Marie's. Walter Morris was sitting at a small
table in the corner, his arm around a very young woman who
gazed at him adoringly. When Jim caught his eye, Walter instantly got rid of the girl.

"We want to thank you for trying to help," Jim said.

"I have a soft spot in my heart for Leah. She was a hot little
thing, most Jewesses are, I've noticed. Oh, McCready, come
now, you're not going to offer to break my nose because I used

to fuck her, are you? Don't be an ass. It was a long time ago. She was very young and naive, but an eager student. I had hoped to raise her to a new level of lasciviousness, but . . . she wouldn't play." He laughed briefly. "Does that make you feel better?"

"Not a hell of a lot!" They eyed each other, then both gave the same tight, grim smile. "But what's past is passed," Jim went on, "and I'm not here to talk about what Leah used to do, anyway."

"I heard you asking if Cavalier had been in tonight. What do you want with Leon?"

Jim leaned forward. "Do you know where he is? I've got to see him!"

"What about? No, it's no use your glaring at me with that mad Irish look. I don't scare easily. You tell me what you want, and if I think it's important, I'll tell you where he is."

"You're a son of a bitch, Morris."

"Tell me something I don't already know. Now. About Leon . . ."

"Well, it appears he's got something on old man Lazarus."

"Ike? Yes, that's entirely possible." He smiled lazily.

"You *know*, you bastard!" Jim reached across the table and grabbed Walter's collar, twisting it. "You'd better tell me, and quick! I don't care if my Irish temper *doesn't* scare you. My Irish fist'll make you feel differently, I can promise you that!"

"Says who? All right, all right! Let go and I'll tell you!" When Jim loosened his grip slightly, the painter continued: "Leon did some paintings of old Ike . . . *personal* paintings."

"Meaning?"

"Cavalier has a business he keeps pretty quiet, painting randy old goats doing it to some young whore. Six different positions, all in miniature . . . so they can be easily tucked away somewhere, hidden from other eyes. Well, he did a series for Ike a year or so ago. He remembered him particularly, because he had 'a vivid imagination,' that's how Leon put it. He told me he actually had a good time watching!

"Well, when this custody trial started, and the guy's name was in all the papers, he figured to squeeze the old man for some ready cash. You know—give me money or I tell what I've got on you."

"The lousy shit!"

"Hey, whoa! Leon just does the painting, whereas your respectable button king picks a little girl, so young the hair's just beginning to grow on her pussy ... practically splits her in half, and gets even hotter when she screams with the pain. Which one's the bastard, *you* tell *me*!"

"Okay, your friend Leon is a prince." Jim released his grasp on Morris's shirt and sat back in his chair. Jesus, Mary, and Joseph, what a picture: solid, stolid, portly Isaac with the neatly-trimmed goatee and his gold-rimmed pince-nez, buck naked and horny, ramming himself into a young girl while another man looked on and—Jesus Christ!—made sketches?

The respectable Isaac Lazarus, merchant, Republican, pillar of the community, president of his synogogue! *And* suing Leah on grounds of moral turpitude! If it weren't so awful, it'd be funny! No wonder he paid and paid. If anyone found out, he'd be ruined. "Maybe your friend will take *my* money and testify for us."

Walter shook his head. "He's gotten a bundle from old Ike. Anyway, he's damned if he wants to testify. Who would ever come to him again, knowing he's likely to squeal? Kodak's damn camera has already horned in on his business!" He gave one of his short, unamused laughs. "Look, I told you I've got a soft spot for Leah. So I'll tell you. Leon kept the pencil sketches of Ike and the girl, studies for the paintings. He might let you have them."

"I wonder how many randy old goats Cavalier's collecting from. Never mind, it's none of my affair. Just tell me where I can find him, and I'll see if we can't make a deal."

Walter named a building on Hudson Street, a good twenty minutes away. "I can't promise he's there ... or he might be busy." Jim was already up and running; when he was halfway to the door, he heard Walter calling: "You'd better have plenty of cash! He doesn't take checks!" Followed by a bark of laughter.

Jim ran all the way—well, he did the best he could, with his two-hundred-twenty pounds and his flat feet. So he was breathing hard by the time he got to the top of the six flights of narrow creaking steps. He knocked loudly on the door and waited.

The door opened a crack and a pale eye looked out. "Who are you and what do you want?"

"I'm Jim McCready and I—"

"Never mind, I know who you are. You're the paramour. What do you want with me?"

"Open the door, would you?"

"I'm entertaining some young ladies right now and they're

. . . not decent." Jim could hear giggling from somewhere inside. "Unless, perhaps, you're interested in joining us? A fiver would do it, and I'd even give you your pick."

"No thanks. I don't want your women. I want the sketches you did of Isaac Lazarus and the girl."

The smooth bland voice took on an edge. "Did he send you?"

"Christ, no! Think, man. We're on opposite sides, he and I. I just need the sketches."

"You don't have enough money."

Jim felt the sweat building up on the back of his neck. "I'll give you a hundred . . . just to borrow the damn things. I'll come back this very night and return them."

"A hundred . . ." The door swung open a bit farther and a swirl of sweet narcotic, opium maybe, drifted out. In the back of the large room were dozens of flickering candles, heaps of pillows, a tangle of pale legs and arms. Cavalier, who had wrapped his loins in a towel, was otherwise naked. "You're sure I couldn't interest you in a little . . . entertainment? No? You said a hundred. Up front?"

"Fifty now, fifty when I return them."

The colorless eyes stared at him. Then Cavalier nodded. "Done. Wait." He shut the door. It felt like an hour before the door opened again and an arm snaked out, holding a sheaf of folded drawing paper. No more words were exchanged, just sketches and money. Jim snatched the bundle and charged down the stairs, praying to God there would be a cab on Hudson Street. He was in no mood to race up to the Broadway Central on foot.

It was quarter to twelve when he got to the front desk of the hotel and insisted that they ring the Lazarus suite. He must have had blood in his eye because the desk clerk, at first officious and superior, began to stammer, and in the end hurried to do what he asked.

Isaac Lazarus, roused from his sleep, was annoyed. "What the hell is going on?" he snarled into the phone.

Jim spoke sweetly, surprised to hear his brogue come sneaking back. "What's going on, dear man, is that I have in my possession some truly interesting pictures that seem to be of you, Mr. Lazarus, and a lady who in no way resembles your lady wife."

On the other end of the telephone there were strange strangled sounds and then a fit of coughing. Hoarsely, Isaac demanded: "Who the hell *are* you and how do you come by my property?"

"Never mind who the hell I am, Isaac my dear. A friend of Leah's, a friend of little Joanna's. Just make yourself decent and bring yourself down to the lobby, where I'll be smoking a cigar and waiting for you. But don't take too long, Isaac, the late city edition at the *American* goes to bed within the hour, and if I don't see you soon, I'll just have to take these here pretty pictures right over there. They'll make copies for the other papers."

Whispered: "Damn you! I'll be there!" The receiver was slammed down.

It wasn't quite over, but Jim found himself grinning, anyway. So he sat down in the big soft chair, lighted himself a cigar, and puffed at it contentedly, letting out the smoke in a series of rings. Jo loved his smoke rings; and now, goddammit, he was going to be able to blow them for her again. He thought of calling Leah; Jesus, she must be pacing the apartment and wringing her hands, wondering where the devil he'd gone to. But he mustn't tell her until he was really sure, until this was all finished.

Isaac Lazarus appeared in front of him before the thought was finished, his eyes wild and his thinning hair tousled from sleep.

"I know you! You're McCready!"

"Right you are! Let's see if you can be smart about other things, shall we? Why don't you sit down so we can talk like gentlemen?"

"Gentlemen! No gentleman would come in the dead of night with larceny on his mind!"

Jim's voice dropped and became deadly. "No gentleman would fuck a child while someone else looked on." He took out his precious pieces of paper, unfolded them, and held them out. "No gentleman would—"

"Shut up, for the love of God, and put those damned things away! What do you want from me? More money? That's fine, you can all bleed me dry and then there won't be any more!" His voice, climbing the register, had begun to quaver.

"Money? Don't be stupid. We don't want your money, you silly ass. We want Joanna back. You and your fine wife kidnapped her in the first place. That wasn't a nice thing to do, Isaac. It made Leah unhappy, and when Leah is unhappy, I become very irritable. I ought to pop you one, right on the button, for the hell you've put that woman through. But if you go to Justice Phelan tomorrow with your lawyers and tell the judge you've changed your mind, you've decided to let Jo go home to her mother . . . well, we'll all just forget the whole thing. And these—" He waved the sheets. "—these will never be given to the press or the judge."

"It wasn't my idea, you know, to take Joe's child, I never even liked the idea. But Bertha . . . when Bertha makes up her mind, she's like an act of God, she cannot be stopped. I don't want another female child to raise—for what? Women are no good for anything important. They just cost you money. I already have one useless female living in my house, eating my food, earning nothing. . . ."

"Zelda?"

Bitterly: "Zelda! The girl no one will have."

Jim wanted to tell the ignoramus how wrong he was about his daughter; but a promise was a promise. "So . . . you'll do it, then. You'll call your lawyer now, with me by your side, and you'll tell him what you've decided."

"At this hour? I can't do that!"

Jim smiled ever so sweetly. "Oh, but I think you *can*."

"She'll destroy me, you know. She'll never, never let me forget this. I'll never hear the end of it, never." There were tears in his eyes. At first Jim thought he meant Leah, and he was puzzled. Then he realized: it was Bertha! The poor schnook. Jim did not envy him the rest of his life. But he knew he had won.

Holding his cigar in his teeth, Jim got up, suddenly bone-weary, but very happy. He nodded at the sweating Isaac, threw an arm across the other man's shoulder, and laughed as he felt him cringe.

"Let's go, Isaac my dear, and have a little chat with your attorney, what do you say?"

19

February 1925

The courtroom was charged with an edgy silence. Everyone, even the reporters jammed into the jury box, sat very still, waiting for His Honor to enter. Leah sat next to Jim, her eyes fixed on the judge's chair. She was holding Jim's hand so tightly, she had lost all feeling in her own. But she couldn't let go; if she did, she felt she would drift away and never find her way back.

Last night, when Jim finally came home, she was fast asleep—she who was so sure she would never be able to let go of her troubled thoughts. He hadn't woken her; in fact, he allowed her to sleep until the last minute this morning. And when she asked him what had been going on, he grinned and said maybe it should be a surprise. It had better be a good one. Today, the judge would make his decision. Fin O'Toole had done his very best, and they had just as many witnesses as the other side; but she knew how bad it looked for her. There was no jury of her peers in this case, to go into a room and argue back and forth. There was only the judge, a devout churchgoer, "a man," Fin explained with a heavy brogue, "who's educated himself out of the shanty Irish into the lace curtain Irish. And Leah, me dear, there's no people in the world quite so sure of their morals and their duty as the lace curtain Irish."

They had all laughed a little, but the uncomfortable truth was that Justice Phelan probably considered her a loose woman, no better than she ought to be, and certainly not fit to raise a child. And when he said it from the bench, she would lose her daughter, her only child, the only family she had left in this world. She closed her eyes and felt the wild beating of her heart. If she had any tears left, she would cry them now, in front of everyone. But she had no more tears.

"Oyez, oyez, all rise!" the clerk cried, and the judge came sweeping in, his black robe billowing out behind him, his freshly shaven cheeks quivering with the vigor of his step.

". . . the Honorable Justice Gerald Phelan presiding!" As the clerk came triumphantly to the end of his pronouncement, the judge, with a wave of his hand, allowed them all to be seated. Leah's mouth went dry with apprehension as she stared at the stern face so high above her. Like looking up at God, she thought: and that wasn't so far wrong, either. This morning, he had all the power of a god to put her life on either one path or another.

The Lazarus lawyer stood. "Your Honor? At this time, I would like to inform the court that my clients—" He paused to clear his throat, clearly not happy. "—my clients would like to withdraw their claim and to halt these proceedings."

The judge frowned and ordered both lawyers to approach. Leah turned to ask Jim what was going on, and she saw a flash of jubilation—there was no other word for it—between him and O'Toole. If this was the surprise, then it *was* good. But what did it mean? What did they want *now*? Fin went to join the other attorney in front of the bench. Leah turned to stare at Jim, who was trying vainly to keep a grin from spreading across his face. Leaning toward her, he whispered: "Keep your fingers crossed, sweetheart. If this is what I think it is, our troubles are over."

She tried to smile back at him, but she was so tired. They were up there, all of them talking. Words, words, words, and what did any of them mean, really? She was so tired of all the words—she, a writer!—so weary of the reporters crowding around her every time she left the courtroom, shouting their outrageous questions, all of them talking at once, pressing in on her, surrounding her, leaving her no room to breathe. Tired, too, of all the images that were swarming up from the depths of her memory, like evil spirits suddenly set free. Justice Phelan spoke and, scraping his chair back, he rose and strode out the door. A loud buzz immediately filled the courtroom, and all the reporters began to write.

"Come on, Leah, he means us, too."

Leah felt a bit unreal.

"Leah! Are you deaf? The judge wants all of us in his chambers. By God, old Isaac's done what I asked, he's really done it! In spite of that termagent he calls a wife! Oh sweet Jesus, what a beautiful morning this is!"

Blinking, she looked at him dopily. "Jim, just what did you *do*, last night?"

"I'll tell you all about it . . . after." He pulled her to her feet and, holding her hand, led the way.

They all took chairs in the judge's chambers and sat without looking at each other. Every eye was fastened on Justice Phelan's scowling face as he pulled in a deep breath and expelled it noisily. "All right, then. Let's hear this again, Mr. Harris."

"Your Honor, my clients have thought long and carefully and have decided to withdraw their suit for custody of the child Joanna Lazarus, and are willing to return her posthaste to her mother's care."

A sound came out of Leah's throat, something between a squeak and a laugh; and the judge turned to scowl at her. She folded her hands in her lap and bit her lips to keep from shouting with joy. They were giving Joanna back to her! It was over, it was really over, and she had *not* lost her baby! She had better keep very quiet; who knew what might make them change their minds again?

"Mr. Lazarus? Mrs. Lazarus?" Justice Phelan very obviously did not care for this turn of events. "Have you anything to add?"

Isaac spoke quickly. "A child belongs with her mother, Your Honor. I . . . I had a dream about my son Joseph, and in this dream he spoke to me. 'Papa,' he said, 'give my baby back to her mother. A child belongs with its mother.' "

"Are you telling me," the judge demanded, "that after all this preparation and after all your trouble and the gathering of all your witnesses, you're withdrawing because of a *dream*?"

Isaac, sweating profusely, wiped at his bald head with a huge handkerchief. "Yes, Your Honor."

"Mrs. Lazarus? You are in agreement?"

Bertha was sitting ramrod straight, her hands encased in white gloves, holding tightly onto her purse. *"Yes."* Her mouth snapped shut, as if to trap any further words that might dare to make their way to her tongue.

Leah stared at them. She felt her mouth dropping open with her amazement, and she closed it. Bertha Lazarus . . . with nothing to say? Impossible. Bertha Lazarus . . . giving up something she wanted? Incredible. What in *hell* was going on?

"Mr. Harris," the judge said. "You have spoken with your clients at length about this matter? You are certain in your mind that this is a decision made freely and of their own accord?"

"Absolutely certain, Your Honor. My clients are not without feelings, you know, and—"

Phelan raised his hand for silence. The judge regarded Jim and Leah, frowning, his lips moving in and out. Then he shook his head impatiently. "Mr. O'Toole . . ."

"Yes, Your Honor."

"If I ever find out there's been chicanery on your part, in any way, shape, or form, you will answer to the Bar Association, sir, I promise you that."

"Your Honor!" O'Toole's voice was a study in hurt bewilderment. "I have done nothing, I swear, nothing at all. I was as surprised as Your Honor is when Mr. Harris called me this morning. You could have knocked me over with a feather, Judge."

"Just remember what I said." A moment of silence. "Very well, then. We will return to the courtroom now."

Leah was in a daze. In a few minutes everything had been turned around, and she could hardly take it in. She didn't hear what the judge said; she didn't even hear the horde of reporters who followed her out of the courtroom and into the corridor, where a redheaded blur streaked across the hall with the speed of a bullet and flung herself into Leah's waiting arms. Oh God, could anything feel better than your own darling girl hugging you? Could anything be sweeter than the sound of her voice?

"Mommy! Mommy! I waited and waited but you never came!"

"Oh, but darling, I did come for you! They wouldn't let me in!"

"I didn't see you!" Jo was crying.

"Sweetheart, I was there, I promise you. I was searching and hunting for you every day you were gone. . . ." She knelt so that their heads were even, wiping the tears from Jo's cheeks, kissing her over and over, talking between kisses. "Jo, darling, you know Mommy was trying to get you back, didn't you?"

"I didn't see you!"

Leah felt someone standing over them and looked up. Zelda stood there, awkwardly, crying. "They told her . . . my mother told her you didn't want her anymore."

"Oh God, that's a terrible lie, Jo. You know Mommy loves you and wants you, forever and ever. Grandmother told you a lie. You believe Mommy, don't you?"

"You never came for me. And I wrote you so many letters."

"Sweetness, I never got them. Oh, your grandmother, if I ever get my hands on her—never mind." She picked up Jo to hold her close. She wished Jo would hug her back. But who knew what other things they had told her? She tightened her arms around Joanna. She would be patient; the child had been through hell.

"Zelda, what happened here this morning . . . did you have something to do with it?" Zelda nodded. "Oh God, how brave, how wonderful of you. How can I ever thank you enough?"

"One day . . . one day, Leah—" Zelda's voice wobbled, although she smiled. "—I'll need your help, and you'll give it."

"You have my promise on that. But—"

The reporters, who had been forced back behind a wall composed of Jim, O'Toole, and a policeman, broke through and made their own wall of bodies and questions around Leah and Jo.

"Leah, do you know why the other side suddenly gave up?"

"How does it feel to win, Mrs. Lazarus?"

"Is it true, Leah, that you're going to bring them back to court on kidnapping charges?"

Voices shouting, flashbulbs popping and dazzling the eyes. The little girl buried her face in Leah's shoulder.

"You can see that my daughter is exhausted from her long ordeal," Leah said. Her face felt flushed with joy and relief. "I will say that we are pleased and gratified that Joanna's grandparents finally came to their senses. And now, please, I'd like to take my little girl home—"

"And you might want to question Mr. Isaac Lazarus, who it seems had a prophetic dream." Jim's voice cut across all the babble. There was a moment's gasp of silence, and then, like a herd of animals, the reporters turned in unison and were galloping down the hall, shouting, "Mr. Lazarus! Isaac Lazarus!"

Leah stood there, laughing. That Jim! And she had her baby back! The long nightmare was finally over. She felt Jim's hand on her shoulder, and she let herself relax against his comforting bulk.

"When are you going to tell me what you *did* to him?"

"How do you know I did anything, and how do you know it was to him?" Jim was laughing.

"Because we saw something in the judge's chambers this morning that's never been seen before—Bertha Lazarus keeping her trap shut. So you must have done something to *him*, and he ordered her to not say a word. I could see her trembling with the need to open her mouth and give us all hell, Judge Phelan included. What did you do, Jim? I'm dying to know."

"I'll tell you the whole story later." Jim threw his head back and roared with laughter. "Sure, Leah, you never know who your friends really are until you get into trouble. No, no, I'll tell all at home, after this little darlin' has been put into her own bed for a nice long rest."

Sleepily, Joanna said, "Tell me a story, Uncle Jim?"

"Sure thing, little lady. All about the Irish kings and the wonderful battles they had."

"Jim!"

"Well, all right, maybe not the battles. But the banquets!"

Leah smiled at him. She was utterly happy and at peace. "I do love you, Jim."

A moment later he said, in a strange voice, "You know, that's the first time you ever said that to me."

"Is it?" She smiled at him and spoke lightly. "Well, you keep on being such a sweetheart, and maybe it won't be the last!"

"How about right now, Leah? Just for practice." They had started walking toward the big front doors.

She stopped and looked him in the eye. "I love you, Jim McCready." And God forgive her if it wasn't quite the truth, the whole truth, and nothing but the truth.

"Me, me, too! I love you, Jim McCready! I love you, Leah Mommy!"

They all laughed. Oh God, it felt so good to laugh again. "And we love *you*, Jo." Leah's arms around Joanna, Jim's arms around the two of them, they stood, all of them together, safe at last. A new beginning, she was being given a new beginning, she and Joanna, and they would make the most of it.

20

September 1939

The day after Labor Day was the first day of school, and the uptown Broadway–Seventh Avenue Express was jammed with CCNY students heading for 137th Street and Convent Avenue. Their laughter and chatter filled the car; one voice especially. It was deep and resonant for a girl, and it penetrated the general din easily. "Chamberlain is a dope," it announced emphatically. "Peace? Oh, sure! That's why all those Stukas came 'screaming out of Poland's clear dawn sky,' unquote. To make peace!"

"Okay, Jo, save the speeches for Prof Abrams's poli sci class! Some of us *believe* Chamberlain!" someone shouted; and the husky female voice laughed along with the others.

Jo McCready laughed easily and often. She was perfectly willing to find herself amusing. But she did not find the German invasion of Poland at all amusing. It worried her mother, too, and her mother was always up on what was happening in the world, especially on what you had to worry about.

"I almost forgot," she countered, her voice heavy with sarcasm. "Henry Ford says there'll be no war in Europe, so I guess Hitler is just a bad dream!" More laughter, but one or two of the adults sitting in the train scowled furiously at her. Too bad, if they thought Hitler was harmless! She didn't, and it was a free country, wasn't it?

The subway screeched to a halt at the 137th Street station and the college students flooded out. Jo McCready got a lot of interested glances. She was used to it; she stood out in a crowd. It wasn't just the thick, flaming auburn hair; nor that she was a lot taller than most girls—over five feet eight. She didn't know *what* it was, exactly, that made people notice her. And she wasn't quite sure whether she liked it or not.

187

People told her she walked "like a man"—whatever *that* meant. They also said she thought like a man, which translated into amazement that a girl could think at all. And a girl who thought about serious topics, like war and poverty and politics . . . well, that girl was obviously not "feminine"—whatever *that* meant.

The hundred or so kids, including her, who had emerged from the subway, turned to climb the long flights of steps that led to the CCNY campus. It was a matter of pride never to get out of breath, and many of them defied the hill by singing favorite radio jingles, like the one for Wheaties or Rinso White, on their way up.

The campus was a pretty one, considering it was in the middle of the city. Built high up on a hill in Harlem, the buildings were all alike: dark stone trimmed with limestone, carved and curlicued, like Gothic castles. In Jo's opinion, CCNY's campus was as nice as Harvard or Princeton, and it was better in one respect: the City College of New York was free to everyone who was smart enough to get in. Every time she got to the top and saw the campus, she felt a defiant thrill. She was one of the true elite, because CCNY got the smartest kids in the United States. The students called it the school of the three spices, after the words engraved on the four gateways to the campus: ADSPICE, RESPICE, PROSPICE. Past, Present, Future.

Jo headed for the cafeteria in the Great Hall, the huge curved building that dominated the campus. Classes hadn't yet begun; and she knew she'd find her best friend, Rhoda, sitting there over a cup of coffee.

Sure enough, she spotted Rhoda's curly black hair in the corner. Several other kids were at the big round table already. Jo had the longest trip—all the way from the Village—whereas most of the others lived in the Bronx or Inwood or the Upper West Side. One day she tried to figure out how many hours she had already spent on the subway, just to get a Bachelor of Arts. It came out to three thousand or something like that! Three thousand hours, sitting on a noisy, bumpy train, wasting time.

But why complain? It was her senior year, and she would soon get on with real life. Real life was photography. That was her true passion. "Just like your father," Mom always said; but that was ridiculous. Her father had died before she was even born, so how could she get her love of photography from him? Although she still used his wonderful 4 x 5 Graflex. He hadn't taken it with him to France. She was so glad she had *something* of him. They also had his collection of *Camera Work*, the magazine published by members of the Photo Secession, years ago. Twenty-two issues, dating from 1908 to 1917, were filled with his wonderful pictures.

But really, neither her father's camera nor his collection of magazines had sparked her interest in photography. It was her aunt Zelda. Zelda had given her her very first camera, which she still had somewhere. A Kodak Brownie. She remembered how excited she had been. The camera she used all the time, the one she was carrying today, was a marvelous handheld Leica. Jim had given it to her for her twenty-first birthday; so it was still brand-new, and she loved it like a newborn baby. She wanted to be the next Berenice Abbott or Eugene Atget; she wanted to chronicle the world the way she saw it.

Everyone at the cafeteria table was talking about their Labor Day weekend. "What'd you do, Jo? Besides take pictures."

"As a matter of fact, I got some great shots at Coney Island. You'd be surprised how people are willing to expose themselves when they're at the beach. It's like they think they're not in their real lives, so they can do any goddamn thing they want!"

"You mean like under the boardwalk?" Jo regarded her joking friends. She loved them, but sometimes she wanted to shake them all out of their silliness. There was nobody her own age she could talk to about serious things, about art, about the world, about the things that bothered her.

"Hey, I went to *Rose of Washington Square* Saturday night," Jo said, changing the subject. "It was weird to hear 'Toot, Toot, Tootsie.' I remember, when I was a little kid, my mother used to put on blackface and get on one knee, just like Jolson, and sing all those songs." She laughed. "One time, a messenger boy came to pick up a manuscript from her, and oh my God, he looked scared to death! Of course, *I* was sitting there in a costume, too, my face covered in makeup. So maybe it was *me* he found weird."

She stopped laughing, abruptly. "It was funny," she said, but her voice had changed, and she busied herself with her books. She didn't like to remember the time in Rye or the trial.

Herb, one of the boys she knew, pulled up a chair and asked, "How can you all sit here laughing when there's war in Europe?"

"My father says there's no war until war has been declared."

"Yeah, but there's a war anyway. Cities were bombed—"

"Yeah, and Hitler blockaded their ports—"

"But we'll never be in it. Don't forget the Neutrality Act."

"Yeah, sure," Herb said, his voice heavy with sarcasm, "and that means Hitler's going to stay neutral? You girls can afford to be philosophical about it—it's us guys who'll be sent over there."

His answer was a chorus of hoots. Jo dug into her purse and brought out a newspaper clipping, unfolding it. "None of this stuff is funny. Any of you see this?"

The story had a small amount of space on page one of the *Times*. BRITISH CHILDREN TAKEN FROM CITIES, the headline said, and Jo read aloud: " 'Three million persons are in first evacuation group, which is to be moved today.' "

"Well, that's smart."

"Wait, you don't understand. They've taken these little kids away from their parents and put them on trains. . . ."

"So what? People in Poland got bombed and killed. Why are you so worried about a few kids who get a free vacation?"

"You don't understand! They put barriers up at the train stations and they wouldn't let the mothers go with them, they wouldn't let them say good-bye. All the mothers were standing there crying. Those little kids must have thought their mothers were giving them away, that their mothers didn't want them anymore!" As she spoke, her voice became more emotional. She stopped abruptly, blinking back tears. "It could happen here, you know. They could come over here and bomb us. And then— Can't you see how horrible it is, to do that to little kids?"

Her friends looked at her, concerned but blank. She had not been able to stop thinking about it, about those mothers and their little kids, not since the story had appeared four days earlier. She didn't care *how* much safer they were going to be, she *knew* they didn't want to go. She knew, too, that they wouldn't feel safe again, not until they were back home, maybe not *ever*.

"Jo, what is it?" Rhoda put a hand on her arm. "You look . . . spooky."

"It's nothing. Just that, when I was a kid, I was taken away from my mother."

There was a stupefied silence. She could see that nobody knew how to take that bit of news. "Taken away? *How*, taken away?"

"Kidnapped." She had kept it a secret for so long; but at this moment, she couldn't imagine why. It was easy to talk about, the words slipped right out.

"Kidnapped! Get outta here!"

"Don't jive us, Jo!"

"I'm not making it up. My grandparents kidnapped me and hid out in a house in Westchester."

"Wow! Was it in all the papers?"

"Yeah."

"Jeez! How old were you?"

"Six. There was a trial, and that was in the papers. Well, my mother and stepfather made sure it was in all the papers—so my grandparents would have to come out of hiding. There were big headlines. 'Kidnap Kid Comes Home.' Stuff like that."

"God, Jo, that must have been exciting!"

"Exciting . . . yeah, you could say that. . . ."

She remembered some of it; and what she recalled was in vivid detail, brightly colored. The little house in Rye had diamond-shaped panes that she found fascinating. Through them, she watched as it snowed and snowed until the whole yard was a thick, glistening white. She and Zelda were allowed to go out into the snow. They held hands and marched around the yard, lifting their legs above the drifts, sinking in up to their knees . . . well, up to her knees. The sky was bright blue, and the icicles, which hung along the roof of the house, glittered and sparkled.

They built a snowman. Zelda showed her how to begin with a small ball that you rolled in the snow, and it got bigger and bigger. And when it was big enough for the bottom of the snowman, you stopped rolling and patted it into shape. The middle was harder because you had to lift up a big snowball . . . but Zelda said it was good packing snow, not too fluffy, and wouldn't fall apart.

They finished the snowman by putting in chunks of coal for eyes and nose and smiling mouth. Zelda stood back and said, "Let's make it a snowlady." So after they patted on a bosom and hair, Zelda put her hat on the snowlady and it looked beautiful.

"Not good enough," Zelda said. "Come on, Jo, we'll knock it down and start again. The next one, we'll get a big spoon and we can shape it so it really looks like a person."

Jo didn't want to knock it down; she liked it. But Zelda kept talking about the new one they would make, and then she went over and punched at the snowlady. A big piece fell out and Zelda began to laugh. "Come on, Jo! It's fun!"

It *was* fun, and it was only a snowlady. They kicked at it and punched at it and it broke apart and crumbled and crumpled. The head tipped sideways and wobbled and then rolled onto the ground, and the hat went flying off. They were both laughing so hard. And when it was all just a big pile of snow, Zelda said, "Come on, let's stamp all over it!" So they marched around in circles, smashing it flat, until finally there was nothing left but a big hole in the snow, and their footprints.

Zelda's face looked feverish and her eyes shone with excitement. Jo found that surprising; Zelda was usually sad and quiet because Grandmother was very mean to her. Grandmother thought she was the boss of everyone, and Jo did not like her. She never listened to you or answered your questions, and she was always telling you not to be a silly child.

"See, I told you it would be fun!"

"Let's do it again, Zelda! Let's do it again!"

But suddenly Zelda nervously glanced over at the house. Jo looked and saw Grandmother's face in the window and she, too, stopped feeling good. Trying to recapture the feeling, she stomped around by herself, squealing and trying to laugh. Then she realized that the snowlady they had destroyed was really Grandmother, and she was happy they had done it.

She was very angry with Grandmother. On Christmas Eve, in the Bronx, they had all been decorating the big tree in the corner of the living room. Jo's job was the tinsel. She loved tinsel—she loved anything that glittered—and she put it over the branches with great care, one or two strands at a time.

But Grandmother got very impatient with her. "Joanna, it's getting very late. I suggest you do that a little faster."

"I want it to be even, Grandmother."

"Even! Look, *this* is how you do it." Grandmother snatched a bunch of tinsel from the box and dropped it over the branches in ugly clumps. "There! You see? *That* way!"

"I hate it!"

"I hope I didn't hear what I think I heard." Grandmother's voice was icy.

"Mother, please, it's Christmas Eve—"

"Zelda, one silly child at a time is quite enough. Do I hear an apology, young lady?"

Joanna wouldn't look at Grandmother. She wished she had a big knife to stick into Grandmother. She wished her mother would come save her. And with that thought, she burst into tears.

Grandmother grabbed her by the shoulders and shook her. "You stop that caterwauling this instant."

Jo wrenched herself away from her grip. "You wait till my mommy comes to get me!"

"Oh indeed? Well, you might as well know. Your mommy is not going to get you and take you home. . . ." Jo stopped crying for a moment, stunned at this statement, and stared at her grandmother. "That's right, you're going to be living with *us* from now on."

"I don't want to live with you!"

"Well, that's too bad, because now *I'm* your mother."

"You're not! You're not! I want my mommy!"

"Don't you talk back to me, young woman. You may want your mommy but, let me tell you something, your mommy does not want a girl who talks back all the time. Your mother said we could have you. She said she didn't want you anymore."

There was a flutter and a choked sound from Zelda: "Mother!"

Grandmother whirled to that sound, glaring, her mouth pinched together tightly. "Your mother isn't too happy about having *you*, either, my dear, but unfortunately, she's stuck with you!"

Zelda's face crumpled as if someone just punched her in the stomach. Jo felt as if she had been punched in the stomach, too; and without warning, like a sudden eruption from the depths of her being, her stomach emptied itself. Vomit came spewing out of her mouth, all over her brand-new velvet dress, all over the Oriental carpet, all over the upholstered chair, all over the prettily wrapped presents.

Joanna looked about with a shudder. Her friends were staring at her, perplexed. "Someone just walk over your grave?"

She was still caught up in her memory; she could taste the vomit in her throat.

"No . . . it's nothing . . . I just . . . I just remembered something I had completely forgotten."

Rhoda said, "Jeez, Jo, you look as if you could kill."

"No. No. I just remembered I was supposed to call my aunt, and I forgot." She could see that Rhoda didn't believe her, but she didn't want to talk about it. She still felt a little nauseous. Usually she was able to keep from thinking about that terrible time, but then something would come back, and the feelings were still there, the terror and the anger.

"God, kidnapped," someone said. "Gee, Jo, I never realized you were famous. Like the Poor Little Rich Girl, what was her name?"

"Gloria Vanderbilt. Only we weren't famous, or rich, or anything like that," Jo said. Her eyes had drifted to the unfolded newspaper story, about the English children.

In her mind she was striding down a country road in England, she and her beloved Leica, taking pictures of those scared little kids, cowering in the strange surroundings, their pinched little faces staring at her . . . at the eye of the camera.

She would take pictures, and when they were published in the newspapers and magazines, the whole world would know what it felt like to be taken away from your mother, from everything you know and love, and sent to a strange place where you don't want to be. Yes, she would show the world that those children had been deserted, not saved. She would convince the world that the hurt was the kind of hurt that would never, ever, go away.

Abruptly she stood, her mind made up. "Rhoda, I gotta get going."

"Going? Where?"

"I gotta talk to my folks. I'm leaving."

"Leaving? For where? We gotta register."

She shook her head. "No. I've got to go. Sorry, everyone."

"Wait, Jo. What about Kessler's Ancient History class?"

"To hell with ancient history! I'm going where history is being made right now!"

"What are you *talking* about?"

"I'm going to England."

"Yeah, yeah, and I'm Queen Marie of Romania!"

"But this is senior year! You're on the prom committee!"

Jo had to laugh. "Prom committee! Are you nuts? How can I stay here and think about the Senior Prom or Prof Kessler's course? A war *is* happening in Europe, you guys. As Herb was trying to tell you before, Hitler is bombing innocent people, and little kids in England are being herded onto trains like animals, and . . . all I know is, I gotta be there!"

She ran out of breath for a moment; and when she paused, she realized all of a sudden that she was filled with happiness. It was what she was born to do: to go wherever things were happening, and capture them to show the whole world.

"Yeah, Jo," one of the boys said sarcastically, "you think you're such a daredevil. But driving eighty miles an hour up around Washington Square Park, or jumping into the fountain in Grand Army Plaza, isn't quite the same as going over and thumbing your nose at Hitler's bombers."

"Honestly, Jo," Rhoda said, pouting. "Ever since you got your driver's license, you think you can do *anything*."

"That's right, that's what I think." She was feeling better and better. "I'm going over there while I can still get there, and I'm going to take pictures of the whole damn business! You'll see, all the newspapers and magazines will want my pictures!"

They all gaped at her, and she realized that they absolutely did not know what to make of her. Herb made a dismissive gesture and laughed—after she'd just stood up for him! "Just because the *Daily News* bought your pictures of that accident—"

"Anyway, your mother will never let you go," Rhoda put in.

Well, that *really* was a scream! Jo laughed. "Are you kidding? She's always gone everywhere she pleased to get a story, she won't tell me I can't do the same! And she always took me along with her, a little kid! One time, we were in the slums and it was getting dark. And this guy came up to us and said, 'Give me your money or I'll kill you.' And you know what my mother did?"

"Gave him her money?"

"Not on your life! She *yelled* at him. She really did; she told him to get the hell out of her way! That poor guy never knew what hit him. He just stared at her and let us pass. Let me tell you something, my mother isn't afraid of *anything*."

She paused, looking at her friends, thinking *So long, everyone, I'm on my way.* "My mother, stop me from going?" she said, shaking her head and picking up her purse and camera. "Uh-uh! I'll bet you a hundred bucks she'll pack my bag!"

21

February 1940

The letter was typed hastily with a lot of mistakes and cross-outs. So like Jo, Leah thought, always plunging ahead, always in a rush. It began, "Happy New Year to All!" *Happy New Year* . . . and it was the middle of February. Nearly six weeks for mail to make its way across the Atlantic from London to New York. Well, she shouldn't be surprised. England was at war, and the ocean was thick with German submarines, preying on British ships.

Leah had raced upstairs with the thick envelope, eager to read what her daughter was up to; but now that she had settled into her favorite chair near the fire, she put off reading it. She was *afraid* to read it, to tell the truth. Even after all these years, the memory was vivid—of Joe's letter, her happiness, and the telegram that followed. Letters from Europe during wartime were an omen of death. But that was ridiculous, sheer superstition, and she knew it. What's more, Jo's pictures were coming into *Story* magazine at a regular rate, and that wouldn't be happening if she had been hurt, now would it?

She was so proud of her little girl. Well, Jo really was still a girl, even though her name appeared under photos in newspapers and magazines. She was a regular at *Story*, which hoped to beat out *Life* as the premier picture magazine in the country. Jo McCready was perfectly willing to help them do it, too. She would go anywhere and do anything to get a good shot, war or no war. She haunted the airfields, talking with the young fliers, focusing her camera on their fuzzy-cheeked faces. So young, so young. She'd even been up in one of their planes several times, which made Leah nervous, but apparently didn't faze Jo. She had written that it was "nothing, Mom, really. The fighter planes only have room for one anyway, and I went up in a two-seater. After I bragged so much about being able to get good shots from the air, Colonel Loftus wanted to see for himself. It was safe as a car, honest."

But Leah knew her daughter; sometimes Jo simply refused to see any danger. As her mother, should she have tried to keep her from going overseas? When Jo came home from school that day and said she *had* to go to England and take pictures of those evacuated children, Leah's first thought had been how much *she'd* like to go, too. They could be a team, with Jo in the countryside, taking pictures of kids, while she talked to the mothers who'd had to watch as their children were torn from them. Leah had found the whole idea electrifying. Maybe she should have been more . . . what? Motherly, maybe . . . told Jo she was too young to go gallivanting off across the ocean into the middle of a war. And maybe she *should* have gone with Jo, no matter how much Jim ranted and raved. But she hadn't and that was that. Anyway, Jo seemed to be having the time of her life.

So what was she sitting here for, telling herself *bubbe-meisers*, old wives' tales, that letters from overseas were bound to bring bad luck! What an idiot! She straightened the flimsy pages and started to read. There were the usual greetings and asking after everyone, and then:

. . . People like to say that when the children got on the trains to leave, they were laughing and smiling, like they were off on hols, as they say here. But the kids I see now in the country are so homesick, oh Mom, it's pitiful because everyone expects them to be so brave and grown-up, and they try hard. Not to mention, they're bored silly because there aren't schools for them yet. At the Duke of Connaught's country estate, there are fifty tots, all very little. They play happily enough during the day, but at night . . . oh the sobbing. It's awful! But I'm not to take pictures of *that*! No, "it might give aid and comfort to the enemy!" But I can shoot the older children, even the ones from the slums of London, who have formed gangs and are running around the countryside beating up the local boys, chasing cattle, stealing whatever they can get their grubby little hands on . . . even throwing stones at the local policemen. Nobody knows quite what to do with them. They're full of lice, pee in the corner of the room instead of in the pot, and complain all the time that they "cawn't stand this bloody plice!"

But I've been told to stop harping on the evacuation, as it's old stuff; so a couple of days ago I came back to London. I've been walking about, getting shots of the preparations for when we're invaded. My favorites are the barrage balloons. They look like great sea lions bobbing about in the sky, their cables singing. They're rather lovely, in a strange way.

I sent *Story* a great shot of Piccadilly at night, but it seems Bourke-White beat me to it . . . hers was in *Life*. You may have seen it; God knows the rest of the United States did. I'm gnashing my teeth. But actually, I can't complain. I'm selling tons more pictures than I ever dreamed of. Now I'm thinking of a story about how women are finally free to do real work. There's the W.V.S.—Women's Volunteer Services—and the WAF, the WREN, and nurses, and, oh I can't even think of all of them; but women are doing absolutely *everything*. Isn't that exciting? Only of course the men really worry about our *morals*, but not very loudly because British men are too polite to be direct. Women getting into pants, that's right up your alley, isn't it, Mom? Come on over; I'll shoot pictures and you can write the stories.

And so we prepare and prepare. And nothing happens. Everyone thought the Nazis would storm the beaches the day after war was declared, but no. They call it the Funny War, or the Strange War, but the one I like best is the Bore War.

The letter ended with Jo's scrawled signature beneath the last line. A lot of her phrases sounded vaguely British, which was just like Jo. She had an unerring ear and a wicked way with imitations. But dammit, she was so young! She probably thought she was immortal.

Sooner or later the bombs would start falling on England; Jim was convinced of it. This one was going to be an air war, and the German Luftwaffe was supposed to be unbeatable. London was bound to be a major target. And then— Leah shivered, got up and threw another log on the fire.

She heard the familiar sound of feet clumping up the steps, and a moment later the key turned in the lock and a deep voice sang the last few lines of "Oh Johnny! Oh!" slightly off-key. No voice could be further in sound and style from the girlish tones of Wee Bonnie Baker that emanated from every jukebox in the city.

"You're early, Zelda. I wasn't expecting you until dinner-time."

"I wanted to change. Cliff's taking me to dinner, and I'm not dressed for the occasion." She gestured to her outfit of slacks, sweater, and thick woolen jacket.

"Occasion? What occasion?" Leah grinned at Zelda's blushing discomfort.

"Cliff said I was ready—now or never, he said. Anyway, he won't be giving flying lessons after next week because, in his opinion, we're crazy not to join the Allies, and so he's going up to Montreal to join up with the RCAF." She spoke quickly, looking away in embarrassment. "They make you a citizen or something, in five days, and then you can go fly a Spitfire in England."

"So. He's leaving the country and taking you to dinner. To say good-bye? To ask you that very important question?"

"Leah! Nothing like that! Well, of course, we *will* say good-bye, but it's kind of a celebration. Since he's leaving and since he said I was ready . . ." She gave Leah a mischievous look.

"You're not going to fly a Spitfire in England with him!"

Zelda laughed. "What an idea! But I did take the test for my license! And passed!"

"*Mazel tov.* But, my God, Zelda, doesn't it scare you to death to fly a plane all alone?"

"No. Yes. No. Sort of. But mostly, no. I've gone up alone before, lots of times. Of course, Cliff was there, on the ground . . . But to be a real pilot at last! It's a dream come true, Leah. I *knew* I would love flying a plane, I *knew* it. And I do! Oh Leah, you have no idea what a great feeling it is, to float up there, far above the world, to look down and see everything spread out like a toy countryside . . . just me and sky and clouds and wind. . . ."

Leah laughed. "So you've told me a thousand times before. Okay, Miss Earhart, and now what? A nonstop flight around the world? A job with Trans-American Airways?"

"I just wish they *would* take women in the RCAF."

Casually, Leah said, "Why don't you go with Cliff anyway?"

"Oh, I couldn't!" Zelda blushed, and busied herself removing her heavy jacket and wool hat.

"Why not, I should like to know? Any woman with the guts and the nerve to chop off her hair and disguise herself as a man so she could get flying lessons, can certainly follow the man she loves."

"Cliff says— Say, do I see a letter from our girl? Let me at it!"

"Hold on! Cliff says what? Come on, Zelda, we hear so much about this paragon, let's hear what he has to say."

"Nothing, really. Just that I'm the spunkiest female he's ever met and . . . Well, he says he's going to miss me." She lowered her eyes from Leah's gaze. "So you see, he doesn't want me going with him. And why should he?" When she looked up again, there were tears in her eyes. "He's years younger than me, and just because we've kissed a couple of times . . . Don't look at me like that, Leah. I've had more than I ever expected out of life, much more. Now, let me have Jo's letter, would you mind?"

As Zelda stood reading, her eyes devouring the pages, Leah couldn't help but marvel. From the scared rabbit who did her mother's bidding to this daredevil . . . Well, it defied imagination.

After the trial, Leah wouldn't allow Jo to see her grandparents again. In any case, once Jo got out of their clutches, she never *wanted* to see them again. But Jo and Zelda had a special closeness; and Zelda sneaked away whenever she could and came to New York on the train. It was difficult; they gave her almost no pocket money, and she had to resort to stealing from her mother's purse. But she did it—and suffered Bertha's sharp-tongued wrath.

"*She* knows where I've been," Zelda had told Leah more than once. "Of course she knows. But I never admit it. I just give her the stupid look—" And here, she would let her mouth hang open and her eyes cross, making Jo laugh."—and I don't tell her *anything*."

Leah often asked her why she didn't leave. "It must be awful for you."

"It's Hell in ten overstuffed rooms. That's what it is. She never tires of letting me know how badly I have failed all her expectations. I turn off my ears and pretend I'm reading, but I hear her anyway. Anyway, it's worse for Papa. . . ." Zelda gave a sardonic laugh. "Papa is beyond the pale, you know. He did nasty things, dirty things, things no lady should ever even have to *think* of, much less see. He tells her if she had only been a normal wife with blood in her veins instead of ice water, he wouldn't have had to resort to whores. . . . Oh, and Leah, when he says that word—'whores'—she runs from him, just turns and *flees*!" Zelda grew serious suddenly, and said, "Which I suppose is what *I* should do. But I'm still too scared."

But then came the Crash. Black Monday. Black Monday saved Zelda's life. As she told Leah later:

"Papa came back from his office, looking rather gray. 'A narrow escape, ladies,' he told us. 'A narrow escape. Levy is ruined. Rosenstein, they say, will be penniless. Horvitz—don't ask. But we will be all right. I had the good sense to put almost everything into diamonds and gold—'

"'Because *I* told you to!' Mama snapped.

"'You really think I sold off my railroads and my utilities because your Gypsy fortune-teller said bad times were coming? Then you're even crazier than I thought!' And back and forth they went.

"So I waited for a lull, and then I took a deep breath and said, 'You won't have to find an apartment with a room for me, because I'm moving out.' I couldn't believe my own audacity.

"Papa leaped right out of his chair, his face turning the color of an eggplant. 'You will not!' he thundered. 'You will do no such thing, young lady!' His voice kept rising with every word. The funny thing is, the angrier he got, the cooler *I* became. 'There's only one reason a young woman leaves her parents' home before she's married, and that's—' he began.

"'Yes?' I said, just as calm as you please. 'What is the reason? It is about sex? Is that it? Well, I'm sure you can inform us all on *that* subject!'

"He said not another word, not one, just let himself fall back into his chair. He couldn't look at me. Mama blustered a bit, saying, 'Well, and you needn't expect us to back you in this ridiculous notion.' And I said, 'Oh, but I *do* expect money, and I think you'll want to give it to me.' I put on what I hoped was a superior smile and said, 'I don't suppose it ever occurred to either of you to wonder just who found those, um . . . little paintings. Or to wonder just who got in touch with Jim McCready. . . . '

"Papa, of course, instantly jumped up and raced over to me, holding his fist under my nose and breathing like a steam engine. But I just stood there and stared him down, and in the end he lost his nerve. I don't know how I did it, but it was grand!"

Leah and Jim had insisted she come live with them—they could find a larger apartment—but Zelda shook her head stubbornly. "I want to make it on my own. I feel like a baby, I don't know anything about cooking or paying bills, and I've got to learn." She got herself a job selling toys at Macy's, and took a room at Webster Apartments, a hotel for working women, where the cost of a tiny room depended upon how much you earned at your job. There, she studied what the other working girls were wearing, and how they made themselves attractive.

In the end, Zelda looked much as she looked right now: a tall, robustly built woman with a strong, pleasant face and close-cropped hair. She favored slacks and man-tailored shirts, which suited her; and, since she worked for Jim, selling ad space by telephone, she didn't feel compelled to wear the obligatory stockings, pumps, and kick-pleated skirt, which was the usual working girl's costume.

At first she just disappeared every weekend on mysterious errands; but finally she confessed that she had started flying lessons, dressed like a man, using the name Zack.

"But now they all know I'm a woman, and it's okay. And Cliff thinks it was really gutsy, that I did that so I could fly. They all feel that way about flying, that it's the best, most important thing in the world."

So this woman, who had once been afraid to leave her parents' house, had been spending every weekend in a small plane, doing tricks, like barrel rolls and loop the loops, and all the rest of what those crazy pilots did. Life was full of surprises.

On the day Jo left for England last October, Zelda had come to the airfield, with a big bag of film, to say good-bye and wish her well. And then she had come back to the apartment on Barrow Street with them, and had never left.

Zelda finished reading Jo's letter and heaved a great sigh. "God, it sounds like she's having such an adventure! She's so lucky, having you for her mother. I can't think of many women who would let their twenty-one-year-old daughter go halfway round the world, into the middle of what will undoubtedly be a war."

Leah smiled. "You sound like Jim."

"Well, he gets to you. Anyway, I think he's right. I think Hitler wants to own all of Europe. Anything for me in the mail?"

"Your usual check from Bronxville." She held out the thin envelope. Zelda tore it open, took out the check and a folded sheet of paper. She held the paper out so Leah could see.

"Blank, as usual. I guess my dear parents have nothing to say to me anymore."

"Zelda, do you ever mind them cutting you off like that? I mean, they're awful, of course, but they *are* your parents."

"I like to try to forget that. I'm sorry, Leah. I know you feel keenly about family, having lost your own so young and all. But honestly, I feel I might have been much better off without those particular parents. I keep asking myself, Why did they treat me so badly? Because I had the bad luck to look like my father, when the others looked like *her*? Well, it doesn't matter. I got out and I'm fine. And, more important, so is Jo." Then Zelda rattled Jo's letter and announced, "That's what I'll do!"

"What?"

"Go to England, where they won't care how old I am, or how inexperienced! That's what I'll do! I'll be a WAF or a WREN or I'll drive an ambulance for the Red Cross. Like Jo says in her letter, women are doing everything over there."

"I still think you should go with Cliff."

"Well—" Flushing a little. "—that's where he's going to end up. In England, flying for the RAF. They have a lot of foreign pilots over there, refugees from Hitler, whole squadrons of Poles, Czechs, and Canadians, too."

"So, you get to England. Fine. Then what? What will you do?"

"Whatever they need me for. Why not, Leah? Look at me—a spinster who can fly a small plane and sell ads. That's about the extent of my usefulness! But now England needs every pair of hands she can get! Who knows, they might even let me fly!"

They probably would put her to work immediately, Leah thought. Zelda was healthy and strong and willing. . . . Why not?

"I'll tell you the truth, Zelda," Leah said. "I'm selfishly thinking I don't want you to go because I'll miss you. But there's a war on, and why should you be any different than your brother?"

Zelda's whole face lit up. "You think I'm like Joe? Like *Joe*? I always loved him so much. He was so full of life and laughter. Oh Leah, that's the nicest thing anyone ever said to me!"

She went over and threw her arms around Leah, hugging her tightly. And Leah prayed silently that she was not someone else who would disappear from her life forever.

22

October 1940

Jo McCready ran, as fast as she could in her high-heeled dancing shoes, across Berkeley Square. It was deserted, except for the blackout wardens in their tin hats, patrolling the dark streets by flashlight. The cinemas and theaters had been closed, the traffic lights taped so only a little sliver of light showed. The street lamps were dimmed and the occasional automobile headlamp emitted only the faintest of glows. A good thing she knew enough to follow the white stripes that had been painted onto the bottoms of the trees and lamp posts.

As she got to the corner of Charles Street, she saw a whole family huddled together for warmth around the flames of a dying firebomb. What a marvelous picture that would make! She wanted to run right back to the flat and get her camera. But she was already late; and she wasn't sure enough of Peter Fielding to know if he would wait for her. The thought that he might *not* be waiting made her insides feel hollow.

She was late because the Jeep had broken down on their way back from the airfield at Church Fenton. The Eagle Squadrons, the Yank glamor boys of the RAF, the beloved volunteer pilots, had just been moved there. Bit by bit they were being shifted closer to London, and they were all excited to think they might finally be allowed to get into real combat, instead of training or flying the occasional escort for a convoy.

But the truth was, as one of them admitted to her after four or five stiff drinks, "We don't know shit from shinola about flying instruments. . . . Hell, most of us learned how to fly in California! But if you try to tell the Limeys there's a place where the sun shines most of the time, they just stare at you as if you were bonkers."

There were many foreign pilots in the RAF; most of them couldn't even speak English. Maybe that's why the American Eagles were so popular. Anyway, back home, they sure sold magazines. *Story* said they'd give her at least a spread, and that was okay with her. But the airfield was way up north, hours away, and then the Jeep broke down! When she finally got back to London, she'd barely had time to change from her trousers and sweater. Tonight she was wearing Pam Watson's dress—and, she supposed, Pam was wearing her green silk, since it wasn't hanging in the closet. Pam was a nurse she had met while doing a story on a hospital in Paddington. They had quickly become chums, and Pam had moved in with her two months ago. They were both tall and slim and could wear each other's clothes. In one move they had doubled their wardrobes, and it was very patriotic, too. Everyone in England was making do, and having a grand time doing it.

She loved the English! They just went on with their lives, calm and cool, as if nothing unusual were going on. They even *walked* to the shelters when the air raid sirens went off. Like tonight, just as she was coming down the front steps from her digs. She'd had to duck into the nearest Underground, where everyone had already settled in cozily, most of them knitting away on scarves and balaclavas for the soldiers, even the men. A few were even curled up in their hammocks, sleeping. She admired the British stoicism, but had a hard time emulating it. Every time the sirens started screaming and wailing, her heart began to thump double-time and her palms went all sweaty. Not that she'd ever let it show!

Peter, though, didn't have to pretend. A week ago, they'd been caught in an air raid. When had they *not*? as Peter said. He was so utterly composed. Of course, he was an airman, one of the brave RAF pilots who went up almost every day in their Spitfires and Hurricanes, to battle the Nazi planes that were trying to bring the British Isles to their knees.

"But they won't, you know," Peter said, smiling down at her, his arm firmly around her shoulders. "We won't be beat. We almost were, actually. The Blitz saved us."

"The Blitz? How?"

"They've stopped bombing the airfields, you know, and that means we've got some breathing space to build up our force once more, build planes and so forth. We were just about decimated. But we're coming back, and don't you worry, we'll beat Jerry."

"How come you English are so . . . so intrepid?"

He smiled at her, amused. "It must be something in the water that gives us that stiff upper lip, darling Jo."

Darling Jo. She ran that one over in her head about three thousand times. Darling Jo. Oh, she hoped he really meant it. God, if he didn't really mean it, she would die, just die! She never let herself even think about how small his plane was, how vulnerable, fighting off the Germans in their Messerschmitts and Stukas. If anything should happen to him . . . !

When she first got to England, almost a year ago, everybody wanted to know when the so-called war was going to start. And then it did, horribly—on Saturday, September seventh, five o'clock in the afternoon. All of London's teatime calm was disrupted by the roar of bombers and explosion after explosion as the bombs fell everywhere. She and Pam were toasting bread over the open flame on the stove and boiling water for tea when the sirens began hooting and screaming. They ran downstairs, in a dither—well, *she* was; Pam seemed cool as a cucumber—and went racing up the street, following the S for Shelter signs. It had been quiet underground, and eerie, not knowing what was happening up on the surface.

They'd found out soon enough, emerging into the dark, smoky atmosphere that stank of something acrid. Fires were burning out of control everywhere, sending waves of heat and black smoke into the sky, blocking out the sun. They were still blazing the next evening—"serving as beacons," the newspapers all said—when the bombers came again. But it couldn't be helped; there wasn't enough water or enough hoses to put them all out. And every night, every single night since then, like a recurring nightmare, the sky was filled with the throb of engines, and the thudding roar of London crashing down, block after block, crumbling and burning, while the ack-ack guns boomed and thundered. And still the English smiled and gave the thumbs-up and sang a popular ditty that said "the King is still is London . . . and the King will *be* in London . . ." They really were the most wonderful people in the world!

The moment the all-clear sounded tonight, Jo began running, and now she was racing down Curzon Street, turning onto Half Moon Street toward the Park Lane Hotel. Love put wings on her feet. At least, that's what it felt like. And at last there was the grand old hotel, its lights dimmed. But inside the marvelous art deco ballroom, she knew, there would be lights and music and dancing. And Captain Peter Fielding of the RAF. Oh how she loved him; it was painful, she loved him so much.

Fifty feet from the front door, she slowed her pace, patted her hair, straightened her stocking seams—last pair of stockings; when these went, she'd have to resort to drawing seams up the back of her legs in black pencil. She hoped she looked tranquil and quite, quite unruffled. She caught a glimpse of herself in the darkened glass. How she had changed, in just one year! From a tomboy coed to a woman dressed up in lavender silk, and breathless at the thought of a man who left her feeling tongue-tied. It wasn't like her, it wasn't like her at all.

The huge ballroom was filled, as usual, with girls in their best frocks, older women in well-cared-for finery from prewar days, and uniforms, many many uniforms. The orchestra, five women in dainty tea frocks with lace collars, was playing "The White Cliffs of Dover," which had become the most popular song in London. In her head she sang along: " . . . there'll be love and laughter, and peace ever after . . ." Everyone's dream, these days.

There he was, sitting with the others at a round table across the room. He was so handsome, in that pale, dreamy English way, with chiseled features and a long thin aristocratic nose. He was very tall and thin, ever so slightly stooped—as if he was too diffident, too polite, to tower over ordinary mortals. She found everything about him elegant: his long narrow fingers, his long narrow feet, the way his uniforms remained uncreased, no matter the circumstances. He was the opposite of everything she had grown up with; and she couldn't believe that he, with his Oxford education and his air of sophistication, found her attractive.

Peter was twenty-six years old to her twenty-two, but he seemed years older. His father was an *earl*—it was just too glamorous for words. King Charles II gave the title and property to Peter's great-great-grandfather or somebody, for service to the Crown. "Service to the Crown": the very sound of those words conjured up a fabulous world of enchantment, a world of money and privilege, a world that beckoned to her as if she belonged, only she didn't know it. Like the princess in a fairy tale who had been under a spell.

If her mother could hear her thoughts, how she would laugh! That's why she hadn't told her about Peter yet. Instead she'd written to Zelda. Jo knew Zelda would understand what was happening to her. Hadn't Zelda waited until she was nearly forty to find love? Or was it that love had found her? They weren't even married! Somehow, none of it seemed to fit Zelda; but there it was. Zelda had written back, telling her how wonderful it was to be with the man you loved. "Here's my advice, Jo, for what it's worth. If you find the man for you, don't you hesitate for a minute. Don't let anyone tell you you're too young. They told me I was too old, and look how I fooled them!"

But Jo knew her mother would react differently. "You really think you're the frog princess, waiting for the handsome prince's kiss?" she'd say. "You've got it backward, as usual." And she'd give Jo a look of amusement that said, We both know you aren't serious. But she was! She thought it must be marvelous to belong to a family that went back for hundreds of years, living in the same place, without change or disruption. Imagine if your father were Lord Somebody, like Peter's father was Lord Fielding, and everyone said, "Yes, m'lord" and "No, m'lord!"

Not that Peter would ever be. He had explained it to her very carefully. "I'm a second son, dear Jo, and second sons simply don't count. My brother Edward will inherit Nether Althorpe *and* the title *and* the income, whereas I shall be plain Mr. Fielding, left to find my way in the world somehow, without a sou."

As if she cared! All she cared about was that he not slip away from her and leave her life suddenly barren. As if the intensity of her thoughts spoke to him, Peter's head turned in her direction and he spotted her. Getting up and striding across the room to her, he took both her hands in his and smiled down into her eyes, saying, "I was terribly worried, Jo dear. I thought—but never mind. You're here and that's all that matters."

She smiled back at him, her heart fluttering, longing to kiss him, *really* kiss him. But one didn't do that, it seemed. He always kissed her good night, of course, but very gently and sweetly. He was so restrained, such a gentleman. She often felt like an awkward child next to him. And she certainly wasn't going to spoil things by flinging herself at him.

"The Jeep broke down. And then the sirens went off, just outside Berkeley Square—"

"Never mind. Come dance with me so I can hold you close."

Oh God. She melted into his outstretched arms and they danced cheek to cheek. He had told her it was marvelous that she was tall enough so he didn't have to bend over. She pressed her cheek against his, reveling in the feel of his lean taut body so close to hers.

"You look so lovely in that color. What do you call it? Lilac? Lavender? It's . . . ethereal, somehow. It's my favorite color. How did you know that? And you smell like lilac, too. You always manage some sort of magic, don't you?"

Jo couldn't answer him; she didn't know what to say, and anyway, her voice was caught in her throat. Love was happening, it was happening to her; it was really happening. Boys at home always found her daunting—she was too tall and too opinionated—and she had become convinced that she was going to go through life without anyone ever loving her. She held her breath and turned her head slightly, so that her lips were pressed against his face.

He pulled back a bit, and she thought, That's right, dummy, push yourself on him and send him running. But his eyes were filled with tenderness as he gazed down at her. "I want to memorize the way you look right now. I'll carry it with me all through the week, while I'm . . . working. Your lovely long throat, and that wonderful tumble of hair, the color of autumn leaves—" He pressed his lips against her hair. "—and the marvelous smell of you, let me remember it, too, to keep me sane until I see you again."

He was planning to see her again. That was all she wanted in the world; that was pure happiness.

"You're going away again, Peter?"

"It's just a spot of night flying. But I don't want to see a worried frown on that pretty face. So wipe it away. There's a good girl. Nobody is going to get me. I know how to fly between the flak, you know. Now that I have you, I've turned lucky."

"That's how I feel, too."

"You darling." He pulled her close for an instant, then released her and said, "But you must tell me what you've been doing this past week. You lead such an adventuresome life."

She paused. Ever since the Air Ministry made a deal with *Story* magazine to use her photographs as part of the history of British aviation, she'd been terribly aware of her new responsibilities. She'd stopped writing any sort of details home to her mother. Even so, Leah had written her that one of her last letters had arrived looking like ticker tape, all cut up by the censors. But, for heavens sake, this was *Peter*, an RAF pilot. "I spent three days at Church Fenton, with the Eagles, and before that, at Aston Down, for a story on some American fliers. . . ."

"I've heard good things about your flyboys, crude though they might be. Now darling, don't take that the wrong way. We're damned grateful for their help, let me tell you."

"Well, the flyboys at Aston Down aren't crude, Peter. And they're not part of the Eagle Squadrons. They're part of the Army Air Corp. And they're Negroes. A whole unit of Negro pilots. I had no idea there *were* any Negroes in the Air Corps! I don't think anyone did. So I expect all the news services will pick up my piece after it appears in *Story*. It's horrible, the way Negro people are treated, even pilots. All you have to do is talk to them and you soon see that— Peter? Is this all just too boring?"

But she knew the tightening of his face wasn't boredom, it was reprimand. Every once in a while she got hints of prejudice in Peter, and she would wonder how he'd react if she told him she wasn't an Irish-American girl, as her name indicated, but a Jew. The British could be, well, kind of funny about Jews. The moment she had those thoughts, however, she felt disloyal and pushed them away. She'd tell him eventually. But right now she only wanted to be with him and enjoy her happiness.

"Boring? How could you bore me, Jo? You're by far the most interesting woman I've ever met. . . . You have no idea how vapid our well-bred English girls can be! But you're independent, fearless! Not only that, you always know the words to all the songs!"

They laughed, although she felt just the littlest bit uneasy, as if they were laughing at her mother. When she had showed him the issues of *Hit Parader* that Mom sent her every month, with the words to the most popular songs, he had found it hilarious and "terribly American." That wasn't quite fair; the pubs were always full of voices lifted in discordant but enthusiastic song. And it was a breather from the Blitz, to see the old familiar covers and feel the roughness of the cheap paper and read through the newest lyrics, imagining the tunes in her head.

"You're the fearless one, going up into the night sky to be shot at, night after night! I'm just a photographer."

"A lovely photographer . . ." he murmured, giving her a twirl. "A photographer of such divine, angelic innocence . . ." Who cared what he meant? It sounded so nice, especially in his accent. Peter liked to dance, so they stayed on the floor, while the little orchestra bravely made its way through the latest hits, like "The Last Time I Saw Paris," everybody was singing that, and a haunting tune called "The Nearness of You." And, of course, the omnipresent "A Nightingale Sang in Berkeley Square."

The music stopped and they went to join the others at the table. A bottle of champagne was turned upside down in its bucket, and from the flushed faces and superbright smiles, Jo decided, it was not the first to be emptied.

"Here she is, safe and sound!" Peter announced; and the others lifted their glasses to her. The two men were Peter's pilot friends; she'd met them before. Nigel and Everett . . . what strange names the British gave their children! She was so happy Peter's name was Peter. Pamela was there, of course. Jo and her roommate usually double-dated.

And there was a new girl—"This little beauty is called June," Nigel announced, his arm firmly around her shoulder. A bit of a floozy, by the look of her, Jo thought. June had on far too much rouge and her lipstick was a deep red, almost purple, all wrong for her milky, freckled skin. Her pink dress was a bit too tight, and her upswept hairdo featured a great many little flowers and bows. She put out a languid hand to Jo and said, "So pleased to meet you," only the last two words came out as "meecher." She hiccuped in the middle of the sentence, putting her hand to her mouth and giggling, so the ladylike effect was ruined.

Pam and Jo exchanged a look. June was probably not a day over sixteen and no better than she ought to be. That Nigel, he ought to be ashamed of himself. Poor little cockney kid, out on the town and out of her depth.

They had just lifted their glasses to the orchestra, for making such a noble effort, and Jo had just gulped down some of the sweet warm wine, when the wailing and shrieking of the air raid warning began again. They all got to their feet without fuss—all but June, who began to whimper. "Oh, I can't. I can't. I can't move. They'll get me for sure this time." Nigel tugged at her to get up, to no avail. "They got me whole family," she blubbered, tears leaving mascara trails down her cheeks. "Everyone, Mum, Dad, me sister Katie, me brothers, all. One bomb and all gone, all gone, all gone!"

Jo stood staring at her, feeling a shock of recognition. The floozy wasn't a floozy; she was a child. A child who had lost her mother, her father, everyone. "I was with me old granny, you know, she gets terrible scared of the noise, you know, and when I got home . . . nothing was there, nothing, nothing but a great black hole!"

Without thinking, Jo was at her side, an arm around her shoulder, saying, "I know how that feels . . . I lost my family once. That is, I thought I'd lost them. But you've got to carry on. Listen, my mother tells me she listens every night to Edward Murrow—he's an American correspondent— on the wireless, and you know what he said . . . ?" She was urging the girl to her feet as she talked, and June was so intent on her voice, she began to move. "He said 'the little people in the little houses are the unknown heroes of this war.' You and your family are heroes, all of you, and you must carry on. . . ."

They all headed for the shelter, through the hotel kitchens and down among the laundries and furnaces and storerooms in the basement, where one hoped the bombs would not reach. Jo felt awful; she had been so busy feeling superior to June, and meanwhile the girl had been hiding the most awful grief. And she was so young; back home, she'd still be in high school. Jo found herself becoming annoyed with the other hotel guests, who cast derisive looks in June's direction because she was openly crying. Well, they weren't teenagers all alone in the world, Jo thought fiercely, tightening her hold on the girl. They didn't know what it felt like to suddenly be abandoned by everyone you loved and trusted.

The shelter was in a large underground laundry, with a dozen stone tubs lining one wall. The other equipment had been taken away, and there were two lines of cots, each one made up with sheets, eiderdown quilts, and a pillow. Overstuffed chairs had been brought down, and little tables, each one with an ashtray and a lamp. Some people had carried bottles of wine with them and were preparing to continue the party; others curled up on the cots to sleep.

As for Jo, she knew there would be no sleep for her, so she took a chair, sharing it with the frightened girl. She had been separated from Peter, who, with Pam and the two other men, was crammed into two chairs, directly across from her. If it weren't for his tender gaze on her, she would have been very unhappy. But that look in his face, that look of—did she dare to think it?—that look of *love*, that made everything all right.

June, clinging to her, asked her meaningless questions like "When will it be over?" and "Will there be bombs?"

Peter answered, in his dry, calm voice. "No telling how long it will last. Jerry likes to play games at night."

"I can't stand it 'ere. I feel I'm suffocating. What if they bomb the 'otel, we'll all be trapped 'ere, trapped!"

Peter said, "Being in a shelter can have its bright side. Joanna and I met in the Underground during an air raid. . . ."

He gave Jo a knowing look, and she felt as if she were melting. It was at the Charing Cross tube station, shortly after the Blitz began. She was still scared out of her mind, and showing it. He was lounging, alone, against a wall, looking handsome in his uniform, smoking a cigarette, until the volunteers began passing out mugs of tea and biscuits. He started to help them. He didn't ask could he; he didn't make a big fuss about it. He just took a tray and bent courteously over each person in turn, ending with Jo, who was sitting on the floor, hunched up and miserable.

"Here. It's the last cup. You look as if you could use it."

"Thanks. I can."

She felt a little jolt when their eyes met, and maybe he did, too, because he said, "I wonder if there's room next to you. I'll sit and keep you company, shall I?"

Later he told her that she looked so frightened, he just wanted to take care of her. They talked all night. Jo told him how she came to London. He was terribly impressed that she had been unafraid of the danger; and he was also impressed that she sold to *Story* and newspapers. He even thought he remembered one of her pictures that had been printed in the *Picture Post*.

"Good for you!" he said, peering at her in the dim light. "God, I don't suppose there's been a woman in my family who's done real work since . . . well, unless you count breeding horses."

He had gone to Oxford! He had taken a "first"! She wasn't really sure what that was, but she could tell it was good. He told her he'd been raised to go to Oxford and take some sort of genteel job that didn't *look* like a job.

"I'm not supposed to work, you know. It's infra dig."

"Infra dig?"

"Beneath my dignity, don't you know. But it really is not very comfortable, not knowing what I'm to do with the rest of my life. Like King Edward, you know, waiting donkey's years for his job to come vacant . . ." He smiled and added, "But of course, you don't know English history. I keep forgetting you're a Yank."

But what really stuck in her mind, when he walked her home after the all-clear, was that he wasn't like the other soldiers she'd met. He didn't back her into the nearest corner and put his hand up her dress. He didn't climb all over her, insisting that he had to have her, that he might be a goner tomorrow.

He took her hand and walked her to her flat and kissed her on her forehead. She was confused. It was nice that she didn't have to wrestle with him, but still . . . Didn't he like her? And although she had only known him a few hours, the thought that she might never see him again made her chest squeeze up in pain.

She hadn't changed her mind since that first night, either. She gazed across the shelter at him and longed to be near him. Little June had fallen asleep and was snoring lightly, slumped heavily on Jo's shoulder. The others apparently had partied themselves out and were sleeping, like puppies, all curled up around each other. Peter gestured to Jo to extricate herself and come to him. A thrill coursed through her veins. Carefully, she moved June and eased herself away. Peter held his arms out to her and she snuggled next to him. When he bent to put his lips next to her ear and whisper, "I think perhaps I'm in love," she turned her head, and they kissed, such a sweet and tender kiss.

A moment later the all-clear sounded and people began rousing and stretching. Peter whispered that they should leave the others to sleep or not, as they pleased. They went out together, tiptoeing, arms around each other's waists. In the street the dull glow of fires could been seen in the distance, but not, thank God, close by. They began to walk back to her digs.

They strolled along in silence, Peter's arm around her waist, her head resting against his shoulder. After a few minutes he said, "I'd like to show you something, Jo. Are you too terribly tired?"

"No, no, I really don't want tonight to end."

He kissed her forehead and, taking her hand, began to walk very fast, turning corners and crossing streets so quickly, she couldn't keep track of where they were. Since there were no street signs or directionals anymore, you either had to know your way around or make a good guess. So she wasn't sure where they wound up—a darling little mews near Whitehall and the river. He stopped in front of an old house and dug into his pockets for keys.

"Is this yours, Peter?"

"No, the flat belongs to a . . . friend of mine. Chap I knew at Oxford. But he's Navy and he's off somewhere. Anyway, we're not going into the flat, but—never mind, let it be a surprise."

The surprise was a little garden up on the roof, high above the city. They stood without talking, his arm around her shoulders, gazing over a scene that was all shades and tones of darkness: deep black, black, almost-black. You felt rather than saw the other rooftops nearby. The streets were almost invisible, although the Thames was a ribbon of reflected moonlight, curling through the gloom. A searchlight or two split the sky, then disappeared. It was very quiet. Jo realized, after a moment or two, that she was listening for the sound of planes.

"It's . . . it's beautiful, Peter."

"Yes. It *does* have a macabre kind of beauty, doesn't it."

They were silent again, and then he cleared his throat and said, "Joanna, I think perhaps it's time we thought about you coming to Nether Althorpe . . . meet the mater and the pater and so forth. What do you think? Is it all too daunting?"

"No . . . I mean, yes, I'd love to come. When?" Her mind went skittering, thinking ahead to assignments and train schedules and deadlines. Next weekend was out, but perhaps the one after. . . .

"Actually . . . I don't know. I'd like it to be soon, of course, but . . . I guess it might have to wait until after Jerry's been beaten off. I was hoping that you might . . . well, wait for me, actually. You know, not see any other chaps. Could you consider it?"

Jo held her breath and stared out over the dark city. Did he . . . Had he really said it? *He wanted her to wait for him.*

"Does that mean we're engaged?" It just came blurting out of her mouth. "Oh dear!"

Peter laughed and put his arms around her, tucking her head between his shoulder and his chin. "Yes, my lovely naif, I imagine that's exactly what it means. Would you, could you, will you?"

"Oh, Peter, of course! It's a dream come true!"

He bent his head to her—at last! she thought, a thrill creeping up her spine, at last!—and pressed his lips to hers in a soft, sweet kiss. Jo waited for it to change, to heat up and become deeper. She moved closer, making a little sound in her throat, and opened her mouth slightly, waiting, waiting.

He pulled back. It was absurd, but she felt rejected. His arms were still tightly around her, but she felt as if he had shoved her away. Obviously, she did not know the right way to behave in these circumstances, and a shamed heat climbed to her face.

"I'm sorry, Peter, I don't mean to be . . . forward, whatever," she said, struggling to pull away from him. "But I thought . . . I thought since we're engaged, that you would want . . . want to . . . that you would want to make love to me." There! She'd said it.

For a moment he did not look handsome and charming, but like a bleak and uninterested stranger, all the emotion drained from his face. Now she'd done it, with her big mouth. She should have known that no elegant sophisticated man, no son of a lord, would be able to love her for long.

But then the strange look left his face and he held her tightly, stammering apologies, saying, "Dear Jo, dear darling Jo, forgive me, please forgive me."

"No, it's my fault, you must forgive *me*."

"Jo, listen, please. I do love you so much, you must believe me. It's just that . . . well, it's difficult to say, in this modern day and age . . . I'm a bit old-fashioned, you see, and . . . Actually, I'd like to wait for our wedding night. Do you mind terribly, darling? Waiting, I mean, for our wedding night?"

Oh, the darling! The sweet darling! Jo flung her arms around his neck and held on tight. "Of course not, Peter, of course not. I love you, too. I'll wait as long as you say."

23

April 10, 1941

Christ, what a week! Jo collapsed onto the sprung couch and kicked off her shoes. She was too weary even to look at the mail; and the mail was her lifeline to everyone she cared about. It took an effort to stretch her arm to the radio and snap it on. The strains of "I'll Remember April" came wafting out, and she smiled. How many times had she and Peter danced to that song? But that only reminded her how much she missed him!

Groaning a little, she pushed herself up from the sofa and onto her feet, only to plop back down. It had been a long and arduous three days at Martlesham Heath, following P/O William Walling, a pilot officer with an Eagle Squadron, taking pictures of his every move. She had focused her camera on P/O Walling eating, being briefed, drinking beer in a pub, flirting with the local girls, chatting up the local men, sleeping. She even had one of him being awakened before dawn to go up on a mission. Bill Walling was very good-natured about it. He was on top of the world because, after nearly a year in England, being shifted from one training field to another, the Yanks in Eagle Squadron 71 had at last been sent down to Eleven Group on the east coast—the Group that flew the really tough missions across the Channel.

"Now, maybe we'll see some action!" he crowed. "That's what we all came here for!" He had a boyish, snub-nosed face, with freckles and a wide grin. *Picture Post* would eat it up. *Picture Post* was another *Life* imitation—like *Story*, only British. Jo had sold them little until the Air Ministry did their "press event," to convince the British public how wonderful the Eagle Squadrons from America were. The Eagles had come to England without military training, boys who had spent their teens hanging around the barnstormers, doing odd jobs in exchange for flying lessons, not even knowing how to salute. For a while the going had been rather rocky. But there were three squadrons now, and most of them had even learned how to behave like officers and gentlemen.

On the seventeenth and eighteenth of March the Air Ministry had every reporter and photographer in the British Isles there, talking to them, shooting pictures of them, shaking their hands, and thanking them for coming to help. After her photos for *Story* were picked up by a lot of newspapers, she got a call from *Picture Post*, telling her they'd like "the same story, only different." They went for her idea of focusing on just one pilot, which she thought would be a cinch. She didn't know the Eagles got along on two or three hours sleep a night; and right now, she was bleary-eyed with fatigue from keeping up.

Maybe a bath would make her feel more human. Or maybe she should see what was in her mail. Mail would take much less effort. Pam had stacked everything neatly on the table, separating them by type. No doubt, the way she laid out the scalpels and such for the surgeons? Jo flipped through the pile. Bills. A reminder to save tin and bones. Tin, she understood, but *bones*? She didn't even want to imagine what old bones might be used for.

Oh good, a letter from Zelda, up north in either Ireland or Scotland, where her friend Cliff had been sent to teach green kids in the RAF how to fly. Zelda wasn't allowed to say precisely where; once she had tried, but it came out, "here in the hills of CENSORED, just a few CENSORED from CENSORED." Jo hoped to go visit her. It would be easy to hop a ride from one of the pilots she knew. One of the Eagle squadrons was up in Eglinton, in Northern Ireland, and Cliff was surely stationed near there.

Ah, and here was one of the large envelopes from the photo lab, delivered by hand. She wondered which batch of pictures these were. She'd taken a whole roll of faces . . . just faces, close up, and she was hoping they would spell out the indomitable spirit of England, without words. She ripped the envelope open and pulled the prints out. On the top a little boy with large unreadable eyes stared out at her. He held tightly onto his ripped and filthy teddy bear. Jo closed her eyes briefly. It was the series she had shot in hospital; that little boy had no legs anymore. She shuffled through the rest. All kids, kids with bandages, casts, crutches. And all of them so perfectly behaved, so uncomplaining, so solemn. Children who had burrowed their way out of piles of rubble, past their mothers' dead bodies sometimes . . . !

She shouldn't torture herself taking such pictures. But that's what *Story* wanted. The magazine loved her photo stories about British families, and it had become her speciality. They said it made a nice change from soldiers and sailors and guns and tanks. They said Americans were hungry to know how ordinary people got along during the Blitz; what kind of lives they led. So, though she never would have *chosen* to take pictures of wounded children, now the Home Front was considered Jo McCready's major area of expertise.

About a month and a half ago, she had been out for an early stroll with her Leica—usually she used the Graflex; the Leica took good pictures, but when they were blown up in developing, they had a graininess she didn't care for. Anyway, she was just having a look-see around London, not really working, and the Leica was small and lightweight. She came across a block that had been bombed the night before, and swarming over the debris were a dozen rescue workers, in their trench coats and tin hats with the big white R. They were carrying bodies, helping the wounded onto stretchers. So she began snapping away.

When those negatives were developed, one of the pictures was of a sweet little girl who had turned on the stretcher as they carried her by, curious to see what Jo was doing. She was smiling, tentative but friendly. A crude bandage had been wrapped around her head, half covering one eye, little wisps of blond hair curled around her face, which was smudged with blood. She was hugging a battered velveteen rabbit, which also seemed to look straight at the camera. An irresistible shot.

The magazine certainly thought so, too. They gave the little girl and her velveteen rabbit a full page, and it was picked up by some government agency and made into a painting—a poster begging for aid to Britain. So her little girl was cutened up and posted all over the U.S.—and the money poured in. And Jo McCready was almost famous; or would have been famous if anyone gave a hoot about who took the picture.

She put the stack of pictures down, again fighting tears. She stared at herself in the mirror, willing away her grief and sorrow. She had to keep a distance from all of this, or she'd be no good as a photojournalist. And she *was* good; she knew that now. Then why didn't she feel better about it? Just look at her, she was haggard and drawn and her eyes were positively pink with fatigue! She looked as if she had been out on a three-day drunk.

She glanced at her wristwatch. That, at least, made her smile. It was a Mickey Mouse watch; a child's watch, with a big round face and Mickey's gloved hands pointing to the hour and minute. Jim had given it to her before she left. "I figure Mickey'll bring you back to us, safe and sound." And then he had blown his nose noisily so she wouldn't know he was crying.

There she went again, her eyes misting up. Dammit! She really needed a change of scene. Well, she was about to get it. She was going to meet Peter's parents, finally, after all this time. She was so worried, she kept putting it out of her thoughts. She would do now. She had a couple of hours before Peter came to pick her up, and the weather was beautiful. It was one of those magical, clear, fragrant days that happen every so often in April. "Oh, to be in England, now that April's there" . . . isn't that what Browning wrote? She would take a walk. Grabbing up her keys, she ran down the stairs. Halfway down, she realized she hadn't taken a camera; she hesitated, then ran back and got it. What if she missed something really wonderful?

Outside, the air was sublimely soft, the sky looking as if it had been scoured to a bright clear blue. Bright sunshine, no clouds; tonight's bombing would be devastatingly accurate if there was a moon. She had to stop thinking about the war. But how could anyone stop thinking about it when it was there, without letup, every single night for seven months!

Okay, what should she think about? Peter. Her nice, lovely Peter. He'd been in hospital for a short while until two days ago. Shrapnel in his shoulder and arm from a German gunner who just barely missed killing him. Her heart squeezed up. But he did miss and Peter was fine. So fine, in fact, that they were going to send him back up after his week of furlough. She hadn't seen him since he'd been let out, but she would see him later today.

They were going to Buckinghamshire, to Nether Althorpe. About time! a little voice in her head said, and she told it to shut up. That little voice had been nagging her a lot lately. Why, it wanted to know, hadn't she been invited to the memorial service for Peter's brother Edward? Edward, the heir-apparent; Edward the brave and the beautiful, who had been cut down in his youth by Rommel's Afrika Corps. Why had she been left out of the whole thing, when she was going to be Peter's wife? Peter hadn't said a word about it until after the service had been held.

He had taken her to tea at Brown's Hotel, where all the elderly matrons in their prewar frocks watched them fondly, because he was so handsome in his uniform, and she was so young, and they were so much in love. He would not let go of her hand, and there was a strange glittery look about him. She knew something was up, but he just chatted on and on until she finally said, "Peter, what *is* it?" and he flushed crimson.

"Edward was killed in action," he blurted.

"Edward? Your brother, you mean?"

"Yes, my brother."

"Killed in action? How? When?"

Peter grimaced. "When? We don't know, actually . . . sometime last month. His tank blew up . . . and he was in it."

"Oh Peter, how horrible!"

"Yes, a nasty way to die. And I shall miss him. We're . . . we *were* very different, but we . . . respected each other, I suppose you might say. And—" Here he leaned over to kiss her lightly, causing the ladies at a nearby table to smile benignly upon them. "—and I'm really sorry he never saw what an angel I found . . . an angel in trousers."

All at once Jo was self-conscious about her slacks. She always wore them; many women did nowadays. Peter saw her look down at herself and said, "I love you in pants, darling. Of course, I'd suggest that you wear skirts while you're at Nether Althorpe. Mother is very much a nineteenth-century person."

It took her a minute, and then she got it. He was going to be taking her home to meet his folks. "You mean . . . ?"

"Precisely. I mean it's more important than ever that you meet my family, now that I shall inherit."

Shame on her, for looking to see whether he was perhaps a bit too happy about inheriting. "When's the funeral?"

"The funeral? Oh. Edward, you mean. Actually, there won't *be* a proper funeral unless they ship the body back, and I doubt that. And . . . of course, there *was* a small memorial service in the chapel at Nether Althorpe."

"There was?" And I wasn't asked to come? The words were right on the tip of her tongue and she bit them back.

"Just a small family gathering, you know. There aren't many of us left." He stared off into the distance, gloomily, then turned to her and smiled. "But now, you see, you shall be

Lady Joanna and ride to hounds with the Althorpe Hunt and
open the church fetes and . . . and so forth." He looked at her
so hopefully, she couldn't stay mad. But it had hurt.

"Lady Joanna . . ." she tried, and then giggled. It struck her
as silly. And then they had both laughed, and she told herself
not being asked to the memorial service hadn't meant a thing.

So why was she feeling so . . . doubtful, so dubious? All
right, all right. Enough of that. What was *wrong* with her these
days? She should be as happy as a lark. She needed a vacation.
She needed a drink. She needed—

Her mother! Jo stopped dead in her tracks. There was a
woman who looked exactly like her mother, stepping smartly
down the street, waving at her and shouting, "Jo, Jo! It's me!"

Oh my God, it *was* her mother. Only it was a Leah Lazarus
she'd never seen before. Her mother was usually dressed like
somebody else: a Gypsy, maybe, or a Parisian waif or a Turkish courtesan. But *this* woman was the very picture of the
modern woman, in her fitted gray suit, crisp white jabot at the
neckline, jaunty veiled hat atop her neatly rolled pompadour.
Jo could only stare in astonishment . . . amusement . . . and finally, admiration.

"Mom! Mom! What are you *doing* here? You're an answer
to a prayer!" She ran, laughing, into her mother's embrace.
With a shock, she remembered that she was quite a bit taller
than Leah. "Where on earth did you drop from?"

"A clipper flight, just like you took last year." Her mother
pulled back a bit. "Let me look at you, my world-famous photographer. Oh dear, you seem to be all grown up. And I
brought Hershey bars. You'll be too old for them."

"Like hell!" Jo burst out, and they both began to laugh.

"Sweetie pie, everyone who reads *Story*—I won't mention
the dreaded name of that other magazine—knows that choco-
late will buy you just about anything you want in war-torn England. Of course, I was joking. I thought they called this *merry*
old England. . . . Don't they kid around, in your gang?"

"Not in the same way." Jo felt a pang. Did she and Peter
ever kid around? Well, never mind, she loved being with him.
"But why are you here? In England, I mean."

"Why, to see my one-and-only child, sweetie pie, what
else?"

"A story, that's what else."

"Well . . . in fact, Jim's fallen madly in love with the way
you photograph people in crisis. So he sent me here on

assignment—for his newest magazine. *In Hiding*, it's called, can you believe it? But the stories delve a lot deeper into motives and politics and unspoken promises than most. In fact, that's why I'm here . . . in this particular neighborhood, I mean. I'm looking for Thirty-five-A Lyall Street, top floor."

"Well, you were walking in the wrong direction. If you'll turn around and go about seven blocks, you'll find it."

"What a lucky wrong turn, Jo. Oh my God, don't look like that! I was coming to see you. I sent you a telegram. Obviously you didn't get it. I tried phoning you, too, but there was no answer. In fact, I even have dinner reservations made for us tonight at— Is something wrong?"

"No, no. I'm just not sure . . . I may have to leave London." Peter would be coming to get her in a little over an hour; what was she going to do? "So what's at Thirty-five-A Lyall Street, Mom?"

"A family called Leibowitz. A man and wife and their child. They've just escaped from Germany, via a very elaborate underground, and have a horrible story to tell. Jo, Hitler is rounding up Jews and shipping them off to death camps. They're called work camps, but they're not. Smoke rises every day from those camps, and the stench of burning bodies."

"Ugh, Mom, stop! You're giving me the willies!"

"Yes, it's awful, isn't it?"

"It can't be true! They'd never get away with it!"

"Oh, Jo, I only wish it couldn't be true! But surely you know that there's no limit to the horrors people can dream up to do to other people. And the Leibowitzes were there. They bought their way out of Poland into Germany, were smuggled out of Germany into Holland, and sneaked out of Holland onto a cargo plane that brought them here in the dead of night. What a story! And I'll be the first to report on it! You just wait till the American press gets hold of it! We'll shine such a glaring spotlight on what the Nazis are doing, they'll *have* to stop."

The cloud was lifted from Jo's spirits as she listened to her mother, talking just a little too fast, as usual, full of passion and fervor. That's what life was really about: doing things that mattered. Not worrying about an invitation to a memorial service.

"Listen, Mom. You know that RAF officer I've mentioned in my letter?"

"Peter the pilot? Yes . . ."

"Come on, I'll walk you to Curzon Street, and we'll talk." They set off. "And then I'll have to run. See ... well ... I'm meeting his family this weekend. At their manor house in Kent. And he's coming to get me in about an hour."

Her mother stopped walking. "Forget Curzon Street. They're not expecting me at any particular time. Does meeting his family mean what I think it means?"

"I want to marry him, Mom. Oh, please, you have to like him. I know you'll like him—you'll *love* him. He's so wonderful ... but you'll have to get used to him. He's not like us, all mouth and a yard wide. He's ... God, he's going to be a *lord*, Mom, and I'm going to be a *lady*!"

"You mean ... as in a title. Are you joking, Jo?"

"No, Mom, isn't it a scream? The family has been in the same manor house for three hundred years. Isn't it wonderful?"

"You think it's wonderful?" her mother said carefully.

"Well ... *yes*, I think it's wonderful. But that's because I'll be with Peter." She couldn't bring herself to tell her mother how she felt, how badly she ached for the solidity of a family so ancient that their roots went far back into history. She and her mother were rootless; she knew nothing of her mother's forebears, but how could she look her in the eye and tell her that? Leah had always avoided talking about her family. She always said things like, "Oh, we're not interesting at all." And then quickly changed the subject.

"I'm crazy about him, Mom."

"I'll give the Leibowitzes a call ... how do you say that here? I'll ring them up. British English is all very nice; but I must say, when people tell me they'll knock me up, it makes me just a little bit nervous." They laughed. "Anyway, I'm coming home with you. I think I'd better meet Peter the paragon before it's too late. I didn't mean that the way it sounded. But I really should cast my eyes on him, don't you think?"

"Oh, I want you to! I want you to!" As they walked to her flat, Jo gave a sidelong glance at this American dynamo marching along next to her, trying to see her through Peter's eyes. She was sure Leah was unlike any mother Peter had ever known in his life. Leah was great; she had a lot of pizzazz, and she certainly was good-looking. She didn't look her age, either; her dark glossy hair had only one or two stray strands of white, and her skin was still taut and unwrinkled. But what would he *think*? How would he react to a mother so unmotherly, still as full of herself as any young girl?

Up in the flat, sitting over cups of tea, her mother reached into her purse and took out a small box. "Listen, Jo. I have something for you. It always brought me luck. I should have given it to you before you came over here, but . . . well, better late than never."

Jo opened the box, sure she knew what it was. And she was right. It was Mom's locket, the one she wore before every big story and for every major event. Tears rose in Jo's eyes; the locket was her mother's most precious possession.

"Do you like it, Jo?"

"Like it? I'm thrilled, Mom. I'm . . . honored." She blinked and a couple of tears slid down her cheek. "Sorry."

"Quit that, or you'll have *me* bawling. Well, put it on, put it on. If you're going to meet the in-laws, you'll need all the luck you can get."

Jo ran her finger over the oval surface. The engraving of flowers had been worn down but was still visible. She opened it and smiled at the two girls. The photos had aged a bit with the years, but you could still see that the dark one with the sparkling eyes was her mother. When she was a little girl, Jo had been allowed to open the locket and look at the pictures; she knew that her father had taken them. Her father. She *had* no father, except maybe for Jim.

"I don't look a thing like you, Mom. Isn't that funny?"

"You look exactly like my mother."

"I *do*?"

"The spittin' image."

"You never told me that."

"You never asked."

"But . . ." She had to look away. Shouldn't she have been told her own history? What had her grandmother been like? Were they alike? She had so many questions. Too many for now. "Thank you for the locket." She slid it over her head. "I hope it's good luck. I'm so nervous! They're very upper crust and very county . . . that's landed gentry to a Yank, Mom. What if they don't like me?"

"If your young man is what he should be, he won't give a hoot *what* his parents think of you."

"I hope—" But then, Peter knocked on the door, their special signal, the dit-dit-dit-*dot* that stood for vee for victory, and she ran to open it. As always, her heart skipped a beat when she saw him. He bent to kiss her and then, catching sight of

Leah, straightened up. "Don't tell me. This is your mother, isn't it?"

"Yes. Mom, this is Captain Peter Fielding. Peter, my mother, Leah Lazarus."

"Lazarus?"

"I have kept my own name, Captain Fielding . . . Peter. It's easier that way, since I use it professionally."

"Ah yes, you're a writer, aren't you?"

She put out her hand to be shaken. "And you're to be a lord, as well as an RAF pilot." She was twinkling up at him.

"Both correct. Yes. Well, I'm so glad to meet you." Taking her hand, he kissed it. "You know that Jo and I are driving up to Buckinghamshire? To my parents' house for the weekend?"

"Yes, and I insisted upon meeting you before you left."

"And *I* insist that you come *with* us."

"Of course not. Isn't this the first meeting? Oh no, I couldn't intrude on that!"

"No, really," Peter said. "They're quite accustomed to unexpected guests. And . . . well, England's not quite so war-torn once you get out into the country. The servants are all still there. No need to think you'd be a bother. The only thing I might warn you about is—they've always lived in the manor and are rather stuffy, you know," he confided, as Jo stared at him in disbelief. He never talked this way about his family to her! "It will do them a world of good to meet you two and see the sort of women the United States turns out! Beautiful, intelligent, *and* spunky!"

Leah laughed. "Well, if you put it that way . . . how can I possibly say no? But what do *you* think, Jo?"

Jo had one small moment of jealousy, thinking that her flamboyant mother was going to steal the limelight from her; then she thought, Why not? Let them stare at Leah Lazarus; let them think what they wanted. Her mother never had given two hoots in hell for what people thought. And then maybe they'd leave her and Peter alone. Actually, it would be fun to have her there.

"Oh, a help, Mom, definitely a help. At least they'll realize I wasn't found under a cabbage leaf."

"Oh, I wouldn't take bets on *that*," Peter said, and they all laughed. Suddenly Jo's spirits lifted. Peter was lighthearted; he was even making little jokes, and he liked her mother. She took hold of the gold locket. Her mother was right, it *was* a lucky talisman.

24

April 1941

They had been in the car about an hour. At first the landscape was depressing, as unscathed neighborhoods alternated with bombed-out blocks and sandbag walls. Even with all the destruction, there was plenty of traffic, so Peter scooted the tinny little Morris Minor up lanes and down alleys and around circuses, trying to get out of town by his own special "shortcut." Finally they were riding along a narrow, bucolic winding road.

Leah sat tucked tightly into the back with her valise, hoping to get to know the lean young man with his fair hair and ascetic look, maybe just a little. She couldn't imagine what he and Jo had in common. But there was no chance for real conversation; the car made a frightening amount of noise. Oh, at first they shouted at each other. Leah told Peter how everyone back home listened to CBS every night, to catch Ed Murrow with "London Calling."

"There's something about his voice," she yelled. "Something that makes you *see* what he's talking about. Of course," she added, "he's nothing next to your Mr. Churchill!" And she quoted: " 'Do they not realize that we shall never cease to persevere against them . . .' " imitating Churchill's plummy tones, hoping to get a laugh. But Peter only gave a brief smile and drawled, "Ah, yes, Winnie. He seems to be quite eloquent . . . something nobody expected of him, I believe." Chastised, she sat back and kept her mouth shut.

The young couple did not talk to each other, either, not *about* anything. They played games. First, he tested her on her knowledge of England's war planes; so for ten minutes Leah half listened to the list: Hawker Henley, Handley Page Hampden, Lockheed Hudson, Hawker Hurricane . . . Then Jo sang songs in a not-bad British accent. Some of them Leah had heard: "Roll Out the Barrel" and "We'll Hang Out Our Washing on the Siegfried Line." Jim had brought the sheet music for that one home to her, he found it so hilarious.

Finally, bored, Leah studied the lush meadows and great old trees of Buckinghamshire as they went bumping past. The ditches were filled with daffodils, crocuses, and something that looked like a purple haze. The English countryside might have been in an entirely different country, it was so removed from the war.

Peter half turned his head, at one point, slowing down to give Leah a quick course in the British gentry. Nether Althorpe House was the seat of the Fielding estate, and the little town that belonged to it was also called Nether Althorpe. The original house, of something and wattle, had burned to the ground in eighteen-something and this was the "new house—Tudor style, I believe you Americans call it. We call it 'black and white.' The house contains twenty-seven rooms, including the kitchens and dairy, and is located," he went on, in a singsong she assumed was supposed to be funny, although he never cracked a smile, "two miles west of Wing and three miles southeast of Epworth Buzzard."

As he finished his recitation, he swung through a pair of huge open gates, then drove down a wide avenue of tall trees, going much faster than was absolutely safe, in her humble opinion. So this is how the nobility lives, Leah thought, as the little car screeched to a halt in the cobbled yard. Nether Althorpe was a house of plaster and timber so huge and rambling, she couldn't take it all in.

And standing outside, dwarfed by the huge carved front doors, were a man and a woman. "The butler and the head parlormaid," Peter explained as he opened the driver's door. He leapt out and greeted the servants warmly. Leah and Jo were introduced and taken upstairs to be unpacked and settled.

Later, Leah stood gazing out of the window in the huge, paneled, gloomy library of the Fielding manor house, glad to be alone for a few minutes before rejoining "the others." They had finally been greeted by Reggie and Dilly, Peter's parents, a few minutes earlier in the drawing room. Everyone was so formal, even Peter. Leah had expected to see him throw his arms around his parents—well, at least around his mother—but they saluted each other as civilly and distantly as strangers, shaking hands. Peter's mother offered her cheek to be kissed. And then he beckoned to Leah and Jo. It was hard to warm up to the Fieldings. They were *old*; Lord Fielding had to be in his sixties and quite a drinker from the look of his nose and the large paunch. And Lady Fielding—"Oh, please, you must call me Dilly, everyone *does*"—while still trim and shapely, with cloudy pale hair, had pallid watercolor eyes that looked as blank as a child's. She was faded now, but Leah could see the ethereal blond beauty she must have once been. Peter took after her.

Conversation had been stilted and formal—well, that was to be expected, wasn't it? No matter *what* Peter thought, it must be unsettling for them to suddenly have Jo's mother in their house. Leah exclaimed over the shabby-looking furniture, the fireplace that was big enough to roast an ox, and the grounds. Outside, the light was waning, but one section of the long sweeping vista of lawn was still lit by a golden glow. A double line of topiary animals, shrubs sculptured into fantastic shapes—"begun, oh, donkey's years ago, in my great-grandmother's time," Lord Fielding had told her—led the eye down to the lake's edge. What was the lake called? "Why, nothing at all," Lady Fielding had said, obviously amused. "It's the lake on this manor. Although I imagine we could call it Lake Fielding, should we care to." And she had tittered at her own wonderful wit.

On the pretext that she had to use the bathroom, Leah had taken the opportunity to wander a bit on her own—and to get away from the high-pitched voice of her hostess. Other guests were coming, and she was expected back in the solarium for drinks. They seemed to want for nothing. Apparently, even in wartime England, if you were rich enough you could live the way you always had.

But she was determined to see at least a little of the house herself, and so she had ended up in this library, which smelled strongly of leather and dust. On the outsized Queen Anne desk stood a silver picture frame, and in it the photo of a young officer with the delicate features of his mother. This must be the brother recently killed in action. Edward, wasn't that his name? There was no matching photo of Peter; in fact, no picture of Peter at all. When Leah heard the sound of voices and Jo's above them, she decided she'd better get back to the party.

Everyone was standing around a small table that held tiny glasses of sherry, and as soon as Leah came in and took one, Lady Fielding—Dilly—prettily toasted her American guests. And then they trooped into a large gloomy dining room, where a table that seemed the size of a tennis court was set with beautiful old china and silver and linens. The huge chandelier, hanging from rafters so far above them, gave out a dim yellowish light. Very bad for the complexion, Leah thought. Even her beautiful daughter looked ghastly.

They were six: Lord and Lady Fielding—Reggie and Dilly—Peter, a very subdued Jo, herself, of course, and—a nice surprise—a thin, bearded Frenchman named Emile Le Boucher, a very mysterious and charming man. There was a sexy twinkle in his eye. Unfortunately, he wasn't seated near her; Dilly put him at her right, and Leah was at her host's right, too far away to make conversation.

There was much more food served than she had been led to expect, especially after London restaurants, which were out of everything. Apparently, they raised a lot of their own stuff, and didn't have to depend upon the greengrocer or butcher. A very nice burgundy was served with the goose, and a good thing, because everything was undercooked and lukewarm. But the wine was excellent, there was plenty of it, and after several glasses everything became quite palatable and the company almost entertaining.

Lord Fielding asked her what she was doing in England, and when she told him, he stared at her, speechless. "Oh, surely not!" he exclaimed, and turning away, addressed himself to his son and ignored her. A while later he leaned toward her and asked, "What did you say you do . . . back home in the States, I mean?"

"I'm a writer."

"Jolly good. I enjoy a good woman writer—Jane Austen, Georges Sand."

"George Eliot, you mean, dear," said Lady Fielding. How in the world had she heard their conversation, when she seemed so busy talking to Monsieur Le Boucher?

"I don't write novels, Lord Fielding—"

"Reggie. You *must* call me Reggie. I insist."

"If you like, fine. Reggie. I write articles for magazines."

"Oh, surely not!" And once again he removed his somewhat bleary-eyed attention from her. By this time she had counted ten refills into his wineglass—he kept the cut-crystal decanter by his right elbow. There was no way to beat him to the decanter, but on the other hand, every time he poured for himself, he refilled her glass, too.

And in the meantime, the nice-looking Frenchman, who might possibly want to carry on an adult conversation with another visitor from a faraway land, was far, far away. When they had been introduced, he had leaned close and murmured, "Of course, Le Boucher is just a nom de guerre, *ma chère madame*." And gave her a look that put a little shiver down her back. *Le Boucher*. The Butcher. A war name, he had said. She was intrigued.

As for her daughter, she didn't know *what* to think. Jo, wearing a frock that looked like something meant for a ten-year-old, puffed sleeves and all, sat meekly across the table, gazing adoringly at Peter, who hardly gave her a glance. Whenever Peter's mother deigned to speak to Jo, she was so eager to answer, she nearly stammered. And halfway through her reply, Dilly's vacant eyes would wander away and she'd say something to someone else. It was all very strange. She'd never seen Jo act this way, never. Except, of course, with Bertha Lazarus. But that was long ago. Dinner was a stilted affair, and, it seemed ages before Reggie suggested they have an after-dinner drink in the drawing room.

They all got up from the ornately carved chairs and removed themselves to the drawing room, a cavernous place where one fire burning in a huge stone fireplace hardly made a dent on the chill dampness. Leah was offered "gin and it" and gladly accepted, though what "it" was, she hadn't the vaguest idea. And nearly spit it out; it tasted like medicine. But she discovered that you quickly got used to the bitterness, and the gin made a nice warm glow in your head.

Then they all took seats on the Victorian furniture and had a conversation. It was like decoding a foreign language. Lord and Lady Fielding spoke mostly to their son, and mostly of county gossip: marriages, affairs, people cut out of other people's wills, and every single person had one of those remarkable British nicknames. Listening to endless talk of Buffy and Pip and Boots was very boring, Leah decided.

And it wasn't a whole lot better when they switched to talk of horse breeding and hunts—and rationing. Rationing was everyone's pet gripe, rationing and the shortage of everything worthwhile. Bicycles and alarm clocks had to be repaired over and over; and there was also a shortage of repairmen. Technical palm oil was used to make margarine. Technical palm oil! It sounded like something used to repair bicycles and alarm clocks.

Leah was becoming quite annoyed with Captain Peter Fielding. Where was his announcement that he had found the love

of his life and that they were planning to be married? Where
were his fond glances at the nervous Jo? Where was there *any*
sign of normal human emotion among the three Fieldings?

Soon, other guests came bursting in—three men in tweed
jackets, bringing with them the scent of the cold outdoors—
and suddenly the room was alive. She could almost *smell* the
change in atmosphere, it was so palpable. One of the men
called out, "After you, Claude!" and the man behind him answered, "No, after *you*, Cecil!" All three Fieldings burst into
laughter.

Dilly was instantly on her feet, trilling out welcomes and in-
troductions; and no one was named Claude *or* Cecil. Either
I'm *really* tired, Leah thought, or I've missed something.

The tall, stooped older man with the long gentle face was
Bertie Delacourt. The younger man was very different in
looks, with hair as thick and eyes as dark and gleaming as a
young bull's; and heavy with muscle, his thighs straining
against his pant legs. That smoldering volcano was Bertie
Delacourt's son Chauncey, called Chummy. *Chummy!*

The third was perhaps twenty-two, skinny and drawn. Using
a cane, he limped across the room. He kept tossing his head
back to get a lock of his long hair off his forehead. He was
Philip Merritt, Pip, the next-door neighbor but one, Dilly dith-
ered, actually one estate down from the Delacourts. "Wounded,
as one can see, in action, the brave darling."

However, it was not the brave darling she fluttered around,
it was the muscular and disgustingly healthy Chummy, her
hands dancing and darting like a pair of pale birds, offering
him tidbits of cake, gin, ale, brandy. He accepted her ministra-
tions with a lordly indifference. He seemed used to it.

Pip accepted a glass of brandy and drained it in one ˈgulp.
His attention was focused on the sofa near the fire where Peter
sat with Jo. Pip seemed unable to take his eyes from them.
Gazing at her daughter, now animated, her hair glowing copper
in the firelight, Leah thought she couldn't blame him for staring. Jo was lovely. A tight look pulled down Pip's mouth.

Pouring another large tot of brandy into his glass, Reggie
said, "Pip is how we know Emile, you see. Pip's plane was
shot down over Normandy . . . wasn't it, old chap? And he sur-
vived. Miracle, they say. Some peasants found him crawling
through the woods and saved his life. And then, dear Emile
brought him out of Occupied France, right under the noses of
the Nazis. Good show, what?"

Murmuring her agreement, Leah turned to study the Frenchman anew, only to find him studying *her*; and when he lifted his glass in salute, she found herself blushing. There was something about him . . . something a bit dangerous and interesting that caused a bubbling in her veins that hadn't been there for years.

As if he could read her thoughts, Emile got up to refill his glass, and bent to her. "May I get you a drink, madame?"

"Leah. Please don't be so formal. No thanks, but perhaps you could explain something to me?"

"But of course, madame. Leah."

"What was that Cecil and Claude routine, just before?"

He laughed. "The British humor!" He rolled his eyes, looking very French. "It is a BBC program, madame, very childish, but exactly to the English taste."

She pretended to be shocked at his remark.

"Forgive me, I forget that I am not in France." He sat down next to her, adding in a low voice, "Which is a shame."

"Really, Monsieur Le Boucher? And why is that?"

"Leah! Did you not say no formality? And now you call me monsieur? For shame!"

"Emile. Why is it a shame we aren't in France, Emile?"

"Because in France, dear lady, eventually I would carry you upstairs and make wonderful love to you."

Leah blinked. She knew he was flirting, but hardly expected such an outright proposition. He put a hand over hers and said, "Excuse me, I beg. I am being perhaps . . . precipitous. But this is wartime, my dear Leah, and who knows what tomorrow may bring? Believe me, tonight you will hear many doors creaking open, so careful, so quiet. But I hear—how do you say it?—the tiptoes along the hall. . . ."

Leaning very close to her, so close she could smell the soap he had used, Emile murmured, "The young Chauncey, he comes here often, and in the night he creeps into my lady's chamber." His eyes widened in mock innocence. "He is a horse breeder . . . for the races. Perhaps they talk of the horses. Or perhaps of breeding . . ."

"Well, I say good for her," Leah exclaimed. "God knows enough old men chase after girls young enough to be their daughters!"

"Then you forgive me for being so—how do you say?—blunt."

"How could I do otherwise, with so charming a man?"

There, she could give as good as she got. He picked up her hand and pressed a kiss on it . . . on the palm, which caused a disturbing sensation to shoot up her arm.

But once he left her side, there was nothing but more interminable talk of horses, foaling, and putting down. That, and the "gin and it," was making her quite groggy. Long before the others were ready to call it an evening, Leah excused herself to go to her chilly bed with the skimpy blanket and the flat pillow. How Jo thought she would be able to live in this place was beyond her! Let her have a fling with her young man, and then decide if she really wanted to marry him and be a part of this family forever.

Peter's parents seemed very calm and casual about every goddamn thing—even about the death of their older son—not to mention the fact that their only remaining child went up in a small plane on a daily basis, to get shot at by other men in small planes. Their composure bordered on lack of interest, in Leah's opinion; but who was she to talk? She hadn't lost a child, her country was not being bombed every night. Maybe that's what you had to do when things became too much to bear: you gave a weekend party where you entertained a mixed bag of guests; and you behaved as if nothing out of the ordinary was going on.

Someone had unpacked her valise and hung up her clothes. That was nice, she thought, yawning hugely. Her new silk pajamas were neatly laid across the bed. She sat on the bed and bounced on it a little, wondering how in the world she would ever get to sleep on its unyielding surface, and with the room so cold. . . .

And the next thing she knew, she was opening her eyes to morning light. In her sleep she had pulled the blanket around herself; but she was still fully dressed.

Later, after a cold bath, she wandered around downstairs until she found the breakfast room—the sideboard laden with gently steaming chafing dishes—but no sign of a human being anywhere around. "The others are about to go out into the meadow, madam," the elderly maid informed her frostily as she poured a second cup of coffee. "*They* et an hour ago." Looking at Leah as if to sleep past seven in the morning was a certain sign of moral turpitude.

Everyone was in the courtyard, seven or eight men and two women, all carrying their shotguns—rifles?—Leah knew nothing about weapons. Lord and Lady Fielding. No Peter, no Jo.

No Emile, either, more's the pity. Once again, she headed for the library and was soon engrossed in Jane Austen.

Luncheon consisted of a quantity of potatoes mashed with "marge," small birds shot that morning and quickly roasted, so quickly that when she stuck a fork into her half bird, the juice ran bloody. Did all of England eat underdone meat? Leah wondered. Jo and Peter were there; and she thought Jo seemed more lively today. Maybe in the night he had tiptoed into her room? Emile, it seemed, had taken a car and motored into the village to send a wire. He would return later. She missed him.

"What does Emile do, exactly?" Leah asked, and found two pairs of accusing eyes blazing at her. "I'm sorry. Is it . . . a secret?"

"Emile came from France, via the Underground. We don't know *what* the chap does, only that he saved Pip. So of course we feel we should extend him our hospitality," Peter announced.

"Well, Peter, I'm sure we're happy to do our part for the war effort. But, if you ask me, Monsieur Le Boucher is a Jew," Lady Fielding said, wrinkling her nose.

Leah would have spoken, but she felt eyes boring into her, and she turned to find Jo silently imploring her to be quiet. She said nothing; she promised herself, however, there would be a good long talk with Jo later. This was an impossible situation for a Jewish girl, no matter how irreligious. And no matter how she felt about Peter, Jo was going to have to extricate herself before she made the mistake of her life.

25

That Night

She had no idea what time it was when the door was—ever so carefully, ever so quietly—opened. The knob turned so noiselessly, it seemed to be turning itself. She opened her eyes, instantly awake, and saw through the worn lace curtains that it was deep into the night, a moon casting its magical blue light through the window, making lacy patterns on the coverlet.

She felt rather than saw him, and then he was there, reaching for her, pulling her into him, bending his head to find her mouth, and finding it. Oh yes, finding it! Warm lips, his mustache, warm tongue, probing and exploring, sucking and licking at her mouth and then her throat and then—the covers thrown back, the pajamas stripped off—her breasts and her belly and her thighs. . . . She moaned, and a hand, laid gently over her mouth, quieted her.

He smelled of . . . something, something wonderful, she didn't know what. Her senses were reeling and spinning. His tongue was everywhere, his fingers, his mouth, his hands. She was on fire, frantic for him, panting like an animal. And then at last, with a jolt like an electric shock, he entered her, and she could feel herself flooding. Leah wanted to scream, but even as he moved closer, farther, deeper, she knew she must not.

When he came, his buttocks pulsating under her hands, he collapsed onto her, kissing her throat, ears, nose. Oh God, that was heavenly. So it was true, what they said about Frenchmen and their educated tongues. And then she froze: What if it wasn't the Frenchman?

Quietly, he began to laugh, whispering: "I can't find your mouth," and of course it was Emile, the accent unmistakable.

There was a candle on the nightstand, she remembered. After a great deal of fumbling and fumfering around in the dark, she managed to get it lighted. He was sprawled out, on his back, his mighty cock lying soft and limp in its bed of fair curly hair. The same blond hair covered his chest—but it did not hide the heavy, bumpy scars. She ran her finger over one, and he said, very low, "I was captured once," as if she had asked a question.

"By the Germans?"

"By the Germans, who else? They do not play nicely. Especially not if . . ." He lifted his penis for her inspection; and she realized suddenly that he was circumcised. "But don't look that way, dear Leah, I escaped . . . as you can see."

"And now you help downed airmen escape. You're very brave."

"Yes, I suppose I am. It comes as quite a surprise to me. I had no idea . . . well, I never *had* to know whether or not I could withstand torture . . . or run through the night, dodging Nazi bullets. In most times, in most lives, such things are not tested."

He looked so sad. Leah reached out and smoothed a lock of hair from his forehead. "Well, you've certainly been tested and *not* found wanting. And, as a Jew, you're taking an even bigger chance than most."

"I don't 'look Jewish,' whatever that means. So I hide it." He grinned impishly and ran his hand over her breast. "Unless, of course, I *cannot* hide it."

"Listen, Emile. I heard the Fieldings talking . . . they know you're a Jew."

"The Fieldings! They know nothing. They see Jews in every corner and under every bed! In fact, I believe they may be Nazi sympathizers——" He stopped talking abruptly. "You must pay no attention to me. *I* see the Boche in every corner!"

Leah thought she really had to talk to Jo. She wouldn't give Emile away, but what kind of a mother would she be if she didn't try to warn Jo?

Perhaps her silence alarmed him; his voice had a sharp edge to it. "I forget. You are a journalist."

She leaned over and gave him a light kiss on his mouth. "A journalist, yes, but a Jew before that. And, in fact, a woman first." She straightened up. "You know I'm a writer; so why did you come tonight?"

"I came to you tonight," he said, reaching out to pull her into him, "because I could not resist. You looked so delicious." Bending his head to kiss her: "And you *are*. You are." As he proceeded to prove how edible, every coherent thought fled her brain.

Jo knew the exact time when she padded out into the dark hallway. There was a cuckoo clock somewhere downstairs, and every time that stupid wooden bird popped out and made its stupid noise, it woke her. It was four A.M.—*ack emma*, as she had learned from Peter—and she was now wide-awake, and not even a good book to read. She was heading downstairs to look for the library.

She felt slightly guilty, creeping about in the middle of the night. But, she told herself, this was going to be her home, and one day it would actually belong to her . . . well, almost; to Peter. So why shouldn't she wander around? In fact, she might go into the pantry and see if there was something to nibble.

She had only picked at her dinner; Peter's parents made her so nervous.

Her heart speeded up when a bedroom door creaked open. She flattened herself against the wall. Not that it would do any good. It was probably Dilly, and she could just imagine Peter's mother giving her the fish eye and saying, in that vague way, "Hungry, at *this* hour? A *book*? To *read*? At this hour? Oh dear, you Yanks really do have odd habits, don't you?"

Thank heaven it wasn't Dilly. It was a man, in his pj's, walking very quietly. Tiptoeing, actually. She shrank back even farther against the wall, hoping he would go the other way; she would be very visible in her white nightie—her very expensive and revealing white nightie—packed in the hopes that Peter might change his mind and knock softly on her door.

The man went only a short distance and opened another door, disappearing inside it. Good. Jo continued down the hallway. But when she got to the door where she had first seen him, and saw a flickering light inside, she realized suddenly that it was her mother's room. Her mother had been visited by a man! A man she hardly knew—it had to be that Frenchman—and they had probably . . . oh, how disgusting! My God, they had just met tonight!

Without knocking, Jo opened the door and slipped in, closing it quietly behind her. Her mother, her thick curly hair out of its pins and falling across her shoulders, was belting her robe.

"Who was that?" Jo demanded, surprised at the harshness of her voice.

Her mother turned, startled. "Don't you believe in knocking?"

"Did *he* knock?"

Her mother's voice was ultracalm, a tone Jo recognized as disguising deep anger. "I would say that's none of your business, Joanna. What are you doing spying on me, anyway?"

"I wasn't spying on you. I couldn't sleep and I caught him leaving." She wrinkled her nose. "This room stinks of sex!"

Leah regarded her. "You should be smacked for that, Jo. What's going on? Why are you so angry?"

"Where does Uncle Jim fit into this little . . . adventure?"

"Don't you worry about Jim. Jim and I are okay. Since you don't know anything about our lives, suppose you just calm down. Do I ask you questions about you and your pilot?"

"He wants to wait until we're married!"

"And you sound mad as hell about it," Leah murmured.

To her surprise, Jo heard herself say, "I am." She plopped down on the edge of the bed and burst into tears. A minute later, feeling her mother's arms around her, she began to cry even harder.

Her mother let her cry for a while, and when she was calmer, said, "Listen to me, Jo. Maybe this isn't such a good idea."

"What isn't?"

"Marrying this man."

"You never call him by his name. It's 'this man' or 'your flyboy.' His name is Peter!"

"Peter, then. Maybe you should think twice about marrying Peter."

"I love him and he loves me."

"Jo, the family is anti-Semitic—"

"That's rot!" Jo burst out. She stared at her mother. "So why don't you tell me *really* why you don't want me to marry Peter."

"I'm telling you really, Jo."

"I think you're jealous. . . ."

"Jealous? Of what?" Her mother gave an irritating little laugh. That did it: if it hadn't been for that condescending laugh, the one that said 'You're stupid,' she wouldn't have gotten so angry.

"Of me, because I'm young, in love, and my life is just beginning. Because I'm going to be rich, with a title and ancestors—"

"Oh, Jo! You know better than that."

"Just because I feel at home here!" That was only half true and she knew it; but she could no longer stem the tide of words. "Just because I've finally found a family!" Bull's-eye! Her mother's eyes filled with tears. "*You* never gave me a family. Big deal, you don't believe in marriage! How do you think that made *me* feel? I've never had a father, never! I've hardly had a mother!"

"Jo! You've had me your whole life! I took you with me everywhere!"

"You never came for me! When Grandmother took me away, I never heard a word from you. You never tried to call. You never wrote me a letter. You just let me go!"

"Jo, that's not true! You know that's not true! We tried and we tried to find you! It was a nightmare."

"I was all alone! Grandmother was the boss of everybody, and I hated her and you didn't want me anymore! If you had wanted me, you would have found me. You would have gone without food and without sleep until you found me!"

"I did, I did! Jo, for God's sake, what *is* this?"

"This is the truth, Mother, dammit! This is the truth!" Jo couldn't stop it; she began sobbing again. "The truth! You let them take me away! I've never been able to forgive you for that!"

There was silence for a few minutes, and when her mother spoke again, it was in a very different voice. "I did not leave you. You were taken from me. My heart ached every minute. I never had a full night's sleep until you were home again. You weren't left! If you want to know what left is, try to imagine your mother taking your hand and leading you to the train station and handing you over to a stranger and then disappearing forever. Imagine that!"

Jo turned to look at her mother. Leah was dry-eyed but very pale. "Mom! Your mother did that to you?" Leah nodded.

Jo put a hand on her mother's arm. "I'm really sorry, Mom, I'm sorry she did that to you. Is *that* why you never talk about your family?" Her mother nodded, her eyes lowered.

"Do you realize what that did to me?" Jo said. "I have no history, none! Peter's family has been in this same house for centuries! There are pictures of all of them. He knows stories about all of them. He's part of something! I'm not part of anything! He has ancestors. I don't have a family I know anything about. When I marry Peter, I'm going to be part of a real family."

"But Jo, you have *me*!" Her mother's lips were quivering. She'd better not start crying; that was not fair. But she did. The tears poured down Leah's cheeks, though she wiped them away with the back of her hand.

Jo couldn't stand watching her mother's helpless tears; she didn't know what she was supposed to *do*. "Don't pull that trick on me!" she cried. "Don't try to make me feel sorry for you. We're not talking about you now. We're talking about me, and about *my* happiness! Peter is sweet and good, he makes me feel taken care of. He's so gentle and kind. You think it's some kind of joke, that we haven't slept together. Well, I think it's wonderful. I think it shows how important our marriage is to him. His parents' politics don't matter to me—"

"Jo, of course it matters! Listen to yourself. Of course it

matters! What's going to happen when they find out you're Jewish?"

"They're not! Hell, I'm not *really* Jewish! You never raised me to be Jewish. I don't even know what it means, for God's sake!"

"You're Jewish," her mother said in a very tired voice. "Don't worry, to anti-Semites, you're Jewish, all right?"

"You don't *know* they're anti-Semites. Anyway, it won't matter. I'll *make* them like me. I want this so badly, Mom, can't you understand? I need so much to *belong* somewhere!"

"Dammit, Jo, didn't you learn *anything* from me? You need to belong to *yourself*! You—"

Jo got up, filled with resolve. "You'll never see my side of it, will you? Well, I'm sorry, but my mind is made up."

"And what about your photography?"

"Right now, Peter is the most important thing in my life. I know you've never felt that way about anyone, but maybe there's something wrong with *you*, Mom. Have you ever thought of that? Maybe you're the odd one, and *I'm* the one on the right track."

"Oh, Jo, I feel this is such a big mistake. . . ."

"Well, that's too damn bad. I'm going to marry him and live right here, at Nether Althorpe. And I'm going to be ecstatically happy. And if you don't like it, you can just lump it. You can just leave on the first train back to London, tomorrow . . . this morning! I'd just as soon you did, anyway, before my future in-laws find out about your . . . your promiscuity."

"You *are* a little prude, aren't you? That's not how I raised you. Never mind. You've already broken my heart. . . ."

Her mother got up and began to get dressed, her back to Jo. "It might interest you to know that your future father-in-law offered to come visit me here in bed this evening—"

Rage swept over Jo like a cold shower. "You have no sense of decency, do you?" she hissed, getting to her feet. She could feel her whole body shaking.

Leah turned. "No sense of decency? *Me?* I didn't ask him if *he'd* like a spot of fun!"

"You're lying, you're lying. You just want to be right. You always have to be right. Well, I'm not listening!"

"I thought you were so big on truth, Jo."

"You're not going to spoil it for me! I won't let you! I want you to leave! I want you to pack your things and get out of here and leave me alone to live my life the way *I* want!"

Jo slammed out of the room and stood in the hall, her pulse hammering in her throat, trying to get herself under control. She waited for her mother to come after her, to prove once and for all that she really wanted her daughter. But her mother did not come for her.

So be it, Jo thought, her heart an ice-cold block in the middle of her chest. So be it. Peter would just have to be her whole family.

26

June 1941

The chapel was small and dim and, to be truthful, a bit damp; but never mind. It was her wedding day, the sun was shining for the moment, and a beam of light had actually found its way through one of the stained-glass windows to throw trembling splotches of ruby and emeralds and amber onto the stone floor. Lovely!

The vicar was in his seventies, and garrulous. Jo had long since stopped listening to him. In fact, she was trying terribly hard not to laugh as he kept losing his train of thought; and she peeped over at Peter, to share her amusement. But Peter would not acknowledge her sideways glances; all she could see was his remote profile, his eyes fixed steadfastly on the minister.

Jo wondered for the umpteenth time just why so few of Peter's friends and relatives had come to see him married. There *were* an aunt and an uncle: Helen and George Holdsworth from Kent, near Maidstone, wherever *that* was. And their daughter Dinah, a sulky eleven-year-old already taller than her mother and extremely self-conscious about it. Also present and sitting, hands folded in laps, were several ladies from the village of Althorpe. There was an old couple, neighbors apparently, another lord and lady. And the neighbors who came over almost every evening: Bertie Delacourt, Chummy Delacourt, and the gaunt, limping Pip Merritt.

"Don't you have other cousins, Peter? Where are they?" she had asked. But his response, said with a smile and a pat to her cheek—"We English aren't big on family, darling"—didn't satisfy.

"After we're married, will you really talk to me?" she asked wistfully. "I want to know what you're thinking, Peter. I want to know *you*."

"Perhaps you won't really want to know me, my sweet Jo."

"Peter, what a dreadful thing to say!"

"Oh God, I'm sorry. Of course it was a dreadful thing to say. Look, darling . . . how do I explain this to you? The English middle class is extremely suspicious of family. Yes, I know it sounds peculiar, and I suppose it is. But it's true. We send our children out of sight and out of mind, just as soon as we can. Nanny and nursery, then public school, then university or the military. You remember the evacuation of children from London—well, of course you do, it's what brought you to England. Middle-class men thought up that scheme, and they were absolutely astonished to find that the working class was fiercely against it. What—people unwilling to part with children? How terribly odd!"

He laughed a little, but she didn't. It was undoubtedly true, but she didn't like to hear it. It made her feel cold all over. Would Peter feel that way about *their* children? Would he want to get rid of them just as quickly as he could?

"You won't do that, will you, Peter? Send our children away where they'll be frightened and alone?"

"Not if you don't want it," he said, pulling her into his embrace.

Of course, she shouldn't complain about the meager showing of his family . . . where were *her* people? Of her friends in England, only Pam had been able to come. She'd found someone to take her duty for her; but she was going to have to rush back to London. The boys at the airfield were "otherwise occupied," as Peter had put it in his dry way. Zelda and Cliff had sent a telegram wishing Jo and Peter "all happiness." And that was it, for family. She was determined *not* to think about her mother. Every time she did, she started to cry. Leah should be here, on her daughter's wedding day. But they hadn't made up. And that meant Jim wasn't here, either. At least *he* should have come, no matter what her mother said to him. Jo had taken his name. He should be here to watch her give it up.

She was sorry now that she had said all those terrible things to her mother. She hadn't realized they were still there, in her mind, just waiting to pop up. That time with her grandparents in Westchester, that awful time . . . Sometimes she had dreams about it, worrisome dreams that woke her in the middle of the night sweating, her heart pounding. But the dreams always faded, leaving nothing behind but a faint feeling of dread. And now, whenever she thought of her quarrel with her mother, she was uneasy. She wished it had never happened. Some things were better left buried. So her mother wasn't married; so what? She and Jim had been together so long, they were as good as! And besides, Jo had long ago forgotten they weren't strictly legal. Her in-laws, of course, had no idea. God, if they ever found out!

But that did *not* excuse her mother's behavior. No decent woman would have allowed a stranger into her room. Just thinking about it made Jo mad. What if Peter or his parents had been up and had seen that Frenchman leaving her mother's room! What would they have thought? It was typical of her mother not to care; but she might have thought of her daughter's happiness!

If her mother had apologized for putting her into such a position, if her mother had only written and said she was sorry . . . But that hadn't happened. The first V-Mail letter that had come, Jo tore open so fast, she made a long jagged tear across it. She was expecting . . . she didn't know *what*. But she didn't get it. The letter from her mother was amusing, full of gossip and tidbits of news, nothing that might be censored, of course. But no apology, not even a regret that she had left so hurriedly.

Jo had ripped the letter into tiny pieces, and when other letters came, she tore them up without reading them. Let her mother see what it felt like, to have *her* feelings ignored.

Jo stole another look at Peter. He would never treat her the way his father treated his mother. He was so sweet, so romantic. They would cuddle together in the old sofa in the drawing room, watching the flames in the fireplace, sipping sherry, and he would talk about the children they would have, the jolly times ahead of them. "The line will continue. Oh, my darling Jo, the line will go on, and all because I have found you." Then they would kiss and kiss and her heart would melt. She only hoped she deserved his devotion.

The Reverend Hawkes asked Peter to place the ring on her finger. She turned to face her beloved, with all her love shining out to him. But his eyes were lowered and his hand trembled as he slid the ring on. Poor darling, so nervous. Didn't he know she would love him forever, no matter what? And when the vicar asked her if she was ready to stick by Peter through sickness and health, for better, for worse, until death did them part, she nearly shouted out her "I will!" That brought Peter's head up, and his eyes finally met hers and he smiled.

It was chilly in the garden, even with the sun shining bravely and the daffodils blooming against the stone wall. But Dilly had been determined they should toast the newlyweds out "under God's own blue skies." So there they huddled, the women's hair blowing out of the neat rolls and pompadours, and the vicar's robes whipping about his legs.

"Oh dear, it does look like rain, doesn't it? Well, my dears, let us drink to the newlyweds' health and happiness, and then in to tea by the fire!" As Dilly spoke, Speakes, the elderly butler, limped among them, pouring out tiny amounts of sparkling wine.

"To Peter and his bride, may they have many sons!" That was Lord Fielding. Jo thought, And what about daughters? Don't *we* count? But she knew the answer. No, girls did not count. Girls could not inherit. And when Jo had asked why not, "After all, you did pretty well under Queen Elizabeth and Queen Victoria!" Dilly just looked at her oddly.

And now Reg was calling for three cheers. Hip, hip— hooray! Hip, hip—hooray! Hip, hip—hooray! Peter bent to Jo and gave her a long, lingering kiss, while they all applauded and laughed. Jo closed her eyes and thought, I'm in an English garden. I'm married. I'm Lady Fielding. I'm wearing a dress made from Peter's great-grandmother's dressing gown, and I'm about to go in with the vicar and townspeople and have high tea. A wave of absolute happiness washed over her. When she opened her eyes, she saw Peter's smiling face above her, and above him, wisps of cloud racing away. Good-bye clouds, good-bye rain, Jo thought. This is my wedding day, the happiest day of my life. No rain allowed.

Inside, the fire was blazing, and the warmth felt heavenly. Thin sandwiches and several kinds of plain cake and scones were offered. "Raisins!" the vicar cried. "Wherever in the world did you find raisins?" And then he colored and apologized, because one *never* asked where one's friends or relatives or parishioners "found" their various forbidden, rationed good-ies.

"The raisins in the scones must be a gift from God!" Peter quipped. Jo gazed at him. He could be a "clever lad," as the vicar had called him at some point during that interminable sermon.

She was determined to be happy this afternoon, with a room full of guests wishing her well, a table laden with good food, a fire crackling on the hearth. If it hadn't been for all the war talk, you'd never know you were in a nation being bombed nightly and threatened every day on the radio from Germany.

The latest talk was of Hitler's declaring war on Russia. "The fellow's mad, of course," Bertie proclaimed. "Quite mad! Look at Napolean, what? The whole thing's impossible!"

"He's taken over every other country he wanted," said one of the ladies. "Why not Russia?"

"Damn thing's immense, Polly! Look at a map, what?"

Lord Fielding agreed. "Fellow's made a major mistake there!"

"But darling," cried Dilly, "doesn't he have several armies all marching at once? How can those poor Russians withstand it? And you know," she added, as a gossipy side thought, "they aren't trained soldiers. They killed off all the nobility . . . so sad. It hasn't been the same since the Revolution, you know."

"The Russian winter, Mother," Peter said, sipping at his scotch and water. "You'll see . . . Jerry will seem to be win-ning just so long as it's warm. And then . . . he'll be soundly beat."

And Pip added, in a lugubrious tone, "They'll all die in the Russian steppes, in the snow. But at least then the war will be over."

"Oh Pip, that's utter nonsense! You won't see an end to this war until our so-called friends, the Yanks, get off the pot—"

Someone shushed the speaker, creating an awkward silence. At that point, Jo wandered off to look out the window at the watery landscape. Did they imagine that she minded being thought of as "the Yank girl"? Well, she didn't, and anyway, she had just been seized with the most unusual notion: that she should not be drifting about this drawing room in Bucking-hamshire in a made-over wedding dress. She should be putting on trousers and trench coat, packing her gear, and hitching a plane ride to the Russian front. *Someone* with a camera was going to go there and shoot the whole thing. She thought it would probably be Margaret Bourke-White, but why shouldn't it be Joanna McCready Fielding?

She stood by the window, not really seeing anything, frozen with indecision. In her mind she saw herself running from the room, tearing up the stairs two at a time, changing her clothes, and coming back down to announce to the stunned and astonished assembly that she was terribly sorry to interrupt her wedding festivities, but there *was* a war on, you know, and it was her job to put it down for history.

But when she turned from the window and saw Peter across the room, she stopped. She loved him. She had never known anyone like him. Nobody like him had ever noticed her; nobody like him would ever notice her again. She had lucked out, and if she didn't grab her chance, she would grow old and lonely, all alone.

There were more shrieks of laughter now. Someone was acting out a recent ITMA show and they were doubled over about the Minister of Aggravation and Mysteries and the mayor of Foaming-at-the-Mouth. Even a man who had taken a first at Oxford could shout, "I go—I come back," and weep with helpless laughter. As Peter was doing right this minute. He was . . . so adorable. She was so lucky to have found him. The vision of herself on a snowy battlefield with her beloved Leica just faded away.

She wished her mother were here, to see her get married, to see how happy she really was. And then she nearly laughed aloud. Because she was standing alone, staring out at the endless rain, wishing her wedding guests gone and blinking back tears. Her mother would say, I told you so, I told you it was a mistake to marry him. Or worse, she'd find it all terribly amusing. Well, to hell with her mother!

Today was her wedding day, and there should be stupid dirty jokes and endless toasts . . . she should be dancing cheek to cheek with her new husband! Her wedding guests had stopped joking and had turned back to the favorite topic of all: the war. The war!

She was Mrs. Peter Fielding now—Joanna McCready Fielding—and it was time she tended to her company. A big smile on her face, Jo turned and cried out, "Who can find some dance music on the radio? We should all dance at a wedding, shouldn't we?" To her utter amazement, everyone applauded and agreed. Pip limped over to the big old set in the corner to see if he could tune in one of the London hotels.

Dilly fluttered over to give Jo a vague kiss on her cheek. "Poor darling, this hasn't been much of a party, has it? Never mind, the christening for the first son will make up for it. The war will be over and rationing will be off and we'll have plenty of everything . . . and . . . oh dear, Chummy needs me, do excuse . . ."

Plenty of everything. It sounded lovely, but Jo knew it wasn't quite true. Peter had explained it all to her, about the laws of 1925—or was it '26—that instituted death duties . . . "and how nobody could keep their large holdings because the moment the old lord died, half the place had to be sold to pay the tax inspector. Not to mention that there was very little cash now."

So they only had two farms instead of thirty, and only part of the woods and only three orchards and one topiary garden and two ponds, where there used to be miles and miles of Fielding property. But since the Fielding property seemed endless and huge to Jo, all such talk of poverty made no sense. She had grown up in four rooms . . . and even *that* wasn't theirs, they didn't own it.

"The Last Time I Saw Paris" came over the radio, and everyone in the room began to sing and change partners. There were smiles all around, and Jo's heart lifted. It was turning into a real party. Peter, an arm still around her waist, turned to where Pip sat by the fire, alone.

"Pip, old chap, come have a turn around the floor with my bride. Oh do, old fellow, it will do you worlds of good."

Pip flushed deeply, and Jo could feel the color climbing in her own cheeks. He always scuttled away, like a shy animal, if she happened to come near him. And when she tried to strike up a conversation, his eyes never met hers.

"Jo doesn't mind your game leg, do you, darling?"

Jo said, as sincerely as she could manage, "Of course not. Would you care to dance, Pip?"

He pushed himself up and put his arm gingerly on her waist, barely touching the fingertips of her other hand. He so obviously did not want to do this. Was it his bad leg . . . or was it her? Actually, he didn't move badly; the limp was much less pronounced than when he walked. And he had a nice sense of rhythm. But he held her at arm's length and, even now, refused to meet her gaze.

"Pip, why don't you like me? I like *you*." The words just popped out.

He blushed, started to speak, stopped and then burst out with: "Damnation!"

"Pardon me?"

"I say! I *am* sorry, Joanna. I didn't mean you. I'm a goose. I like you, of course I like you. I . . . look here, Peter and I grew up together, he's my oldest friend. We went to Sandringham together, hated it together, came down from Oxford together, joined up together. . . . D'you see, just a little? The shock, I mean . . . the surprise, to suddenly find him engaged. Coming back here was difficult enough, what with the pitying looks and so on . . . but in a way, you see, I was hoping that everything else would be the same. Silly of me, wasn't it, wanting time to stand still. No, wanting it to move backward—to a happier time, I suppose."

This long speech had come gushing out of him, without pause, and so earnestly. She almost couldn't believe the sudden change.

He stopped dancing and looked directly at her. "See here, Joanna, let me be truly honest. I've been terribly angry at you—for messing up the sameness, you see. I've been an idiot. Can you ever forgive? Do say yes. I feel so foolish."

How could she resist? She threw her arms around his neck and gave him a big hug. "Of course. Nothing would make me happier."

"Good." He stayed tense in her embrace, so she let go and stepped back. "Then, as a friend, I'll admit my leg is giving me bloody hell right now. Would you mind . . . ?"

"Oh no! Please, sit down. Let me get you a drink." He did look pinched and pale. He must be in dreadful pain . . . and all she could think of was her own hurt feelings! When she got back with his drink, he downed it in one gulp.

"Much better, thanks ever so. But go along, Joanna, your guests will be missing you."

Nothing could be further from the truth, Jo thought, looking around the room at the animated little groups. *A stranger at my own wedding. What a stupid state of affairs.* She felt she'd made great strides with Pip; he had actually told her something real, right from the heart. They might even end up being friends, given enough time.

Then Peter came for her. "I claim my bride," he said, with such a glow about him, her heart melted all over again. Everyone said the Brits, especially the country people, were impossible to get to know, that it took forever to be invited

anywhere. But that wouldn't happen to her. She was Peter's
bride. She belonged.

They didn't go upstairs to their bedroom until nearly midnight. They climbed the stairs, her heart thumping away like
crazy, Peter yawning. She hoped . . . well, she didn't know
what she hoped. Oh yes, she did! She giggled, and Peter, tightening his arm around her waist, said, "What?"

"Nothing, darling. Just . . . I can't believe we're really married!"

"Well, we are, we are, and it's forever." He stopped right
there on the stairs and took her in his arms and they kissed,
such a melting, lovely kiss. She was flooded with her happiness.

The bedroom had been all prepared for them: a fire blazing;
the bedclothes turned back invitingly; his pj's laid out on one
side. And on the other side, her nightgown and negligee, white
with frothy lace.

Peter closed the door. "Well . . ." he said. "Here we are."

"Yes. Here we are." They both stood, irresolute and shy, unable to move on to the next thing—whatever that was. Jo had
a notion that she should disappear into the bathroom and reappear in her nightclothes, and that Peter should do the same.

"I'll go get dressed . . . undressed . . . dressed. . . ." She
stumbled over the words and then began to laugh. "Oh, Peter,
aren't we the fools? We're *married*!"

"Quite right." He was laughing, too. "So why don't you get
dressedundressed and I'll pour us each a tot of brandy."

"Oh, that would be wonderful." She all but ran to the bathroom, and once there, took extra pains with her appearance,
brushing and rebrushing her hair, pinching her cheeks for
color, putting on lipstick and then wiping it off so that only a
blush of pink remained. She stared into the mirror. Was she a
beautiful bride? Nobody had said so. She didn't look exotic or
unusual; she looked Irish, with her auburn hair and green eyes
and high cheekbones. Maybe the English didn't think Irish was
beautiful. Peter thought she was beautiful. She was sure he did.

When she came out from the bathroom, feeling very self-
conscious in the revealing silk, he looked at her and bit his
lower lip. "My God, but you are gorgeous. I *have* had a bit of
luck, haven't I?" He had changed and was in pj's and a navy-
blue silk robe. He looked so elegant.

She ran to him, throwing her arms around him. "I'm the
lucky one, Peter," she said into his neck. "Some days, I have

to pinch myself, because I can't believe my luck." He bent to her, kissing her deeply, and together they fell onto the bed. She could feel herself becoming dizzy with heat and love; and she pressed herself to him. Peter pushed the negligee from her shoulders, pulled down the skinny little straps, and freed her breasts. Immediately he put his lips to a nipple and began kissing it, making her feel breathless and strange. He moved his lips up to her throat and to her lips, pushing his fingers deep into her most private place. It wasn't long before she was writhing on the bed in a frenzy, wanting, wanting—

"Oh God, Peter, darling, please, please . . ."

Jo waited for him to enter her. She knew she should feel something: a jolt, a shock, a . . . she didn't know what. But he reached down and once again his fingers entered her and oh, it felt so good. She lifted her backside to get that delicious sensation even deeper inside. He pushed his hips against hers, faster and faster, and she found herself matching his movements, his rhythm. Now, she kept thinking, now, Peter, *now!*

"Oh Jo, I'm so sorry, darling. I'm so sorry. I don't know what—I can't—oh dear God, I thought— Jo, can you ever forgive me? You know I love you, but— I will make it up to you, I'll— Jo, please say you understand. Forgive me."

Her eyes were wide open, staring up into the darkness, seeing nothing. Forgive him for *what*? Make up for *what*? But really, she knew. He hadn't got hard. She tried to blink back the tears that crowded her eyes, but they slid down her cheeks anyway. What had happened? He had seemed so passionate. What had she done? Something had gone wrong and it must be her fault.

He was making horrible sobbing sounds into her shoulder.

"Of course," she soothed, "darling, of course, Peter, of course, of course . . ." she murmured into his ear. "Don't worry about it. I love you. I'll get better at it, you'll see. It'll all be better, and I love you. We're going to be just fine."

27

April 1944

They walked out of the theater into the bright sunshine and the
bustle of Piccadilly. Jo blinked and shook her head, trying to
clear it. She loved seeing films in the daytime—it made her
feel young and wicked, as if she were skipping class—but it
always left her disoriented for a few minutes.

"God, what an experience. Who would have thought Shake-
speare could be so . . . so modern?" she said.

Elias smiled at her; his eyes were exactly level with hers.
She liked that. There was none of this tipping one's girlish
head back and gazing up adoringly at the big strong man sort
of thing. They were on equal terms—in everything.

"I knew you'd like it," Elias said, very pleased with himself.
"He's an extraordinary actor, Olivier. And that was a glorious
Hamlet, don't you think?"

"I had never pictured Hamlet as muscular and good-looking.
I've never pictured Hamlet as . . . a real person. But now that
I've seen Olivier, I can't imagine him any other way."

"Who . . . Olivier?"

"No, silly . . . Hamlet." They grinned at each other. Ever
since they had become lovers, Jo had begun smiling again.

It was just dumb luck, meeting each other. If she hadn't
started roaming the countryside near Nether Althorpe, camera
in hand, looking for something to fill up her empty life; if she
hadn't taken a dozen pictures into London, looking for frames
to put them in—old, cheap ones mostly; if Elias hadn't been
meandering through Covent Garden market, looking for old
photographs to add to his collection . . . If, if, if. But it had all
happened, just like a novel, only better because it was real. Because it was *them*.

"Where to now?" Elias asked, imitating a British accent. "Lyons for a cuppa?"

"Not thirsty," she said.

"A sandwich, then?"

"Not hungry."

"Ah. Well, then, back to my flat and to bed."

"Righty-ho, mate," she said, using her best and broadest accent. "For a spot of rub and tickle, hey?" His answer was to pull her in tightly against him. She could feel herself getting wet already, her heart speeding up in anticipation. Soon, soon, she would feel his mouth, his lips, his tongue . . . oh God, his cock, his stiff, hard, erect rod. Something dear old Peter could not usually manage. Peter didn't like to talk about it, but she had gotten a mumbled admission from him last year that, no, he had never found the act of sex very satisfying. He said he felt passion, and with effort he had orgasms, but it was rare for him to get really hard. And when she suggested he might want to see a doctor about it . . . well, she might as well have said, "Why don't you print up a notice in the London *Times*?" So he did nothing and he could never really do it. But Elias Blanchard could. Oh God, yes, could he ever!

In the beginning Peter had tried valiantly to be a real husband to her. But it usually ended the same way, with him sweating and swearing, only half hard; and she, staring up at the dark ceiling, waiting for it to be over. And yet, one of those times, Sarah was conceived. Somehow, a sperm made its way up that long narrow passageway and found a waiting egg. And she had her beautiful darling little girl, born in April of '42, while Peter was away on duty. Sarah looked like a baby doll, with wide light eyes set far apart and a fuzz of dark hair.

The name was Peter's idea; Jo never would have suggested it. To her, it sounded biblical, old-fashioned, and, yes, let's face it, Jewish. But Reg's Mum had been Sarah, though she was called Sally her whole life. That's where Jo put her foot down. No Sally. Sarah was her name, and Sarah she would be called.

Jo would never forget Peter's first look at his daughter. He looked joyfully stunned, if such a thing could be. He stared down into the cradle—a family heirloom, naturally—at the little pink bundle with its flower face, and smiled with pure happiness. Putting out one gentle finger, he touched her satin cheek. "My daughter," he said softly; and then he turned to Jo and added, "Our daughter. I shall never be able to thank you enough."

"For what?"

"For giving me this child."

"She's only a girl and cannot inherit."

"Ah, Jo, that's unworthy of you."

"You're right, Peter. I apologize. And I'm terribly happy we have her. I don't mind at all she's not a boy."

"Nor do I. We're a family," he said, and once again that smile of unadulterated delight spread over his face, and she realized he had thought he would never father a child. Poor Peter.

She spent every waking moment with Sarah, and nobody could object, because she was nursing. That was an embarrassment to everyone, and she was expected to do the dirty deed in the privacy of her own bedchamber, which delighted her. They left her alone, at least. She wasn't supposed to be able to get pregnant while she was breast-feeding, and yet she did. She supposed it had happened in much the same way as Sarah's conception, during one of those rare times Peter got hard enough to do something.

Timothy Peter Fielding was born on New Year's Day, 1943. It was a hard labor; he was a breech, and by the time he finally was born, Jo was exhausted. She took a look at him to make sure he was all right, turned her head and fell asleep.

Peter got leave to come home for Timmy's christening, preening himself and parading around with "my son and heir" as if he'd done it all himself. There was a spate of jokes about his sexual prowess and potency . . . how he'd managed to put a loaf in the oven while the first was still cooling, that sort of thing. And he ate it up. Everyone brought elaborate gifts of silver and silver gilt: cups and plates and spoons and mugs and porringers, as well as tiny pistols and tiny riding crops. She found herself annoyed by his display of self-congratulation.

She said not a word to anyone, just held it all in. A mistake, of course. And the next time Peter struggled to have sex with her, she found herself saying, "Oh, and I thought you were so damned manly, Peter. I thought you had some magic potion, to have produced a son." The minute she said it, she could have bit her tongue out, he looked so hurt. So she apologized and snuggled up to him, hugging and kissing him, pretending to be excited.

He kept saying it was probably only nervousness . . . it was overstimulation . . . it was exhaustion. And she kept saying maybe it was something medical; but *that*, he wouldn't hear of.

And it never got much better. She even used some of the techniques she found in Lord Fielding's collection of pornography—Peter knew where the books were hidden—but nothing helped, not even when she did exactly what Peter said would excite him.

And then Peter began to berate her. "I'm horny as can be," he would say. "There must be something wrong with you. And I'm getting damned tired of this humiliation." When Timmy was three months old, Peter began to sleep in another room when he came home.

She believed him. She really thought that there was something she was doing—or wasn't doing. Or maybe there was just something off-putting about her. She *had* been a tomboy as a teenager. But once she met Elias, she learned how quickly and urgently a man could respond to her. And Elias assured her that he was far from unique, that she was really an attractive woman.

To think they might never have met. It just happened. She had come in to London on the train, as she often did when Peter was on duty. It was last summer, during an English heat wave, which meant the temperature got to seventy.

She had just finished a series of twelve photographs of the woods and meadows of Nether Althorpe, and had given herself the job of finding old frames for them. God knows she had nothing *real* to do. Dilly and Reg still ran the household—very unusual, Peter explained, because in normal times they would have moved out of the big house, leaving it to the new heir and his wife . . . "but the war, you know." Oh yes, the war, she knew!

So she had no responsibility in her own household. A nanny, Brenda MacPherson, had total charge of the two children, and there she was, idle, bored, restless. So she began to take pictures again—it was not considered quite the thing; but to hell with them. What did they expect her to do: fill her life with arranging the flowers in the chapel, or running the jumble sale at the church? And her pictures were good, dammit! Well, of course they were good. It was so strange, how she had to remind herself that only a few years ago she had been on her own in England, dashing about the countryside in a Jeep, taking on dangerous assignments, selling her photographs everywhere. How quickly she had taken on protective coloration. How thoroughly she had made herself into the perfect picture of Lady Joanna. But she wasn't really Lady Joanna. What she really *was*, she was determined to find out.

And that was how she happened to be wandering about the Covent Garden stalls, rummaging through piles of frames. She was holding her favorite picture in her hand, an eight-by-ten of the meadows. Shot through the very edge of the forest, so that the picture was dark and mysterious at its edges, opening up into a center of serene and misty sunlight. The clouds had parted, letting through four or five rays of light that morning, making it look like all those pictures of God speaking from heaven. It was a lovely picture; she felt good every time she looked at it.

Well, and there she was, not at all glamorous, her long hair pulled back and tied with a scarf, wearing slacks and one of Peter's old sweaters and a rather worn mac because it had been threatening rain when she left Althorpe station. Rooting through a pile of dusty old frames—sneezing a lot, too—she found a rather nice frame. It was not too ornate, but had some interesting doodads cut into the corners. She held the photograph behind it, to see how it looked.

And this voice, this really nice male voice with just a hint of a French—or was it Italian?—accent, said: "I say, that's really outstanding!"

She turned, startled. "Yes, it is rather pretty, isn't it? I'd give a shilling for it, provided it would clean up nicely."

He laughed. "Not the frame, mademoiselle. The photograph. I am something of an ... expert, you see, and it's quite fine. Might I look more closely, do you think?"

"Madame," she corrected.

He looked at her oddly and when she said, "What? *What?*" he just shook his head and said, "Nothing, I thought when I first saw you that we had met, but I was wrong." He was already engrossed in studying the picture. Funny thing, she felt the same way: that she had met him before. She didn't recognize his face; it was something about his voice.

"You called me mademoiselle," she said. "But you see, I'm an old married woman with children."

"By chance, are you an old married woman with children who marches about the shires of England with a four-by-five camera, taking splendid pictures of misty meadows in the early morning hours?"

"Yes, that's exactly who I am." She couldn't help smiling, he was so jolly and friendly.

"Excellent. Come have tea, and perhaps we can do some business."

Now it was her turn to say "Excuse me?"

Again he laughed. "Ten thousand pardons, madame. Allow me to introduce myself. I am Elias Blanchard, dealer in art. Oh yes, quite legitimate, I do assure you. I am not—what do the Yanks say?—picking you up. Do you have other photos with you? Would you be willing to let me look them over? To try to sell them?"

"Nobody buys photographs as art! And, monsieur . . . sir . . ." What in the world was he up to, this smiling, smooth-talking man with the smashed nose and the long scar down one cheek and the too-long, rather lank dirty blond hair. What was his game?

"So spirited, so American, so, forgive me, *young* . . ." he murmured, looking terribly amused. "I consider you an artist, madame. And by the way, are you aware that you have smudged your face, handling these ancient frames?"

"Oh, dear—" She began to wipe at her nose and chin, but what was the use, without a mirror? To her utter amazement, no, stupefaction was a much better word, this perfect stranger reached into a pocket and brought out a snowy white handkerchief, with which he proceeded to wipe off the dirt, as if she were a small child. She was so astonished, she just stood there and let him clean her face. But apparently her surprise was obvious, for when he had finished and looked her over, he burst into laughter.

"You will please forgive me, mademoi—madame. You had a look on your face . . . a look I have seen on my five-year-old niece who wishes I would go away and stop bothering her. I should have asked your permission. I have been at war, as perhaps you can tell, and my ways are still a little . . . rough, perhaps. Without subtlety. But now you are quite, quite clean, and fit to be seen in, for example, a little café I saw on my way from the tube stop. Some few souls in England realize that there is art to be had from the camera, dear lady, and several of them are my customers. May we at least talk a little? I will show you all my bona fides, and then perhaps the suspicious look will fade from your pretty face."

Jo blushed. It had been donkey's years since anyone had paid her a compliment. Englishmen, she had discovered, were not demonstrative . . . at least, not the Englishmen *she* saw every day. The British were a strange race: repressed and stilted

and secretive, but somehow admirable in spite of it. She eyed
this engaging stranger—she had to admit, the interested glint in
his eye was very seductive—and decided, Why not? It was
only a cup of tea, after all.

But after all, it was not only a cup of tea. They started to
talk as he led the way to the café, and they never stopped, really. She found herself becoming very animated, expressing
thoughts and ideas she had only vaguely been aware of. And
now, out it all came: her pictures for *Story*, her Eagle Squadron
stuff, her pictures of children hurt by war, of families coping
despite war. Her hopes, her dreams, her ambitions. Everything.
"And then . . ."

"Yes? And then?" He laid his hand over her briefly, and her
heart began to race. "And then?"

"And then . . . well, I met Peter and, well, I fell in love."

"And that is the end of your story, Joanna? You met Peter
and you fell in love?"

"And got married, of course. And had children. And . . . and
here I am."

"And your husband? Where is he?"

She knew she was treading on very shaky ground. Nonethe-
less, swallowing hard, she said, "I think he was over Essen last
night, although of course I can't be sure. He's RAF . . . a pilot."

"Essen . . . ah yes, the new night assaults. It seems the British are indestructible. They are going to win the war, you
know." Once again his hand covered hers, and his voice lowering, he added, "But your husband, I think, is losing you, am
I not right?"

She longed to tell him everything, just spill her guts; let it
all out. But she couldn't! Not to a stranger, a man who had, after all, just picked her up in the flea market. To her chagrin,
her eyes filled with sudden tears. His hand tightened on hers.
She should thank him for tea and catch the next train.

Instead, when he suddenly said, "Come. We are leaving
now," she obeyed. Like a puppet on his string, she followed
him through crooked lanes and narrow back streets, until they
came to a wooden fence with a gate. He opened the gate and
there, hidden away from view, was a mews, six tiny houses
that had once been stables. He took out a key, opened the door
to the last one, and taking her hand, led her up a narrow flight
of stairs.

At the top of the stairs he drew her inside. Then standing

very close to her, he peeled the coat from her, letting it drop to the floor. His also fell to the ground. All the time, his eyes never left hers. His eyes glowed, rapt but not feral.

"You are a beautiful woman, Joanna," he murmured, "and soon you will believe that. Yes, soon, very soon." As he spoke he took her hand and put it firmly on his belly, where there was a long, hard protrusion. Her gasp told him everything he wanted to know. Five minutes later they were entwined on his bed, panting, moaning, thrashing, rolling about. When he finally pushed himself deep into her with a grunt, she yelled out, "Yes! Yes! Yes!" and he laughed. And thrust himself in again and again until he had her screaming, and then sat himself on the edge of the bed and had her impale herself. Rivulets of sweat ran down her sides and her back and from under her breasts. She was soaking wet everywhere, inside and out, and he was indefatigable, smiling into her eyes as he lunged and plunged and jabbed and stabbed his great bursting thing into the very center of her being. And when it was over, and they both came in a series of shudders, she lay in the damp sheets with his streaming body still glued to hers, and she knew what she had been missing all this time. And she was furious with Peter, for cheating her and then making her take the blame.

She fell asleep, they both did, and when she came awake with a start, it was dusk and she was filled with guilt and remorse. She had been away all day. She leapt up and raced into the tiny W.C., using a dampened towel to wash herself off. When he knocked on the door, she cried out, "I'll be out in a minute! Don't come in!" Wrapping herself in a skimpy towel, she sidled out, her bare back against the wall.

He laughed and then stopped abruptly. "Ah, but Joanna, that was . . . it was *magnifique* . . . it was smashing, as the English say. Why do you act this way? I think it has been a very long time since a man made beautiful love to you."

How could she tell him it was never? Oh God, and she had allowed herself to be seduced—so easily!—by a sexy Frenchman who probably haunted Covent Garden, hoping to see some absent soldier's wife, preferably one who looked sex-starved and naive.

"I must be off. I'm late, they'll worry." She could hardly bring herself to look at him.

He muttered to himself in French, then said, "Joanna, I am very attracted to you, I was from the first. I do not make a habit of seducing every woman who browses the stalls, looking for a bargain. No, I do not look for a bargain in sex. It . . . happened. It was meant to be. It will happen again."

At the last sentence he came up to her and put a hand on her cheek, turning her head, forcing her to look at him. And the terrible thing was, the moment she did, she was ready to jump right back into that damp and sweaty bed and start all over again.

"Yes," he said, sounding satisfied, "it will happen again. And it will be even better." And he kissed the tip of her nose.

Well, he had been right, hadn't he? There was no way, having tasted such delights, that she could stay away from him. And it had been so easy, especially since he really was interested in her work, and had put her photographs on display in his gallery. Nobody questioned her going into town to have "business meetings" with her representative. In any case, nobody cared where she went or how long she stayed. She had done her job and had presented the Fielding family with an heir. Now she could busy herself any way she chose and no questions asked.

Reg and Dilly had found her odd from the very beginning. It wasn't only her early morning tramps in the dewy misty fields with a camera, of all the things. They had looked askance at the amount of time she spent with Sarah, playing games with her and reading stories and drawing pictures. Dilly had hired Nanny MacPherson the minute Timothy was born, and insisted that Jo "take it easy." As a result, Jo had somehow never made the same connection to her little boy as she had to Sarah. Timmy was a sweet little thing, but placid and pale, unlike his vivid and temperamental sister.

Jo couldn't help resenting him because, once he was born, the Fielding's interest in Sarah, who was bright and full of life, ended. To make it up to Sarah, Jo paid the little girl extra attention, and when Timmy clamored for it, she found herself becoming irritated. What an unnatural mother she was! Oh God, this whole marriage had been one big mistake, from beginning to end.

But now, at least, she was free to take the train down to London, even though Reg made many snide comments about his daughter-in-law "flogging her little snaps on the streets of London," as if she was some stupid amateur housewife. But after all, she *had* sold two pictures, damned if Reg could figure out why. So he contented himself with his stupid jokes and made no move to stop her.

Jo wondered whether Dilly guessed why her son's wife visited her art gallery so frequently, and why she stayed in the city so late. Jo had long ago guessed where Dilly spent long hours, in the afternoons, when she was supposed to be exercising the horses. Once, bringing a message to the stables from the vet, Jo had found the place deserted. She walked around, hoping to find a stablehand having a quiet lunch in the back; and instead had heard, from upstairs over the tack room, the unmistakable sounds of two people in the throes of passion. And then, clearly, she heard Dilly's voice urging Chummy on to greater efforts, yes, darling, yes, my angel, yes! And Jo had fled.

One day, not long after that, wandering around the house aimlessly, she had drifted into the pantry and had overheard Cook talking to Nancy MacPherson. "Had her eye on 'im since he was twelve, she did. And by the time he was fourteen, she 'ad seduced the lad and was 'avin 'im service 'er regular like. . . ."

"Did you ever!" said Nanny.

"Insatiable, she is. A regular what'd'youcallit . . . nymphomaniac." A sly little chuckle. "There's them as says she wore 'is Lordship's thing to a nubbin, so's it's no use to nobody." The two women had a good laugh over that one, and the cook added, "But it's a damn shame, *I* say, for 'e's enchanted, like, the young cock. 'Is father wants 'im to marry, but 'e can't, not 'e. She 'as tricks to keep 'im, as no decent woman knows."

Jo had tiptoed away from that one. She wondered idly if the story was true. . . . Oh, not that it was so unnatural for a young man to screw an older woman, but that Dilly had gone after Chummy while he was only an adolescent.

Elias nudged her and said, "Here we are. Why are you just standing there, staring into space? I thought you were so eager to make love!" He laughed.

They were at the mews; she had just walked along like a wind-up toy, not knowing where she was, lost in memories.

"I am, I am." She leaned over to give him an open-mouthed kiss. His response was, as always, instantaneous and ecstatic.

She pulled away from him, laughing. "Let's go upstairs. Poor Peter . . . to think he'll never know. And what an unkind joke, to give him that name, when his peter won't work . . . when it peters out all the time."

Jo caught the four-sixteen back to Althorpe, feeling wonderfully relaxed and hugging her newest secret to herself. Elias thought she was ready for a show. He was prepared to give over the entire back room of the gallery to her work, to call the press, to send out leaflets and letters . . . the works.

"I want you to bring in your strongest stuff, do you understand, Joanna? No pretty flower gardens, no sweet old ladies, nothing that will make people feel all warm and fuzzy. Grit, that's what's wanted."

"Ugly old ladies, with warts on their noses?"

"Yes, dammit, if that's how you see England."

"Oh, Elias, what's the use? Nobody will buy them."

"But we don't care, *ma belle*. We only want the bigshots to look and to see and to—how do you say it?—take you seriously."

"My in-laws will never get it."

"To the devil with your in-laws."

As her train pulled into the dark and empty little station, she had decided she agreed. To the devil with what anyone thought; either she was an artist or she wasn't. It was time to stand up and be counted. But God, it was scary!

When she let herself into the house, there wasn't a sound anywhere, and she wondered what had happened to everyone. Then she remembered the church fete. The children had been looking forward to it for weeks, and plans had been made for the entire family to go. She could have saved herself the taxi fare and walked to the church from the station. Well, as long as she was here, she might as well freshen up.

She took the stairs two at a time, smiling still at her memories from the afternoon. And then, at the top, she stopped dead in her tracks. Sounds from one of the bedrooms, strange strangled sounds. She tiptoed nervously down the hallway. A dim wavery light was coming from under the door of Peter's room. But Peter was on duty. So, what could be . . . ? She listened again, but the sounds had stopped.

She opened the door, peeking around it in case he was there and sleeping. And her heart nearly stopped beating, for there on the bed, entwined and doing unspeakable things, their naked bodies washed by the light of three fat candles on the dresser, were her husband—and another man!

She must have made a noise, because both heads rose up as one, and two pairs of eyes stared guiltily at her. It was Pip. The other man was Pip, and all she could see was his mouth, all wet and shiny. She turned suddenly and bolted down the hall to her own room and her own bathroom. She knelt over the toilet bowl, trying to vomit, *needing* to vomit . . . but nothing would come up, though her gut convulsed over and over again.

Finally her stomach stopped churning and she stood, feeling weak and depleted, but realizing that with her quick look into that room, her whole life had changed completely. She had to change her clothes and get into the village. She felt crazy and disoriented. Peter had turned her world upside down and topsy-turvy. She kept seeing them, writhing on the bed, moaning—oh God, it was horrible. Horrible! She didn't want to think about it. She wanted only to be with her children, and get ahold of her sanity again.

She got out of her clothes, throwing them in a heap onto the floor, and then scrubbed herself with a cold sponge, shivering but needing to feel clean. Quickly, she pulled on fresh clothing and raced down the hallway to the stairs.

"Jo! Joanna! Wait! Please, Jo!" Peter's voice.

"Don't come near me!" she shouted, surprised at the hysteria in her voice. "Don't come near me!" Down the stairs she flew.

"Jo, for God's sake, can't we talk about this?"

"No!"

"But . . . what are you going to do?" His voice was plaintive and panicked, all at the same time. She swallowed fiercely. She was not going to let this destroy her, she was *not*.

At the bottom of the stairs, pausing only long enough to snatch up her mac and scarf, she yelled back, "I don't know, Peter. I really don't know!"

28

May 1945

"Bang! Bang! I got you, you lousy Nazi! Die like a dog!"

"Woof!"

"You aren't *really* a dog, Timmy! And you can't say anything; you're dead!"

"Am not!"

"Timmy, you *have* to be dead! Remember, when we planned it?"

"Not dead! Don't *wanna!*" Heartbroken sobs.

"Children, children, for heaven's sake, you're giving me a splitting headache!" Dilly trilled. "And anyway, you sillies, the war is over. No more war games!"

"But Gran—"

"Good grief, child, hasn't Nanny taught you manners? MacPherson! MacPherson!" she shouted. "Where *is* that woman when she's wanted? Never to be found!"

"I'll find her," Jo said. "I'm in need of a breath of air, anyway." Talk about splitting headaches, she thought, the constant sound of Dilly's voice was giving her a killer-diller.

Just then Nanny MacPherson *loomed* in the doorway, which was very strange, Jo thought, considering she was a tiny thing. But inside—an Amazon, with a will of steel. MacPherson snapped her fingers, and both kids instantly got up and started for the door. Like trained animals, Jo thought. Not at all her idea of how children should be treated; but she had to remember that they were English and she wasn't; that they would be here their whole lives.

"Give Mummy a kiss before you go!" Jo called out. They both came trotting back eagerly; but not, she noted sadly, before checking with Nanny first. She hugged them both extra tight. If she wasn't careful, they'd grow up feeling she'd ignored them, and she mustn't let that happen!

What kept haunting her was how Peter had tried to warn her—the day of the wedding, wasn't it?—that the British don't like being close with their children . . . and made sure to keep them out of sight. She had been so shocked, and now look: she was sitting here and letting it happen. But that was how it was done in upper-crust British society; the children had to learn sooner or later, she thought.

"Ah, and here are the men, back from their ride." A strong smell of horse preceded the four of them.

"Now, you'll see," Reg said as they came pushing through the French doors, heading for the decanters. "Churchill will be voted out, got rid of, just like that!" He snapped his fingers.

"Nonsense, dear fellow." That was Bertie. They were always on opposite sides of any argument. "He kept our chin up, he kept our spirits up. Nobody will want to let him down now, will they?"

"Wrong, old chap, bloody wrong. You mark my words . . . Irish?"

"Scotch today, I think."

"Where's Chummy?" Dilly interrupted. "And really, Reg, I wish you would watch your language when there are ladies present."

"Awfully sorry, m'dear. I forget. As for Chum—he's 'round here somewhere," Reg said. "Now don't you worry your head about him, Dilly dear, and do stop fussing."

Reg plopped himself down into a leather chair. "Merry month of May, what? Roosevelt dead, Hitler dead, war over, Churchill on his way out—pish, pish, Bertie, just wait until there's an election and you'll see! It's a new world, ladies, a brand-new world, and I say let's drink to it." He held his glass aloft.

Chummy walked in at that moment and cried, "Wait till I have a glass in my hand to lift!"

Laughter at that. Then Dilly got up to fix his drink, and decided the ladies should drink, too. So it was several minutes before all glasses were filled and raised to toast "the new world and whatever wonders it may bring. I promise you this, ladies and gentlemen, we have seen the end of an era. From now on, it's a new game, with new rules and new players."

"Reg!" his wife protested. "That's so gloomy, darling! We've won, you know!"

Jo was bemused. New game, new players, new rules. And she had barely got used to the old ones! The only England she knew, really, was wartime England. What would it be like now, in peace? Peter had been away, on duty—or so he said—so much that she had no idea what it might be like to have him around all the time. Forever, she reminded herself, or anyway, till death did them part. What would she *do*? What would *he* do? Raise horses? Oversee the tenants? Oh my God, what would *they* do?

It simply had not occurred to her that one day the war would be over and life would return to normal—whatever *that* was. And now here it was. The day had come. Was she supposed to lie in her marriage bed alone, trying not to think about what she had seen that afternoon? Was she expected to look the other way as Peter and Pip mooned after each other? When he did whatever it was he did when he wasn't in her bed? And what if he insisted they try again to have a normal marriage, as he'd already done several times?

Most importantly, would she be expected to give up her lover, now that her husband was around? She knew one thing for certain: she could not bear to have Peter's hands on her, or his lips . . . not any part of him.

For six months now she had not so much as looked at her camera, but spent her time working on the church ladies committee, playing the Gypsy fortune-teller in last Sunday's fete; supervising the village women as they sorted out things for the jumble sale; even going to church with Peter, on the occasions when he came home for a visit.

It suddenly occurred to her that now she would have to spend an hour in that chapel with Peter every Sunday of her life. If there was a God, she thought, He must be doubled over with laughter at *that* prospect.

She had decided to give up on photography, after the fiasco of her show at Elias's gallery last September. She had reprinted many of her favorite shots of blasted London and had traveled into the country to get others. They named it "Britain Indomitable," and when the pictures had all been matted, framed, and hung on the gallery walls, she had walked back and forth, loving them; feeling such pride; thinking, *I* did this, I really did.

She thought people would find them poignant: the soccer game in the bomb crater; the wall half torn away in the Blitz, revealing a ruffled boudoir; the family sitting to table, saying grace in a makeshift shack built from rubble; an elderly priest kneeling over a wounded youngster.

But most of the critics did not find her photos moving. One called her pictures "unfeminine" and another had announced himself "disgusted by the emphasis on the ugly and unsightly." The night she stood in the partially darkened gallery as they dismantled the show, her arms full of her work, she began to weep. Elias took the photos, put them down, and, grasping her shoulders, looked deep into her eyes.

"You shouldn't care. Sales aren't what matter. The critics aren't what matter. This was only your first show, and everyone knows the English don't know good art when they see it. Wait till I take these to Paris! As soon as the war is over. I promise you! The French understand! But I think, first I'll have them made into a book . . . or maybe, wait, no, take the show to Amsterdam, and to New York—places where you'll be appreciated!"

But she was too hurt to hear him. She had put her best work out for the world to see, and the world had spit on them. Enough was enough. Elias pointed out that not *every* critic was negative; several found her full of promise, although one hoped she would find "subjects more suitable to the female sex."

"Remember what we promised ourselves?" he urged. "That we wouldn't care what anyone thought?"

"Oh fine, Elias! But who is it getting reviled? Us? Or just me? You know how Peter's parents reacted!"

Reg had pronounced her work "ugly rubbish." Oh, he didn't mean her to hear it—maybe—but she had heard it. She also heard Dilly soothing him, reassuring him that Joanna would settle down to a normal life as soon as her husband was home.

"I'm just glad my mother didn't come and see my public humiliation!" Jo told Elias. But she was lying; she wished Leah had come. She wished her mother had at least sent her a telegram or a letter. But there was only silence. She had waited too long to make amends, she guessed. "But I'll never have to worry about her snubbing another show, because there won't *be* another!"

"Ah, Jo, you don't really mean that."

But she did. She had meant every word. Only now, in the damp and chilly drawing room of Nether Althorpe, she was beginning to see her future as endless evenings of boring din-

ners, of stupid village gossip . . . oh God! What had she done
to herself?

She turned her head to regard the others in the drawing
room: Chummy sitting low in an armchair; Dilly, curled up in
her kittenish way at his feet. And hunkered close by the fire in
the cracked leather chairs, backs turned to the two lovers—
deliberately?—the two older men, the decanter within arm's
reach, harumphing and galumphing their same old debates. She
need only add Peter to the picture . . . oh yes, and Pip, chatting
like the old friends they were, and maybe with their eyes holding quite a different conversation.

There it was: her life, with one important person missing.
Herself. How was she going to face years of this and not go
crazy?

And suddenly the thought blazed before her, as if written in
neon: GO HOME. She could go home. But of course that was
crazy. What was she talking about? She couldn't "go home."
This was her home. She was a married woman, the mother of
two; she wasn't a child anymore; and she and her mother had
not spoken in years.

In any case, Peter would *never* stand for her taking the children to the States; especially not his son and heir. Where
would she go and how would she earn a living, with two small
children clinging to her skirts? No, no, it was quite impossible.
And what about Elias? Elias, who took her into ecstasy, where
for a short time she could forget everything. How could she
leave him, forever?

Jakes, the elderly butler, came shuffling into the room.
"Lady Fielding . . ." he ventured. Both Jo and Dilly turned to
him. He cleared his throat and corrected himself: "Lady
Joanna."

"Yes, Jakes?" She jumped to her feet with surprise.

"A visitor, m'lady. A foreign female person."

Curious, she hurried to follow him. Not someone Jakes considered quality, or he would have referred to her as a *lady*. One
of the church women . . . no, Jakes knew all of them by name.
Pam? But what about Pam would cause the old snob to label
her a female person?

There, in the great hall, looking around with interest, was a
tall broad-shouldered woman, a stranger in a baggy tweed suit
and sturdy walking shoes. Her thick salt and pepper hair had
been cropped even with her chin, and she wore no jewelry.
What could she be wanting? And then she turned to Jo. Her

strong face, robust and tanned, had only a hint of lipstick on the wide mouth. Not a pretty face, but a nice one.

"Jo! You can't have forgotten me?" Ah, the voice—the voice was unmistakable.

"Oh my God! Zelda! Aunt Zelda!"

They rushed at each other and embraced tightly. The tweed jacket was scratchy and Zelda smelled of the outdoors, of heather and grass. "Oh Zelda, I'm so happy to see you! So happy! I was just thinking about home and missing it! Oh God, I'm so glad you're here! I can't tell you how glad!" And suddenly burst into tears.

Zelda stopped. "Whoa!" she said, surprised. "You're gonna make me think you're crying at my cheap tweed suit! Well, it's all they had. Usually, you know, I'm in coveralls, or at the very least, slacks. Oh Jo, please, please, tell me it's not this suit!"

Jo shook her head, beginning to laugh in the middle of the unexpected and wild weeping. *No, no, it's not you. It's me,* she wanted to say; but her voice wouldn't work.

Zelda's voice changed, became tender. "Shall I sing to you, kiddo? That always used to make you smile."

"Oh God, Zelda, I'm sorry." Swallowing hard and swiping at the tears, she finally managed to talk. "You don't have to sing to make me smile. See? I'm smiling." And to her surprise, she was. "You know what, though? I don't know any of the new songs! Do you believe that? Leah Lazarus's little girl, not knowing all the words?" Once again tears threatened.

"Well, we gotta get you singing again, kiddo!"

"You said it, Zelda! You said a mouthful." She grabbed the warm, callused hand and held onto it for dear life. How wonderful to see her! Time had dealt kindly with Zelda—time and the cropped hair fluffed out over her cheeks, which made less of the heavy chin. She wasn't exactly beautiful, but she *was* attractive. She looked competent, brisk, and—what was that look?—happy. Happy, that was it. An emotion Jo had not felt for a very long time.

"Cliff and I get all the American music on the shortwave. 'A hubba hubba hubba, hello Jack, well a hubba hubba hubba, just got back.' " She sang a bit off-key, just like always, which made them both laugh. "Yeah, it's been a long, long war, kiddo. Speaking of which, how's your hubby? Is he coming home soon?"

"Funny you should ask . . . I was just thinking about that. But come on into the drawing room and meet my in-laws—"

"First things first, kiddo. I've never seen your kids!"

For some reason, the tears began again. She heard a sympathetic noise from Zelda, and felt her aunt's hand around her shoulder.

"No, no, don't worry about me, Zelda. I'll be fine, honest. It's ... it must be homesickness. I haven't seen anyone from my family in a long time. Come on upstairs to the nursery."

As they started up the stairs, Jo noticed Jakes, still standing unobtrusively in a far corner of the great hall, his hands folded in front of him, his bright beady eyes following them with interest. Oh God, what did he make of all this? Her sobbing and weeping like a lost child at the sight of a strange woman. He'd probably run into the kitchen the moment they were out of sight, and give his report to Cook.

Both children turned startled faces at the unexpected intrusion. As for Nanny, her lips tightened just a trifle as she said, "We were about to have tea, m'lady."

"Well, we'll just join you in a cup of tea," Zelda boomed, ignoring Nanny's hard looks and striding right in. "Hi, kids, I'm your great-aunt Zelda. D'you think we'll all fit in a cup of tea?" She waited, but the two round pairs of eyes regarded her solemnly. No smiles. Well, they were too young to get jokes, weren't they? Sarah was just past three, and Timmy was still a baby. "I've come down from Scotland to celebrate V-E Day with my family," Zelda went right on, ignoring the fact that her gag had fallen flat.

"You don't sound Scottish," Sarah protested. "You don't sound like Nanny, and Nanny comes from Scotland."

"Well, I've only been staying in Scotland. I come from the U.S.A., just like your mum."

"What are you doing in Scotland?"

"Knitting balaclavas and doing farm chores, mostly. But every once in a while they let me gas up the planes." That got them; they stared up with new respect at this apparition who, however strange, had something to do with aircraft.

"Do you fly a airplane, like Daddy?"

"Don't I wish! I am a pilot. Yes, that's right, really, truly, cross my heart and hope to die. But they haven't let me fly a plane here, although sometimes they let me drive a lorry. Oh aye, a wee lassie lak me isna ta be trusted aboot great machines that fly oop in the sky!" she added with a twinkle. Now the children both giggled, their eyes flitting to Nanny for the okay. Suddenly Jo remembered how Zelda had always been good at imitations, as was she herself, come to think of it. Zelda could sing just like Al Jolson or Bing Crosby. She used to do Amos and Andy, too, and most of the other characters on the show. And she could do a wicked caricature of Grandmother Bertha's voice and manner. Recalling it, Jo giggled, too. That was something *else* that had gone from her repertoire lately: giggling.

They stayed in the nursery for tea, hunkering down on tiny nursery chairs to do so, and pretending to love the pudding, which was soupy and tasteless. Jo thought of the wonderful meals her mom used to concoct: pancakes and bacon with real maple syrup; or thick soup made from everything in the kitchen, eaten with slabs of fresh pumpernickle slathered with butter; or lamb chops with baked potatoes ... whatever they felt like. Her poor children were being raised on gruel and pap and thin slices of white bread. No wonder they were both so slight and pale! She'd have to talk to Cook.

Nanny was so obviously disapproving, Jo stayed on longer than she really wanted to, out of spite. Brenda MacPherson often seemed to forget who paid her wages, seemed to forget she was there to serve, not to glare and heave great sighs of impatience. Finally Jo took pity on her and said, "Come on, Zelda, we can't keep you a secret much longer. I'm sure Jakes has spread the word in the scullery, that we have a guest, and the guest has been taken to the *nursery* first!"

"That's bad, huh?"

"The worst!" They laughed. It felt good to laugh; it felt good to be with another American, to be with her own family. They dared each other to slide down the long curved banister but in the end settled for a race down the stairs. Which Jo barely won.

So they were both a little bit breathless and still laughing when they stepped into the drawing room. All four heads turned as one, like puppets pulled by a single string, to see what on earth the commotion was all about.

"Joanna's *aunt*? But ... how terribly strange, that we haven't met you before now."

"Well, I was in Scotland with my friend, who has spent most of the war teaching RAF pilots. He's with the RCAF. I'm a volunteer general dogsbody. We wanted to come down for the wedding, but it was not on, as you English say. And then ... well, to tell the truth, we did a bit of traveling, thanks to the Air Ministry, and weren't available. I really cannot say more than that."

"Your, ah . . . *friend*," Reg said pointedly. "A man, I presume?" When Zelda nodded, he went on: "Is he here with you?"

"No, I'm afraid not. He's in London. At some meeting with some high mucky-mucks. I took the opportunity to come here. . . . Well, actually, I took the train from Victoria Station, as all opportunities were closed."

Jo giggled; nobody else did. They stared at Zelda much the way the children had: as if she were a visitor from another planet—a planet that didn't smell quite right, from the looks of them. And that made her giggle even more.

In a few minutes Jo excused them both, saying she wanted to show Zelda the horses before she had to get back, and they escaped.

They tramped up and down in front of the stalls, patting the gentle heads that poked out, and talking talking talking.

"Your friend Cliff . . ."

"Clifford Armbruster. Major Clifford Armbruster, if you please." Zelda blushed a bit. It was endearing.

"You're happy?"

"Oh, very! You don't know what—never mind, kiddo. Let's just say I count myself lucky, finding love so late in life. Your mother says—"

"My mother. How is she, Zelda?"

Zelda clucked a bit. "Not a bit happy that you've estranged yourself so completely."

"Me! Well . . . I admit I started it. . . . It was stupid, I admit that, too. But I sent her a letter about the show—the show of my photographs—and I never heard from her, not one word. So I figured she was still mad at me."

"Gee, kiddo, she wrote me that she was really excited about your show and was trying to get herself a seat on a plane. But it was almost impossible, you know. They bump you if some general or admiral or Secretary of Whatsis wants to go to London . . . and usually *somebody* important does. But I know she was hoping!"

"Well, all I know is, I never heard anything from her." If they kept talking about it, Jo knew she'd start crying again. "Let's hear more about your . . . your guy, your . . . boyfriend?"

"My lover, Jo. It's okay, you can say it. Although he's been saying maybe we should get hitched when we get back home."

"Married! Oh, Zelda, how exciting! Can I be your bridesmaid, or bridesmatron, or whatever?"

"Sure thing, kiddo. *If* we get married. I don't know if marriage is for me."

"Oh, you will, you will, I just know it! So tell me about him. Come on, give!"

Zelda laughed. "Well, first of all, I guess he's not anyone's idea of a dreamboat—except for me, of course. But he's a helluva guy and a helluva pilot. Flying's in his blood, you know. His father was one of the old barnstormers—the guys who came out of the Lafayette Escadrille after W.W. One and couldn't stop flying. His dad was killed in a crash in 'twenty-three, doing some kind of triple loop or something that had never been done before. The other guys at the airfield, they took on Cliff, like a foster son. So, his manners are sometimes just a little rough. But inside, he's a real gentleman, with real soft feelings."

"He sounds like he might deserve you, Zelda. How did you meet? Either Mom didn't say or I wasn't interested. But I am now."

Zelda leaned up against one of the stalls and folded her arms. "I went up to a little airfield in Westchester, in White Plains, to see if I could get lessons. I even cut my hair, and went to the Salvation Army store and got men's clothes and a cap and . . . Well, I told them my name was Zachary. I shouldn't say 'them'—it was Cliff I talked to. And he said, sure, he'd give me lessons, but he'd better warn me, not everyone was gaited to fly."

"What made you want to?"

"You knew Amelia Earhart was my idol. I couldn't tell you why—maybe because flying in the sky, so light and free, was the exact opposite of my life. Well, when she disappeared . . . I don't know . . . I just said to myself, It's now or never, kiddo."

"And so you learned to fly," Jo prodded. "Dressed like a man."

Zelda laughed and, pushing herself away from the wall, began to pace again. "Let's walk. I've spent too many hours on a train. Yes, dressed like a man, thinking I had him fooled. We became good buddies, you know. It got so I just swaggered in, without my heart missing a single beat. And then, when I wanted to get my license, Cliff took me into his office and shut the door and poured us each a shot of rye whiskey and he said, 'Look, Zack. I don't know your real name, but I do know you're a woman. And you're going to need some ID if you want—' "

"That's all I heard, Jo. I felt myself turn fiery red. I was so horribly humiliated. All this time, I'd been so cocksure—excuse the pun—and all this time, I hadn't fooled *anyone*. What an idiot I was! I ran out of the office and got a train back to the city and I didn't go back."

"Oh, Zelda! But how did he find you?"

"He didn't find me. How could he? I only knew I wished he would. So I got all dolled-up, mascara, lipstick, crepe dress, stockings, Cuban heels, even a little hat with a veil! Nobody's ever seen me look like that, not before, not since!" She hooted with laughter. "But it was worth it, to see the look on Cliff's face, to hear the way he said, 'Zack!' like it was a prayer. Well, he didn't waste a minute, just reached out and kissed me and then, cool as a cucumber, said, 'Like I was saying, if you want a license, you'll need ID and some more airtime, so when would you like to start?' "

"And that was it?"

"The rest, like they say, is history."

"God, Zelda, that's the most romantic story I've ever heard. What does Cliff look like?"

"He's shorter than me and younger than me and weighs ten pounds less than me, and he's not Jewish—I'm not sure which damned him the most in my mother's eyes. Of course, she threatened to have a heart attack, and damned if my father didn't, instead!"

"Is he . . . did he . . . ?"

"Dead? Die? Yes, Jo, three years ago. He left my mother a very rich widow, which pleased her immensely. And within the year, she was married to one of his competitors. So now she's Mrs. Harvey Newman, consort of the zipper king, with a mansion on Long Island. I understand she devotes herself to Mr. Newman's children and grandchildren, who have the good taste not to be freaks of nature—unlike some people I could mention."

"Oh, Zelda, she was awful to you, wasn't she?"

"Yeah, you could say that. But hey, that's a long time ago, so don't go feeling sorry for me, Jo. You just make sure *you've* got what you really want."

"I hope you don't think I made a mistake," Jo heard herself saying stiffly, "just because I cried when I saw you. It was only that I hadn't seen you in so long."

"Kiddo, you looked and sounded miserable. . . . Hey! Never mind! I've forgotten it. Just . . . take care of yourself, will you?"

"I guess I'll have to, since nobody else has ever bothered!"

"Aw, Jo . . . go easy on your mother, why don't you? She really loves you, and she always did."

They were walking back to the house, and Jo avoided answering. She had to call for a taxi to come fetch Zelda and take her to the train station; the family automobile was once again inoperative and was waiting for the one mechanic in Althorpe to come home from the army.

But Zelda would not be diverted. "Your mother, kiddo. And Jim. They both care about you. Always did. Don't forget that."

"My mother! She was always working on a story. She lived the Bohemian life, dragging me all over the place. She let your mother take me away. She had boyfriends, never got married . . . What kind of an upbringing do you think that was, for a kid? A mother who's constantly busy, or distracted, or traveling, or in love, or involved in some cause or other! No thanks. That's why I married Peter, really. Because his family's been here forever and the life is stable and normal and—"

She stopped dead, dumbstruck. What in hell was she saying? That her life at Nether Althorpe was stable and normal and happy and peaceful? What sort of fairy tales was she telling herself, for God's sake? That she was different from her mother! That she wasn't making the same mistakes! Hell, she was just like her mother, she saw that now.

"Hey, kiddo, snap out of it. What's wrong?"

"What's wrong? I'm not sure, Zelda. Maybe everything." This struck her funny, for some strange reason, and she began to laugh. "And maybe nothing. Tell you what, though. I'll let you know just as soon as I figure it out."

29

September 1946

The great lawn, spread out on either side of the old church, was very festive, with its colorful tented booths and bright home-sewn banners flying and flapping in the breeze. Lady Joanna Fielding looked about her with satisfaction. The ladies had outdone themselves, and the fine weather would bring out everyone within a fifteen-mile radius. They should collect quite a few shillings and pence for the Church Tower Fund.

She glanced down at the notes in her hand, rehearsing her little speech. . . . Ladies and gentlemen, honored guests, Vicar Blahblah, welcome, we are delighted to see so many and so forth, in such a worthy cause etcetera etcetera, and now, a few words from our own beloved Vicar Hawkes, and then a graceful inclination of the head, three steps backward and finished. It was the first time Jo would open the fete; usually Dilly did the honors. But Dilly had insisted—"Now that our dear hero is back home, it's time you took on all the duties of the lady of the manor, Joanna dear."

Jo had smiled dutifully. Dear hero indeed. If dear Edward hadn't been blown to bits in his tank in North Africa, dear Peter would hardly be welcome to *visit* Nether Althorpe, hero or no hero. He'd be just the younger son, counting for exactly nothing, and expected to go quietly away and get along somehow. And they, all of them, including Sarah and Timmy, would be poor relations. Poor relations were a cut below the servants, discussed on a yearly basis to see whether or not they were "suitable" to be invited for the Christmas festivities.

In fact, as had been pointed out to her more than once, now that the war was over and Peter was home for good, Dilly and Reg were expected to move out of their large apartment— which by rights belonged to the lord and lady of the manor—

and go live in the second-best rooms down the hall. And consider themselves lucky there was still a place for them at Nether Althorpe.

Standing in the rich golden sunlight, Jo shivered. The longer she stayed in England, the more alien she felt. Well, it wouldn't *be* much longer, she'd made up her mind to that.

The only reason she was still there was because Peter had begged her: "Just one more chance, Jo darling, give us one more year. I do so want it to work out." Well, it had been over a year, more like a year and a half since she had agreed.

Somehow, the days and weeks had melted into months and there never was a right time to make her move. When Peter first came home, he was so exhausted, so thin and pale, she didn't have the heart. Then the children got chicken pox, one after the other, and then they both had measles, and Timmy was terribly ill. Jo spent whole days in his darkened room, singing and telling him stories. When they were over that hurdle, she was simply exhausted.

So when Peter came to her, his eyes soft with regret, and begged her forgiveness, she was too tired to argue.

"I hate being this way, darling, really, so awfully much. Perhaps if we tried something . . . novel." Oh God, she thought, what now? She dropped her eyes, sighed and said, "For instance?"

"Well . . . perhaps if you took it in your mouth . . . oh, Jo, do forgive me, but I do so want . . ." His voice trailed off with shame.

She wanted to laugh and cry, all at the same time. Did he think she had never heard of fellatio, that she had never done it, that it would disgust her? How little he knew her, she who had tried everything that came from the fertile imagination of Elias Blanchard, and loved it all!

For a while, out of compassion, she tried all sorts of things: dressing in men's underwear, turning over and having him take her from the back. That worked—sort of—for a while. And then there was that wonderful day when he suggested, very hesitantly, that perhaps the three of them—what three?—why he and Jo and Pip, of course; he found the idea of sharing her with Pip terribly arousing. The blood rushed to her head.

"Over my dead body, Peter, do you hear me? What a disgusting idea! And you actually thought I'd *go* for it? Get out!"

After that, he never came into her room at night; and she had heaved a great sigh of relief that it was over at last.

Sighing now, Jo went to the platform, erected under the thick and gnarled limbs of an ancient oak, to give her speech. For a moment she admired the picture framed by a crook in the old tree: a branch with its jagged-edged leaves made a stark outline for the green and gold distant meadow where two ponies and two men stood out in sharp, shadowed relief. One of the men was Peter. She averted her eyes from her husband in habitual distaste and began her speech, letting the practiced words come out automatically.

". . . and now, our dear vicar, Mr. Hawkes, will ask the Lord for His blessing on our autumn fete," she finished. Stepping aside for the old man, she held his elbow to make sure he didn't trip on one of the huge tree roots. There was a spattering of applause. Just then a cloud that had been cutting off the sunshine moved on and a blaze of light warmed the lawn.

"I think the Lord has just given us His blessing," quavered Mr. Hawkes. More applause. Laughter. A general bustle as, ceremonies over, the crowd prepared to enjoy themselves.

"Mummy! Mummy! May we go on the ponies?" Sarah came running to her, her eyes shining, Timmy on his chubby legs puffing along behind. Sarah loved horses, and the grooms said she was a natural. Jo had made up her mind to have her take instruction. If she had a talent, it should be fostered.

"Of course you may. Now, Sarah . . ." She knelt so their eyes were level. "I know you aren't frightened a bit, and that you like to trot. But your brother copies you, and if you go too fast, he'll go too fast and he'll just plop right off."

The little girl giggled a bit, but then pouted. "Why can't Timmy do something by himself, Mummy? Why does he always have to come along? Then I can't do what *I* like! It isn't fair!"

"We have to protect those who are younger and weaker—"

"And dumber!"

"Sarah! Timothy is not dumb, he's just little."

"Am not little! I'm big!" Timmy came running up and flung himself at Jo. "Aren't I, Mummy? Aren't I a big boy!"

A voice from above them said, "Certainly you are, Timmy, a great big boy, and Daddy will take you on the big horse!"

Peter reached down and lifted Timmy away from her. He doted on the child, who was a miniature of himself, with his sandy coloring and pale, expressive eyes.

"Take me, too, Daddy! I can ride, I know how!"

"Now Sarah," Peter said gravely. "You know what we've

discussed about jealousy. I shall take Timmy on my horse because he can't ride alone. You can, and you shall go on the pony."

"But Daddy, it's not *fair!*"

"Now stop pouting ... it's most unattractive, you know. 'There was a little girl, who had a little curl right in the middle of her forehead,' " he quoted, even though he knew Sarah hated it. " 'When she was good, she was very very good, and when she was bad she was horrid.' "

"I'm not horrid! I'm not!" Two bright spots flared up on her cheeks and her little fists clenched.

"Little girls who yell and scream in public are generally considered horrid." And he was gone, with large definite strides, Timmy riding on his shoulders.

Jo looked after him, hating him. Everyone said he "favored the little one," as if it were perfectly all right. Well, it wasn't. Sarah was his child, too. Just because she was a girl—! Jo couldn't stand it. She had to *do* something about the situation. She had to think, to plan, and to start moving, for God's sake.

"Mummy ..." Sarah was tugging at her skirt.

"Go with Nanny, darling."

"But Timmy gets to go on—"

"Sarah, darling, I know it's not fair, and I intend to do something about it. But right now, I really would like you to go with Nanny, understand? You're a smashing rider. You can show the others how it's done. Go ride the ponies. Will you do that, please?"

Jo didn't wait for an answer, but hurried away. She would put a call in right this minute to a steamship line. She had some money put aside. This ... this *charade* had come to an end.

Genevieve, the vicar's daughter, was cozily ensconced in the office with her friend Polly Crawford. The two women were sipping at cups of tea and nibbling from a plate of digestive biscuits, gossiping in low voices. As soon as Jo appeared, they both jumped guiltily to their feet and began to apologize, their words tripping over each other. Oh, Lady Joanna, they had no idea ... they weren't due at the jumble table until three ... would she like to join them ... They'd be right along. ... Oh, the telephone. Oh, yes certainly, just give them a moment to clear away ...

"No, no. No, *really*. You've both worked *so* hard, you deserve your cup of tea and your rest. My telephoning can wait,

really it can. I'll just go back out and make sure our Gypsy
fortune-teller's shown up."

It was wrong, it was all wrong! She wasn't Lady Joanna
Fielding; hell, she wasn't lady *anyone*! What was she doing
here, where she didn't belong?

Out in the sunlight, she looked around at the charming little
village, the charming little green with a babbling brook running through it, the charming old church with its rotting bell
tower, the charming fete which she, in her flowered frock and
leather pumps, had opened. Had *opened*! Playing at lady of the
manor was for Dilly. She should have been prowling around
with her Leica. When had she stopped being herself and become a character in an English story? And immediately, she
thought of the family portrait.

Last New Year's, Peter had insisted they have a family picture taken, by a traveling photographer. He had been after her
to take it, but she had refused. "I'm not a portrait photographer," she told him, and he seemed to accept that. So they all
got dressed up in their finery and posed on the least worn of
the sofas and smiled until their jaws ached. The photographer,
William Wordsworth—"yes," as he told them with his nervous
laugh, "like the poet"—scampered about, arranging legs and
fluffing out skirts and tucking in stray hairs, and finally disappeared under his big black cloth, inviting them to watch the
birdie. But every time she looked at the picture, hanging in the
drawing room in its large gilt frame, she felt sick.

What a good-looking family they were: the tall, slim, fair father, handsome though thinned down, and never mind his sad
eyes; the tall handsome mother with her high cheekbones and
large breasts and full, dissatisfied mouth, her hair a glossy
pageboy. The little boy, the image of his father, his hair cut
like all little English boys' hair, in a medieval bob with bangs,
his legs neatly crossed, his hands on his knees, such a good little boy. And the little girl, the stranger in their midst, so dark,
so exotic, with her wild, curly black hair; her vivid face. She
would grow to be a beauty, that one, but she looked alien. Everyone commented on it, and Reg called her his little Eyetalian
or little Turk. She looked like Joe Lazarus; like he did in the
pictures Jo had studied so carefully when she was a child, as
if she could get to know the father she'd never known if she
stared hard enough. Sarah looked Jewish. It was a great joke,
Jo thought. But it wasn't a joke. She had run away from herself, from everything she was, and this was her punishment, to

be in this strange land, married to a stranger, and wondering how to survive.

They were all back at the manor house in time for tea. As Jo started up the stairs for her bedroom, Jakes called to her.

"Madam, the postman delivered this today. He said the King's government apologizes to you."

She reached out to take a tattered and battered and torn letter . . . V-Mail, just barely legible, looking as if it had gone through the entire war. The postmark was over a year old; well, that happened every once in a while. And then she recognized her mother's handwriting and ripped it open. It was the letter Leah had sent her, saying she would do her damnedest to get to London for Jo's show but it was almost impossible. "Whatever I try, whoever I ask, I'm given the same response: 'Hey lady doncha know there's a war on?' But I know it will be great; you were good when you were five years old. . . ."

Jo stopped reading; she had to. She and Leah had been writing to each other ever since Zelda's visit in '45. But that this particular letter should come, on this particular day, when she had just been making up her mind she had to leave . . . ! It was a sign, an omen. She turned and went right back down the stairs, into the little closet under the staircase where they hid the telephone—as if there were something slightly shameful about the instrument. Transatlantic calls took forever, but never mind that. She had all day, she had all night. She tried to figure out what time it was in New York, if it was teatime here. Was it seven hours later? Earlier? Six? But she was too excited to add or subtract.

Then she sat on the stairs, and had Jakes bring her a cocktail while she waited for the operator to put the call through. Right here, madam? Yes, Jakes, right here, on this step.

She was on her third gin and lime, her head just beginning to buzz a bit, when the phone sounded its double ring. Up she jumped, and shouted "Yes?" into the mouthpiece, her heart banging away like a drum.

Then she heard her mother's voice, also shouting: "Jo! Is it really you? Oh God, is it *really* you?" And they were both bawling like a couple of babies, and it felt *so* good.

"I'm coming home, Mom!"

"Did I hear right? Did you say you're coming home?"

"Yes, I'm coming home! Home! Right away, as soon as I can!"

And just then the lot of them came into the hall—Peter and his parents—and stood there, staring at her. Peter was frowning. She waved them to wait a minute and ended the conversation, saying she'd send a telegram with details.

"Whatever are you talking about, darling?" Peter's voice sounded calm, but she thought she saw panic in his eyes. She no longer cared.

"I've decided—" she began, but the sounds of running feet and excited voices stopped her. They all turned as Nanny MacPherson came running into the hall. "M'lady! M'lady! Come quickly! Sarah has fallen from a horse!"

They followed her at a dead run, through the dining room, through the scullery and the kitchen and out the kitchen door, where they stopped. A sheepish groom, pale and sweating, was just coming up, carrying the little girl in his arms. Jo heard herself whimpering but she found she could not move; her legs were frozen.

"She's alive, m'lord, m'lady. Knocked cold, she was . . . What was she doing on Thunderbolt?"

"Thunderbolt!" Peter's face turned crimson. "Who let her get onto Thunderbolt. You know nobody is allowed to ride him save myself and Mr. Thornber!"

"Yes, m'lord. Nobody let her. She must have come creeping in by herself, when we were havin' our tea, like. . . ."

"Oh dear God!" That was Nanny. "While I bathed Timothy."

At last Jo was able to move. She held out her arms for Sarah, and the groom shifted his burden to her. As soon as Jo had her, Sarah stirred and her eyelids fluttered. "She's coming to!" Jo called. "Let's get her inside. And for God's sake, somebody call the doctor!"

As they walked, Peter fell in beside Jo, reaching out to touch Sarah's cheek. "You know why this happened, don't you?" Jo demanded. "Because you took Timmy on a horse and snubbed her, absolutely snubbed her."

Stubbornly: "I explained why to her. She's old enough to understand."

Her voice laced with scorn, she answered, "Obviously, Peter, you are wrong. Does this look like she understood? Or does it look like she decided to take matters into her own hands?"

"Headstrong and stubborn, just like her mother."

"Better than a poseur, like her father."

They glared at each other. There was no love left, Jo realized, none at all.

"Mummy . . . ?"

"Yes, darling, Mummy is here. I'll take care of you. The doctor is coming. Does anything hurt?" She hurried away from him, holding her child tightly, fiercely, protectively against her bosom.

Much later, Dr. St. John came, and prodded and pulled and poked and pronounced one hip broken, one collarbone broken, plus a few bruises. He said what a lucky young lady she was that nothing worse had transpired, and did that teach her not to mount a horse much too big and powerful for her little hands? He certainly hoped so. She would be abed, oh, one or two months, probably, and after that . . . well, no excitement for a while, that was his advice. Certainly no riding.

"Have you any idea how she got such an idea into her head?" the doctor asked.

Jo pulled in breath, wondering how to phrase it nicely, when Nanny began instead: "She fancies herself a rider, Doctor, ever since the head groom told her she had a natural talent. She *is* good around horses, but she hadn't even begun her lessons. She was told this afternoon she couldn't ride a horse, she'd have to be content with a pony ride. If you ask me, that was more than enough for Miss Sarah. She *will* be willful, Doctor, well beyond her years."

"Well, Miss Sarah," said the doctor, bending over her, "if you'll take my advice, you'll listen to your elders and betters and you won't end up being bored in your bed during the fine weather."

The little girl did not answer, but gave the doctor a baleful glare. She was totally unrepentant, Jo saw. In a flash she knew that the moment she was free to get out of bed, Sarah would get back up on a horse . . . Thunderbolt, more than likely. Damn Peter, damn this whole country with their progeniture and their worship of the male of the species, damn it all! What chance did a female have? Sarah was right. It wasn't fair.

It wasn't until later, when she finally flopped down onto her bed, drained and weary, that Jo realized what this meant. Once again, she would have to put off leaving. For the next couple of months she would have to continue to play Lady Joanna—and then it would be Christmas, and then Boxing Day, and on and on and on. Damn! Was she doomed to stay here forever?

30

March 1947

Sex alone was what Jo longed for these days, waited for, *lived* for. In Elias's arms, in his bed upstairs over the gallery, she could forget her misery for a little while. For a little while she could stop her brain from running round and round in tight little circles.

When she was writhing and moaning under Elias's expert stroking, there were no thoughts at all in her head; there was nothing but sensation—and blessed forgetfulness. At those times, she loved Elias—maybe needed him was closer to the truth, but it felt like love.

Today, though, they had exhausted themselves and were lying together on his bed. The gray, almost dirty-looking March light made the sheets look soiled, and bleached all the color from Elias's skin. He looked like a corpse suddenly, and with a twinge of nausea, she turned away from him and stood up to get dressed.

He slitted his eyes open and asked, "Where are you going, Jo?"

"Home."

Sitting bolt upright, he said, "Home! But it's still early!"

She could hardly look at him. "I—I'm not feeling well."

"What is it? Do you need a doctor?" He was so caring, so tender, even in the most passionate moments. It made her feel guilty, that she was so . . . restless, edgy, discontented.

"For God's sake, Elias, every time I'm a bit down in the mouth, I'm not *ill*!"

"You needn't snap at me."

"I'm sorry." And she *was* sorry; but she felt no better for being regretful. She slithered the slip over her head. "I'm in a terrible mood, Elias. It's best if I just leave."

"If you say so." He lay back down onto the bed and on his side, his head propped in his hand, gazing at her.

"You see? You don't really want me here! You're glad I'm leaving, so why not admit it?" she said.

He rolled over onto his back, closing his eyes. "You're spoiling for a fight. I won't join you. I'm a lover, not a fighter." Usually she laughed at that line; this time she didn't.

He *was* a wonderful lover. What had changed her mood so suddenly, from melting pleasure to distaste? She thought she knew. When they had finished and were lying there, still joined, smiling at each other, he'd said, "I can't ever remember being with another woman who could arouse me so often, so quickly."

She had laughed, pushing her face into the thick gray hair on his chest. "And why do you think that is?"

He thought for a moment. "In bed, you are so passionate, so hungry, so wild, but on the outside, so different—the picture of the British lady, controlled, polite, repressed."

She had said, still laughing, "Oh, Elias, that's not *me*, I'm not any of those things." Then, unexpectedly, tears sprang to her eyes. "I used to sing. We sang a lot."

Elias had looked at her quizzically; he didn't get it. And that made her really start to cry. He had held her, murmuring comforting words; but there was no comfort for her now. The world had gone bleak and black. He didn't really know her, that was the trouble. She wasn't a real person to him, just convenient cunt. They hadn't discussed her work in *weeks*. Hell, they rarely talked these days, just fell into bed.

Just thinking about how eagerly she had come here today, throwing her clothes off as she walked in the door, rubbing up against him, moaning and wet before he had even really touched her . . . ugh! she disgusted herself.

Quickly, she pulled her clothes on, and combed her hair with her fingers, not even bothering to glance in the mirror. Elias stayed on the bed, not speaking, not moving; he might have been asleep. She knew better, but it suited her to let him pretend. She bent over him to kiss his cheek, and left quickly.

Soon she was on the train once more, heading home. *Home!* What a strange word for a place she was beginning to loathe. No, actually, it was herself she was beginning to loathe, wasn't it?

All the time Sarah had been bedridden, much of that time in pain, Jo had convinced herself that she had to give the child time to heal before she tried to leave. So, she had buried her problems in caring for the little girl, soothing her when she whimpered with the pain in her sleep, reading to her, dreaming up projects. She moved a cot into Sarah's room for the duration, so she could stay the night. And when Sarah went stumping about the house on crutches, she told herself that it would be too cumbersome and uncomfortable for her to travel. And now that Sarah had mended—even the slight limp had disappeared—Jo persuaded herself that keeping the child happy, and giving her riding lessons, took precedence over her own disquiet.

Oh, yes, she told herself story after story. It was too hot, it was too cold, it was too soon, it was too late. Peter would hate her, Peter would love her, Peter would be nasty, Peter would cry. It all meant she should not leave yet. But she hated staying! She spoke to her mother and Jim every Sunday on the telephone—when they could get through—and each time, as soon as she put the receiver back on the hook, she began to weep with homesickness.

When the train pulled into her station, by some miracle the lone taxi was there. She climbed in and let her mind go blank. Usually she sat back and replayed the hours with Elias in her head, like a loop of movie film that ran the same scenes over and over. Today she didn't want to remember. She just wanted to . . . what *did* she just want to do?

When she let herself in, there was no sign of Jakes, although she could hear the murmur of voices from the kitchen wing. Letting her coat fall onto a chair, she decided that what she wanted to do at this particular moment was build herself a large drink.

As she walked into the drawing room, she saw that Peter was there, slouched in one of the big chairs, his stocking feet stuck out toward the small fire that burned in the grate. She was surprised to see him. Lately, he rarely appeared for dinner, and when he finally came home, usually late at night, she could hear him stumbling down the hallway, muttering to himself.

He said nothing when she came in today; but when she walked up to him, he lifted his eyes to her. A strong smell of Irish whiskey surrounded him.

"Why, hallo, Joanna. Fancy meeting you here!" He chuckled. He didn't *sound* particularly drunk. "We don't see much of you these days, m'dear."

"That's nonsense, Peter. *I'm* always home for dinner."

"As I am not, yes, quite right, quite right. I am a bounder and a cad."

"Peter—" She didn't want to go through this routine with him; she had no patience for it.

As if he read her mind, he said, "I'm sorry, Jo, I do try to wring pity out of you, don't I? Well, I won't, I promise. Do stay. I'll make you a drink, shall I? And try to behave."

"That would be nice." Gingerly, she sat on the chair opposite, noting that he pushed himself up with no difficulty and was even steady on his feet. Drinking heavily but not yet *schnockered*? The Yiddish expression, straight out of her years at CCNY, surprised her. Those were the days! God, life had been simple back then, simple and sweet and she had been too young and dumb to realize it.

Peter snapped on the huge console radio that sat in one corner. "At five o'clock," he said, "the American sector in Berlin broadcasts the latest hits from the U.S.A. Let me see if I can tune them in. . . ." And suddenly, there was a blast of sound that Jo instantly recognized as Benny Goodman's "Sing, Sing, Sing!"

"That's prewar," she said, laughing. "Not the latest hit, you poor ignorant limey."

He laughed, too. "American songs all sound alike to me!"

We're almost having a good time together, Jo thought. How very strange.

"Dance?" he invited, bending over her with her drink.

"After this?" she answered, lifting her glass.

"Whatever you like." Shrugging, he plopped back into his chair.

Jo sipped at the gin and vermouth, savoring. It was terribly strong, but what the hell, she could use a little help today. Three sips later her head was light and airy and the world looked a whole lot better. The song on the radio was one she hadn't heard before. "Laughing on the outside, crying on the inside, 'cause I'm still in love with you . . ." lamented the crooner. For some reason, that struck her as terribly funny and she began to laugh.

Peter, opposite her, took gulps of his drink and regarded her steadily. When she stopped laughing, he remarked, "You're home earlier than usual."

"I finished my business in London."

"No lingering at the shops? No high tea at Brown's? I thought you loved London."

"I do, Peter. But it's not as if I'm a tourist. . . ."

"No. Quite. You're my wife, aren't you?"

She was instantly on the alert. The last phrase had a sharp edge to it, she thought.

Sure enough, he put his glass down and licked his lips. "Come here, my devoted spouse, come here and give your husband a kiss."

Nothing could appeal to her less. And she had raced out of Elias's digs so fast, she hadn't showered. The thought of going to Peter smelling of sex . . . ! She shuddered.

"Oh, surely it isn't *that* distasteful, is it, Jo? Or is it?" He sat forward, arms resting on his knees, peering at her. "Ah. Of course. You've just come from your lover, haven't you?"

"Don't be disgusting!" Her heart began to beat very fast. Had he known all along?

"Well, perhaps I don't find that so disgusting . . . perhaps it excites me, the thought of you with another man, another man with a nice big thick cock. . . ."

"Peter, for God's sake!"

"You can tell me how it feels, when he pushes it into you, how it fills you up. . . ."

"Peter! Can't you shut up?"

"No. Look." He patted the large bulge on his belly.

"Can't you see, Peter, it's the thought of another man's cock that excites you? For God's sake, why don't you *admit* it?"

"Me? A poof? You must be mad."

She got up from the chair and started to walk away, but he stuck out his foot and she stumbled over it, falling in a heap on the floor. She wasn't hurt, but the breath was knocked out of her, and when he loomed over her, she felt a shiver of fear. "Peter!"

He straddled her, unbuttoning his pants, and his massive erection stuck out, quivering. The reek of whiskey was overpowering. "Peter, for God's sake, the servants!"

"To hell with the servants, to hell with God! You're my wife and I demand my congojal . . . my conjuju . . . my conjugal rights!"

Sickened, she pushed at him and he lost his balance, falling to the floor and rolling away from her. Scrambling to her feet, she fled. What if Dilly and Reg had walked in? What if Jakes had walked in? What if the *children* had come in?

She ran up the stairs and into her room. The first thing she did was turn on both taps in the ancient bathtub, so she could climb in and soak the whole scene out of her memory. Then she would start to make plans, because obviously something *had* to be done, and quickly. It was time to end the masquerade.

Later on, when the children had been bathed and were ready for their tea, Jo let herself into the nursery and told Nanny firmly, in a voice that brooked no argument, that she wanted to speak with Sarah and Timmy *alone*, if you don't mind. Nanny's pursed lips and stiff back said that yes, indeed, she *did* mind, but that she was a long-suffering servant and would do as she was told.

Both children were curious but not alarmed. "What is it, Mummy? Has somebody died?" Sarah asked; and Jo remembered that the last time she had done this—come into the nursery and demanded private time with her own children—was when one of the kitchen maids had been killed in an auto accident.

"No, darling, nobody has died. But I do want to talk to you both about something terribly important. It will be a big change for all of us, but it will be heaps of fun." They both stared at her, waiting, so she took a deep breath and plunged in. "We're all going on a lovely trip to the United States. Won't that be nice? And you'll see your granny Leah and grampy Jim, and Mummy will take you all over New York City and we'll choose a good school and—"

"And Daddy will take us riding."

Jo took another deep breath. "No, darling, Daddy won't be coming with us."

"Then I won't go!" said Sarah firmly.

"I won't go!" Timmy echoed.

Jo looked at them, surprised. She had known it would be touchy, but she had not counted on an insurrection.

"No, Mummy, no! We don't *want* to go live in nasty dirty New York City where there are bad gangsters who shoot you! We want to stay right here at home!" Sarah's face had become quite pink with emotion.

"Where on earth did you get those ideas? Gangsters are certainly not going to shoot you! I grew up in New York City and no gangsters ever shot me!"

"Nanny says," Timmy said, very pleased with his knowledge.

"Nanny told us," Sarah backed him up. "Nanny says the women in New York City are no better than they ought to be. She says there are giant skyscrapers with nightclubs where wicked people dance all night, and nobody believes in Jesus. Nanny says if we ever went to such a sinful city, she would worry about us every moment."

"Oh my God," Jo murmured. Nanny had created a whole separate little world up here in the nursery, and it wasn't any sort of world she wanted *her* kids growing up in. Wicked people! Nightclubs! Gangsters! Nanny obviously got her information from grade-B movies.

"See here," Jo said, looking deeply into their faces, "Nanny has never been to New York City, so she doesn't really know. And none of it is true. That's not what it's like."

"Is! Is so! Nanny says!" That was Timmy. And Sarah chimed right in, her lower lip pushed out defiantly. "Nanny wouldn't lie, Mummy. Nanny would never lie to her two darlings."

The last sentence was so obviously a direct quote, including the holier-than-thou tone, it made Jo feel ill. Oh save me! she thought, No, better than that, let me save Sarah and Timothy before they're both turned into Scots Presbyterian bigots.

"Maybe not," she mollified. "Maybe not. You've known for ages that we were going on the boat to New York one day, and you've never objected before. Nanny wouldn't lie, perhaps, but she *could* be mistaken, you know."

Timmy stubbornly shook his blond head, but Sarah gave the matter some thought. Finally she said, "I know! We can take Nanny with us and then she won't worry!"

"What a lovely idea!" Jo said, thinking: over my dead body. "We'll talk more about that later. Right now, I want to tell your Gran and Gramps about our trip. . . ." She bent to kiss them. "So you have tea with Nanny now and it will be our little secret, okay? And we won't even think about it until the time comes, how's that?"

They had looked so forlorn. She almost stopped and turned to go back upstairs and take it all back. But she mustn't be turned from her resolve, not this time. Once they were there, they'd soon love Greenwich Village—she always had—and forget Nether Althorpe and this house where nothing was really what it seemed. One day they'd both thank her.

In front of the closed door to the drawing room, she stopped and braced herself. They were not going to let her go without a battle, she realized. But she could do it. The martini Peter had mixed for her was still buzzing pleasantly in her head. Maybe she had been born one drink under par, she thought, and giggled a little. There. If she could make a joke, even a poor one, she was in control.

She had already decided to wait until all parties were sufficiently oiled with before-dinner drinks before she broached the subject. So, she would just go in, have a drink with the rest of them, and—before they ate—break the news.

To her surprise, Peter was still there, slumped down in the sagging chair before the fire, a glass of whiskey resting on his flat belly, cradled in both hands. He did not move or turn his head when she entered, but he knew it was her.

"I say, Jo . . . I'm sorry about . . . about all that nonsense, before. I don't know what got into me. . . ."

She went to the sideboard and carefully made herself a drink, thinking of what she wanted to say to him.

"Jo?" he prodded.

"Yes, Peter, I heard you—you're sorry. Well, I'm sorry, too. Sorry it's come to this. Sorry our marriage is such a . . . such a mess."

She could heard him sitting up, feel his body tensing, even with her back turned. "No, Jo! Don't say it!"

"Say what?"

He got up and came to her. "Damn it, Jo, don't play with me. What are you saying about our marriage?"

Now she turned to look at him. It was the least she could do: look him in the eye when she told him. "It's over, Peter, surely you can see that."

He shook his head, his eyes squeezed shut. "Don't say it, don't say it, please, Jo."

"Peter, for God's sake, you *can't* want to keep up this pretense."

His eyes flew open. "Oh, yes, I do, I do, you have no idea. Please, Jo, don't do this to me. Don't leave. What will I tell . . . how will I explain . . . ?" His eyes glistened with tears. Jo wanted to turn away from the sight, but she owed him at least that much honesty.

"You can explain it any way you like, Peter. Tell them I've been unfaithful and you kicked me out. I'll be the villain. That's okay. But I can't do this anymore. I can't stand by and watch my children turn into small-minded strangers, and I—"

"Not . . . the . . . children." He spoke through gritted teeth. "You may not have them. They're mine!"

"They're mine, too, Peter, let us not forget that."

"You . . . you can go if you must. But not my children. No." He was quite pale, and sweat had broken out on his forehead.

Try and stop me, she was about to say. But just then Reg and Dilly came waltzing in, chattering away a mile a minute about a foal and the vet; and both Jo and Peter turned to them, putting on false smiles. As if, Jo thought, they were naughty children, hiding their mischief from the grown-ups. But goddamn it, she thought, *we're* grown-ups, too.

She tried to wait until Dilly stopped talking for a minute; or, that being impossible, took a breath. But it was not going to happen, not with two new foals and a horse that had to be put down. Her horses were one of the few things in this world that could consume Dilly's concentration utterly.

So Jo just said it, abruptly, brusquely, briskly, bluntly. "Peter and I are separating."

Now she had their attention. Two dropped jaws, two shocked, disbelieving expressions.

"No!" Reg spoke first. "No, that's quite impossible. Fieldings don't divorce."

"Reg dear, Joanna didn't say *divorce*. She said *separate*. Quite different, you know." Dilly turned to Jo. "But where will you *go*, my dear?" Her voice was soft with false concern.

"Perhaps it's Peter who's going," Jo said, more sharply than she had intended.

Again Reg barked out a "No! Impossible!" and then backed it up with a barrage of negatives. Couldn't be, mustn't be, unheard of, quite impossible, not done, utter nonsense, errant rot . . . She stopped listening after a moment.

"But yes, I'm afraid so. Yes. We are separating. And you're right, Dilly, I'm the one leaving. For home." She waited for the little smile to appear on her mother-in-law's lips, and then added: "With my children, of course."

Then the outburst was of three voices, crisscrossing each other. She didn't have to listen to know what they were saying. She just sat in her chair and sipped her drink. At one point she looked over at Peter, trying to catch his eye. Come on Peter, she thought at him, tell them you're miserable with me. Tell them I'm not a good wife, that you'll be *glad* to see the back of me. But Peter just sloshed the whiskey around in his tumbler, watching the circular movements as if they held the answer to all questions.

"Look," she said, mostly to Dilly, "I've never really fit in here. It's never been right. Remember, when I met Peter, I was a war photographer, taking pictures for magazines, taking *chances*, taking *risks*. Country life . . . well, I'm not suited for it, you can see that. I should be out there, working, not presiding at fetes."

"Well, my dear, if you must, take your little pictures. Nobody is *forcing* you to be part of the social scene. But . . . you know, divorce is just not in it. We simply cannot allow—"

"I'm afraid you have nothing to say about it. My mind is made up."

"That's as may be," Dilly said sweetly, after a moment's thought, "but you know, Joanna, we cannot let you take Peter's children all the way across the Atlantic."

"*Our* children," Jo said sweetly through gritted teeth. She mustn't lose her temper. "And I am, after all, the mother."

"What is that supposed to mean?" Reg blustered.

"Nothing, except that, in the case of disagreement, I believe the law always gives children to their mother," she said, hoping she was on firm ground.

"Utterly impossible, British law—" Reg began.

"Now, Reg, do calm yourself, dear, you're looking quite crimson, you know. Joanna, I can quite see how postwar life may seem a bit tame to you. It happens to all of us. But when the bloom is off the rose, why, we just find new interests. . . ." Like adolescent boys, Jo thought nastily.

"I've heard enough," Reg announced, getting to his feet and stumping to the sideboard, where he poured himself a generous amount of Irish, tipped his head back and tossed it down his throat. "Now, see here, Joanna, enough is enough, what? We've heard you out. We've sat through your temper tantrum. Now it's time to behave like a lady and settle into your marriage. You might at least give it a *try*." He glared at her from under his brows.

Thought fled from her brain, she was so angry. She felt herself rise to her feet. "A try!" she cried. "A try? I've been doing nothing *but* trying, for years! It's nothing to do with *me*, Reg. It's not me who's got the problem. It's Peter! Look at him sitting over there, butter wouldn't melt in his mouth, but he won't look at me, he won't look at you, he won't face *anything*! Tell them, Peter, goddammit, *tell* them!"

She ran over and took him by the shoulders, shaking him. "Tell them!" She could hear the gasps behind her. "Tell them, Peter! I've been a wife without a real husband! Tell them!"

"Leave him alone!" Dilly shrieked. "How dare you, you're nothing better than a—"

Jo whirled around and stared at her mother-in-law, who was shaking with rage. "Don't you dare say it," she said. "Not *you*, of all people. Don't you dare!"

"You're a hateful, low-class liar. There's nothing wrong with my son!"

"Oh, really? Why don't you ask him? Ask him how he knows exactly when each of the children was conceived. Ask him about Pip, and ask him about the interesting leather paraphernalia he keeps in his dressing table drawer. Ask him if any of it does any good—"

"That's quite enough!" Reg's bellow could be heard for miles, Jo thought. In a lower tone, he went on, "Very well. If you must leave, then go. And you can take the girl with you. But Timmy stays. He is, after all, the heir apparent, and must be with his father to learn about running the estate."

"That's not all he'll learn!"

Dilly marched up to her and slapped her across the face; it happened so quickly, Jo had no time to duck or move. "There are no words," Dilly hissed, "to describe what you are."

"Oh yes, there are." Jo put her palm to the stinging cheek and locked eyes with Dilly. "But there's one in particular you should know. *Jewish.* I'm Jewish, Dilly—on both sides of the family. McCready is my stepfather's name. Do you know what that means? It means your grandchildren are Jewish. Any child born of a Jewish mother is *automatically* Jewish!"

Dilly's eyes rolled back and, with a small sigh, she slumped to the floor in a faint. Reg ran to her, kneeling by her side. He turned his head to glare at Jo. "I hope God punishes you," he said.

"Whose God?" Jo said. She could feel the blood pumping through her veins; for the first time in years, she felt really alive, really *herself*. "Yours? Or mine?"

"Enough, Jo." At last Peter was looking at her. His eyes were empty. "Enough," he repeated. "You win. You can go. Yes, with the children." He gave a dismissive wave of his hands. "Just leave. I can't fight you anymore."

31

July 1947

The air was soft and balmy, filled with gentle breezes; and at seven in the evening, the sky was just beginning to turn purple at its edges. The rest, streaked with faint banners of cloud, was a pale blue with a slice of even paler moon hanging low over the horizon. Only the water was dark, a dark deep green, with tiny sifted sparkles dancing in it. Jo could imagine drifting slowly down through those twinkling depths, rocked by the ceaseless motion of the water, as she was rocked by the gentle movements of the ship.

"Mummy! Mummy! Come on! They rang the gong ages ago!"

"And I'm hungry, Mummy!"

Jo bent and scooped Timmy up in one swift move. "You! You're always hungry!" Just as quickly, she put him down and went to give Sarah a hug. But Sarah, sulking, twitched away from her.

Jo stifled a sigh. She wished Sarah would stop acting up. They were just a day away from docking in New York, and by now you'd think the child would have realized that her tantrums weren't going to change anything. God knows she was doing everything possible to make Sarah happy! She'd had them all put into the same stateroom, so that neither of the children would wake up in the night, frightened, wondering where they were or where she was. They even sat with her at dinner, although generally all the children on board ate together, with a couple of nannies to watch over them.

She realized it was hard on them, leaving the only home they'd ever known and going to a strange land; and she was willing to sacrifice her own comfort to show them she understood. But try to make Sarah Fielding happy! It was hopeless. No matter what you did, she wanted that extra bit more.

Still, Jo was determined not to let Sarah—or anything—spoil her own joy. She was so terribly happy, it was shameful. She couldn't let the children know; they loved their father and their grandparents and their Nanny and all of Nether Althorpe. So she couldn't jump up and down and holler with elation. She couldn't walk around with a silly grin on her face, or dance around the stateroom. But inside, she did. She was on her way to her own life. She hadn't fully realized what a prison her marriage had become. Poor Peter. But she didn't have to consider Poor Peter anymore. She was *free!*

"I thought I saw a porpoise," Jo said. The children loved seeing the animals leaping gracefully out of the water and cavorting in and out of the wake of the big ship. "But there wasn't one," she added quickly, before Timmy demanded they wait to catch another glimpse. "Come on, Sarah. I'm sure you're hungry, too."

Holding their hands, she entered the *Concordia*'s main saloon. She was aware of the picture they made: the tall, slender young woman and the two children, so different. The little girl, so fiercely dark, her eyes a bright, surprising blue edged with thick black lashes. The little boy, so blond, so fair, so English. She knew they were a mystery; she was aware that all over the dining room people murmured behind their hands as Lady Fielding and her children walked by. She found herself gliding along, her head high and her eyes straight ahead . . . as if to the manor born. What a joke! But the joke was on *them*, that was the thing.

At Table 4, First Officer Clyde Phipps came to his feet as soon as he spotted them. Jo smiled to herself. First Officer Phipps was providing a bit of amusement for her on the voyage. First class was jammed—everyone who had the money was dying to travel again, to get away from all reminders of war. But, of course, it was jammed with the very rich—and that meant she was by far the youngest adult at her table, if you didn't count Clyde Phipps. Her fellow diners were elderly and cranky, with many complaints and a great deal of boring conversation.

Jo would never have chosen to travel first class; but Dilly had insisted. It wouldn't do, she said, for anyone to see their family traveling second class. Joanna and the children were, after all, *Fieldings*. Sure, Jo thought: *Fieldings* who were running away from Nether Althorpe, *Fieldings* who would probably never return, *Fieldings* about to be divorced. Her mother-in-law was either stupid or perverse . . . or maybe just deluded.

First Officer Phipps helped Timmy and Sarah into their seats and then handed Jo into hers. He was in his early twenties, slim and blond, always impeccable in his gleaming white uniform, the perfect gentleman. She knew that he had been seated with her on purpose—hell, on *orders* to keep Lady Fielding occupied and contented. Well, she didn't need a good-looking young officer for that; she was filled with buoyant joy without any outside help. Still, he helped pass the time, and he was a terrific dancer.

Lately he'd been growing amorous; and she doubted the captain had made *that* part of his job. She had noticed, the last couple of days, how he held her a bit closer when they danced, relinquishing his embrace a bit more reluctantly each time. It was pleasantly titillating to wonder how he would be, this evening, she thought; whether he would press on or decide it just wasn't worth the trouble. It passed the time. And she felt she needed a little practice with someone safe before she went back into the real world, a divorcée having to grapple with real men.

Dinner passed agreeably enough. Since Mr. Phipps was especially attentive, Jo took pleasure in turning her back on him and paying attention to her children. She could feel his consternation, and it gratified her to know she still had some feminine wiles. When the music for dancing started and Clyde turned to her with a smile, she said, "Not just yet." And then he did a wonderful thing: he asked Sarah for a dance. The look on the little girl's face was something to see! So enchanted with the whole idea! Jo wished she had brought her camera to dinner.

Out onto the dance floor they went. Clyde, carrying Sarah, did all the dancing and twirling. It was adorable, and Sarah really loved the dipping and swaying and turning. The orchestra was playing, "Papa, Won't You Dance with Me," a lively tune and a big hit in the States, Clyde said. He sang the words to Sarah and she laughed, but suddenly she wasn't laughing anymore, she was crying.

Clyde brought her back to the table, looking completely out of his depth. "I don't know what brought it on," he said. "She just suddenly started to bawl."

Jo took the little girl onto her lap, smoothing her hair and trying to soothe her. "Darling, whatever is the matter?"

For a while Sarah couldn't even talk, and then it came out. "I miss my daddy!" Because of the song title, Jo guessed. What a bore. Jo wondered how long that sort of thing was going to go on; and how long she was going to be able to put up with it without losing patience.

But she wouldn't show a thing in front of the kids. The very next song, she took them both out onto the dance floor, and they held hands in a circle and bounced around. That put them into a good humor. Sarah didn't even pout and ask to stay just a little while longer when Jo announced bedtime. In the cabin, she stayed with them longer than usual, telling them two bedtime stories instead of one.

She was feeling quite satisfied and maternal when she let herself out of the stateroom and started back for the main saloon. Suddenly, Clyde Phipps loomed out of the darkness.

"What's going on, Jo?" he demanded.

"Excuse me?"

"Why suddenly the cold shoulder? I don't appreciate that."

"And I don't appreciate your nasty tone, either," she snapped. "You needn't worry, Clyde, I'll give your captain a very good report on you. You kept the lonely Lady Fielding company and were a perfect gentleman."

She tried for a grand exit on those words; but he blocked her way. "You've been leading me on, *Lady* Fielding."

"Flirting, perhaps. But not, believe me, leading you on."

He lowered his voice to a hissing whisper. "You were ready to go, last night. I could feel you trembling when we danced."

"You're out of your mind. Now please move and let me pass."

"Ever since the first night, you've been asking for it." He grabbed her and pulled her into him, his mouth coming down onto hers like an attack. One hand curved around her buttocks and pushed, so she could feel the rock-hard protuberance; the other hand crept up her front, trying to get ahold of her breast.

Jo froze for a moment at the sudden assault, and then she became furious. Who did he think he *was*, with his talk of leading him on and asking for it? She resented the groping hands that treated her so roughly, and she struggled to escape the tongue he pushed into her mouth. She thought she heard the stateroom door open behind them. Oh God, the children! Frantic, she reached down for his erection, and when she had hold of it, she squeezed as hard as she could. Cursing softly—he dared not draw attention to them—he let her go and backed away. Quickly, she slipped back into the safety of the stateroom, locking the door behind her.

In the darkness she heard Sarah sobbing. Oh Lord. Well, she couldn't just let it go; she would talk to the child. She sat on the edge of Sarah's bunk, speaking softly.

"Sarah, did you see Mr. Phipps kissing me?"

Sobs.

"Listen, darling, he was very naughty to do that. I pushed him away and told him never ever to do that again."

More sobs, and a strangled voice: "He was . . . he put his hand . . ."

"I know, he was not being nice, and I hated it. I *hated* it. Do you hear me? But I'm fine, he didn't hurt me. So please, do stop crying. I'm fine. I promise."

"You dance with him all the time."

"Oh, Sarah, that's totally different!"

"Not different! He hugs you!"

Oh Lord. "Sarah, listen to me, I didn't want Mr. Phipps to hold me and kiss me. He was not a gentleman, and I . . . I'm going to tell the captain, and Mr. Phipps will be punished. All right?"

"You were kissing him."

Jo had been smoothing Sarah's hair. Now she stopped. The child was being an absolute pill! What did she mean, using that accusatory tone on her mother? Jo felt doubly assaulted— first by the horny Mr. Phipps, and now by her own daughter. She wanted to shake Sarah. She'd tried so hard not to let her children feel deserted or neglected, and this was the thanks she got!

"Honestly, Sarah, I don't know *what's* got into you. You've been out of sorts this entire trip. I told you that I pushed Mr. Phipps away and that I was very angry with him. You're just going to have to believe me, that's all!" She paused, waiting for a response, but there wasn't one. "For God's sake, we're not going to the moon, we're not going to prison. We're going to New York City, a very beautiful and exciting place where Mummy grew up. You're going to see Nana Leah and Uncle Jim, who love you to pieces, and everything's going to be just perfect. I swear, I don't understand you at all!"

There was another long silence, and then: "Mummy?"

At last! "Yes, darling?"

"Do you still love Daddy?"

What in hell could she *say*? *No?* It was the truth, but so blunt and ... well, cruel, actually. *Yes* would be dishonest. "Well, darling, actually ... you see ..." she stumbled; and then said, "Why do you ask?"

"Daddy still loves *you*! He doesn't want a divorce! He told me! And *I* don't want a divorce, either!" And the flood gates opened once more.

Oh, that consummate bastard! Getting a five-year-old child to take sides! Playing on her sympathies, the bastard!

"I'm sorry, darling, I really am. Nobody ever *wants* a divorce, you know, but sometimes it just has to be. When you're all grown up, you'll understand better. And I know it's hard to leave everything behind in England, but I promise you, you're going to love New York."

Muffled: "Won't!"

"Oh, Sarah—!" But what was the use? It was like talking to the wall. Jo got to her feet, annoyed, and started to undress. But when she was in her pajamas, she knew she was too keyed-up to go to sleep. So she belted on a robe and tiptoed to the door, thinking that moonlight shimmering on the endless watery vista would surely lull her and make her sleepy.

Her movements on the carpeted floor were silent; still, as soon as her hand was on the doorknob, she heard Sarah's quavery voice: "Mummy, where are you going?"

"For God's sake, Sarah, only right outside. I'm in my pajamas and robe. I'm not going anywhere! You're as snoopy as Nanny!" She regretted the last words as soon as they were out of her mouth; but it was too late. From Sarah's bunk came the sound of stifled sniffling. Without another word, Jo left, closing the door firmly.

She was in the way; she knew it. Mummy didn't want her, no, nor Timmy, either. It was just like Nanny said. Nanny, brushing her hair one hundred strokes—"never more, Sarah, and never, never less!"—saying, "If I live to be a hundred, I shall never understand why your mother thinks she must cart you away, over the ocean, away from everything and everyone you love. What in the world is she going to *do* with you? She doesn't know you the way Nanny knows you! My poor little lamb, what will become of you in that wicked city? Oh, what *could* she be thinking of?"

Just the thought of Nanny's voice, so familiar, so dear, and now so far away, made the tears come even faster. She sniffed them back, but at least she didn't have to be absolutely quiet, because Mummy had gone out, slamming the door behind her. She had made Mummy angry. She was always making Mummy angry. Well, Mummy made *her* angry, so there! She and Timmy had a plan. When they got to New York to Nana Leah's house, they would find the telephone and they would call Nanny and tell her to come get them. Nanny had her own telephone laid on especially for them, for Sarah and Timmy, and she told them, "If you ever need me, you have only to call and I'll come running, whether your mother wants me or no!"

Oh how she missed Nanny! Nobody brushed her hair, or scrubbed behind her ears and made her face shiny clean, like Nanny did. Nobody told them stories about Robert the Bruce and her daddy the war hero like Nanny did. Sarah turned to bury her face in the pillow; she was crying so hard, she might wake Timmy, and he was still a baby. He'd get scared, like he did the last time she woke him. But why couldn't Mummy take Nanny *with* them? She asked Nanny that a million times. But Nanny just folded her lips in tight and said, "Never mind, it's not for children to know." So, of course, they knew. Mummy hated Nanny and was jealous of her. Sarah had overheard Nanny complaining to Granny about it once. It must be true, because just saying she missed Nanny made Mummy ever so angry.

Sarah also knew Mummy had sent Nanny away. On Monday night Nanny kissed them both good night, just like always, and put out the last light and, when she opened the nursery door, waited for her and Timmy to call out: "Good night. Sweet dreams. See you in the morning, bright and early!" And Nanny answered, like always, "Good night and sweet dreams to *you*." And she put her head down on the pillow, knowing all was right with the world—even though she was going thousands of miles across the great ocean—and fell asleep.

But in the morning, it wasn't Nanny who opened the drapes, crying, "The birds are cheeping and you're still sleeping!" No, it was dumb Margaret from the scullery, putting down the breakfast tray with such a clatter that it startled her out of sleep.

"Where's Nanny?" she scolded. "Nanny always brings us our breakfast."

Margaret dipped a curtsey and said, "Gone, miss. Nanny's gone."

"Gone! What do you *mean*?"

"Gone, miss. To Scotland, so Cook said."

Sarah hardly remembered what happened after that. She ran downstairs as fast as she could, into the kitchen, demanding to know where Nanny was. She could not believe that Nanny, her Nanny, would just go away without saying good-bye. But they all looked at Sarah with very sad eyes, and said it was true.

Now she took her face out of the pillow, where it was becoming quite hot, and wiped at her wet cheeks on the sheet. Then came the part she didn't like thinking about. She had "gone wild," that was what Cook said; and Mummy had to be waked up to do something about her.

She hated this boat. This *ship*. Hated the way it swayed and dipped, hated the horrid sounds, the creaking and the groaning. Why did she have to be here? Why did she *have* to do what Mummy said? It wasn't fair! She hated Mummy, hated, hated, hated her! She hated Timmy, too. He'd already forgotten Nanny.

The tears stopped; they always stopped if she thought about hating. Her head ached and so did her eyes. Tomorrow they were going to be in New York, she reminded herself, and tomorrow she would be able to get to a telephone and call Nanny.

In the meantime, she would put herself to sleep singing the pretty song on the music box Daddy gave her when she was two. "Lullaby . . . and good night," Sarah whispered to herself. Singing something so familiar from the nursery made her feel close to Nanny, and safe. . . . Her eyes fluttered closed, and with a sigh she drifted into her dream.

As soon as the tugs came alongside, tooting merrily, while everyone on decked cheered and waved, the mighty throbbing engines were turned off. The sudden silence rang in Jo's ears, along with the thudding of her heart. Coming home! She was so elated, she felt she could float the rest of the way. There was the lady with the lamp, coming closer and closer, her strong arm reaching into the bright blue sky. So beautiful! Tears stung at Jo's eyes. She hugged her children close.

Home. Jo had no idea what kind of a house her mother and Jim had bought. Nor why, for God's sake. Who would leave the charm of Greenwich Village for *Brooklyn*, of all the damn places! But her mother said the Village had changed—for the worse, she said—and it was becoming horribly expensive. And Brooklyn Heights was right across the river, very pretty, and cheap. "A lot of writers live there. It's like the Village used to be," her mother insisted. "And we have a whole house. Not a huge house, but it's all ours. Better than trying to squeeze everyone into the apartment on Barrow Street." Maybe so; but when Jo thought of home, the apartment on Barrow Street was what she imagined. Willow Street in Brooklyn Heights was a string of words with no mental picture to accompany them.

She'd have to get used to lots of changes. Fiorello LaGuardia was deathly ill. New York without LaGuardia? How odd that would be. Her mother had sent her a piece she did for *Women's Gazette* or maybe it was *Good Housekeeping*, a sweet little memory piece about the way LaGuardia used to campaign in all the different immigrant neighborhoods, speaking the language of each one as he went ... including fluent Yiddish. New York with no Mayor LaGuardia was like thinking of the U.S. without FDR. But FDR had been dead for three years, and she had to get used to thinking of President Truman. The Truman Doctrine. The Marshall Plan. Christian Dior. Lots of new names. Leah had written an article for *McCall's* about Dior, too, called "The So-Called New Look Is Old as the Hills."

Jo glanced down at the dress she had chosen this morning, a voile print in yellow and gray, very pretty, its skirt almost at her ankles. What did her mother write in the article? "Here we go again! The men come back from the war and the women go back into corsets and long skirts that don't allow their legs to move freely." It was a hoot. Jo was amazed the women's magazines would even print it; but Leah said they weren't quite so stodgy as they used to be.

As the tugs pushed them west, toward the Hudson River side of Manhattan, Jo kept pointing out things to the kids, the Battery and the piers and all the ships, and in the distance, the Chrysler Building and the Empire State Building. "Look," she kept saying, "look, look, look!"

They were going to land at Pier 60, at Fortieth Street. "Oh, kids, it's going to be super! Nana Leah told me she got us tickets for the theater. Sarah, you'll love New York theaters, there are so many, just like London. We're going to see the very latest shows. *Brigadoon. Finian's Rainbow* ..." What else had Leah mentioned? "*Annie Get Your Gun.* With Ethel Merman, oh, she's great! It's going to be lovely!"

Jo picked up Timmy so he could see, and when Sarah whined that *she* couldn't see, either, Jo wasn't even irritated. She was so happy to be out of that nightmare marriage and back home where she belonged! She put Timmy down, saying, "And now a turn for Lady Sarah!" and picked up her daughter, feeling for the first time since they'd left England pure love for the child.

"Sarah, we have a piano in the house and a new record player and three radios. I'll give you piano lessons, so we can play duets, and we'll sing all the new songs from Broadway. We always sang all the songs when I was your age, and now we will again!"

Her heart was thumping like crazy as the huge ship, as ponderous as an elephant, slowly bumped and lurched against the wooden pier. All the whistles were tooting and horns hooting and everyone was yelling and shouting at the tiny people below.

Jo began to cry, and Sarah hugged her. "It's going to be fine, Mummy, really it is." Then, after a pause, she asked, "But is it always this hot?"

Jo put her down, laughing with relief and happiness. "It's only this hot in the summer. But never mind, never mind . . . Oh my God, there they are! Look, Sarah, look, Timmy, it's Nana Leah and Uncle Jim, see? Down there, she's the lady with dark hair like yours, Sarah. See the lady in the very long red dress with the flowers on it? And the straw hat with the red flowers? See? And the big man wearing a boater?"

Her mother was dressed in the very style she had excoriated in print not so long ago. Jo laughed. It was just like her!

"She doesn't look like a granny!" said Sarah.

"That's right, my pet, and she doesn't *act* like one, either!" She picked Sarah up again. "You're going to *love* her!" She was jolted by the intensity of her emotions. She tightened her grip on Sarah, and the little girl whimpered. "Mummy, you're getting me all sticky, please put me down!"

Jo could hardly hear. She could hardly feel; she was only dimly aware that Timmy was wrapped around her legs. Leaning over the railing, she shrieked: "Mom! Jim! Up here!"

At last they saw her and waved madly, and she had to fight not to burst into tears. She was home, she was home, she was *home!*

"Come on, kids, let's start moving. It's hot, but never mind. We'll go bathing . . . in the ocean! I'm going to take you to the most beautiful beach you ever saw—wide and smooth, all soft sand. I'll get you spades and buckets and you can dig to your hearts' content. We'll go on such wonderful rides, the same ones I went on when I was a little girl. The carousel! The Cyclone! Loop the Loop! Then we'll walk on the boardwalk, where you can buy any toy you want!"

"Where, Mummy?" Timmy asked, tugging at her skirt. "Brighton?"

She laughed and laughed. "No, silly goose! Not Brighton! We're in the good old U.S.A.! The land of the free and the home of the brave! The best country in the world! And New York is the best city in the world, and we're going to go to the best beach in the world. I promise you, before we do anything else, we'll all go to Coney Island!"

32

August 1947

The radio was on in the kitchen—it was always on, all day long. Right now, the lilting strains of "How Are Things in Gloccamorra" filled the room. Seated at the table, a linen towel tied around her neck, Sarah sang along, her bowl of cereal and glass of orange juice forgotten.

"Your breakfast," Jo reminded her, fanning herself briefly with a section of the *Times*. The second section, open to the Help Wanted, Female, ads, sat on the table in front of her. But it was just too hot and humid to even look. What the hell could she do? What the hell was she good for? There wasn't one listing for a photographer, not even a lab assistant. She couldn't type or take shorthand or do anything that employers seemed to want from women, which wasn't much, in her opinion. But she had to find *something*. They couldn't live off Leah and Jim forever! "Eat your breakfast, Sarah," she repeated without much force.

To tell the truth, she enjoyed listening to Sarah sing. Sarah was a natural at music. She could learn any song from one hearing, was always right on pitch, and naturally, considering the family she came from, remembered all the words. But Jo had a feeling it was more than just a family trait; she thought the kid was talented. As soon as she had a job, she'd see about getting her music lessons. She waited until the song was over and then said, "Very nice, very good. Now finish the Rice Krispies, please."

"They're not going snap crackle pop anymore."

"That's because they're soggy, Sarah. You let them sit in the milk too long."

"Well, who needs their breakfast cereal making all that noise? Snapping and crackling and so forth? Hoo! It's more than *I* could bear, this hour of the morning." Jim came through the doorway, redolent of Old Spice, and chose the chair next to Sarah. He always filled up a room, all by himself. He had great presence, beyond the fact that he was big and burly and had blazing white hair. Eyeing him now, Jo thought what an interesting model he would make, if she could get him to sit still.

"Myself, I like a cereal that sings," Jim said, giving Jo a little wink. "Didn't I just hear a bowl of cereal giving a rendition of 'Gloccamorra?' "

Sarah giggled. "That was *me*, Uncle Jim."

"Oh, was it now? I thought, considering the brogue, it might have been Irish oatmeal."

"Oh, Uncle Jim!" More giggling. He was great with the kids, Jo thought, not for the first time. Better than her mother. Hell, better than *their* own mother! Jo seemed to be out of sorts all the time now; she who had been so overflowing with joy and happiness the day they landed. She couldn't figure out what had happened to her high spirits. Smothered by heat, humidity, and boredom, maybe.

"Now why don't you try some nice cornflakes, Sarah darlin'. Look how pleasantly they sit in the bowl, smiling up at you, and never a cross word. Not like those bad-tempered rice things that make rude noises while you're trying to eat!"

"Oh, Uncle Jim! You're so silly!" Sarah was openly pleased to have his total attention. Timmy wasn't at the table this morning; he hadn't been for the last couple of days. Right now he was sleeping, after a restless night. His fever had gone up to 102 degrees at midnight; but at dawn, when Jo woke up, cramped from sitting on the old rocker, the flush was gone and he was covered in sweat. It must be a summer cold. If his temperature didn't go up again today, she decided, she'd cancel the pediatrician.

"Silly?" Jim repeated. "Indeed I am, and glad of it. Being silly is good for you, you know." He gave Sarah that very straight, solemn gaze that let her know he was on her side. "Maybe later, when he wakes, we can go upstairs and be silly for your brother. That should make him all better in no time."

"Please eat your cereal, Sarah," Jo said. "If there's one thing we don't need around here, it's another sick child."

A cheery voice from the doorway said, "What do you mean, another sick child? I just checked Timmy and he feels almost normal."

"NanaLeah!" Sarah ran to her and hugged her around her legs. Jo gazed at her mother in wonderment. The woman never seemed to sweat . . . hell, she never aged! Well, she had no gray in her hair, and that alone would make her look younger; but it was the way she stood so straight, and that little bounce in her walk. And the energy level. Sometimes it made her tired just watching her mother race from one thing to another. She was all dressed up this morning, in a soft crepe dress, and she carried a straw hat with a perky little veil on it.

"Careful, child, you'll rumple my dress, and I have to look absolutely perfect and ladylike when I meet with the editor of *Good House*. God, it's hot. Are you hot, Sarah? Yes? Why don't you get her some lemonade, Jim?"

"I can't have lemonade for breakfast!" Sarah said.

"Who says? Didn't I just invite you?"

"My mummy says—"

"Oh that's right, make me the bad guy!" Jo protested. "Mom! You should be ashamed of yourself. You never let *me* have lemonade for breakfast when I was Sarah's age."

"Well, I was young and dumb. Now that I'm young and smart, I realize how stupid it is to think we can eat only certain things for breakfast. Just think about it. We all insist on orange juice, like it was holy. Well, aren't lemons and oranges related? They're both citrus fruits. So what's the difference?"

Leah headed for the refrigerator and brought out the pitcher, half full of lemonade. "There we go! And I'll have one, too. Jim. What the hell! It's so hot! I heard you up in the night, Jo."

"He had a hundred two in the night, but it broke this morning."

"Good. You look awful. Don't worry so much. It's just a summer cold."

"I hope so." Nobody wanted to speak the dreaded words. Nobody wanted to say "infantile paralysis" out loud. Just thinking about it made Jo's heart thump in slow, thick beats. Polio was every mother's fear. Like a tiger crouched in the darkness, polio was ready to spring and destroy; you never knew exactly when or exactly where. And she had taken her kids to Coney Island to swim! In the middle of polio season! But it was the ocean; there had been no warnings on the radio. It wasn't infantile paralysis, of course it wasn't.

Timmy was probably pining away for Nether Althorpe. She'd taken him away from the only life he'd ever known. And what did she bring him to? A shabby old house in Brooklyn, for Christ's sake! What had she been thinking?

Her mother pulled out a chair and sat, spreading her skirt out carefully. "Hand me the *Times*, would you, Jim?" She was an avid newspaper reader, and she read nearly the entire thing.

"Oh, how dreadful! Listen to this! Here's a story about eight men who were in a Jap internment camp during the war, and now six of them have committed suicide. Apparently they made a pact as prisoners, that if they weren't happy when they got home, they'd—"

"Mom! Don't you think you could find something better to read aloud at breakfast? Something a bit more . . . suitable?"

Her mother frowned, then realized Jo was talking about Sarah, who was leaning forward in her chair, all ears.

"Oh. Sorry," Leah said. She read silently for a moment or two and then said, "Oh, dear!" She read aloud: " 'The condition of former mayor Fiorello H. LaGuardia became increasingly grave last night' . . . oh dear . . . 'not expected to regain consciousness and—' "

"Does that mean he's going to die?" Sarah asked.

"Mom!"

"Oh God, I'm sorry. Yes, Sarah, Mayor LaGuardia is probably going to die. But he lived a good life, a wonderful life, and that's what counts." She shot Jo a look that said *Okay?* and added: "Can I help it if the papers put the bad news on the front page?"

"I always thought LaGuardia was immortal somehow," Jim said, wiping his mouth and getting up from the table. "I keep forgetting that O'Dwyer's the mayor, don't you, Leah?"

"Absolutely." But she was deep into the newspaper again, and waved without looking up when Jim left. Sarah bounced up from the table to follow him to the door for a kiss; then she went upstairs to play.

"So what takes you into *Good Housekeeping* this morning, Mom?"

"A new assignment. I'm not so sure I'll take it, since I'll have to go out to Long Island a lot. God, I wish I'd learned to drive. Well, too late now, and anyway, where would we keep a car? But what a schlepp!"

"Sounds like heaven to me."

Her mother gave her a narrow-eyed scrutiny. "You're bored," she announced. "Well, as soon as the children are settled in, you'll be able to get back to work. Now that the war's over, the women's magazines will be booming. As soon as Timmy's better, why don't you call Irene Fairchild at *Woman's Gazette* and see what they need in the way of photo stories? Say—" She grinned. "—I have an even better idea! We sign up as a team! As a matter of fact, we could start with the job they gave me today, Jo. I write the story, you take the pictures."

In spite of everything, Jo felt a stir of anticipation. "What's the assignment?"

"Levittown."

"What's a Levittown?"

Leah laughed. "It's a brand-new idea, Jo, it's called—wait a minute, I'll remember it—it's called *prefabrication*. They make parts of houses ahead of time, see, and ship them out to where there's a lot of land. Then they build the houses—hundreds at a time—all exactly the same! They can do it so quickly that, according to this press release, they'll have a new village in just a month or two. So returning GIs will have housing!"

"Oh, I get it. Levittown's the name of the new village."

"Right. You wanna guess the name of the builder? It's going up right now, way out in Long Island somewhere." Her voice took on a dramatic tinge as she continued: "This way, every G.I. Joe and his family can have the American Dream for a mere, I forget exactly, three thousand dollars . . . something like that."

"You want me to take pictures of *houses*?"

"No, silly, not houses. People. I want you to snap away while I interview four all-American families who've already signed on the dotted line and are anxiously waiting for their houses to be finished."

"What kind of houses?"

"I don't know. Small, I think. But with modern bathrooms and kitchens . . . and listen to this, Jo, it's not just going to be a bunch of houses sitting out in the Long Island potato fields. No, they're building a whole *town*, with playgrounds and schools and shopping streets; it's brilliant!"

"Maybe I should sign up."

"Jo! Shame on you! You'll always have a home with us."

"Sorry, Mom. I didn't mean it. I think. Oh Christ, I don't know *what* I think anymore. Nothing's going the way I expected!"

"Nothing ever does," Leah said with a little laugh. A moment later, her tone careful: "Are you regretting you left Peter?"

"God, no! Never! You have no idea how stultifying my life was."

"Oh, don't I? I was in that house, and even that brief visit . . . not my taste. Well," she added, leaning over to give Jo's knee a pat, "you're here now and that's what matters. Oh, look, it's raining, they said scattered showers. I'd better take an umbrella when I go. Wouldn't do to have my hair a mess." She patted her thick hair, which was tucked into a French roll.

"Well, I, for one, am grateful for showers. Anything to cool off this damn city."

"The *Times* says relief is expected. And if you can't believe the good gray *New York Times*, what can you believe?" Leah went back to the paper, reading the ads and chattering on. "Lunch at Longchamps . . . cold fresh salmon, only $1.75, we'll have to try it." Jo wasn't really listening—until her mother said something about Jim.

"What was that?"

"I said I plan to buy Jim a new tie, a striped rep, at Rogers Peet. It's four bucks, but what the hell. They're paying well for this Levittown story. And I have to make up with him, anyway, so . . ."

"I should think you *would* make up with him. You've been landing on him pretty hard lately, Mom. When you're not treating him like the furniture."

Her mother sighed deeply and stared out of the window. "Yes," she said finally. "Yes. I know I've been not so nice. But he seems stuck in the thirties. Maybe the twenties. We had such fun back then. We were such . . . *pals*. We shared things and we went through hell together and—" She stopped and laughed. "God, I don't know about men, Jo. They're so resistant to change. They want everything to just stay the way it always was. But nothing does. Thank God."

Again she laughed, and then sobered. "Nobody's radical anymore, not like he remembers. There's no *need* to be! There's no place to go, in this country, but up and up and *up*. You'll see, we'll get bigger and richer and better all the time. The war's over and we won! People have plenty of money now; and all they want is to get back to normal."

Jo couldn't help laughing. "Surely not *you*, Mom? You've never been one for being *normal*."

"I know, I know. But you don't have to live it to write about it. And if the women's magazines want normalcy extolled, I'll be happy to oblige—for a price. It's Jim who won't budge."

"I can't believe you're that cynical. You've always had such high ideals."

"Well, Jo . . . maybe I'm not so cynical. But right now, I'm the one paying the bills around here . . . and, hey, if you want to know, at Jim's office, too. He hates it, I know he hates it. Even so, you'd think he could give me a thank-you now and then, wouldn't you? But no, not him. His male pride is all wounded. So instead of getting mad at the world that went ahead without him, he gets mad at me, keeps yelling at me that I'm selling out! If he keeps it up, I don't know what will happen to us."

"Oh, Mom, you're not going to *leave* him! You love him!"

"Of course I love him! What does that have to do with it? Love, as you should know, does *not* conquer all. He's turning into a stubborn, opinionated old geezer, right before my eyes. I'll tell you, I don't know how much longer I can live with it."

"That's very funny, you know? When I was debating whether I should leave Peter or not . . . Well, I asked myself what *you* would do, and I figured you'd never, ever, stay in a marriage that was a mess, with a man you didn't really love. So I decided I wouldn't, either. And now here I am, telling you you can't do that!"

"Hey! Wait a minute. Jim's a good man and he's always come through for me when I needed him. How could I leave him now, when he's *already* down? It's just . . . oh hell, I don't know—"

"You're bored," Jo said. It took her mother a minute to realize Jo was only tossing it back at her. Then they both laughed.

"Maybe. I find myself recalling other days, like that time in

London ... remember how we bumped into each other in Sloane Square?"

"Remember? I'll never forget! What a surprise! And I'd just been thinking about you. . . . It was like an answer to a prayer!"

Her mother beamed at her. "Really? God ..." She stopped talking and her eyes misted. "I didn't know ... I didn't know if I'd be welcome, just showing up without warning like that. I told you some cockamamie story about coming over to interview ... well, it was partly true. But really and truly, I was getting the hell away from New York. I ... I had been having an affair. I thought I was really in love—for the second time in my life." After a long pause, she added, "The first was your father." Another pause.

"But it was impossible. He had a wife. Children. A public position. Too many problems. So ... I ran away. . . ."

"What happened to him? Did you ever see him again?"

Leah shook her head. "I discovered it wasn't true love, after all. In England I found I was able to forget about him." She smiled in a certain secretive way, her eyes dropping coyly.

"Mom! That French Resistance fighter—the one who was visiting at the manor house! The one I was such a self-righteous prig about," Jo added dryly. And then the whole scene suddenly flashed in front of her, and with it, total knowledge. That French Resistance fighter ... shave off his beard and mustache, cut his hair short, add a couple of years, and voilà! Guess who?

Leah looked up and gave her a smile. "That's the one, the one you were such a self-righteous prig about."

"God, I'm sorry. I was so young, and sure I was right."

"Forget it. It's all water over the dam now. God, I wonder where he is now? Emile Le Boucher. Emile the Butcher." She shivered a little. "There was that hint of danger about him, remember? The iron fist under the velvet glove. It made him so attractive, didn't you think so?"

Jo got up from her chair and walked to the stove, unable to look at Leah. "Attractive?" She made her voice sound casual. "I don't think I even noticed what he looked like! I was so nervous, meeting Peter's parents, seeing the way they lived. All I could think about was whether Peter would still want me after he saw me in his home. Everything else is a blur."

"Your eyes weren't so blurred that you couldn't see Emile leaving my bedroom."

"Yes. Well, to tell you the truth, I was probably jealous. Peter had just given me a chaste kiss good night . . . *very* chaste." But she didn't want to get into *that*. "So, this French guy . . . he made you forget the man in New York . . . and then?"

"I stayed on an extra ten days . . . with him, in London."

"And you never told me! Mom!" Worse, *he* never told me. Because, of course, there was no question about it. Emile the Butcher and Elias Blanchard were one and the same. She and her mother had shared a lover! Oh God, it didn't bear thinking about!

"It was wonderful. Well, making love is always better in wartime. There's the added excitement that this might be the last time ever. And then . . ." Leah ducked her head, fighting a smile. "And then, of course, he happened to be quite a sexual athlete." She paused, blushing a little. "You know . . . the kind of man who can go on and on. He told me he learned the trick from an Arab friend, of keeping an erection for hours and hours—"

"Hours and hours! Mom!" She had to keep her eyes from revealing anything.

Her mother gave her a defiant look. "They say that the young Ali Kahn knew how to do it, too."

And someone else, as well, Jo thought, feeling slightly stunned. Elias. Elias, who could make love for hours, and who had said that an Arab chieftain had told him how it was done—in exchange for his revolver. El-Imsak, that's what he called it. El-Imsak . . . Elias, with his French accent and his little limp and his way of changing the subject whenever she tried to find out about his past. Her heart began to thump. Oh, that bastard!

"What happened to him, do you know?" Jo asked in her best noncommittal voice. "After those ten days, I mean. Unless, of course, all those hours and hours did him in!"

"Nothing romantic. He was called away on a mission, while we were together in London. He was going to parachute behind the lines somewhere, probably in France. So off he went, with a wink and a smile. 'See you in a few days,' he said. But I never saw him again. I waited a whole week, and then one afternoon the phone rang and I ran for it, sure it was him, but it was a voice I'd never heard, a woman saying, 'Mrs. Lazarus, linger no longer. Your friend has been killed.' And then she hung up.

"And that was it. That was the end of it. I couldn't get it

into my brain. He had been so . . . alive. I must have packed and made all the arrangements, because I did get back to New York. But I don't remember a thing. It was like sleepwalking.

"Not that it would ever have lasted—of course not. He was much younger than me. And we were so different. Still . . . I think of him sometimes, to this day. And sometimes I wonder . . . Sometimes I'm sure they were just giving me the cover story and he's still alive. I thought, a few times, of running an ad in the personals in the London *Times*, but it just seemed too silly."

I should tell her, Jo thought. She even opened her mouth to do it. But she couldn't. "And you came back to Uncle Jim."

A deep sigh. "I came back to New York. And to Jim, sure. But . . . well, you'd have to know our history, Jo, Jim's and mine. I had planned to tell him about it. It seemed only fair. But I didn't have the heart to do it. So I kept my mouth shut and let it slide. We did okay, Jim and me, but now—" She shook her head. "I don't know. I just don't know. If I suddenly heard from Emile Le Boucher . . . I just might go running to him."

Worse and worse. Jo's head was whirling. She was going to have to do *something*. But then, from upstairs, she heard Timmy whimpering and all thought fled. With surprise, she realized that for ten or fifteen minutes she'd forgotten all about Timmy and her terrible fear of polio.

"Oh God!" she said, and began to run.

"Jo, please, don't worry so. Don't panic!" her mother called after her. "He's going to be fine, really, he's going to be fine!"

But a week later Timmy wasn't fine. He seemed to get better, but then his neck got stiff and then the fever came back, and now he lay in the bed by the window, struggling for his every breath; his scrawny little chest quivering with each effort. He couldn't be so sick, he couldn't! She hadn't brought them all across the ocean for some stupid germ to interfere! No! They had to have their fresh start, their second chance!

God, it was hot! It was unbearable! The air was so heavy with humidity, every breath was difficult. But how could she even *think* that, Jo wondered, when her sweet Timmy was suffering so much! Sitting in a straight-back chair brought up from the dining room, every muscle tensed, sweat trailing down her backbone under the thin cotton dress, Jo tried to tease up a breeze with the fan her daughter had made for her.

Mom had taught Sarah how to fold oaktag back and forth to make a fan. After the first one, Sarah felt so accomplished she wouldn't stop. And now they had a ten-year supply of fans. But it did kind of stir up the air.

It was nearly eleven o'clock. Dr. Weeks had said she'd try to be there at ten, but she had a lot of house calls to make. A lot of kids were sick. "It's always like this in August. Polio season."

Polio! Dread word. Braces, wheelchairs, iron lungs, horrible. Please God, not polio, anything but that. Again Jo glanced over at Timmy. He looked awful. He was pale, anyway, but now he looked positively bleached and his face glistened with sickly sweat. Jo got up and, for the hundredth time, wiped his face and neck with a damp washcloth.

She shouldn't have let them go in the water. Everyone said that's how kids got infantile paralysis: swimming. But surely that only meant public pools where the same water stayed there day after day ... not the clean, ever-changing Atlantic Ocean! And the day they went to Coney Island was the *worst* in the entire heat wave, all the papers agreed. Trust her to pick the hottest day in ten years to take her English kids, who'd never known the temperature to go above seventy, out into the blazing sun!

"Mummy, I'm *hot!*"

Sarah again. She'd told her and *told* her to stay downstairs; to stay, for God's sake, out of Timmy's room. "We don't know what he has," she had explained. But Sarah would *not* stay away; every ten minutes or so she was back in the doorway.

"We're *all* hot, Sarah. It's a heat wave. And didn't I tell you that you *must* keep out of this room?"

"I'm not in the room." Indeed, she was standing on the doorjamb, her toes carefully positioned just in back of the threshold.

"Sarah, come on, you know quite well what I mean! You shouldn't be anywhere *near* here! How many times do you have to be told that we don't want you to get sick—"

"You said you'd play Old Maid with me."

"After the doctor comes, I said. Remember?"

"Why hasn't the doctor come? Doesn't she know Timmy is sick?"

"She's very busy, Sarah. There are lots of sick children she has to see." Christ, she shouldn't have said that. She didn't want

Sarah worrying. Maybe she should stop saying she didn't want
Sarah to get sick.

"How many?"

Exasperated, Jo said, "Sarah, please. How am I supposed to
know how many? I know what . . . you can go down and play
the piano."

Stubbornly: "You told me it was too noisy when Timmy is
asleep."

"Well, now I'm telling you it's okay."

"I want to stay with *you*, Mummy."

"Sarah, for God's sake!" Sarah's face scrunched up and she
began to cry. "Oh Lord. Come here, baby. Don't mind
Mummy. I'm just worried about Timmy. Come, sit on Mummy's lap." But two minutes of the damp warm weight was
more than enough and she said, "Get down now, Sarah, it's too
hot to cuddle."

"May I have lemonade?"

"At lunch . . . . oh Lord, Sarah, please don't start crying
again, would you?" She stood up and sent the child sliding off
her lap.

"I want my Nanny!"

Jo looked down at the dark head, the curls tight in the humid air. How was it possible to love and hate a person all at
the same time? "You want to know something? *I* want your
Nanny, too!"

"That sounds like you need *me*." Her mother was standing
in the doorway, like a miracle in a blue dress. "And I happen
to know a guy named Jim who's waiting downstairs to teach
a certain little girl how to play poker."

"Poker! Mom!"

"Never you mind. The kid's great at cards. Might as well
teach her a game that's useful in the big world. Old Maid!
That's for children, right, Sarah?" In a minute the little girl, all
smiles, was clattering down the stairs calling for her uncle Jim.

"How's it going, Jo?"

"How do you think?"

"I know, I know. I remember that knot of dread sitting in the
middle of the chest, when they kidnapped you. God, I thought
I would die of the waiting, of the not knowing."

"You always seemed so tough and strong to me when I was
a kid. Except once, now that I think of it."

"Only once? I remember a lot more times than that!"

"During the trial. I don't remember much about that time. It was all so crazy and they were always trying to keep everything from me. And . . . I kept waiting for you to come and get me. . . ."

"Don't you understand yet? It was all legal mumbo-jumbo, writs of this and that. I wasn't *allowed* to even get *near* you until that damned judge said so." Leah's voice became bitter. "That horrible woman. She wanted you to hate me."

Like a movie unreeling in front of her eyes, Jo suddenly saw the corridor of the courthouse, felt the pinch of the Mary Janes she had outgrown. Her grandmother's hand gripped hers like a vise; it hurt as she tugged at Jo, pulling her down the hall . . . pulling her *away*, Jo suddenly remembered. Because her mother was there, reaching out, calling her name, unable to come any closer, unable to move. "Jo! Joanna! Jo, baby! It's Mama! I love you!" Her voice anguished and clogged with tears, *Her mother, helpless.*

"Mom. I suddenly realize. I was *scared.* By Grandmother, naturally, but really, more by your being powerless. I always thought you were invincible. In a way, it was easier to believe that you didn't try hard enough. . . . Oh God, how awful!"

"That's right, it was."

"I'd completely forgotten that I even *saw* you trying to get to me . . . isn't that weird? Why would I forget a thing like that?"

"Ask Dr. Freud."

"No, none of that malarkey for me, thanks just the same." Jo checked the sleeping Timmy. He was still struggling to push air in and out of his lungs, and it scared her. She looked away, made herself not think about it. She'd wait for the doctor to get here.

"Funny, but seeing him in the bed, I suddenly remember—"

"Yes, Mom?"

"Nothing. No, not nothing." She sucked in an audible breath. "I grew up in an orphanage, Jo. My mother left me with them because she couldn't take care of me. People did that back then."

"An orphanage? So that's why you always ducked stories about your childhood. Poor Mom!"

"Not 'poor Mom,'—no, they were very kind. It wasn't a bad life at all, once I got used to it. And everyone else I knew was in the same boat. We even had a public school *inside* the orphanage. I was a good student. In fact, the year I was thirteen, the Superintendent of Schools gave me an award, for being—

let me see if I can remember the exact words—for being 'one of the best that ever was brought up in an institution.'

"I was going to be a schoolteacher. And, in fact, when I turned fourteen, the usual age they dismissed you from the orphanage and sent you out into the world to make your own way, they asked me to stay on. They said they would educate me."

"Mom, how wonderful. You must have been terribly bright."

"I'm sure I was. Didn't I have a terribly bright daughter?" They smiled at each other. "But it was Miss Shapiro who encouraged me. Betsy Shapiro. How I loved her! I thought she was so beautiful! I wonder if she really was. Who knows? She was in charge of all the 'clubs' they formed when I was around eleven or twelve. It was the very latest word in child welfare. Miss Shapiro made sure we learned typewriting and cooking and housekeeping—and do you know, Jo, we jumped at the chance to learn them! That's how tedious and unchanging life was there.

"You know what else I suddenly remember? They gave the boys music lessons, because they had a marching band. No girl could hope to learn to play an instrument. But girls could memorize all the popular songs and sing them. So, of course, we did. And Miss Shapiro even tried to make a choir out of us." Leah laughed. "God . . . Betsy Shapiro. I haven't thought of her in . . . oh, ages."

"What happened to her?"

There was a long silence. Then, "She died. She got TB and was spirited away to a sanitorium in the middle of the night. That's how they did things. Children weren't supposed to know anything. One day, she was there, my teacher, my friend, my encouragement. The next day, poof! Disappeared. Look at me! Do you believe . . . tears? Betsy Shapiro must have died in . . . it must have been nineteen seven or eight . . . and look at me!" She sniffed and dabbed at her cheeks with the back of her hand.

"Mom, I'm so sorry!"

"That's why I left at fourteen. I couldn't bear to finish high school without her. Let that be a lesson to you, Jo. If I'd stayed, I'd be a schoolteacher today, instead of a writer."

The doorbell's insistent buzz made them both jump. "The doctor!" Jo cried, and went clattering down the stairs, almost falling in her rush. She nearly embraced Dr. Weeks in her relief at seeing her.

The pediatrician's sharp eyes took it all in, and she said, "Why don't you get us some iced tea, while I go upstairs to look at . . . Tim?"

"Yes. Timmy."

"Well, Timmy and I will get along just fine." She had already started up the stairs. "His room?"

"In the back."

The doctor nodded. She knew her way around all the old houses in Brooklyn Heights. A tall broad-shouldered woman, who looked a lot like Eleanor Roosevelt. She always made her house calls accompanied by one of her dogs. The dog sat quietly on the stoop, waiting for her. Dr. Weeks was the best there was, everyone knew that.

Jo went into the kitchen and began to pour iced tea. They kept a jar of it, cold, in the fridge. It didn't occur to her not to obey the doctor; but she forgot to make a glass for her mother and had to do that. At last she had the three sweating glasses on a small metal tray, with lemon wedges, ice cubes and long iced tea spoons that tinkled against the glasses as she climbed the stairs.

Sarah called up the stairs. "Mummy, you should see what I—"

"Sarah, you'll have to wait, sweetie. The doctor's here."

"But Mummy, I only—"

"Later."

Without waiting to hear more, Jo hurried into the bedroom. And instantly knew something was dreadfully wrong. Her mother's face was drained of color and tears were streaming down her face. The doctor looked so sad as she patted Leah's hand.

"It's infantile paralysis, isn't it?" Jo heard her own voice as if it came from somewhere else, harsh and overly loud.

"Looks like it," Dr. Weeks said. "Where is your phone? I'll call Brooklyn Hospital and have them send the ambulance. . . ."

"Downstairs . . . in the hallway. Ambulance?"

"He may need an iron lung." The doctor hurried down the stairs.

"Iron lung . . ." Jo could do nothing but repeat the words, like a parrot. She leaned against the door, still balancing the little metal tray, and felt the tears coming. "Oh God, why?"

"There's no reason for something like this," her mother said, her voice sharp. "Don't start blaming yourself or thinking it's some kind of godly retribution."

"I brought him to this country."

"He could have gotten sick in England. You did what you thought best. What *was* best, Jo."

"And now he has—oh Lord!—infantile paralysis! Did you hear the doctor? Iron lung, she said. Iron lung!"

"She also said she hoped it wasn't bulbar . . . whatever *that* is."

"It can't be any worse than my baby in an iron lung! Oh God!" Cries came out of her, torn from her gut. "How can I tell Peter? How can I ever explain? How can I ever forgive myself?"

Jo stood at the doorway, wracked with sobs that hurt her chest. At some point her mother took the tray from her nerveless hands. Jo watched as the men with the stretcher came to get Timmy and rolled him gently from the bed. She saw how small and thin and pale he was, and heard the harsh sounds of his struggle to breathe, but only through a blur of tears and panic.

And then the sounds stopped. Just like that. The attendants exchanged looks, put the stretcher down, and bending over Timmy, began pushing at his chest.

"Stop! You'll hurt him!"

"Jo, take it easy, they're trying to help."

Time froze and everything began to happen in slow motion. The two men, taking turns, the strange rattling noises, the doctor taking the stairs two at a time, kneeling, giving orders. And then shaking her head, just shaking her head, very slowly.

"No! No!" With some surprise, Jo realized it was her voice shrieking like that.

"Please sit down, Mrs. Fielding." It was the doctor. She shook her head, bracing her back against the door frame. The light eyes bored into hers. "There is nothing we can do."

"The iron lung!" Jo heard herself begging.

"Not even the iron lung would have helped. At least he is no longer suffering. I am so sorry." Arms went around her.

There were more words, but she couldn't hear. There was a roaring in her ears, in her whole head. Timmy was dead, no, it could not be. And then she felt herself sliding down, her back still against the door frame, sliding down until she was crumpled on the floor. She beat her fists on the wooden planks until she was able to feel pain.

"What have I done?" she wailed. A small warm body flung itself onto her. Sarah. She held her child, whose entire body was shaking with sobs, held onto her for dear life.

"What have I done? Oh God, what have I done?"

33

September 1951

In the darkroom, nobody bothered you; if you were a person given to drifting and dreaming, you could drift and dream. The darkroom, down in the basement in an old bathroom not far from the washing machine, was a safe place. When the door was closed, everyone in the house knew it was off-limits. Jo welcomed the inviolate privacy, enjoyed the red-tinged hush; liked watching as the images slowly began to appear under the solution, like watery apparitions. The little radio on the shelf, tuned to WNEW, played George Shearing or Frank Sinatra or Sarah Vaughn. It was a radio station in limbo, Jo thought; listening, you'd never know it was 1951.

The print darkened in the developer, first an image so faint you couldn't tell what it was, then an outline, then it filled in feature by feature. And there she was: the woman in Jersey City, with her neatly pageboyed hair and her tightly corseted body, her mouth wide open, shouting, the face distorted, a smear of lipstick on one tooth. Jo reached down and, with one fingertip, rubbed up the dark mouth and then the stripes in the tiny American flag the woman clutched. An American mom, waving good-bye to her son who was going off with the army to fight communism in Korea. The woman was joyous, even delighted. She was proud. "And don't come back till you beat them!" she had yelled. Not a thought in her empty patriotic head that her boy might be shot and killed, Jo mused, or that they might send him back in a box; that this might be the last time she ever saw him.

Oh shit. Tears were leaking from her eyes. She couldn't think "son," she couldn't think "dead," without this dreadful unbidden weeping overtaking her. Timmy had been dead four years. Her baby, her sweet good-natured little boy. Dammit. Now she couldn't see a thing in the developer; she had to stop *doing* this, stop torturing herself. You'd think after four years the grief would have dried up. But the tears still came. They came by themselves, at the oddest times. When she was brushing her teeth in the morning; as she was falling asleep; in the peaceful aftermath of good sex, even. Not that there was much of *that*.

The only thing that stopped the endless mourning was work. Not developing and printing—all alone in the darkroom, it was too easy to let her mind wander—but the real work: the plane trips to catch American families at work and play, or to cover parades or conventions—anywhere there was a story with a picture in it. She'd been all over the country. If they'd create spaceships, she'd go take pictures of Buck Rogers on Mars!

She concentrated on the photo, and the tears stopped. She pulled the Jersey City woman out of her bath, hung the print up to dry, and went on to the next one. And started to laugh. Backlit and misty, it was a dramatic female profile, cigarette held to lips, eyes lowered, hair covered by a turban, the face so deeply shadowed you couldn't tell who it was. But she knew. It was her mother.

Leah had taken to writing sexually provocative articles—not dirty, but . . . what was the word? titillating—for *Playboy*. "What Women Really Want" or "Why Women Long to Be Part of a Harem." Titles that promised more than Mom was actually willing to deliver.

The editors apparently thought it a great joke, having a woman write for their cock-centered magazine, with its frank letters to the editor, its nude photos of very large-breasted, very young girls, its advice to the sexlorn. But they were good to Leah, good, and careful not to call a spade a spade or a cock a cock. Leah came home from those meetings laughing. "Oh, if they only knew I used to pay the rent by writing pornography!"

Well, the men who bought the magazine ate it up; and lots of letters had come in asking for a look at "Lady Pamela Harding." So, a little embarrassed, but determined, Mom had come to her and said, "Look, this is crazy. But will you help me out here? They want a picture."

"Of you?"

"You needn't sound so surprised! Of *course* of me ... but not really. Sort of."

Leah had explained how she wanted to be disguised. "But, nothing uncovered, you understand. I'm too old for that. Just sexy. They are positively obsessed with sex over there." She rolled her eyes. "Men!"

Jo thought a minute, then said: "Dietrich! Updated, but with her mystery and ... glamor!"

Leah had enjoyed hamming it up for the camera. She wanted to keep writing for *Playboy*; they paid top dollar. "They say it'll soon put *Esquire* out of business," she remarked. "Well, it certainly will if they keep paying this way for talent."

Jo took the mysterious-lady print out of the developer and squinted at it. Yes, it was good, and no, you couldn't tell who it was. Or how old she was, for that matter. Jo laughed again; she had smeared Vaseline over the lens; it really did make for an interesting erotic effect, and at the same time hid unwanted lines and wrinkles. *Playboy*'s readers should be storming the editorial offices to meet "Lady Pamela"! A lot of luck to them!

Reaching over to where several rolls of negatives were stored, Jo searched for the old roll she'd found last month. It was film she'd shot in London during the war. It had been hidden in the fold of a corner in her gadget bag, undeveloped, all those years. As soon as she had seen the negatives, she realized they were taken during the Blitz. And when she spotted several precious shots of Edward R. Murrow—one of them as he was broadcasting from the top of the BBC tower, vulnerable but defiant—she had been elated. She recalled how frantically she had hunted and searched for that roll of film; finally, she'd just given it up for lost.

But there it was, the whole roll. She was so excited to find that chunk of her past, especially since the prints had turned out to be as good as she'd hoped they would be. Later, as she spread them out on the kitchen table to study them, a terrific idea came to her.

Back down to the darkroom she'd gone, poking around until she found another set of negatives from the war years: bomb craters; explosions blooming in the night sky like poison flowers; bombed-out houses; a flower pot, whole and complete with plant, sitting in rubble. Then she superimposed Murrow onto the war scenes he'd always described so eloquently, and made eight-by-ten blowups. They were quite wonderful, she thought, a little strange and ghostlike, but really fine.

She had put them into a folder, marked it "In the Mind of Murrow," and sent it straight off to Elias at the gallery in London. He'd wired her immediately, just one word: MORE!

Elias. Whenever she thought of him, she saw him naked, hairy, stiffly erect. She shivered a little. There was nobody else like him, nobody. She felt guilty lusting after him when she wasn't in love with him, just because he could make love for hours—until you begged for mercy, and then he would laugh and make you come again. A couple of times a year she flew to London, supposedly to take pictures and check in with the gallery. But what she really did, for a week or two, was fuck her brains out.

The first time she had seen Elias, after she realized he was probably her mother's mysterious Emile Le Boucher, she felt a bit strange. It was difficult enough to think about your mother in bed with *any* man . . . but with your own lover, almost impossible. All the way to London she'd wondered if she'd be able to do it . . . wondered if she'd still find him sexy. She should have known better. As soon as she walked into the gallery and saw him, she felt the same old excitement.

Later, sitting cross-legged on his bed feeding him lo mein from the carryout Chinese place down the street, tingling pleasantly in all the places she liked to tingle, Jo decided she was going to ask him straight out. "Elias," she planned to say, "how come you never told me about you and my mother?" But the words had stuck in her throat. What a coward she was!

It was time, she decided, as she studied the negatives, to pay another visit to England. She hadn't been there for, what? Two months? No, longer. She would make plans as soon as she had finished her current project. And she wouldn't *ask* him; she'd *tell* him that she knew Elias Blanchard and Emile Le Boucher were the same man.

Squinting in the dull red light, Jo looked to see what else the old film had that she could use.

She found herself looking at a negative of Peter—a young, handsome Peter, leaning against his little roadster, smiling into the camera. She remembered the day she had taken that snap; it was the day he had confessed his love for her, stammering a little, endearing himself to her with every hesitant syllable. She remembered her heart pounding in her chest, the adoration almost suffocating her. Lord, what a naive ninny she had been! She could not bear to look at it. She remembered how he had seemed to her then: strong, purposeful, brave, intelligent, charming, stable, rooted, *safe*. Lord, how young and dumb and wrong she had been!

She had not seen Peter in years, although he wrote. About twice a year, she'd get a long chatty letter in his schoolboy hand. In fact, these were not precisely *her* letters; they were always addressed to both her and Sarah. But she always went through them first, just in case he had written something strange. Of course, he never did; they were just ordinary gossipy ramblings.

The taxes had become horrendous and the mater refused to face facts, wouldn't give up anything. He was determined not to lose Nether Althorpe, so other things had to be lost, ha ha, like the silver holloware and the Turkey carpets. Did she know that memorabilia from Victoria Regina's Golden Celebration were worth thousands of pounds? The pater was a regular at the local pub—one might say *too* regular, and had already had a heart attack, a small one, nevertheless the medico had given him orders—no more scotch whisky, no more cigars. But she knew how the pater was; one couldn't tell him anything, one did the best one could. And he was scraping together the fare for Sarah to come visit during her next school hols, just when were they again?

He'd written the same thing for five years, claiming he was scraping together the fare for Sarah to visit; but somehow he never managed to scrape hard enough. Last summer, in exasperation, Jo had sent the child over for a month, with her own money. She had lied—God knows why—and told Sarah that Daddy had sent the fare. For years Sarah had been saying, "When Daddy sends for me . . ." making all kinds of little-girl plans. So of course she was thrilled. You'd have thought she was going to heaven!

Jo had no idea what had transpired over there last July, but when Sarah came back, she didn't talk much about it. She gave vague answers to their questions and kept saying everything was okay, Daddy was okay, the grandparents were okay, Nether Althorpe was okay, London was okay.

Jo tried, very carefully, to probe Sarah about Peter's social life.

"Does Daddy have a . . . a lady friend?"

"There were lots of ladies at the fete." An irritated toss of the head.

"I know, Sarah, but I meant . . . a special friend?"

Sarah gave her a look of deep disgust. "How would *I* know?" she said. "We don't talk about that stuff."

"Does he seem happy?"

"He's okay. They were all okay and it was all okay, Mummy. I wish you'd stop asking me about it all the time." After a pause, she added: "Daddy *never* asked me about you!"

So Jo stopped asking, but she had to admit she was terribly curious. Peter must have changed, of course, but how? He would have aged slightly. She imagined him pale and vague, something like Dilly, fussing from one thing to another, dropping things behind him, never getting anything *done*. Sarah's Christmas gifts were a good example. Every year since they had left, he wrote Sarah a special, separate note sometime in the autumn, asking her what she would like for Christmas: Now think carefully, darling, it must be very very special. And she would think and think and then a note would be sent back to Buckinghamshire with a list.

And he always lost the list, or forgot, or simply didn't want to be bothered, and so called a department store in London and ordered a doll to be sent. Every Christmas a proper English girl-doll with stiff painted smile would arrive and Sarah would bite her lip and try to smile. But the plain fact was, she didn't like dolls. Sarah liked to listen to music on her radio, alone, with the door shut and locked; or sit at the piano, picking out tunes. She wanted a guitar, and Jim said he'd get her one for her tenth birthday. What in the world did Sarah dream about? Think about? Jo could not even imagine. She found Sarah a peculiar child, and that beautiful little face seemed blank to her.

Now, Jo heard her mother coming down the basement stairs—you could hear the clack of her high heels a mile away—singing a very sexy rendition of "Come Ona My House," à la Rosemary Clooney. She even sounded a little like her. She banged on the darkroom door.

"Come on, Jo, when I left three hours ago, you were down here hiding away. And now I come back and you're still here? Enough already! Come on, come upstairs and have a drink with me. I need to complain to someone."

Oh, terrif. Just what she needed. How about *her*? Didn't her mother think *she* had anything to complain about? Oh, to hell with it. Leah's complaints were usually amusing anecdotes.

"I'll be up in a mo'!"

"I'm making very, very dry martinis . . . no wait, we're out of olives. Make that Gibsons. I'm sure we have onions." The high heels clack-clacked up the stairs.

When Jo came up into the kitchen, she had to blink. After several hours in the darkroom, even normal light seemed blinding.

"God, you look like a—whaddayacallit—like a troglodyte. . . ."

"A . . . what?"

"One of those troll creatures who live beneath the earth." Leah was bustling about, with the gin bottle and the vermouth bottle; but Jo could see she was upset. She was running her fingers through her hair, which had recently been clipped into a poodle cut. Every movie star had one, but Leah Lazarus was the first woman in Brooklyn Heights to have done it. It suited her; she was a very good-looking woman, and, as usual, did not look her age at all. But she was *certainly* bothered about something.

"What's up?" Jo asked. "You look upset."

"Upset? *Upset?* That's hardly the word for it!"

"Wait a minute. Let *me* play bartender. Sit down and tell me all about it." Swiftly she poured a generous portion of Bombay gin into a thick glass, plopped three onions in, and waved the vermouth over it. But the wan little martini joke didn't get even a smile.

"What's wrong, Mom?"

Leah took a hefty gulp of her drink, shuddering a little as it went down. "What's wrong? What's wrong is that the *Redline Newsletter*, with all its Red-hating garbage, is sitting in huge piles on the reception desk at the *Woman's Gazette* editorial floor. And when I went in to see Irene Fairchild, she was distinctly cool."

"Cool? But Irene Fairchild *loves* you."

"Yes, yes, I know. Irene Fairchild loves me and loves my work. Except that today she actually asked me if it was true I once belonged to the ACLU. And whether Jim McCready is, ahem . . . 'still a friend of yours.' I just stared at her. She knows—they all know—that Jim and I have been living together for years! So I said yes, we were still, ahem, friends, and what did that have to do with the ACLU? 'Well, Leah dear,' she says, cool as a cucumber, 'you *are* aware Jim is being investigated? We've had, um, people in here asking about him, and about you, too, Leah dear.' "

Her mother paused, drank, and then, in a phony high voice, repeated, " 'And about you, too, Leah dear.'

" 'And just what does Jim McCready or the FBI—or the House Un-American Activities Committee, for that matter— have to do with our meeting?' I asked. Sweet as pie, you understand.

" 'Why nothing, dear, nothing at all. I just thought . . . well, you know . . . the Red Menace . . . the Bomb . . . well, we in the information industry have no choice but to be ever vigilant.'

"And then, Jo, the bitch—'information industry,' my foot!— handed me back my manuscript, smiling, and told me she was so sorry, but the head office in Ann Arbor had decided *not* to continue with my 'Life Around the Country' series. They were going to add fashion pages to the magazine. And the head office wanted to see make-overs—*make-overs*, Jo—and, oh God, Jo, the woman babbled on and on, while I sat there, realizing I was being given the shaft! And she had the lousy goddamn nerve to tell me I was certainly free to take the material to any of the other shelter books or women's publications. Ha! I'll bet you anything I'm on *their* list, too!"

"Maybe not, Mom. *Somebody* has to still be sane."

"Don't be sure! You know how Jim's advertisers have all dropped out all of a sudden, and now the crazies are after *me*. I have this horrible sneaking feeling I'm going to find myself without any work, and very soon! And all because of that goddamn *momzer* McCarthy you want to go take pictures of!"

"I don't want to take pictures of him. I've been given an assignment to do it. Come on, Mom, Joe McCarthy's news."

Her mother made a terrible face, and took another gulp of her drink, then got up and poured, liberally, from the gin bottle. "I'll make you a bet that all my assignments dry up within the next few months. Dammit, I'll have to go back to the little magazines, or worse, to the pulps—at ten cents a word! *That* won't pay the mortgage! Maybe I should just go back to writing porn."

"Mom! Don't even say it!"

"Hey! I was damn good at it, better than any of those men! And you can get that look off your face, Jo. Let's just say I have a vivid imagination, okay?" She laughed, instantly looking many years younger, and Jo felt relieved.

"In the meantime, there's always *Playboy*," Leah said. "I hope. Oh, there's mail for you. From England. I put it over there, next to the toaster."

England! And she had just been thinking about Elias. Unless it was one of Peter's rambling missives. Oh please, not that. She was relieved to see Elias's elegant European hand on the envelope.

"You *can* refuse an assignment, you know," her mother went on. "Especially when the subject is the new version of Attila the Hun—"

"When I get finished shooting Senator McCarthy, he'll wish to God it had been a gun instead of a camera!" Her mother looked dubious; so Jo shrugged and bent to her letter from Elias.

When the front doorbell rang, Jo pretended to be concentrating on her mail. Let her mother go. Anyway, Elias loved her Murrow pieces. He had put them in the window, and there was a great deal of interest. He thought he should come over to the States with them; he thought there was bound to be a good market over here since Murrow was now a big thing on the telly, with his *See It Now*.

Jo's eyes moved swiftly over the pages; not a single personal word, damn him. Still . . . to sell her pictures, actually sell them, as *art*, oh Lord, that would be heavenly.

Thinking she heard the unmistakable cadences of Elias's deep voice coming from the front hall, she shook her head. Things were really bad when she began to hear voices. But the sounds did not stop so she stepped out into the hallway.

It was Elias! Big as life and twice as natty with his Saville Row suit, standing by the doorway, Leah's hands gripping his arms. "Now, Leah, now, Leah . . ." he was murmuring. "You must calm yourself, I have much to tell you."

"Much to tell me! I'll say! I thought you were *dead*, Emile! They told me you were dead!"

"Wartime. You understand."

"But you're here. I don't know how you found me, but you did and you're here! Oh Emile, it's like a sign, a portent. You couldn't have come at a better time!"

Leah was so involved in her own excitement, she obviously did not notice his discomfort. He said, "Leah, please calm

yourself, it's not a portent, there's something you should know.
I—Listen, Leah, I had no idea you were here."

"But this is my house! How . . . ?" Her voice faded and she
stepped back, away from him. "What . . . ?"

At last he looked over Leah's shoulders and found Jo's eyes.
He fought a smile and then gave a distinctly Gallic shrug. Jo
said nothing. Let him explain. Of course she hadn't mentioned
to him that she was living with her mother; she had carefully
avoided any mention of her mother. He never asked her anything; he wasn't interested in the details of her life. He'd gotten himself into this predicament, let him wiggle out of it.

"Leah, I had no idea—" he began, and immediately gave it
up. "Joanna," he said, "would you please explain?"

"Jo!" Leah cried, whirling around. "How does Jo— Oh,"
she said in a flat voice, the color draining from her face.

Shit. Jo shot him a hard look and then said, as pleasantly as
she was able, "Mom, I had no idea you knew Elias."

"Elias?"

"Elias Blanchard. My London agent. My gallery."

Tightly: "I knew this man as Emile Le Boucher."

Brightly, innocently: "Really? Oh, of course. The Resistance
fighter who was at Nether Althorpe when Peter and I became
engaged. Am I right?"

"That's right." Her mother's eyes were narrowed as she
looked quickly from one to the other of them.

Elias began to speak, stammering a little in his haste. "You
see, Leah, we met—purely by accident—Jo and I. At Covent
Garden, going 'round the booths. She was looking for a frame
for one of her photographs. I was already running the gallery,
you see. I—I recognized her, as Peter's fiancée, his *wife*, actually, and I was going to remind her of our brief meeting that
weekend. But I could see she didn't know who I was, didn't
remember me at all, and . . . I must have been too embarrassed
to press it . . . and so . . . she never realized . . ." His voice
dribbled off.

There was a thick, loaded silence.

"I see," Leah said after a moment. "I see. Of course. You're
here to see Jo, not me. I—It was foolish of me to think so. But
I was so shocked to see you standing in the doorway after all
these years of thinking you were dead. Who knew?" She
laughed. "I'm a foolish old—no, make that middle-aged—
woman! But I'm happy you're alive."

They all laughed—Jo with relief—and Elias took Leah's

hand, pressing his lips to it. "You look as marvelous as ever, you know."

Leah turned to Jo, smiling brightly. If she was hurt by it all, you would never know it. "Jo, come greet your guest, why are you standing back there? Emile—sorry, Elias, of course—you'll stay with us." Now she blushed, and laughed again, in a way that made Jo conscious of the fact that her mother had guessed that she and Elias were lovers.

Then, crowding in behind Elias, came Jim with Sarah in tow. Jo saw at once that he was weaving just the tiniest bit, and Sarah's eyes, filled with sadness, confirmed that he had been drinking. Not a whole lot, just enough to take the edge off. Poor Jim, struggling to make the world stand still. Jim had no audience anymore for his radical views . . . and what was worse, with this guy McCarthy on the rampage and everyone scared shitless of communists, his ideas only made trouble for him. He was elderly, and tired, and America had changed on him.

Leah guided Jim into the center of the hallway, and Jo could see by the whiteness of her mother's knuckles how hard she was holding him. He must be numb, not to feel it.

"Jim, you're home early!" Jo cried. "And we have a guest!"

Jim pulled himself together with a kind of shiver, pulling his shoulders back, rubbing his hair with his hands and clearing his throat noisily. He put a big grin on his face.

"A visitor. Well, visitors are always welcome in this house!"

Leah's face was a study in contained anger; but give her credit, she managed a smile, managed to introduce Elias, although she forgot his last name and called him Boucher. And then, her hand still gripping Jim's arm—a thinner arm now, Jo realized with a shock, on a smaller, thinner man—Leah helped Jim up the stairs.

Jo watched them for a moment and then turned back to Elias. Well, here he was. Never mind why; he was here, and boy, did she need him. She stepped close to him and lifted her face for his kiss. But he gave her a warning frown, and, startled, she turned to see Sarah standing in the corner, leaking tears. It made Jo crazy.

"What *is* it, Sarah?" For heaven's sake, she'd seen Jim worse than that!

"You forgot me."

"Sarah! I didn't forget you. How can I forget you, when you're always underfoot, weeping?"

Now crying openly, Sarah ran up the stairs. Elias gave Jo a look and opened his mouth to speak, but she cut him off with a chop of her hand. "Do you mind? I know I'm a dreadful hag, but sometimes that child is a pain in the neck." With the words came the sudden realization that she had promised to meet her daughter after school, to shop for new shoes. Oh Christ!

"That's all right, Jo. I only came to discuss business."

Elias's tone was icy, distant, and she felt, like a cold wind blowing, something alter, irrevocably, irretrievably. Her blood ran cold, as cold as his tone; and she knew, just as if he had said it, that nothing between them would ever be the same again.

34

Christmas 1951

Nobody would be home. Nobody was *ever* there to say hello when she came in from playing. Sometimes NanaLeah might be in the kitchen and just not hear her—she was always singing along with the radio—but usually she was out working on a story or something. Mummy was always down in the darkroom; and if you disturbed her while she was in the darkroom, she got very mad. It used to be that Uncle Jim made sure to come home early, so they could play poker, or he'd watch and applaud while she put on a show. He said she sang like an angel . . . but not lately. Lately he stayed out a lot.

And anyway, the person Sarah was *really* hoping to see was Elias. She had a twinge of guilt because she knew it hurt Uncle Jim's feelings, that she loved Elias. Well, she couldn't help it. Elias was so nice to her. He said she had the devil in her eyes; she didn't know what it meant, not really, but she knew it was good to have the devil in your eyes. She still loved Uncle Jim. But Elias was different, and anyway, she had to get

Mummy married. Then *she'd* be like everyone else, because she'd have a new father.

"A new father? How do you get a new father?" her friend Lucy had wanted to know earlier, when they were playing in the snow. Lucy was dumb about some things.

"Silly, your mother gets married, that's how."

"Your mother's already married," Lucy said.

"No, she isn't. She's divorced, and that means she can get married to someone else. . . ."

Lucy made a funny face. "Somebody else . . ." she said. "That's so weird. And having a *new* father—what a drag. Of course, it's better than no father at all. . . ."

"I still have my real father," Sarah said, suddenly angry at Lucy. "And he loves me—more than anything. It's just that—that—there's no room for me at Nether Althorpe." And she'd stopped making the snow fort with Lucy right then, and headed home. She'd said she had to go to get her Christmas present from England. But she didn't even know if there would be a present this year.

Running up the hill from Squibb Park, she crossed all her fingers inside her mittens and prayed that he remembered. It could even be a doll, only please God, let him not forget again. Pretty soon it wouldn't matter, because Elias would be her new daddy after he married Mummy.

Her mother said don't call her "Mummy" anymore, it was an affection—something like that. *Affectation*; that was the word.

"You haven't lived in England for years, Sarah, there's no need to cling to British speech. It sounds phony. Call me 'Mommy,' for God's sake. Or even better, Mom."

I'm *not* going to call her "Mom," Sarah decided as she let herself into the front hall. She slammed the door, hard; but nobody heard. As usual. She took off her new ski jacket and began to wrestle with the leggings, and then she had to sit down because the boots had to come off first. She loved her new boots; they had a zipper instead of buckles and looked so grown-up.

No, she was not going to call her "Mom." If it couldn't be "Mummy," which is what *she* wanted, then what? Mother. That's what she'd call her. And her mother could like it or lump it. Sarah didn't know exactly what that meant, but it sounded good and tough.

She started toward the kitchen when she heard the sound of

voices from the living room. They never used the living room;
NanaLeah was always saying she didn't know why she spent
good money on a big house when everyone always hung
around the kitchen. Well, *she* did, too. Even her Underwood
portable was there, on the table, unless she'd stuffed it into the
bread box. Once, when Sarah asked her why she kept her typewriter in the bread box, NanaLeah looked startled for a minute,
then said, "Because it fits!"

Lucy's mother was always saying it must be so stimulating
to live in such a creative household. "My, but you must lead
such an interesting life over there," Lucy's mother said. Sarah
didn't think so; and she didn't think Lucy's mother meant it
nicely, either.

Sarah Fielding was sick of interesting. She wanted a regular
life. She wanted a grandmother who looked like a real granny,
like Lucy's, with wrinkles and white hair. And she really
wished Uncle Jim would stop drinking and be like he used to
be.

Lucy liked coming over to play, but Sarah always felt funny
when other kids came over because they asked so many questions. And so did their mothers. She knew, even though their
faces were smooth and kind, that they were thinking mean
things. She hated her family being so . . . so unusual. She'd
said that once. And both of them laughed at her, Mummy—
Mother—and NanaLeah.

It was their voices, in the living room, mostly NanaLeah,
and there was something about the way she sounded that made
Sarah tiptoe very very quietly so they wouldn't hear her.

"Oh God, what is Jim *doing* so long? I told you that man
would ruin the country, and he *has*."

"Who—Jim?"

"Don't be such a smartmouth, Jo. You know damn well who
I mean. That scourge, McCarthy!"

"Jim isn't taking a long time, Mom. The committee is taking a long time, asking him the same dumb things over and
over, hoping he'll name names."

"Jim will never cave in."

"Well . . . the human instinct for self-preservation is pretty
strong. Oh, don't look at me that way, Mom. I don't think Jim
is a quisling. But these days, who knows what *anyone* might
do?"

"You're right, you're right, and I know it. I just don't *want*
to know it. This country is going crazy! California with a state

loyalty oath! And have you seen the comic books they have now? Heroes jabbing out communist eyes with ice picks? This is what they give children to read! I'll tell you something, if I didn't remember so clearly how I felt at my first sight of the Statue of Liberty, how everyone on that ship cried with relief to *be* here . . . if I didn't have that memory, I'd be ashamed to be an American!"

Sarah crouched by the doorway, barely breathing. She loved it when NanaLeah got going on something . . . when her voice rang out and her eyes flashed. It was thrilling. But she almost never did it if she knew Sarah was listening; she'd stop and say, "Oh my God, the child. Don't mind me, sweetie pie. I just get carried away."

"I've thought of moving to Sweden, Mom. But then I'd have to learn *Swedish*, and hell, I don't know how the Swedes do it! People are so scared . . . even the college kids. Lord, I remember when I was at CCNY, we were all dying to get out and change the world! Well, there's no more of that. No wonder they're called the silent generation. All they want is to get good jobs and make money. And go on panty raids. *Panty raids!* Did you ever hear of anything so ridiculous? Biz Ad— Business Administration—that's what they're all going in for. Hand me some more tinsel, would you? And maybe we should turn on the lights. It's getting dark in here."

"If it's dark, then where's Sarah?"

"At Lucy's. Thank God for Lucy."

"Why do you say that? I think Lucy is a little priss."

"Oh, she is. Just like her mother. But she's Sarah's only friend. And I must admit, I don't know *what* to make of Sarah. I could understand a loner, I'm one myself, but she really carries it too far. I don't think she likes people, Mom, I really don't."

NanaLeah laughed. "That's nuts, Jo. Of course she likes people. But she doesn't seem to *need* them. She's just . . . an individualist." She laughed again. "Like us, in fact!"

Individualist. Sarah liked the sound of that; it sounded big and important. It was a much nicer word than loner; and she made a mental note to remember it. But it was time to make a lot of noise so they'd know she was there. She didn't like overhearing her mother talk about her; it made her feel squeamy.

"Jim?" NanaLeah called out, and then, just a little bit disappointed, said, "Oh, hello, sweetie pie. I thought maybe it was Uncle Jim, back from . . . his meeting."

"I was wondering if you'd get here in time to help us trim the tree," Mummy—*Mother*—said.

"You said you'd wait," Sarah argued.

"I said we'd wait until three and then we'd start. It's three forty-five. You *know* I have theater tickets tonight."

"Is Elias going, too?"

"Elias left today," her mother said after a pause. Her voice was tight, as if it didn't want to leave her throat.

"Left?" Sarah repeated. But he hadn't even said good-bye!

"Yes. He had to get back to London. He has a business there, and if he's not there, it all falls apart." Her mother was talking so fast, Sarah knew there was something she wasn't saying.

"You're not going to get married," she said sadly.

Her mother turned so fast, she almost fell off the little stepladder. "Married? Whatever put *that* notion into your head? Elias and I never—I wouldn't—Sarah, that's just ridiculous! Where did you get the idea we were going to get *married*?" Her mother's face was pink and she looked angrier with every word.

"But you always went to sleep together, and Lucy told me that meant you'd get married."

"Lucy's a twit!"

"Jo!" NanaLeah said, annoyed. "Come here, Sarah, come to me. *I* can see where you got the idea Elias and your mother might get married, but you should have asked, you know."

She held out her arms, but Sarah was too humiliated to be comforted. She could feel her face getting hot.

"I'm sorry, Sarah," Mummy said. "I know you love Elias. I . . . I love him, too. I thought maybe—but it just wasn't meant to be. He's my agent. He sells my photographs. Or at least, he *tries*." She sighed loudly. "It was time for him to go back, so he went. And Sarah . . ." She waited a minute, thinking hard. "And Sarah, I don't think you should wait for me to get married again. It's not going to happen. Oh Lord, don't cry, please? Try to understand. I'm no *good* at being married."

Her mother looked like she was about to cry; but then she shook her head and smiled. "I know what! *You* get married and I'll try very hard to catch your bouquet. I'll practice!"

Sarah had to laugh. She always had to laugh when Mummy got silly. "Oh, Mummy, *I* can't get married! I'm too little."

"You don't seem so young to *me*. Why, I think I spy a gray hair here in your head—" But now she was laughing, too, and so was NanaLeah. They were all feeling good; Sarah liked it when they were all feeling good together.

"Anyway," her mother went on, "Elias left you a lovely present—no, no, you'll have to wait until Christmas morning—and he said he'd send you a long letter from London. And we saved the bottom of the tree for you. We just did the top. And the tinsel. You know how you hate doing tinsel."

"It takes too long."

"If you do it right." Her mother always insisted that tinsel be placed on the branches a few strands at a time. If you threw a big bunch on, the way NanaLeah and Sarah and Jim liked to do, she got fussy. So everyone let her do it herself.

Sarah concentrated on finding her favorite ornaments. There was an old tin Santa Claus, and a carousel horse painted with red and green that her daddy had sent her one year. He said he'd ship her a new one every year, but it was the only one. And she loved the Italian glass balls; they were so fragile and beautiful. They looked like soap bubbles, as if they would pop if you blew on them.

"Look outside. It's snowing. How pretty it looks, in the street lamp, like lace."

"I hope it snows and snows and snows," Sarah said. "Right up to the windowsills." They had been studying about the Blizzard of '88 in school; children had gone sledding out of their bedroom windows, right here in Brooklyn Heights, that's how high the snowdrifts were! Oh, if it would only happen again!

"Don't wish too hard for something," NanaLeah said. "You might get it! Not too many years ago, in 'forty-seven, we had one helluva blizzard. Don't you remember? You were big enough. Remember how nothing moved. How slippery it was in the street? Don't you remember how we tried to take a walk, with you on your sled, only I kept falling down? God, that was some snowfall! It *was* pretty, that I'll admit. But we ran out of everything. We ended up eating tuna fish and canned baked beans, breakfast, lunch, and dinner!"

Just then the doorbell rang. And rang and rang, all impatient. Sarah noticed how her mother and NanaLeah exchanged quick glances. She knew what *that* meant. Uncle Jim had been drinking again and had forgot his keys. He was doing that a lot lately. Sarah crossed her fingers. She hated when Uncle Jim stumbled and forgot what he was saying; or else he got very angry and stomped around the house, yelling and shaking his fist.

Both women went to the door. But it wasn't Uncle Jim. Sarah heard a woman's voice, very deep and gruff, shouting, "Ho, ho, ho, and a Merry Christmas to all and to all a good day! Do you have room for a stranger at this inn?" And shrieks of delight. She had heard that voice somewhere before. So she went to see.

NanaLeah was laughing and crying all at the same time, and hugging the lady at the door, and saying, "What heaven did you drop from?" Gusts of snow came swirling in through the open door.

"Which heaven do you think? Scotland, of course. Here, let's get this door shut or you'll be making snowmen in here." She was a tall woman with short gray hair that stuck out from under the bright red tam. She was big, too, and looked even bigger wrapped in a huge red plaid shawl. "No, Cliff's not with me. As a matter of fact . . . well, we've decided it's time to part."

"After all this time?" her grandmother said. "Well, come right in and make yourself at home! It's wonderful to see you!"

Now it came back to her. That woman had come to Nether Althorpe once and it made Mummy very sad when she left. Even Nanny had said, "Now there's a decent body, if you please, and quite amusing, too." What *was* her name? Something unusual.

Then the visitor noticed her and threw up her hands in mock surprise. "It's little Sarah—only not so little anymore, are you, kiddo? A good thing I didn't get you a teddy bear. I see you're well beyond stuffed animals. But I did bring you something— here you go, kiddo, see how you like it." She had bent over a large canvas bag and pulled out a brightly wrapped package.

Sarah heard Mummy say, "Now, Zelda, you needn't—" Zelda. That was her name!

And Zelda said, "You hush now. I brought *you* something, too, never fear."

Sarah ripped the Christmas paper from the package. It was from Harrods. The best store in the whole world, she remembered *that*. Inside the box was a dark crimson leather box that opened with a snap. And inside! She couldn't believe her eyes. It was a manicure case and it had absolutely everything in it. Tiny scissors, nail file, pusher, everything! And a series of little bottles. Nail polish! In wonderful grown-up colors. Not blue and green and yellow, like in the Chen Yu magazine ads she loved studying. But four different reds and three pinks and a bottle of remover and cotton pads. Oh, it was super! Super *duper*! It was so grown-up. Oh, Lucy would just turn green and *die* of envy.

Zelda laughed loudly. "I think she likes it!" she said.

Sarah looked up. "Oh, yes, I love it!"

"I could see. Well, have fun with it, kiddo."

"She's a little young for nail polish. . . ." NanaLeah said; but then she smiled at Sarah and said, "Oh, forget it. It's a gift!" She turned to Zelda and said, "Only ten years old and already starting to try different hairdo's and to pose in front of the mirror."

They were busy for a few minutes, hanging up Zelda's coat and all talking at once, and then Mummy ran into the kitchen to make coffee—"No, no tea, thanks just the same," Zelda said. "I never did take to it. A nice big cup of good strong American coffee will set me up just fine. And . . . have English muffins made their way across the Atlantic yet? Or scones? Never mind, whatever you have will be fine, just a bite. Oh, good! I'm here in time to help trim the tree! Excellent! The weather cooperated, too."

Zelda began to sing "White Christmas," and she sounded so much like Bing Crosby that Sarah had to stare, which made Zelda laugh. "It's a little talent of mine, kiddo. Called impersonation. Say . . . we're related, you know. Maybe you have it, too. Here, try some of Der Bingle. . . ." And she began to sing a song with a lot of ba-ba-ba-boo's in it. Sarah shook her head.

"Come on, kiddo, at least give it a try. Try 'White Christmas.' You know that one, don't you?"

Sarah knew "White Christmas." She knew the words to all the songs. Everyone in this house did, even though nobody ever played the upright piano in a corner of the living room, except her, and she didn't *really* know how. She began to sing the song, and then faltered as a strange look came over Zelda's face.

"No, no, don't stop." When Sarah finished the song, Zelda said, "You have a gorgeous voice, you know that? They giving you lessons on that?" Gesturing with her head to the piano. "No? Well, we'll see about that. You should have lessons."

"Uncle Jim is giving me a guitar for Christmas. And I'm learning the violin. In school. They have an orchestra."

"Violin! Well, that's okay for some, but give me a piano any day of the week, kiddo. You sit down at a piano and start tickling the ivories, you've got a crowd around you, listening and singing and tapping their feet. Of course, a guitar could be good, too. And hey! It's a lot easier than a piano to take on a picnic!" She was a funny lady. Nice. "Ah, here's my coffee. Good show!" Her voice went from American to British, just like that.

Zelda forgot to say anything about music lessons, though. Sarah was disappointed but not surprised. Grown-ups were always forgetting their promises to kids; she'd learned that long ago.

"Jim's *where*?" Zelda asked, sipping at her hot coffee, slurping it a little.

"HUAC . . . House Un-American Activities Committee."

"Where do they live? In Un-America?"

NanaLeah snorted. "That says it, all right. I can't get work, and Jim's advertisers have all left. Where it's all going to end, I don't know!"

"Well, not to worry, as far as money. I have plenty. Oh yes, Leah, tons of it. My father left me a bundle. My mother hired herself five lawyers and tried to say he wasn't in his right mind, that he intended her to have it all, but the judge wouldn't buy. So, if you need help . . . hey, here I am."

"Yes, Zelda, here you are. And that reminds me, you promised to tell us *why* you're here, instead of Scotland with your fella."

Zelda laughed. "He wanted to get married and I didn't. So finally he gave me an ultimatum. Either wedding bells or good-bye. I gave it a lot of thought, I really did. But it wouldn't have worked. Since the end of the war, women in Britain are expected to stay at home, wear a frilly apron, and have babies." She laughed again. "I'm a bit long in the tooth for *any* of that! Anyway, it wouldn't suit." She sighed. "So, I left. I felt awful about it for a while. But now I realize I'm just freed up."

"What are you going to do?"

Zelda leaned back in the easy chair. "Buy myself an airfield."

"Excuse me?"

"That's right. There were quite a few, before the war, up in Westchester and Dutchess counties. I'm going to look for one and hope there's a hangar and an airplane or two left. I figure

I can give lessons and do crop dusting . . . and give a couple of flyboys jobs. A lot of them hate civilian life. They liked being up there in the wild blue yonder—believe me, I know that feeling—and now there's nothing for them to do."

"Zelda, you're a character," Mummy said. She was smiling a lot with Zelda here, and that made Sarah feel good. Her mother had been in a bad mood. Maybe, it suddenly occurred to her, her mother had wanted to marry Elias and *he* was the one who didn't want to!

She didn't have time to examine that thought closely, because Jim came stumbling up the steps outside, sliding on the slippery snow and swearing at the top of his lungs.

"Good God, you could hear him in Canarsie," NanaLeah grouched. She got up in a hurry, to go get him. "Jim's been drinking a lot lately, Zelda. Don't be shocked when you see him."

Sarah jumped up, too. She would save Uncle Jim from NanaLeah's wrath. Sometimes, if she got him to look right into her eyes and she talked real fast, he'd snap out of it right away. Then he'd ask for hot coffee, and run the cold water in the kitchen and duck his head under the faucet, shivering and calling out to Jesus, Mary, and Joseph to come to his aid.

Today he wasn't too bad, even though he smelled strongly of whiskey. But he was already apologizing. "Leah, it was a nightmare, a goddamn nightmare. I couldn't b'lieve this was America. I said to them, I can't b'lieve I'm in the Unide States of 'merica." He was, Sarah decided, about half drunk.

Sarah took his hand and began talking very loudly about Zelda. He heard her; he grinned, pleased. "Zelda Laz'rus, the last of the great ladies. . . . Lemme give Zelda great big kiss. . . ."

He hadn't stamped all the snow off his shoes, so he slid a little. Sarah braced him but he was very heavy, even though he had got very thin. And sometimes he forgot that she was so much smaller than he and he *leaned*.

But today he was not bad. He straightened up and said, "I'm okay, sugar, I won't fall. Just a bit dizzy, 'sall."

Zelda was okay; she grinned at him and shook his hand and pretended he wasn't drunk at all. Just like us, Sarah thought. Once when Lucy was visiting, Uncle Jim had come in. He was pretty bad, stumbling and tripping over his own feet. It was awful, and Lucy didn't pretend.

"Is he *tipsy?*" she had said, right out loud. "It's not even Saturday night!"

"He's not tipsy," Sarah had lied. "He's sick. And you'd better go right home or you'll *catch* it!"

She smiled to remember how Lucy had scampered out, as fast as her fat little legs would carry her.

NanaLeah called out, as he headed for the crystal decanters, "Jim! I really think—"

He turned and gave her such a beautiful smile, saying, "Ah, Leah, just now when you called my name, I was put in mind of you when we were first in the Village, do you remember? Eating with the crowd every night? And now that I'm looking at you, I see that you haven't changed at all. Has she now, Zelda?"

NanaLeah gave him a hard look, but she didn't have a chance to say more because Zelda began talking about the olden days. Usually, her grandmother joined right in. But today NanaLeah sat on a footstool, one leg crossed over the other, tapping her foot impatiently. Sarah got a funny feeling; something bad was going to happen.

"Uncle Jim, we need you to put the angel on top of the tree," Sarah said, leaping up and talking as fast as she could, hoping . . .

But NanaLeah gave a chop of her hand, and Sarah sat back down. "Okay, Jim. Enough stalling. What happened?"

"What happened where, Leah darlin'?"

"Jim!"

"You know. The usual. They asked questions. Over 'n' over 'n' over. Was this me, in this picture? Was that you, in that picture? Was that us, at a rally in Union Square in 'forty-one, for the Russian War Relief?"

"And what did you tell them?"

"What did I tell them? The truth, Leah. Sweet Jesus, in 'forty-one it was *patriotic* to give aid and comfort to the Russians. They were our allies. What was I going to say? No, that's not me. That's not Leah Lazarus. That's two other people who happen to look exactly like us? Is it my fault, Leah darlin', that all of a sudden the Soviet Union is our enemy? I told them the truth. I looked them straight in the eye and—"

"Jim. You didn't give them any names." And when he did not answer, she persisted. "You didn't, did you? You wouldn't be such a—well, you wouldn't. Would you? Jim?"

Uncle Jim sat forward in his chair, both hands cupped

around his glass of scotch whiskey, staring into its depths. For a long time he said nothing and he didn't move; it was almost as if he wasn't even breathing. And then he pulled in a big noisy breath and let it out and then he tossed off the rest of his drink.

"Leah, listen. They have a list. A list of names. It has everyone on it, everyone who ever joined a union or signed a petition or gave a dollar to a cause!"

Her grandmother came to her feet, her fists clenched and her whole body leaning toward him. "Did you betray your friends?"

"No, Leah, I did not! They already knew everything. Every fucking thing. Excuse my French, ladies. They had pictures, they had minutes of meetings, they had affidavits. I betrayed nobody. I didn't have to. They already knew it all, had everyone's name, hell, they had my subscriber lists from way back! There was nothing I could tell them—"

"Oh my God, how they must have been laughing at you when you left—at what an easy mark you were, soaked in cheap scotch, not telling them to go to hell! Oh, you nogood *momzer!*"

NanaLeah looked as if she would march right over to him and shake him; but she just stood where she was. She was trembling; so was her voice; but her eyes were fierce. Jim began to whimper in the back of his throat and his hands went out in supplication.

"All your advertisers, all your writers, all your *friends* who have stood by you through thick and thin . . . did you deny you knew them? Me, too, I was on the list, wasn't I? And you never said I don't know what any of those people did! I don't know a damn thing and be damned to you! That's what *I* would have said!"

"But I did. Anyway, I think I did. I told them they were mistaken . . . I'm sure I told them that."

"You've got no guts left! You've given in to the thought police, that's what you've done. You betrayed us all with your silence, you lousy nogood." NanaLeah raised an arm and pointed to the door. "Out!" she commanded. "Out of here! I never want to lay eyes on you again. You have no heart, no soul, no honor!"

Jim came to his feet, tears streaming down his cheeks, and his loose jowls shook. Sarah couldn't stand to look at him like that. She ran to him and put her arms around him. As much as he seemed to have shrunk, these past years, he was still very tall and her head came about to his belt buckle. She couldn't reach all the way around him, so she wrapped her arms around his legs.

"Sarah, get away from there!"

"Please, Leah, try to see reason, would you?"

"Reason!" Now her voice was ice cold. "I cannot bear to *look* at you. The sight of you sickens me. Sarah, let go of him! Get out, Jim! And don't come back!"

Jim leaned forward, "Leah, listen, listen, Leah—" He was not balanced and he began to teeter. Sarah could feel his tears falling into her hair; she was crying, too, and trying to make her grandmother hear her. How could she be so cruel? How could one afternoon mean the end of so many things in the world? Elias, gone . . . and now Jim, too?

"No, no, no!" Sarah cried, and hugged his leg as hard as she could. She would keep him here until NanaLeah changed her mind.

Jim swayed to one side and lost his balance. He hopped on one foot, trying to straighten himself, then reached out to grab whatever was closest. It was a branch of the Christmas tree, and it was no support at all for him. Over he went, and Sarah with him, the tree falling over both of them. He fell on his side, one leg pinning her to the ground, while everything went flying through the air: tinsel, ornaments, her beautiful favorite glass ornaments, falling and crashing and smashing.

Sarah felt she could not breathe, and she called out. But who could hear her? Everyone was hollering and screaming and running back and forth. She could hear her grandmother's voice, weighted with disgust:

"Men! You just can't rely on them, especially a *schicker*!"

Sarah lay, trapped, her cheek pushed into the rough carpet, Jim's weight heavy on her. Zelda's voice came close: "Hold on, Leah. I don't think it's the drink." Then her tone sharpened. "Oh God, he's having a heart attack. Get a doctor!"

"The hospital! The ambulance!" her mother said, sounding afraid.

Sarah heard her mother running out. Above her, NanaLeah was sobbing, saying, "Oh, Jim, I didn't mean it, you *know* I didn't mean it, you *know* what a temper I have! Come on, Jim, just open your eyes! Oh God, he can't be having a heart attack! He can't!"

A heart attack. Was Uncle Jim going to *die*? And in her

head, like she did whenever she was really frightened, like when there was a strange noise in her darkened bedroom or something, she began making up a song in her head. Most of her songs didn't have much of a melody or else she'd use phrases from a favorite tune, but they were *her* songs. This one went, "Uncle Jim is big and strong and living long, and they're all wrong, he will not die." He couldn't die and leave her, like Timmy! She began to cry.

"Just a minute, sweetie pie, take it easy, we'll have you free in just a—oof!" The weight was gone and her grandmother lifted her up. "Are you all right? Move your fingers. Move your legs. Good." Sarah wanted to ask if Uncle Jim was going to die, but she couldn't stop crying. "Can you stand up on your own?" NanaLeah asked, and put her down.

Her mother came running in. "They'll be here in two minutes. Oh my God, this is horrible! Jim! Can you hear us?"

"Hush, Jo. The child."

Didn't they know she had already heard everything? Couldn't they see she was *already* scared? She ran up the stairs to her room, to her record player, closing the door carefully behind her. She knew exactly what she needed to hear. Her special music. The records were nearly worn out, she had played them so often; but she took very good care of them, putting them in their paper jackets, cleaning them regularly. That way, they would last forever.

After Timmy died, her mother sat in her room a lot, rocking in her rocking chair, playing these songs over and over on her record player, sometimes singing along with them and crying. And Sarah remembered so clearly sitting on her mother's lap, held in her arms, hearing the beautiful haunting songs. "He's gone away for to stay a little while . . . but he's comin' back, if he goes ten thousand miles . . ." That was her favorite. She would close her eyes and let the tears fall from under her lids and let the music wash over her, let the words tell her the lie she wanted to hear about her little brother. "But he's comin' back, if he goes ten thousand miles."

Later Mummy told her that the singer was named Jo Stafford and the songs were folk songs. Funny name for such lovely sounds. Songs people had been singing since forever, Mummy said, handing them down from mother to daughter without even writing down the notes. And when, later, Sarah asked if she could have those Jo Stafford records, Mummy's

eyes filled, but she smiled and said, "From mother to daughter,
just like I said."

Today Sarah lowered the arm of the record player carefully
and the music began. She'd sing the words and then maybe
Uncle Jim would be "coming back," and not leave her here all
alone.

35

June 1960

The audience was absolutely silent, as if it was holding its collective breath while she sang. Sarah was pleased. This was
what she lived for: the hushed and attentive listeners in front
of her, a baby pink spot lighting her, and the music, the haunting and mournful sounds of the folk airs that plain people had
made up and sung and changed over centuries. Beautiful
songs, laments, most of them. They suited her.

". . . All my trials, Lord . . ." she sang in the voice someone
had described as smoky, ". . . 'Soon be over."

The auditorium of the High School of Performing Arts was
packed—tonight was the third and last performance of the Senior Showcase. The old brick building had once been an elementary school, and everything in it was scaled for younger
kids, including the tiny auditorium. The dancers hated the minuscule stage; but it was perfect for a folksinger, and Sarah
Fielding was a folksinger, for sure.

Funny, until her mother had explained, all those years ago
she hadn't even known what a folk song was. She thought
"Big Rock Candy Mountain," was "hillbilly music." The next
song she could remember was "Greensleeves." Well, she knew
that wasn't hillbilly music; it was just plain gorgeous. Her
mother noticed her picking out "Greensleeves" on the piano—
get that, her mother actually noticed something she was doing,

and didn't make a sarcastic remark about it—and she got an old album from her record collection.

"Here," she said. "You'll like these." It was all folk music: "Black Is the Color" and "Ten Thousand Miles" and "Over Yandro" and a bunch of others. By the time Timmy got sick, that album was almost worn out from her playing it over and over. Singing of other people's sadness somehow made her feel better about her own.

It was funny about singing. In her real life, she had never been able to make friends easily. And when she first came to Performing Arts, it was worse than ever. She knew she was considered good-looking, but too particular and snobby. Actually, she was shy; always worrying that nobody would like her. But when she sang, she was unafraid; she could look anyone right in the eye. While she was singing, she was able to hypnotize her audiences, whether she was on one of her jobs— singing at a birthday party or, once, a bar mitzvah—or doing a pickup show at some makeshift theater way downtown. The best of all so far was the job she had last summer at Sam Katz's Summer Hotel and Resort in the Catskills. It wasn't as big or as fancy as the other hotels, but the guests all loved her singing. She never had to buy a meal the whole summer, or pay for a movie. Even those large, noisy Jewish families would shut up when she sang. "And that, *bubbele*," Sam Katz told her, "is a bigger miracle than the parting of the Red Sea."

Even here, at school, sometimes she'd be practicing and look up and find a whole group gathered around her, listening and staring at her, as if they were in love. Especially boys.

Boys thought she was beautiful—"Small wonder," Nana-Leah said, "since you *are*"—and they were always hanging around. She always picked a boy out of the audience to sing to, even a boy sitting hand in hand with his girlfriend. That was okay. Boys tended to forget their girlfriends when Sarah Fielding sang to them. They'd just sit there and goop at *her*.

Zelda had said it first—that she had power. Her mother always snorted and said, "Power, yeah, sure. She's boy-crazy, Zelda. She flirts with *everything* in pants." Sarah wanted to throw something at her mother when she said things like that, but never mind. Soon she'd be out of that house and away from them all. Zelda just answered, "More power to her, then!" And stuck her tongue out at Mom. Then they both laughed.

I'm not boy-crazy, Sarah thought, moving into her special

rendition of "Ten Thousand Miles." She knew that men couldn't be trusted—just look at all the men she ever loved, how they all left her one way or another. So obviously she had to find a way to be in control. She *did* have power, too, in her eyes and her voice. She could make any boy look at her— unable to take his eyes off her—just by singing and staring at him.

Like now. In the front row an interesting-looking older man—God, he must be twenty-five, not really a boy—was sitting hunched forward, looking intently at her. He hadn't moved in five minutes; he seemed almost hypnotized. She sang straight to him, focusing her big-eyed gaze on him, and he stared back. She couldn't tell if he was tall or short, but he was broad in the shoulders and his hair was a mop of light curls. Blond? He reminded her of the musicians at the Newport Folk Festival, with his big mustache and casual clothes. He wasn't old enough to be someone's father; maybe a big brother, although he was sitting alone. He was very good-looking. As she studied him, she saw his lips curl in a little smile and she nearly missed a beat, and then she decided she didn't really want to hypnotize him. He was too old; it was only fun, really, with boys her own age. Sometimes she could watch them getting all hot and bothered. Just from her singing.

She began to understand about her power the day of her audition for Performing Arts. Only that first time, it hadn't been on purpose. She was so tied in knots and so tense, her voice felt as if it wouldn't come out, and she decided that if she sang to one particular member of the jury, looked at him through the whole song, she'd forget to be nervous. And to her utter amazement, the teacher became slightly uncomfortable and he blushed. So she really turned it on, smiled and batted her eyelashes, and he got even more uncomfortable. Finally he interrupted, a little too loudly, "That's fine, and now will you please give us 'Sebben, Crudele'?" The jurors often switched you from song to song on your list, to see if you really knew everything you listed. But she saw the other two teachers give him a look of surprise. And when she came back the next day, for her callback, he was nowhere in sight. Now she knew his name, Gilbert Redondo; she had had him for chorus and the Madrigal Singers. And she still made him nervous.

The last notes of the song faded away and Sarah sat very still, as she always did as the end of a set, her head bent over the guitar, the long hair hanging like a curtain. And then she looked up, flinging her hair behind her shoulders, and smiled. Her eyes were wet; she always cried a little when she sang "Ten Thousand Miles"; it made her think of Timmy and Uncle Jim. And that's when the audience always went crazy, shouting and stomping and whistling. That's the part she loved. Not because they were yelling for her, but because she had touched them with her voice; she had moved them, had made them feel exactly what she was feeling. That was the best power of all.

Tonight she looked out over the packed auditorium to find her mother and NanaLeah and Zelda. There they were, and Sally Moon, too. Her piano teacher. She grinned at them and waved and the four of them stood up, each holding up a red rose. Well, not quite. A flash of light in her eyes told her that Mom was taking pictures, and without thinking about it very much, Sarah turned her head so her mother could get a profile and then switched positions again. She was going to need photographs when she went to get a job in one of the Village clubs.

Not that they knew she was planning to get a singing job. As far as the three women in her family were concerned, Sarah was headed for Juilliard in the fall, and would be spending her entire summer practicing lieder and Italian songs. Only Sally Moon knew what she wanted to do and Sally was on her side. For years Sally had lent her records of Odetta and Leadbelly and John Lee Hooker. They had spent half the piano-lesson time listening, trying to play and sing along. Sarah loved all of it. Ray Charles singing "Sweet Georgia Brown," and Harry Belafonte and Pete Seeger. Sally was her first audience for folk songs, and she got all excited and told Sarah she was a natural. "You've got that certain something, Sarah, I'm not kidding. A little . . . I don't know . . . sob. A catch in your voice."

For a long time Sarah had fun singing the blues and jazz tunes. She taught herself the guitar so she could accompany herself. Then she heard Segovia play flamenco and classical music, and began to copy that, too. After listening to Bach and other baroque composers, she thought maybe she'd study to be a classical guitarist. Or become a concert singer who specialized in the sixteenth century. "And starve," Mom said. But when Sarah answered, "If I have to!" Mom gave her a funny look and nodded. "Well, well . . . So we have an artist on our hands."

Last summer, Sally Moon had taken Sarah to the Newport

Folk Festival. A damp, sweltering hot August, with the audience sitting in a haze of mist. It rained every day, so that the water crept into all the tents; tents filled with folksingers and banjo pickers and fiddlers and gospel groups. And, oh God, the music! Who cared about the weather! She saw Pete Seeger; it was an epiphany, tall skinny Pete Seeger, dressed like a workman, so easy and at ease, the voice coming out of him like breathing. And there was a new singer, a girl her own age, Joan Baez. She had a voice so pure and so simple that Sarah found her chest aching with jealousy. She felt she could never be as good as Joan Baez . . . yet at the same time, she was burning to be better than Joan, to be written up in all the papers as the greatest thing to come along in a decade.

When she came back from Newport, Sarah realized that all that other stuff was nice, but not what she really wanted. She was a folksinger; she just hadn't been sure before. She practiced at school; she didn't want to disappoint NanaLeah and Mom, who thought she was heading for a classical career. She knew eventually she'd have to tell them, but not yet.

Not until after this weekend, for sure. This weekend, right after graduation, she was piling into Joe Caldone's old Buick along with five or six other kids, and heading up to Rhode Island for this year's Newport Folk Festival. There, she'd hear them all again—John Lee Hooker and Pete Seeger and Joan Baez and Odetta and Mahalia Jackson! Mahalia Jackson—now that was really power. Sally always said that power came from the heart. "If you believe what you're playing or singing, it will have the power to move people."

Now, all over the auditorium, Sarah saw people standing up—not just her family—standing up and shouting and clapping like mad. The power of song. Hell, the power of Sarah Fielding. Why not? Joan Baez had first billing *every night* at the folk festival this year, and she was only nineteen. This kind of applause was what Sarah had been waiting for.

She tried to get off the stage three times, but they cheered and hollered "More! More! More!" She recognized certain voices, her grandmother, a couple of friends, a teacher or two, shouting as loud as they could; but there were plenty of others screaming, too. After three encores she ended with a surprise: "My Man's Gone Now" from *Porgy and Bess*. When she had finished, the audience seemed to take a deep breath, and then they clapped and clapped, and she ran off the stage because, in a minute, she was going to bawl.

He was there—the curly-headed man from the front row—waiting for her. Funny, she wasn't even surprised. He didn't say a word, just grabbed her shoulders and kissed her.

"Sarah Fielding, you're wonderful! You have to come with me."

"Where?"

"Boston. Cambridge. Harvard Square. There are dozens of coffeeshops there. Baez sang in Harvard Square, at Gerdes, that's where she got her start."

"Boston!" She didn't know anyone in Boston, had never even been there.

"Don't you understand? You're fabulous. You're a natural. And I'm going to make you famous."

"Who *are* you?"

He laughed, throwing his head back. He had a wonderful laugh. "Excuse me, I got so excited, I just forgot my manners." He picked up her hand and bent over it, pressing a kiss onto it. "Allow me to introduce myself. I'm Barry Jordan, entrepreneur, music lover, and the owner of the Quarter Note, a brand-new coffeehouse on Harvard Square."

"Are you offering me a job?"

"Are you accepting?" His eyes danced with laughter. He had wonderful eyes.

Before she had a chance to answer, NanaLeah, Zelda, Mom and Sally Moon descended upon her, handing her the roses, and all trying to hug her at once. When she looked around again, Barry Jordan was gone, and she wondered for just one moment if she had dreamed the whole thing.

36

November 1960

Of course, he hadn't just disappeared the night of the Senior Showcase. Barry Jordan had only stepped behind her grand-

mother, waiting, ready to come out and charm all those women
who hovered around her. He was amused by them: by
NanaLeah, who was letting her graying curly hair grow out of
the short cut, and whose skirt was fashionably short; by Zelda,
in her pantsuit; and even by Mom, tall and lanky and freckled,
little squint lines at the corners of her eyes, as if she had spent
her life at sea, looking out toward a distant horizon.

"No wonder you're so . . . unique," Barry said to her. "You
come from a family of uniques." She had to study his face, to
make sure he wasn't making fun of them. But his dark eyes
were warm, so she decided it was a compliment.

He invited them all out to dinner, to Peter Luger's for
steaks. Who wouldn't want to go to Peter Luger's, the best
steakhouse in the world, full of old-world charm and cranky
waiters who had grown old there? The restaurant had been
tucked under the Williamsburg Bridge since the Brooklyn
Bridge was built, and it still held on to its Gay Nineties' flavor.
They all looked at each other, NanaLeah, Zelda, and Mom, and
accepted his invitation, and he swept them outside into a cab.

The restaurant was terribly crowded with mafiosi and
Brooklyn politicians and just plain people, and they had to wait
an hour for a table. Barry kept ordering drinks from the bar, so
they were all feeling quite happy by the time they sat down.

Sarah was in a daze of admiration and wonder. She couldn't
concentrate on any of the conversation; all she could do was
look at Barry Jordan, study his face, watch the movements of
his lips, the crinkling of his eyes when he smiled. He seemed
so sophisticated, in charge. The steaks came. He cut his into
small pieces; Sarah remembered that, but did not recall eating
hers. When they left, the steak was gone, so she must have, but
she had no memory of the meal, only of him. She couldn't believe he had just fallen out of the sky and into her life.

In the cab on the way home, to Willow Street, Barry talked
to the three women very earnestly, explaining how Sarah was
a major talent—she remembered those words, in particular:
major talent—and how she needed a showcase, a real one,
with a real audience. How he was going to be her agent, and
book her all over Boston. Her mother's face was a study in
skepticism.

"Sarah always escaped into music whenever something
bothered her," Jo said. "She'd run up the stairs and you'd hear
her door slam and then, loud enough to wake the dead, the music."

"Really? What kind of music?"

"Oh, that depended on what she was interested in at the time. The blues. Jazz. Baroque. Giuliani. Bach. Pete Seeger. Muddy Waters." Barry just laughed.

"I remember one time," her mother said, "when she was concentrating on Ray Charles. Day after day and night after night, that's all you'd hear from her room. The same songs, over and over. So I asked her, 'Sarah, what's bothering you?' And you know what she said?" Without waiting for an answer, her mother went on. "She said, '*You're* bothering me, Mom.' That was it."

Sarah remembered her mother's face, in the cab, when she told that story, her lean face with the prominent cheekbones and the proud nose. Her mother looked strong, powerful, even though her tone was a little sad. She looked like someone who knew what she was doing with her life. Sarah remembered that, because she felt the same way. Or at least she was sure that wherever Barry Jordan wanted her to go, she was going to go.

Barry Jordan did not charm her family; they were scared of him, especially Mom. She made him stay in the cab when they got home. "You can come over tomorrow," Jo said, in a voice that brooked no resistance. And as soon as the four of them were up the front steps and safely inside, she said, "He's too damn slick, too sure of himself." She turned to Sarah and said, "I see myself in you . . . I see a young, rather naive young woman who thinks she's smarter than she is . . . who knows nothing of life, but thinks she does. Is beguiled by promises. We don't know if he can get you jobs, Sarah."

"Hush, now, Jo," NanaLeah said. "Listen to me. No matter how much it reminds you of . . . whatever . . . it's not the same. It's never the same. She has to test her wings."

"Promise me you won't go until you've thought about it," Mom said, fierce and red-faced. "Promise, Sarah. Please. He's handsome and charming, and I'm scared to death for you. So, don't do anything this minute, okay? Okay?"

Sarah promised. But later that night, very late, she heard a knock on the front door. Not the bell, a knock. She might have imagined it, it was so soft. But it came again. She knew it was him. Only *he* would know she would never be able to sleep, that she would be in her room, still dressed, staring at the ceiling and thinking about his enthusiasm, his praise. He was there when she went down, and he drew her out, pulling her into his embrace and kissing her deeply. She pushed him away.

"Okay. All right. I'm coming with you. But I have to get my guitar."

And leave a note, she did not add. Hastily scrawled, it said: *I have to go. It will be fine. Please don't hate me.*

Sarah fell asleep in his car, never stirring until he pulled in front of his building in Cambridge and killed the motor. The silence must have awakened her; her eyes flew open and for a minute she couldn't figure out where she was. Her neck was stiff and her right foot asleep, and *she* wanted to be asleep. But then he bent over and put his warm lips on hers, and it was like getting a transfusion. She was suddenly totally awake and alert.

"Where are we?"

"Home." He laughed. "Cambridge, Massachusetts. Look, this is where I live. Where *we* live now."

"Oh, God."

That made him laugh harder. "Come on."

They walked up two flights of stairs, dimly lit, and he fumbled with his keys and swore, and then they walked into darkness. He flipped a switch, and when the light went on, Sarah looked around. It was only one large room, part living room, part kitchen, with a curtained doorway at the far end.

"Home, sweet, home," Barry said, and yawned, stretching mightily. "Well, you don't have to unpack, and I don't want to." He dropped his stuffed duffel bag onto the floor. "So let's go to bed." He put an arm around her and together they walked to the door with the curtain. Behind it was a tiny room completely filled with a mattress heaped with quilts and pillows.

Barry took her into his arms and kissed her. She could feel his erection; she was accustomed to that. Whenever she danced with a boy, it was there. They always pushed their hips into hers; Barry did it now, and with one hand he pulled her close to him. And then he started to take off her clothes.

She struggled with him. It didn't do any good. Teenage boys were hot as pistols, everyone knew that, and girls were supposed to be very cautious with them. But they always stopped if you said no. Now, she said no, Barry didn't pay any attention. He stripped her and pushed her down onto the bed, on her back, and lay half on top of her while he unbuckled his belt and unzipped his fly and, oh my God, she thought, when his monster penis was freed and sticking out, thick and stiff and dark red, looking like a weapon of war. Oh my God.

"Barry, listen. No, really . . ."

He held her tightly, he kissed her mouth and her hair and her neck and her breasts and her belly, and her senses went flying away. She had never felt anything like it, never before. He pushed his fingers into her and, to her shame, she pushed her hips up to meet his fingers. She was breathing so hard her mouth was dry. And then he was on top of her, reaching down and pushing that great big thing into her. It hurt, it felt like something was tearing, and she yelled, and then suddenly it didn't hurt. It was . . . it was . . . it was . . . And she stopped thinking altogether.

She had always wondered what the big deal was, about fucking. Well, she had certainly found out—two or three and sometimes four times a day since the day they arrived. Barry told her she was something else, something special, she was one in a million. But other times he told her she was just a little slut. "How come you like it so much?" he'd say, a mean look on his face.

"Because I love you." And the mean look would wipe away. He'd smile and kiss her and say, "Tell me how much you love me, baby. Tell me."

But she was getting tired of all that.

"You brought me here to push my career, remember? To take the place of Joan Baez. Well, Baez has gone to California and now she has this top-selling record! And what've *I* got after all this time?" Sarah asked him one day toward the end of November.

"You're no Baez, you know."

"You bastard!" Sudden tears filled her eyes. She did not want to cry; he'd only call her a baby. But he was so unfair! She packed them in at the Quarter Note, and at the concerts he arranged for her at Harvard, B.U., Boston College, Northeastern and Wellesley. God, there were so many colleges in Boston! When the word got out, the smaller schools began asking for her, too. She was very well known, and all right, so she wasn't Joan Baez, but she never said she *was*. She only wanted a chance at the big time. She knew she could make it, if Barry would only give her a chance. But he was always stalling.

Not only that, but the other night, after her set, he dragged her into a hall and pushed her against the wall so hard she lost her breath.

"Barry, what's wrong? What *is* it?" He had such a fierce look, she half expected his fist to smash into her. "Barry!"

"I saw you, making eyes at that jock. At Table Three."

"Barry, are you crazy? I wasn't making eyes. I was singing to him. You know that's what I do."

"Not anymore it isn't."

"It helps with my nervousness."

"Pick some other way. I don't like the way they all look at you, like they'd like to eat you with a spoon." And then his voice changed and he leaned forward to kiss her in the curve of her neck. "I'm the only one gets to eat you with a spoon."

As always, she melted, dissolving into desire, her bewilderment and indignation forgotten. Until now.

"I think you're trying to hold me back, Barry."

Barry put down the copy of *Variety* and said: "You're working, aren't you? You work all the time. You're making good money. Which is more than most singers of antiques can say."

"Where's my invitation to the next folk festival?"

He laughed.

"Damn it, Barry, you're the one who told me I'd make it big! So, tell me, what have I got?"

"Me! You've got me!"

"When am I going to have a record contract? Why wouldn't you let Al Grossman talk with me? Everyone knows that Big Al means the big time. Maybe I could be at this year's folk festival. Maybe I could have a record contract."

"You read too many stupid articles in the papers. I'm saving you, I'm building you up."

"You're hiding me! You don't *want* me to be successful because then I might not need you!" She was sure she was right.

He sneered. "Maybe you're not good enough . . . ever think of that?"

"Oh, you bastard!" She needed to do something, anything. If she didn't, she really *would* use this knife. Wildly, she looked around. There was a pile of dirty dishes on the kitchen counter. There was *always* a pile of dirty dishes. She picked one up and threw it. It went whizzing by Barry's head, and he ducked, flinching. That made her laugh, especially when the dish shattered into a thousand shards, flying and spraying. She threw another, and another, and another, while he stood there, at first startled and then clapping and urging her on.

When the dirty dishes were gone, she turned and opened the cupboard and one by one threw every single dish—they were cheap painted glass, white with pink bands—against the wall, where they smashed and splintered, sending pieces flying through the air.

When they were all gone, she stood there, breathing hard, and he came to her and kissed her hard, unzipping his fly and putting her hand on his engorged cock. He pulled her to the bed, where they made love, fast and frantic, both of them yelling wordlessly.

But after it was over and he was snoring, flat out on the bed, his jockey shorts twisted around his knees, Sarah's eyes were wide open and staring at the ceiling. What was she doing here? How did she get here? Nineteen years old and playing coffeehouses on a college campus, living with a man who was terribly jealous. And what did she have to look forward to? More of the same?

Sarah moved herself off the bed very quietly and put on her panties. Barry hadn't bothered to undress her further, so she was all set to go, in her long skirt and crocheted sweater. His jeans, he'd thrown halfway across the room. She crawled over to them, and reaching in the back pocket, took out his wallet and grabbed the money. Then she tiptoed over to pick up her guitar case. She'd have to leave all the clothes she'd bought here; fuck them. Fuck *him*. He'd never humiliate her again. Good-bye, Barry.

Quietly, she put on her duffel coat and her woolly hat and let herself out. The stairs creaked, but what could she do? She ran down as fast and as lightly as she could, with a chill on her spine as she waited for his hand to come down on her at any moment. But it didn't, and she let herself out into the gray November twilight, feeling as if she'd just been let out of jail.

When she got to Harvard Square, she stopped and counted the money she'd taken from his wallet. Over two hundred dollars! That meant she could get a cab. She climbed into one; but when the cabby asked, "Where to, miss?" she realized she had no idea what she was going to do.

She tried to think rationally, but couldn't. She was too scared, and she kept looking out the car window, expecting to see Barry running after her with blood in his eye. "The train station," she said. When the words came out of her mouth, she knew where she was going: back to New York, to a *real* city. Back home. Oh, how she wanted to go home.

God, she couldn't go home, not after the way she left. They must hate her! NanaLeah would give her hell and then forgive

her. But her mother . . . her mother was so angry all the time,
particularly at her. And right now she just couldn't face her
mother being mad at her, telling her how stupid she'd been,
how she should have listened to them, should have gone for
her audition at Juilliard. She didn't want to hear it!

Suddenly she had it. She'd call Zelda. Zelda would understand. Zelda was a peach. Zelda would talk to them. She'd call
Zelda from Penn Station. . . . Maybe she'd live with Zelda,
who had a couple of rooms in an old Quonset hut at her airfield. Zee-Plane, that was the name of Zelda's airfield and flying school, and she said it was doing real well. She gave
lessons, and lately she had enlarged the landing strip so that
more planes could land there. She'd built a second hangar so
she could rent space to the rich people who wanted to own a
plane. Sarah let herself drift and dream a bit, about learning to
fly, helping Zelda around the hangar, practicing her guitar between times.

And maybe she should go to Juilliard, sing song cycles, take
theory and composition, get herself an education. Whatever.
But whatever it turned out to be, she promised herself, it was
going to be *her* choice and *her* decision. No more going along
with what some guy said. She had learned her lesson!

37

November 9, 1965

Sarah bent over the guitar, so that her long curly hair hung
down, hiding either side of her face. Closing her eyes, she let
her voice break a little as she sang. "Where are you? . . .
Where have you gone without me?" A throb in the voice, not
quite a sob.

The crowd in the Bitter Bean usually kept right on talking,
that's what singing in a Village café was like . . . but for this
number, they stopped their chitchat. Couples reached for each

other's hands and all their starry-eyed gazes were fixed on her. Maybe she wasn't cut out to be a folksinger; maybe she should do more torch songs. Her audiences seemed to go for them in a big way ... including the ones she wrote; the good ones, anyway. One of these days she was going to do a set of nothing but her own stuff. She'd come out in something slinky with sequins, instead of her usual costumes. Lately her look had been Russian, short, short skirt, high shiny boots, and one of those Cossack shirts, buttoned up to the high neck; or sometimes she'd be a Gypsy with huge hoop earrings, millions of bracelets, and flashy prints all mixed up. But as a torch singer she'd wear rhinestones in her ears and toss her hair back and make them shut up and listen to her, really listen. And then you'd *really* hear some applause!

The set was half over, and she segued into "Ten Thousand Miles"; it was their reward for keeping quiet, for gazing up at her with all that love shining out of their eyes. She needed that love.

Where *was* he? His compadres were already seated at their usual table; the big round one near the front window, the table closest to her. They had loosened their ties and were getting noisy as they ordered new rounds and started talking about their cases. Well, they deserved a little recreation. Assistant D.A.'s had it tough—Hawk had told her enough stories, so she knew it was true. "Every day they had to go out and slay dragons," as he put it, "and we have to *win*, Sammy." Hawk always called her Sam or Sammy. At first it annoyed her, because she was convinced he couldn't be bothered to remember her name. But now she realized it was a sign of affection ... maybe even more.

Her heart speeded up at the thought of him, so she switched to another song, for a boffo ending. She vamped a little, then picked up the tempo and began "Matty Groves." She'd get them all singing along and then she'd end the set. It would be five minutes early, but Andy would just have to understand. She wasn't a jukebox, for God's sake, she was a human being.

And right now she was in love. In love with the most fascinating man in the world. Even his name was thrilling: Hawk. Hawk Diamond, Assistant District Attorney, New York County, right-hand man to Frank Hogan, the D.A., and next in line to head a division. Maybe Appeals, although Hawk shook his head over that.

"I like beating them up in court. I like putting those bastards

away. It gives me a hard-on!" He talked tough, hell, they all
did, all the D.A.'s. He liked talking sexy, reveled in it, liked
watching people pull back, shocked, for an instant, but they
would lean forward again right away, smiling and pretending it
didn't matter, because everybody wanted Hawk Diamond to be
their friend. Sarah didn't mind either; she often said shocking
things, too. It put people off balance, which was exactly where
she wanted them.

Well, not Hawk. She wanted Hawk Diamond to be her love,
her one and only, her beloved. He was so . . . She didn't have
the words to describe what was so exciting about him. He was
dark, very dark, and not everyone found him handsome, the
way she did. He had almond eyes and thick black hair cropped
to a dark cap that came to a vee on his forehead. His cheekbones were high and prominent, his mouth wide, his nose "like
the blade of an ax"—his own words.

His real name was Howard. She asked his pal, Burt Golden,
if they called him Hawk because of his nose, and Burt
laughed.

"No, sweetheart, Diamond is called Hawk because when he
goes after them in the courtroom, he's like this—" Burt thrust
his head out, narrowing his eyes. "—like a bird of prey, see?
Hawk has that killer's instinct; that's why he always wins. But
you watch out. He's dangerous to pretty girls like you." She
found that exciting, too; she liked a little danger in her men.

She sang the saga of Mattie Groves's bad luck looking out
the window so she'd spot Hawk the minute he crossed the
street. He always showed up sooner or later, pulling his chair
around so he had an unobstructed view of her. He'd sit and
stare at her, smiling a little, his eyes intent. When he first
started coming in, he did that for weeks, without ever buying
her a drink or trying to speak to her. It made her crazy. And
then one evening, when her set was done, he'd crooked his finger and she'd just floated off the stool and over to his table, as
if she were hypnotized. And it had been like that every week-
night since.

Where *was* he? The only thing she could see in the windowpane was her own reflection. Artie had her sit in the
window. At first it was awful, but she had come to enjoy the
admiring stares; the way so many guys did a double-take and
then came right in. People told her she looked like Elizabeth
Taylor.

She knew she was beautiful, and so what? All it did was

make men behave like animals. But she knew how to handle them; she'd had plenty of practice, beginning with Barry the bore. He'd come running to New York after she left him, pleading for her to come back to him. But she told him to get lost, she'd look out for herself, thank you very much.

And she did. She took care of her own business. She'd been singing six nights a week at the Bitter Bean for two years now; and Artie said business had doubled. Of course, her mother always asked her when she was going to get a *real* job. Mom was still disappointed about Juilliard; why couldn't she give it a rest? She had gone for her audition, in the summer of '61. She'd been taking lessons again with Sally Moon, and her technique had developed by leaps and bounds. One hot Wednesday in August she presented herself at Juilliard, and was sent to a waiting room where four other would-be singers sat, looking nervous and agitated. "How long?" she asked; but nobody knew. And then a man came out of the audition room looking as if he might vomit, and suddenly she thought *she* might; the room was stifling and she was sweaty. So she left.

Mom wouldn't let her forget that she had been "this close, *this close*" to a really meaningful career—maybe in opera. Hell, her mother was always so scornful about everything she did; what did she think *she* was doing that was so goddamn wonderful? Running around the world taking pictures. Big fucking deal! She was hardly ever around, and when she was, all she could do was put Sarah down. You'd think she'd *want* her daughter to be a success.

Even when Sarah found her own apartment, even then, Mom had something to sneer about. She looked around and made a remark about how many mirrors there were. Could she help it if looks were so important when you were in show business? If you went on an open casting call, you were in competition with hundreds of other girls, all of them pretty, all of them talented. You had to look terrific to get attention, to get your big break.

And it might happen soon, her big break. Sarah was pretty sure she was going to get a part in a new Off-Broadway show. She went on casting calls just about every day, but the one to-day was different. This morning, after she sang a little, instead of waving her off, the three people sitting down below huddled for a minute or two and then the producer asked if they had her phone number. She just *knew* they had liked her, that she'd be offered a part. The only thing she had to decide was whether or not she was willing to strip to the waist.

She wasn't ashamed of the way she looked naked, and she had really nice boobs . . . or so they all told her. The producers said that singing and dancing nude was a . . . what was it? Oh yeah . . . they said it was a *statement*. It was meant to shock people into an awareness of how we're all members of the human race, stuff like that. Of course, it was really about shocking people into buying tickets.

But how to explain it to her family? NanaLeah would pitch a fit! And she could imagine what her mother would have to say! Well, too bad. If Hawk didn't show up in the next minute, she decided, she'd do it. And if he did? Well, she'd think about it some more.

Suddenly, like an answer to her prayers, there he was. She glanced down at her watch. Five-twenty; he and his pals usually came in just before five for the cocktail hour set. He was running; good, that meant he was worried that she might be mad. He had said something yesterday about them maybe grabbing a bite to eat tonight. Almost a date! And he knew he was late and he was hurrying—to *her*. She wanted to jump up and down and shriek with her joy; but instead she pretended she didn't see him, just let her eyes slide over him, turned so that her back was to him when he came in, and slowed down the song.

Hawk did not go to the D.A.'s table. He stood at the bar, staring at her, waiting for her to finish, to turn around and see him.

When she did turn around, he was standing right in front of her, that odd half smile on his lips. "Sorry I'm late, Sam." She loved his deep bass voice; it gave her the shivers. She had a thing about voices. Once, she told him he'd make a wonderful actor, and he laughed. "What do you think I do now, Sammy? It's all theater!"

"Late? For what?" She refused to smile. Let him squirm.

A shrug. "Oh well, if you don't remember . . ." He turned away.

"Wait! Do you mean . . . about having dinner tonight?"

Hawk leaned forward so that he was very close to her, disturbingly close. "Listen, Sam, we've got something going here—" He ran one finger casually up her arm, and the entire arm turned to goose bumps. "—so do me a favor. Don't play games with me, okay?"

She could not find her voice, so she nodded.

"Okay, then. Come on." He crooked his finger at her, and she got off the stool, leaned her guitar against it, and followed him to the big round table. She had two more sets before she was through for the night. But right now, she had twenty minutes ... twenty minutes of heaven with Hawk Diamond.

The other young attorneys all greeted her by name and shoved their chairs together to make room for her. She could feel admiring eyes on her, eyes that didn't quite have the guts to stare, because she was with Hawk. She was the only girl at the table, but she didn't have to worry. They'd never dare get fresh; she was a star and she was Hawk Diamond's ... what? Date? New conquest? Just friend? She knew she wanted to be Hawk Diamond's girl, in the worst way.

She'd never felt like that about any guy. Men always came after *her*, sometimes sweetly, often not. And Hawk hadn't done anything except stare at her, smiling that strange half smile of his, and motion for her to come over to his table between sets. They'd never seen each other outside of the Bitter Bean, nor shared more than a cup of cappuccino. But she wanted him, that she knew, wanted him in a fierce burning way she hadn't felt in a long time.

Sarah figured that every single man at the table at the Bitter Bean was looking at her and wishing he could get her naked and alone—everyone but Hawk. Hawk she wasn't sure of; that's what made him so fascinating.

She looked at him now, talking, his long-fingered hands as alive as two animals, his black eyes snapping. "And then Judge Roberts said 'Just what do you think you're up to here, Mr. Diamond?' and I said, 'Your Honor, with all due respect, I'm up to here with how these Gypsies fleece our good tax-paying citizens.' " The other D.A.'s laughed, but Sarah didn't bother to listen to any more; he talked about getting the Gypsies all the time. She didn't understand *why* he had to get them; they came into town, rented empty stores, put up curtains, and told your fortune. But Hawk said they were thieves and con artists and he was going to get them if it was the last thing he ever did.

"And besides, Sammy, it makes wonderful copy." He was a celebrity, kind of; and one of the political columnists—in the *Mirror*, she thought—said he was after Frank Hogan's job. Although when she asked him about that, Hawk found it funny. "Nobody will ever get Frank Hogan's job until he points his finger at someone and says, '*You.* You're the next D.A. of New York County!' He's indestructible and unbeatable, and only an idiot would even *think* about trying to unseat him, Sam." And he had put one finger on the tip of her nose, a simple gesture but one that caused great havoc inside her. She had been waiting ever since, for him to do that again; it had felt so . . . so loving.

She wished he'd stop schmoozing with his buddies and pay some attention to her before it was time for her next set. She cast a surreptitious look at her wristwatch, the good gold one NanaLeah had given her for her twenty-first birthday.

"By all rights, you should be getting the locket this year," her grandmother had said, "but your mother says it's her lucky charm, and she's in so many dangerous situations, especially now with all the riots and the shootings over civil rights—"

"Don't worry about it, NanaLeah." What did she care about some old locket? She knew the whole story of it, God, she must have heard it three gazillion times. But it was just a locket, and she didn't even find it pretty. The engraving was almost worn off, and it was too big. Of course, she'd never say that to NanaLeah; to her, that locket was as precious as the Hope Diamond.

All of a sudden all the lights went out in the place.

"Help! I'm going blind!" someone shouted; and everyone laughed.

"Come on, Artie, pay your Con Ed bill, why don't you?" More laughter. At the same time, you could hear a lot of shouting and carrying on from back in the kitchen. And Artie yelling for someone to tell him where the devil they'd put the fuses!

"You really did it this time, Artie! Didn't pay for the streetlights, either!" Hawk called out.

Everyone began talking, and at once there was a crowd around their table, looking out the window. Of course it wasn't dark yet, but there were no lights, except for car headlights. Everything else—streetlights, traffic lights, store lights, apartment lights—had been snuffed out.

"Where's the phone?" a male voice shouted. "My brother's with Con Ed. I'll call him and find out what's going on."

"Hell, my roommate's with the *Daily News.* That's a better source!" There was a lot of talking and joking and then the second voice called out, "Hey! He says it's *everywhere*! The whole fucking city's out!"

"Bring out the candles, Artie! We'll stay here and buy your booze until they fix the damn thing."

"No such luck, people. Electric heat."

There was a big groan at that news. "Oh well," Sarah said, trying to hide her disappointment. No supper with Hawk tonight! "I guess I'd better get started walking home. The subway'll be a *zoo*."

"The subway's electric, too," Hawk said in her ear, "and the buses will all be jammed. But listen—"

Outside, there was a cacophony of horns bleating and blaring. She looked out and began to laugh. Nobody knew what in hell to do without traffic lights, and cars were stopping all at once and trying to move all at once. As a result, the worst traffic jam she'd ever seen was right there in Sheridan Square; hundreds of cars at a standstill, unable to move in any direction.

"Oh God," she said, giggling. "What are they going to *do*?"

"Stay there until the cops come to tell them where to go. Where do you live, Sammy? Down here?"

"Don't I wish! Columbus and Sixty-ninth."

He whistled softly. "Quite a walk. Well, I'll join you, at least as far as Penn Station. That's where I get my train."

"Jersey?"

"Long Island." He offered no further details, and she felt silly about asking.

"I'll be glad to have company," she said, keeping her voice calm, although her heart was thumping so hard she was afraid he would hear it.

She was actually *with* him. They walked along together, talking about how different the city looked, heading toward Union Square where Hawk thought it might be easier going. Sarah found it all exciting—doubly so because they were so anonymous in the growing darkness. "I guess this is how it was before electricity . . . before gas lights, too," she said.

"Yeah. They had guys who used to walk the town all night long carrying a lantern and yelling out, 'Four o'clock in the morning and all's well!' Now you know why. It's spooky. Brrrrr."

"I kind of like it," Sarah said. "It's like when there's a big blizzard and suddenly the city's all quiet and covered in white and nothing's moving. . . ."

Hawk laughed and touched her shoulder, leaving a burning

sensation. "I'd say it's exactly the opposite from quiet and white!"

"Yes, but what I mean is, it gives you a whole new way to see the city. It makes everything new, all of a sudden."

"You can write a song about it," he said. He moved closer to her, so that his left arm was just behind her right arm. They were walking slowly, and Sarah adjusted her pace so he could stay there, tucked in behind her. "I like your songs," he said.

"Thank you. I wish someone would record them."

"Someone will."

"You know what my grandmother would say to that? She'd say, 'From your lips to God's ear!' "

"My grandmother, too," Hawk said, and laughed. Without any fuss, his hand found hers, and he laced their fingers together. Sarah thought she might stop breathing, but she kept on talking, though she was certain she'd never remember later what she'd said. All she could think about was: We're holding hands. It felt so right. She had never felt so right with any man.

Most cafés and restaurants were still open—groceries, too—using kerosene lanterns and candles. One hardware store had a line of flashlights upended and lighted. People were gathering anyplace there was light. As they passed one bar, two guys yelled for them to come on in and bring the guitar. So they went in, and Sarah played a song, and the bartender poured them each a tot of brandy, and then gave her an extra shot when he heard she had to go all the way to Lincoln Center. Everyone assumed she and Hawk were married; and that was okay with her.

They stayed on Broadway—since it cut across the city diagonally and would take them west—passing through the printing section and then the button section and the hat section and the paper-goods section, talking about everything, about nothing, all the time. They were holding hands, and he walked very close to her, very close, and she kept sending inarticulate, almost wordless prayers up to heaven; she wasn't sure for what except she didn't want him to leave. Please, let him stay; don't let him get on a train and go to Long Island tonight.

Just before Penn Station, just as she was steeling herself in case the miracle didn't happen, Hawk stopped walking. "Hey, Sam, you know what I just realized?" he said, and his voice was loaded with excitement.

"No, what?" She held her breath. Please. Please.

"The LIRR is electric. I can't take my train, I can't take *any* train. And you know something else I just realized?" Mute, she shook her head.

He bent so his cheek was against hers. She could feel his lips moving, barely brushing her skin. "I just realized I'm *delighted* I can't take the train. Delighted? Hell, I'm elated!"

"Me, too," she said.

"Which one?" Now he put his finger on the tip of her nose, gazing down at her so tenderly.

"Everything. Me, too, happy, elated, delighted, everything!"

"If you didn't have that guitar slung over your shoulder, I'd pick you up and swing you around, Sammy my girl!"

Letting the guitar slide off and fall to the ground, she smiled up at him. And he picked her up, held her tight, and turned around and around and around, crowing with laughter.

When he put her down, they both knew not to kiss, not yet. Instead they just stood there, grinning at each other like idiots, and talked about having a drink to celebrate. They didn't say celebrate *what*; they didn't have to. So they stopped off at an Irish bar near Thirty-eighth Street and ordered a beer, joining the others there in toasting every Irishman they could think of, including the entire Kennedy clan, "and the President, God rest his soul!"

"The President . . ." everyone murmured; and that changed the mood of the place, so they split.

Out in the street, Hawk took her guitar and put his other arm around her shoulder, so she could hold him around his waist. They fit perfectly, walking silently in step.

"I cried," Hawk said.

"What?"

"When Kennedy died. I guess nobody will ever forget where they were when they got the news. I was on the third floor of the courthouse, running because I was late, eating a hot dog—my lunch—and somebody yelled out, 'Kennedy's been shot! In Dallas! They think he's dead!' I remember I came to such a sudden stop, I almost fell over. I couldn't believe it; I couldn't make my mind take it in. . . . So, Sammy mine, where were *you* when you heard?"

Sammy mine, he had said.

"Where was I? In bed, with my poli sci professor!" The instant the words were out, she regretted them. It was the answer she gave everyone because, of course, everyone always asked that question sooner or later. And it happened to be true.

From the first class, she'd known she didn't have to waste any time studying for the American Dream 1776–1916. She knew all she had to do was be extra nice to gorgeous, dark Mister . . . what the hell *was* his name?

Anyway, it was a pretty funny place to be, but she shouldn't have said that to Hawk, not when they were being so close and romantic.

He wasn't shocked. He squeezed her and said, "Oh Sam, you are the most fearless woman I've ever known! In bed with your poli sci professor! Oh God, that's great. That's so great! No wonder I love you!"

The next thirty blocks, she walked in a daze of bliss and jubilation. He'd said "I love you"; well, not quite like that, but it amounted to the same thing. Didn't it?

They never stopped talking, but her mind was racing ahead, racing up the stairs to her apartment, running in the door, slamming it shut, turning to him, melting into his embrace, the two of them falling slowly slowly slowly onto the bed, tearing each other's clothes off. Oh, she was sure there would be no soft, slow, gentle stuff, not for them, they would be kissing hard, biting each other's lips, kissing each other everywhere, and then—

"Some guys really get it off pretending to be cops," Hawk was saying.

"Huh?" Coming out of her daydream, she stared at him, amazed to see him fully dressed, in his overcoat, his muffler wrapped around his neck, her guitar slung over his shoulder.

"Wake up, Sammy baby." He laughed. "The guys in the street. Directing traffic. Watch the fat one. He looks like he's dancing."

At Columbus Circle two men had appointed themselves traffic cops. Hawk was right, the big fat guy was terrific. He twirled and ducked and spun around like a top, waving cars on with his hands, halting them with a single gesture. He was surprisingly graceful, and they stood there studying him so long she began to shiver.

"Cold?" Hawk said. "Me, too. Let's run. It's not far . . . Sixty-ninth Street, you said? Then I plan to warm you up good."

She shivered again, but it wasn't with cold. They began to trot up Central Park West because it was prettier, laughing because, pretty or not, it was now almost invisible in the dark.

"I must be getting old, Sammy. Phew! A couple years ago, I could've run the whole distance," he said, out of breath.

"Carrying a guitar and dragging me along behind you?"

"Ah, Sam, with you, I feel I have wings on my feet. But I guess that's just the way you make me feel."

Oh God. Oh God. She was so happy, she felt she could choke with it. "Come on!" she cried, grabbing his hand and starting to run again. "We can do it!"

At Sixty-ninth they turned toward Columbus, and Hawk put his arm around her waist to pull her to him. "Almost there, Sammy, almost there," he murmured. Her answer was to snuggle herself in even closer. When they passed the Fleur de Lys, the neighborhood French restaurant, it was blazing with candlelight. The manager called out to her:

"Mademoiselle Sarah! *Venez!* Come in! We are giving our favorite customers glasses of wine!"

She would have gone, but Hawk grinned at the man and said, "Next time, monsieur. I'm in a bit of a hurry."

The manager winked and laughed and said, "*Vive l'amour!* But excuse me, mademoiselle, you will be unable to see inside your building, *n'est-ce pas*? One little minute . . ." And he came out a moment later with a fat white candle and a book of the restaurant's matches. "*Voilà!* And you shall have light!"

When they got to her building, she said, "This is it, right over Austin's Drugstore. Not very fancy . . ."

"It will be beautiful," Hawk said, his voice heavy with meaning.

"Yes," she said. "Oh, yes."

They ducked into the hallway, where he lit the candle and she led the way, holding it well out in front of her. The flickering light cast long, grotesque shadows ahead of them; it was amazing, how her familiar stairway suddenly became full of pitfalls. She tripped a couple of times, and each time Hawk said, "Take your time. I'm right behind you."

And at last there they were, in front of her door. As she turned the key in the lock, she felt him press his body against hers, just a little, just enough so she could tell how excited he was, and she thought, Thank you, thank you, thank you for giving me this night.

38

March 1966

Pregnant! Oh Christ, no! Sarah squeezed her hands together in her lap and stared at the doctor's bland, tired face, willing him to take it back. But instead he smiled and said, "You're young and healthy, Mrs. Danton. You shouldn't have any problems. If you smoke, you should stop, and keep your alcohol intake down and, please, watch what you eat. We don't like our ladies to gain more than eighteen pounds, and you've already put on half that." A little shake of the head. "I wish you'd come to me right away, instead of waiting three months."

Her head was buzzing, drowning out all his words but *three months*! She couldn't be that pregnant! Hawk would *kill* her. He told her a thousand times he'd rather use rubbers—"then I'm sure we're covered," he'd say, laughing at the pun—but she preferred the diaphragm. She liked feeling the heat of him, his skin; liked him to know exactly how wet she got for him.

He'd accuse her of forgetting the diaphragm; but she hadn't. She hadn't! She hardly knew when it was in; sometimes she'd forget about it and leave it in for days. And then, even when she took it out and washed it, she put it right back in. Always ready. And she really had to be. Always ready, that is. Hawk was wild for sex; he might suddenly show up at her place four o'clock in the morning—any time of the day or night. She'd be doing her laundry in the afternoon, or coming back from a casting call, or fast asleep in the middle of the night, and suddenly he'd be there, with that hot, hungry look. Oh, the look of him when he was aroused! She loved his wanting her so much. So, lately, she always had the diaphragm in. God, could *that* be the reason this had happened? Oh God, what was she going to *do*?

"Mrs. Danton? Are you all right? Do you feel faint?"

"No. No, I'm okay. I wasn't . . . we weren't planning on this. I use a diaphragm."

"Are you sure you didn't forget it? Sometimes . . ." He cleared his throat delicately, lacing his fingers together on top of the polished desk. "Sometimes in the, ah, heat of the moment—"

"No. No, I'm sure I didn't." She was damned if she'd say more.

"Well . . ." The doctor smiled. "Nothing is a hundred percent perfect. But don't worry, you'll soon get used to the idea. And in six months or so . . . you'll have your baby, and believe me, you'll be very happy it happened."

Outside his office she leaned against the wall and let the tears come. Oh Christ, what was she going to do? She had to get rid of it. How could she not have realized she'd missed so many periods? Three months! Three goddamn months! She felt so fucking stupid. It hadn't occurred to her until she noticed she was nauseated *every* morning . . . that, plus the fact she had put on so much weight. Last week it finally hit her that she could be pregnant. Even then she managed to convince herself it was something else . . . until today, of course. Now she couldn't pretend any longer.

She had to get rid of it. But how was she supposed to find an abortionist? She'd ask Hawk; the D.A.'s knew everything and everyone. Oh Christ, he couldn't take her to an abortionist. It was against the law. He'd lose his job. He'd be disbarred. What a mess! She had to get rid of it. She knew he would leave her if she didn't, and life without Hawk Diamond wasn't worth living.

That first time, the night of the Big Blackout, they had started undressing each other as soon as they were inside, letting everything just drop to the floor. She remembered treading on clothes, tripping over them as they stumbled to the bed, kissing and caressing, moaning and whispering endearments. They had been in such a hurry, and when he pushed into her, she felt she had been waiting for him her whole life; it was like coming home.

Though that was four months ago, she still remembered how she woke up in the morning, realizing even before she opened her eyes that he wasn't beside her. She remembered the panic that swept over her, afraid he had left without saying good-bye, afraid that she'd only been an easy lay for him and that she would never see him again.

She had sat up, whimpering a little, blinking at the light. And then she saw him, standing by the window, looking out.

"Is the power back on?" she asked, keeping her tone casual, hiding the wave of relief that swept over her.

He turned from the window, smiling. He was naked except for a towel wrapped around his loins. "Well, hello there, little Sammy, my big surprise. Ho, look at this. Just seeing you does it." He laughed as his erection slowly lifted the towel.

It *was* a funny sight. She laughed, too, and then he made a fierce face and, growling in his throat, threw himself on the bed on her, nuzzling her neck, biting her lightly, sending shivers down her back. He slid right in, she was so slippery, and oh God, he felt so good, so *right*. The night before, it had been frantic the first time, delirious and grasping. The next time it was slow and delicious, and after that they tried everything they could think of, standing up, sitting down, in the rocker, on the toilet seat. But in the morning, it had been fierce and fast and over too quickly.

He rolled away from her, groaning, a big grin on his face. "Oh, Sam, it hasn't been this good . . . in years and years." She pushed away a little zing of jealousy. She wanted him to say it had *never* been so good; but that was crazy. He wasn't a kid, he was twenty-nine years old; he'd had dozens of girls.

"Yeah, it went on sometime in the middle of the night." For a minute she didn't know what he was talking about. And then she got it: the electricity. "I woke up early. You looked so peaceful sleeping, I didn't want to bother you. I kept the radio low."

As he stretched lazily, she admired his lean body, his chest and belly covered in black hair, his legs surprisingly muscular. She remarked on that, and he said, "Yeah, squash. And tennis." She put her hand out to stroke the flat stomach. Instantly his cock stirred, but he lifted her hand away.

"No, no, Sammy, not now. I've got to get back to the office. To reality." He groaned and lifted himself up onto one elbow, leaned over to give her a light kiss, and leapt off the bed.

"What time is it?"

"Quarter to eight. I've *really* got to get going." Over the back of the sagging easy chair she'd picked up at the Salvation Army store, she saw his clothes, neatly folded. He must have retrieved them as soon as he got up.

She rolled onto her side and watched him as he dressed.

"The worst blackout ever . . ." He was not looking at her; he was gazing into the mirror, tying his tie, smoothing his close-cropped hair with his two hands. "Not just New York, but the entire Northeast . . . nine states, I think they said, parts of Canada, too. Thousands of people were trapped in the subways." He shuddered. "That, I couldn't have stood. I'm a little claustrophobic." His eyes, in the mirror, found hers, and he winked. "Here I am, telling you all my secrets. You'll dump me if I'm not careful."

"Never!" she said forcefully; and his mouth made a kiss for her. Her heartbeat speeded up. She loved him, she *loved* him!

"Remember the last time this happened? 'Sixty-one? I'll never forget it. I was in a skyscraper and the elevators all went out. Twenty-six flights. You think walking down is going to be easy, but not on a day when it's ninety-six degrees in the shade!"

"I remember," Sarah said. "I was only a year out of high school."

He turned, startled. "High school! Jesus Christ, am I a cradle robber? How old *are* you, Sam?"

"Old enough!"

That made him laugh, and he came over, sitting on the edge of the bed, stroking her hair and smiling at her. "Oh Jesus, I can't help myself, I gotta have you again."

He made love to her, completely dressed from the waist up. It made her giggle when his tie moved up and down on her face, keeping time with his movements. He filled her entirely, he was wonderful. She began to quiver and shake uncontrollably, and, his eyes glazed with heat, he urged her on until they exploded together.

She must have dozed, because when she next opened her eyes, the light coming in the window was bright with sunshine. Once again he was standing by the window, buckling his belt, gazing down into the street.

"Oh Christ!" Sarah said, and he whipped around.

"What?"

"Well . . . now when people ask me what I was doing the night of the Big Blackout . . . I'll have to say I was making love with the most wonderful man I've ever met."

"I'll keep those words with me all day." He kissed her briefly, saying if he gave her a better kiss, he'd never leave. "I'll call you later." And she lay on her bed, loving the aching throb between her legs, listening to the fading sound of his footsteps moving down the stairway, missing him already.

She had died a thousand deaths that day, waiting for him to call. Why, she asked herself a thousand times, hadn't she said, "When will you call me? *When*, later?" Why hadn't she pinned him down to a time; then, at least, she'd known for sure, and wouldn't have to pace back and forth in her little room, unable to keep her eyes off the telephone. He still hadn't called when it was time to go to work. And he didn't come into the Bitter Bean later. But none of the attorneys did, so she figured they were all still at the office. But why didn't he call?

He didn't call until way after midnight, after she had cried her eyes out and had finished a whole bottle of dago red by herself, sitting cross-legged on her bed.

"Sam, listen, I want to see you again. I really . . . I *need* to see you again." He spoke so low, she could hardly hear him. "I'm a goner, I'm a lost soul, Jesus Christ, I am in such trouble!"

"Don't freak out. Tell me," she said.

"I can't talk right now but . . . we have to talk."

"Okay. We'll talk. Not tonight, I guess."

"Tonight? Christ, no. I'm—I mean, it's impossible tonight. But tomorrow. Tomorrow I'll come into the Bean and we'll catch a bite after your last set. Okay?" And then he didn't even wait for her to answer. "Gotta go," he whispered, and hung up.

She knew, with thickly beating heart, that it was going to be something terrible, whatever he wanted to talk to her about. All the next morning, she fought the fear that threatened to smother her. She wrote a new song, about the blackout, calling it "Hawk Man," and then she figured that might be bad luck, so she changed it to "Bird Man," but that sounded dopey so she changed it back.

Finally, she went to a movie, *The Sand Pebbles*. She picked it because it was supposed to be great, but she didn't really watch it. She sat alone in the dark and thought about Hawk. He hated her because she went to bed with him; Christ, he wasn't like *that*, was he? She'd never got those vibes from him. But if it wasn't him being turned off, then *what*? The draft! Oh God, maybe he was going to go to Vietnam and get killed! She gave up and left the movie long before it was over.

At last it was time to go down to the Village. Singing helped; working the audience made her stop thinking about anything else but their faces, the eyes trained on her. She sang her new song, "Hawk Man" about two strangers who meet in the dark and fall in love. They loved it, they kept asking her to sing it again. She was right in the middle, singing ". . . and he turned to her and said,/Oh, babe, get back to bed/'cause I just gotta have you again. . ." when Hawk came in. She had missed seeing him cross the street! It flustered her, meeting his eyes suddenly, when she was singing about him . . . about them, and using his very words to her.

He heard it; he got it. He stopped dead in his tracks, staring at her, just staring. She faltered, just for a second, but recovered quickly and went on with the song, tearing her eyes from his and casting her big broad impersonal smile all around the room.

She took her break early. She knew she didn't want to hear what he was going to say, but what the hell, the sooner she heard it, the sooner it would be over.

"Hi, Hawk, where are the others? I'll have a double bourbon . . . Jack Daniel's, please," she said as she sat down.

"I thought you didn't drink when you're working."

"Well, tonight I do."

"Okay, okay. Whatever you want, I want you to have it." He held her eyes, very serious.

It just came out of her mouth. "I want *you*, Hawk."

He didn't frown; he didn't get up and leave. "I know, I know. And . . . what I have to tell you isn't easy."

"Shit," she said. "I know what it is." And, quite suddenly, she *did* know. "You're married."

He nodded. "Yes. But it's not how you think." The drinks came and he sipped at his. Sarah took a great gulp, waiting for the boubon to hit her stomach and send a nice wave of buzzy fuzzy warmth to her brain, so this wouldn't hurt so much.

"Look, here's how it is. I deflowered her, my wi—Marilyn, when we were both fourteen. We were in junior high together—we're from the same neighborhood."

"Where?" she asked, inanely.

"Inwood. Uptown in Manhattan. Working-class neighborhood."

"Anyway . . ." she prodded. "You deflowered her."

"Yeah. She was in love with me. I was . . . shit, I was horny. I was fourteen. All I wanted was to get into some girl's pants, for Christ's sake. Get laid. But you know what, Sam? Love *is* a tender trap. I couldn't shake her, couldn't make her stop loving me. I went out with other girls, laid other girls, but all the time, there she was, with her big blue eyes, waiting for me, loving me ... oh shit!" He put his head in his hands and stopped talking.

Sarah hardened her heart. She was *not* going to pity a man who was about to blow her away; she was not going to make it easy for him.

"We both went to CCNY, and she was exactly the same. Always waiting for me ..."

"And you took advantage of her."

"That's right, Sammy baby, I was a typical rotten weak-minded male. When I was between girls, there was always Marilyn. And she was always so fucking *grateful* when I showed up, always so full of fucking *rapture*. And she was so sure of her feelings, so ... I don't know ... so steadfast. She told me she could never love another man. 'I'm a one-man woman,' she'd say, 'and you're the man for me. There'll never be anyone else.' I have to tell you, Sam, there's something terribly seductive about that kind of unwavering constancy. It makes you feel like a goddamn Greek god!" His voice shook a little and he gulped at his drink.

"Okay. I just want to get this told. I want you to hear the whole thing, okay? I got into Columbia Law. One of the top three! You can't imagine how I felt ... I mean, this was my way out of Inwood and all that it stood for—nosy neighbors, never having enough money, apologizing to people for where I came from!" Again his voice quivered with agitation. "And it was a way to get away ... from her."

Hawk's voice trailed off and his eyes went out of focus, staring across the room, at nothing, his face stormy. She signaled to the bar for another round, and as soon as the drinks arrived, Hawk came to with a start.

"Sorry, Sam. So, where was I?"

"Columbia."

"Yeah. Well, Marilyn was always talking about getting married, and I always put her off. But she came over just after I got my acceptance, and when she started in on me about when we were going to get married, I told her, 'Never! That's when! I'm going to Columbia Law School.'

"Well, she threw hysterics, screamed and cried and threw herself around, and tore at her face with her fingernails. She was like a crazy woman. All I wanted was to get the hell out of there. But, Jesus, I couldn't leave her like that. So I said okay."

"Okay?"

"Okay, I'd marry her. I know, I was a fucking coward, right? But I didn't know what *else* to do. And the real hell of it was, the minute I said it, she turned off the hysterics. Just turned it off. Just like that."

"But you married her anyway."

"But I married her anyway."

"Well, so long, it's been good to know you, like it says in the song." She got up.

He grabbed her wrist, pulling her back down into the chair. "Please, Sammy, don't do that to me. You haven't heard the whole story yet. I'm crazy for you, I've never felt like this about any woman, ever, not in my whole life. That's why I'm being totally honest with you. I want you to know every god-damn thing about me, even the lousy stuff, and then I want you to love me anyway."

She stared at him, her eyes filling with grateful tears, her heart singing. He loved her. He loved her. "Tell me the rest."

He pulled in a deep breath and let it out noisily, holding up two fingers for two refills. She didn't dare drink any more—she had two more sets to do—but she didn't want to interrupt him. Artie was giving her the hairy eyeball: *pick up the guitar and start, already*. She shook her head and gave him the hairy eyeball right back.

"I married her. She wanted a big wedding, we had a big wedding. She wanted a honeymoon in Bermuda, we had a honeymoon in Bermuda. But I told her, when we got home, that this was not a marriage of love, that I didn't love her."

"Christ, she must have freaked out," Sarah said.

"Freaked? She was out of her mind. And I said, 'So if you don't like it, get the marriage annulled.' "

"She wouldn't," Sarah supplied.

Now he laughed, a sour kind of laugh. "She wouldn't." He stopped talking, staring out blindly into space.

"So," he resumed in an entirely different tone, draining his scotch and picking up the new one, "you've heard the whole thing."

"But you cheat on her."

"Sam, it's not cheating. She knows. I've never hidden it from her. I'm completely open and honest." He gave that strange bark of a laugh again.

"How could you keep it up all these years, Hawk? It seems . . . I don't know . . . so cruel."

Harshly: "It's meant to be."

"Hawk, this toughness, this is a side of you I'd never have imagined. I'm not sure I like it."

"Sammy, this is the side of me that earned me my nickname, the side of me that wins every case, the side of me I hope *you'll* never see. But of course you won't. You'd never resort to a cheap trick like that. And in any case," he said in a voice suddenly soft with tenderness, "I've never felt the way I feel about you, never. I think it may be l-l-l—" He threw his head back and laughed. "See? I can't even say it, it's so strange to me. But I have this feeling that you can change all that, Sammy my girl."

He leaned across the table, his face very close to hers. "Say you care. Say I get to take you home tonight and feel your satin skin against mine, feel the silk of you when I slide in. . . ."

She had gotten excited; it was terrible, right there in the Bean in front of Artie and everybody. So she gave Hawk a playful slap and laughed and fell so deeply in love with him, right then and there, that she knew she'd never never find her way out again.

And she didn't care. They had never looked back. They saw each other almost every night, and often during the day, too. They just couldn't seem to get enough of each other. Sarah hadn't known a man and a woman could feel this way. Her mother's boyfriends had always seemed so dispensable, so easily replaced; and she still couldn't forget NanaLeah's harsh words to Uncle Jim—even though, after the heart attack, she took tender care of him for months . . . until he had the one that killed him.

Sarah had always thought that's just the way it was: men were creatures who drifted in and out of your life, as wispy as dreams. When you wanted a family, you got married because, otherwise, it said "Illegitimate" on your baby's birth certificate. Love? Sarah couldn't remember it ever being mentioned.

She hadn't dreamed you could be so obsessed with another person that sometimes you wished you could swallow him, suck him into your body and carry him around inside you, you wanted to be that inseparable. And now she was going to have to tell him that the diaphragm had failed and she was pregnant. He'd think it was just another dirty trick to get him.

She was aware that people were staring at her, wondering if they should stop and help the strange young woman who leaned against the wall of a building on Horatio Street, weeping. She roused herself and began to walk. She had to figure out what she was going to do. She had to find an abortionist; but how? Nobody she knew had ever needed one. Her mother was at Berkeley, taking pictures of the war protestors.

"There's never been anything like this before," Jo had told her, all excited. "And I've got a feeling it's going to be historic." Anyway, her mother was always more interested in big ideas than she was in her own child; no way would Jo fly back from California just because she was in trouble. Her grandmother was a possibility—very little in life shocked or shook her up—but Sarah hated disappointing NanaLeah.

Besides, if she was going to do it, Hawk Diamond was going to be with her. She could take anything if he was with her. She would tell him tonight, when they were having their nightcap at Marie's Crisis before heading uptown. It would be a heavy thing to lay on him, but it was his baby in her belly.

She told him as they were finishing their drinks. He turned absolutely white—no, a greenish gray—and then the color flooded back into his face, dark and ugly. He looked as if he might explode.

"I'm dreaming, right? You didn't just say you're pregnant."

"Hawk, I don't know how it—"

Tightly: "You *are* pregnant. Cunt!"

He frightened her, to call her such an ugly name. He looked so fierce and strange, she hardly recognized him. "Hawk! It's not my fault! I didn't do it on purpose!"

"I'll bet you didn't, I'll just bet you didn't conveniently forget the fucking diaphragm." His words felt like slaps.

"I knew you'd think that, but I didn't." Tears flooded her eyes.

"Oh, cut the crap," Hawk said. "I assure you my heart is hard—harder than my cock. Tears don't move me, Sammy. But tricks make me madder than hell."

"It's not a trick, Hawk. For God's sake . . ." She couldn't help it, her eyes kept filling. "I love you. I wouldn't do anything to hurt you."

"Then how in hell did you get pregnant?"

They were both using harsh whispers, their eyes locked.

"I don't know! I told you! It was an accident. The doctor said that lots of accidents happen with diaphragms."

"Not to me, they don't, I can tell you that."

That got to her. She felt anger rising in place of the sick

anxiety that had been sitting, like a rock, in the middle of her chest. Fuck him! "Well, for your information, Mr. Diamond, I wasn't planning to *have* it. I'm telling you because . . . well, I want to be just as open and honest as you are." That got him! "And I didn't notice a star shining in the east."

"A star . . . ? Oh. Very funny. Very cute." But now he was relaxed; the fury had left him. "Okay, Sammy, what's done is done. I could find you an abortionist—I know where—but I don't know."

"What do you mean, you don't know? We've *got* to."

He reached out for her hand, fondling the fingers idly as he talked. Not looking at her face. "I'm sorry I lost it. I just can't stand to think another woman has tried to fuck with me. I promised myself Marilyn was the first and the last bitch who'd ever do *that* to me. I couldn't stand that, Sammy." He looked at her, his eyes pleading. "You're different from the others. The thought that you were just ordinary, trying to back me against the wall . . . I'm sorry. It'll never happen again." He leaned over and gave her a tender little kiss on the tip of her nose.

"Oh, Hawk, I do love you!"

"Good. Then you'll have my baby."

"Have it!"

"Yes, have it! And now that I've said it, I like the idea even better. Our baby, our little boy. Oh, if he gets your looks and my brains! Oh shit, what if he gets my looks?"

"And my brains?"

"Just a joke, Sam. Your brains are fine with me." He was grinning; he looked so happy! She wanted to be happy *with* him.

"But Hawk, how can I have a baby? Christ, you're a married man. What will we call it? And how do I tell my family?"

"We'll call *him* Adam Diamond, of course. And what'll you tell your family? You'll tell your family you're going to marry a lawyer with a big nose and a bad attitude."

"Marry? But Hawk—"

"No, this charade has been going on long enough! I don't know why I didn't leave her sooner! Well, yes, I do know. Because I was never in love before and she was a great excuse for not getting involved. But now I'm involved; I want to be involved. . . ." He leaned close to her and spoke softly, his breath warm against her skin. "I want to be as involved as a man can get—for life."

She pulled back, to look him in the eyes. "Hawk, do you *really* mean it? We'll get married? To each other?"

"No, to three other people." He seemed joyously giddy. "Yes, I really mean it, and yes, we'll get married, and yes, to each other."

There was a breathless moment before it hit her, that all of her dreams were about to come true.

"Oh, Hawk!" She lifted her lips and they kissed, more and more deeply, until nearby patrons began to stamp their feet and whistle in appreciation. In the middle of their passion they both began to laugh; they were laughing when they pulled apart. They were so perfect together! Now she could tell him all about her visit to the doctor on Horatio Street, how the nurse eyed her with suspicion, how she stood outside and cried, how the people stared.

Oh, it would make a good story to tell him when they were relaxed after making love, lying side by side on the bed with their fingers intertwined. She couldn't wait to tell him! And Hawk would laugh and say, "What do you expect, when you dress out of a rag bag?" He always made fun of her Indian things and her tie-dyes, but she knew he liked the way she looked, and, even better, loved the way other men looked at her, knowing she was his.

Hawk slapped a ten-dollar bill down on the table and stood up, pulling her to her feet. "Come on, Sammy baby, I want to take you home and make love to both of you. I want to go home with you and begin the rest of our life together!"

39

August 1967

The Summer of Love, they were calling it, the Summer of Love in Hashbury, in the Haight, in beautiful San Francisco; and she was here, she was part of it, she could dig it. Hey, man, this was It, the beginning of a whole new world, where love would take the place of money, and war, and all the struggling in the world.

"Love," she said aloud, dreamily; and the others repeated, "Yeah, man . . . love." She knew exactly what they meant: that love would conquer all the evil, the fear, and the greed, and that love would end the war. It was a trip, living with so many people alike, where understanding was instant and complete. You didn't need all those words anymore, especially when a joint was being passed around.

She'd been here, in the pad, since June. And she loved it. The Haight-Ashbury scene was all about peace and love and freedom, and it was a turn-on. There was no crime, no rules, no jealousy, no money. The Grateful Dead lived there, and they put on free concerts all the time. People, like, danced in the streets. It was all free; everything was free. You could get free food from the Diggers' store. The flowers in Golden Gate Park were for everyone, even though the non-hip people complained. The hippies told them, "Flowers belong to God, not the city." It was a new spiritual dawn, and everyone was there.

She had a feeling she would end up somewhere like this, the first time she had seen the Flower Children in New York, at a big anti-war rally at the UN. Her mother was covering it, of course, for some big-time magazine; and her grandmother never missed a left-wing demonstration.

It was the usual scene, with yelling and jeering and booing and hating; with the *anti*-anti-war people on the sidelines while the anti-war people marched. Her mother went tear-assing all over the place, grouching that she ought to be in Vietnam with the real action instead of where it was all safe and boring. She thought her mother was nuts. If she thought it was boring, what was she doing, hanging upside down to get a particular shot? And as for safety, well . . . the people who found it amusing to throw rocks and bottles at the marchers didn't mind hitting a few reporters and photographers, too. They couldn't tell the difference. Her mother had been knocked down and bruised more than once, in her supposedly safe, boring assignments.

It didn't take Sarah long to wish she had stayed home. She wasn't an activist, that's all there was to it. None of this had any meaning for her; and she really didn't see what good all these activists milling around were going to do for people half a world away, who were getting bombed and killed. You kept seeing the same faces at these things, over and over. A whole lot of noise and what was the good of it?

And then, all of a sudden, along came the Flower Children with their flowing skirts and long hair and gentle expressions, carrying daffodils and calling out, "Flower Power!" One carried a sign that said, "Make Love Not War." A feeling swept over her, that *they* were the only real people here, and everyone else, with their signs and clenched fists and their slogans, were the crazy ones. She knew right then and there, she had found her people, *her* cause.

She had landed in San Francisco on the seventeenth of June, along with about fifty other new friends she'd made on the long trip. Everyone wanted to be part of the Summer of Love. They all loved to sing and they were all against war. They all dressed like her; it was groovy. Everyone in tie-dyes and beads and Indian earrings, and all the guys with ponytails, and everyone so cool. The official opening of the whole summer was the Solstice Festival and she was just in time for it.

She thought she'd have to look and look for a place to stay, but as soon as she got off the city bus at the corner of Ashbury and Haight, this guy came up to her, a real cute guy, and he invited her to stay with his family. She kind of stared at him until he explained his family was, like, other kids, sharing a pad.

"You can crash with us, as long as you want." He told her he'd take her around the festival, too. "A bunch of us are going to watch the sunrise from Twin Peaks. Wanna go?" Was he kidding?

Later, when someone called to him, "Grady! Grady Ward!" she realized she was walking hand in hand in a strange city with a strange man, feeling good, feeling safe—and she didn't even know his name! Heavy!

Everyone at the pad was cool, too; they all hugged and kissed her and said she was truly welcome—especially since she had a guitar. Doris played the flute and now they could have real music.

"What other kind of music do you have?" Sarah asked, looking around for a record player or something; but the place was just about empty, only mattresses piled on the floor, covered with shawls and Indian bedspreads and like that.

She was so naive! Everyone laughed and laughed; and Grady squeezed her and said, "The music of the spheres, lady, the music of the colliding heavens . . ." And when she still didn't know what he was talking about, he said: "Tripping, Sarah. Blowing your mind, dropping acid. Then you hear celestial music."

"Yeah," one of the guys said, "if you have a good trip, the Angel Gabriel himself is blowing horn." And they all chimed in, telling her how wonderful it was, the gorgeous colors you saw, the beautiful people you talked to. Of course, if you had a bad trip . . . Everyone fell silent.

"If you have a bad trip—?" Sarah prodded.

Well . . . nobody wanted to put a scare into her, but one guy thought he was on a diving board and took a half-gainer into the highway below. But, hey! That was, like, freaky.

"It's ecstasy, there's nothing like it!"

"I saw Jesus, I talked to him!"

"I became an eagle and soared in the sky, looking down on the beautiful blue and green earth! I grooved with the entire world."

"You gotta try it! It's, like, beautiful!"

But first they wanted to sing. So she sat down on the floor and began to play her guitar, and someone lit a joint and passed it around. Later, when it got dark, they went out onto the street to panhandle.

"You all do it?" Sarah asked Grady, astonished. "You all go out every day and beg for money?"

"Hey, we're a tourist attraction! They have buses full of squares, staring out the windows at the freaks. You know how they advertise the tour? They say it's the only trip to a foreign country right inside the borders of the U.S.A. So we hold out our palms and the touristas, they cross them with silver!" And he laughed. Grady laughed a lot, sometimes at nothing.

She wasn't so sure, her first night in the Haight, that she would want to stay. The place was none too clean; they were none too clean; and the begging made her feel ashamed.

But then the next morning they all went out together, before dawn, with only a faint pearly glow on the horizon and all the streetlights still on, everything still and calm. And as they walked, they were joined by dozens and then hundreds and finally by so many other kids, on their way to Twin Peaks, you couldn't even count them. And everyone so calm and so happy and so loving.

Later, there was music and singing. The bushes were filled with paper flowers, the big wooden stages were filled with bands: The Dead, Big Brother, Quicksilver. All day long there was the sound of music and clapping and singing and laughter, and one group sat crosslegged in the meadow chanting "Om." There were jugglers, and dancers and musicians. So many people—but no bumping, no swearing, no drunken brawls, just love, and the sweet smell of pot. Joints were for sale everywhere and LSD, mescaline, methadrine and a whole lot of other stuff. Grady asked if she had any bread, and by this time she knew he meant money; and she did. So they bought five joints and they smoked as they walked. Pretty soon she was feeling wonderfully mellow. Everything looked beautiful. Diggers were barbecuing lamb and frying burgers in shovels; the smell made her ravenous.

"I'm starving!" she said, and Grady laughed.

"You've just got the munchies! But don't worry—there's food for everyone." They walked to the Diggers and said they were hungry, and the girl cooking handed her a hamburger—it was free. "Food belongs to the people," the girl said; and Sarah gobbled it down.

Next time, she thought, I'll bring my guitar and I'll be sitting on the grass, playing and singing, and people will stop to listen to me. I'll write a song about this festival, I'll call it "Solstice Love."

For just one minute sometime during the long endless beautiful day, she thought, Mom should be here, taking pictures of *this*. And then she stopped. She didn't want to think about Mom or her grandmother or . . . or anything that had happened before. She just wanted to *be*.

Well, there was one thing about the Hashbury: you could be any goddamn thing you wanted and nobody bothered you. After the Solstice Festival, there was no doubt in her mind that she was staying, just as long as she could. Eleven people, six girls and five guys, lived in the apartment, and they were all cool. Nobody was attached to anyone else—around there, people didn't own other people. What did Grady say the other night? "All the girls are my wives and all the guys are my brothers. This is life, the way it was meant to be. This is love." And everyone crowded around him to touch him and hug him.

She liked Grady the best of all the guys, but she would never say it. You weren't supposed to have a favorite; but he was the nicest in bed, he always smelled good, and he took his time, not like some of the others, rushing it and then rolling away. Also, he was the only guy who noticed that she wasn't exactly turned on during sex.

"This isn't your thing, is it?" he said once.

"You kidding? I love it! And you're, like, the greatest."
Quickly, she started to rub his cock, moaning and saying, "Oh
just look at that gorgeous thing."

But he took her hand away, shaking his head. "Nope.
You're, like, somewhere else when we're doing it." Grady was
smart. He had dropped out of Harvard in the middle of the
year to come to the Haight, he said, even though his father had
then disowned him.

"Who needs his millions?" Grady said. "They haven't made
him happy. He's got ulcers and high blood pressure and he
works all the time." And everyone said, Yeah, man, and said
how they'd try to get disowned, too, if they had an old man
with millions. Grady felt bad, that his father couldn't understand what was happening, how the times were changing. He
thought he might write a book about this summer so that his
parents, and everyone else, too, could see that they weren't just
rebellious kids. They were changing the world! He was ready
to start the book—if he ever got his typewriter out of hock.
One of the best things about being there was that there was no
hurry about anything; the future was going to meet you, sooner
or later.

"Hey, Sarah . . ." The voice came from behind her: Jock.

"Mmmmmm?" This grass was *good*.

"So how'd *you* get here? You were a coffeehouse singer in
New York. That's cool. So why bug out?"

"Man trouble, man." The juxtaposition of "man" and "man"
struck her funny, so she repeated it, laughing. For the first time
since she got on that bus, the thought of Hawk didn't make her
heart hurt. "Yeah. Man trouble."

"He, like, dump you?"

"Like a load of garbage, man." Oh, she was wonderfully
witty today. She giggled. "Like yesterday's trash."

"Hell . . . happens to everyone."

"Everyone five months pregnant?"

It took her a few minutes to realize there was a strange silence in the room, that everyone was staring at her.

"Pregnant?" Karen said. "You have a kid, Sarah?"

"Sweet little baby girl. Sweet." She had trouble remembering what Annie looked like. She was round and pink-cheeked,
with a mop of dark hair, like hers. Like Hawk's. Damn him,
the dirty rotten bastard. "Dirty rotten bastard," she said.

Karen, surprised, asked: "Your baby?"

"No. No. Him."

"The baby. How could you leave her?"

"She's too little to bring here."

"We'd all take care of her!"

"Yeah, man, we'd've helped out!"

Sarah's heart was warmed. They were the best, the very best, the most loving people. "Sorry I didn't bring her. Next time."

"Yeah. Next time." To celebrate this thought, Sam lit up a new joint and passed it around. Acapulco Gold, the very best.

Sarah inhaled, sucking the sweet smoke deep into her chest and her lungs. This was the way to live, no worries, no tensions, and especially, no dirty rotten bastards to break your heart.

They had made such plans, Sarah and Hawk. They'd looked at furniture ads and walked through all the department stores on Thursday nights, talking about what they'd do and how they'd live when they were together all the time. He still went home for weekends; he said he had to gradually build up to leaving.

"You don't know Marilyn," he said, shaking his head. "She can be . . . daunting. You have to get her at just the right time. You know what I mean." She didn't know what he meant, but he was the love of her life, the smartest man she'd ever known, the best of all of Frank Hogan's men, the other A.D.A.'s said so. If he could put all those criminals behind bars—they said he never lost a case—then he could do a simple thing like end a loveless marriage.

Inside her, their baby was growing and moving around, and it even became exciting, now that the morning sickness was over. She could feel the little arms flailing away, bumping her under the ribs, and when she told Hawk, he reached out for her and held her close. He would put his ear to her belly and call out: "Baby! Baby, it's Daddy! Put up your dukes and fight *me*! Be a man!" And they'd both roll around on the bed, laughing.

In the middle of her fifth month, he called her on a Sunday night—very unusual. She never heard from him when he was in Long Island. He wouldn't even tell her the name of the town he lived in. One day she asked him and he turned to her with such a look that she never asked again. Anyway, what did it matter?

"Sam, we have to talk."

She kept it light, even though he sounded weird. "So talk!"

"No, I mean we *really* have to talk. Meet me at Rienzi's in ... let's see ... an hour and a half."

The minute he walked in, her heart began a sullen throbbing. She wanted to bolt and run; she thought wildly of locking herself in the ladies' room. But she was frozen, petrified with fear.

Hawk didn't smile at her. He lifted two fingers in greeting and came to sit across from her, just looking at her for a few minutes. Then he reached out for her hand. The whole time he talked, he held onto her hand tightly, his eyes wet. "Oh Jesus, Sammy ... I can't, I can't, I just can't."

"Can't what, Hawk?" She knew, her heart freezing solid within her chest. She knew.

"Can't ..."

"Can't *what*, Hawk?" She was gathering strength; despair was stiffening her spine and her resolve. She would not cry.

He cried. Tears streamed out of his eyes, and when she just looked at him, unmoving and unmoved, his shoulders began to shake.

"Marilyn threatened to kill herself if I left her."

"And you believe that?" she said, laughing nastily.

"I do ... and I don't," he said. "What if she means it? I can't take that chance. What if she did it?" He shuddered. "What if she left a note?"

Sarah pulled her hand away from his. "Now I get it," she said, amazed at herself, amazed that she was not weeping or begging. In a strange way, she had been almost expecting this. "If she left a note, blaming you ... goodbye to your brilliant career, right? No more next-in-line to Frank Hogan, right? You know what, Hawk? You disgust me! I can't believe I ever wanted to marry you! I can't believe I ever wanted to have your child!"

"Aw, Sammy, don't say that, please, please don't say that!"

"Call me Sarah. That's my name. Look at me and listen to what I'm saying. I don't want your child."

"I knew you'd feel that way. I don't blame you. I know a doctor. He's clean, he's legit. I'll pay for it, I'll pay for everything, and then we'll—"

"You bastard! You're so fucking ignorant! It's too damn late for an abortion! I don't want this baby, but I'm damn well gonna have to have it. Hey, maybe it'll look like you." She gave him a hateful smile. "If it does, I'll bring it to the office, to visit, let Mr. Hogan get a good look at it."

"Sammy! Sarah! Sweetheart!"

Her voice was a growl. "Don't you dare! Don't you dare call me sweetheart—or anything else, for that matter. You're a shit and I hope you die."

She turned on her heel and walked out. He called after her, his voice trembling and breaking. At her last words, he looked as if he'd been punched in the stomach. That was triumph, that was worth everything, she told herself, heading up Broadway. But after a few blocks, as her feet began to hurt, and her hands began to turn blue from the cold, the realization hit her. I'm alone, I'm really alone.

Remember the family motto: You Don't Need a Man to Take Care of You. Oh yeah, sure, and now what? Now where? Now who? I don't *want* anyone else! I want Hawk Diamond, and now I'll never, never have him! And the tears she had been holding back by sheer willpower began to pour down her cheeks.

Taking another hit from the joint, she said, "Never again, I told myself, never love a man again."

"Oh wow, Sarah. What a bummer. But anyway, you had the baby, so you got something out of it."

That's what everyone thought—everyone but her. Days would go by and she would forget all about Annie. She hadn't even named her. She had called her Baby until NanaLeah yelled at her and told her she wasn't normal. If Sarah wouldn't name her own child, NanaLeah said, then *she* would. "Go right ahead," Sarah had said; and her grandmother picked up the baby and announced, "I name you Anna Diamond, and you'll be called Annie, after my very best friend who died too young. May you honor her with your life."

Maybe NanaLeah was right; maybe she wasn't normal. After the birth, Sarah had felt empty, cold and empty. She didn't want to see the baby; they made her. And when they put the tiny red thing, wrapped in a pink blanket, into her arms, she felt nothing for it. She stared at it and stared at it, waiting for something to happen, something magical called Mother Love. But there was nothing; and maybe the infant knew it, because she screwed up her face and began to scream, and Sarah called out to the nurses to take it away.

"I want to give it up for adoption," she told them, but NanaLeah, like, *freaked*. "Over my dead body!" she said in a real weird voice. Sarah had never seen her grandmother so mad. NanaLeah grabbed her shoulders and shook her. "In this family, we take care of our own. We . . . don't . . . abandon . . . our . . . children! Do you understand me?" It was scary. All she could do was nod. So the baby came home with her.

She was never easy with the decision. Sometimes, in the night, she would wake up suddenly, thinking, I'm a mother. I have a daughter. But she was never able to make herself believe it.

It was NanaLeah who loved Annie and fussed over her all the time. Everyone loved sweet little Annie; but whenever Sarah looked at the flower face with the almond eyes and black curly fuzz, her heart hurt. It was *his* face. She hadn't wanted to have her in the first place, and if that rotten cold-hearted *momzer* hadn't lied to her, she wouldn't have a baby on her hands. Whenever she said anything about the way she felt, they all shushed her: NanaLeah, Mom, even Zelda. "Oh, you can't mean that!" they'd say. "You'll see, you'll fall in love with her." Well, if they were so crazy about this baby, they could *have* her! That's what she figured.

So, secretly, she saved up from her job. She didn't tell anyone her plans, no one at all; and one afternoon, she left the house on Willow Street with her guitar and backpack and she just never went back. Instead, she got on a Greyhound bus heading for San Francisco . . . and, like, here she was.

"Yeah," she said. "I got a daughter."

"Wow! That's, like, so cool!" That was Jonathan; he was a sucker for all that kind of stuff: puppies and babies and flowers.

"What's cool is having you guys for friends," Sarah said, and her eyes filled with tears. She meant it, she realized. They had all come here, from all over to belong to something and now they did. They all belonged, and it was the greatest!

40

September 1967

Sarah leaned her head against the cool windowpane and watched the countryside go by, mile after mile of swaying expanses of golden brown grain; wheat, she supposed. Every once in a while a house broke the monotony. Usually unpainted and weathered to a soft gray, sitting all by itself, without even a tree to shade it, the house looked naked and alone. She thought the houses looked like little girls left behind, solitary and sad.

Stupid. They were only Nebraska farms. She was just nervous about going back, about what would happen. What would they say to her? Her mother, if she was even home, which was doubtful, would be disgusted. But her grandmother . . . NanaLeah would *kill* her.

"How could you just walk out and leave your child behind without a thought?" Sarah could just hear her. Could she explain to her grandmother that she felt about a hundred years older than when she left a few months ago; that the Haight and everything it stood for had changed her totally? She could just imagine the look on NanaLeah's face: that doubting, exasperated, what-story-are-you-trying-on-me-now look.

But truly, she was a different person now; and the proof was, she was heading back home, sitting on this Continental Trailways bus, staring out of the window at Utah and then Wyoming and now Nebraska—instead of sitting on the grass in the Panhandle, playing and singing with her friends.

Then suddenly, that weird thing happened again: she began to trip. She squeezed her eyes shut and prayed hard that this would be just a tiny one. And it was. Just a hint, just some flashing colors, her father's face for an instant, and then it was gone. She leaned back in the seat, weak with relief, sweating, tears flooding her eyes. It had been rotten of her to run away and leave her baby without a word, but did she really deserve this kind of punishment? She'd only dropped acid one time, just once. That had been enough! But pieces of the trip kept coming back, attacking her when she least expected it. Some of the older hippies who'd been dropping acid for years had tried to reassure her, saying sometimes it happened. Yeah, you never had to do it again and you'd still be tripping, even years later! It didn't help to know she was not alone.

There was no way to be in Hashbury during the Summer of Love and not drop acid. No way. It was what you did in the evening, after dinner. It was what you did at night, for entertainment. Everyone did it, period. So when Grady soaked the tabs in LSD and handed them out, she took hers obediently and put it on her tongue. And was almost instantly plunged into the past.

She was in England, at Nether Althorpe, and she was fourteen, still a kid, but grown-up at the same time, visiting Daddy for a summer vacation—"the long hols," Daddy called it—and thrilled to pieces that her father was a lord, that the servants called her Lady Sarah. Helping take care of the horses, riding every day, out over the gentle green hills and along the edge of the forest. And getting to see Daddy every single day, getting to know him.

Well, it was hard to know him; he was very quiet, and when he did talk to her, it was vague and general. He kept forgetting how old she was, but he was a bit absentminded, she told herself. Still, he was very very sweet, and she was determined to love him.

She had visited once before, when she was eleven, and her grandparents were still alive. There were a million parties, and people all over the place. She wasn't given much attention then, but at least it was lively. The second visit, however, was very different. Her grandparents were dead, buried and under the chapel in the family crypt with all the other Fieldings. Daddy took her to see the marker, and as they were leaving the chapel, he said, "This is where we were married, you know, your mother and I. Right here." He had brought her there when she was eleven, too, and he had told her the exact same thing then.

That second visit, there were no parties, none at all. "We don't entertain, these days," her father told her. "Too much of a bother. And the neighbors are not . . . not too understanding."

Whatever *that* meant. The next-door neighbor, Pip, the pale man with the limp, was living there. He had moved into the manor house, and had a room of his own upstairs, next to Daddy's.

Pip did not like her; she knew that the minute they shook hands and said hello. Though he said pleasant words, his eyes were angry. But when she mentioned his animosity to her father, he said, "Oh dear me, no, you're wrong, Sarah, of course you're wrong. Pip loves you, just as I do."

Pip loved her, yeah, sure. That's why, every time he saw her, he had something bad to say about her. "Really, Sarah, a lady shouldn't *tromp* on the stairs." "Did your mother neglect to tell you to sit straight?" "Really, don't they *have* fish forks where you come from?"

"No, they don't!" she shouted at him that time. "Where I come from we don't think we have to have a special fork for fish. Where I come from we're not so ridiculous!"

He stared at her, tightening his lips to a thin line. "I daresay you'd find yourself ridiculous if you could look in a mirror right now." And when she got up from the table and left, nobody called for her to come back.

One day she said to Pip, "I wish you would stop telling me what's wrong with me all the time," and he said, "Certainly, Sarah." After that he would turn, very elaborately, to Daddy to complain about her. "Sarah's table manners are really quite . . . American, aren't they?" he'd remark; or, "Little girls are no longer taught to be seen rather than heard," stuff like that. He never again spoke directly to her; and the worst part was the sniffity smile, with his nose wrinkled as if he were smelling something bad.

Daddy told her it was her imagination. "Pip is only trying to help. Now let's have no more tittle-tattle."

Then one evening, at dinner, she became aware of those pale eyes staring at her hands, staring and staring. Finally she put down her fork and knife.

"What is it, Sarah?" her father said. "Don't you like beef and kidney pie?"

Then Pip spoke up. "Cook is getting tired of trying to please Miss Sarah's strange American taste, Peter. You might ask your, ah, daughter if she wasn't taught to eat what's put before her."

She was fed up. "I'll eat, if you'll stop staring at me," she said, looking straight at him. Her heart was hammering; she'd never stood up to a grown-up that way, and she almost expected to be sent from the table.

That smirky smile again. She *hated* it! "Peter, I ask you," Pip said, "how could one help staring when a person at table is eating like a . . . a *peasant*. All that shifting of the fork from one hand to another . . ." He gave a delicate shudder.

"You're horrible . . . horrible!" she yelled. She had *had* it. "You're the worst person I ever met! You never stop picking on me. Well, it's my daddy's house, not yours, and you'd better *stop* it!"

She really thought her father wold take her side and make Pip stop. But as she sat there, waiting, her father stood up looking very grim, his eyes boring into her. "Apologize to Pip, Sarah."

"Me? Me, apologize? I haven't done anything wrong! He picks on me! I *am* your daughter, aren't I?"

Stiffly, he said, "At this moment, my dear, I must say I don't much like admitting it. I am ashamed of you."

"Well, to hell with you. *And* him, too! I'm not apologizing!"

She was delighted to see that Pip's face was red with anger. She wished she could think of more things to say that would really get to him. But her father walked over to Pip and, putting an arm around Pip's shoulder, said, "There, there now, dear Philip, don't excite yourself." To Sarah, in a much different tone, he added: "Don't make me choose between you and Pip, Sarah. You won't like the results. I suggest you apologize. And quickly."

"I won't!"

"Well, then . . ." her father said. As she watched in horror, her father turned and with one finger under his chin, tipped up his friend's face. They gazed at each other with tender smiles, and then, horribly, unbelievably, her father bent down and they kissed! A long, loving kiss! She knew exactly what it meant—and it felt like a punch in her stomach.

She ran from the dining room, up the winding stairs and into her room. Tears of rage and pain and revulsion poured from her eyes. She waited for her father to come upstairs after her, to comfort her and make her feel better. But he never did.

The next morning she packed her bags and left. Her father made the arrangements, sent a wire to New York to tell them she was coming, even carried her bags to the big square taxicab. But it was Cook, her going-to-church hat fastened firmly on top of her head, who went with her on the train and saw that she got on the right plane. Cook muttered to herself, shaking her head and clucking her tongue. But when Sarah tried to talk to her about it, she tightened her lips and said, " 'Tis not my place to pry and gossip, Lady Sarah, and you needn't try changin' my mind, neither."

Sarah could hardly remember the flight back to New York; she felt dazed, as if she had been hit over the head. She only wanted her mother. She wouldn't tell her what had happened, she couldn't tell *anyone*, but now she understood why her mother had left England in such a hurry all those years ago.

In order to feel better, she began to make up a story about why she had left early. She made up a wonderful holiday, and Pip wasn't even there. So she was able to come out of Customs with a smile on her face and a tale all ready to tell, ready to hug her mother, make up with her, maybe even become friends. Only her mother wasn't there.

NanaLeah was waiting, but she was in a hurry—"The traffic was horrendous and come on, come on, otherwise we'll be stuck for hours in the rush hour"—and when she finally noticed that Sarah was not happy, she became impatient.

"Now don't sulk, Sarah, please, you know how I hate that. You *did* come home all of a sudden, you know, never mind if anyone here had other plans! I guess you've forgotten that your mother's in Melbourne covering the Olympic games. I almost went myself, so count yourself lucky that *anybody's* here."

Day after day Sarah pushed the bad stuff away, adding more details to her fantasy. Soon the made-up visit felt much more real than what had happened.

Until that night in the Haight, when she tripped. Then she relived the whole thing, only then it was like she was both herself and Pip, and she could feel her father's wet mouth and his probing tongue and it was *horrid*.

When she stopped tripping, her knuckles were raw and she felt as if her soul had been ripped into shreds. They told her later that she screamed and screamed and beat her fists on the floor.

She never tripped again. She faked it . . . palmed her tab when they were handed around, pretended to put it on her tongue, waited until everyone else was tripping and then beat it. Usually she'd grab her guitar and go somewhere quiet and make up songs, singing them for her own enjoyment. And when people walking by stopped to listen and threw dimes and quarters into the open guitar case, well, she wasn't going to stop them.

That money, she did not share with the others. That money did not go into the cracked teapot on the shelf above the stove. That money, hidden away, had bought her ticket back East.

As the bus moved on across another state line, Sarah began to trip again; she saw Pip's horrid face with its squeamy smile and those tiny little teeth, and she recoiled. Please, please, no, she prayed, let this stop, please. If you'll make it stop, I'll apologize to NanaLeah a million times, I'll be good, I'll go back to work, I'll be meek and mild, I'll love my baby and I'll never leave again. Just let it stop.

And like a miracle the horror stopped and she was just sitting on a Trailways bus in the middle of the night, the wheels rumbling on the highway, someone at the back snoring like crazy, a train with dozens of tiny lighted windows zipping by in the distance, like a dream.

She made a promise. She would do anything, whatever she had to, only she would make it up with her family. She curled up, closed her eyes, and began to make up a story about why she had decided to come back home.

41

April 1968

The mailman started up the front steps. As Sarah got up to run out and take the thick bundle from him, she realized that Annie was still hanging onto her leg, sucking her thumb with that filthy piece of blanket she loved so much.

"Dammit, Annie, will you stop *clinging*?" Sarah demanded. When the baby puckered up her face and prepared to cry, her voice got even sharper. "And stop crying! Oh, all right, come on, let me carry you and we'll go outside and get the mail."

Annie allowed herself to be picked up, but before Sarah

could open the door, she heard *thunk! thunk! thunk!* Three
batches sailed through the mail slot, scattering all over the polished wood floor.

"Annie, you'll have to let go so I can get the mail. Annie!
Don't cry, okay?" Awkwardly, the child still clinging around
her neck, Sarah knelt and retrieved the envelopes and magazines. With Annie still holding on, she walked back into the
kitchen. She didn't even glance at the pile, that was bad luck.
If she looked, hoping for a letter from Grady, there wouldn't
be one. If she didn't care, *then* it would be there. She went
through elaborate pretenses to show the fates how little she
cared. And what the hell good did it do? For the past three
weeks—not a word from that bastard!

She plopped Annie into her high chair and put a handful of
raisins on the tray. That would keep her busy for ten minutes.
The little girl picked up each raisin separately, examined it,
turned it over, squooshed it, and only then did she put it in her
mouth.

Sarah poured the last of the coffee from the pot; Christ, it
was thick, it probably tasted like burnt grounds. But what the
hell, it was dark and it was hot. First she separated the magazines and put them in a pile; NanaLeah had subscriptions to
every magazine ever published. Well, of course, it was what
she did for a living, but still ... *Bluebook*? *Vogue*? Not to
mention all the ones from England—*Queen* and *Punch* and
some sort of snooty country thing, with pictures of houses like
Nether Althorpe. She shivered at the thought of the house in
Buckinghamshire.

Ah, the *real* mail! A leaflet on the Peace Corps. A card
saying that Mrs. Mailer had cleaning women for hire. Norman Mailer's mother lived in the neighborhood, and so did
he. Something from the Poor People's Campaign, wanting
money, no doubt; something from the Brooklyn chapter of
SANE, ditto; a check for NanaLeah from the *Nation*, she could
tell because the envelope had a window, and not a check from
McCall's, no window. Lots and lots of bills, A&S, Con Ed,
Brooklyn Union Gas. And then, at last, a thin envelope with a
real stamp, not a postage meter thing. Her heart began to race
with anticipation. A letter! But it wasn't from Grady, it was
from her mother. The GPO was San Francisco, but Jo Fielding
was in Vietnam, finally, after months of trying.

When Sarah had arrived home from San Francisco last fall,
her mother was not here, as expected. But Jo wasn't in Viet-

nam yet—the government didn't want her to go, or something.
She was in a much more dangerous place: Newark, in the middle of the riots. Just like she'd been in Detroit, when they
rioted there, and in Watts. Jo was always in the thick of things.
In Sarah's opinion, she was an excitement junkie. She was a
grandmother, for Christ's sake, what the hell was she doing
hanging out of airplanes and putting herself into cross fire.
And for what? A picture that would appear in a newspaper or
magazine, to be glanced at once and then used to wrap the garbage! And her mother thought that she and her hippie friends
were crazy!

That's what Jo kept saying. Whenever she was around,
she'd look her up and down and sigh. "Your whole generation
is out of its collective mind, you know that?"

"Why? Because we believe in loving each other, and hate
all these wars and riots and things?"

"Yeah, yeah, 'Make love, not war.' Very eloquent. But what
do any of you *do*, for God's sake, to maybe *create* peace and
love, to maybe change some of the people in this country from
hating so much? God, if you'd been with me in Selma, in
L.A.—"

"I know all about it. You've only told me maybe fourteen or
fifteen times. Did a person have to be in Selma, Alabama, to
get your respect, Mom? Does a person have to be someplace,
getting killed? Anyway," Sarah added after a moment, "we're
making changes. Look at the resistance. Look at all the burned
draft cards. Who do you think organized Stop the Draft week?
Christ, Mom, you and NanaLeah still say 'Negro,' instead of
'black'! *We* sleep with them!" Her mother just shrugged and
gave her a shit-eating smile; she wished she had said "fuck,"
like she wanted to.

NanaLeah was just as bad; all uptight about "young drop-
outs who should know better, lying in the streets and passing
out from drugs, instead of doing something about the state of
the world."

"NanaLeah," she told her, "you're so set on me *doing* stuff,
on getting *involved*. So tell me, what good does it ever do? Do
we still have war and hate?"

"Nothing gets done on talk alone."

"That's the millionth time I've heard that one," Sarah said.

"You're not too old to be put over my knee, young woman."

Well, that made her bust out laughing, and then so did her
grandmother. But it was clear that the women of her family

were without a clue. They didn't realize that nonviolence was the way to peace; look at Ghandi, for Christ's sake.

"What we need is a different philosophy," Grady would always say. "No more God who's a big white guy in the sky with a white beard and a bad temper. No, we need Buddha or Krishna, a philosopher who teaches us to live in peace and harmony and fuck all this competitive shit!"

She always loved it when Grady got going on one of his favorite subjects. He was brilliant, a genius probably. He said that's what was driving his old man up a tree, that he was "wasting" himself. She wondered what his father had done when Grady burned his draft card.

He wrote her a long letter about it, after they did it; he and seven other guys, in Golden Gate Park. They called all the newspapers and TV stations and lots of them came. He had clipped a picture from the *Oracle*—because it was the biggest, he said—and sent it in the letter. There he was, fist in the air, his mouth wide open like he was yelling. Not very peaceful, Sarah thought; and then told herself she didn't *know* that Grady was angry, it just *looked* like it; he might have been yelling: "Hell no, we won't go," or something.

Grady wouldn't have gone to India, would he, without telling her? He was always talking about going to what he liked to call the Indian subcontinent. Sometimes he was an awful show-off. So he went to Harvard, so what? And fuck him. He didn't have to write to her if he didn't want to.

"Men stink, Annie," she said; and the baby gave her a big raisiny grin. Sometimes she was so cute! On impulse, Sarah got up and gave her a big kiss. Immediately Annie raised her arms and said, "Uppie, uppie." Give them an inch, they'll take a mile.

"No uppie, uppie right now, sweetie. Mommy has to—oops!" The phone rang. Usually she just let it ring, because it was always for NanaLeah. But it might be Grady, although where would he get the bread to make a long distance call? Still . . .

She picked up and said, breezily, "Yes?"

"Sammy, don't hang up, for Christ's sake. Don't hang up on me please, *please*. Just talk to me, would you?"

She slammed the receiver back down, her heart racing. When she first got back, she'd gone to work at the Bitter Bean again. She had expected Hawk to walk in the door every single night, expected his voice to be on the other end of the phone

every single day. Then one of the A.D.A.'s told her he'd left
the D.A.'s office and gone into private practice out on Long Island.

"Oh God, Hawk," she said aloud, and she could hear the
longing in her own voice. What a fucking weakling she was!
The man was a turd, a piece of shit, not worth even thinking
about!

The phone rang again. She let it ring. At last it stopped, and
she scooped the baby up out of the high chair. "Let's go to the
playground," she said; and Annie repeated, in her high baby
voice, "Pay-gwou'."

"That's right, pay-gwou' . . . you like that, right? Can I tell
you a secret, Annie? I hate it! I hate the mommies, talking
about their little hubbies who work until eleven at night, and
the latest recipe for dip or beef Wellington and their kids'
BMs. I *hate* the fucking Pierrepont Street playground, Annie.
But look how nice I am. I'm going to take you there. You can
go into the sandbox and get all nice and dirty, and somebody's
little kid can bop you with a shovel and you can bop *him* with
a shovel—"

The phone rang. Her heart began hammering. No. No. No,
she wasn't going to answer it.

She answered it. She didn't say a word, just stood there,
breathing, listening to him breathing, loving him, *loving* him.
Still. Still loving him, dammit.

Finally he spoke. "Sam . . . Sarah. Sarah, Sarah, how I
wish—" And then his voice broke. "Sarah, forgive me, please,
please, forgive me."

"Forgive?" Her voice came out rusty, like it hadn't been
used in a million years. "I only want to forget you." But I
can't, she thought. I can't forget you because every time I look
at Annie, with her beautiful odd almond eyes, I see you; every
time she grins at me, that dimple appears next to her mouth
and I see you.

"Oh God, I love you!"

"Yeah, Hawk, I know all about it." She heard the anguish in
his voice. T.S. He had stayed with that crazy woman for the
sake of his career, and then he'd left the D.A.'s office anyway!
So he had sacrificed her—and Annie, too, of course—
sacrificed both of them, for *nothing*!

Swallowing, she drew in air and began, very softly, to sing.
As always, when Sarah sang, the baby cooed as a kind of ac-
companiment. It was Carly Simon's song about the child that

had his eyes and her smile. She sang the last line very slowly, "Reminding me that we fell in love for just a little while. . . ."

On the other end of the line, Hawk made a strangled sound and then the line went dead.

"You fuck!" Sarah mouthed into the phone. Carefully, she replaced the receiver, forcing the tears back by sheer will. The fuck, the no-good shit! She was better off without him; they were both better off without him.

When the phone began ringing again, she just ignored it. She changed Annie's diaper, and still the phone kept ringing. Then it stopped and she could breathe again. As she put Annie into her stroller, the *New York Times* headlines caught her eye: U.S. BOMBS HAIPHONG . . . U.S. BOMBS HANOI RAIL YARDS. Where was Mom, anyway? In the middle of the bombing, without a doubt. Where had she put that letter from Vietnam? She'd have to go look for it. She began to read the story: "General Westmoreland said that the antiwar protests 'gives the enemy hope that he can win politically what he cannot accomplish militarily.' " Oh great! You couldn't disagree with the fucking general or you were a fucking traitor!

When the telephone began its insistent shrilling again, she realized she had been standing there the whole time, waiting for it, not wanting to go to the park.

She snatched up the phone and yelled, "Just leave us alone, okay. Just go away and do your thing and leave us the fuck alone!"

"Oh wow! Sarah, is that you? But what, am I kidding? Who the fuck else would it be? Hey, beautiful, what's happenin'?"

"Grady!" Christ, had any man's voice ever sounded so beautiful? "Grady, I'm so fucking happy to hear your voice, you can't imagine!" She was grinning. Oh, thank God, thank God!

Grady laughed like crazy. "Where do you think I am, baby?"

"The Haight. San Francisco, where else?"

"I'll tell you where else! In a great pad on Greene Street!"

"Greene Street? Where's that?"

"In New York City, you stupid broad! In a great pad! Jesus Christ, Sarah, it's a *commune*—it's a fucking *commune*, and it's so goddamn beautiful, I can't even describe it. You gotta come over."

"When?"

"When? Now, of course. This minute. Christ, I've missed

you. Get right over here so I can hug you and kiss you and . . .
oh Christ!"

Little happy bubbles were rising in her chest, making it hard
to breathe. "Listen, Grady. Are you listening?"

"I'm listening."

"You may have just saved my life, Grady."

"Come over right now—I'll give you directions—and bring
your baby. We all want to meet her."

"All?"

He laughed like crazy. "Sarah, Sarah, we're starting a commune, you dig? A beautiful place where we can all love each
other and live off the land and forget all about Vietnam and the
stupid politicians."

"On Greene Street in New York?"

Again he laughed. "No, we're just crashing here for a couple of nights. We've—dig this, Sarah—we've *bought* a place
in Cold River, Connecticut, an old farm. Yeah, a real farm with
fields and orchards and barns and everything, and we're all
gonna live there together. You'll come with me, won't you? I
came to get you, that's why we're in New York. . . ."

"Yes. Yes, yes, yes. Of course I'll come."

"And the baby. There'll be plenty of little kids. She'll love
it. And we'll love *her*."

"Oh God, it sounds so fantastic! I'll have to tell my grandmother. . . . But she's cool, she won't try to stop me. Not if I'm
taking Annie with me. But I have to tell her first. So, Grady,
give me directions and we'll be there in a little while. Oh,
Grady! I've been dying here, I've been withering away, you
have no idea. We're coming, so wait for us!"

42

November 1968

Wrapped in a quilt that was nearly as cold and damp as her skin, Sarah sat in front of the fireplace, picking at her guitar and *willing* the damp kindling to finally catch, dammit! Get hot! Then she could put on some of the big pieces of lumber they'd picked up from an old, falling-down barn "up the road a ways," as the local folk said.

"Up the road a ways," she sang, putting on her best rural New England twang. "Up the road a ways . . . that's where the hippies stay/But we don't talk to such as they . . . 'Cause all they do's drug out all day. . . . Oh Christ!" she said to herself. "That's awful. My mind is turning to Jell-O." She pondered for a moment, then added, "Green Jell-O," and shuddered, hitting the guitar strings to make discords. That's exactly how she felt.

It had been, like, so *beautiful* last summer when they first got there; everything perfect. Romping in the fields, picking daisies and raspberries and black-eyed Susans that just grew wild in the fields. Skinny-dipping in the pond . . . yucky-mucky bottom, but, ah, the feel of the cool water, like silk on sun-heated skin. Sometimes they'd make love hidden in the tall grass, she and Grady.

She had written a song called "Summer Everlasting," and she put into it the heat of the endless lazy days, the golden haze hanging over the fields that stretched into the distance behind Ivy Hill Farm, the long starry nights, the scent of patchouli, the velvet feel of grass on bare feet, the kiss of the sun on your body, the children browning like cookies.

But now! It was so fucking cold in here! There were a million chinks and cracks in the walls, and the frigid air crept in all night as the fire died. The men kept saying they were going to plug up those leaks, but they never seemed to get around to it. And last night, it snowed. Alan and Grady, who were supposed to be splitting logs, got carried away as the heavy snow piled up and they made snow sculptures, and never got around to the wood. So now every window in the house was decorated with thick frost, and you could see your breath in the air.

Breath. The word reminded her, with a squeezing in her chest, that Annie was sick. The baby had finally fallen into a deep sleep, her mouth open, sometime early in the morning. You could hear her heavy breathing; but that was better than *not* hearing it. Sarah had dozed off a couple of times without realizing it, and had come to with a start, thinking, *I don't hear her breathing.* Her heart would start a heavy drumbeat, shaking her chest—as if her whole body were quaking. She was filled with a nameless fear—and then suddenly her dread had a name. Timmy. She hadn't thought about Timmy for years; there were times when she forgot she had ever had a little brother. That raspy wheezing, with the little squeak in it, had brought it all back. She found herself praying—*praying*, for Christ's sake. Please, don't let her die, don't punish me again. Weird.

Then, at last, Annie shifted on her mattress, made a deep loud sigh, and fell into a very different kind of sleep. As spacey as she was, Sarah could see that Annie was better. The baby's skin still felt hot, but it was damp instead of that terrible dry, searing heat that burnt the palm of your hand.

Finally Sarah allowed herself to burrow into the big mattress with its pile of quilts and try to sleep. Outside, a pale rim of light edged the horizon. Christ, she had been awake all night! It was her job to get the fire going this morning, and so she forced herself out onto the foot-numbing floor, teeth chattering as she put on extra layers of clothing. The baby was sleeping so soundly, Sarah had a moment of fear, but when she put a hand on her, Annie stirred. She was alive. Well, of course she was alive. Babies didn't die anymore.

But when she went to poke up the fire, there weren't any logs and goddamn little kindling. She had to go out herself to get some, and water, too. When she came back in, she found Grady and poked him with her foot. He opened one sleepy eye and muttered something. She said, not caring who heard, "Get the fuck up, Grady, and chop wood. You guys were so busy playing in the snow, you forgot people can fucking *freeze* in here!"

Grady held his arms up to her, like, come kiss me good

morning. She gave him another kick. "Annie nearly died in the night," she said. "Get *up*, dammit, and chop wood!" Well, he jumped up then, and she glared at him. "And get Alan, too."

"You borrow somebody's balls this morning?" Grady muttered. Then he took another look at her and added, "Only kidding."

She tried to forget the cold, and fed the hungry little flames some bigger bits of wood, cut-up limbs of saplings and those junk trees, the cottonwoods. The fire flared up, but it wouldn't make much difference anyway. The big room with its long narrow windows just ate up heat. If you sat right next to the fire, you could get warm, but the minute you moved even a little ways away from the fireplace—frostbite. Nevertheless, it was better in front of the fire than anyplace else, except maybe the kitchen.

She could hear pots clattering; someone was starting breakfast. Good. She was hungry this morning. Last night's meal had been pretty fucking meager: a stew of sprouting potatoes and what they could salvage from a load of rotting turnips and carrots left in back of the market in Cold River. They had run out of salt, so it tasted terrible.

Longingly, she recalled the wonderful meals they'd had last August and September. The guys had been hired by a couple of local farmers, to take in the harvest; and they got paid in food: tomatoes, corn, beans, and cabbage; eggplants, grapes, apples, peaches . . . Christ, it made her mouth water just thinking about it. And they'd thrown in bags of cornmeal and flour, too, and eggs. The farmers liked hippies; they thought "the youngsters at the old Collins place have the right idea." Not like the townies, who were down on all strangers and stared at them when they went into Cold River, their eyes cold and suspicious.

Hell, they should be glad somebody lived here. The house was two hundred years old and, like, falling down. At first it had seemed kind of romantic. Not anymore, not with no heat, no running water, no toilets. They'd built a privy in back of the house, near the woods; although now, with it so cold, most of them peed in a bucket in the front hall closet.

When she'd gone outside earlier, to gather kindling for the fire and fill buckets from the pump, she had put on the one really warm coat they owned, a sheepskin jacket, somewhat the worse for wear, that the minister's wife had brought over along with some other warm hand-me-downs. The jacket had obviously belonged to a very large man, and everyone took turns wearing it. At this point her feet were permanently iced, in spite of the two pairs of socks she wore day and night. She'd put on a pair of man's work shoes, the high kind, but there weren't any laces, so they flopped around her ankles.

Since it was summer when they first got there, nobody had thought to bring heavy boots. Or long johns, wool socks, heavy jackets, or anything like that. Nobody had thought of anything, except the excitement of having a place of their own, a *farm*, with a pond and an old peach orchard. They were going to live off the land, simplify their lives, and go back to nature.

When they had first seen the place, driving up the hill on the narrow dirt road, the house sitting at the crest, with an arc of big oaks and maples at its back, a stone wall stretching out on either side, they were thrilled. Glossy green ivy, a profusion of leaves and tendrils, covered the stone fence. The day was soft and beautiful, the sky blue and the clouds white and fluffy. The seven adults and three kids all had the same reaction. They loved it. They piled out of the station wagon and stood in the road, grinning and laughing.

"Ivy Hill Farm," Grady said. He was holding Annie in one arm, his other around Sarah's shoulders. "That's our place, people, holding out its green leafy arms to welcome us."

They yelled and hollered and ran the rest of the way up the hill, climbing onto the wall, sitting there and joining hands to show their solidarity. "It's an omen," Holly said. Holly was there with Andy, whom she had met in the Haight, and their infant, a boy they were calling Moon Ray—Ray for short.

"A good omen. Look how green it all is. Green is good." That was Lou, short for Louise. Lou's man never showed up to meet her in New York so she came on with James, who was a member of the Broome Street commune and was ready for a change of scene. Lou had a child, too, a little girl named Cinnamon, the same age as Annie. That was one thing Sarah just couldn't get with: the weird names. But hey, if it was what they grooved on . . .

"Green is good," they had all agreed, and Sarah made up a ditty right then and there about how good green was; a tune so simple everybody was able to join in and sing. That was before they all discovered that those gorgeous green vines were poison ivy.

Nobody had brought any calamine lotion, of course, and a

lot of Sarah's money went for large bottles of the stuff, until Holly and Andy got talking with an old woman down the road, who knew how to cure things with herbs. After that, whenever they got poison ivy, which was pretty often, they just dosed themselves with poultices of garlic or green-bean leaves or a potion of baking soda and water.

Once she started, Holly really got into the herbal remedy thing; she spent a lot of her time roaming the fields, picking things and cooking them up and trying them out. Holly could mix you a shampoo or a cure for your menstrual cramps or a remedy for burns. They needed that last one; nobody had ever really cooked over a wood fire before, and there were lots of accidents. The men made fun of Holly, and Grady called her Witch Woman, but she did a lot more good, in Sarah's opinion, than the men, who never cooked or even picked up after themselves.

In the beginning they had all decided that they were not going to fall into the middle-class traps that had made such a mess of their parents. Women would be equal with men; everyone would share everything, including the chores, including child care. But that's not how it had ended up. What they had here at Ivy Hill Farm was business as usual. The men still went out hunting and slaying, and the women still stayed home and tended to the chores and tried to look pretty for the men when they came back. Sarah often thought about, but never mentioned, how she had grown up in a household that was more progressive than Ivy Hill Farm!

Just then James came in, like an answer to a prayer, his arms loaded with logs for the fire, big ones, wearing the old sheepskin jacket and a triple layer of mittens. He smiled at her—James was always smiling, but then, James was always stoned, so why not?—and said, "Morning, Sarah. I thought I smelled you when I put the jacket on." He had come into bed with her sometime during the early morning hours, kissing her neck and pulling her legs apart, his hard penis pressing into the soft flesh of her thigh. That's all she remembered; she must have fallen back asleep.

James put the armload of logs down near her and leaned over to kiss her lightly. "There's oatmeal," he said. That meant Holly was cooking. Holly was into oatmeal, not that there was much of anything else. Sarah moaned.

"What's the matter?"

"Nothing. Just hungry for some real food."

"Hell," Grady said, coming into the room in his long johns, wrapped in a quilt, yawning and shivering, "we'd have some real food if you chicks had thought to can all that stuff last summer. Jesus, when I think of how much we had to throw out—!"

"We should have *canned* it?" Sarah said, not knowing whether to laugh or throw something at him. "Who knows how to can, for Christ's sake?"

"Canning is something chicks are supposed to know."

Sarah turned her back on him. Grady was beginning to freak her out, with all this talk about peace, freedom, and fulfillment for everyone . . . except chicks. The simple life, it seemed, was simple for everyone except women. The guys went out and chopped wood and built things and then sat back and lit a joint and relaxed. When was the last time she had relaxed, between the chores and the laundry, which had to be done by hand, and the cooking and the kids? Not to mention the constant demands for sex. What made it worse was there were only three women—Lou, Holly, and Sarah—and four guys. Grady, of course; Andy, who was Holly's old man, most of the time, anyway; James and Alan.

Alan was . . . strange. There was something . . . different about Alan. The other guys were laid-back; he was intense. Sometimes Sarah thought she could see sparks flying from his eyes. He had thick black hair and his pale blue eyes could bore right through you. When he made love, he was rough, grunting and groaning and yelling the whole time, until he was finished.

Sarah didn't like him; in fact she was scared of him. He was a bomb that hadn't gone off . . . yet. Still, sometimes in the evenings, he would sit cross-legged in front of the fire, his eyes closed, reciting poetry by the hour, all from memory; and then he was transformed. He had a beautiful voice. Those times, she would think she was crazy to find him frightening.

"Mama, Mama, Mama!" Two little-girl voices, in unison. In they came, in their funny little bunny suits, Annie and Cinnamon: one dark head, one platinum-blond; one curly-haired, one straight. They both came running up to her, leaning into her on either side. Annie's curly hair was damp with sweat; the fever must have broken for good. Sarah let the quilt fall from her shoulders to put her arms around them. She was instantly cold, but if she didn't hug them, Grady would be sure to have something to say. He was always telling her what a lousy mother she was, asking her what the hell happened to her maternal instinct.

She knew she had a problem with Annie. Annie was the image of Hawk, even to the beautiful full-lipped mouth. Whenever she looked at Annie, she was reminded of everything she had lost. But Annie was a sweet baby, and smart, too. She'd already learned, at two, that she could get everyone's attention by doing or saying things that would make them laugh.

"Laughter is love, isn't it, Annie?" Sarah said, thinking what a good song title that was. She gave the little girl a kiss and rumpled her hair. "You're a funny little thing."

"Why's *she* so funny?" Grady demanded. "*You* think applause is love, and they're the same, laughing and clapping." Then he wrinkled his nose. "Woof! I smell a diaper that needs changing."

"If you don't like it," Sarah said, "*you* change it! For a change," she added, and laughed at her own pun.

He laughed, too, but he didn't move. Annie ran to him and held her arms up, piping "Gwady, Gwady!" but he shook his head and said, "Not now, Annie baby. Mama will change your diaper and *then* Grady will pick you up." He yawned again. Sarah wanted to throw something at him; but what was the use?

"Let me lay this on you, Sarah," Grady said. "You go to Middington with Annie and maybe Cinnamon, too—yeah, one on either side, that'd be good—and sign up for Welfare."

"Welfare!"

"Hey, why not? We can use it. There's no work in the winter."

"*You* sign up for Welfare! I thought we were here to get away from the horrors of government and the capitalist system, the 'money morality.' And you want me to go begging!"

"Hey! It's for the babies, Sarah, not for us. They don't give you that much. I'd go, believe me, but nobody's heart is going to go out to an able-bodied male. A chick, though, with two adorable little girls . . ."

Sarah picked up Annie and got to her feet. "Maybe," she said, and started walking out.

"That's my girl."

"I said *maybe*, I didn't sign any contract! And I'm not *any-one's* girl, you got that?" Fuming, she marched out, Annie tucked firmly in the circle of one arm, while Grady called after her, "Whatever happened to your sense of humor, Sarah?"

As she changed Annie's diaper, she thought about going on welfare. She didn't want to; it was degrading and demeaning. Grady's dad sent him an allowance, and a check came every month for James, too. They'd been bugging Holly to make a lot of her herbal potions, so she could sell them in town. Not so *they*, the men, could sell them. Oh, no, that was a job for a chick! Going on Welfare was a job for a chick! Changing shitty diapers was a job for a chick!

"Annie cold, Mama!"

"I'm almost done, baby. Gotta get your tushie clean."

"Gotta get Annie's tushie cwean!"

"That's right."

Sarah finished pinning the diaper, and pulled the warm bunny suit back up and zipped it. It was filthy, she noticed, and the zipper was ripping away from the fabric. She'd get Annie a clean one and sew up this one.

She picked up the baby and walked past the kitchen, filled with steam from the kettle and the warm, homey smell of oatmeal bubbling on the stove, and into the utility room, which was so cold the air hurt your nostrils. The only utility in the room was a pair of old wooden laundry tubs. On the floor was a large pile of dirty clothes, and above the tubs, a wooden shelf with a few clean items. She rummaged through them, but there were no bunny suits. Dammit, that meant she would have to come in here and freeze her ass off while she scrubbed baby clothes on the washboard and her hands turned into two blocks of ice. Tears formed in her eyes.

Well, she was going to have some breakfast first. She reentered the kitchen's welcome warmth and took out two bowls. Holly was there now, stirring her caldron of oatmeal.

"Morning, Sarah. Good morning, Annie."

"Holly, Holly!" Annie's arms went up. "Holly want a cwacker!" she said, waiting for Holly to laugh. One day she'd overhead someone imitating a parrot and had misunderstood and went running to get a cracker for Holly. Everyone had laughed so hard that now she said it every time she saw Holly.

Holly took her and gave her a kiss. "Funny little girl," she said. "Just for that, how about some sugar on your oatmeal?"

"Sugar!" Sarah repeated, surprised.

"Shhh. I always hide some of the food from the men. They're such pigs."

"They are, aren't they?"

"That's because we're all stuck inside together. No place to hide." After a moment of silence Holly added, "I'm pregnant."

"Oh Christ."

"Yeah. I'm thinking of splitting. It's hard enough taking care of Moon Ray and all the cures and stuff. . . ."

"Christ, Holly, if you leave, we'll all die of something horrible. Dysentery or bubonic plague."

Holly laughed and flung her head so that her long hair flipped behind her back. "Listen," she said, and stopped, looking around, as if for spies.

"What? Go ahead."

"Don't, like, say anything, okay? About me splitting. Because, well . . . I don't plan to take Andy along, and anyway, I'm going to get an abortion and you know how Andy is about abortions. Evil, wicked, against nature. God, he's as bad as one of those hellfire-preaching parsons that used to come to my hometown."

"Yeah, I thought we came here to get away from all that," Sarah said.

"Listen, Sarah, I've been thinking. You remember what happened when I suggested maybe we should eat three meals a day, like regular people?"

Sarah remembered. The men had hooted in derision. They liked having stuff cooking all the time, so they could just wander in and eat whenever they felt like it. The trouble was, they'd eat and then leave the dirty dishes for guess who?

"Yeah, I remember," Sarah said. "I remember we got nowhere."

"Well, it got me to thinking. How is our life here any different than a housewife's? It isn't. It's just that we're all, like, doing the drudgery together instead of each one of us inside her own little house. And you know, if you're some guy's wife, instead of a *chick*"—her voice loaded the word with all the anger Sarah had been feeling—"if you're his wife, you get a house, a car maybe, a refrigerator/freezer, the latest appliances, some semblance of comfort, you dig? And, hey, even a prostitute gets cash up front. But when you're nothing but a *chick*, you get nothing but fucked. So, as soon as I get some bread together, I'm on my way—"

She stopped speaking suddenly; her face paled. As Sarah stared, Andy came striding in, his face contorted, his long hair flopping over his eyes. "You're on your way to the fucking death chamber, you bitch!" he yelled. And smacked Holly with the flat of his hand so hard that she went sprawling against the table.

Sarah screamed. Holly was still holding Annie, who had started to cry. But Sarah didn't dare get between them and the livid Andy, who was so beside himself, he was dripping saliva. Like a mad dog, she thought. She knew he had a short fuse, but this was *crazy*.

In another moment he had whipped around and was gone, only pausing in the doorway to say, "You try to leave, dyke, you'll find yourself in a ditch. You can't get away from *me*!"

For a stunned moment the two women just stared at each other. Then they both began to weep. Annie, seeing tears, began to howl. Sarah ran to Holly and they hugged each other, Annie in the middle, all three of them sobbing. Nobody came in to calm them, and when they had calmed down, there was nothing in the next room but an ominous silence. Not a word was spoken about what had just happened. Holly put Annie down, and the baby went toddling off, hiccuping. "G-wady! G-wady!"

Sarah let her go. She had to think, she had to think hard. She spooned oatmeal into a bowl, pushing it into her mouth and swallowing without tasting it. That whole scene was fucking crazy! And why was everyone just pretending it hadn't happened? Why hadn't Grady come in to help Holly—Grady, so intelligent, so . . . so *decent*? What was happening to all of them?

For one horrible moment she felt as if she had just stepped off the edge of something and was falling through space with sickening speed. But then she began to plan. There was one thing for sure; she had to get out of this crazy place.

43

January 1969

Today was the day. The Farm didn't feel like home, not anymore. Grady was finished with her; and she was finished with him, too. "Chicks should be seen and not heard," he'd said, laughing. "And you've got a big mouth." They all laughed, the guys; they thought it was so fucking funny. Wait till they found out she'd taken all the money! She'd like to hear them laughing *then*! She didn't know why she'd stayed so long, anyway, sneaking off into the woods with the other girls so they could bitch about the men without danger . . . working like a fucking slave! Hell, she hadn't even picked up her guitar lately. If she didn't do something pretty soon, she realized, she'd forget how to make music.

So, today, just as the sun was coming up, she dressed a sleepy Annie in two or three layers of heavy clothing, and pushed one hundred dollars in crumpled bills into her backpack, along with half a loaf of bread, two oranges, and two baby bottles of water. With her guitar over her shoulder and Annie riding in a hip-sling of blankets, she split—out of Ivy Hill Farm, right on Route 82, heading for Route 1, the Boston Post Road. Her stay here was over, it was done, she was on her way home. And she was wearing the single piece of warm clothing they had—the secondhand sheepskin coat. Let 'em freeze! The thought made her smile. She'd actually *done* something and she felt pretty goddamn good.

That good feeling did not last for even a mile. Route 82 was empty of any kind of life. Not a car or a truck came by. She might have been all alone in the world, the lone survivor of an atomic war. The road wasn't paved, it was tarred, and slick with patches of ice. Her throat hurt and there was a banging in her head—dammit, she should have taken a couple of

413

aspirin—and she was getting dizzy. Maybe she'd caught the flu; they'd all had it, all but her. For a minute she thought maybe she should turn back; but then she reminded herself of what was waiting for her at Ivy Hill Farm and she just kept plodding along.

Once, she heard a motor and stopped, expectant. Whatever kind of vehicle it was, it would stop for a woman and a baby. With great relief, she waited. But the car turned off before it got to her and she had to keep walking.

At last, she hit Route 1. She could feel the cold numbing her cheeks and neck, and her hands were stiff in the work gloves. But Annie was sound asleep, a dead weight on her hip and shoulder. Here on the Post Road there were cars, plenty of them; but none of them would stop. A couple of times they slowed down and she could see a face, peering at her; and then, with a roar, good-bye. Christ! she must be a fucking *mess*.

She remembered a little general store near here somewhere; she could get herself a cup of coffee and some aspirin, maybe use the toilet and wash her face, ask about a bus to New Haven.

She started walking again, but she must have chosen the wrong direction, because the little store just wasn't there. Every curve in the road, she convinced herself it would be right around the bend; but it wasn't. She passed up a luncheonette; she wasn't sure they'd serve her. They were supposed to be building a McDonald's soon; how she wished it was here right now. She really had to pee bad. So she scrambled off the road, scanning the evergreens to see where it was thick enough to hide her. But then she went sprawling into a snowy ditch. For a moment she lay there without moving, and then the baby cried and she realized how easily Annie could have been hurt. Jesus! But Annie just shifted and fell back asleep, and even the guitar was okay. Sarah had twisted her ankle or something, because when she started to push herself to her feet, it twinged fiercely. She began to cry. Dammit, why was everything going wrong? Was this a, like, sign, that she was supposed to stay at the farm and take whatever was dished out to her?

Somehow she got to her feet, picked up Annie and the guitar case, and managed to limp behind the thick trees, spread her legs, and empty her bladder, just stand there and let it go. Christ, it felt so good.

Back to the Post Road. She thumbed for a while. No good.

Then she held the baby so people could see her. Nothing. Her arms began to shake with fatigue. To hell with it. She plopped herself down on a rock by the side of the road—too damn weary to go on. She put her head down on the guitar case; she'd close her eyes for just a minute, she decided. The baby was still fast asleep; little kids could sleep through anything.

And the next thing she knew, a strange man's voice was saying, "Miss? Miss? You okay? You *alive*?"

What a stupid question! "Of course I'm alive. I have a pulse, don't I?" she grouched, without opening her eyes.

"You were right, Sharon!" the man called out. "It's not a vagrant—it's a girl! And a baby!" More softly he added, "You don't look so hot, honey, if you really want to know. Your old man throw you out?"

Now she opened her eyes, but all she could see was a black silhouette against the glaring sky. Her head felt a bit fuzzy but the headache was mostly gone. "He wasn't my old man . . . and, no, he didn't throw me out. I left." Her voice woke Annie who, as usual, came wide awake all at once.

"Mama! Annie is hungwy! Annie is aw wet! Yuck!"

The stranger laughed. "You're a pistol, aren't you, little girl? What's your name?"

"Annie Dymin."

"Annie Dymin?"

"Annie Diamond," Sara said. She spelled it out. It had been a long time since she'd even had to *think* about Annie's last name, much less say it. When she found out that NanaLeah had put Hawk's name on the birth certificate, she had been so pissed! She raised hell, demanding that her grandmother change it to Fielding!

"I will not," NanaLeah had said. "You didn't give two cents for that baby when she was born. You didn't give her a name, so *I* did. And if I gave her her father's name, so what?"

Sarah had moaned; she couldn't even remember telling NanaLeah the father's name; but she must have. Whenever anyone wanted to know the baby's name, she told them "Annie" and let it go at that. At the farm, they mostly didn't use last names.

"Well, Annie Diamond, how do you feel about letting a strange man change your diaper in a car?"

Annie didn't even hesitate. "Okey-dokey," she said, eliciting more pleased laughter from him.

Sarah felt him lift the baby from her side, heard him going

through the backpack looking for a diaper. It was so nice not
to have to think about it, not to have to think about *anything*.
She must have dozed off because the next thing she was
aware of was someone trying to get her to sit up, and female
laughter. Not mean laughing. Nice.

"Who'd believe a little slip of a thing like that could be so
heavy?" the woman's voice said. She was trying to help Sarah
to her feet. She had a husky voice, what some people would
call a whiskey voice, but nice. "Come on, honey, try to help.
We're gonna walk just a few steps to the car and then you can
fall asleep again."

"My guitar . . ."

"I've got the guitar."

"The baby . . ."

"Jake's changing your baby. Don't you worry about a
thing." She didn't want to sleep anymore; she wanted to be
awake and look at these people, but the moment she hit the
backseat, leather, soft and smooth and warm, she was out.

Later, without opening her eyes, she was suddenly *there*,
totally conscious and knowing exactly where she was: in the
backseat of a big fancy car. In the front, Sharon and the man
called Jake were chatting.

". . . and if he gets his name above the title, so do I, Jake.
I'm the one who gave him this break. He has a helluva
nerve."

"Sharon, sweetie, if you don't know that this business is
full of ballsy guys, then there's something wrong with you.
And believe me, there's nothing wrong with you. But look,
he's the hot new item in town, the latest sex symbol, whereas
you—"

"I'm chopped liver all of a sudden?"

"No, babe, of course not. But you know how it goes. Especially these days. It's the box office, babe."

The woman's voice got icy cold. "And I'm not a draw, all
of a sudden?"

"Sharon, Sharon, don't get uptight. The last two pictures
didn't gross enough to—"

"All right, all right!" Suddenly her voice changed. "Sorry,
sweetie, it's not your fault that I'm getting old."

"You're *not* getting old. Only in Hollywood would a girl of
thirty-four be considered over the hill. Look, babe, as far as
I'm concerned you're still numero uno. And you *are* getting
three hundred thou. *That* ain't chopped liver!"

They were show biz! They were *Hollywood*, and she was a movie star! Oh my God! And here she was, Sarah Fielding, in the back of their fancy car, looking like a truck had run her over!

She struggled to sit up, running her fingers through her tangled hair, pulling it in back of her ears.

"I haven't thanked you yet, for saving my life." Sarah said. Her voice was surprisingly strong, and for the first time in a long long time, she realized she wasn't, like, worried about anything.

"Well, well, so you're awake." Sharon turned to face the backseat and Sarah was disappointed that she didn't recognize the pretty face with the long, shimmering blond hair and the perfect features. "I must say, you look a helluva lot better than you did before." She narrowed her eyes and studied Sarah. "You're very beautiful, aren't you? When you're not freezing to death."

"You're in the movies!" Sarah blurted.

The woman grinned. "You recognize me?"

She looked so pleased, Sarah hated to say no. She hesitated.

"Never mind, honey, that's okay." The woman laughed. "You ever go to horror flicks? You know, 'The Mummy Returns,' 'The Mummy Dies Again'...? No? well, I'm in a lot of those. I'm that brand-new category, the character ingenue. It's the way I shriek, so elegant. My parts call for me to shriek a lot." She laughed again. "But hey, it buys me the goodies I love!" She held up her hands—her beautiful, smooth, white, unmarked, manicured, pampered hands—and wiggled them. Light flashed off several diamonds and a whole lot of gold. Sarah could only stare. She had not seen jewelry in so long, she had forgotten how bright it was, how intensely it sparkled.

And with a sudden fervent hunger, Sarah wanted it, wanted it all. The gold jewelry and the cared-for hands and the squeaky-clean shiny hair, the easy laughter, the nice clothes. She still knew mink when she saw it. Even the opalescent blue eye shadow: she wanted that, too. The whole time while she had been laying across the glove-leather seat, trying not to feel her sore throat, her icy feet, her thumping head, she had been listening to their conversation. And she had thought, I wish that could be me.

Now, it had changed and it repeated in her brain, like a

theme: *Should be me. Should be me.* She had talent. She had looks. Why shouldn't *she* be sitting in the front seat of an expensive car, flashing her jewelry and being nice to some poor slob she'd picked up at the side of the road?

It was like waking up from a long, long dream. She knew what she had to do, and for starters she had to make up with NanaLeah and her mother. She had to go home.

"Are we going toward New Haven, by any chance?"

"We're going to New York. We already passed New Haven—we're in Fairfield County. You live in New Haven? I could turn around."

"No. I live in New York, in Brooklyn Heights. But I thought . . . I'd get a train or something. I . . . I haven't been home for a while. I don't want to shock my grandmother or my mother; I should call first, get cleaned up."

Sharon didn't hesitate for an instant. "Next exit, Jake, pull off and we'll find a place, a place with a phone and a ladies' room. . . . You hungry, honey?" Sarah nodded. "A restaurant. Find us a restaurant. We'll get you cleaned up and fed and you can call your family and forget the train, we'll take you home. Door-to-door service, right, Jake?"

Jake was a surprise to Sarah. He was short, shorter than Sharon, and not really good-looking. He had sandy hair and a crooked nose and he was skinny. But Sharon hung on him like he was Marlon Brando. He *was* nice, playing with Annie and cracking jokes. He ordered her double cheeseburgers, double french fries, a large Coke, coleslaw on the side. Nothing had ever tasted so good, nothing. Sharon fed little bites to Annie, who kept opening her mouth like a little bird for more. Jake kept the baby on his lap, talked to her, and sang to her. At one point, Sharon looked over at Sarah and said, "You're lucky, you know that? No, I don't think you do. You have this little doll. I can't have kids—" Her voice broke and she blinked rapidly, but a couple of tears slid down her perfect cheek, anyway.

Sarah almost said, "You want her? Please, take her. Because I can't take care of her. I'm a terrible mother." She actually had to bite her lips to keep the words from coming out of her mouth. She wanted to tell Sharon the whole story. Sharon would understand, Sharon wouldn't tell her she was a horrible person. But then she realized that probably Sharon would think she was rotten, even if she didn't say it. There was something unnatural, no, monstrous, about a mother who actually thought of giving her baby away!

And she decided she'd wait to call home until they were in the city. She was so nervous about it; but if she was already in Brooklyn, they couldn't tell her to go away, could they?

When they all got back into the car, Annie popped right off to sleep and Sarah took out the guitar and looked it over, grieving because the bridge was broken.

"You ever play professionally?" Jake asked.

"Yeah. Some. In Cambridge, at a coffeehouse called the Quarter Note. And in the Village, at the Bitter Bean. I do mostly folk songs and I write my own stuff."

Well, he said he wanted to hear something, he kept insisting, so she sang him "Summer Everlasting," and when she finished, he nodded and turned his head to Sharon and then nodded again.

"Listen, kid. Your voice has something, you know what I mean? Something special. Plaintive, kind of. It has that folk-music sound, smoky and sad. If you've got a bunch of songs like the one you just sang, why don't you look me up and I'll get you auditions. I'm a manager, an agent, kind of. . . ." He met her eyes in the rearview mirror. "You think I'm handing you some kind of line, don't you? Well, I'm not. Sharon here is my wife . . . and my client, too."

"And I liked your song, too."

"Where are you? The Brill Building?"

"The Br—? Oh. No, honey, I don't do business in New York anymore. But you'll come to the Coast, and when you do, you look me up, you got that? This is on the level, kid. You look me up and I'll take care of your career."

"Okay. Thanks a lot." But her heart sank. How did he think she was going to get to California, for Christ's sake? She had a hundred dollars in her pocket, a baby on her hip, and not much else. But she couldn't help feeling excited when the car got onto the FDR Drive going downtown to the Brooklyn Bridge, and all the familiar sights unwound as they maneuvered the twists in the road.

She had always loved seeing New York this way, hidden and then revealed and then hidden again, as the road followed the curve of the river, disappearing into dark tunnels, emerging back into the light. Then they came around the last curve and suddenly the skyscrapers in downtown Manhattan loomed up and there, on their left, curving grandly, majestically, across the river, was the Brooklyn Bridge, its stone arches etched against the sky.

She must have made a sound, because both Jake and Sharon
started to laugh, and Sharon said, "Good to get home, isn't it?"

"God, I hope so."

"Don't you worry," Sharon said, "your mother and your
grandmother will be so glad to see you and Annie, they won't
care what you've done."

But she made them leave her off at the candy store a block
from home. She got out and took the guitar and the backpack
and Annie, hating to lose Jake and Sharon, hating to see them
go.

"I don't know how to thank you. Honest. I just don't know
any way to show you how grateful I am for rescuing me . . .
us."

"Glad to help. And listen, Sarah Fielding, I meant what I
said before," Jake told her. "Take this. And *use* it when you
get to L.A. Okay?"

"Okay," she said, but she didn't really believe it. He was
just being nice. She slid the card into her backpack, ready to
forget all about it. She smiled at them, and said thank-you
again, many times, and then she waved as she watched the car,
a beautiful, shiny, expensive Jag, drive away, out of her life.

She had to put everything down, including Annie, to make
her call. She was going to close the booth door, but she needed
to watch the baby, who was very curious about everything, so
she kept it open. She put in a dime, her heart thundering loudly
in her ears, and counted the rings. One. Two. Three. Four. Shit,
nobody was home. Five . . . and then that old familiar, "Yes?"
Never "Hello," always that harried, hurried "Yes?"

"NanaLeah—!" She could say no more.

"Sarah? Sarah! Is that you? Is it really you?"

Good-bye to the prepared speech, farewell to the carefully
worded apology and everything else she had thought of. She
burst into noisy tears, sobbing into the phone.

Her grandmother's voice came cutting through. "Sarah. Stop
that and stop it now. Do you hear me? Wherever you are, just
leave and come home. Do you hear me? Come home right
now!"

44

Leah put the last dish in the cupboard and stood in the middle of the kitchen, pushing her anger and resentment away by sheer willpower. Sarah couldn't help it, she had been badly treated in that horrible commune, she had been badly treated by that *momzer* Diamond who had promised to marry her and then backed out, the *hazzer*, leaving her holding not only the bag, but a baby as well.

Still, was that an excuse to drop her clothes on the floor, leave wet towels all over the bathroom, pile dirty dishes and pots and pans in the kitchen sink, never notice when the garbage pails were overflowing? Did she think there was a staff of chambermaids to clean up after her? She was a grown woman and a mother, and she should take some responsibility for herself and her child.

But no. Here it was, one o'clock in the afternoon, and she was still asleep upstairs, her bedroom door locked—*locked*! When Annie woke up, bright and early as usual, calling from her crib, "'Hi, hi, hi, hi! Annie's hun-gwy! Annie wants bwek-fast!" Sarah hadn't even stirred. She didn't care two pins for that child, her own daughter; it was heartbreaking.

And guess who got up out of her bed and gave the baby her breakfast and changed her diaper and put her on the pottie and read her a story and turned on *Romper Room* and gave her lunch and washed her hands and face, and was now looking out of the kitchen window every few minutes, to make sure she was still playing quietly in the sandbox in the yard. Guess who?

Annie was a doll, though a bit unusual-looking, with almond eyes of such a pale gray they almost looked transparent, and heavy dark eyebrows and lashes. Her hair was thick and black and kinky.

"Was her father a black man?" Leah had asked Sarah once, and Sarah turned on her as if she had just offered to shoot her.

"And what if he was?"

"What if he was?" Leah repeated. "If he was, then he was. Did I say I objected?"

"I wouldn't give a damn if you did!"

"Excuse me, I only asked. One day, she'll want to know about her father. Are you going to snarl at her, too?"

"You want to know about her father, NanaLeah? He was a handsome, charming, lying bastard, an assistant district attorney, a *landsmann* of yours, too . . . from Russia. His folks, anyway. He looks like you'd imagine Ivan the Terrible looked." And then, in one of those lightning-fast changes of mood she specialized in, Sarah began to laugh. And when she stopped laughing, she said, "Sorry, NanaLeah, I don't like thinking about him, much less talking. And yes, Annie looks just like him."

Of course, since then Leah had learned all she needed to know about Hawk Diamond. He'd been an A.D.A.? So, sue her, she made a few discreet inquiries. She had a friend here and there, in City Hall. He was married—the stupid girl, didn't she know they never leave their wives? He was considered brilliant, this Hawk—good. And, for whatever difference it might make to God, if there was such a person, he was Jewish. He had done a terrible thing to Sarah, terrible, leaving her at the last moment, pregnant and alone. But dammit, why couldn't Sarah forget about it and get herself together? If she wasn't bitching about him, it was her mother.

Yes, Jo was always away on assignment. Well, that's what happened when you were the best: everyone wanted you. Sometimes Leah had trouble remembering where Jo was, on any given day. She had finally come back from Vietnam, which meant Leah didn't have to have palpitations every time the newspaper headlines said there was another offensive, a big bombing, an all-out attack. But Jo was never home for long. And 1968 was the year everything that could go wrong, went wrong; so every week she was flying somewhere else. To Los Angeles, where Bobby Kennedy was killed. To Memphis, where Martin Luther King was killed. To Chicago, where the police acted like the Gestapo, where Mayor Daley decided to declare war on thousands of kids.

Jo had come back from the riots at the Democratic Convention in Chicago with a black eye, a bruise on her cheek, and haunted eyes. She had spent two night in jail, and when she came back last fall, she looked almost as bad as Sarah had. Exhausted, weary, and battle-scarred. After Chicago, Jo had said that she wanted to be finished with violence. "Maybe I'll take pictures of babies," she said. "Or nice old people." Yeah, yeah.

And where was she now? Up in Massachusetts, trying to get the whole story on Chappaquiddick and Ted Kennedy and that poor unfortunate girl. It was a *shandah*, what had happened to that whole family, the Kennedys. It was either bad luck or—what did the Greeks call it?—hubris. Thinking you were so special that the usual rules didn't apply. There weren't any pictures for Jo to take: the girl was dead, the senator had gone on television to apologize; it was over. But Jo was fascinated with it; she said she might even do a book about it. What drove Jo to seek out all the horrors of the world, Leah didn't know; but she obviously preferred dealing with other families' problems. Jo had no time, it seemed, for her daughter and granddaughter.

"Too bad, because that leaves just me," Leah muttered to herself, glancing out the window again to make sure Annie wasn't toddling into trouble. But the child had remarkable powers of concentration; she hadn't moved. She could work on a sand castle for an hour, patting it into shape, changing it, carefully adding pebbles and blades of grass. She was a good, patient little girl—with, of all the things, a wicked sense of humor!

Yesterday Annie did a tinkle in the pottie on her own, but for some reason she decided it would be a very interesting thing to empty the pot onto the floor.

When Leah discovered the puddle, she scolded her, with her best stern look. "Never, never, never," she said, "*never* dump the pottie on the floor."

Annie nodded, her face serious. "Okay, NanaWeah."

Later in the day, Leah walked into the bedroom and immediately smelled urine. "What did you do, Annie?" she demanded. "Did you dump the pottie on the floor, after NanaLeah told you no-no?"

Annie gave her a mischievous smile. "No dump pottie onna fwaw. Dump pottie onna *bed*!" Well, she shouldn't have, but Leah *had* to laugh. And the child *knew* she was being funny.

Nevertheless, Leah thought with a heavy sigh, Annie shouldn't have to be brought up by her great-grandmother. I'm over seventy, she thought. Never mind how much over seventy; I don't look it and I don't feel it. I still turn out articles, and I have all my teeth. But that doesn't mean I'm good for a two-year-old.

From upstairs came the unmistakable sound of that smoky liquid voice, singing. So the Queen was finally awake. What was the song? Oh yes, the one that sounded like gospel music . . . "You Make Me Feel Like a Natural Woman." Leah found herself humming along. Softly, of course. Who could compete with the gorgeous instrument in Sarah's throat? She sighed. Maybe Sarah was so difficult because of her talent. Maybe if the craziness was taken away, the talent died? Who knew? Well, at least she sang for her child. The baby would toddle up to her and say, "Mama take wequest," and Sarah would laugh and say, "Okay, baby, what's your request?" And she would sing whatever Annie wanted, which was usually "Over the Rainbow," though lately it had been "A Boy Named Sue."

The phone rang and Leah ran for it. Jo, maybe? She wished Jo would come back and *stay* back for a while. Maybe *she* could handle Sarah. Leah was at a loss.

A familiar husky voice shouted: "Leah! Hello! How *are* you?" Zelda couldn't bring herself to believe that long-distance was the same as a local call, and she always shouted. You had to hold the receiver at arm's length so as not to go deaf.

"Zelda, darling, you don't have to yell, I promise you. I may be getting old, but my hearing's still okay." It was amazing, how good it made her feel to talk to Zelda. Zelda's head was screwed on straight, as they used to say.

"I'm dropping by in a week! Next Tuesday. On my way to the *Lucky Fortune*. That's a ship!" Zelda shouted and laughed. "Cliff left me so much money, I didn't know what to do with it all! So before I get too old, I'm taking a trip around the world!"

"Good for you."

"Want to go? You'd better, before *you* get too old—just in case that ever happens!" More guffaws.

"Believe me, I'd love to set sail for the other side of the world." Leah sighed. "But I can't. You don't know what's been going on here, Zelda."

"Tell me! Nothing bad?"

Leah gave me a little laugh. "Sarah's up to her usual—

ignoring Annie, moping around. She's so restless, so unsettled."

"I thought she would settle down after that commune."

"Fat chance, Zelda! And she hardly *looks* at the baby. Her own child!"

A sound alerted Leah, and she stopped abruptly, turning to see Sarah, face like a thundercloud, standing in the doorway. "Listen, Zelda, can I call you back later?"

"You'll see me in a week. Save your money."

Leah replaced the receiver carefully and turned, equally wary. She would wait and let Sarah attack, or she could beat her to it.

"Well, so here you are at last," Leah said quickly. "I thought you were never going to get up for breakfast, and here it is, one-thirty, so I guess you'll be wanting some lunch."

"What I want, NanaLeah, is for you to stop talking about me all the time. I'm sick and tired of hearing myself painted as a total disaster!"

"I'd like to know what else you'd call it, giving up a good job and a good home to live out in the middle of nowhere, working like a peasant and having nothing! You weren't so self-righteous when you called me from the candy store!"

"All right, all right!" Sarah brushed past her and opened the refrigerator door, taking out the orange juice and pouring herself a large glass. She gulped it down thirstily. She really was a sensationally beautiful woman, Leah noted, not for the first time. She used almost no makeup; she didn't need it, with her vivid coloring and her black, black hair, which now hung down in ringlets almost to her tush. She was wearing an Indian shirt, very thin, many shades of blue shot with gold threads, a long blue skirt, many strands of African beads, and around her head a scarf tied Indian brave style. She was breathtaking.

"Annie tried to wake you, four or five times, Sarah. You wouldn't budge. It frightens her when you don't wake up."

"I can't help it if I don't wake up. I'm not doing it on purpose, for Christ's sake!"

"If you wouldn't stay out half the night, you wouldn't need to sleep half the day. You're a mother, Sarah, you have a small child who needs you, it isn't right—"

Sarah banged the glass down on the kitchen counter, angry color staining her cheeks. "I didn't want to have her, and believe me, I'm sorry I did. I do the best I can."

"You're doing nothing. That's the best you can do?"

"The minute I got back, you took Annie away from me. Ever since we got here, you've been making all the decisions about her—what she eats and where she goes and when she naps. You just took over, and now you're telling me I'm a lousy mother? Well, maybe I am. I learned from an expert!"

"What are you saying?" Leah's heart began to pound.

"I'm saying I never had a mother worth shit."

"Hush your mouth!"

"She was always gone. She still is. You think she gives a damn about me?" Sarah gave a harsh laugh.

It was eerie, Leah thought, and sickening, to hear Sarah say of Jo what Jo had said of Leah all those years ago. It had never stopped echoing in her head; it was so unfair. She had never abandoned Joanna; she had taken her everywhere.

"Your mother loves you," Leah said. "Why do you think she ran from that horrible place in England. To save her children."

"My mother didn't rescue me! Us! She was saving herself! My father preferred men, so she ran away! You think she paid us any mind at all, at Nether Althorpe? Even there she was gone all the time, taking pictures, or in London with her lover, coming back at all hours. You know who my *real* mother was? Nanny MacPherson! And I wasn't even allowed to say goodbye!" Tears began to stream down Sarah's face. With her hands, she wiped them away, but they still came. In a choked voice she added: "I'll tell you why my mother brought us here ... so my father couldn't have us. That's the only reason."

Leah gazed on the beautiful face, so contorted with self-pity. She should feel sorry for Sarah, but she didn't have the patience anymore. "You are an ingrate, Sarah Fielding."

"I'm an ingrate. Swell. So where is my mother right now, when I certainly need her, tell me that. Never mind. I'll tell *you*. She's off, doing her own thing, just like she's always done."

"At least she's doing important work. Do you know how many of her pictures are in the permanent collections of museums? Listen to me, Sarah, when the names of famous women are listed, your mother's is among them."

"I'm not impressed," Sarah sneered. "You think every selfish act is justified if it's quote important work unquote."

"You sound like a child, Sarah, an unhappy bad-tempered child. When you were small, your mother was here. She made sure she never took dangerous assignments until you were grown. Why do you insist upon making up stories? *You* were never abandoned in an orphanage."

All the color drained from Sarah's face, leaving her ashen. "Please, not that tired old story again, okay?"

Leah felt as if a knife had gone straight into her heart. She could not speak. Tired old story, was it?

"My friends are picking me up in a few minutes. I'll be upstairs, getting my things together."

Now Leah exploded. "To listen to music in a cow pasture! To smoke that filthy stuff and get high! For this you leave your child! What's wrong with you, Sarah? You're a grown woman!"

"You're right, I *am* a grown woman. So what I do is none of your business. You don't want me to leave Annie? Okay, I'll take her with me. What's the matter—you tired of her already?"

It was only by effort of will that Leah did not smack that lovely face. She kept her arms down, but her fists were tightly clenched.

"Me, tired of that funny, adorable little girl? I suggest you look in a mirror if you want to see who's tired of that child. Look into yourself if you want to see who took and who handed over. . . ." She gestured to the window. "Why don't you look out there and see her, happy, playing, wanting only a little attention from her mother. It doesn't even occur to you, does it?"

"Dammit, that's why I left the farm! Because it was impossible to take good care of her there. Hell, I left because of Annie!"

"That's not what I hear when you're talking on the telephone with your so-called friends!"

Sarah paled even more. Her lips looked white. "What do you mean, 'so-called'? My friends are my friends. Dammit, you think everything in my life is shit!"

"Watch your tongue!" Leah's tone was stern, but inside she was quaking. She had the feeling this argument had gone too far, too many things had been said that could never be taken back. "Look, Sarah, I'm only thinking of you—"

"Well, I'm sick and tired of you trying to run my life and making nasty cracks about all my choices. Yes, I'm going to a concert. It's going to be the greatest rock music festival *ever*. I've been thinking maybe I ought to get out of folk music, and I need to listen to rock. It's very important to me, but that doesn't mean a thing to you! Well, too damn bad. I've had my plans for weeks and I'm going. No *way* am I going to miss it!" She strode out of the kitchen, her face stormy. Without so much as waving out the window to little Annie!

The words came shooting out of Leah's mouth. "Maybe you shouldn't bother coming back, then!" For a moment she thought of running upstairs to apologize, to tell Sarah she didn't really mean it. But to hell with her. She was a self-centered and cold-hearted girl, and there would be no apology from her. As Sarah herself would say, *no way!*

45

May 1970

"Wee-ah, am I going to go to nursery school *today*?" Annie clung hard to Leah's hand while trying to skip ahead. She wanted to leave and wanted to stay, all at the same time. "Zelda, am I?"

Zelda, holding her hand on the other side, exchanged a look with Leah. "We've told you a hundred times, school is next fall. Today you're going to *look* at the nursery school and the teacher."

"Will the teacher wook at me?"

Both women laughed, and Leah answered, "Yes, sweetness, the teacher will look at you, too."

Annie considered this, her eyes narrowed as they did whenever she thought deeply. "Will I be pretty?"

They laughed again. "Absolutely!" Zelda said. "You'll be better than pretty—you'll be smart."

"I want to be pretty."

"Okay," said Leah, "you'll be pretty."

"And smart, too," Zelda added defiantly.

" 'Will I be pretty?' Where do they get their notions, at such a young age?"

"If she looks at television for ten minutes, Leah, she knows a woman is required to be beautiful, for God's sake. It's up to *us* to make her realize that's not all there is to being female."

"I suppose so. I only hope we're up-to-date enough for the nursery school. I only hope Miss Haggerty doesn't think that we're lesbians, like everyone else in this neighborhood does."

"Well, can you blame them?" Zelda chuckled. She made a gesture meant to include her trousers and shirt, her very short gray hair, her lack of makeup or jewelry. "An ugly old woman who always wears pants living with a beautiful old woman who turns herself out with great style! In Brooklyn Heights, that's tantamount to an admission of guilt!" She laughed again. "To hell with them, Leah, isn't that what we decided?"

"Sure, sure. But I don't want us to ruin Annie's chances of g-e-t-t-i-n-g i-n. This is Junior League territory—or so *she* always said."

"Leah, Leah, you could call Sarah by name. She *is* Annie's m-o-t-h-e-r, after all."

"I swore I would never say her name again as long as I live, and I won't. Any woman who would just disappear, just *disappear* without a word, not even a postcard—"

"Don't get your bowels in an uproar, Leah. What's done is done—it's been almost a year. And we're almost there, so pull yourself together for Miss Haggerty."

There was a moment of silence. Neither woman noticed Annie looking at them, observing everything. Then Leah said, "You're right. What I have to figure out is what to tell the teacher."

"How about the truth?"

"You want to know something, Zelda? You just said a mouthful!"

"What is Zelda eating? I want some!" the child demanded.

"Nobody's eating anything." Leah knelt to examine Annie, make sure she looked like the kind of little girl the nursery school wanted. She was very unusual for this WASP neighborhood. Whenever Leah took her to the playground, she couldn't help noticing how Annie stood out among all the blond heads.

"Let me see how you look, sweetie. Your face is clean, that's good. Your nose is cute, that's good. Your dress is red, that's *wonderful.*"

Annie giggled and picked up the skirt of her sun dress. "Bwoo," she said, and gave Leah a mischievous look. She knew all her colors; and she knew that when she pretended not to, it made Leah laugh. In any case, for the past week she had refused to wear anything that *wasn't* red.

Leah gave her a hug. "You're a card, aren't you? Well, you're just about perfect, so let's go in."

The school was four large rooms inside a big church. They went in a side door and down a long hallway. Offices, meeting rooms, cloak rooms, a kitchen even. Funny church, Leah thought.

In the nursery school—you could tell it by the pastel walls and bright posters—a pretty young woman with dark curly hair and a big smile greeted them. Focusing on the toddler, she said, "This must be Anna Diamond. Hello, Anna, I'm Miss Haggerty."

"She's always called Annie," Leah said.

"Annie. What a pretty name. Why don't you come play in the block corner with Miss Hope, Annie, while I talk to your . . . grandmother?"

"Great-grandmother." Only the barest flash of astonishment, quickly hidden. The teacher disappeared into a classroom, Annie clinging to her hand and gazing up at her with awe. Miss Haggerty came back a few minutes later and led them to an office.

"Before we fill out all the forms and answer all the usual questions," Leah said, talking very fast, "I think it would be helpful if you knew a little bit about us. Zelda is my sister-in-law—" Well, almost, even though she and Joe had never actually gotten married. "—Annie's great-great-aunt . . . is that enough greats? Zelda owns an airfield in Westchester and lives with us. I'm a writer, freelance."

"Tell me about Annie," Miss Haggarty said.

Leah cleared her throat. "She lived on a commune for a while, and then they came back home to the Heights, but her mother—my granddaughter—went off to that rock concert in Woodstock and . . . well, she never came back."

"Never came back!" The voice was still soft and even, but the eyes widened. "How terrible for Annie . . . for you, too. I'm sorry."

Leah was amazed to find tears springing to her eyes. She hadn't cried at all over Sarah's disappearance. First she'd been too worried, then she'd been too frightened, and finally too angry. She blinked the tears back and forced herself to smile. "To tell you the truth, I'm not sure whether to be sorry or not. She was never much of a mother."

"Some women aren't, you know. My own mother—" The young woman stopped abruptly and looked down, swallowing hard.

Leah leaned over the desk and put her hand on Miss Haggerty's. "Mine, too," she said. Their eyes met. "My mother left me on a train platform." She could not go on. Maybe it runs in the family, she thought, throwing daughters away.

Miss Haggerty reached for a tissue, blew her nose, and handed one to Leah. "I wasn't left on a train platform. My mother had a nervous breakdown when I was six years old, and I didn't see her again until I was twenty." She smiled and shook her head. "I don't know why I'm telling you all this . . . we only just met."

"It's the eyes," Zelda announced.

"Pardon?"

"Leah's eyes. They're sympathetic, and they fasten on you like there's nobody else quite so interesting in the whole world. Everyone talks to her. That's why her articles are so good."

Miss Haggerty grinned. "I *knew* that name was familiar. Leah Lazarus. You write for all the women's magazines. I love your stuff." She giggled. "Only . . . I pictured you about my age."

"She is," Zelda said. "Inside." And they all laughed. Then Miss Haggerty folded her hands in front of her and sat up very straight. The official interview was going to resume.

Leah had always made up her mind that Miss Haggerty could be told the whole sorry story. Well, almost the whole thing. It was nothing she *wanted* to recall. God knows.

When Sarah did not reappear at the end of the Woodstock weekend, Leah's first response had been disgust. No doubt her granddaughter had found some man to bed with, all thoughts of her child flown to the winds. Sarah always had been boy-crazy. For a teenager, it was understandable, but that a grown woman should go running off every time something in a pair of pants beckoned . . . !

When by Wednesday, there was still not a word from her, Leah called the Bitter Bean. But the owner knew nothing, and he was furious. She had never come in for work on Tuesday— after he'd given her the weekend off!—and he still didn't have a singer to take her place! "She's such a flake!" he lamented.

"Gorgeous voice, but I can't keep taking her back and taking her back, only to have her bug out on me *again*. She'll never get another job *here*, I'll tell you that!"

The police, too, were less than helpful. The sergeant she spoke to at the Eighty-Fourth Precinct sounded pleasant enough but worn-out. "Lady, you know how many young people run away nowadays? Right now I've got, let's see, one, two, ten, *thirteen*—I've got thirteen missing persons, and they're all under thirty." He snorted. "And they say not to trust anyone over thirty? Who's on the missing persons list, them or us?"

"Isn't there *anything* you can do?"

"Do you think she's hurt, or has been abducted?"

"I don't know what to think. No, I don't think anyone kidnapped her. It's just—" She wanted to say "she's never done anything like this before," but that would be a lie. "—she has a child," she finished. "A three-year-old."

"That's different. Give me some facts." And they went through it together. "What was she wearing when you last saw her? ... Who was she with? ... Where was she headed? ... Are you sure she got there? ... Has she ever disappeared before and then come back?"

"Never mind. Never mind. She could have gone anywhere!"

"I'll put out an APB on her ... but even then, she'd have to do something to get picked up by the police wherever she is. You see what I'm saying?"

Yes, she saw what he was saying. Leah hung up and put her head down into her hands. Oh God, what now? And into the middle of her thoughts came the insistent ringing of the front doorbell.

It was Zelda, in twill pants and sensible shoes, a huge handbag slung over her shoulder, a grin on her face. "I've got a bottle of bubbly so we can say bon voyage and— What's wrong?"

"Sarah. She went to her rock concert and never came back."

"Woodstock? She was at Woodstock?"

"Yes, Woodstock." Leah grasped Zelda's arm. "Listen to me, Zelda, she's *gone*, disappeared. She left her child here and just vanished into thin air! I get so damn mad, and then I think, but what if she's been murdered? And then I think, if she hasn't been murdered, *I'll* do it! What am I going to do, Zelda?"

"You're going to sit down and I'm going to bring you a glass of brandy and then *I'll* deal with it."

"Three days later," Leah told Miss Haggerty, "I woke up and realized Zelda had missed her boat."

Zelda laughed. "My trunks went to England without me."

"And she's been part of the household ever since."

There were nursery school papers to fill out. Dates, places, names. A form for Dr. Weeks to fill out. A checklist. The foods Annie liked or disliked. Sleep habits, favorite toys, interests. "And you should know that Annie's a little ham," Leah said. "She'll do anything to get a laugh."

"I can think of a lot worse traits! I think Annie will do just fine in our afternoon threes. They're a little older than the morning class, just that little bit more sophisticated, and able to concentrate. And most of them have given up the afternoon nap, like Annie."

A few minutes later they were back on Cranberry, heading for Willow, Annie skipping ahead, then circling back to tell them some fascinating bit of news about "my skoo" ... the cubbie where she would keep her things and the "dwessup corner" and the "woft." At least they wouldn't have a problem getting her to go.

"God, Zelda, she's only three. Do you realize how many more of these firsts we have to go through before she's off to college? Kindergarten. First grade. Junior high. High school. College. Her period. Boys. Oh God, boys! I'd forgotten all about boys!"

Zelda began to laugh, saying, "Leah, you look so comical. Boys aren't a *tragedy*!"

"Who told you *that* lie?" But she had to laugh, too.

It was good to laugh again. Those first months when she was still hoping to find Sarah, the dreams had begun: trains roaring into the station, her mother getting smaller and smaller and finally evaporating, fading into nothingness. She would awaken, bolt upright, shivering horribly, her entire body cold and clammy with sweat. She was afraid to fall asleep again. All the years that had gone by since her mother left her ... and still it hurt.

"Don't you sometimes wish you could go back and do it over again?" she asked Zelda.

"Do *what* over again?"

"Your life."

"Don't be silly! It was hard enough doing it once, Leah, who wants to repeat it?"

"I meant . . . make it better, do it right."

"Ah, Leah, if we only could. But I think that if we were given the power to go backward in time, probably there would be some kind of law against changing anything. *Baschert* is *baschert*."

"Our fate is our fate?" Leah repeated. "We're all prisoners of our life? I'm not sure I like that idea. I always thought free will was the way to go."

They were back at the house, the baby climbing eagerly up the front steps. She always wanted to be the first one to the door; it was very important to her. Luckily, she only had two old ladies to beat so she always won.

The phone was shrilling when they walked in. "Okay, okay, keep your pants on," Leah muttered, running to it. "Yes?"

"Don't you ever say hello, Mom, like the rest of the world?"

"Jo! Where are you?" Recently, one of the intellectual magazines had been sending Jo to college campuses all over the country, to cover the student strikes that were popping up everywhere. A very different attitude these kids had, Leah thought, from her day, when the teacher was revered and you'd no more tell the school what to do than you'd tell God Himself.

"California. L.A. Listen, Mom, I've found Sarah."

"Really?" Leah said in her coolest tone. "How does she look?"

"Oh, I haven't actually *seen* her yet. What I meant was, the private eye found her, remember I told you I'd hired one? Well, he found Sarah Fielding . . . let me read from the report. 'Subject living with male called Guy Faison, both working the streets in Melrose'—that's a section of Los Angeles, Mom— 'playing guitar and singing'—that's how I know it's her. They're living hand-to-mouth, never in one place for very long. . . . They crash with friends or move into abandoned buildings. . . . Now they're in a bungalow in a lower-class neighborhood, sharing with six others . . . and like that."

"All right, Jo, no sense your skipping the bad news."

Leah heard a long weary sigh. "She's stoned all the time. They're on drugs, that means."

"Give me some credit, Joanna. I know what stoned means."

"Anyway, I drove out there, and they had just left, yesterday or the day before. But I have another address, a house on a beach about an hour from here. The potheads in the bungalow thought like, man, they're not sure, but maybe, like, she went *there*. What a generation! Are any of them just normal, regular people? Don't mind me, Mom, I'm just tired and disgusted. Anyway, I'm on my way out to this, like, beach house."

"Jo, stop for today, okay? Get a good night's sleep first."

"I can't stop until I find her. *Then* maybe I'll get a good night's sleep."

"Jo, when you find her, what do you think you're going to do? Tell her it's time to come home?"

There was a moment of silence, and then Jo gave a brief, humorless laugh. "You're right. I don't know why I'm chasing her this way, since it probably won't do a bit of good when I find her. But Mom . . . she's my daughter, you know? And in spite of everything, I care about her."

"Will that get her off drugs, Joanna? Will your caring turn her into a responsible human being?"

"Maybe. Who knows? In any case, I *have* to find her, I have to at least try."

"Of course you do," Leah said. Like I had to find you, she thought. God, what a family! Maybe this is what Zelda meant when she said *baschert* is *baschert*. Maybe they really *were* all doomed to keep repeating the same terrible story, over and over. "Of course you do," she repeated, shaking off her sadness. "But Jo, listen, I don't want her back in this house."

"Mom, come on!"

"No, I mean it. I can't forgive her for what she did. Today, I took Annie to the nursery school, to register her. That's why."

She could hear Jo give a little sigh of exasperation.

Too bad. Call me *pisher*, Leah thought defiantly. So I have standards! "You find me stubborn," she said. "But that's how it is. I'm sorry."

"Yeah, yeah, me, too, Mom. It's just . . . when I think of the life we led, of everything that's happened to us, my God! I'd think you, of all people, would be ready to give her a break."

Leah leaned against the hallway wall and stared at the wallpaper. How was she going to ever explain to Jo? "She . . . abandoned . . . her . . . child," she said, very slowly and clearly. "I know you thought you were abandoned, too, but you weren't."

"Mom! I stopped blaming you ages ago! I don't feel that way anymore. But I do remember what it was like to be young

and mixed-up. And hey, she didn't leave Annie on a train platform to be taken by strangers!"

"I never forgave my mother, you know that? Never! You
want to chase around California looking for Sarah, be my
guest. But she is not welcome here, not until she proves she's
changed. You think you can save her soul, but I've got news
for you, my darling, nobody can save her but herself. But go
ahead. I can't stop you anyway!"

"I just hope you don't have to be sorry someday," Jo went
on, "for turning your back on her this way."

"I didn't run away. Twice, yet! I didn't leave my child, without a word to anyone. I've nothing to be sorry for!"

"Oh, great, that's very loving and understanding!"

At the same moment, they both hung up.

Jo looked at the telephone, staring at it as if it might speak to
her and tell her what to do. She didn't feel right, hanging up
like that, without saying good-bye, even. But Mom did it, too.
Her hand went out to the phone, then stopped, then went out
again, stopped once more. No. First she'd find Sarah and bring
her back here and see what had to be done: a doctor or a hospital or maybe just a hot bath and sleep. After she had Sarah,
she'd call her mother, tell her whatever there was to tell—and
make up. She didn't particularly feel at fault. In fact, she
thought her mother was being stupid. But Jesus, the woman
was seventy-five years old. How could you fight with someone
that age?

Wearily Jo pushed herself up from the chair. She was so
damned tired; she'd been on the run for the past three months.
When she looked at herself in the mirror this morning, she had
been shocked. The face that looked back at her was the lined
face of a middle-aged woman. Is that what she was? She didn't
feel that old, especially not in Paul's arms. She hadn't told her
mother about Paul; well, it could wait. Everything could wait,
while she went running all over the place after her nutsy
daughter.

She called Paul's office. He was out on a shoot, so she left
him a message, to meet her at their favorite restaurant at eight.
Then she grabbed her purse, a well-worn tan leather shoulder
bag that held everything, and the map. The car was parked
right outside. She got in, opening all the windows to let the
heat out. Christ, she was sticking to the seat! She opened the
map the P.I. had given her, folded it carefully to the section

that would lead her on the freeway to where Sarah was staying, where the private investigator had tracked her. Them. Sarah and a male, both on drugs. Oh Christ! Why was she even bothering?

The car radio was already on, tuned to a station with the least amount of talk. Right now they were playing Beatles' music; that was fine. She liked the Beatles, surprise, surprise. Paul couldn't get over it. "I'm not *that* ancient," she told him, her heart giving that little squeeze. He wasn't that much younger than she was—only nine years—but it made her nervous. She was sure that any minute now he'd take a good look at her and take off. She still didn't know what he saw in her. He told her she reminded him of Katharine Hepburn: "all good bones and hidden sexuality." And when she protested, he just laughed and said, "Let's just say I go for freckles and let it go at that." Oh, but it was hard to let it go at *anything*. Having Paul was getting a second chance at love, and she was a nervous wreck.

She slammed on the brakes. She'd gone right by the entrance to the freeway. Damn it, she had to stop drifting off; she had to pay attention. Forget Paul, she told herself, right now you're searching for your dropout daughter. Thinking about Sarah, trying to imagine her doped up and scrawny, gave her such pain, she had to close her eyes for a moment. She stopped the car and put her head down on the steering wheel.

Damn it, what was *wrong* with that girl? She'd wracked her brains, trying to figure out when Sarah had changed from a sulky but essentially good kid into an irresponsible druggedout wacko. But there was no reason. She had everything: a stable family—okay so her father was a bit weird, but she hardly ever saw *him*—a great voice, and all the encouragement any kid could ask for. Not to mention that she was stunning. She was blessed, for Christ's sake! How could she destroy her life?

"Dammit, Sarah," Jo said aloud, starting the car and moving onto the freeway. "We always loved you. You always got whatever you wanted. When you didn't go to Juilliard, nobody yelled. When you went running off to Boston, nobody yelled. When you had a baby without being married, nobody yelled. So why, Sarah? Why are you punishing us? What did we *do* to you?"

There was surprisingly little traffic at this hour. She'd probably get to where Sarah was supposed to be "crashing" in less than half an hour. Half an hour, and she very well could be holding her daughter in her arms, taking her back—no matter *what* Mom said—to the Heights, to a normal life.

She glanced in the rearview mirror, pulling out to pass a car going under thirty miles an hour, glancing over to see who in the world could be driving so slowly. It was an elderly man, leaning forward to peer out the windshield, his hands tightly gripping the wheel. He looked scared to death, but determined. What a brave old character. And what a picture that would make!

So she was in the left lane, accelerating, laughing a little, when a pickup across the divider, heading in the opposite direction, suddenly swerved, took a leap and came flying through the air, straight at her. She caught a glimpse of two pale, scared faces in the front seat.

Oh my God! Jo thought. They're going to hit me! But they can't, they can't! I've got to—

46

February 1975

"Why the hell do I feel so guilty?"

"You tell *me*, Sarah," said the cool expressionless voice behind her. Christ, she hated this setup: she, prone on the couch, staring at the ceiling, and he, legs crossed, sitting like God in judgment over her, in that thronelike chair. "Why do you feel so guilty?"

"Because I'm a shit. Because I like feeling guilty. Because— I don't know. If I knew, dammit, I wouldn't be *here*, would I? I thought you were supposed to *help* me, for Christ's sake. Not just sit there and repeat everything back to me!"

"A man is in love with you and wants to marry you. This seems to make you uncomfortable," Dr. Rosenberg said, ignoring her outburst. He usually did. She hated *that*, too. Come to think of it, what in hell was she doing here? She hated everything about it. But the thought of walking out, of not having this couch to lie down on or this invisible person to reflect herself back to her—like the talking mirror in *Snow White*—made her feel as if she'd just plunged over an abyss. She *hated* that feeling.

"Abysmal must come from abyss?" she remarked. "When something is abysmal, doesn't it mean empty, yawning danger right in front of you?" His answer was silence. "I guess that means you don't feel like having a linguistic discussion, right?"

"I find it interesting," Dr. Rosenberg said, "that those particular words come to your mind so often. And you often dream about falling into an empty space. Shall we talk about that?"

"No. I need a *little* privacy. Well," she added after a moment, "actually I was thinking about the mirror in *Snow White* . . . you know, 'Mirror, mirror on the wall, who is the fairest of them all?' And I was thinking maybe I'd write a song about it."

"Do you want to know if I think you're the, ah . . . fairest of them all, Sarah?"

"No, Dr. Rosenberg, actually, I don't. I know I'm beautiful. People have been telling me that since I was little. Not people, men." She laughed. "And yes, I guess that means I think men aren't people. Maybe I'll write a song about *that*!"

"You've had trouble with your composing lately, haven't you?"

It was the truth, but she didn't feel like discussing it. Anyway, she was sure it was just a passing phase. "I'm into a different kind of song . . . torch songs. Sad, smoky songs of love lost . . . the man that got away, that kind of thing. Torch singing used to be very popular. Who knows, maybe I can revive it. I already decided that's what I'll use on my next album. Jake thinks it'll sell a million, and Jake is almost never wrong about things like that."

The doctor cleared his throat delicately. "Really? I thought you were going to make an album called . . . *On My Own*, wasn't it? And if I remember correctly, torch songs are almost always songs of total dependence."

"Every song I sing doesn't reflect my *life*, for Christ's sake. I was browsing through a secondhand store and I came across a bunch of old Jeri Southern records. They were a quarter apiece so I bought them. The songs appealed to me. When I sang them for Jake, he went apeshit. End of story. And anyway, Dr. Rosenberg, didn't Freud say that sometimes a cigar is only a cigar?"

He didn't answer her; he rarely did, when she tried to be humorous. One session, he had told her that her attempts at humor—yeah, she got the full weight of *attempts*—were only a defense mechanism. "I have a grandmother who could give you an argument about *that*," she'd wanted to tell him; but she didn't. She didn't talk much about her family. She knew her mother was dead. And, God, NanaLeah! Could her grandmother have . . . ? No, no, of course not. Someone would have told her.

"Do you think you *are* on your own?" The voice again. "Maybe you don't think so. Maybe that's why you're not going to do that album. Perhaps that's why you found those old recordings so appealing?"

A wave of anger, as solid as a shock, went through her. Damn him. Well, she wasn't going to answer. Let him say something. But he could outlast her in the silence department, any day. And it was *her* money, so she might as well talk.

"The women in my family have always been on their own. It's in the blood. Did I ever tell you none of us ever got married . . . ? Well, my mother did, actually, but it only lasted a few years, and then we left England and . . . I lost touch with him. . . ." Her voice dribbled off as she realized that, once again, she was telling a lie. That lie.

"So you think you don't want to marry your manager because it isn't done in your family."

"Of course I don't think that! I think I don't want to marry Jake because . . . well, because he wants to marry me. That sounds like me, doesn't it? Only wants what she can't have." Softly she sang: "Oh what you want and sing your song for . . . it turns to dust and ashes and rust . . . the moment you get what you long for. . . ."

"Is that one of your songs?"

"You know damn well that's one of my songs! From two years ago, for your information!" She shifted on the couch, restless and annoyed. "And I don't want to marry Jake because he doesn't turn me on anymore, and I don't want to marry Jake because I'm guilty, guilty, guilty!"

"Ah," Dr. Rosenberg breathed. "Ah, here we are again, back at your guilt . . ."

He kept on talking, but she turned him off. She knew what he was going to say and then what she'd answer and then what he'd ask, and that she'd snap at him because by that time, she'd be angry again. Why did she ever think that coming here and spilling her guts out was going to help her? Another man, telling her what to do with her life. Jake Marcus was another one, her manager and agent. And her lover, let's not forget that one. Even in bed, Jake was in charge, now that she thought about it.

Christ, she could make a list: the A&R man at Elektra records, the concert booking agent, her dentist, her doctor, her shrink, her vocal coach, her acting coach, her guitar teacher. She was always finding some man to lean on and depend upon, and then she'd end up being furious because it was another man, telling her what was best for her. When was she going to *learn*, for Christ's sake? She had a sudden flash: she was a man junkie, she was fucking addicted to men.

Look how fast she had latched onto Guy Faison. What the hell did he have, besides good looks and muscles and a big cock? That now-famous day at Woodstock, when it rained and the field turned into mud, she had slipped and fallen. She was covered with slimy cold muck, and when she tried to get up, she kept sliding and her wet skirt was so heavy, it just dragged her down. And then a pair of arms came from heaven, lifted her up, carried her to a tent, and wrapped her in a dry blanket. That was Guy, twenty-one years old, college dropout, drummer without drums and cabdriver without cab. He had nothing but his strength and his sex, and because of that—well, that and some really good hash that put her in La La Land for a couple of weeks—she clung to him, trailing along with him, high as a kite, all the way to the Coast.

Eventually Guy ran out of cash and hash—both at the same time. And when she crashed, when she opened her eyes and knew once more who she was, it was a beautiful sunshiny October morning in Venice, California, and she was lying on a damp mattress in a falling-apart beach shack having her brains fucked out by a blond man she only dimly recognized.

When he was finished, she said, "Who are you?"

He laughed and laughed. Then he said, "I wondered when the hell you were going to come down. Man, have you been flyin'!"

"You mean I've been acting stupid!" she snapped, getting up.

"No, no. Honest. You've been fine. But high. And see? I

kept your guitar nice and safe. You got a really fine voice, you know that?"

"I've been singing?"

"All the time! Man, you should see how people gather around. I tried to get some bread out of them so we could rent ourselves a *real* room. But you wouldn't let me. Man, you really carried on about love and brotherhood and shit, and you got so mad, I gave up, you know? Because I didn't want you running off on me. You and me are really fine together, fine like wine. . . ." He reached over and encircled her ankle with his thumb and forefinger. He was a huge man, she saw, big and tall and heavily muscled.

"How about balling again?" A little tug and she was pulled off balance, tumbling to the mattress and enfolded in his embrace, her face pressed against his bare skin. When he spoke, she could feel his voice, rather than hear it, vibrating in his chest. "Swing low," he murmured, "sweet chair-ee-*yot!*" and lifting her easily, thrust himself into her with one smooth, slick move. She would have fought, but actually it felt good, and pretty soon she was writhing on the mattress, biting his shoulder and screaming.

Just going along with the whole thing was so simple. So she just went along. They led the simple life. They ate a little, screwed a lot, smoked hash when they could afford it and pot when they couldn't, sometimes some Angel Dust. Every night, they went out with the guitar, and she played and sang and he passed the hat.

They made their way up the coast and decided to stay awhile in Los Angeles, where they worked a corner near a hotel, hoping a cop wouldn't come along and make them move on before they collected enough. They got much more bread in the richer neighborhoods. People would make them promise to buy *food* and to see a *doctor* and stuff, and give them five or ten dollars instead of a few coins. Of course, they always promised.

But this one night, a couple walked by without even glancing at them. That was pretty unusual, so Sarah was following them with her eyes. And then the woman, a tall slender blond who looked vaguely familiar, suddenly stopped and grabbed her companion's arm. In a minute they were back and the blond woman was staring at her. Sarah stared back; she looked so familiar, her name was right on the tip of Sarah's tongue.

The blond woman said, "We picked you up in Connecticut

a couple of years ago, didn't we? On the Boston Post Road. Gave you a lift to New York. Brooklyn. Your name is Sarah and you had your little girl with you. I always wondered how things turned out. . . ." And then her voice petered out and she looked embarrassed. All at once, Sarah was aware that her feet were dirty and her dress torn. "You're very thin," the woman went on. "Are you okay? How's your little girl?"

"She's great. She's with my family. I wanted to go on the road and see if I could make it. . . ." The lies came so easily. Yeah, now she remembered them, rich and remote, but really nice, up there in the front seat of the fancy car. "But . . . you can see . . . I didn't quite hit the big time. . . ." She felt herself swaying a little and noticed that the world was beginning to go into a slow spin.

"When did you last eat, for God's sake?"

"I . . . don't know." When did she last eat? she asked herself. She couldn't think. She tried to smile reassuringly at the blond woman, and then felt her knees turning to water.

"Jake!" the woman shouted, and the swarthy man next to her reached out and caught Sarah. "Jake, get her to the car. This girl needs food and a bath, and probably a detox center."

Sarah remembered repeating that word, detox, to herself, over and over—for some reason, it struck her funny—and then she passed out. Jake Marcus carried her away, while Sharon Spellman, the movie actress, took her guitar. And Guy said nothing—not even good-bye.

"Sharon was so good to me," she said to Dr. Rosenberg. "Christ, she did everything . . . took me to the doctor, and made sure I ate, and got my guitar restrung, and took me shopping, and put me into detox . . . Christ, she saved my life! She saved my miserable life, and how do I repay her? I boff her husband for two years! I make him so crazy, he thinks he wants to marry me! While she's taking me to my drug-free meetings every goddamn week! *That's* why I feel guilty, and you know it! Because she's been like a mother to me, a *mother*!"

As always, whenever she said that word, "mother," the tears came ripping up out of her gut somewhere, flooding out of her, choking her. Oh Christ, how she hated weeping in this office! She felt so exposed, so ashamed! Concentrating hard, she sat up, willed the tears to stop, blew her nose and took several deep breaths.

"Are we finished, Sarah?"

Sarah stared at him; a short, rather dumpy man, balding, always pushing his black-rimmed glasses back onto the bridge of his nose with his forefinger. "Is there some kind of fucking *law* that says I can't sit up? What if I want to talk to you face-to-face?"

"You're angry," he said in that implacably impersonal voice.

"You didn't answer my question. As usual."

"It's all right to be angry, Sarah."

"I'm not angry."

"I see anger." The expression on his broad, tanned face had not changed at all. What in hell was she doing here?

"You don't see anger, Dr. Rosenberg, because I'm not angry."

"Don't you think all of your anger out—"

She didn't let him finish, but sprang to her feet, holding both arms out straight, palms up, as if to deflect his words before they could reach her.

"I thought it was *okay* to be angry, Doctor! I thought we agreed I have *reason* to be angry! I may be fucked up, but I haven't lost my memory yet. No, and I haven't lost my mind, either! I'm tired of you telling me how I feel all the time. I know how I fucking feel!" He shook his head slowly, looking at her with sad, placid eyes.

"We *are* finished, Dr. Rosenberg, as a matter of fact," she said, feeling five pounds lighter. "Since you asked."

"You haven't left like this in six months, Sarah. Perhaps you'd like to think about what has made you so anxious."

"*You* have made me so anxious! Send your bill. I'll pay it, but I won't be back!"

As she strode out of the room, she heard him saying, "We'll see." *We'll see!* As if she were five years old! She slammed the door behind her as hard as she could. Just like a five-year-old, and she had to laugh at herself.

There was a little park across the street from his office, three benches, four palm trees, a bed of scarlet flowers, and a phone booth. She headed for it, wishing she had a drink. But she had promised Jake she wouldn't drink. She had to stay straight and sober until the album was finished.

The car would come for her in half an hour, and she would be able to see it pull up in front of the professional building where Dr. Rosenberg and three other shrinks had their offices. She sat down and eyed the telephone booth. All that crying had brought back memories. Suddenly she could see her grandmother, holding a tiny black-haired girl in her arms. Shit, she *never* let herself think about Annie! But all of a sudden she was trying to figure out how old the baby was now, wondering if she still looked like Hawk.

She couldn't think about Hawk, it always made her crazy. She had to think torchy thoughts, prepare her mood for her recording session, pretend she was Piaf. Piaf had a great voice; but the Little Sparrow was always singing about the man who pushed her around and she still just loved him. Piaf could make you think, Yeah, that's how it should be. Maybe she should get married and try to be normal, for a change, go back for her child, get in touch with NanaLeah.

NanaLeah . . . Sarah tried the thought the way she might bite down on a sore tooth, gingerly, warily. Annie. Annie Diamond. She burst into sudden tears. "My baby . . ." she found herself sobbing. "My baby, my baby . . ." Where in hell was this stuff *coming* from?

The last time she'd discussed calling home, with Dr. Rosenberg, she went through the same thoughts. In the end she said to him, "I know I should, I want to, but I just can't!" And he said, "You may never be able to do it. Perhaps you don't really want to see your family again. We can explore that."

"No, we cannot explore that!" she had exploded. "There you go again, telling me what I think and how I feel, like you know better than me who I am. I hate that!"

"Your way of dealing with difficulties, Sarah, has always been to run away."

"Well, now I'm not running away. I'm *here*, aren't I? For Christ's sake, keep your fucking fingers out of my head!"

Sarah stuck her tongue out at the stucco building across the street. To hell with who you think I am, doctor, she thought, I'm going to do it. Now.

She marched to the phone, lifted the receiver, dialed the phone number.

Her heart was hammering. Christ, it took long enough! And then the rings. One. Two. What if nobody was home? Three. And then a woman's voice said, "Hello!"

It wasn't NanaLeah, and it wasn't a child's voice, either. "Who's this?" Sarah said.

The voice was tinged with amusement. "Who wants to know?"

And then Sarah knew. "Hello, Zelda."

"That's *my* name. What's yours?"

Sarah licked her suddenly dry lips. "Sarah." It came out nearly a whisper.

"God in heaven!" the woman said, but she had lowered her voice. "Sarah? You mean Sarah Fielding? Our Sarah?"

"Yes, your Sarah. What are you doing at Nan—my grandmother's? Is she all right?"

"Oh yes, she's fine, never better. I live here now, ever since . . . Oh, Sarah, I'm so sorry. Nobody knew where you were at the time. And after you got to be famous, Leah wouldn't allow me to contact you. . . . Never mind. Look. Sarah. You need to know. Your mother . . . is gone. She was killed in an automobile accident."

"I know," Sarah said, her eyes filling. "My agent told me, but it was months later. Too late for me to come home for the—" Her hand flew to her chest, where she could feel her heart racing. "I'm sorry! Now I'll never have the chance—" She couldn't go on.

"Jo found you, you know. Let's see, it was almost five years ago . . . 1970. She was on her way to you, Sarah, she wanted to bring you home. She was very happy that she found you, Sarah, you should know that."

"Oh God, and I never saw her—"

"It was a terrible accident. . . . Two boys from West Texas, in a pickup truck, blind drunk. All of them died."

Sarah gave a cry of pain, clutching the telephone box with one hand so she wouldn't fall. Hearing it from Zelda, she felt as if she were just finding out for the first time. It was so awful, the sense of loss and emptiness. "Oh God, I'm so sorry, I'm so sorry. . . ."

"I wanted to let you know, about the funeral and all, but we couldn't find you. It was all over the newspapers and in *Time* magazine and in *Look*, and it was even on television. To tell you the truth, I'm surprised it took you months to find out."

"I . . . I . . . was out of it. I was . . . sick, I was sick, but I'm better now, I'm clean, I'm straight, oh Christ, I'm so sorry! Let me talk to NanaLeah!"

"Oh, Sarah, I don't know—"

"Please. I know she's probably still mad, but I'm a different person than the one who ran away from home all those years ago. Just put her on."

"I warn you . . . never mind. Here she comes. . . ."

Faintly, Sarah could hear NanaLeah's voice, impatient, preoccupied. And then, suddenly, the imperious "Yes?"

"NanaLeah! NanaLeah!" Nothing from the other end. "Yes, it's really me. It's Sarah, NanaLeah, it's Sarah, and I want to see you!"

There was a moment of profound silence, and then, at last, her grandmother's voice. "You terrible girl, how dare you call after you've ruined so many lives? See me? I never want to hear your voice again!"

Sarah stood very very still, even after the click, even after the buzz of the dial tone. She stared, unseeing, across the street, unable to make her mind work. Finally she realized she was till holding the receiver and, gently, she put it back in the cradle. Her heart was hammering hard; she could feel it knocking against her ribs. Now she really *was* all alone in the world.

That was the abyss she was so frightened of; she could feel herself plunging over the edge and hurtling through empty space. She clutched the side of the telephone booth for dear life, telling herself to take it easy. You're fine, she said to herself, you're Sarah Fielding, you're a star, you've had a hit single, your last album went to the top of the charts, there's no abyss, you're rich and beautiful and famous and there's nothing to be afraid of.

Like an automaton, she pushed away from the phone booth and blindly headed back across the street, to the dim office with its slatted shadows on the floor, to Dr. Rosenberg. She had to stop lying to him; she had to start from the beginning. She had to do it quickly and she had to do it right. Before she died of loneliness.

Epilogue

June 18, 1990

On the boardwalk at Coney Island, a fresh breeze blew in from the ocean to cool the hot June day. A dozen or more people strolled along in the summer sunshine, mostly old women wrapped in sweaters, and young mothers in jeans pushing baby carriages.

Two women stood together at the rail; but instead of gazing out at the ocean and the broad bright horizon, they had turned to face inland, where they could see the deserted pavement of West Twelfth Street; catch a glimpse of the elevated tracks of the B train at the far end; and, on the boardwalk, study a line of small wooden concession stands. One, cheerful in sea-blue paint, proclaimed itself to be Sideshows by the Seashore. A smaller sign invited the public into the Coney Island Museum.

Maybe she could take Leah in there, Annie thought; maybe the old pictures would make her smile. Before she could suggest it, Leah sighed and said, "Annie darling, this is just the remnants of what used to be a fantasyland, a place of such glamor, such excitement . . . ! I never thought I'd live to see it like this. Never!"

Annie Diamond regarded her great-grandmother and decided that maybe it wasn't such a good time to go into the museum. Not that Leah was losing it, not even at ninety-six. So okay, she was wrinkled, but she still had her act together. Today, in honor of her birthday, Leah was decked out in silk pants and a print tunic top, Gypsy earrings and a dozen bangles of different colors. She'd had her hair cut short in the back, but the rest of it was thick and fluffy—white, of course—with a wave dipping over her forehead. She still cared about how she looked.

"You're *gaw*-jiss, you know that?" Annie said, putting on the heavy Brooklyn accent they both liked to affect whenever they were in danger of getting too emotional.

"You, too, dahlink. I love your rags."

"Leah! My skirt is *not* rags! The hem is ragged on purpose! Everything about the way I look is on purpose, you know that."

"Miss Downtown," Leah said, making a wry mouth.

"*Ms.* Downtown, if you don't mind." They laughed. That's why she loved Leah; it didn't matter that she was as old as God, her sense of the ridiculous was still intact. And to a stand-up comic like Annie Diamond, that was pure gold. In fact, it *was* pure gold; "I was talking the other night with my great-grandmother . . ." That was her *schtick*, how she started her routines. It sure got their attention.

"When *I* lived downtown," Leah said, "back when it didn't have a capital letter and was just the lower East Side, we worked like hell *not* to look the way you do, Annie darling."

Annie's thick, wild, black hair was down to her waist. She wore pale, almost white, makeup, fake eyelashes, kohl liner, deep red lipstick, and a long skirt with a heavy leather belt; a vest purloined from an old men's suit; a derby hat tipped over one eye: weird but interesting. That's how she wanted to look. Leah knew it; she was just yanking her chain a little.

"Hey, Weeah, pretty I'm not."

"Hey, Annie, you're better than pretty. You're stunning."

"Yeah, yeah, yeah."

"You know you are!" Leah said, irritated. "You must know how often people turn to stare at you."

"They turn to stare at freaks, too. I'm sorry; I don't mean I'm a freak. I'm okay. But pretty I'm not."

Pretty, she wasn't, although—if her genes had been kinder to her—she could have been. She might have looked like her mother. Oh sure, she knew who her mother was, although her great-grandmother never mentioned her. Years ago, Zelda had come quietly into her room one afternoon and said, in her usual blunt way, "Annie, it's time someone told you about your mother." She still remembered how stupefied she had felt. Sarah Fielding, the singer! Not the kind of music she usually went for, but hey, her *mother*! She went running to Sam Goody's to find a Sarah Fielding album, to get a really good look at her. And what she saw on the cover made her heart swell with pride and then almost immediately sink. Sarah Fielding was obviously one of the world's beautiful women, and her daughter didn't look a *thing* like her.

For a fleeting moment Annie had wondered if *that* was why her mother had run away from her, because she was such an ugly baby.

She never spoke about it to Leah, of course; she couldn't. Leah wouldn't allow her mother's name to be spoken, wouldn't talk about Sarah at all, not even to curse her out. So Annie studied her own reflection, not really liking what she saw. All that kinky hair, which did whatever it wanted, would never stay straight and smooth like her best friend Julia's. Those funny eyes that slanted—well, at least they were gray with golden flecks, that was something—the hawk nose, the cushioned lips. A funny face. Well, since she wasn't a beauty, like her mother, she'd better be something else. Hey! How about funny? Funny face, funny mouth, right?

A breeze came in from the ocean, sending hair and skirts flying. Leah shivered and said: "Annie thought *she* was homely, too . . . the other Annie, darling."

"Yes, I know."

"She was wrong, too. . . . Oy, we stood here, Annie Bernstein and I, on our sixteenth birthday—you know we had the same birthday. Of *course* you know we had the same birthday, I must have told you this story a thousand times when you were little! Sixteen, Annie! How many birthdays have gone by since then, and here I am, still!"

"Yes, and that makes me very happy." She squeezed Leah's hand.

"You want to know something? It's not such a completely happy thing, to live so long. Zelda's gone, a year already. So many, gone. When you get to be as old as I am, it can be lonely."

"Try not to think about the losses, Leah. Think about all the people you still have. Me, for instance."

"Don't worry, Annie darling. I'm not going to get all depressed and weepy. Although, I must admit, lately I sometimes get lost in my memories. This morning, I got to thinking about Jim, that I should have had more *rachmonos*. . . . So he had one moment of weakness: he'd been my strength for so many years! How could I have been so cruel to him? And for just a moment there, I thought, I'll tell him I'm sorry I said all those wicked things. And then I remembered he was dead thirty years."

"I wish I could have known him."

"You should have. You should have known my *first* love, Joe Lazarus. His name, I took, even though we never did get married. I met him at Coney Island. So this place is doubly important to me. Every year, I try to come back on my birthday, as a remembrance. And you know, I'm always so shocked and surprised at how it's changed. Who *dreamed* that such a dazzling, fantastic place could just vanish, nothing left but a few rusting relics!" She shook her head, looking around sadly. "We thought it would last forever. . . . I should have known, when Annie died . . ." Her voice cracked, and when Annie looked, she was blinking back tears. "Look at me, I still cry when I think of her, falling all alone through the air, frightened, she

must have been so terrified. . . . I only hope she died the minute she landed, that she never had to feel alone. I should have
been with her. . . ."

"Leah, what a terrible thing to say! Do you wish yourself
dead?"

"No, no. I mean that if we had only been together, she'd
still be alive!"

"Well, that sounds more like you, at least. But excuse me,
I doubt very much she'd be alive today. Not too many people
get to be your age—not to mention with all their marbles."

"You're right, Annie darling. I should consider myself lucky.
But it's obscene, to be ninety-six. Ninety-six! God, if I'm not
careful, I'll live those one hundred and twenty years Jews are
always wishing on each other! Oy, if they realized that their
knees would stiffen, their sex life would evaporate, their memory would shrivel, that they'd turn into a mass of wrinkles and
sagging flesh . . . maybe they'd wish for something a whole lot
better!"

Great! Annie thought. In fact, perfect. I'll do a whole schtick
on *ein hundert und zwanzig yur*. She'd have to translate it, of
course . . . maybe get in a few cracks about a *shriveling* sex
life—knees could shrivel, but your sex life should stiffen—oy,
as Leah would say. Pretty awful.

She'd start as usual: "I was talking to my great-grandmother
the other day . . . yes, really, I honestly have a great-
grandmother." Then she'd pause and let them applaud, they always did, as if she got the credit for Leah's longevity. "She's
ninety-six, yeah, that's right, ninety-six, and she'll still dance
you to your knees . . . and at her birthday party, someone stood
up and gave the usual Jewish toast—'A hundred and twenty
years!' and she said, 'Oy, Annie dahlink . . .' " She always
gave Leah this Yiddish kind of accent in her act, even though
Leah really had no accent at all. But would anybody believe
you could have a Jewish great-grandmother without a Yiddish
accent? Anyway, she also gave herself a Brooklyn kind of accent you never heard in Brooklyn Heights, but hey, that's what
people liked to think Brooklyn sounded like.

Anyway . . . " 'Oy, Annie dahlink, if they realized that your
knees stiffen, your memory disappears, your sex life evapo-
rates, your looks . . . don't ask—!' " Then she'd slide right
into, "Hey! I'm only twenty-three . . . already my knees hurt,
I have no sex life, and as for looks, well, see for yourself! But

I was hoping things would get better!" And they'd laugh. God, they'd better laugh!

"Maybe I shouldn't feel so sad about Coney Island," Leah said. "Maybe even an amusement park doesn't want to live too long. When all your friends have died, where are you going to find new ones—at the local old age home?" Annie gave her a big laugh. "Maybe Annie Bernstein was lucky, who knows? At least she didn't have to go through any more heartache. Poor sweet Annie, she thought no man would ever want her, she was such a *miese* . . . oy."

"She wasn't so plain as all that, I hope," Annie said.

"Tell you what. Why don't you look for yourself. I've been saving this for a long time. . . . When Jo was killed, the police sent back everything they found in her motel room, and there it was, in her camera case. I was sorry that she hadn't been wearing it—she always said it was good luck for her—but then I realized that now it was *bad* luck, especially with her daughter run away from us, the one who should have had it. So I put it away. But it's time, Annie, time you had it. You'll wear it and it will bring *you* luck."

Leah rummaged in her purse and came out with an old box, its black nearly worn away. Annie took it, thinking, Bad luck. So that's why I was never allowed to touch it. All those times I played with her jewelry, trying it on and hearing stories about the olden days. But whenever she opened up this box, Leah would always say, "Nah, not that, that's too heavy for a little girl to wear." She never got to handle it or look at the pictures inside.

As Annie opened the box, her eyes filled with emotional tears. Awesome, that Leah should pick this particular birthday to give her the locket. Because, tucked in the bottom of her bag, she had its mate, the very one that had been stolen from Annie Bernstein's neck, to give to Leah tonight, as a surprise.

She had spotted the locket in the window of Linda Horn's antique place on Madison Avenue. Her heartbeat speeded up when she spotted it. It was just like the one in Leah's jewelry box, only all shined up and lying on black velvet. At first she shook her head, thinking, Nah, it *couldn't* be. But it *had* to be. She had gone in and asked about it. The saleswoman started talking a mile a minute. "It's a charming old piece, isn't it? Turn of the century, I think . . . Wait a minute, let me get it for you . . . there's an inscription . . ." Talking while reaching into the window and turning back to the shop with it. "See? On the back."

And there it was, exactly like Leah's, except of course for the name. *To Annie ... 6–18–10 ... Friends Forever.*

Shivers went racing down Annie's spine. It really *was* the same, it really was. Out of nowhere, just by chance, here it was, after who knew what adventures? Oh, she'd give her right arm—well, maybe a finger—to know where it had been since 1911. She clicked it open carefully, hoping to see the pictures in it; but of course they had long ago been tossed out.

"You know, this is weird. This locket belongs in my family. My great-grandmother has the mate to it. She and her friend gave them to each other."

"Oh my, how thrilling. So of course you must have it."

"Of course." Her heart sank when she heard what it cost; but what the hell? So she had to break the bank to buy it.

"Oh, Weeah," she said now, blinking rapidly. "I love it. Of course it will bring me luck." Afraid she would cry, she gave Leah a big hug. "So, let's see what my namesake looks like." She opened the locket. The pistol with the dark hair and snapping eyes, she would have known anywhere. And the other girl, so fair and ... tentative, that's how she looked, not quite smiling, not quite sure of herself.

"She wasn't homely, just very pale," Annie said. "If she had used some makeup—a little mascara, some eyeliner—"

Leah snorted in disdain, as Annie had known she would. "Makeup! Who had makeup in those days? You had to pinch your cheeks and bite your lips. You had to develop that special something called personality." She looked over at the open locket, regarding the two young faces. "So maybe she wasn't a great beauty, but there was something sweet about her, something that shone through. She was beautiful *inside*."

"Inner beauty doesn't do much to keep the phone ringing, Weeah," Annie said wryly. "As I know only too well."

"I know you always say how ugly you are in your act, Annie, how you never get a date. But ... you don't *mean* it?"

Annie sighed and, taking Leah's arm, began to walk back toward where she had parked the car. "Honestly, Weeah? Well, honestly, I find I can't tell the difference between my life and my act these days. It's a little creepy."

She had put a new bit into her routine that went over real well. She went on in an outrageous getup, so Downtown it was impossible. Cheers and whistles came from the audience as she twirled around, letting them admire her. And then, after she pirouetted and preened a minute more, she stopped, waited for quiet, and said, "You know, I'm wanted by the Bloomingdale's police." They always screamed. Then she'd put on a police voice. "Excuse me, miss, but are you aware your hemline is three inches above the allowable limit? I'm afraid we'll have to take you in."

They loved it, especially the women. Then she'd ask if there was a woman in the audience who didn't hate her body. More laughter. "Men don't have this problem, you know. Men walk around all the time—have you noticed?—*naked*. They think their bodies are just fine! No matter *what*." More laughter.

Maybe she'd change it a little, stay off men. Maybe she'd say something about going into Alexander's to buy a dress so she could shop at Bloomie's ... or how Bloomie's made her feel short and fat: "I have to find a K mart to feel good about myself again."

"But you're beautiful!" Leah was insisting, like she always did. "No, you're better than beautiful, you're—"

"Funny!"

Leah slid her a sideways look. "You always did think making people laugh was the way to make them love you. But that's not what I was going to say. You're ... wait a minute, let me get the exact right word. You're striking. It's more than a pretty face, you're ... unusual. Oh, and P.S., yes, you're funny."

"Yeah, I am." They strolled in silence for a moment. "The question of the moment, Weeah, is: *How* funny am I?"

"What kind of a question is that? Funny is funny. You need a report card all of a sudden?"

"I need your input."

"So tell me and I'll put in."

Annie laughed. "I don't know why I'm laughing," she remarked. "This is serious ... so serious, I think we'd better sit down."

"That *is* serious."

They took a bench, this time looking out over the broad beach to the sea. Behind them a group of elderly people were singing in Russian, and Leah tipped her head to hear them better, smiling.

"Lots of Russians here now," Leah remarked. "I never

thought I'd live to see *that*, either. But go on, darling, tell me your news."

"A producer named Max—yeah, that's his real name—has asked me to do a one-woman show. Off-off-off Broadway, Leah, so don't get too excited."

"What a wonderful idea!"

"Sometimes I think it's wonderful and sometimes I think it's the pits. I have this stomachache over it. I'd have to give up my day job—"

"Yo. Giving up selling CDs shouldn't give you a stomachache."

"*Yo?* You're giving me a *yo*? On your ninety-sixth birthday?"

"I can give you a yo if I feel like it, Annie. I can also give you advice. Go for it!"

"But I still have to pay my rent."

"You'll have a piece of the action, won't you?"

"Leah, every word out of your mouth is astonishing me, do you know that? Yes, I'll have a piece of the action. Is not Herb Cohen my manager? Would he let me do a show in a garage without a piece of the action?"

"It's what you've been dreaming of your whole life, Annie, practically, since you were a little thing and put on shows in the living room for Zelda and me. Go for it!"

"Yes, but listen, Leah, *what if I fail*? What if they hate me? What if I get lousy reviews?"

"Listen, darling, you come from a long line of women who went for it, and we didn't do so badly. Two different publishers are interested in my book, and I just got a very nice check from Random House, for Jo's pictures. They're publishing a big coffee-table picture book—*World War Two Through the Lens*, they're calling it—and they wouldn't dream of making such a book without Jo Fielding's photographs, they told me."

"And . . . ?" Annie prompted. Really, Leah was too much! How much longer did she think she could pretend that Sarah Fielding, with her platinum records, gorgeous face, and quick-change lovers, didn't exist? Every week some rag had a story about her.

"And what?" All sweet innocence.

"And there's my mother, who hasn't done badly herself. She's at least notorious."

"Her, I don't want to talk about. I want to talk about you.
You're young. You're free. What's that saying in Latin? Carpe
diem. Sieze the day."

"And I always thought it meant fish with Vietnamese
sauce."

"Don't make me laugh, Annie. This is serious. You don't really think you'll fail? Come on, be honest. This is me you're
talking to."

"Oh Leah, I doubt I've thought about it at all. I'm going on
instinct, and instinct says it's right. It doesn't make any sense,
but it keeps beckoning to me—come on, come on, do it, do it."

"Then you should. Let me tell you a little story, my darling,
about beckoning, about instinct. But I need to stretch my legs."
They began to walk slowly along the boardwalk, past the Wonder Wheel and the Cyclone, toward Brighton.

"It was so long ago . . . 1951, maybe. Before Jim died . . ."

It happened right after Emile—*Elias*, as he called himself—
appeared at the house, and she discovered that the fabulous
lover who'd haunted her dreams had also been her daughter's
lover. Leah didn't know if she was jealous or outraged or just
plain hurt. And talk about feeling old! Of course, she was fifty-
six, no spring chicken; but she didn't look it. Didn't feel it, either, not usually. But after she made a complete fool of herself,
flinging herself at Emile only to discover he hadn't even
known she was there, well . . .

But on a bright brisk golden day in October, 1951, with the
wound still fresh, she had decided to defy the years. Her hair
was still long, and instead of twisting it up, she left it loose
and went out and bought herself some new clothes. She took
a train into Manhattan, and went to see *Guys and Dolls*—in an
orchestra seat, expensive as it was.

When she got back to the Heights, she was feeling so buoyant, and the day was so beautiful and sparkling, she just
couldn't go home. So she kept walking down Henry Street,
through the Heights, through Cobble Hill, until she hit Union
Street. Great! She'd do some shopping at the Italian delis:
fresh proscuitto, homemade mozzarella, a bread. She'd make
herself an impromptu sandwich to eat when she got home.

She was bouncing along with her purchases, feeling goddamn good about life, when she felt eyes on her. A man,
standing stock-still on the sidewalk, was openly staring at her:

a man in his forties, perhaps, on the short side, stocky, muscular, heavily tanned, with thick, prematurely white hair. Italian,
she'd bet, and quite handsome. Her eyes met his momentarily,
and her heart gave such a jolt, she stopped walking. Oh, she
caught herself and looked away and kept going, but her heart
was racing and her cheeks felt hot.

He came after her. "Pardon me," he said, and when she
turned, he gave her the sweetest smile. "I don't want to be
fresh ... I don't want to frighten you. But you so beautiful."

"Thank you," she said, and then blurted, "So are you."

He laughed, comfortable with himself and with the rather
strange compliment.

"Well ..." she said, not knowing what in hell to do with
this very curious confrontation. "I'd better get going."

"No, wait. Please. Have lunch with me."

She tried laughing gaily, but it didn't quite work. "I've
bought my lunch already," she said, gesturing with the paper
bag from the deli.

"Good. We can have a picnic. I have wine. It's a beautiful
day, we can eat outdoors."

She tossed her head and said, "Why not?"

"Come," he said, and, natural as he could be, reached out
and took her hand. It was amazing, the shock of something
like electricity that shot up her arm. This was crazy, this was
insane, and the craziest part of it was, she was going to do it.
If she didn't, she felt she would always regret it.

His name was Angelo, he was a stonemason. "My father
and my grandfather, they were both stonemasons, and they
taught me."

He had a small shop on Sackett Street, and they ate at a
stone table in the grassy yard that was his showroom, with
planters, angels, saints, birdbaths, and benches scattered about.
They tore the bread and stuffed it with meat and cheese with
their hands and licked their fingers afterward. And they drank
from a bottle of Chianti. They talked and talked, although later
she could never remember what they said and doubted he
could. Talk was not what it was about, and they both knew it.

They made love in his workroom, on a mattress he had
pushed into one corner, covered with soft old quilts. It was as
natural as breathing; once he had undressed her and had run
gentle hands over her entire body, they never exchanged a

word, although he had his eyes open and fastened on hers the whole time.

When they were both too exhausted to continue, the sun was setting in a blaze of crimson over the East River. "Oh dear," she had said, "I'd better run. They'll be wondering what happened to me, at home." She giggled, adding, "They should only know!"

"I will drive you, in my truck."

"Oh no, no, Angelo, that's not necessary. I *want* to walk. And the Heights is a small neighborhood, they gossip."

"Here, too," he said with a grin. "Tomorrow, I promise you, my friends will all ask what I was doing so long in the workroom with the beautiful woman."

"Your friends *saw* us come in here?"

He laughed. "I didn't see any of them. I saw nobody. But that makes no difference. They will all know, anyway."

"It doesn't matter," she said quickly, getting dressed. "I mean, we won't be seeing each other again."

"No? Why not?"

Because it would spoil the magic. Because we're from two different worlds. Because this was beautiful because it just happened, spontaneously, and it was good, but what it was is what it is. She said none of this to him.

"I'm a married woman," she lied, averting her gaze from the disappointment in his dark eyes.

". . . And the next day, sometime before daylight, the stone angel appeared, next to the front door, right where it is now. I never moved it. I thought, why shouldn't I see him again? Here was proof that he was smart enough to find me and subtle enough to let me make up my own mind. I was tempted, believe me. But it was too perfect, the way it was. Sweet, simple, silent, secret . . . So I didn't. And so, it stayed perfect."

"So what you're saying is seize the day . . . and the guy, too. Let's not forget him!"

"Taking chances to do what you want is what it's about!"

"There *is* something I want to do, Weeah, so I'm carping diem. I want to talk to you about my mother."

"It's *my* birthday," Leah said with a laugh. "And I say no."

"Good try, Leah, but no go. Maybe this has something to do with your birthday. No, really, Weeah, I need you to listen. All those years when you were keeping her a secret, Zelda told me everything. In fact, I know who my father is, too."

Leah's lips tightened perceptively, but she said nothing.

"You were a wonderful mother, you and Zelda. I couldn't have had a happier childhood. But there comes a time when you just *have* to know who you come from. . . . In fact . . ." Long, long pause.

"In fact?" Leah prodded.

Quickly, Annie said, "In fact, I tracked down my father, and I've seen him." Time enough for the other news a little later.

"Seen him! That's more than I ever did! When?"

"Last year . . . three times. Three dinners. One at the Four Seasons, one at the Quilted Giraffe, and the last one . . . right in the Heights, at the River Café."

"Such fancy restaurants . . ."

"He can afford it. He's a Criminal Court judge." She stopped at this point and leaned on the railing, looking out at the ocean. "I look just like him, did you know that?"

"I was told. I never saw him, never. Did you know that?"

"I was told." They smiled at each other, very careful.

They had recognized each other instantly, on the street in front of the Four Seasons. It was summer, and he was wearing an elegant Italian linen suit, a Ralph Lauren shirt, no hat on his beautifully barbered gray hair. She thought it might be him, simply because he was standing there, obviously waiting; and then he turned and it was such a shock, she stopped walking. She was looking at her face—her face with five o'clock shadow. She just stood there, staring at him, and then she noticed that he had a stupefied look on his face, and she thought, Now we *really* look alike, and began to laugh.

What was so wonderful was, he laughed, too. He strode over to her and put a hand on each shoulder, smiling at her. "The resemblance is startling, isn't it?" he said. "And yet, I feel I don't have the right to kiss you."

She nearly bawled. "Sure you do," she said, and leaned over to kiss his cheek. He kissed her back and squeezed her shoulders and then tucked her arm into his and led her into the restaurant.

It was like that all evening. He was warm and welcoming, not at all nervous or unsure. She didn't remember what they ate; she hardly looked at her plate.

He told her he regretted never knowing her, regretted her mother's refusal to see him or talk to him, to try again.

"I always wanted to marry her, did you know that? No? I'm not surprised. My first wife—Marilyn, the one who threatened to commit suicide—well, she finally did it, in 'seventy-two. And that's the first time any of us realized she was—had been—a sick woman. I should have put her into treatment in the first place, and then divorced her, and then married your mother. But back then, we didn't recognize mental illness so quickly. I always thought it was me, something I'd done. God, I loved your mother. Sarah."

They talked and they talked that night, and when the dinner was over, from across the table, he lifted her hand to his lips and kissed it tenderly. "Please, may we have dinner again, Annie?"

"Of course. Of course." He was her father, her *dad*. She had a dad at last. And he was so open and forthcoming, so affectionate and charming. She didn't want to say it aloud, but she felt she loved him already.

But then, in their second meeting, he leaned across the table and interrupted her in the middle of a story about her last gig.

"Annie, you're so bright, why are you wasting your life trying to make dumb audiences laugh in fifteen-minute segments?"

She laughed. "I like making audiences laugh in fifteen-minute segments. And it's actually more like twelve. I mean, you have to be really *fast!*"

But he didn't smile back at her. "Why not have a real profession?" And then, great big smile on his face, he sprang it. "I'll pay for you to go to law school! The whole thing—your tuition, housing, food, spending money, the works! How's that?"

She could see he was waiting for her to fall to her knees in gratitude. And all she could think was, how could he think she'd *want* that? It was the *last* thing in the world she'd want! But she tried to imitate his reasonable tone and said, "Well, this is a brand-new idea. I've never considered being a lawyer."

He grinned. "Then I'm glad I brought it up. Consider it now, why don't you? You're certainly smart enough! And you'd be a great litigator. You know, that's where I made my reputation. In Frank Hogan's office."

"Yes, I know," she said. His face was shining with his eagerness to please. She couldn't say no just like that, so mean, so final. "Let me think about this, okay?"

"Don't think about it too long, honey, or we'll be too late for registration." Registration! He was really serious! He handed her a thick envelope with all the applications and info for Columbia Law. "My alma mater," he said. "I have, ah . . . a little pull there. Hawk Diamond's daughter? Nothing to it!"

She knew she didn't want to go to law school, and tried to tell him in a subtle way; but he wasn't listening to her. He was so excited with his own ideas and his own plans. She wanted to love him, to keep on loving him, but she had a sick feeling in the pit of her stomach.

When she met him a week later at the River Café, she had a little speech all rehearsed, all about how grateful she was, how in his debt, how delighted that he cared about her, but. *But.* She had opened the crammed envelope and crumpled the pages a little, to make it look as if she'd gone through them and given this law school thing a great deal of thought. And on top she had put the *Village Voice* review of her act at Catch a Rising Star. It was a rave. Well, of course it was, he might say, what other kind of review would she show him? And she'd say, I haven't had many, but they've all been good. *This* is what I'm good at. *This* is what I want. If you love me and want to help me . . .

But he pressed her hand and refused to take the envelope. "Not yet," he said. "No, no, let's enjoy a wonderful meal first, and the view here is fabulous. I made sure they gave us a table next to the window." She turned dutifully to see the dinner boats and ferries and barges moving on the river, the drop-dead view of the Manhattan skyline. Had he forgotten where she had *lived* her whole life? She'd seen this same view about three gazillion times.

She told him what she wanted to drink and then leaned forward, making her voice earnest. "Look, er . . . look, Dad." God, it was hard to say, but he had insisted. "I really think we should talk about this now. I mean, it's been on my mind a lot and—"

"On my mind, too. But indulge me. Wait until dessert." He grinned. "I may have the best dessert of all for you."

Uh-oh, she thought. Uh-oh.

And she was right. His big surprise turned out to be that

he'd gotten in touch with the dean of the law school, he'd pulled strings, and she could get into law school and then take the LSAT's later. And he sat back, grinning, so pleased with himself.

She stammered and stuttered, looking for a nice way to say no; but finally all she could do was blurt it out. "I don't *want* law school. I don't want to be a lawyer. . . ." As his lips tightened and the eyes narrowed, she got nervous. "I'm very grateful to you for thinking of me, for wanting to do so much for—"

"Are you sure you really *understand* what I'm offering you, Anna?" His voice jabbed at her, sharp and cutting.

"Of course I understand, and it's so terribly generous. But honestly, all I want is . . . well, what I'm doing."

"That's no career for a daughter of mine! I've gotten to know you, Annie, you're bright, very bright. You have a legal mind. I can't just stand by and watch you dismiss what could be a brilliant career. And for what—?" He made a dismissive gesture, a gesture that took being a stand-up comic and put it out with the trash.

Annie found herself cringing. She was getting mad, but *he* looked menacing. He had a look on his face that said he'd like to hit her. And then he smiled—or at least, tried to smile—and she realized he had no idea his rage was showing. He thought he was being reasonable and rational and *charming*!

"Look, sweetheart," he said, "all I'm asking is that you *try* it my way . . . give it a year. I'll pay for the whole thing, so what do you have to lose?"

"Only everything I really want out of life. I appreciate what you're trying to do. But I wish you'd try to see my side of—"

"You're exactly like your mother—totally irresponsible."

"What do you know about my mother? When's the last time you saw her? And what do you know about *me*? You never even cared enough to find me. *I* had to go chasing after *you*! You want to send me to law school? Where were you with the child support when I was a kid?"

"And you're a bitch like her, too," he said. He threw some money on the table, pushed his chair back, and left. Annie sat and finished her coffee, waiting for her heartbeat to get back to normal and for the tears to go back where they came from.

* * *

"At first, I liked him a lot," she said, answering Leah's question. "But it didn't work out. You know, his wife finally did commit suicide, but by that time my mother had disappeared. . . ."

"Probably in that commune where they didn't even have toilets . . ."

Annie laughed. "Weeah, it was a long time ago. My mother has plenty of toilets now, believe me, she's a rich woman. As a matter of fact, she's *flush* . . . yuck, yuck, get it?"

Leah sniffed. "I've read about her in those horrible tabloids. I know she has money."

"I think my father could have found her if he'd tried hard enough. He's a control freak. You know, the kind of guy who has to be the boss, the one boss, the only boss."

Leah laughed. "So what else is new, darling? Men have always thought that's the way it should be! For all the good it does them! We know who really runs the world."

"Yeah, women like you." Annie gazed at Leah, ninety-six years old today, still gorgeous, still full of beans, telling her great-granddaughter a story about great sex she'd had forty-odd years ago. What a broad! Flooded with love, Annie put her arms around Leah and hugged her tightly.

"I love you, too, Annie darling."

Separating, they grinned at each other. To hell with it, Annie thought, to hell with waiting until some preordained moment at dinner tonight. Now was the time to give Leah the locket.

"Weeah, I've got a present for you."

"Oh darling, that's lovely, but at my age, what could I possibly—" She caught sight of the box, so similar in size and shape to the one she'd just presented to Annie. "Open it for me, Annie."

Annie sprang the clasp, and there it was.

"Oh my God!" Leah cried, and burst into tears.

"Weeah, I'm so sorry, I wanted to make you happy!"

"I am, darling, I am!" She took the locket and turned it over, reading the inscription, then pressed it to her cheek. "Oh, Annie, what a gift! It's like you've given my dear friend back to me . . . I can finally close the book, she can now rest in peace. Annie, where did you find it?" But she didn't wait for an answer. She put it around her neck, smiling through her tears. "You're a doll, Annie Diamond, you always have been. I'll tell you something, Annie. I'm glad I lived long enough to see you grow into a lovely, funny, bright woman. That makes it all worth it!"

"Me, too, Weeah." Now Annie's eyes were brimming. If she wasn't careful, they'd be spending this entire day weeping. "Come on, boss, it's time to start back."

But when they got into the car, Annie didn't start the engine. "Weeah . . ."

"Go ahead. Give me the bad news. You think I can't tell by your face? Like you got caught with your hand in the cookie jar!"

"Not bad news. She's coming today."

"Who's coming today?"

"Sarah. My mother. She's coming for your birthday. Now, take that look off your face."

"What look? I'm just not so sure it's such a good idea, that's all."

"Oh, Weeah, do you think we can fool each other anymore?"

"Okay. I think it's a bad idea."

"And *I* think the bad idea is all the years of separation and silence. Weeah, all we have is each other, our family. Zelda's gone, Jo is gone. We lost them, there's nothing we can do about it. We can't get them back. But today you can get Sarah back . . . *I* can get my mother back."

"I don't know . . ." Annie put her hand over Leah's. "How did you find her, to invite her, anyway?" Accusatory.

Deep breath. Then Annie admitted she'd been to see her mother, too. Out on the Coast. "When she came running to the door . . . when we were finally face-to-face, it was funny. I had it all planned, to yell at her, give her hell. But as soon as I saw her, I just began to cry, and she put her arms around me to comfort me, and it was really funny because she's so tiny and I'm so tall and her head was pressing into my bosom. She thought it was funny, too, so the first thing we did was laugh and cry together. Not a bad beginning."

Long pause, then, "What's she like?"

"She's . . . very beautiful. But you already know that. It was different for me. I saw her pictures in magazines and on album covers. But in person . . . you'd never guess her age, never."

Proudly: "It runs in the family."

Annie laughed. "She looks a lot like you. And she misses you, Leah, she says you were really her mother."

Leah sniffed. "She's wrong, you know. Jo was a *good* mother to her, and that's the truth."

"Oh, Leah, what's *truth*? We all see things differently."

"Have you been in therapy?" Sharply.

Annie laughed. "No, Leah, I'm just smart."

A sigh from the other seat. "She was always so angry. Your mother. I never understood her. Even when she was happy, there was, underneath, a note of . . . discontent. Only music made her calm. . . ."

"Yeah, she says that, too. She says her music was her medication, her antidepressant. She suffered a lot, Leah. She hated being on drugs, hated that whole life. She really loved my father—she says he was the love of her life. If he had left his wife, like he promised, and married her, her whole life would have been different; if—"

"If, if," Leah said with a smile. "If my grandmother had wheels, she'd be a cart. Sarah's life was her life, and let me tell you something, she's not the only one who suffered. You—"

"Me? Me, with two doting mamas?" Annie laughed. "I had a great childhood, Leah."

"And yet you think you're ugly."

"Nothing's perfect!" Pause. "My childhood was fine, Leah. Really. And it's still fine. Look how I use you in my routines all the time, and you never object." Pause. "She's funny, too."

"Sarah, you mean?"

"Yes, Sarah. She's funny and she's smart. And she *has* been shrunk. She says she's still struggling to become . . . Who isn't?"

Leah looked away. "You know, we were all abandoned by our mothers, one way or another. I've often wondered, is that it, that we're doomed to repeat whatever was done to us?"

"Not doomed, Weeah. It ends here, today." There was a long silence. "Does that mean you'll see my mother?"

Leah didn't answer. She turned to Annie suddenly and said, "I think this is the last time I'll come to Coney Island on my birthday."

"Bite your tongue!"

"Oh, I intend to stay alive, darling. But enough already! It's a dead place, it's more worn-out than I am—why do I need to see it? Let the memories stay where they belong. The present moment is quite enough for me, not to mention the future. So let's go home. Hey! It's my birthday, and I want to celebrate with my family! Yes, okay. Annie, with you and with Sarah, maybe we'll get our new beginning."

And Annie, turning the key in the ignition, repeated: "A new beginning . . ."